Resounding acclaim for

ROBIN HOBB
and

FOREST MAGE

"[A] master fantasist."
Baltimore Sun

"Gloriously original . . . typical of one of the most fascinating fantasy writers alive. The Soldier Son can be read as a political satire . . . but on a more personal level it is profoundly perceptive about the challenge faced by the honorable, brave and good . . . Rich in character and plot . . . this is the kind of fantasy that Anthony Trollope would have written if he lived now."
Times of London

"Hobb excels at constructing worlds and people who are fully fleshed out . . . A master storyteller."
Publishers Weekly

"A talented writer who uses all her creative powers to bring a story to life at breathtaking pace."
Birmingham Post (UK)

"Drawn in delicate, vivid language . . . A fine example of how to avoid middle-book slump."
Booklist

"Anything by Robin Hobb deserves serious attention."
Contra Costa Times

By Robin Hobb

THE FARSEER TRILOGY
Assassin's Apprentice
Royal Assassin
Assassin's Quest

THE LIVESHIP TRADERS TRILOGY
Ship of Magic
Mad Ship
Ship of Destiny

THE TAWNY MAN TRILOGY
Fool's Errand
Golden Fool
Fool's Fate

THE SOLDIER SON TRILOGY
Shaman's Crossing
Forest Mage
Renegade's Magic

WRITING AS MEGAN LINDHOLM

Harpy's Flight
The Limbreth Gate
The Windsingers
Luck of the Wheels
Wizard of the Pigeons
Reindeer People
Wolf's Brother
Alien Earth
Cloven Hooves

The Gypsy (with Steven Brust)

ROBIN HOBB

FOREST MAGE

An Imprint of HarperCollinsPublishers

EOS

An Imprint of HarperCollins*Publishers*
10 East 53rd Street
New York, New York 10022-5299

Copyright © 2006 by Robin Hobb
Excerpt from *Renegade's Magic* copyright © 2008 by Robin Hobb
ISBN: 978-0-06-075829-5
ISBN-10: 0-06-075829-5
www.eosbooks.com

First Eos paperback printing: December 2007
First Eos special printing: September 2006
First Eos hardcover printing: September 2006

HarperCollins® and Eos® are registered trademarks of HarperCollins Publishers.

Printed in the U. S. A.

10   9   8   7   6

To Alexsandrea and Jadyn,
my companions through a tough year.
I promise never to cut and run.

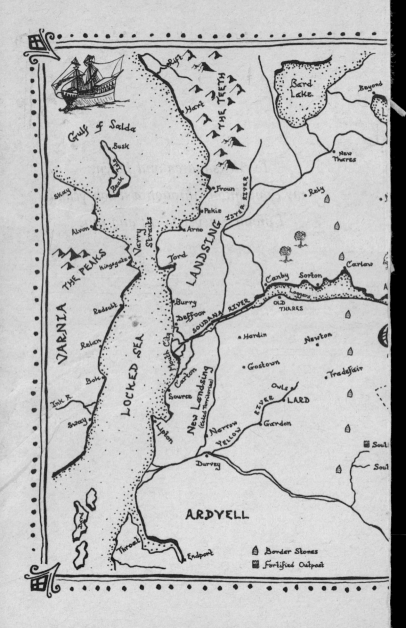

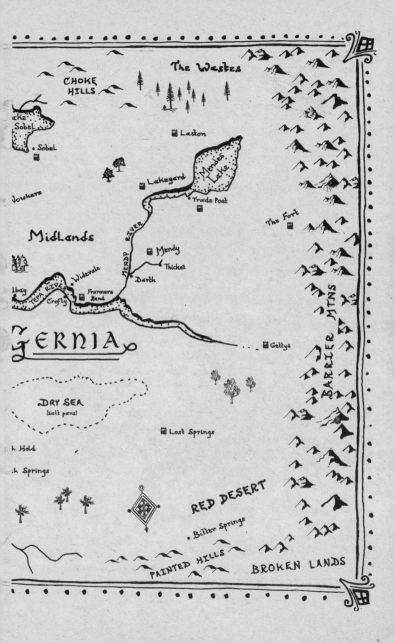

CONTENTS

ACKNOWLEDGMENTS

The author wishes to acknowledge David Killingsworth for providing the insights that helped make Nevare a whole person.

FOREST MAGE

CHAPTER ONE

FOREST DREAMS

There is a fragrance in the forest. It does not come from a single flower or leaf. It is not the rich aroma of dark crumbly earth or the sweetness of fruit that has passed from merely ripe to mellow and rich. The scent I recalled was a combination of all these things, and of sunlight touching and awakening their essences and of a very slight wind that blended them perfectly. She smelled like that.

We lay together in a bower. Above us, the distant top of the canopy swayed gently, and the beaming rays of sunlight danced over our bodies in time with them. Vines and creepers that draped from the stretching branches above our heads formed the sheltering walls of our forest pavilion. Deep moss cushioned my bare back, and her soft arm was my pillow. The vines curtained our trysting place with their foliage and large, pale green flowers. The sepals pushed past the fleshy lips of the blossoms and were heavy with yellow pollen. Large butterflies with wings of deep orange traced with black were investigating the flowers. One insect left a drooping blossom, alighted on my lover's shoulder, and walked over her soft dappled flesh. I watched it unfurl a coiled black tongue to taste the perspiration that dewed the forest woman's skin, and envied it.

I lay in indescribable comfort, content beyond passion. I lifted a lazy hand to impede the butterfly's progress. Fearlessly, it stepped onto my fingers. I raised it to be an ornament in my lover's thick and tousled hair. She opened her eyes at my touch. She had hazel eyes, green mingling with soft brown. She smiled. I leaned up on my elbow and kissed her. Her ample breasts pressed against me, startling in their softness.

"I'm sorry," I said softly, tilting back from the kiss. "I'm so sorry I had to kill you."

Her eyes were sad but still fond. "I know," she replied. There was no rancor in her voice. "Be at peace with it, soldier's boy. All will come true as it was meant to be. You belong to the magic now, and whatever it must have you do, you will do."

"But I killed you. I loved you and I killed you."

She smiled gently. "Such as we do not die as others do."

"Do you yet live then?" I asked her. I pulled my body back from hers and looked down between us at the mound of her belly. It gave the lie to her words. My cavalla saber had slashed her wide open. Her entrails spilled from that gash and rested on the moss between us. They were pink and liverish-gray, coiling like fat worms. They had piled up against my bare legs, warm and slick. Her blood smeared my genitals. I tried to scream and could not. I struggled to push away from her, but we had grown fast together.

"Nevare!"

I woke with a shudder and sat up in my bunk, panting silently through my open mouth. A tall pale wraith stood over me. I gave a muted yelp before I recognized Trist. "You were whimpering in your sleep," Trist told me. I compulsively brushed at my thighs, and then lifted my hands close to my face. In the dim moonlight through the window, they were clean of blood.

"It was only a dream," Trist assured me.

"Sorry," I muttered, ashamed. "Sorry I was noisy."

"It's not like you're the only one to have nightmares." The thin cadet sat down on the foot of my bed. Once he had been whiplash-lean and limber. Now he was skeletal and moved like a stiff old man. He coughed twice and then caught his breath. "Know what I dream?" He didn't wait for my reply. "I dream I died of Speck plague. Because I did, you know. I was one of the ones who died, and then revived. But I dream that instead of holding my body in the infirmary, Dr. Amicas let them put me out with the corpses. In my dream, they toss me in the pit grave, and they throw the quicklime down on me. I dream I wake up down there, under all those bodies that stink of piss and vomit, with the lime burning into me. I try to climb out, but they just keep throwing more bodies down on top of me. I'm clawing and pushing my way past them, trying to get out of the pit through all that rotting flesh and bones. And then I realize that the body I'm climbing over is Nate. He's all dead and decaying, but he opens his eyes and he asks, 'Why me, Trist? Why me and not you?' " Trist gave a sudden shudder and huddled his shoulders.

"They're only dreams, Trist," I whispered. All around us, the other first-years who had survived the plague slumbered on. Someone coughed in his sleep. Someone else muttered, yipped like a puppy, and then grew still. Trist was right. Few of us slept well anymore. "They're only bad dreams. It's all over. The plague passed us by. We survived."

"Easy for you to say. You recovered. You're fit and hearty." He stood up. His nightshirt hung on his lanky frame. In the dim dormitory, his eyes were dark holes. "Maybe I survived, but the plague didn't pass me by. I'll live with what it did to me to the end of my days. You think I'll ever lead a charge, Nevare? I can barely manage to keep standing through morning assembly. I'm done as a soldier. Done before I started. I'll never live the life I expected to lead."

Trist stood up. He shuffled away from my bed and back to

his. He was breathing noisily by the time he sat down on his bunk.

Slowly I lay back down. I heard Trist cough again, wheeze, and then lie down. It was no comfort to me that he, too, was tormented with nightmares. I thought of Tree Woman and shuddered again. *She is dead,* I assured myself. *She can no longer reach into my life. I killed her. I killed her and I took back into myself the part of my spirit that she'd stolen and seduced. She can't control me anymore. It was only a dream.* I took a deeper, steadying breath, turned my pillow to the cool side, and burrowed into it. I dared not close my eyes lest I fall back into that nightmare. I deliberately focused my mind on the present, and pushed my night terror away from me.

All around me in the darkness, my fellow survivors slept. Bringham House's dormitory was a long open room, with a large window at each end. Two neat rows of bunks lined the long walls. There were forty beds, but only thirty-one were full. Colonel Rebin, the King's Cavalla Academy commander, had combined the sons of old nobles with the sons of battle lords, and recalled the cadets who had been culled earlier in the year, but even that measure had not completely replenished our depleted ranks. The colonel might have declared us equals, but I suspected that only time and familiarity would erase the social gulf between the sons of established noble families and those of us whose fathers could claim a title only because the king had elevated them in recognition of their wartime service.

Rebin mingled us out of necessity. The Speck plague that had roared through the academy had devastated us. Our class of first-years had been halved. The second- and third-years had taken almost as heavy a loss. Instructors as well as students had perished in that unnatural onslaught. Colonel Rebin was doing the best he could to reorganize the academy and put it back on a regular schedule, but we were still licking our wounds. Speck plague had culled a full generation of future officers. Gernia's military would feel that loss keenly in the years to come. And that had been what the Specks intended when they used their magic to send their disease against us.

Morale at the academy was subdued as we staggered forward into the new year. It wasn't just the number of deaths the plague had visited on us, though that was bad enough. The plague had come among us and slaughtered us at will, an enemy that all of our training could not prevail against. Strong, brave young men who had hoped to distinguish themselves on battlefields had instead died in their beds, soiled with vomit and urine and whimpering feebly for their mothers. It is never good to remind soldiers of their own mortality. We had believed ourselves young heroes, full of energy, courage, and lust for life. The plague had revealed to us that we were mortals, and just as vulnerable as the weakest babe in arms.

The first time Colonel Rebin had assembled us on the parade ground in our old formations, he had ordered us all "at ease" and then commanded us to look around us and see how many of our fellows had fallen. He then gave a speech, telling us that the plague was the first battle we had passed through, and that just as the plague had not discriminated between old nobility and new nobility, neither would a blade or a bullet. As he formed us up into our new condensed companies, I pondered his words. I doubted that he truly realized that the Speck plague had not been a random contagion but a true strike against us, as telling as any military attack. The Specks had sent "Dust Dancers" from the far eastern frontiers of Gernia all the way to our capitol city, for the precise purpose of sowing their disease among our nobility and our future military leaders. They had succeeded in thinning our ranks. If not for me, their success would have been complete. Sometimes I took pride in that.

At other times, I recalled that if not for me, they never would have been able to attack us as they had.

I had tried, without success, to shrug off the guilt I felt. I'd been the unwilling and unwitting partner of the Specks and Tree Woman. It was not my fault, I told myself, that I'd fallen into her power. Years ago, my father had entrusted me to a Plainsman warrior for training. Dewara had nearly killed me with his "instruction." And toward the end of my time with him, he'd decided to "make me Kidona" by inducting me into the magic of his people.

Foolishly, I'd allowed him to drug me and take me into the supernatural world of his people. He'd told me I could win honor and glory by doing battle with the ancient enemy of his people. But what confronted me at the end of a series of trials had been a fat old woman sitting in the shade of a huge tree. I was my father's soldier son, trained in the chivalry of the cavalla. I could not draw sword against an old woman. Due to that misplaced gallantry, I had fallen to her. She had "stolen" me from Dewara and made me her pawn. A part of me had remained with her in that spirit world. While I had grown and gone off to the academy and begun my education to be an officer in my king's cavalla, he had become her acolyte. Tree Woman had made that part of me into a Speck in all things but having speckled skin. Through him, she spied on my people, and hatched her terrible plan to destroy us with the Speck plague. Masquerading as captive dancers, her emissaries came to Old Thares as part of the Dark Evening carnival and unleashed their disease upon us.

My Speck self had seized control of me. I'd signaled the Dust Dancers to let them know they had reached their goal. The carnivalgoers who surrounded them thought they had come to witness an exhibition of primitive dance. Instead, they'd breathed in the disease with the flung dust. When my fellow cadets and I left the carnival, we were infected. And the disease had spread throughout all of Old Thares.

In my bed in the darkened dormitory, I rolled over and thumped my pillow back into shape. *Stop thinking about how I betrayed my own people*, I begged myself. *Think instead of how I saved them.*

And I had. In a terrible encounter born of my Speck plague fever, I had finally been able to cross back into her world and challenge her. Not only had I won back the piece of my soul she had stolen, but I had also slain her, slashing her belly wide open with the cold iron of my cavalla saber. I severed her connection to our world. Her reign over me was finished. I attributed my complete recovery from the Speck plague to my reclaiming the piece of my spirit she had stolen. I had regained my health and vitality, and even put on flesh. In a word, I had become whole again.

In the days and nights that followed my return to the academy and the resumption of a military routine, I discovered that as I reintegrated that other, foreign self, I absorbed his memories as well. His recollections of the Tree Woman and her world were the source of my beautiful dreams of walking in untouched forest in the company of an amazing woman. I felt as if the twin halves of my being had parted, followed differing roads, and now had converged once more into a single self. The very fact that I accepted this was so, and tried to absorb those alien emotions and opinions, was a fair indicator that my other self was having a substantial impact on who I was becoming. The old Nevare, the self I knew so well, would have rejected such a melding as blasphemous and impossible.

I had killed the Tree Woman, and I did not regret doing it. She had extinguished lives for the sake of the "magic" she could draw from their foundering souls. My best friend, Spink, and my Cousin Epiny had been among her intended victims. I had killed Tree Woman to save them. I knew that I had also saved myself, and dozens of others. By daylight, I did not think of my deed at all, or if I did, I took satisfaction in knowing that I had triumphed and saved my friends. Yet my night thoughts were a different matter. When I hovered between wakefulness and sleep, a terrible sorrow and guilt would fill me. I mourned the creature I had slain, and missed her with a sorrow that hollowed me. My Speck self had been her lover and regretted that I'd slain her. But that was he, not me. In my dreams, he might briefly rule my thoughts. But by day, I was still Nevare Burvelle, my father's son and a future officer in the king's cavalla. I had prevailed. I would continue to prevail. And I would do all I could, every day of my life, to make up for the traitorous deeds of my other self.

I sighed. I knew I would not sleep again that night. I tried to salve my conscience. The plague we had endured together had strengthened us in some ways. It had united us as cadets. There had been little opposition to Colonel Rebin's insistence on ending the segregation of old nobles' and new nobles' sons. In the last few weeks I'd come to know better the "old noble" first-years and found that, generally speaking, they were little different from my old patrol. The vicious rivalry that had separated us for the first part of the year had foundered and died. Now that we were truly one academy and could socialize freely, I wondered what had made me loathe them so. They were perhaps more sophisticated and polished than their frontier brethren, but at the end of the day they were first-years just like us, groaning under the same demerits and duty. Colonel Rebin had taken care to mix us well in our new patrols. Nonetheless, my closest friends were still the four surviving members of my old patrol.

Rory had stepped up to fill the position of best friend to me when Spink's broken health had forced him to withdraw from the academy. His devil-may-care attitude and frontier roughness were, I felt, a good counterweight to stiffness and rules. Whenever I lapsed into moodiness or became too pensive, Rory would rowdy me past it. He was the least changed of my old patrol mates. Trist was no longer the tall, handsome cadet he'd been. His brush with death had stolen his physical confidence. When he laughed now, it always had a bitter edge. Kort missed Nate acutely. He bowed under his grief, and though he had recovered his health, he was so somber and dull without his friend that he seemed to be living but half a life. Fat Gord was still as heavy as ever, but he seemed more content with his lot and also more dignified. When it looked as if the plague would doom everyone, Gord's parents and his fiancée's parents had allowed their offspring to wed early and taste what little of life they might be allowed. Fortune had smiled on them, and they had come through the plague unscathed. Although Gord was still teased by all and despised by some for his fat, his new status as a married man agreed with him. He seemed to possess an inner contentment and sense of worth that childish taunts could not disturb. He spent every day of his liberty with his wife, and she sometimes came to visit him during the week. Cilima was a quiet little thing with huge black eyes and tumbling black curls. She was completely infatuated with "my dear Gordy," as she always called him, and he was devoted to her. His marriage separated him from the rest of us; he now seemed much older than his fellow first-years. He went after his studies with a savage determination. I had always known that he was good at math and engineering. He now revealed that in fact he was brilliant, and had till now merely been marking time. He no longer concealed his keen mind. I knew that Colonel Rebin had summoned him once to discuss his future. He had taken Gord out of the first-year math course and given him texts to study independently. We were still friends, but without Spink and his need for tutoring, we did not spend much time together. Our only long conversations seemed to occur when one or the other of us would receive a letter from Spink.

He wrote to both of us, more or less regularly. Spink himself had survived the plague, but his military career had not. His handwriting wavered more than it had before his illness, and his letters were not long. He did not whine or bitterly protest his fate, but the brevity of his missives spoke to me of dashed hopes. He had constant pain in his joints now, and headaches if he read or wrote for too long. Dr. Amicas had given Spink a medical discharge from the academy. Spink had married my Cousin Epiny, who had nursed him through his illness. Together, they had set out for his brother's holdings at distant Bitter Springs. The sedate life of a dutiful younger son was a far cry from Spink's previous dreams of military glory and swift advancement through the ranks.

Epiny's letters to me were naively revealing. Her inked words prattled as verbosely as her tongue did. I knew the names of the flowers, trees, and plants she had encountered on her way to Bitter Springs, every day's weather, and each tiny event on her tedious journey there. Epiny had traded my uncle's wealth and sophisticated home in Old Thares for the life of a frontier wife. She had once told me she thought she could be a good soldier's wife, but it looked as if her final vocation would be caretaker for her invalid husband. Spink would have no career of his own. They would live on his brother's estate, and at his brother's sufferance. Fond as his elder brother was of Spink, it would still be difficult for him to stretch his paltry resources to care for his soldier brother and his wife.

In the darkness, I shifted in my bunk. Trist was right, I

decided. None of us would have the lives we'd expected. I muttered a prayer to the good god for all of us, and closed my eyes to get what sleep I could before dawn commanded us to rise.

I was weary when I rose the next morning with my fellows. Rory tried to jolly me into conversation at breakfast, but my answers were brief, and no one else at our table took up his banter. Our first class of the day was Engineering and Drafting. I'd enjoyed the course when Captain Maw instructed it, despite his prejudice against new noble sons like me. But the plague had carried Maw off, and a third-year cadet had been pressed into duty as our temporary instructor. Cadet Sergeant Vredo seemed to think that discipline was more important than information, and frequently issued demerits to cadets who dared to ask questions. Captain Maw's untidy room full of maps and models had been gutted. Rows of desks and interminable lectures had replaced our experimentation. I kept my head down, did my work, and learned little that was new to me.

In contrast, Cadet Lieutenant Bailey was doing rather well instructing Military History, for he plainly loved his topic and had read widely beyond his course materials. His lecture that day was one that engaged me. He spoke about the impact of Gernian civilization on the Plainspeople. In my father's lifetime, Landsing, our traditional enemy, had finally dealt Gernia a sound defeat. Gernia had had to surrender our territory along the western seacoast. King Troven had had no choice but to turn his eyes to the east and the unclaimed territories there. Nomadic folk had long roamed the wide prairies and high plateaus of the interior lands, but they were primitive folk with no central government, no king, and few permanent settlements. When Gernia had begun to expand east, they had fought us, but their arrows and spears were no match for our modern weaponry. We had defeated them. There was no question in anyone's mind that it was for their own good.

"Since Gernia took charge of the Plainsmen and their lands, they have begun to put down roots, to build real towns rather than their seasonal settlements, to pen their cattle and grow food rather than forage for it. The swift horses of great stamina that sustained the largely nomadic peoples have been replaced with sturdy oxen and plow horses. For the first time, their children are experiencing the benefits of schooling and written language. Knowledge of the good god is being imparted to them, replacing the fickle magic they once relied on."

Lofert waved a hand and then spoke before the instructor could acknowledge him. "But what about them, uh, Preservationists, sir? I heard my father telling one of his friends that they'd like to give all our land back to the Plainsfolk and let them go back to living like wild animals."

"Wait to be acknowledged before you ask a question, Cadet. And your comment wasn't phrased as a question. But I'll answer it. There are people who feel that we have made radical changes to the lifestyles of the Plainsmen too swiftly for them to adapt to them. In some instances, they are probably correct. In many others, they are, in my opinion, ignorant of the reality of what they suggest. But what we have to ask ourselves is, would it be better for them if we delayed offering them the benefits of civilization? Or would we simply be neglecting our duty to them?

"Remember that the Plainspeople used to rely on their primitive magic and spells for survival. They can no longer do that. And having taken their magic from them, is it not our duty to replace it with modern tools for living? Iron, the backbone of our modernizing world, is anathema to their magic. The iron plows we gave them to till the land negate the "finding magic" of their foragers. Flint and steel have become a requirement, for their mages can no longer call forth flame from wood. The Plainsmen are settled now and can draw water from wells. The water mages who used to lead the people to drinking places along their long migratory routes are no longer needed. The few wind wizards who remain are solitary creatures, seldom glimpsed. Reports of their flying rugs and their little boats that moved of themselves across calm water are already scoffed at as tales. I have no doubt that in another generation, they'll be the stuff of legend."

Cadet Lieutenant Bailey's words saddened me. My mind

wandered briefly. I recalled my own brief glimpse of a wind wizard on the river during my journey to Old Thares. He had held his small sail wide to catch the wind he had summoned. His little craft had moved swiftly against the current. The sight had been both moving and mystical to me. Yet I also recalled with wrenching regret how it had ended. Some drunken fools on our riverboat had shot his sail full of holes. The iron shot they had used had disrupted the wizard's spell as well. He'd been flung off his little vessel into the river. I believed he had drowned there, victim of the young noblemen's jest.

"Lead can kill a man, but it takes cold iron to defeat magic." My instructor's words jolted me from my daydream.

"That our superior civilization replaces the primitive order of the Plainsmen is a part of the natural order," he lectured. "And lest you feel too superior, be mindful that we Gernians have been victims of advanced technology ourselves. When Landsing made their discovery that allowed their cannon and long guns to shoot farther and more accurately than ours, they were able to defeat us and take from us our seacoast provinces. Much as we resent that, it was natural that once they had achieved a military technology that was superior to our own, they would take what they wished from us. Keep that in mind, cadets. We are entering an age of technology.

"The same principle applies to our conquest of the Plains. Shooting lead bullets at Plains warriors, we were able to maintain our borders by force of arms, but we could not expand them. It was only when some forward-thinking man realized that iron shot would destroy their magic as well as cause injury that we were able to push back their boundaries and impose our will on them. The disadvantages of iron shot, that it cannot be as easily reclaimed and remanufactured in the field as lead ball can, were offset by the military advantage it gave us in defeating their warriors. The Plainsmen had relied on their magic to turn aside our shot, to scare our horses, and generally to confound our troops. Our advance into their lands, gentlemen, is as inevitable as a rising tide, just as was our defeat by the Landsingers. And, just like us, the Plainsmen will either be swept away before new technology, or they will learn to live with it."

"Then you think it is our right, sir, to just run over them?" Lofert asked in his earnest way.

"Raise your hand and wait to be acknowledged before you speak, Cadet. You've been warned before. Three demerits. Yes. I think it is our right. The good god has given us the means to defeat the Plainsmen, and to prosper where once only goatherds or wild beasts dwelt. We will bring civilization to the Midlands, to the benefit of all."

I caught myself wondering how much the fallen from both sides had benefited. Then I shook my head angrily, and resolutely set aside such cynical musings. I was a cadet in the King's Cavalla Academy. Like any second son of a nobleman, I was my father's soldier son, and I would follow in his footsteps. I had not been born to question the ways of the world. If the good god had wanted me to ponder fate or question the morality of our eastward expansion, he would have made me a third son, born to be a priest.

At the end of the lecture, I blew on my notes to dry them, closed up my books, and joined the rest of my patrol to march in formation back to the dormitory. Spring was trying to gain a hold on the academy grounds and not completely succeeding. There was a sharp nip of chill in the wind, yet it was pleasant to be out in the fresh air again. I tried to push aside my somber musings on the fate of the Plainsmen. It was, as our instructor had said, the natural order of things. Who was I to dispute it? I followed my friends up the stairs to our dormitory, and shelved my textbooks from my morning classes. The day's mail awaited me on my bunk. There was a fat envelope from Epiny. The other cadets left me sitting on my bunk. As they hurried off to the noon meal, I opened her letter.

Her letter opened with her usual queries about my health and schooling. I quickly skimmed past that part. She had arrived safely in Bitter Springs. Epiny's first letter about reaching her new home was determinedly optimistic, but I sensed the gap between her expectations and the reality she now confronted. I sat on my bunk and read it with sympathy and bemusement.

The women of the household work as hard as the men, right alongside the servants. Truly, the saying that "Men but work from sun to sun, woman's work is never done!" is true of Lady Kester's household. In the hours after dinner, when the light is dim and you might think some rest was due us, one of us will read or make music for the others, allowing our minds to drift a bit, but our ever-busy hands go on with such mundane tasks as shelling dried peas or using a drop-spindle to make thread of wool (I am proud to say I have become quite good at this chore!) or unraveling old sweaters and blankets so that the yarn can be re-used to make useful items. Lady Kester wastes nothing, not a scrap of fabric nor a minute of time.

Spink and I have our own dear little cottage, built of stone, as that is what we have an abundance of here. It used to be the milk house, and had fallen into disrepair after the last two milk cows died. When Lady Kester knew we were coming, she decided that we would relish a little privacy of our own, and so she had her daughters do their best to clean and tighten it up for us before we arrived. The inside of it was freshly whitewashed, and Spink's sister Gera has given us the quilt that she had sewn for her own hope chest. There is only the one room, of course, but it is ample for the little furniture we have. The bedstead fills one corner, and our table with our own two chairs is right by the window that looks out over the open hillside. Spink tells me that once the late frosts have passed, we shall have a vista of wild flowers there. Even so, it is quite rustic and quaint, but as soon as Spink's health has improved, he says he will put in a new floor and fix the chimney so that it draws better, and use a spoke shave to persuade the door to shut tightly in the jamb. Summer approaches and with it warmer weather, which I shall be grateful to see. I

*trust that by the time the rains and frosts return, we
shall have made our little home as cozy as a bird's
nest in a hollow tree. For now, when the cold wind
creeps round the door or the mosquitoes keen in my
ear at night, I ask myself, "Am I not as hearty as the
little ground squirrels that scamper about during the
day and have no better than a hole to shelter in at
night? Surely I can take a lesson from them and find
as much satisfaction in my simple life." And so I make
myself content.*

"Yer cousin wants to be a ground squirrel?" Rory asked
me. I turned to find him reading over my shoulder. I glared
at him. He grinned, unabashed.

"That's rude, Rory, and you know it."

"Sorry!" His grin grew wolfish. "I wouldn't have read it,
but I thought it was from your girl and might have some in-
trestin' bits in it."

He dodged my counterfeit swipe at him and then with
false pomposity warned me, "Better not hit me, Cadet! Remember, I outrank you for now. Besides, I'm a messenger.
Dr. Amicas sent word that you were to come and see him.
He also said that if you don't think his request to visit him
weekly is sufficient, he could make it a direct order."

"Oh." My heart sank. I didn't want to go see the academy
physician anymore, but neither did I want to annoy the iras-
cible old man. I was aware still of the debt that I owed him.
I folded up Epiny's letter and rose with a sigh. Dr. Amicas
had been a friend to me, in his own brusque way. And he'd
definitely behaved heroically through the plague, going
without rest to care for the dozens of cadets who fell to the
disease. Without him, I would not have survived. I knew
that the plague fascinated him, and that he had a personal
ambition to discover its method of transmission, as well as
document which techniques saved lives and which were
worthless, and was writing a scholarly paper summing up
all his observations of the recent outbreak. He had told me
that monitoring my amazing recovery from such a severe
case of plague was a part of his research, but I was dismally

tired of it. Every week he poked and prodded and measured me. The way he spoke to me made me feel that I had not recovered at all but was merely going through an extended phase of recuperation. I wished he would stop reminding me of my experience. I wanted to put the plague behind me and stop thinking of myself as an invalid.

"Right now?" I asked Rory.

"Right now, Cadet," he confirmed. He spoke as a friend, but the new stripe on his sleeve still meant that I'd best go immediately.

"I'll miss the noon meal," I objected.

"Wouldn't hurt you to miss a meal or two," he said meaningfully.

I scowled at his jab, but he only grinned. I nodded and set out for the infirmary.

In the last few balmy days, some misguided trees had flowered. They wore their white and pink blossoms bravely despite the day's chill. The groundskeepers had been at work: all the fallen branches from the winter storms had been tidied away and the greens manicured to velvet.

I had to pass one very large flower bed where precisely spaced ranks of bulb flowers had pushed up their green spikes of leaves; soon there would be regiments of tulips in bloom. I looked away from them; I knew what lay beneath those stalwart rows. They covered the pit grave that had received so many of my comrades. A single gravestone stood grayly in the middle of the garden. It said only, OUR HONORED DEAD. The academy had been quarantined when the plague broke out. Even when it had spread through the city beyond our walls, Dr. Amicas had maintained our isolation. Our dead had been carried out of the infirmaries and dormitories and set down first in rows, and then, as their numbers increased, in stacks. I had been among the ill. I had not witnessed the mounting toll, nor seen the rats that scuttled and the carrion birds that flocked, despite the icy cold, to the feast. Dr. Amicas had been the one to order reluctantly that a great pit be dug and the bodies be tumbled in, along with layers of quicklime and earth.

Nate was down there, I knew. I tried not to think of his

flesh rotting from his bones, or about the bodies tangled and clumped together in the obscene impartiality of such a grave. Nate had deserved better. They had all deserved better. I'd heard one of the new cadets refer to the grave site as "the memorial to the Battle of Pukenshit." I'd wanted to hit him. I turned up my collar against a wind that still bit with winter's teeth and hurried past the groomed gardens through the late afternoon light.

At the door of the infirmary I hesitated, and then gritted my teeth and stepped inside. The bare corridor smelled of lye soap and ammonia, but in my mind the miasma of sickness still clung to this place. Many of my friends and acquaintances had died in this building only a couple of months ago. I wondered that Dr. Amicas could stand to keep his offices here. Had it been left to me, I would have burned the infirmary down to scorched earth and rebuilt somewhere else.

When I tapped on the door of his private office, the doctor peremptorily ordered me to come in. Clouds of drifting pipe smoke veiled the room and flavored the air. "Cadet Burvelle, reporting as ordered, sir," I announced myself.

He pushed his chair back from his cluttered desk and rose, taking his spectacles off as he did so. He looked me up and down, and I felt the measure of his glance. "You weren't ordered, Cadet, and you know it. But the importance of my research is such that if you don't choose to cooperate, I will give you such orders. Instead of coming at your convenience, you'll come at mine, and then enjoy the pleasure of making up missed class time. Are we clear?"

His words were harsher than his tone. He meant them, but he spoke almost as if we were peers. "I'll cooperate, sir." I was unbuttoning my uniform jacket as I spoke. One of the buttons, loosened on its thread, broke free and went flying across the office. He lifted a brow at that.

"Still gaining flesh, I see."

"I always put on weight right before I get taller." I spoke a bit defensively. This was the third time he had brought up my weight gain. I thought it unkind of him. "Surely that must be better than me being thin as a rail, like Trist."

"Cadet Wissom's reaction to having survived the plague

is the norm. Yours is different. 'Better' remains to be seen,"
he replied ponderously. "Any other changes that you've noticed? How's your wind?"

"It's fine. I had to march off six demerits yesterday, and I
finished up at the same time as the other fellows."

"Hm." He had drawn closer as I spoke. As if I were a
thing rather than a person, he inspected my body, looking in
my ears, eyes, and nose, and then listening to my heart and
breathing. He made me run in place for a good five minutes,
and then listened to my heart and lungs again. He jotted
down voluminous notes, weighed me, took my height, and
then quizzed me on all I'd eaten since yesterday. As I'd had
only what the mess allotted to me, that question was quickly
answered.

"But you've still gained weight, even though you haven't
increased your food intake?" he asked me, as if questioning
my honesty.

"I'm out of spending money," I told him. "I'm eating as
I've eaten since I arrived here. The extra flesh is only because I'm about to go through another growth spurt."

"I see. You know that, do you?"

I didn't answer that. I knew it was rhetorical. He stooped
to retrieve my button and handed it back to me. "Best sew
that on good and tight, Cadet." He put his notes on me into a
folder and then sat down at his desk with a sigh. "You're going home in a couple of weeks, aren't you? For your sister's
wedding?"

"For my brother's wedding, sir. Yes, I am. I'll leave as
soon as my tickets arrive. My father wrote to Colonel Rebin
to ask that I be released for the occasion. The colonel told
me that ordinarily he would strongly disapprove of a cadet
taking a month off from studies to attend a wedding, but
that given the condition of our classes at present, he thinks I
can make up the work."

The doctor was nodding to my words. He pursed his
mouth, seemed on the verge of saying something, hesitated,
and then said, "I think it's for the best that you *do* go home
for a time. Traveling by ship?"

"Part of the way. Then I'll do the rest by horseback. I'll go

more swiftly by road than on a vessel fighting the spring
floods. I've my own horse in the academy stables. Sirlofty
didn't get much exercise over the winter. This journey will
put both of us back into condition."

He smiled wearily as he settled into his desk chair. "Well.
Let's pray that it does. You can go, Nevare. But check back
with me next week, if you're still here. Don't make me remind you."

"Yes, sir." I dared a question. "How is your research pro-
gressing?"

"Slowly." He scowled. "I am at odds with my fellow physi-
cians. Most of them persist in looking for a cure. I tell them,
we must find out what triggers the disease and prevent that.
Once the plague has struck, people begin to die quickly. Pre-
venting its spread will save more lives than trying to cure it
once it has a foothold in the population." He sighed, and I
knew his memories haunted him. He cleared his throat and
went on, "I looked into what you suggested about dust. I simply cannot see it being the cause of the disease." He seemed
to forget that I was merely a cadet and, leaning back in his
chair, spoke to me as if I were a colleague. "You know that I
believe the onset of the plague and the swiftness of its spread
mean that sexual contact cannot be the sole method of con-
tracting it. I still believe that the most virulent cases stem
from sexual contact . . ."

He paused, offering me yet another opportunity to admit
I'd had carnal knowledge of a Speck. I remained silent. I
hadn't, at least not physically. If cavalla soldiers could con-
tract venereal disease from what we dreamed, none of us
would live to graduate from the academy.

He finally continued, "Your theory that something in the
dust that the Specks fling during their Dust Dance could be a
trigger appealed to me. Unfortunately, while I did my best to
gather data from the sickened cadets before they became too
ill to respond, the disease took many of them before they
could be questioned. So we shall never know exactly how
many of them may have witnessed a Dust Dance and breathed
in dust. However, there are several flaws in your theory. The
first is that at least one cadet, Corporal Rory Hart, witnessed

the Dust Dance and had absolutely no symptoms of plague. He's an unusual fellow; he also admitted to, er, more than casual contact with the Specks themselves, with no ill effect. But even if we set Rory aside as an individual with exceptionally robust health, there are still other problems with your theory. One is that the Specks would be exposing themselves to the illness every time they danced the dance. You have told me you believed that the Speck deliberately sowed this illness among us. Would they do it at risk to themselves? I think not. And before you interrupt—" he held up a warning hand as I took breath to speak, "—keep in mind that this is not the first outbreak of Speck plague that I've witnessed. As you might be pleased to know, the other outbreak I witnessed was close to the Barrier Mountains, and yes, the Specks had performed a Dust Dance before the outbreak. But many of their own children were among those stricken that summer. I can scarcely believe that even primitive people would deliberately infect their own children with a deadly disease simply to exact revenge on us. Of course, I suppose it's possible that the dust does spread the disease, but the Specks are unaware of it. Simple, natural peoples like the Specks are often unaware that all diseases have a cause and hence are preventable."

"Maybe they face the disease willingly. Maybe they think that the disease is more like a, uh, like a magical culling. That the children who survive it are meant to go on, and that those who die go on to a different life."

Dr. Amicas sighed deeply. "Nevare, Nevare. I am a doctor. We cannot go about imagining wild things to try to make a pet theory make sense. We have to fit the theory to the facts, not manufacture facts to support the theory."

I took a breath to speak, and then once more decided to give it up. I had only dreamed that the dust caused the disease. I had dreamed that it was so and my "Speck self" believed it. But perhaps in my dreams my Speck half believed a superstition, rather than knowing the real truth. I gave my head a slight shake. My circling thoughts reminded me of a dog chasing its own tail. "May I be dismissed, sir?"

"Certainly. And thank you for coming." He was tamping

more tobacco into his pipe as I departed. "Nevare!" His call
stopped me at the door.

"Sir?"

He pointed the stem of his pipe at me. "Are you still
troubled by nightmares?"

I fervently wished I'd never told him of that issue. "Only
sometimes, sir," I hedged. "Other than that, I sleep well."

"Good. That's good. I'll see you next week, then."

"Yes, sir." I left hastily before he could call me back.

The spring afternoon had faded and evening was coming
on. Birds were settling in the trees for the night, and lights
were beginning to show in the dormitories. The wind had
turned colder. I hurried on my way. The shadow of one of the
majestic oaks that graced the campus stretched across my
path. I walked into it, and in that instant felt a shiver up my
spine, as if someone had strolled over my grave. I blinked,
and for a moment a remnant of my other self looked out
through my eyes at the precisely groomed landscape, and
found it very strange indeed. The straight paths and careful
greens suddenly looked stripped and barren to me, the few
remaining trees a sad remnant of a forest that had been. The
landscape was devoid of the randomness of natural life. In
true freedom, life sprawled. This vista was as lifeless and as
unlovely as a glass-eyed animal stuffed for a display case. I
was suddenly acutely homesick for the forest.

In the weeks following my recovery, I had dreamed of the
Tree Woman, and in my dreams I was my other self, and she
was beautiful. We strolled in the dappling light that fell
through the leafy shade of her immense trees. We scrambled
over fallen logs and pushed our way through curtains of
vines. Fallen leaves and forest detritus were thick and soft
beneath our bare feet. In the stray beams of sunlight that
touched us, we both had speckled skin. She walked with the
ponderous grace of a heavy woman long accustomed to
managing her weight. She did not seem awkward, but majestic in her studied progress. Just as an antlered deer turns
his head to maneuver a narrow path, so did she sidle past a
network of spiderwebs that barred our way. The untidy, un-
mastered, lovely sprawl of the forest put her in context.

Here, she was as large, lush, and beautiful as the luxuriant life that surrounded us.

In my first vision of her, when the Plainsman Dewara had told me she was my enemy, I had perceived her as very old and repulsively fat. But in the dreams I'd had following my recovery from the Speck plague, she seemed ageless, and the pillowed roundness of her flesh was abundant and inviting.

I had told Dr. Amicas about the occasional vivid nightmares I had. I had not mentioned to him that my erotic dreams of the forest goddess far outnumbered the horrid ones. I always awoke from those dreams flushed with arousal that quickly became shame. It was not just that I lustfully dreamed of a Speck woman, and one of voluptuous fleshiness, but that I knew that some part of me had consorted with her, in passion and even love. I felt guilt for that bestial coupling, even if it had occurred in a dream world and was without my consent. It was treasonous as well as unnatural to mate outside my race. She had made me her lover and tried to turn me against my own people. A dark and twisted magic had been used to convert me to her uses. The threads of it still clung to my thoughts, and that was what pulled my soul down to those dark places where I still desired her flesh.

In my dreams of her, she often cautioned me that the magic now owned me. "It will use you as it sees fit. Do not resist it. Put nothing you care about between you and the magic's calling, for like a flood, it will sweep away all that opposes it. Ride with it, my love, or it will destroy you. You will learn to use it, but not for yourself. When you use the magic to achieve the ends of the magic, then its power will be at your command. But at all other times," and here she had smiled at me and run a soft hand down my cheek, "we are the tools of the power." In that dream, I caught her hand and kissed the palm of it, and then nodded my head and accepted both her wisdom and my fate. I wanted to flow with the magic that coursed through me. It was only natural. What else could I possibly want to do with my life? The magic coursed through me, as essential to me as my blood. Does a man oppose the beating of his own heart? Of course I would do what it willed.

Then I would wake and, like plunging into a cold river, my reality would drench me and shock me into awareness of my true self. Occasionally, as had happened when I passed through the shade of the oak, the stranger inside me could still take control of my mind and show me his warped view of my world. Then, in a blink of my eyes, a truer perspective would prevail, and the illusion would fade back to nothingness.

And occasionally there were moments when I felt that perhaps both views of the world were equally true and equally false. At such times, I felt torn as to who I truly was. I tried to tell myself that my conflicting emotions were no different from how my father felt about some of his vanquished Plainsmen foes. He had fought them, killed them, or defeated them, yet he still respected them, and in some ways regretted his role in ending their unbound existence. At least I had finally accepted that the magic was real. I had stopped trying to deny to myself that something arcane and strange had happened to me.

I'd reached my dormitory. I took the steps two at a time. Bringham House had its own small library and study area on the second floor. Most of my fellows were gathered there, heads bent over their books. I ascended the last flight of stairs, and allowed myself to pause and breathe. Rory was just coming out of our bunkroom. He grinned at me as I stood panting. "Good to see you sweating a bit, Nevare. Better drop a few pounds or you'll have to borrow Gord's old shirts."

"Funny," I gasped, and straightened. I was puffing, but having him needle me about it didn't improve my temper at all.

He pointed a finger at my belly. "You popped a button there already, my friend!"

"That happened at the doctor's office, when he was poking and prodding at me."

"Course it did!" he exclaimed with false enthusiasm. "But you'd better sew it on tonight all the same, or you'll be marching demerits off tomorrow."

"I know, I know."

"Can I borrow your drafting notes?"

"I'll get them for you."

Rory grinned his wide froggy smile. "Actually, I already have them. They're what I came upstairs to get. See you in the study room. Oh! I found a letter for you mixed in with mine. I've left it on your bunk."

"Don't smear my notes!" I warned him as he clattered off down the stairs. Shaking my head, I went into our dormitory room.

I took off my jacket and tossed it on my bunk. I picked up the envelope. I didn't recognize the handwriting, then smiled as the mystery came clear. The return address was a letter writer's shop in Burvelle's Landing, but the name on it was Sergeant Erib Duril. I opened it quickly, wondering what he could be writing to me about. Or rather, having someone else write to me about. Most reading and all writing were outside the old cavalla man's field of expertise. Sergeant Duril had come to my father when his soldiering days were over, seeking a home for his declining years. He'd become my tutor, my mentor, and toward the end of our years together, my friend. From him, I'd learned all my basic cavalla and horsemanship skills, and a great deal about being a man.

I read the curiously formal letter through twice. Obviously, the letter writer had chosen to put the old soldier's words in more elegant form than Duril himself would have chosen. It did not sound at all like him as he sympathized with my illness and expressed fond wishes that I would recover well. Only the sentiment at the end, graciously phrased as it was, sounded like advice my old mentor would have given me:

> Even after you have recovered from this dread epidemic, I fear that you will find yourself changed. I have witnessed, with my own eyes and often, what this devastating plague can do to a young man's physique. The body that you so carefully sculpted for years under my tutelage may dwindle and serve you less well than it has in the past. Nonetheless, I counsel you that it is the soul of a military man that makes

him what he is, and I have faith that your soul will
remain true to the calling of the good god.

I glanced back at the date on the envelope, and saw that
the letter had taken its time to reach me. I wondered if Duril
had held it for some days, debating as to whether or not to
send it, or if the letter writer had simply overlooked the missive and not sent it on its way. Well, soon enough I'd see
Sergeant Duril. I smiled to myself, touched that he'd taken
the time and spent the coins to send me this. I folded the
paper carefully and tucked it away among my books.

I picked up my jacket again. From the chest at the foot of
my bed, I took my sewing kit. Best to get it done now, and
then study. As I looked for the place where the button had
popped off, I discovered they all were straining, and two
others were on the point of giving way.

Scowling, I cut the buttons off both my shirt and my
jacket. I was absolutely certain that my newly gained bulk
would vanish in the next month or two as I grew taller, but
there was no sense in failing an inspection in the meantime.
As I refastened the buttons with careful stitches, I moved
each one over to allow myself a bit of breathing space. When
I put my shirt and jacket back on, I found them much more
comfortable, even though it still strained at my shoulders.
Well, that couldn't be helped. Fixing that was beyond my
limited tailoring skills. I frowned to myself; I didn't want my
clothing to fit me poorly at my brother's wedding. Carsina,
my fiancée, would be there, and she had particularly asked
me to wear my academy uniform for the occasion. Her dress
would be a matching green. I smiled to myself; girls gave
great thought to the silliest things. Well, doubtless my mother
could make any needed alterations to my uniform, if the
journey home did not lean me down as I expected it to.

After a moment's hesitation, I cut the buttons off my trouser waistband and moved them over as well. Much eased, I
took my books and headed down to the study room to join
my fellows.

The scene in Bringham House library was much different
from our old study room in Carneston Hall. There were no

long trestle tables and hard benches, but round tables with chairs and ample lighting. There were several cushioned chairs set round the fireplace for quiet conversation. I found a spot at a table next to Gord, set down my books, and took a seat. He glanced up, preoccupied, and then smiled. "A messenger came for you while you were gone. He gave me this for you."

"This" was a thick brown envelope, from my uncle's address. I opened it eagerly. As I had anticipated, it contained a receipt for my shipboard passage as far as Sorton, and a voucher written against my father's bank in Old Thares for funds for my journey. The note from my uncle said that my father had requested he make my arrangements for me, and that he hoped to see me again before I left for the wedding.

It was strange. Until I held the envelope in my hand, I had been content, even satisfied to stay at the academy. Now an encompassing wave of homesickness swept over me. I suddenly missed my whole family acutely. My heart clenched as I thought of my little sister Yaril and her constant questions, and my mother and the special plum tarts she made for me each spring. I missed all of them, my father, and Rosse, my older brother, even my older sister Elisi and her endless good advice.

But foremost in my thoughts was Carsina. Her little letters to me had grown increasingly fond and flirtatious. I longed to see her, and had already imagined several different ways in which I might steal some time alone with her. For a short time after Epiny's wedding to Spink, I had entertained doubts about Carsina and myself. My parents had chosen my fiancée. On several occasions, I'd had reason to doubt that my father always knew what was best for me. Could they truly select a woman I could live with, peacefully if not happily, the rest of my life? Or had she been chosen more for the political alliance with a neighboring new noble, with the expectation that her placid nature would give me no problems? I suddenly resolved that before I returned to the academy I would know her for myself. We would talk, and not just niceties about the weather and if she enjoyed dinner. I would discover for myself how she truly felt about being a soldier's bride, and if she had other ambitions for her life. Epiny, I thought with grim humor, had ruined women for me. Prior to meeting my eccentric and modern cousin, I had never paused to wonder what thoughts went through my sisters' heads when my father was not around to supervise them. Having experienced Epiny's sharp intelligence and acid tongue, I would no longer automatically relegate women to a passive and docile role. It was not that I hoped Carsina secretly concealed an intellect as piercing as Epiny's. In truth, I did not. But I suspected there must be more to my shy little flower than I had so far discovered. And if there was, I was resolved to know it before we were wed and promised to one another to the end of our days.

"You're a long time quiet. Bad news?" Gord asked me solemnly.

I grinned at him. "On the contrary, brother. Good news, great news! I'm starting for home tomorrow, to see my brother's wedding."

CHAPTER TWO

HOMEWARD BOUND

My departure from the academy was neither as swift nor as simple as I had hoped. When I went by the commander's office to inform him that I had my ticket and was ready to leave, he charged me to be sure I had informed each of my instructors and taken down notes of what assignments I should complete before my return. I had not reckoned on that, but had hoped for freedom from my books for a time. It took me the best part of a day to gather them up, for I dared not interrupt any classes. Then my packing was more complicated than I had planned, for I had to take my books, and yet still travel light enough that all my provisions would fit in Sirlofty's saddle panniers.

It was some months since the tall gelding had had to carry anything besides me, and he seemed a bit sulky when I loaded the panniers on him as well. In truth, I was as little pleased as he was. I was proud of my sharp uniform and fine horse; it seemed a shame to ride him through Old Thares laden as if he were a mule and I some rustic farmer taking a load of potatoes to market. I tried to stifle my annoyance at it, for I knew that half of it was vanity. I tightened my saddle cinch, signed the ancient "hold fast" charm over the buckle, and mounted my horse.

My ticket told me that my jank would sail the following evening. There was no real need of haste, yet I wanted to be well aboard and settled before the lines were cast off. I went first to my uncle's home to bid him farewell, and also to see if he had any messages for my father. He came down immediately to meet me, and invited me up to his den. He did all he could to make me feel welcome, and yet there was still some stiffness between us. He looked older than he had when first I met him, and I suspected that his wife, Daraleen, had not warmed toward him since Epiny's wild act of defiance. Epiny had left their home in the midst of the plague to hurry to Spink's side and tend him. It was a scandalous thing for a woman of her age and position to have done, and it completely destroyed all prospects of her marriage to a son of the older noble houses.

Epiny herself had been well aware of that, of course. She had deliberately ruined herself, so that her mother would have no option but to accept Spink and his family's bid for her hand. The prospect of a marriage connection with a new noble family, one with no established estates but only raw holdings on the edge of the borderlands, had filled Daraleen with both chagrin and horror. Epiny's tactic had been ruthless, one that put her fate into her own hands, but also severed the bond between mother and daughter. I had heard Epiny's artless little sister Purissa say that she was now her mother's best daughter and jewel for the future. I was certain she was only repeating words she'd heard from her mother's lips.

So when my uncle invited me to sit while he rang for a servant to bring up a light repast for us, I remained standing and said that I needed to be sure of being on time for my boat's departure. A sour smile wrinkled his mouth.

"Nevare. Do you forget that I purchased that ticket at your father's behest? You have plenty of time to make your boat's sailing. The only thing you have to worry about is stopping at the bank to cash your check and get some traveling funds. Please. Sit down."

"Thank you, sir," I said, and sat.

He rang for a servant, spoke to him briefly, and then took his own seat with a sigh. He looked at me and shook his head. "You act as if we are angry with each other. Or as if I should be angry with you."

I looked down before his gaze. "You'd have every right to be, sir. I'm the one who brought Spink here. If I hadn't introduced him to Epiny, none of this would ever have happened."

He gave a brief snort of laughter. "No. Doubtless something else, equally awkward, would have happened instead. Nevare, you forget that Epiny is my daughter. I've known her all her life, and even if I didn't quite realize all she was capable of, I nevertheless knew that she had an inquiring mind, an indomitable spirit, and the will to carry out any plan she conceived. Her mother might hold you accountable, but then, Epiny's mother is fond of holding people accountable for things beyond their control. I try not to do that."

He sounded tired and sad, and despite my guilt, or perhaps because of it, my heart went out to him. He had treated me well, almost as if I were his own son. Despite my father's elevation to noble status, he and his elder brother had remained close. I knew that was not true of many families, where old noble heir sons regarded their "battle lord" younger brothers as rivals. Spink's "old noble" relatives had no contact with him, and had turned a blind eye to the needs of his widowed mother. Certainly a great deal of my aunt's distaste for me was that she perceived my father as an upstart, a new noble who should have remained a simple military officer. Many of the old nobility felt that King Troven had elevated his battle lords as a political tactic, so that he might seed the Council of Lords with recently elevated aristocrats who had a higher degree of loyalty to him and greater sympathy for his drive to expand Gernia to the east by military conquest. Possibly they were right. I settled back in my chair and tried to smile at my uncle. "I still feel responsible," I said quietly.

"Yes, well, you are the sort of man who would. Let it go, Nevare. If I recall correctly, you did not first invite Spink to my home. Epiny did, when she saw him standing beside you at the academy that day we came to pick you up. Who knows? Perhaps that was the instant in which she decided to marry him. I would not put it beyond her. And now, since we are discussing her and Spinrek, would you tell me if you've heard anything from your friend? I long to know how my wayward daughter fares."

"She has not written to you?" I asked, shocked.

"Not a word," he said sadly. "I thought we had parted on, well, if not on good terms, at least with the understanding that I still loved her, even if I could not agree with all her decisions. But since the day she departed from my doorstep, I've heard nothing, from her or Spinrek." His voice was steady and calm as he spoke, but the hollowness he felt came through all the same. I felt an instant spurt of anger toward Epiny. Why was she treating her father so coldly?

"I have received letters not just from Spink, but also from Epiny. I will be happy to share them with you, sir. I have them with me, among my books and other papers in Sirlofty's pack."

Hope lit in his eyes, but he said, "Nevare, I couldn't ask you to betray any confidences Epiny has made to you. If you would just tell me that she is well . . ."

"Nonsense!" Then I remembered to whom I spoke. "Uncle Sefert, Epiny has written me pages and pages, a veritable journal since the day she left your door. I have read nothing there that I'd hesitate to tell you, so why should you not read her words for yourself? Let me fetch them. It will only take a moment."

I saw him hesitate, but he could not resist, and at his nod I hastened down the stairs. I took the packet of letters from Sirlofty's panniers and hurried back up with them. By then, a tempting luncheon had been set out for us in the den. I ate most of it in near silence, for my uncle could not resist his impulse to begin immediately on Epiny's letters. It was like watching a plant revived by a rainfall after a drought to watch him first smile and then chuckle over her descriptions of her adventures. As he carefully folded the last page of the most recent missive, he looked up at me. "I think she is finding life as a frontier wife rather different from what she supposed it to be."

"I cannot imagine a greater change in living conditions than leaving your family home here in Old Thares for a poor cottage in Bitter Springs."

He replied with grim satisfaction in his voice, "And yet she does not complain. She does not threaten to run back home to me, nor does she whimper that she deserves better. She accepts the future that she made for herself. I am proud of her for that. Her life, indeed, is not what I would have chosen for her. I would never have believed that my flighty, childish daughter would have the strength to confront such things. And yet she has, and she flourishes."

I myself thought that "flourish" was far too strong a word to apply to what Epiny was doing, but I held my tongue. Uncle Sefert loved his unruly daughter. If he took pride in her ability to deal with harsh conditions, I would not take that from him.

I was willing to leave Epiny's letters with him, but he insisted I take them back. Privately, I resolved to rebuke her for making her father suffer so; what had he done to deserve such treatment? He'd given her far more freedom than most girls of her age enjoyed, and she'd used it to arrange a marriage to her own liking. Even after she had publicly disgraced herself by fleeing his house and going to Spink's sickbed, my uncle had not disowned her, but had given her a modest wedding and a nice sendoff. What more did she expect of the man?

As I bade my uncle farewell, he gave me a letter to my father and some small gifts for my mother and sisters, and I managed to find room for them in my panniers. I made a brief stop at my father's banker in Old Thares to change my check into banknotes, and then went immediately down to the docks. My ship was already loading, and I was glad I had arrived with some time to spare, for Sirlofty received the last decent box stall onboard the vessel. My own cabin, though very small, was comfortable and I was glad to settle into it.

My upriver passage on the jankship was not nearly as exciting as our flight downriver had been the previous fall. The current was against us, and though it was not yet in full spring flood, it was still formidable. The vessel used not only oarsmen, but also a method of propulsion called cordelling, in which a small boat rowed upstream with a line threaded through a bridle and made fast to the mast. Once the small boat had tied the free end of the line to a fixed object such as a large tree, the line was reeled in on a capstan on the jankship. While we were reeling in the first line, a second towline was already being set in place, and in this way, we moved upriver between six and fifteen miles a day. An upstream journey on one of the big passenger janks was more stately than swift, and more like spending time at an elegant resort than simple travel.

Perhaps my father had intended that part of the journey to be a treat for me, and an opportunity to mingle socially. Instead, I chafed and wondered if I would not have made better time on Sirlofty's back. Although the jankship offered all sorts of amusements and edification, from games of chance to poetry readings, I did not enjoy it as I had the first time I'd taken ship with my father. The people onboard the vessel seemed less congenial than the passengers my father and I had met on our previous journey. The young ladies were especially haughty, their superciliousness bordering on plain rudeness. Once, thinking only to be a gentleman, I bent down to retrieve a pen that had fallen from one young lady's table by her deck chair. As I did so, one of my ill-sewn buttons popped from my jacket and went rolling off across the deck. She and her friend burst out laughing at me, the one pointing rudely at my rolling button while the other all but stuffed her handkerchief in her mouth to try to conceal her merriment. She did not even thank me for the pen that I handed back to her, but continued to giggle and indeed to snort as I left her side and went in pursuit of my wayward button. Once I had reclaimed it, I turned back to them, thinking that they might wish to be more social, but as I approached them they hastily rose, gathered all their items, and swept away in a flurry of skirts and fans.

Later that day, I heard giggling behind me. A female voice said, "Never have I seen so rotund a cadet!" and a male voice replied, "Hush! Can't you tell he's with child! Don't mock a future mother!" I turned and looked up to find the two ladies and a couple of young men standing on an upper deck and looking down at me. They immediately looked away, but one fellow was unable to control the great "haw" of laughter that burst from him. I felt the blood rush to my face, for I was both infuriated and embarrassed that my weight was a cause of so much amusement.

I went immediately back to my stateroom, and attempted to survey myself in the tiny mirror there. It was inadequate to the task, as I could only see about one eighth of myself at a time. I decided that they had been amused by how tight my uniform jacket had become on me. Truly, it had grown snug, and every time I donned it after that, I feared that I cut a comical figure in it. It quite spoiled the rest of the voyage for me, for whenever I attended one of the musical events or cultural lectures, I felt sure that the ladies were somewhere in the audience, staring at me. I did catch glimpses of them, from time to time, often with the same young gentlemen. They all seemed comfortable staring at me while avoiding my company. My annoyance with them grew daily, as did my self-consciousness.

Matters came to a head one evening when I was descending the stairs from one deck to the next. The stairs were spiraled to save space, and quite tightly engineered. My height as well as my new weight made them a bit tricky for me. I had discovered that as long as I kept my elbows in and trusted my feet to find their footing without attempting to look down, I could navigate them smoothly. Even for a slender passenger, the stairs did not allow users to pass one another. Thus, as I descended, a small group of my fellows were waiting at the bottom of the steps for me to clear the way for them.

They did not trouble to lower their voices. "Beware below!" one fellow declared loudly as I trod the risers. I recognized his voice as the same one that had declared me pregnant. My blood began to boil.

I heard a woman's shrill and nervous giggle, followed by another male voice adding, "Ye gads, what is it? It's blocking the sun! Does it wedge? No sir, it does not! Stand clear, stand clear." I recognized that he was imitating the stentorian tones of the sailor who took the depth readings with a lead line and shouted them back to the captain.

"Barry! Stop it!" A girl hissed at him, but the suppressed merriment in her voice was encouragement, not condemnation.

"Oh, the suspense! Will he make it or will he run aground?" the young man queried enthusiastically.

I emerged at that point from the stairwell. My cheeks were red but not with exertion. There I encountered the familiar foursome, in evening dress. One girl, still giggling, rushed past me and up the steps, her little slippers tapping hastily up the stairs and the skirts of her yellow gown brushing the sides of the stair as she went. Her tall male companion moved to follow her. I stepped in front of him. "Were you mocking me?" I asked him in a level, amiable voice. I cannot say where my control came from, for inside, I was seething. Anger bubbled through my blood.

"Let me pass!" he said angrily, with no effort at replying.

When I did not answer him or move, he attempted to push by me. I stood firm, and for once my extra weight was on my side.

"It was just a bit of a joke, man. Don't be so serious. Allow us passage, please." This came from the other fellow, a slight young man with foppishly curled hair. The girl with him had retreated behind him, one little gloved arm set on his shoulder, as if I were some sort of unpredictable animal that might attack them.

"Get out of my way," the first one said again. He spoke the words through gritted teeth, furious now.

I kept my voice level with an effort. "Sir, I do not enjoy your mockery of me. The next time I receive an ill glance from you or hear you ridicule me, I shall demand satisfaction of you."

He snorted disparagingly. "A threat! From you!" He ran his eyes over me insultingly. His sneering smile dismissed me.

The blood was pounding in my ears. Yet, strangely, I suddenly felt that I was in full control of this encounter. I cannot explain how pleasing that sensation was; it was rather like holding an excellent hand of cards when everyone else at the table assumes you are bluffing. I smiled at him. "You'd be wise to be thankful for this warning from me. The opportunity will not come again." I'd never felt so dangerous in my life.

He seemed to sense how I dismissed his bluster. His face flushed an ugly scarlet. "Make way!" he demanded through gritted teeth.

"Of course," I acceded. I not only stepped back, but also offered him my hand as if to assist him. "Be careful!" I warned him. "The stairs are steeper than they appear. Watch your footing. It would be a shame if you stumbled."

"Do not speak to me!" he all but shouted. He tried to cuff my hand out of the way. Instead, I caught his elbow, gripped it firmly, and assisted him up the first step. I felt the iron of my strength as I did so; I think he did, too. "Let go!" he snarled at me.

"So glad to help you," I replied sweetly as I released him. I stepped back two steps, and then gestured to his companions that they should follow him. The girl rushed past me and up the steps, with her companion a stride behind her. He shot me a look of alarm as he passed, as if he thought I might suddenly attack him.

I was walking away when I heard a shout above me, and then a man's roar of pain. One of them must have slipped in his panic. The woman mewed sympathetically at whichever man had fallen. I could not make out his words, for they were choked with pain. I chuckled as I walked away. I was to dine at the captain's table that evening, and I suddenly found that I anticipated the meal with a heartier than usual appetite.

The next morning, as I enjoyed a good breakfast, I overhead gossip at our table that a young man had slipped and fallen on the stairs. "A very bad break," an old woman with a flowered fan exclaimed to the lady beside her. "The bone poked right out of his flesh! Can you imagine! Just from a missed step on the stair!"

I felt unreasonably guilty when I heard the extent of the young man's injuries, then decided that he had brought them on himself. Doubtless he'd missed a riser; if he hadn't mocked me, he would not have felt obliged to use such haste in fleeing from me.

When next I caught sight of their small party in the late afternoon, the young man I had "assisted" on the stairs was absent. When one of the women saw me, I saw her give a gasp of dismay and immediately turn and walk off in the other direction. Her friend and their remaining male companion followed her just as hastily. For the rest of the voyage they assiduously avoided me, and I overheard no more remarks or giggling. Yet it was not the relief that I had hoped it would be. Instead, a tiny niggle of guilt remained with me, as if my bad wishes for the fellow had caused his fall. I did not enjoy the women being fearful of me any more than I had enjoyed their derision. Both things seemed to make me someone other than who I truly was.

I was almost relieved when our jank reached the docks at Sorton and I disembarked. Sirlofty was restive after his days belowdecks, and displeased at once more having to wear his panniers. As I led him down the ramp to the street, I was glad to be on solid land again and dependent on no one but myself. I wended my way deeper into the crowded streets and out of sight of the jankship.

Along with my ticket and traveling money, there had been a letter from my father that precisely detailed how my journey should proceed. He had measured my journey against his cavalla maps, and had decided where I should stay every night and how much distance I must cover each day in order to arrive in time for Rosse's wedding. His meticulous itinerary directed me to spend the night in Sorton, but I abruptly decided that I would push on and perhaps gain some time. That was a poor decision, for when night fell, I was still on the road, hours short of the small town my father had decreed was my next stop. In this settled country of farms and smallholdings, I could not simply camp beside the road as I would have in the Midlands. Instead, when the night became too dark for traveling, I begged a night's lodging at a farmhouse. The farmer seemed a kindly man, and would not hear of me sleeping in the barn near Sirlofty, but offered me space on the kitchen floor near the fire.

I offered to pay for a meal as well, so he rousted out a kitchen girl. I expected to get the cold leavings of whatever they'd had earlier, but she chatted to me merrily as she heated up a nice slice of mutton in some broth. She warmed some tubers with it, and set it out for me with bread and butter and a large mug of buttermilk. When I thanked her, she said, "It's a pleasure to cook for a man who obviously enjoys his food. It shows a man has a hearty appetite for all of life's pleasures."

I did not take her words as a criticism, for she herself was a buxom girl with very generous hips. "A good meal and a pleasant companion can stir any man's appetite," I told her. She dimpled a smile at me, seeming to take that as flirtation. Boldly, she sat down at the table while I ate, and told me I was very wise to have stopped there for the night, for there had been rumors of highwaymen of late. It seemed plain to me that she had gone far beyond her master's orders, and after I watched her clear up my dishes, I offered her a small silver piece with my thanks for her kindness. She smilingly brought me two blankets and swept the area in front of the hearth before she made up my bed for me.

I was startled into full wakefulness about an hour after I had drowsed off when I felt someone lift the corner of my blanket and slide in beside me. I am shamed to say that I thought first of my purse with my traveling money in it, and I gripped it with my hand beneath my shirt. She paid no mind to that but nudged up against me, sweet as a kitten seeking warmth. I was quickly aware that she wore only a very thin nightdress.

"What is it?" I demanded of her, rather stupidly.

She giggled softly. "Why, sir, I don't know. Let me feel it and see if I can tell you!" And with no more than that, she slipped her hand down between us, and when she found that she had already roused me, gripped me firmly.

I was no more prudish than any young man of my years. If I had been chaste before, it had been more from lack of opportunity than any inclination to virtue. I'll admit that I gave a passing thought to disease, for the academy had lectured us more than once on the danger of coupling with cheap street whores. But I very swiftly and easily persuaded myself that this girl in such an outlying farmstead had probably not known many men and thus had little chance of disease.

There followed a night I have never forgotten and seldom regretted. I was fumbling at first, but then that "other self" seemed to awaken inside me, and I discovered that he was not only experienced but skillful at bed games. I knew when to tease with a tickling touch, and when my mouth should be hard and demanding. She shivered under me, and the small moans that escaped her were music to me. I did experience some awkwardness, for although the rounded contours of her body seemed like familiar territory to me, I was not accustomed to dealing with the bulk of my own belly. Ruefully, I had to admit to myself that my weight gain was more than a trifling matter, but I refused to let it become an obstacle for us. Toward dawn, we parted with many kisses. I fell into the sleep of exhaustion, and morning came much too early for me.

If I had been able to think of any excuse, I would have fabricated a reason to spend another night. As it was, the same kitchen maid offered me a huge breakfast and a very fond farewell. I did not wish to embarrass her by treating her as if she were an ordinary whore, but I did slip some money under my plate where she would find it when she cleared away the dishes. I bade the farmer and his wife farewell, and thanked them earnestly for their kind hospitality. The farmer repeated the kitchen maid's warning about highwaymen. I promised him I'd be wary and saddled up Sirlofty and went on my way with an entirely different opinion of myself than I'd had the day before. As I made the "hold fast" sign over my cinch buckle, I suddenly felt myself an adventurous traveler experiencing life on my own for the first time. It was exhilarating, and a welcome change from the self-consciousness I'd felt on the jankship.

The day passed quickly. I paid small attention to the road or scenery, but instead pondered every moment of the night before. I confess that I derived as much pleasure from imagining telling Rory and the fellows about my dallying with the farm maid as I did from recalling it. In early afternoon, I reached the town that my father had listed as the next stop on my itinerary. Despite the hours of daylight left, I decided I would overnight there, not only because I'd had two warnings of highwaymen but also because I'd had no sleep the night before. I found a likely inn and bought myself a meal, then retired to my small room and slept until early evening. I occupied myself for a time with updating my journal, but when that was completed, I still felt restless. I longed for an adventure such as I'd had the night before.

I went downstairs, hoping for some company, music, and lively conversation. Instead I found only a few fellows swilling cheap ale and a grumpy innkeeper who obviously wished his customers would either spend more money or take themselves elsewhere. I was half hoping that some girl of easy virtue would be wiping the tables, as there always was in poor Caleb's lurid papers, but there was not a female anywhere in sight. When I went out for a stroll about the little town, I found the streets deserted. I told myself it was probably just as well, and returned to my inn. After three beers, I went back to my bed, and fell asleep.

My next few days of traveling passed without incident. My father had very accurately judged the distance Sirlofty could cover in a day. One night I took lodging at a hostelry with several obvious whores ensconced in the taproom. I plucked up my courage to approach the youngest, a slight woman with a halo of yellow curls around her face. She was wearing a pink gown trimmed with plumes all around its low collar. Thinking to be clever, I opened my conversation by asking her if the feathers tickled.

She looked me up and down, and then said bluntly, "Two silver bits. Your room."

I was taken aback. In all the stories I'd heard from Trist or read in Caleb's magazines, whores were flirtatious and flattering. I had expected at least some conversation. "Right now?" I asked stupidly, and she immediately stood up.

There was little I could do then but lead the way up to my

room. She demanded my silver in advance, tucking it down the front of her dress. I was unbuttoning my trousers when she took me firmly by the upper arms and backed me toward the bed, pushing me onto my back. I was not averse to this, even when she said, "Don't think I plan on being on the bottom side of you. A heavy bloke like you could break a girl's ribs!"

With that, she bundled her skirts up around her hips to reveal her nakedness and straddled me as if I were a horse and very quickly finished me. Afterward, she lifted herself from my body, and shook her skirts out as she stood by the bed. I sat up on the bed with my trousers around my ankles. She walked to the door.

"Where are you going?" I asked in confusion.

She gave me a puzzled look. "Back to work. Unless you've another two silvers to spend?"

I hesitated, and she took it as a "no." Sneering slightly, she said, "I thought not. Fat men are usually tightfisted with their money." Without another word, she let herself out. I stared after her in shock, numbed and insulted by her words. As I fell back onto my bed, I suddenly realized I'd just learned the difference between a very friendly kitchen maid and a real whore. Remorse and trepidation closed in on me, and I decided I could use a good washing. Before I fell asleep that night, I resolved to stay away from common prostitutes. Sternly I reminded myself that I was as good as engaged, and had a duty to keep my body free of disease for Carsina's sake. Nonetheless, I was glad to have finally gained some experience in that essential area.

The farther east I traveled each day, the less settled the land became. On the last leg of my journey, I entered the true Midlands, and followed the King's Road as it somewhat paralleled the river. The quality of the new high road varied greatly from stretch to stretch. There were supposed to be way stations at regular intervals, to offer clean water, a resting place, and food to the king's messengers. Some of these were small hamlets, but most were meager places of doubtful shelter with little to offer an ordinary traveler. The worst was little more than a hut swayed to one side with a roof that threatened to collapse at any moment. I learned to be sure my water bags were full and that I had provisions for a noon meal before I departed from my lodging each morning.

Once I passed a long coffle of prisoners and guards headed east. Rather than being flogged or losing a hand for their crimes, these men would become forced labor pushing the King's Road ever closer to the Barrier Mountains. After a term of work, they'd be given land and an opportunity to begin life anew. Thus, in one stroke, the king offered the felons a second chance, advanced his road building, and peopled the new settlements of the east. Nonetheless, the shackled men I passed did not look as if they were anticipating a new life, while the wives and children riding behind the coffle in mule-drawn wagons looked even more dismal. Dust coated their faces and clothing, and several babies were wailing as Sirlofty and I cantered past them. I will never forget one small boy who sat near the tail of the wagon, his little head jogging miserably with every jolt of the wheels. I thought to myself at the sight of his dull eyes, "That child is near death." Then I shuddered, wondered how I could even imagine I knew such a thing, and rode past them.

My cavalla cadet uniform, I am sorry to say, suffered from constant wear. The buttons strained on my chest and the seams at the shoulders and thighs threatened to give way. Finally I bundled it up as best I could and packed it away in my crowded panniers. After that, I wore my ordinary clothes, which were actually much looser and more comfortable for such a journey. I had to admit that I'd put on flesh, and more than I thought I had. I was hungry as I rode, for such exercise consumes a man, and yet I was grateful for the short rations I was on. Surely I'd be my lean and fit self again by the time I reached home.

CHAPTER THREE

SPINDLE DANCE

The deeper I went into the Midlands, the more familiar the land became to me. I knew the prairies and plateaus, the green smell of the river in the morning, and the cry of the sage hens. I knew the name of every plant and bird. Even the dust tasted familiar in my mouth. Sirlofty seemed to sense that we were nearing home, for he went more eagerly.

One midmorning, I reined in Sirlofty and considered an unexpected choice. A crudely lettered sign on a raw plank leaned against a pile of stacked stone by the side of the road. "SPINDLE DANCE" was spelled out on the coarse slab. The roughly drawn characters were the work of a hand that copied shapes rather than wrote letters. A rough cart track led away from the well-traveled river road. It crested a slight rise; its hidden destination was beyond that horizon.

I debated with myself. It was a diversion from my father's carefully planned itinerary, and I did not know how long a detour it might prove. Yet I recalled a promise from my father to show me someday the monuments of the Plainspeople. The Dancing Spindle was one of them. I suddenly felt it was owed to me. I set the rein against Sirlofty's neck and we turned aside from the road.

The trail was not badly rutted, but enough traffic had passed this way that it was easy to follow. When I reached the top of the ridge, I found myself looking down into a pleasant little vale. Trees at the bottom indicated a watercourse. The cart track sidled down to the trees and then vanished into them.

Smelling water, Sirlofty quickened his pace and I allowed him his head. When we reached the brook, I allowed him to water freely, and knelt to quench my own thirst. Refreshed, I remounted and rode on. The cart track followed the brook for a short way and then crossed it. I resolutely pushed aside worry over how much time I was wasting. An inexplicable excitement was building in me; I felt compelled to follow the trail.

We followed the track as it climbed up out of the valley, over a rocky ridge and onto a rather barren plateau. A short distance away, the plateau gave way abruptly to a substantial canyon, as if some angry god had riven the earth here with an immense ax. The trail plunged down sharply to the distant floor. I reined in Sirlofty and sat looking down at a strange and marvelous sight.

The cracked earth of the canyon walls displayed seams of colored stone, sparkling white and deep orange and red, and even a dusky blue. A roofless city, the walls worn to knee-high ridges and tumbled rubble, floored the canyon. I wondered what war or long-ago disaster had brought the city down. Dominating the canyon and dwarfing the city at its base was the Dancing Spindle of the Plainsmen. No tale could have prepared me for the sight. The immense pillar leaned at a sharp, impossible angle. I shivered at the sight.

The Spindle was named for the woman's spinning tool, and in truth it resembled a rounded rod with tapered ends, but of such a size that it beggared comparison. It had been chiseled out of red stone striated with bands of white. One end towered high above the canyon floor while the other was set in a deep depression in the earth, as if it drilled a bed for itself in the stony ground. The spiraling white stripes on the pillar and a heat shimmer rising between me and it created a convincing illusion that the Spindle was truly spinning.

The monument cast a long, black shadow over the ground at its base. The lone building that had survived whatever had slain the rest of the city was a tower edged with winding steps that spiraled up to almost reach the lower side of the tilted spindle's topmost tip. For the life of me, I could not see why the Spindle had not toppled ages ago. I sat on my horse grinning and enjoying the deception of my eyes. At any moment I expected the spinning Spindle to waver in its gyration and fall to the earth, spent.

But it did not. As I started down the steep wagon track that led to the canyon floor, I was surprised at how well the illusion held. I was so intent in staring at it that I almost didn't notice the ramshackle hut built in the spindle's shadow. It hunched on the edge of the depression that cradled the tip of the spindle. The surrounding ruins were of stone and clay, but the dilapidated cottage was more recently built of slabs of rough wood, gone silver with weathering. It looked abandoned. I was startled when a man emerged from the open door, wiping his mouth on a napkin as if my arrival had interrupted his meal.

As I rode closer, he turned and tossed the cloth to a Plainswoman who had followed him out to stare at me. She caught it deftly, and at a sign from her master, the servant returned to the hut's dubious shelter. But the man came toward me, waving a large hand in an overly friendly way. When I was still a good way off, he bellowed at me, "So you've come to see the Spindle?"

It seemed a ridiculous question. Why else would anyone have followed the track here? I didn't respond, for I did not feel like shouting a reply to him. Instead, I rode steadily forward. He was not deterred.

"It's a wonder of primitive design. For only one hector,

sir, I will show it to you and tell you its amazing history! From far and wide, from near and far, hundreds have come to behold its wonder. And today you shall join the ranks of those who can say, 'I myself have seen the Dancing Spindle and climbed the steps of the Spindle's Tower.'"

He sounded like a barker outside a carnival tent. Sirlofty regarded him with suspicion. When I pulled in my horse, the man stood grinning up at me. His clothes, though clean, were shabby. His loose trousers were patched at the knees, and scuffed sandals were on his large dusty feet. He wore his shirt outside his trousers, belted with a brightly woven sash. His features and language were Gernian, but his garments, stance, and jewelry were those of a Plainsman. A half-breed, then. I felt both pity and disgust for him, but by far the largest measure of what I felt was annoyance. The sheer size and unlikeliness of the Spindle moved me to awe. It was majestic and unique, and I could not deny the soaring of spirit that it woke in me. I wanted to contemplate it in peace without his jabbering to distract me.

I thought the man a fool when he reached for Sirlofty's headstall to hold my horse while I dismounted. Didn't he recognize a cavalla steed when he saw one? Sirlofty, long schooled against such a tactic, reared and wheeled in one smooth motion. As he came down, he plunged half a dozen steps forward to be clear of the "enemy." I pulled him in quickly before he could launch a savage kick at the man. Dismounting, I dropped his reins and he stood in obedient stillness. I looked back at the half-breed, expecting him to be shaken by the experience.

Instead, he was grinning obsequiously. He shrugged his shoulders and lifted his hands in an exaggerated gesture of astonishment. "Ah, such a mount, such a proud creature! I am full of envy at your fortune in possessing him."

"Thank you," I replied stiffly. The man made me uneasy, and I wished to be away from him. His Gernian features contrasted with his Plainsman mannerisms. His choice of words and vocabulary were those of an educated man, the guttural notes of a Plains accent almost completely suppressed, and yet he stood before me in his worn sandals, his clothes little better than rags, while his Plains wife peered out at both of us from the shadowed doorway of their hovel. The contrast made me uncomfortable. He drew closer to me, and launched into a rehearsed monologue.

"No doubt you have heard of the fabled Dancing Spindle, the most enigmatic of the five great monuments of the Midlands! And at last you have come to behold for yourself this marvel of ancient stonework. How, you must wonder, did the forerunners of the Plainspeople, with their simple tools, create such a wonder? How does it balance and never fall? How does it create an illusion of motion when seen from a distance? And what, I am sure you ask yourself, did such an amazing creation signify to those who wrought it?

"Well, you are not alone in asking these questions, sir! Learned scholars and philosophers and engineers have all, in their turns, ruminated upon these mysteries. From as far as Skay and Burry they have come, and I who share the heritage of both the Plains and Gernia have been pleased to assist them, just as I will gladly enlighten you, for the modest sum of one hector!"

His glib pitch reminded of the singsong cant of the freak show barkers on Dark Evening in Old Thares. The memory of that evening and all that followed flooded through me. I pushed aside his pleading palm with the back of my hand and stepped away from him. He flinched at my touch, although I was not rough.

"I've come to see a rock formation that was doubtless mostly carved by the forces of nature, and only embellished by your people. I do not need to pay you to see what is right before my eyes! Please stay out of my way."

For an instant, his eyes narrowed and I thought he would snarl at me. Then his eyes widened, and to my surprise, he mimed another of his elaborate shrugs. He gestured toward the towering stone, making a small bow as he did so. "Do as you will, sir," he said. Then he bowed again and backed away from me. I stared after him, puzzled, for I had detected no sarcasm or rudeness in his words.

But as he turned away from me, I lifted my eyes and perceived the real reason for his sudden loss of interest. Creaking down the steep trail was a team and wagon. The open wagon had been decked out as if for a holiday outing. A sunshade of bright yellow was suspended over its passengers. A banner painted on the side of the wagon proclaimed, "SEE THE WONDROUS SPINDLE!" Within, a dozen passengers of all ages sat on cushioned benches, the ladies holding parasols against the spring sunshine. As my erstwhile guide hastened toward them, I saw my error. I had stumbled into his commercial endeavor unawares. Now that his true prey had arrived, he was forsaking me for a richer prize. That was as well with me. I turned my back on the tourists' arrival and set my attention on the Spindle.

It was taller than the tallest building I'd ever seen, and far more massive. My eyes traveled to the towering tip, and then down the rod. It appeared to dwindle to a single sharp point touching the ground. I walked to the edge of the depression that cupped it and looked down. The sides of the bowl sloped steeply down, and the narrow point of the Spindle was lost in deep shadow, like a giant pen plunged into an inkwell. The whole structure leaned at a sharp angle, not touching the sides of the well, apparently supported by a small joining hidden within the well. That ran counter to my engineer's instincts. How could such a small anchorage of rock support that weight? Even at this closer perspective, it still maintained its illusion of motion.

For a time I stood there, my neck craned, staring down at the Spindle's tip in the deeply shadowed bowl. What had seemed when viewed from a distance a fine point in proportion to the gargantuan spindle was in fact a substantial girth of stone. Where it disappeared from sight in the depths of the hole it had seemingly drilled in the earth, the cylinder's girth was still as wide as a watchtower's base. It must have been still. If it hadn't been still, the grinding of the stone tip against the depths would have been deafening, as if a giant mortar and pestle were at work. But my gullible eyes still insisted that the Spindle spun. I shook my head to clear it of the optical illusion and tried to focus my mind on the real puzzle: What kept it in place? Given its mass and how it leaned, why hadn't it fallen ages ago?

I had been certain that a closer view would reveal the trick of it. But now, standing as close to the base as I could get without tumbling into its well, I was as puzzled as ever. A lone tower edged with winding steps spiraled up to almost reach the lower side of the tilted spindle's topmost tip. I resolved that I would hike to the standing tower and climb the stairs. It looked as if the tower came so close to the Spindle's tip that I could actually put my hands on it, to prove to myself that it could not be rotating. All thoughts of keeping this side trip to a brief detour had vanished from my mind. I would satisfy my curiosity at all costs. I lifted my eyes to pick out the best route over the broken land and immediately saw a faint footpath across the stony earth. Obviously, I was not the first gawker to have such an ambition. Confident that Sirlofty could mind himself, I left him standing and followed the track.

When my path led me directly beneath the spindle and through its shadow, I went with trepidation. At the heart of the shadow, the day seemed to dim. I could swear I felt a distant chill wind, manufactured of the Spindle's turning, brush my cheek. I felt in my chest rather than heard the deep rumbling of the Spindle's eternal motion. The ghost wind seemed to slide a hand across the top of my head, stirring an uncomfortable memory of how the Tree Woman had caressed me. I was glad to step out of that shadow and away from those strange fancies, even though the day now seemed brighter and the sun too hot on my skull.

My path was not straight, but wandered through the broken walls and sunken roads of the fallen city that intersected my route. The stubs of the walls gave witness to the half-breed guide's claim that the Spindle was a manmade wonder, for some were built of the same reddish stone as the spindle and still bore odd patterns, an alteration of checkering and spirals, at once foreign and familiar. I walked more slowly, and began to see the suggestions of sly faces eroding from leaning slabs of wall. Hollow mouths fanged with now dulled teeth, carved hands reduced by time to blunt paws, and voluptuous women whittled by the wind to become sexless boys teased my eyes.

I climbed up on one corner of wall and looked around me from that vantage point. I could almost make sense of the tumbled walls and collapsed roofs. I jumped down and once more began to thread my way though . . . what? A temple town? A village? A graveyard of ancient tombs? Whatever it was, it had fallen, leaving the spindle and its tower to lord it over the time-gnawed remains. How could a folk with tools of stone, bone, and bronze have shaped such a vast creation? I even considered giving the guide a hector on my return, to see if he had a believable answer to the question.

When I reached the base of the tower, I discovered two things. The first was that it was in much poorer condition than it had seemed from the distance. The second was that it was not a proper building at all. It consisted only of a spiraling stair that wound up and around a solid inner core. I could not enter the tower at all; I could only ascend to its peak by the outer stair. A crude barrier of ropes and poles had been thrown up in front of the tower's first step, as if to warn people off. I paid no heed to it. The lips of the stairs were rounded. The center of each step dipped, tribute to the passage of both feet and years. The walls of the stair's core had once been tiled with mosaics. Glimpses of them remained: an eye and a pair of leering lips, a paw with claws outstretched, the fat-cheeked face of a little child with eyes closed in bliss. Round and round I climbed, ever ascending. I felt a giddy familiarity yet could recall no similar experience in my life. Here, in the mosaic, the head of a red and black croaker bird gaped its beak open wide. There a tree, arms reaching up to the sun with its face turned to its rays. I had passed it by a dozen steps before it came to me that a tree should have neither arms nor a face. There was graffiti, too, the ever-present proclamation that someone had been here, or that someone loved someone forever. Some of it was old but most of it was fresh.

I expected to grow weary with the climb. The day was warm, the sun determined, and I was carrying more flesh than I'd ever had in my life. Yet there was something exhilarating about being up so high with nothing between me and a sheer drop to the rocky ground below the spire. With every step I took, the music of the spinning Spindle grew louder; I could feel the vibration in my bones. I felt the wind of its passage on my face. There was even a peculiar scent that I knew was generated by the stone's movement, a warm smell, delicious, like singed spices. I stopped watching the stairs and looked up to the Spindle. I could see the striated stone core. It, perhaps, was still. But there was a hazy layer of air or mist that surrounded the Spindle, and it spun. I cannot explain the fascination and delight that this woke in me.

The top of the tower culminated in a platform the size of a small room. A low stone wall edged it, but on one side a crack had corrupted it and the stone had eroded away to an uneven mound only about the height of my knee. I walked to the center of the platform and then stood, looking straight up at the tip of the Spindle above me. I am a tall man, but its stony heart was still out of my reach. It puzzled me. Why had they built this spire, to bring someone so close to the wondrous monument and still have it be out of reach? It made no sense. The wind of the spinning stuff's passage was warm on my face and redolent with spice.

I took a moment and stared out at the view. The ruined city was cupped in the canyon. The sightseers had disembarked from the wagon and stood in a respectful mob around the half-breed. I knew he was speaking to them, but not a sound reached my ears save the soft hum of the turning Spindle. I gazed up at it. I suddenly knew I had come here for a reason. I reached a slow hand up over my head.

Suddenly, a voice spoke nearby.

"Don't touch it."

I jumped and looked to see who had spoken. It was the Plainswoman from the guide's hut, or someone very like her. She must have followed me up the steps. I scowled. I wanted no company. My hand still wavered above my head.

"Why not?" I asked her.

She came a step closer to me, cocked her head slightly, and looked at me as if she had thought I was someone she knew. She smiled as she said jestingly, "The old people say it's dangerous to touch the Spindle. You'll be caught in the twine and carried—"

My fingers brushed the spinning stuff. It was mist, said

my fingers; but then the gritty stone surface swept against my hand. I was snatched out of my skin and borne aloft.

I have watched women spinning. I had seen the hanks of wool caught and drawn out into a fine thread on a spinning wheel. That was what happened to me. I did not keep my man's shape. Instead, something was pulled out of me, some spirit or essence, and was drawn as fine as yarn and wrapped around the immense Spindle. It twisted me as it pulled me into a taut line. Thin as string I was, and I spiraled around it like thread. My awareness was immersed in the magic of the Spindle. And in that immersion, I awoke to my other self.

He knew the purpose of the Spindle. It pulled the widely scattered threads of magic out of the world and gathered them into yarn. The spindle concentrated the magic. And he knew the spire's purpose. It gave access to the gathered magic. From here, a Plainsman of power, a stone mage, would work wonders. This spinning spindle was the heart of Plains magic. I'd found it. This was the well that not only the Kidona but all the Plainspeople drew from. The suppressed other self inside me suddenly surged to the fore. I felt him seize the magic and glory in the richness of it. Some he took into himself, but there was only so much this body could hold. As for the rest, well, now that he knew the source, no Plainsman would ever unleash this magic against the Specks of the mountains again. I'd see to that. All their harvested magic was at the tips of my fingers. I laughed aloud, triumphant. I would destroy—

I strained, striving to grip what I could not see. It was too strong. I was abruptly flung back into my body with a jolt as shocking as if I'd been flung to my back on paving stones.

". . . to the edges of complete power. It is not a journey for the unprepared." The Plainswoman finished her sentence. She was smiling, sharing a silly old superstition with me.

I swayed and then folded onto my knees. I saved some of my dignity by collapsing back onto my heels rather than falling on my face. My hands, I saw, rested on faded patterns carved into the stone. She frowned at me and then asked, more in alarm than concern, "Are you ill?"

"I don't think so," I replied. I took a deep steadying breath and became aware of a voice lecturing. It was coming closer.

I was dizzy and I did not want to turn my head, but I did. The guide advanced slowly up the steps. He had donned a straw hat that gave him a comical dignity. Behind him came a gaggle of sightseers, the hardy ones who had made the climb. One woman held her parasol overhead. Two others fanned themselves against the day's warmth. There were only two men in the party, and they seemed to be escorting the young ladies rather than here by their own inclination. A dozen boys and girls traipsed along behind the adults. The girls were trying to imitate the ladies but the lads were exhibiting the universal signs of bored boys, nudging one another, scuffling to be first onto the platform, and parodying the guide's posture and remarks behind his back.

"I beg of you all to be most careful and to stay well away from the edge. The wall is not sound. And to answer your question, Miss, the spire has four hundred and thirty-two steps. Now, please lift your eyes to the Spindle itself. Here you will experience the clearest view of it. You can now see that the illusion of motion is created by the use of the striated rock. At this distance, of course, the illusion ceases and one can see that the spindle is fixed in place."

Without standing up, I turned my eyes to the spindle again. "It spins," I said quietly, and heard, aghast, the distance in my own voice. "For me, it spins." Despite my effort to clear my voice, I sounded like Epiny when she spoke through her medium's trance. That other self inside me struggled for ascendance. I suppressed him with difficulty.

"You are not well, sir." The Plainswoman stated this with emphasis. I sensed that she spoke to inform the others of my situation. "You should leave here."

I stared at her. I had expected her to urge me to rest or offer me water. Instead, her gray gaze was narrow with distrust. I closed my eyes for a moment.

"I don't know if I can," I said. I had been about to do something, something of vast importance. I could not get my bearings. My pulse beat in my ears. I staggered to my feet and then blinked at the scene around me. Only a moment had seemed to pass for me, but the tourists were not as I had last glimpsed them. The guide had concluded his lecture and was pointing out over the valley, answering questions for an earnest young man. The other sightseers likewise stood beside him looking out across the wide vista. Two of the women had opened sketchbooks. The parasol woman was working from an easel her male companion had carried for her, her watercolor already sketched and half-painted. He stood behind her shoulder, admiring her skill. An older woman had gathered the girls around her and was repeating the key points of their tour. One dutiful boy held a sheet of paper against a block of stone as a stout older woman made a charcoal rubbing of the bas-relief etched there. The guide turned away from his party and started toward me.

The Plainswoman had remained beside me. "What's happening to me?" I asked her. She knit her brows and shrugged at me. She stood by me, almost as if I were in her custody.

The guide approached me with a sanctimonious smile. "Well? And have you satisfied your curiosity, sir? I am sure you must be very impressed with the winds that managed to sculpt these wondrous carvings."

His sarcasm was justified. Possibly that was why it angered me. "I'm leaving," I announced. I heaved myself to my feet. I was turning away when I felt a sudden wave of queasiness. The earth seemed to rock under my feet. "Is it an earthquake?" I asked frantically, although I suspected that the unrest was within my own body. I lifted my hands to my temples and stared bleakly at the guide and the Plainswoman. They regarded me with alarm.

A terrible whine like an ungreased axle shrieked through my ears. I turned my head in search of the source of it. To my horror, three of the boys had gathered at the center of the platform. Two acted as support to hold a third aloft. Thus lifted, the middle boy could reach the stone of the spindle. He had taken out a sheath knife and set the blade to the stone. As I watched, he tried to scratch a line into the ancient monument. The self that the Tree Woman had tutored stabbed me with fear. There was danger, vast danger, in suddenly loosing that magic.

"Stop!" I shouted the warning. Against all common sense, I expected to see the young fool snatched up and away by the momentum of the spindle. "Don't do that! Stop that immediately!" The iron was tearing the magic free of the spindle in wild, flapping sheets. It could go anywhere, do anything. I was deafened and dizzied by its buffeting, but the others apparently felt nothing.

The boy stopped, glared at me, and said scornfully, "You're not my father. Mind your own business."

The moment he had lifted his knife from the stone, the screeching had stopped. Now, as he deliberately set his blade to the monument, it began again. As he bore down on the iron blade, the sound soared in volume and pitch. I clapped my hands over my ears against the harsh shriek. A ghostly smoke rose from the point at which blade met stone. He seemed oblivious to all of it.

"Stop!" I roared at him. "You don't know what you're doing, you idiot!"

Now every member of the touring party had turned to stare at me. For myself, I did not know how they could be immune to the shrieking of the spindle as the cold iron bore into it. Wave after wave of vertigo washed through me. The humming of the Spindle, a constant that had been so uniform I had scarcely been aware of it, now warbled as the blade's contact slowed its turning. "Make him stop!" I shouted at them. "Can't you see what he's doing? Can't you sense what he's destroying?" My hidden self warned me of magic unraveling around me. I felt the tattered threads of it score my skin as it dispersed into the empty air. It felt like tiny swift cuts with a razor-sharp knife. It threatened me; it threatened to strip from me all the magic I had so painstakingly stored away.

"Stop him, or I shall!" I made the threat, but the wavering of the magic unbalanced me. It wasn't just the air; it was the reality around me that seemed uneven and fickle. I didn't think I had the strength to swat a fly. Nonetheless, I moved to stop the boy.

I must have looked like a madman as I lurched and staggered toward the young fool who was whetting his blade on ancient magic. The women had lifted their hands, covering their mouths in horror. The two boys supporting the vandal staggered back, one dropping the leg he had supported. One young man stepped forward as if he would protect the boy from me. Only one matron, the one making the rubbing, added her voice to my protest. "Stop that, you young hooligan! I brought you here to teach you about primitive culture, not to have you ruin it! Stop defacing these ancient works! Your father will hear of this!" She dropped her charcoal and advanced on the lad. Behind her, her assistant rolled his eyes wearily.

With a surly snarl, the boy flung the knife down so hard it bounced. "I wasn't doing anything! Just making my initials to show I'd been here, that was all! What a fuss about a stupid striped rock! What's it going to do, make it fall down?" He turned to glare at me. "Are you happy, fat man? You've got your way! I never even asked to come on this stupid outing to look at a stupid rock!"

"Jard? Where are your manners?" the matron snapped. "Regardless of the man's mental condition, he is your elder. You should speak to him with respect. And I have warned you before about your endless carving on things. It's disrespectful. If you cannot behave any better than that, and if Ret and Breg have nothing better to do than assist you in being a fool, then I think it is high time we all left! Boys and girls. Gather your things and follow me. This has *not* been the outing that I had expected it to be. Perhaps all of you prefer to sit in the classroom and study from a book rather than see the real world. I shall remember that the next time I think of taking you out."

There was a chorus of whines and dismayed denial from her students, but she was adamant. The guide shot me a vicious look. Plainly I had ruined his trade for the day. The other tourists were folding sketchbooks and taking down the easel. I caught sideways, uneasy looks from them. They seemed to think I was mad, and the guide apparently shared their opinion. I did not care. The boy stooped to snatch up his knife, and then made a rude hand gesture at me before he followed the others to the top of the winding stair. As before, the guide went with them, offering them many warnings about going carefully and staying close to the inner edge of the steps. After a time, I became aware that I was alone on the top of the tower, except for the Plains-woman. I felt as if I were caught between dreaming and wakefulness. What had just happened?

"The Spindle does turn," I said to her. I wanted her to agree with me.

Her lip curled in disgust. "You are a madman," she told me. "A fat and stupid madman. You have driven away our customers. Do you think we get tour wagons every day? Once a month, perhaps, they come. And you have spoiled their pleasure with your shouting and your threats. What do you think they will tell their friends? No one will want to come and see the Spindle. You will destroy our livelihood. Go away. Take your madness elsewhere."

"But . . . don't you feel it? The Spindle turns. Lift your hands. You'll feel the wind of it. Can't you hear it? Can't you smell the magic of it?"

She narrowed her eyes at me suspiciously. She gave a quick, sideways glance at the spindle and then looked back at me. "Do I look like a foolish savage?" she asked me bitterly. "Do you think because I am a Plainswoman that I am stupid? The Spindle does not turn. It never turned. From a distance, it tricks the eye. But always, it has been still. Still and dead."

"No. It turns." I wanted someone to confirm what I had experienced. "It turns for me, and when I lifted my hands, it happened, as you warned me it might. It lifted me up and—"

Anger flared in her face and she lifted a hand as if she would slap me. "NO! It did not. It has never turned for me, and it could not turn for you, Gernian! It was a legend. That was all. Those who say they see it turning are fools, and those who claim to have been lifted by it are liars! Liars! Go away! Get out of here! How dare you say it turns for you! It never turned for me and I am of the Plains! Liar! Liar!"

I had never seen a woman become so hysterical. Her hands were clenched in fists and spittle flew from her lips as she shrieked at me.

"I'm going!" I promised her. "I'm leaving now."

The clamber down the circling steps seemed endless. My calves screamed with cramps. Twice I nearly fell, and the second time, I bloodied the heels of my hands when I caught myself on the wall. I felt sick and dizzied. I felt angry, too. I was not crazy, and I resented how I had been treated. I did not know if I should blame the blindness of the other people or the foreign magic that had polluted me and taken me for its own. What was real? What was illusion?

For the moment, the battle for control that I'd had with my other self had subsided. There was no comfort in that. When I'd previously confronted him, I'd been able to set him apart from me, to comprehend him as "other" to myself. There was no such separation now. He permeated my being, and I recognized him as comprising the harder parts of my soldier self. Had Tree Woman deliberately chosen those parts when she had seized a lock of my hair and jerked a core out of my awareness? I stole a cautious peek at that part of my self, as if I were peeking at an adder in a box. I was both fascinated and repelled by what I glimpsed. There were the bits of myself that I'd lacked in my first year at the academy. He was the one who had enabled me to take my petty vengeance on the new noble sons. He had fierce pride and recklessness and daring. He was also ruthless and single-minded in what he would do for his people. The frightening part of that was that it was not to Gernia that he pledged his loyalty, but to the Specks. I'd been imagining that I'd reintegrated him into myself. Now I wondered if the flow were not the other way; was he absorbing my knowledge and memories for his own ends? He'd had a goal up there near the Spindle, one that I still didn't grasp.

I suddenly decided it was time to leave.

The guide seemed to have calmed his customers on the way down. As I followed the path back through the ancient city, I saw that the teacher and her charges had dispersed throughout the ruins. The easel woman was hard at work again. One of the women with a sketchbook was drawing the other as she sat picturesquely beside a tumbled wall. I passed them all, enduring their glances as I did so. Something nagged at me, some task had been left undone, but I recognized that concern as belonging to my other self. Nevare only wanted to be away from that place.

As I drew near to the base of the spindle and the shabby little shack there, I saw the guide again. He leaned in the shade against the wall of his pathetic house and watched me come. I could see him trying to decide if he would say anything to me or would let me pass unchallenged. His furtive glances told me that he both despised and feared me as a madman.

I heard voices. As I passed the edge of the bowl in which the Spindle rested or spun, I glanced over the rim. The boys were there. This time, his two companions gripped his legs while Jard lay, belly down, in the slanting cup of the bowl. His knife was busy again. Large letters proclaimed that Jard had been there. Ret's name was in the process of being added. All three were so intent that they didn't see me staring at them. I looked at the guide and our eyes met across the distance. His face paled with fear. I smiled.

"If my illustrious ancestors had carved this, I'd protect it from young vandals," I advised the half-breed sarcastically.

He narrowed his eyes and opened his mouth to respond. But before he could, one of the boys holding Jard's legs yelped, "It's that crazy fat man! Get out of there, Jard!" At the same moment, he helpfully let go of Jard's leg as he sprang away and fled, intent on saving himself from my supposed insanity. Jard, supported now only by Breg's grip on his other leg, gave a wild yell as he suddenly slid deeper into the bowl. He flailed his arms wildly, seeking a grip on the smooth surface and finding nothing. Breg, surprised by Ret's desertion, was himself tugged to his knees at the edge of the bowl. "I can't hold him!" he wailed. I heard a tearing sound and saw the fabric of Jard's trousers starting to give way.

In two steps, I reached the rim of the Spindle's bowl. I flung myself to my knees and reached to grab Jard by the knees. He screamed and kicked at me, evidently thinking I intended to tear him from Breg's grip and let him plunge headfirst into the Spindle's well. I didn't. I hauled him back to the lip of the bowl. He jabbed his knife at me, still struggling against his rescue. My blood seethed with anger at his insolence. I seized his wrist and slammed it flat against the stone of the bowl. His knife flew free. An instant later, I had dragged him back over the edge and to safety. I released him and tried to stand up. Magic was singing triumphantly through my blood. Something was happening, something vast and not of my volition, but of my doing all the same. The forest mage within me laughed wildly, victoriously, and then slid back into the leafy shadows of my subconscious. I could not discern what his victory was, and then I did.

Even as the other tourists were running toward me, and Jard fled sobbing to his teacher, I watched his knife sliding down the bowl toward the unseen depths at the center. As the bowl became steeper, the knife slid faster across the polished stone. When it entered the darkness of the center, I felt my heart stand still.

The half-breed had seized my hand and was pumping it while stuttering out his thanks and apologizing for misjudging me. The fool. I heard Ret shouting to the rapidly gathering tourists that, "No, it's all right, he didn't try to hurt Jard, he saved him! Jard nearly fell headfirst into that hole. The man pulled him out." Jard was sobbing like a small boy as he clung to his teacher. I alone seemed to hear the terrible grinding noise at the edge of the world. The blade of the knife had wedged beneath the Spindle's tip. I knew that tip existed, deep inside the well the magic had drilled for all those years. The vast momentum of magic met the iron knife and wedged against it. The Spindle ground to a halt. I felt the moving magic foul and tangle, thwarted by a small iron blade. I sank down and pressed my brow to the edge of the stone bowl. It was like the death of the wind wizard all over again, but this time I could not claim innocence for myself. What had I done? What had the forest magic done through me?

"Best leave him alone!" I heard the guide say. "I think the man just wants to be left alone."

Then all sound halted around me. Like the harsh kiss of a sandstorm, the harnessed magic of the Plainsmen suddenly burst free and scattered. For a blink of my lifetime, I swear the world went black and still. Raw power abraded my senses and engulfed me. I struggled to stand, to lift my arms to defend myself from it.

When time started up again, I seemed again to have fallen behind the rest of the world. The guide had rounded up his tourists and was herding them back toward their wagon. Several of them glanced back at me and shook their heads, speaking quickly to one another. The knife boy was already sitting on a wagon seat. Ret said something to Breg and they both hooted with laughter. Jard's brush with death was already a joking matter for them. They had no idea of what had just happened.

The flash of anger I felt subsided before I even felt its heat. Surely the sun had moved in the sky? I gave my head a small shake and let my clenched fists fall to my sides. My arms ached. My nails had left deep red indentations in my palms. I had no idea how long I had stood there. I did know what my Speck self had done. The Dancing Spindle no longer danced. The magic of the Plainspeople was broken. I found Sirlofty. It was all I could do to clamber onto his back. I held onto the horn of the saddle as I kicked him into a lope and fled that place. The driver of the wagon shouted at me angrily as I passed his team on the steep trail. I paid him no mind.

By the time I reached the road again, I had almost recovered. The farther I went from the Spindle, the clearer my head became. The forest mage inside me ceased his chortling and grew still.

Evening fell, and I pushed Sirlofty on, journeying through the dusk to make up the time wasted in my foolish detour. I wished I'd never left the road. I tried to stuff what I'd discovered back into the darkness, but it rode with me now. I shifted in my saddle and felt it slip under me. Gently I reined Sirlofty in; I dismounted as if I were as fragile as an eggshell. With a feeling of ineffable sadness, I tightened the cinch on my saddle.

It was the first time in my life that I'd ever had to do that.

Night was deep by the time I reached the town. I found an inn that would admit me. Before I fell asleep, as had become my habit, I wrote carefully of the day's events. Then I scowled at the words. Did I really want these wild thoughts in the first volume of my soldier son journal? Only the teaching that it was my duty to record what I observed each day comforted me.

In the days that followed, I did not again diverge from my father's itinerary for me. I fixed my mind on my carefully planned life, on my brother's wedding, my reunion with Carsina, my education at the academy, my service, and my eventual marriage. My father had mapped out my future as precisely as he had mapped out my journey home. I had no time for illusions, no time to question where my reality ended and someone else's began. I refused to think about the magic of the plains and a keep fast charm that no longer seemed to work. Everyone knew that the magic of the Plainsfolk was fading. There was no reason to blame myself for its demise. With the destruction of the Spindle, that other self in me seemed to subside. I dared to hope that it was the last I would sense of him. I practiced believing that until I was able to think and live as if I were certain it was so.

Although the Midlands are often referred to as flat, they rise and fall with subtle grace. Thus it was that the trees and walls of my father's home were concealed from me until I rode up a slight rise in a gentle bend of the road and suddenly perceived my home. My father's manor was set on a gentle rise overlooking the road. I gazed up at it and thought that it looked smaller and more rustic than when I had last seen it. Now that I knew what the estates and manors of the west looked like, I could see that my father's house was a pale imitation of their grandeur. I could also see how clearly our home was modeled upon my uncle's house. They had made improvements since I'd left for the academy. River gravel had been hauled up to surface the drive, and young oak trees, each little more than a shovel handle high, now edged it. Someday they would be tall and grand, and this would be a fine carriageway to our home. But for now, they looked spindly and forlorn, exposed to prairie dust and wind. Each had a damp circle of soil around its base. I wondered how many years they'd have to be watered daily before their roots reached deep enough to sustain them. This copying of our ancestral home suddenly seemed both sentimental and a bit silly to me.

But nonetheless, it was home. I'd arrived. For an instant, I had the foolish thought that I could pass it by and keep traveling east, on and on, all the way to the mountains. I imagined tall trees and inviting shade and birds calling in the shadowy thickets. Then Sirlofty took it on himself to turn from the main road and break into a canter. We were *home!* We woke dust all up the long driveway from the King's Road to my father's front door. There I pulled him in with a flourish, as our family's dogs swirled around us in a barking, wagging pack and one of the stablehands came out to see what had roused them. I didn't know the man, and so I was not offended when he asked, "Are you lost, sir?"

"No, I'm Nevare Burvelle, a son of the house, just returned from the Cavalla Academy. Please take Sirlofty for me and see that he is well treated. We've come a long way, he and I."

The man gaped at me, but I ignored that and handed him my reins. "Oh, and send the contents of his panniers up to my room, if you would," I added, as I climbed the front steps. I let myself in, calling out, "Mother! Father! It's Nevare, I'm home. Rosse, Elisi, Yaril? Is anyone home?"

My mother was the first to come out of her sewing room. She stared at me, her eyes growing round, and then, embroidery in hand, she hurried down the hall. She embraced me, saying, "Oh, Nevare, it's so good to see you. But the dust on you! I'll have a bath drawn for you immediately. Oh, son, I'm so glad you are home and safe again!"

"And I am glad beyond words to be here again, Mother!"

The others had arrived by then. Father and Rosse looked startled, even when I turned and strode toward them, smiling. Rosse shook my hand but my father held back from me, demanding, "What have you done to yourself? You look like a wandering peddler! Why aren't you wearing your uniform?"

"It needs a bit of mending, I'm afraid. I hope Mother can have it ready in time for Rosse's wedding. Elisi, Yaril? Am I a stranger now? Aren't you going to say hello even?"

"Hello, Nevare. Welcome home." Elisi spoke stiffly, and looked past me as if I'd done something rude and she wasn't sure how to deal with it.

"You're so fat!" Yaril exclaimed, tactless as she had ever been. "What have you been eating at that place? Your face is round as the full moon! And you're so dirty! I thought you'd ride up all glorious in your uniform. I didn't even recognize you at first."

I chuckled weakly, and waited for my father to rebuke her. Instead, he muttered, "Out of the mouths of babes." Then, speaking more strongly, he said, "I'm sure you've had a long trip, Nevare. You're a few hours earlier than I expected you, but I think you'll find your room is waiting, with wash water. After you've cleaned yourself and changed, please come and see me in my study."

I made a final effort. "I'm so glad to see you, Father. It's good to be home."

"I'm sure it is, Nevare. Well. I'll see you again in a few minutes." There was restraint in his voice, and the edge of command. Plainly he wished me to obey him immediately. And I did. The habit of not questioning his authority and commands was still strong in me, but as I washed the dust from my face and hands, I experienced something I hadn't felt before about my father. Resentment. It wasn't just for the way he ordered me about, but for his obvious displeasure with me. I had only just arrived home. Could not he have suppressed whatever it was that annoyed him long enough to shake my hand and welcome me back? Must I immediately fall completely under his domination again? I thought of his rigid itinerary for my journey home, and suddenly saw it not as a helpful aid, but as oppression. Did he or did he not trust me to make my own way in the world?

My anger gave way to a greater frustration as I tried to find some clothing that would still fit me. When I had left for the academy, I had emptied my room. My mother, ever thoughtful of such things, had hung two of Rosse's old shirts and a pair of his trousers in my closet, for my use until my traveling clothes could be washed and pressed. When I put them on, I looked ridiculous. The trousers were too short on me as well as far too tight. I had to let my stomach bulge out over the top of them. Both shirts strained on me. I took them off and vindictively threw them on the floor before putting my travel-stained clothes back on. But a glance in my mirror showed me that they were ill-fitting and dirty to boot. The seams in the seat of the trousers looked ready to part. The shirt was already slightly torn at both shoulders, and barely met over my middle.

Well, I decided, if I must look silly, I would at least be clean. I retrieved Rosse's clothes, put them on, wiped the worst of the dust off my boots, and descended the stairs. The house was silent. My mother and sisters seemed to have vanished completely. I did not even hear their voices in a different room. I tapped at the closed door to my father's study and then walked in. My father was standing with his back to the room, staring out the window. My brother Rosse was there also. He glanced at me and then away, plainly uncomfortable. My father held his silence.

I broke the silence at last. "Father, you wished me to come to your study?"

He did not turn around. He did not immediately reply. When he did speak, he seemed to be addressing the trees outside the window. "Your brother's wedding is scarcely four days away," he said heavily. "How can you possibly think to undo in four days what sloth and gluttony have accomplished in six months? Did you give a thought to anyone beside yourself when you were allowing your gut to become the size of a washbasin? Do you wish to humiliate your entire family by appearing at a festive occasion in such a state? I am humiliated to think that you have presented yourself thus to the academy, to my brother, and to everyone who knew your name on your journey home. In the good god's name, Nevare, whatever were you thinking when you allowed yourself to descend to such a state? I sent you off to the academy a fit and able young man, physically suited to be an officer and a soldier. And look what comes back to me less than a year later!"

His words rattled against me like flung stones. He gave me no opportunity to reply. When he finally turned to face me, I could see that his quiet stance had been a deception. His face was red and the veins stood out in his temples. I dared a glance at my brother. His face was white and he was very still, like a small animal that hopes not to draw the predator's attention to himself.

I stood in the focus of my father's anger with absolutely no idea of how to defend myself. I felt guilty and ashamed of my body, but I honestly could not recall that I had overeaten since I had begun my journey, nor had my pace been what I would call slothful. I spoke the truth. "I have no explanation, sir. I don't know why I've gained so much weight."

The anger in his eyes sharpened. "You don't? Well, perhaps a three-day fast will refresh an elementary truth for you. If you eat too much, you get fat, Nevare. If you lie about like a slug, you get fat. If you don't overeat and if you exercise your muscles, you remain trim and soldierly."

He took a breath, obviously to master himself. When he spoke again, his tone was calmer. "Nevare, you disappoint me. It is not just that you have let yourself go; worse is that you try to shrug off the responsibility for it. I must remind myself of your youth. Perhaps the fault is mine; perhaps I should have delayed your entry into the academy until you were more mature, more capable of regulating yourself. Well." He sighed, clenched his jaw for a moment and then went on. "That cannot be mended now. But the mess you've made of yourself is something I can remedy. We cannot undo it in four days, but we can put a dent in it. Look at me, son, when I speak to you."

I had been avoiding his gaze. Now I brought my eyes back to meet his squarely, trying to mask my anger. If he saw it, he ignored it. "It won't be pleasant, Nevare. Do it willingly, and prove to me that you are still the son I trained and sent off with such high hopes. I ask only two things of you: Restrict your food and demand performance from your body." He paused and seemed to be weighing his options. Then he nodded to himself. "Sergeant Duril has been supervising a crew clearing stones from the land for a new pasture. Go and join them, right now, and I don't mean to supervise. Start working off that gut. Confine your appetite to water for the rest of this day. Tomorrow, eat as sparingly as you can. We'll do what we can to trim some of that off you before your brother's wedding day."

He turned his attention to my brother. "Rosse. Go out to the stables with him, and find him a mule. I won't have one of the good horses broken down by lugging him over broken terrain. Take him out to the new alfalfa field."

I spoke up. "I think I could find a mule for myself."

"Just do what you are told, Nevare. Trust me. I know what is best for you." He sighed heavily, and then with the first hint of kindness I heard from him, he said, "Put yourself in my hands, son. I know what I'm doing."

And that was my welcome home.

CHAPTER FOUR

THE FAST

Rosse and I rode silently out to the work site. Several times I glanced at my brother, but he was always staring ahead, his face expressionless. I supposed he was as disappointed in me as my father was. We said a perfunctory good-bye, he rode off leading my mule, and I joined my work crew. I didn't recognize any of the four men, and we didn't bother with introductions. I simply joined them at the task.

The future pasture was on a sunny hillside by a creek. Coarse prairie grass and buckbrush grew there now. The ground was littered with stones, some loose on top of the earth and others nudging up out of the soil. The larger ones had to be moved before a team and plow could break the thin sod. I'd watched our men do this sort of work before, though

I'd never bent my back to it myself. It should have been well within my ability, but academy life had softened me. My first hour of prying rocks from their beds and lifting them into a wagon first raised and then broke blisters on my hands. The work was both tedious and demanding.

We used iron bars to prise the larger stones from the hard earth. Then each had to be lifted, sometimes by two men, and loaded onto a buckboard wagon. When the wagon was full we followed it as the team hauled the stone to the edge of the field. There we unloaded it in a neat line of rock. It became a rough stone wall to mark the edge of the sown pasture. The other men talked and laughed among themselves. They were not rude; they just ignored me. Doubtless they had decided I wouldn't last long and that there was little point in getting to know me.

Sergeant Duril was supervising the work. The first time he rode by to check on our crew, I don't think he recognized me. I was glad to escape his notice. The second time he rode up to ask how many wagonloads of stone we'd hauled since he last spoke to us, he stared at me and then visibly startled.

"You. Come here," he commanded me roughly. He didn't dismount, but rode his horse a short distance while I walked beside him. When we were out of earshot of the work crew, he pulled in and looked down at me. "Nevare?" he asked, as if he could not believe his eyes.

"Yes. It's me." My voice came out flat and defensive.

"What in the good god's name have you done to yourself?"

"I've got fat," I said bluntly. I was already tired of explaining it. Or rather, I was tired of not being able to explain it. No one seemed able to believe that it had simply happened and that I had not brought it on myself by sloth and greed. I was beginning to wonder about that myself. How *had* this befallen me?

"So I see. But not in a way I've ever seen a lad put on weight! A little gut from too much beer, that I've seen on many a trooper. But you're fat all over! Your face, your arms, even the calves of your legs!"

I hadn't stopped to consider that. I wanted to look down at my body, to see if it was truly so, but suddenly felt too ashamed. I looked away from him, across the flat plain that soon would be a pasture. I tried to think of something to say, but the only words that came were, "My father has sent me out here to work. He says hard work and short rations will trim me down before Rosse's wedding."

His silence seemed long. Then he said, "Well, a man can only do so much in a few days, but the intention is what matters. You're stubborn, Nevare. I would never have imagined that you'd let yourself go like this, but I know that if you're determined to get back to what you were, you'll do it."

I couldn't think of any response to that, and after a short time, he said, "Well, I have to finish my round of the crews. Your da says that a year from now, this will all be alfalfa and clover. We'll see."

Then he tapped his horse and rode off. I walked back to the work crew. They had been loitering, watching us talk. I went back to levering up stones and loading them on the wagon. They didn't ask any questions, and I didn't volunteer anything.

We worked the rest of the day, until Duril rode past again and gave the sign for quitting time. We still had to unload the rock we had on the wagon at the fence line. Then we all rode on the wagon back to my father's manor house. The other men went off to the help's quarters. I entered the back door of the house and went up to my room.

I blessed my mother when I arrived there. She had left out wash water and towels, and some of my old clothes, along with an old pair of Plains sandals. I could see that she had hastily let out the seams of the trousers and shirt as far as they could go. I washed. When I dressed, I found that my old clothes were still snug on me, but they were bearable and far more presentable than Rosse's castoffs had been.

I had come in late and the rest of the family was already at dinner. I was in no hurry to join them. Instead, I crept into my sister Yaril's room.

My father had always said that vanity was too costly a vice for any soldier to afford. In my own room, I had a mirror large enough for shaving, and that was all. My sisters, on the other hand, were expected to be continually aware of their appearances. They each had full-length mirrors in their bedrooms. When I stood in front of Yaril's, I had a shock.

Duril was right. The weight I had put on was distributed all over me, like thick frosting on a cake. No wonder others had been reacting to me so strangely. No part of me had escaped. As I stared at my face, I was certain that instead of losing weight on my journey home, I'd added to it. This was not the face I'd seen in my shaving mirror at the academy. My cheeks were round and jowly, and my chin was padded. My eyes looked smaller, as if they were set closer together. My neck looked shorter.

The rest of my body was even more distressing. My shoulders and back were rounded with fat, to say nothing of my chest and belly. My gut was more than a paunch; it was starting to hang. My thighs were heavy. Even my calves and ankles looked swollen. I lifted a fat hand to cover my mouth and felt cowardly tears start in my eyes. What had I done to myself, and how? I could not grasp the changes the mirror showed me. Since I'd left Old Thares, I'd ridden each day and my meals had been ordinary ones. How could this be happening?

Prior to looking in the mirror, I had planned to go down and join my family at the dinner table, if only for talk. Now I did not. I hated what I had become and heartily endorsed my father's plan. I went to the kitchen, intending to get a mug of water. A kitchenmaid and a cook stared at me, surprised, and then looked aside. Neither spoke to me, and I ignored them. The sight of a bucket of fresh milk temporarily overwhelmed my resolve to fast, and I took a mug of that instead. I drank it down thirstily, and yearned for more. Instead, I contented myself with plain water. I drank mug after mug of it, trying to assuage the feeling of emptiness in my belly. It felt as if the liquid splashed into a void. At last I could drink no more, and yet felt no fuller. I left the kitchen and went upstairs to my room.

There, I sat on the edge of the bed. There was little else for me to do. I had emptied my room before I left for the academy. I had my schoolbooks and my journal from my panniers, but little else. Doggedly I sat down and made a complete entry in my journal. Afterward I sat with no refuge from my nagging hunger or my dismal evaluation of myself.

I could not recall that I had changed any habit that would lead to this result. I had eaten the same rations allotted to any man at the academy mess, and done the same marching. How had I swollen up to this toadish size? Belatedly, it occurred to me that I'd never seen Gord eat more than what was portioned to us at the mess, and yet his bulk had persisted. I had to wonder if mine would do the same. In sudden fear, I resolved it would not. I had three days before Rosse's wedding, three days before Carsina and her family would arrive to be guests. I had three days to do something about my appearance before I was disgraced before all our friends. I firmly resolved that not a morsel of food would pass my lips for those days, and yet oh, how I ached with hunger. I rose abruptly, determined to go for a brisk walk to distract myself. Standing up quickly woke every aching muscle in my back and legs. I gritted my teeth and left the room.

I didn't wish to face anyone. I stood silently in the hallway for a few moments, confirming that my father and Rosse were in his study. My father was talking, his words indistinguishable but his disapproval plain. Obviously Rosse was hearing a lecture on all the ways I had failed the family. I strode quickly past the door of the music room. I heard Elisi's harp and recalled that often my mother and sisters gathered there to play music or read poetry after dinner. I opened the front door quietly and slipped out into the Widevale night.

My father had created an oasis of trees around his house. It was an island of illusion, a way to pretend that we did not live far from civilization on the endless sweep of prairie. Over one hundred carefully nurtured trees cut the wind and screened a nearly flat vista. My father had even had water piped up from the river to form a little pond and fountain for my sisters' pleasure in their private garden. The soft splashing drew me toward their bower.

I followed a graveled pathway through an arched gateway.

The latticework I had helped to erect years ago was now completely cloaked in vines. Small night lamps with glass chimneys hung from the branches of a golden willow, illuminating their silver reflections in the pond's surface. I sat down on the edge of the stone-banked pool and peered into the dark water to see if the ornamental fish had survived.

"Planning to eat one?"

I turned in shock. I had never heard my sister Yaril sound so sarcastic and cruel. We had always been close as children. She had not only been my faithful correspondent while I was at school, but she had also managed to smuggle Carsina's letters to me, so that we might carry on a private correspondence away from our parents' supervision. She was sitting on a wrought-iron bench under a graceful trellis of pampered honeysuckle. Her dove-gray dress had blended her into the shadows when first I approached the pond. Now she leaned out into the light, and anger hardened her face. "How could you do this to us? I am going to be so humiliated at Rosse's wedding. And poor Carsina! This is certainly not what she was anticipating! The last two weeks, she has been so excited and happy. She even chose her dress color to go well with your uniform. And you come home looking like this!"

"It's not my fault!" I retorted.

"Oh? Then who has been stuffing food down your throat, I'd like to know?"

"It's . . . I think it has something to do with the Speck plague." The words jumped out of my mouth as quickly as the idea had suddenly come into my mind. On the surface, it seemed a silly thing to say. Everyone knew that Speck plague was a wasting disease. But the moment I said it aloud, odd bits of memories suddenly fell into an accusing pattern. A long-ago conversation I'd overhead between Rosse and my father combined with the dour words of the Fat Man in the carnival freak show tent in Old Thares. He'd claimed he'd once been a cavalla soldier until the plague had ruined him. Even Dr. Amicas's fascination with my weight gain now took on a darker significance.

But those seemed trivial clues compared to words recalled from a dream. Tree Woman had encouraged my

Speck self to gorge himself on the magical essence of dying people. I suddenly recalled how I had seen myself in that dream; I'd been full-bellied and heavy-legged. Tree Woman herself was an immense woman. In my dreams, my arms could not encompass the rich curves of her body. I felt a disturbing flash of arousal at that memory and thrust it from me, but not before I heard like a whisper in my ear, "Eat and grow fat with their magic." I stood absolutely still, my every sense straining, but all that came to my ears was the gentle splashing of the water and the shivering of the leaves in the evening wind. They were followed by my sister's snort of disdain.

"Do you think I'm a fool, Nevare? I may have had to stay here and be tutored by some silly old woman from Old Thares while you were sent off to the grand city to learn at your fine school, but I'm not stupid. I've seen men who have had Speck plague! And one and all, they have been thin as rails. *That* is what the Speck plague does to a man. Not fatten him like a hog raised for bacon."

"I know what I know," I said coldly. It was a brotherly remark, one that I'd often used to end our childhood arguments. But Yaril was no longer the innocent little golden-haired sister I'd left behind almost a year ago. She would no longer be cowed by a simple assertion of superior knowledge.

She merely sniffed and replied, "And *I* know what *I* know! And that is that you are as fat as a hog and you're going to humiliate all of us at Rosse's wedding. What will Remwar's family think of me, having such a brother? Will they fear that I, too, will inflate like a bladder? I was hoping that this wedding might be a chance for me to make a good impression on his parents, so that his offer for my hand might become formal. But they won't even see me. I'll be eclipsed behind you!"

"I didn't choose this, Yaril. You might stop for one moment to think of my feelings." All the resentment I felt at my father's harsh treatment of me was blossoming into fury at Yaril's childish concern for her dignity. "You're such a selfish little girl. Every letter you sent me, you begged me for gifts.

And fool that I am, I sent them. And now that I've returned home after nearly dying in the filthy city, you disdain me because of my physical appearance. A fine welcome I've received from any of you! The only one who has shown one jot of sympathy for my situation is Mother!"

"And why shouldn't she?" Yaril flashed back at me. "You were always her favorite! And now that you've ruined yourself for being a soldier, she can keep you here with her always! Carsina won't have you, fat as a hog, and when she looks around, she and her family will take Remwar away from me! He was her father's first choice for her anyway. You've ruined it for everyone, Nevare, you selfish pig!"

Before I could even reply to that, she played a woman's trump card. She burst into tears and then ran off into the darkness, sobbing into her hands. "Yaril!" I called after her. "Come back here! Yaril, come back!"

But she did not, and I was left standing alone by the stupid fish pond that I'd helped to build. At the time it had seemed like an enchanting concept. Now I saw it for the folly it was. The fish pond and fountain were completely at odds with the land that surrounded us. To build something that could not be sustained save by daily effort was a vanity and a waste and an insult to the beauty of the true nature that surrounded us. What had seemed a shady retreat from the harsh plains that surrounded our home now seemed foolish self-indulgence.

I sank down onto Yaril's bench and considered the words she had flung at me. She'd been angry and she'd used her best ammunition to wound me. But how much of it was true? Would Carsina ask her father to break his agreement with my father? I tried to worry about it, but a wave of hunger washed through me, leaving me feeling both nauseous and hollow. I rocked forward over my belly and embraced it as if it were an ally instead of my enemy.

I was in that undignified posture when I heard a light footstep on the pathway. I straightened up and prepared for battle, but it wasn't Yaril returning. Instead it was my mother, holding a lantern to guide her steps as she came softly down the walk.

"There you are," she said when she saw me. "Why didn't you come down to dinner?" Her tone was gentle.

"I thought it better to stay away." I tried to make my voice jovial. "As you can see, perhaps I've had too many dinners of late."

"Well. I won't deny that your appearance surprised me. But I did miss you. I've scarcely had a chance to speak to you. And . . ." She hesitated a moment and then went on delicately, "I do need you to return to the house and come to my sewing room with me."

I stood, grateful for an ally. "Are you going to let out my cadet uniform to fit me?"

She smiled but shook her head. "Nevare, that is simply impossible. There isn't enough fabric to let out, and even if I could, it would show badly. No, my son. But I have several folds of a very nice blue fabric, and if I put the seamstresses to work on it tonight, we should have something presentable by the wedding."

My heart sank at the thought that I was hopelessly too large for my uniform, but I squared my shoulders to bear the truth. Presentable. My mother would help me, and I would not look ridiculous at my brother's wedding. "Seamstresses?" I asked, keeping my voice light. "When did we become so prosperous as to employ seamstresses?"

"Since your brother decided to wed. The decision has little to do with prosperity and more to do with necessity. I sent for two from the west two months ago. I was fortunate that I did, for between making new curtains and hangings and bed-clothes for your brother's chambers and ensuring that the entire family would have wedding clothes as well as ball gowns for your sisters, well! It would be impossible for your sisters and me to do that much sewing in such a short time and still have time for all the other preparations."

She led the way, holding her little lantern up to guide us. I watched my mother's trim figure as she stepped lightly along and I suddenly felt monstrous and misshapen, like some great beast hulking after her. The house was quiet as we went down the hall to her sewing room. I imagined that my father and Rosse had settled down to quieter talk and that

Elisi had gone off to bed. I thought of mentioning that I'd spoken with Yaril and she'd run off in tears, but my old habit of protecting my little sister was still strong. My mother would scold her for being outside at this hour on her own. Annoyed as I was at Yaril, I still had no desire to get her in trouble. I let it go.

I had a very uncomfortable session in the sewing room as my mother measured me and jotted down her notes. She frowned as she did so, and I knew that she tried not to be shocked. As she was measuring my waist, my stomach rumbled loudly, and she actually jumped back from me. Then she laughed nervously and went back to her task. When she was finished, she said worriedly, "I hope I have enough blue fabric."

A pang of hunger cramped me. When it passed, I said, "Carsina was particularly hoping that I would wear my uniform to the wedding."

"And how would you know that?" my mother asked with a sly smile. Then she quietly added, "Don't even hope for that, Nevare. In truth, I think we shall have to have a new uniform made for you when you go back. I don't know how you managed to wear the one you brought home."

"It fit me when I left the academy. Well, it was tight, but I could still put it on. Mother, I truly don't understand what is happening to me. I've traveled hard and eaten no more than I ordinarily would, but even since I left the academy, I've put on flesh."

"It's that starchy food they feed you at that school. I've heard about places like that, trying to save money by feeding the students cheap food. It's probably all potatoes and bread and—"

"It's not the food, Mother!" I cut in almost roughly. "I've only gained this weight since I recovered from the plague. I think that somehow the two are connected."

She stopped speaking abruptly, and I felt I had been rude to her, though I had not intended to. She rebuked me gently for lying. "Nevare, every young man that I've ever seen who has recovered from the plague has been thin as a rack of bones. I don't think we can blame this on your illness. I do

think that a long convalescence such as you had, with many
hours in bed with little to do save eat and read, could change
a man. I said as much to your father, and asked him not to be
so harsh with you. I cannot promise you that he will heed
me, but I did ask."

I wanted to shout that she wasn't listening to me. With
difficulty, I restrained myself and said only, "Thank you for
being my advocate."

"I always have been, you know," she said quietly. "Now
when you finish your work tomorrow, take care to wash well
and then come here for a fitting. The ladies will be here to
help me then."

I took a deep breath. My anger was gone, consumed in a
dark tide of dejection. "I shall take care to be clean and inof-
fensive," I told her. "Good night, Mother."

She reached up to kiss me on the cheek. "Don't despair,
son. You have confronted what is wrong, accepted it, and
now you can change it. From this day forth, things can only
improve."

"Yes, Mother," I replied dutifully, and left her there. My
stomach was clenching so desperately with hunger pangs that
I felt nauseous. I did not go up to my room, but went to the
kitchens instead. I worked the hand pump at the sink until
cooler water came, and then drank as much as I could bear. If
anything, it made me more miserable.

I went up to my room and tried to sleep until just before
dawn. I was standing with the rest of the crew when the
wagon came for us, and went out for another day's work.
The catalogue of my misery: blisters, hunger, aches, nausea,
and, roiling beneath it all, a sense of bewilderment and outrage at the injustice of life.

By the second half of the day, I was staggering. When the
rest of the work crew broke out their simple packets of meat
and bread for their noon meal, I had to walk away from
them. My sense of smell had become acute, and my stomach
bellowed its emptiness at me. I wanted to wrestle the food
away from them and devour it. Even after they had consumed it all and I came back for my share of the water, it

was difficult to be courteous. I could smell the food on their breaths when we huffed and strained to lift the larger rocks, and it tormented me.

When we finally received the signal to quit, my legs were like jelly. I did not do my fair share at the final unloading of the wagon. I saw the other men exchange glances over it and felt ashamed. I staggered back to the wagon and barely managed to climb aboard.

When the wagon dropped us off, the other men strode toward the town. I tottered up the drive and into the back door of the house. I had to pass the kitchen. The air was thick with wonderful smells; the cook had begun to prepare the special cakes and breads for the wedding. I hurried away from that torture. My father had not told me to fast entirely. I could, I knew, have a small meal. But that thought seemed a weakness and a betrayal of my determination to change. Fasting wouldn't kill me, and I would return to my normal self that much sooner.

The steps to my room seemed long and steep, and once there all I wanted to do was curl up around my miserable belly. Instead, I stepped into the low tub that had been left for me and washed myself standing. I stank. Now that I was heavier, I sweated more and the sweat lingered in every fold of my flesh. Left too long, the perspiration made a scald mark on my skin, painful to touch.

Rosse's old clothes, freshly washed and newly let out, awaited me. They felt tight and awkward against my damp skin. My cadet haircut had begun to grow out. I toweled it dry and then, mindful of embarrassing my mother, I shaved before I went down to her sewing room.

My mother awaited me with the two seamstresses. The last time I'd been measured for clothing, the tailor had done it and I had been fit and trim. It was inexpressibly humiliating to undress to my small clothes and then have three women hold pieces of fabric against me, pinning the parts together around me. One seamstress glanced at my belly and rolled her eyes in disdain at the other seamstress. I went hot with a blush. They pinned my new clothing around me,

stood back, consulted like hens clucking in a barnyard, and
again surrounded me, moving pins and having me turn and
lift my arms and raise my knees. The fabric was a very somber dark blue, nothing at all like the brave green of my cadet
uniform. By the time I retired behind a screen to get dressed
again, I felt that nothing worse could happen to me.

I climbed up the endless stairs to my room. With grim
determination, I decided to avoid the dinner table entirely.
I did not think I could withstand the wonderful aromas of
cooked food. I went to bed.

In my dream, I was my other self, and I was ravenously
hungry. I recalled with sorrow all of the magic that had been
wasted at the Dancing Spindle. I was proud that I had halted
the Spindle's dance and ended the Plainsmen's magic, but I
regretted that I had not been able to absorb more of it into
myself. It was a bizarre dream, filled with the elation of triumph underpinned with a grating hunger for foods that would
properly nourish my magic. I woke at dawn still feeling both
hungry and vaguely triumphant. The first I could understand;
the latter made me feel ashamed. I shook the cobwebs from
my head and faced my day.

That day was a repeat of the previous one, only more miserable. I felt dull and weak. I was late to meet the wagon, and
it took a great effort for me to lever myself up into the back of
it. Terrible hunger cramps wracked me. My head pounded. I
crossed my arms on my stomach and slumped over them.

When we reached the field and the wagon stopped, I
jumped down with the others, only to have my legs fold under me. The rest of the crew laughed, and I forced myself to
join in. I staggered upright and took my levering bar from the
back of the wagon. It felt twice as heavy as it had the day
before, but I set to work. I tried to jab it into the hard soil at
the edge of an embedded stone, but it only skipped across the
surface. I wanted to shout with frustration. I felt no strength
in my arms. I used my weight instead, and spent a miserable
morning. After a time, I got my second wind. The nagging of
my hunger receded slightly. My muscles warmed up, and I
devoted myself to doing my share of the work. I still walked
apart from the men when they took out their noon packets of

food. My sense of smell had become a special torment. My nose told me all that my mouth was forbidden to taste, and my saliva ran until I thought I would drown in it.

I tried to remind myself that this was not the first time I had fasted, or even the longest time. Certainly in my days with Dewara, I had eaten very sparsely and still retained a leathery energy in my body. I was at a loss to explain why I now suffered so acutely when I had previously been able to discipline myself and endure. I came to a reluctant conclusion. I had lost self-discipline at the academy. From there, I had to make the next logical assumption: that I had brought this on myself. It was foolish for me to go on insisting that since I had only eaten what had been placed before me, I had no culpability for what I had become. It did not matter that my fellow cadets had not gained weight as I had. Obviously what was enough for them had been too much for me. Why had I stubbornly resisted seeing that? Hadn't the doctor attempted to point that out to me when he so carefully asked me what I'd been eating and how much? Why hadn't I taken alarm then, and cut down on my food?

My father was right.

I had only myself to blame.

Strangely, with the guilt came an odd relief. I'd finally found a cause for what had befallen me, and it was myself. Suddenly, I felt I had control again. Before, when I'd been unable to admit I'd been doing anything wrong, the fat had seemed like a curse, something that had befallen me, an effect with no cause. I thought of how I'd wanted to blame it on the plague and shook my head at myself. If that were so, then every cadet who recovered from the plague should have been affected as I had. I took a deep breath and felt the strength of my resolution surge within me. I'd finish out my fast today.

Tomorrow, I'd rise and go to my brother's wedding. I'd face the humiliation that I'd brought upon myself, and I would practice great self-discipline in what I ate, not just on that festive day, but on every day that followed. When I returned to the academy, I intended to go back as a thinner man. And I promised myself that by high summer, I'd be moving the buttons on my uniform back to their proper positions.

With determination strong in me, I returned to the afternoon's work and drove myself relentlessly. I raised and broke new blisters on my hands, and didn't care. I rejoiced at how my back and shoulders ached as I punished my recalcitrant body with hard work and deprivation. I thrust my hunger pangs out of my mind and toiled on. Toward the end of the day's work, my legs literally shook with fatigue, but I felt proud of myself. I was in charge. I was changing myself.

That was my attitude when I returned home, washed, and went down for a final fitting. The seamstresses were both tired and frenetic as they rushed me into my new suit. They had brought a mirror into the room, for my sisters were likewise having the final touches put on their clothes. What it showed me rattled me. I did not look any thinner than I had when I arrived home. The weight made me look older, and the sombre blue made me look middle-aged and staid. I glanced at my mother, but she was preoccupied with picking stitches out of something pink. There was no reassurance for me there. I could not focus on the seamstresses as they pinched and tugged at the fabric, poked in pins and marked lines with bits of chalk. I stared at my own face, round as a full moon, and my stout body beneath it. I did not recognize the miserable man who stared back at me.

Then they all but snatched the clothes off me and chased me from the room, ordering me to return in two hours, for Elisi was waiting her turn. I gathered from their talk that a neckline had gone wrong and would require many tiny stitches to alter. As they turned me out of the room, Elisi rushed in.

I trudged up to my room. Only an hour ago, I had felt I'd recovered control. Now I had to confront that the wedding was tomorrow, and Carsina was not going to find a dashing and handsome young cadet waiting to escort her. No. She'd find me. Fat me. I thought of Gord's girl, and how she seemed to adore him despite his fat. Then I thought of Carsina and didn't even dare to hope for the same response. Gord, I suspected, had always been fat. Cilima had probably never seen him any other way. But Carsina had seen me fit and lean. I hated how I appeared now; how could she not also hate it?

I was light-headed with hunger. All the fasting, all the toiling of the past three days had done nothing. It was so unfair. I tried not to think about all the rich and wonderful things that were simmering in the kitchen or stored in the pantry right now. The wedding day would be at the bride's home. We'd arise early and ride there in the carriage for the ceremony. But the festivities that followed, with dancing and eating and singing, were to be held here at Widevale Hall, and the food and drink necessary to such an occasion now awaited the guests. At the thought of it, my stomach growled loudly. I had to swallow.

I rolled over on my bed and stared at the wall. At the appointed hour, I roused myself again and went back for the final fitting. I wished I hadn't. In the hallway, Elisi rushed past me in tears, calling over her shoulder, "Then I shall look like a cow! That's all that can be said, I shall look like a cow!" As she passed me, she snarled, "I hope you're satisfied, Nevare! But for you and your stupid belly, there would be plenty of time to reset the neckline of my dress!"

Confused and alarmed, I entered the sewing room. My mother was sobbing into her handkerchief as she stood in the corner of the room by the window. The seamstresses, both of them red-cheeked, were endeavoring not to notice. Their heads were bent over their tasks and their needles winked in the lamplight as they diligently sewed. I sensed that I walked into the aftermath of a storm. "Mother? Are you all right?" I asked her gently.

She wiped her eyes hastily. "Oh, weddings! My own was just such a disaster as this one is, right until the moment when it all went perfectly. I'm sure we will all be fine, Nevare. Try on your suit."

"Elisi seemed quite upset. And she seemed to blame it on me."

"Oh. Well." My mother sniffed and then hastily wiped her nose and eyes again. "Well, we had assumed you would wear your uniform, so we did not allow time to sew clothing for you. So there has been less time to work on Elisi's dress, and the pattern for the neckline was quite difficult. That new fashion, with the standing ruffle, has gone all wrong. Still, even without the ruffle, it looks nice. She is just upset. There will be a young man at the wedding, Derwith Toller. He is a guest of the Poronte family. We don't know the Tollers well, but his family has made an offer for Elisi, and of course she wishes to look lovely when she meets him."

I continued to nod as she unwound a long and convoluted tale about a young man who might be a good match for Elisi and the difficulties of the standing ruffle when the lace was wider than what had been ordered and too soft to stand well. I fear it all seemed vapidly trivial to me, but I had the sense not to say so. Privately I thought that if this young man were going to make a marriage proposal based on how well the lace stood up on Elisi's neckline, then he wasn't much of a catch, but I forbore from saying it.

At last my mother's tongue ran down, but strange to say, she seemed relieved to have rattled off her woes to me. I think her telling moved the seamstresses, for one suddenly stood up and said, "Let me have one more try with that lace. If we back it with a piece of the dress goods and use a goodly amount of starch, it might be a pretty effect and make that dratted ruffle stand."

I tried to get away with carrying my suit off to my room, but had no luck. I had to try it on yet again, and although I thought I looked dreary and dull in the mirror, the three women pronounced it a "respectable fit for such short notice" and sent me on my way with it.

CHAPTER FIVE

ROSSE'S WEDDING

W e were all roused when the sky was barely gray. The girls ate in their rooms from trays lest a breakfast mishap soil their traveling dresses. I joined my father and brothers at the table. It was the first time I'd seen Vanze since I'd returned. My priest brother had journeyed home for the ceremony, only arriving last night. My father and Vanze were serving themselves from the sideboard when I entered the room. Vanze had shot up while he was at seminary. Despite being the youngest, he was now the tallest of us.

"You've grown!" I exclaimed in surprise.

When he turned to greet me, his shock was evident. "And so have you, but not taller!" he blurted out, and both my elder brother and my father laughed aloud. After a painful moment, I joined in.

"But not for long," I promised him. "I've been fasting for the last three days. I've resolved to take this off as quickly as I put it on."

My father shook his head dolefully. "I doubt it, Nevare. I hate to say it, but you don't look a bit thinner to me. I fear it will take more than three days of fasting. Have a bite now, to get you through the start of the day. Can't have you fainting at your brother's wedding!" Again they all laughed at me.

His remarks stung me, for all that they were true. Nevertheless, his tone was affable, for the occasion had sweetened his mood. I swallowed the hurt, resolving not to say or do anything that might reawaken his displeasure with me.

I found eggs, meat, bread, fruit, and milk set up on the sideboard. The sight and smell of the food dizzied me. My discipline might have failed me if my father had not been frowning over every morsel I put on my plate. I felt as furtive as a wild animal stealing food. I put a piece of toast on my plate, glanced at my father, and added two small sausages. I took up the spoon for the scrambled eggs. A small frown creased his brow. I took a tiny serving. I decided I would risk his wrath by adding one other item.

It was an agonizing decision. I finally settled on a serving of apple compote. The aroma of the warm, sugary fruit almost made me swoon. I filled a mug with hot black coffee and took my feast to the table. I wanted to fill my mouth with huge bites of food. I wanted to feel the substance of chewing and swallowing a mouthful of eggs and spicy sausage heaped on crisp buttered toast. Instead, I forced myself to divide my meal into small bites and eat it very slowly. I filled my coffee mug twice, hoping the hot liquid would help satisfy my hunger. Yet when my plate was scraped clean of the last crumb, my body still clamored for more. I took a deep breath and pushed my chair back from the table. I would not starve, I told myself severely. This discipline of tiny meals would not last forever, only until I had regained my previous state. Besides, there would be a feast following the wedding today, and I must partake of that to avoid giving offense to the bride's family. Such thoughts were consolation.

I glanced up to find Rosse and Vanze pointedly not looking

at me. My father was regarding me with distaste. "If you are finished, Nevare, perhaps we can depart for your brother's wedding?"

They had been waiting for me while I stretched out my meal. A flush of shame rose to my face. "Yes. I'm finished." I followed them from the room, full of loathing for myself and anger at them.

The carriage awaited us, festooned with wedding garlands. My mother and sisters were already inside. Blankets draped them to keep the dust away from their carefully arranged dresses. There were seven of us in the family, and at any time that would have meant a crowded ride. Today, with the voluminous gowns the women wore and my voluminous body, it was a hopeless fit. Before I could volunteer, my father said, "Nevare, you will ride with the coachman."

It was humiliating to climb up to my seat while they watched. The seams of my new trousers strained, and I could only hope that the stitches would hold. The driver, dressed all in bright blue for the occasion, looked directly forward, as if by gazing at me he might share my shame. My father and brothers managed to fit themselves into the carriage, the door was closed, and we were away at last.

It was a morning's ride to the Poronte estate. For most of the journey, we followed the road along the river, but for the last hour and a half the carriage jolted and bumped along a lesser road that wound its way into the heart of the Poronte lands. Lord Poronte had built his manor on an immense upthrust of stone. It commanded a wide view of all the plains and reminded me more of a citadel than a gentleman's home. Rumor said that he was still in debt to the stonemasons who had come from Cartem to erect the thick rock walls of his mansion. Lord Poronte had taken the motto "Stone Endures," and it was etched into a stone arch that framed the entry to his grounds.

When I look back at my brother's wedding day, my memory shies like a badly trained horse. I felt that every person who greeted me betrayed a jolt of shock at my appearance. At first sight of me, Lord Poronte pursed his lips as if he were trying to restrain a lively goldfish in his mouth. His lady actually lifted a hand to smother a giggle and then quickly excused herself, saying that she must assist the bride in her final preparations. I both felt and saw my family's embarrassment.

A servant led us upstairs, while others followed with the ladies' luggage. A suite of rooms had been set aside for my family to freshen ourselves after our journey and where the girls and my mother could change from their traveling dresses into their wedding clothes. We men more quickly put ourselves to rights. My father and brothers were eager to descend and join the festive gathering. I followed with trepidation.

The Poronte ballroom was not as large as ours, but it was still a gracious room, and at that moment it bustled with guests. The fashion that year was for very full skirts, with layers of fabrics in different tints of the chosen color. From the landing at the top of the stairs, it reminded me of a garden, with the women as lovely blossoms of every hue. A few months ago, I'd have been eager to descend those stairs and find my Carsina among the bouquet. Now I dreaded the moment when she would see me. Reluctantly, I descended the steps. My father and brothers made themselves convivial among the guests. I did not attempt to follow them or to stand near them as they hailed old friends and renewed acquaintances. I did not blame them for disassociating themselves from me.

Everyone I greeted reacted uncomfortably to my body's change. Some smiled stiffly and kept their eyes firmly on my face. Others frankly stared and seemed hard put to find anything intelligent to say. Kase Remwar gave a hoot of mirth and jovially asked me if the cavalla had been feeding my horse as well as it had me. Mockery countenanced as a shared jest was most common among the males of my acquaintance. I forced myself to smile and even to laugh along with them at first. At last, I retreated to concealment.

I sought a quiet eddy in the room. Several large ornamental trellises had been draped with floral garlands to frame the family altar where the couple would make their vows. A few chairs had been placed behind the angle of the alcove. I quickly claimed one. No one approached me, let alone sought to converse with me. This was very different from the triumphant homecoming I had imagined. I had dared to imagine Carsina at my side as I cheerfully told my friends about my studies and life in Old Thares. From my vantage I could quietly observe the gathering. My father was obviously pleased with the day; he was affable and magnanimous. He and Lord Poronte, arms linked, moved through the gathering, greeting the guests. They were a powerful duo, and their alliance through the marriage would make them even more formidable in the Midlands. They paraded as if they were the happy couple rather than their offspring.

Rosse was as nervous as any bridegroom, and endured the jibes and jests of his male friends. They had cornered him near the garden entrance, and from the roars of laughter that burst intermittently from the group, I guessed the crude nature of the banter. Vanze, my priest brother, was a fish out of water. His time at the seminary had accustomed him to a more sophisticated company than prevailed at this frontier manor. He carried his book of Holy Writ with him, for he would assist at the oath-giving of the pair, clutching it like a drowning man holds to a piece of wood. He spoke little and smiled much. I imagined he was already counting the days until he could return to the genteel atmosphere of his school. He had lived so long at his monastery that I suspected it was more of a home to him than our family abode was.

I didn't blame him. I strongly wished I were back at the academy.

I found myself studying people's bodies as I never had before. I had always accepted that with age, men and women became stouter. I had never thought less of a woman whose heavy bosom and rounded belly spoke of years of childbearing. Men of a certain age became portly and dignified. Now I found myself speculating on who was larger than I was and who was smaller. My girth would not have been shocking in a man in his mid-thirties, I decided. It was the coating of fat on a young man that made me so offensive to their eyes A few of the younger men carried substantial bellies, but they did not sport fat on their arms and legs as I did. It made me look indolent and lazy. It was a false impression, for under my fat,

I was as muscular as I'd ever been. I watched the staircase that led to the upper storeys of the house with dread. I longed to behold Carsina, but feared what I would see in her face as she confronted my change. Despite my trepidation, when she appeared at the top of the stairs, I lunged to my feet like a dog that has been promised a walk. She was a vision. Her dress, as she had promised me, was a delicate pale green, with an overskirt of a richer green with trim of darker green that was the exact shade of my academy uniform. It was both modest and provocative, for the high collar of white lace emphasized the delicacy of her pale throat. A small yellow rose was pinned in her upswept hair. My sister Yaril was beside her. A simple change of clothing had transformed her from girl to woman. She wore a gown of rich turquoise, and her golden hair was netted up in an elaborate concoction of gold wire and turquoise ribbons. The cut of the dress revealed her tiny waist and the gentle swell of her hips and bosom. Despite my recent irritation with her, I felt proud of her beauty. Each of the girls wore a bracelet of silver bells for the wedding ceremony.

Kase Remwar appeared as if by magic at the bottom of the stair. He looked up at my sister and Carsina like a dog contemplating unguarded meat. Yaril had set her heart on him, but as of yet, neither of my parents had mentioned any formal engagement. Indignation flashed in me that he dared look at my sister in such a way. I took two steps and halted, a coward. A year ago, my mere physical presence would have reminded him to respect our family, with no threats verbalized. Now, if I bobbed up beside her, I feared that I would look pompous and silly rather than properly protective of my sister's honor. I halted where the trellised flowers still screened me.

I should have known that my sister would have warned Carsina that I was not the dapper trooper that she had seen off to school in the fall. The girls halted strategically midway down the stair. Surely my sister was aware that Kase's eyes devoured her. I felt she immodestly gave him the opportunity to stare. As for Carsina, her eyes roved over the gathered folk, looking for me. My sister leaned toward her and said something. The sneer of it twisted her pretty mouth. I guessed the nature of her remark, that I would not be hard to spot among the crowd. Carsina's smile was uncertain. She hoped that my sister was teasing her, and feared she was not.

Hope congealed in me, replaced by harsh determination. I'd face it and get it over with. I stepped out of my concealment and made my way through the guests to the base of the stair. The moment Carsina saw me, her eyes widened in disbelief and horror. She clutched at my sister's arm and said something. Yaril shook her head in disgust and sympathy. Carsina actually retreated a step before she mastered herself. As she and Yaril descended the stairs, Carsina's face was set in a stubbornly bland expression, but there was despair in her eyes.

As I drew closer, I could almost feel the anger that boiled off her. I bowed to her gravely. "Carsina. Yaril. You both look lovely."

"Thank you, Nevare." Carsina's voice was cool and correct.

"More than lovely, I think." Kase circled behind me to stand next to Yaril. "As beauteous as blossoms. I declare, a man would be hard-pressed to say which of you were more gorgeous." He included them both in his smile. "May I offer to escort you to the altar alcove? The ceremony is soon to begin."

Carsina turned to him with a wide smile. A shadow of discontent passed over Yaril's face. She shot me a look of pure fury, then hastily claimed Kase's right arm. Carsina promptly stepped past me to take his left. Kase laughed with delight, and Carsina tipped her face to smile up at him. Yaril smiled grimly. "I shall be the envy of every man in the room for the next few minutes," Kase proclaimed.

"That you shall," I said quietly, but my hope that I would win some sort of response from Carsina was a vain one. They swept off toward the altar. Most of the people in the room were moving in that direction. I followed disconsolately. When I realized I was scowling, I deliberately straightened my spine and put a pleasant expression on my face. Today, I reminded myself, was my brother's wedding day. I would not let my personal disappointment spoil it for anyone.

I refused to follow the threesome or attempt to join them. Instead, I took a place sufficiently near my older sister Elisi to be recognized as her brother, yet not so close as to embarrass her. She did not look at me. A young man and an older couple whom I judged to be his parents stood not far from her. I wondered if he were the prospective suitor my mother had mentioned.

We all gathered before the good god's altar. Silence descended over the assembly. Vanze and a priest I did not know entered the room. The priest carried a lamp, the god's light, and Vanze carried a large, empty silver basin, the symbol of an end to blood sacrifice. Once, I knew, a wedding would have required Rosse to preside over the slaughter of a bull, a goat, and a cat. Both he and the bride would have had to endure a ritual flogging of three lashes, to symbolize their willingness to suffer for each other. The enlightenment of the good god had changed all that. The old gods had demanded that blood or pain be the coin that paid for any oath. I was grateful such days were gone forever.

Rosse and my parents went to the altar to accept Cecile's pledge. She made a grand entrance, descending the staircase to the ringing of silver bells. Her gown was blue and green, with elaborate sleeves that nearly reached the floor and an embroidered blue train that trailed several steps behind her. Every single woman in the room wore a bracelet of tiny bells, and they raised them over their heads and shook them merrily as the bride descended. Her parents followed her down the stairs. Between them they bore a large basket. As they passed through the crowd, people surged forward to toss in jingling handfuls of coins to wish the young couple wealth in their lives. Among our class, it was merely a charming tradition. Among the lower classes, such an offering might furnish the couple with a goat or a few chickens and truly become a foundation for later wealth.

Rosse and Cecile had chosen a simple ritual for their ceremony. The day was beginning to warm, and I'm sure I was not the only guest who was grateful that we would not be required to stand in witness for too long.

Their fathers exchanged pledges of friendship and loyalty

first, and then their mothers exchanged vows to comfort, help, and refrain from gossip. I stood stoically through them. But when Cecile and Rosse made their pledges of loyalty, trust, and mutual faithfulness, my throat constricted and tears pricked my eyes. I do not know if I wanted to weep because Carsina had betrayed our fledgling love or for my scratched pride. This moment with Carsina should have been mine, I thought fiercely. It should have been a memory that we would cherish through our years together. Instead, I would have to remember always that she had forsaken me at this moment. I set my teeth and forced my lips into a rubbery smile, and when I wiped a tear from my eye, I told myself that everyone who observed it would think it was a tear of joy at my brother's good fortune.

Rosse and Cecile shared the tiny cake of bitter herbs followed by the more generous honey cake that represented the bad and the good times that they would share. Then they turned from the altar and lifted their joined hands. The gathered witnesses erupted with cries of joy and congratulations and the musicians on the dais awoke their instruments. As lively and celebratory music filled the ballroom, the guests cleared the floor and formed a circle for Cecile and Rosse. My brother had never been a graceful dancer, so he must have practiced quite a bit to perform as well as he did. Not once did he step on Cecile's trailing blue train. At the end of the dance, he swept her up in his arms and spun around and around as he held her, making her sleeves and train fly out around them, much to the delight of the onlookers. A single misstep would have sent bride and groom tumbling to the floor, but he managed to set his giddy bride squarely on her feet. Flushed and laughing, they bowed to their audience.

Then came the most important part of the ceremony, not just for Rosse and Cecile but for both families as well. My father and Lord Poronte broke the seals on the congratulatory scrolls that had come from King Troven. As all the gathered folk expected, the scrolls contained a substantial land grant to each family to "celebrate the joyous union of two of my most loyal noble families, and with fond wishes that both your houses will continue to flourish." The land allotted to the Burvelle holdings increased our holdings by a third. The satisfaction on my father's face shone. I could almost see him totting up how much additional acreage the king would gift him as each of his other four children married. I suddenly realized that this was how King Troven encouraged alliances between the new noble houses, thus keeping their loyalty safely in his pocket.

"Please join us in dancing and feasting!" Cecile invited her guests, and to a loud burst of applause, all did just that. The doors to the adjacent dining room were opened wide, to reveal long tables. I was not near the doors, yet I was abruptly aware of the savory aromas of the fresh breads and roasted meats and sweet fruit tarts. A wedding in our part of the country was an all-day celebration. When one traveled long distances for such an event, the host endeavored to make it memorable. The talk and dancing and eating would continue all day at the Porontes' home. Servants would be kept busy constantly replenishing the tables. Many of the guests would spend the night with the Porontes, and then join us at our home tomorrow for a second day of socializing and feasting. At one time, I had anticipated a merry occasion, and had planned several opportunities to be alone with Carsina. I had even imagined stealing a kiss or two. Now I dreaded several days of torment. My stomach growled at me urgently. I listened to it in horror, as if a monster had taken up residence in my flesh and demanded sustenance. I tried to tell myself that I was too saddened to be hungry, but my belly asserted otherwise. The sight of Kase Remwar leading Carsina to the dance floor only reinforced the emptiness I felt. I was famished, I discovered, and trembling with hunger. Never before had my sense of smell seemed so keen. From where I stood, I could tell that the prairie fowl had been roasted with sage and onion, and that the lamb had been prepared Plainsman-fashion, rubbed with wild celery root and cooked in a pot with a tight lid. I thought it the limit of my self-control that I walked around the edge of the dance floor rather than elbowing my way through the dancers to reach the food.

Halfway around the room, I encountered my father talking to Carsina's father. Lord Grenalter was laughing at

something my father had just said. They both seemed very
jovial and convivial. I'd intended to slip past them unac-
knowledged. But as Grenalter drew breath from laughing,
our eyes met. Courtesy forced me to greet him. I stopped,
bowed to him, and then, as I advanced, he said, quite loudly,
"Good god's breath, Burvelle! Is that Nevare?"

"I'm afraid so," my father said levelly. His look told me I
was a fool for having called attention to myself. He forced a
grin to his face. "I think the academy doctor went too far in
putting flesh back on him after the plague. He'll soon have it
off, if I have anything so say about it."

And what could I do, save grin shamefacedly and agree?
"Very soon, sir," I assured him. And then, lying through my
teeth, I added, "The doctor told me that a temporary weight
gain like this is not unknown among plague survivors. He
told me that I should be grateful to have gone this way,
rather than lost flesh and stamina."

"Well . . . I'm sure the doctor would know what he is talking about. Still. It *is* a startling change, Nevare, as I'm sure
you know." Lord Grenalter seemed determined to make me
admit that the transformation was horrifying.

"Yes, sir, it is that. Thankfully, as I've said, it is temporary."

"Well. I suppose we should thank the good god for your
health, and never mind the rest for now."

"Yes, sir. I do that every morning when I awaken alive.
It's not a thing a man takes for granted, once he has experienced the plague."

"Was it very bad, then, in the city?"

And I was pathetically grateful to horrify the poor man
with a lurid telling of just how bad it had been. When I spoke
of the dead stacked like cordwood on the snowy grounds, I
realized that even my father was listening to me. So I deliberately told, with genuine sorrow, of my fellows whose health
had broken so badly that they would never soldier at all, let
alone continue a career at the academy. I finished with, "And
so, of course, ungainly as I find myself at present, you can
understand why I am grateful to have come through the experience with my future intact. And with Colonel Rebin in

charge of the academy once more, I anticipate continuing my studies with more pleasure than ever."

"A remarkable tale! And did they ever find what wayward son of a dog brought plague to Old Thares?" Carsina's father was completely in thrall to my tale now.

I shook my head. "It is suspected that it came to the city with some Specks who were being displayed at a Dark Evening carnival."

"What?" Horrified, he turned to my father. "Had you heard of Specks being allowed to travel to the west?"

"It was inevitable that someone would try to smuggle some to the city eventually," my father said with great resignation. "The greatest folly was that one of them was a female. From correspondence I've had with authorities at the academy, she was the likely source of the plague."

"No!" Carsina's father was aghast. He turned to me, and suddenly a new light kindled in his eyes, as if he had suddenly worked an equation and was appalled at the answer. His eyes appraised me warily. How had I contracted the dread disease? The question was in his gaze if not on his lips, and I answered it directly.

"There are other ways of transmission beside sexual contact," I hastily insisted. "I've been working with Dr. Amicas at the academy, simply because of the unique aspects of my case. Some of my fellows, I will admit, fell to the plague after having congress with a Speck whore. I, sir, was not one of them. Nor, for example, was the young son of the former Academy commander. And of course, my own girl-cousin Epiny was also a victim of the plague."

"And did she die?" I suddenly realized that the circle of my audience had grown. This query came from another listener, a middle-aged woman unwisely dressed in a virulent pink gown.

"No, ma'am, I'm happy to say she did not. Her case was very mild and she recovered with no side effects. Unfortunately, that was not true for the young new noble cadet she married. Cadet Kester was forced to withdraw from the academy. He is determined that he will recover his health sufficiently to return, but many feel that his military career is over."

Several of my listeners now spoke at once.

"I served with Kester! It must be his son. That's a damnable shame! Who else fell to the plague, from the new noble ranks?"

"What saved your cousin from the plague? What herbs did she take? My Dorota is with her husband at Gettys. She and her two little ones. They haven't had it in the household yet, but she fears it's just a matter of time!" There was great worry in that matron's voice as she pushed closer to me.

But the voice I heard most clearly was that of Carsina's father. Grenalter said slowly to my father, "Epiny Burvelle—that would be your brother's elder daughter. She married a new noble soldier son who'll have no career? Surely you told me that your brother planned to marry her to an old noble heir son?"

My father attempted a tolerant laugh. That was when I knew I'd said too much. "Well, you know young people today, Grenalter, especially the city-bred ones. They have small respect for the plans of their parents. And in a time of plague, permissions are given that ordinarily would be refused. Just as soldiers facing battle will sometimes commit acts that they would otherwise recognize as foolhardy."

"Foolhardy. Indeed. I've witnessed a few acts like that," Grenalter conceded heavily. I could tell he was distracted, and I could almost see him totting up and subtracting the advantages and disadvantages of his marital agreement with our family as if he were an accountant. Suddenly Epiny's words about being sold as a bride to the highest bidder didn't seem so melodramatic. Obviously, my weight gain was a debit to the transaction, but an even larger one was that the branch of the Burvelle family in Old Thares had not sold off their daughter to an old nobility family. Did connections and marriages actually carry that much political and social weight, I wondered, and then instantly knew that they did.

"Well?" demanded the woman anxiously, and my mind leapt back to her question.

"Lots of water and rest were the chief treatment, I'm afraid. I wish I could tell you something more specific. Dr. Amicas is making the prevention of the plague his specific area of study. He's a very dedicated man. If anyone can come up with solid recommendation to protect families from transmission, it will be him."

"And which other new nobles perished?" the other man demanded. I recognized him but could not call up his name. He was not a new noble, but was a very successful ranker who had followed Grenalter into retirement much as my father's men had congregated around him. I suddenly realized that men like him would be pinning their hopes on the rise of the new noble class. Old nobles and heir sons would have little respect for a ranker like him. The new nobles who had directly commanded him recognized his worth. And if they came to power, that recognition might extend to his own soldier sons.

So I recited reluctantly the names of those new noble sons who had died from the plague, and those whose health had been badly compromised. When I mentioned that Trist Wissom had lost his health, I was surprised at the collective sigh of sympathy. And I was shocked when I recounted the names of those who had recovered well, and people exchanged glad glances when they heard that Rory and Gord were unscathed. They did not know my fellow cadets, but they knew or had known of their fathers. There was a sense of connection there. The old nobles were right to fear our rise to influence. The real power lay not in the new nobles and their sons who would follow wherever the king led, but in the ranks of the military who felt loyalty and alliance to the new nobles.

"Damn shame what's happened to our academy. Damn shame!" This from the ever-excitable Lord Blair, a little bald man who always bounced on his toes when he spoke. "We needed those young officers, what with the rumors of trouble on the border near Rely. Looks like we might start up with Landsing all over again! You'd be sorry to miss out on that, wouldn't you, Cadet? Fast promotions wherever the fighting's thick, as I'm sure you know."

I was at a loss. I hadn't heard we were skirmishing with Landsing again.

"Gettys is where the real opportunity is!" This from a man I didn't recognize. "The King's Road has been at a standstill for damn near two years. Farleyton went out there to re-place Brede's regiment, but from what I hear, they've not done well. Same problems Brede had. Disease, desertion, and dereliction of duty! The king won't stand for it any-more. I hear he's sending Cayton's horse and Doril's foot to reinforce them. I feel sorry for Farleyton. They were a top-notch regiment not too many years ago. Some say that Get-tys will just do that to a regiment. Disease breaks down the morale and destroys the chain of command. Haren's got the command now. A good enough man for a second, but I'm not sure he's up to ramrodding an operation like the King's Road."

"Colonel Haren's a good officer!" someone else broke in sharply. "Careful what you say about him, man. I served be-side him at the Battle of Dell."

"Gentlemen, gentlemen! Now is not the time for war sto-ries." My father quickly broke in on the lively conversation. "Nevare, I am sure we are all grateful for the information you have shared with us, but let us not forget that we are here to celebrate a wedding! Surely some of you would rather be on the dance floor than listening to tales of disease and death? Or is there so little hardship in our life that we are drawn to such stories?"

He gained a general laugh with that gently bitter question. It was, indeed, part of our common lot that life was harder here on the edges of civilization.

"Let us celebrate life while we can!" one of the men sug-gested. "Death and disease will always be waiting for us." And with that dark toast, my audience began to fragment. Some moved toward the musicians and dancing, others toward the tables of food. Grenalter himself left rather hastily. I surrepti-tiously tracked his flight and saw him join his wife and Car-sina at a refreshment table. I saw him send Carsina off to join a group of other young women, and then take his wife's arm and escort her to a quieter corner. I suspected I knew the topic of conversation. Without intending it, I sought for Kase Rem-war, and found him dancing with my sister. She looked bliss-ful. Remwar, an heir son, had been the Grenalters' first choice as a match for Carsina. Had I just gossiped away my marriage arrangement? And if I had, had I dashed Yaril's dreams as well? I felt queasy.

My father was not consoling. "You should talk less and listen more, Nevare. I will say no more on that topic now, but suggest that for the rest of the day, you become a very good nodder and listener. Keep your tongue from wagging. Why you saw fit to share here such information that you had not previously divulged to me, I shall never know. For the rest of this day, if you must speak, speak only of your brother's happiness and good fortune. If you must speak of gloom, deplore the dry weather we've had!"

With that admonition, he left my side, striding away as if I'd insulted him. Perhaps by his lights, I had. He never liked to be second to know anything. I seethed. It was his own fault. If he had given me a chance to talk to him since my return, he would have known all my news and could have advised me what not to repeat. He had treated me unjustly, but worse, I had foolishly blathered out my tidings without considering if it was wise to do so. I already regretted my lie about what Dr. Amicas had said. I felt sure it was true, but I wished I had not quoted the doctor to give greater authority to my belief. The lie shamed me.

That bleakness of spirit suddenly quenched my hunger. I abruptly felt that selecting the food and taking it to a table and making small talk with my fellow guests would require more energy that I could summon. I glanced back at the dance floor. The musicians still played, and Carsina was dancing with a young man I didn't recognize. He was short, freckled, and didn't dance well, but he wasn't fat. I stood rooted, watching them and trying not to watch them. I saw her laugh at something he said. A perverse part of me dared me to stay in the room and ask her for the next dance. Her certain refusal would end my hope and put me out of my misery.

I loitered there, at the edge of the crowd, building my courage, denouncing it as foolhardy, rebuilding it, deciding that she was promised to me and it was my right to speak to her, losing my courage again . . . never had a dance lasted so long, it seemed. When it ended and her partner bowed over her hand and then stepped away from her, it was all I could do to make myself walk in her direction.

She saw me coming. She fled.

And, fool that I was, I hastened after her, cutting through the crowd to close off her retreat. When she realized she could not escape me, she slowed. I closed the remaining distance between us. "Carsina. I've been hoping to have a dance with you. And a chance to speak to you, and explain what has befallen me."

It was my misfortune that the musicians suddenly struck up a lively tune rather than the stately waltz I had hoped for. Carsina saved herself and me by saying stiffly, "I am weary of dancing at present. Perhaps later."

"But perhaps we could talk now. Shall we walk in the garden?"

"I fear it would not be proper, for we should be unchaperoned."

My smile at her comment was bitter. "That did not stop us the last time."

She looked away from me and gave a vexed sigh. "That was last time, Nevare. *Obviously*, much has changed."

Stung, I replied, "What has not changed is that we are promised to one another. Surely you owe me at least the opportunity to tell you what I've been through—"

"I owe you nothing, sir!" she flared at me. Her companion from the last dance suddenly reappeared, carrying two glasses of wine. His eyes widened with disapproval that I had forced a lady to give me such a stern response.

I warned him off with a glare. "The lady and I are having a conversation."

He was a head shorter than me, but probably thought my weight made me soft. "It did not sound like a conversation to me. It sounded as if she wished you to leave her alone."

"We are promised to one another. I have the right to—"

"Not formally!" Carsina cut in quickly. "And I do wish you to leave me alone."

"You see, sir, the lady has wearied of your company. Be a gentleman, and allow her to withdraw." He stepped bravely between us. He was all long neck and freckled nose. I could have snapped him like a twig. I looked over his head at Carsina.

"Perhaps she should be a lady and do me the courtesy of hearing me out," I said levelly.

"Do you insinuate I am not a lady?" Carsina flared at me. "Nevare Burvelle, you insult me. I shall tell my father of this!"

Anger sang in my blood and rang in my ears. I seethed with fury. Words burst from me, coming from whence I knew not. "And you have ignored me, fled from me, and thus insulted me thrice today, and this shall be the last time. There will come a time before you die, Carsina, when you will crawl on your knees and beg pardon for how you have treated me this day."

Her mouth fell open at my harsh words. She looked, in her astonishment, both childish and common. All the prettiness fled from her face as anger flooded it. I'd said too much, spoken too rashly. I could not have done a more awkward, awful thing at my brother's wedding.

Carsina's face went scarlet. In horror, I saw tears flood her eyes. Her freckled dance partner glared up at me. "Now, see here, sir, I insist—"

"Insist to yourself, then," I said to him, and strode away. But a fat man is hard-pressed to stride with dignity. I tried in vain to compose my face as I departed the scene. Not that many people, I told myself, had noticed our spat. Neither of us had shouted. I glanced back, but Carsina was gone. I felt a moment of relief, until I saw her hurrying up the stairs, both hands lifted to cover her face. Several women turned to watch her go. My own sister was following her. I cursed myself and wondered where that blaze of temper and my ugly words had come from.

I should have chosen to keep my misery and my pathetic hope, I told myself savagely. I left the ballroom for the terrace, and from there descended stone steps to the garden. It was hotter there, not cooler. Many of the flowering bushes had gone yellow with drought; the young trees were spindly and offered no shade. My collar choked me and my jacket was too warm. How could I have been so stupid? Why had

I forced such a confrontation? I should have let her snub me. The next time I saw her, I'd be a thinner man, and there would have been no harm done. She'd have rebuked herself for avoiding me. Now what I had said to her must always stand between us. Uneasily, I wondered if she had fled to her mother. She was already with my sister. I wondered which would be worse for me.

A thick hedge and the sound of a fountain beyond it promised me a shadier retreat. The garden was poorly planned, for I had to walk some distance and follow a turning in the hedge before I found a very small gate. It was closed but not locked. I entered the second garden.

Here, no expense had been spared. I wondered that guests were not thronging it. A paved walkway led me in a meandering spiral toward the heart of the garden. The beds of flowers were lush, despite the heat and dryness of the last week. Bees hummed among the fairy rosebushes and battled the tall lavender for nectar. The fragrance of flowers and the aromas of herbs were heavy in the still air. I passed an ornamental fish pond. Spatterdock opened the fat petals of its yellow blossoms there, and fish transformed from shadow to gleams as they moved in and out of their shelter. Beyond was a dovecote, styled as a quaint little cottage, full of the preening, cooing creatures. The birds were sunning themselves in the fly pen attached to their shelter. I stood there for some time, letting the restful sound soothe me. Then I followed the winding footpath toward the decorative fountain at the center of the garden and the musical splashing of its waters.

I never reached the fountain. A sudden reek hit my nostrils, a stench so bad that I nearly gagged. I turned my head at the same time I lifted my hand to cover my nose and mouth. I could not believe what met my eyes. The altar was white marble, but the top of it was spattered with gore and bird droppings. A brass pole arched over the altar. Suspended from the arch was something that might have been a lovely chandelier, save that the arms of it ended in hooks, not lamps, and a dead dove was impaled on each hook. In the center of the altar, a bird had been split open and its entrails spread for reading. Bloody fingerprints smeared the white feathers.

A black-and-white croaker bird was perched on top of the brass arch, a streamer of dove gut hanging from his beak. Flies and wasps buzzed heavily around the dead birds. They were grotesque. One white dove was more red than white now, its entrails hanging from its pecked anus. As I stared, dumbfounded, a slow drip of blood dropped to spatter on the altar.

This had been done today.

That chilling thought was followed by another. The altar and the hook chandelier were permanent fixtures. Poronte and his family worshipped the old gods on a regular basis. This was a marriage offering. In all likelihood, my brother's bride and her mother and sisters had sacrificed these birds to celebrate Cecile's wedding day.

I had not thought my horror could deepen. But as I stared, transfixed, the unthinkable happened. One bird abruptly twitched on its hook. Its wings shuddered spasmodically, causing the carousel of dead birds to turn slightly. It unlidded a dull eye at me while its small beak opened and closed soundlessly.

I could not stand it.

I had to stand on tiptoe to reach him, and my stretch strained the shoulders of my jacket perilously. I made a grab at him, caught him by the wing, and pulled the gruesome merry-go-round toward me. When I could get both hands on him, I lifted his body from the hook. I'd intended to end his misery by wringing his neck. Before I could, his body gave a final shudder and was still. I stepped back from the altar and looked at my pathetic trophy. The anger I had felt at Carsina suddenly transmuted to fury at the unfairness of it all. Why had this little creature had to die as sacrifice to celebrate a wedding day? Why was his tiny life so insignificant to them? It was the only life he could ever know. "You should not have died." My blood pounded through me, thick with rage. "They were wicked to kill you! What sort of a family has my brother joined to us?"

The bird's eyes opened. I was so shocked I nearly dropped it. It gave its head a shake, and then opened its wings. I did drop it then, releasing it to a fall that it changed into a frantic launch. One of its wings brushed my face as it took flight. In an instant, it was gone. Small downy neck feathers clung to my fingertips. I shook my hands, and they ghosted away to float eerily in the still air. I was not sure what had happened. I looked again at the gory carousel of dead birds and at the smear of blood on my hand. Repulsed, I wiped my hand clean on my dark trousers. How had the bird survived?

I stared too long. In the branches of a nearby bush, a croaker bird suddenly cawed loudly. It lifted its black-and-white wings and opened its red beak wide at me. It had orange wattles on its bare neck; they were fleshy and wobbled cancerously at me as it cawed.

I retreated a step, but he still challenged me with three loud caws. The cries were immediately echoed by a couple of his fellows perched in nearby trees. As they raised the alarm, I turned and hastily walked away. My thoughts were in turmoil. It was one thing to hear tales of what the worship of the old gods had demanded; it was another thing to see a carrion tree set up for their delight.

Did Rosse know of his wife's beliefs?

Did my father? My mother?

I breathed through my mouth as I walked swiftly away from that place. When I reached the lavender beds and the drowsing bumblebees mining them, I stopped. I took deep calming breaths of their fragrance. I was sweating. I'd glimpsed something dark and it filled me with a sudden foreboding.

"Sir. This is a private garden for the family's meditation and repose. The wedding festivities do not extend to this area."

The woman was dressed as a gardener, in rough brown tunic and pantaloons and sandals. A broad-brimmed straw hat shaded her face. She carried a little basket on one arm with a trowel in it.

I wondered if she was in charge of burying the birds. No. From what I knew of those rites, they had to remain as an offering until the elements and the scavengers had reduced them to bones. I met her direct look and tried to read her eyes. She smiled at me politely.

"I've lost my way, I'm afraid."

She pointed. "Follow the pathway to the gate. Please latch it behind you, sir."

She knew. She knew I wasn't lost and she knew about the sacrifice and she guessed that I had seen it. Her eyes moved over me. Her gaze disdained me.

"Thank you. I'll be glad to find my way back."

"You're welcome, sir."

We were so polite. She made my skin crawl. I walked away from her, trying not to hurry. When I reached the gate, I glanced back. She had quietly followed me down the path to make sure that I left. I lifted my hand and flapped it at her foolishly, as if waving good-bye. She hastily turned away from me. I left the garden, closing the gate firmly behind me.

My first childish impulse was to run to my father and tell him all I'd seen. If Rosse and Cecile had not already said their vows, I might have done so. But they were already joined, and my mother and father had given oaths equally binding to Cecile's parents. It was too late to stop them from joining our good name with the heathen Poronte family. I made my slow way back through the first garden and to the terrace. As I went, I decided that I would wait until I could privately pass my knowledge to my father. As the head of our family, he would decide what to do about it. Would it be sufficient grounds for him to contact the High Temple in Old Thares and have the marriage voided? Cecile and the other Poronte family members had called the good god to witness their pledges. Did the sacrifice in the garden mean they did not feel bound by their oaths before the good god? Had they smiled at my parents and mouthed words empty of intent?

On the terrace, people were resting and talking, the women fanning themselves against the rising heat of the day. I kept my smile in place and avoided making eye contact with anyone. No one spoke to me as I passed.

The musicians were still playing in the ballroom. Dancers still spun to their notes. I told myself there was no sense on dwelling on the ugliness I'd witnessed. I'd set it out of my mind until I could consign it to my father's judgment. The spinning dancers made a lovely picture, and I was almost calm when Carsina, apparently fully recovered from our scene, swept by me, once more in the arms of Kase Remwar. I turned and moved on to the dining room.

There, the hubbub of conversation was nearly as loud as the music in the ballroom. Servants bustled around the room, setting out fresh platters of food, refilling glasses, serving people, clearing away dirty plates, and putting out fresh settings. The smells of food assaulted me. My stomach rolled over inside me and my hunger became a sharp ache that reached all the way up the back of my throat. I stood still for a moment, swallowing saliva. My conservative breakfast that morning had not assuaged the insult done to my body by my days of fasting. I felt that I could have cleared one of the laden tables by myself.

Guests were helping themselves and chatting with others as they meandered among the tables, taking a serving of fruit there, a sweet from that platter, and a pastry from another. I knew I could not trust myself. I found an empty chair at a clean setting without anyone near me. It seemed to take decades before a servant noticed me. "May I bring you anything, sir, or would you care to make your own selection?"

I swallowed and had to take a breath. I ached with emptiness. "Could you bring me a small portion of meat, a roll of bread, and perhaps a glass of wine?"

He startled as if I'd flung cold water at him. "And that is all, sir?" he asked me solicitously. "Or shall I select other foods for you and bring them to you?" His eyes roved over my bulk as if disputing my request.

"Just meat and bread and a glass of wine. That will be fine for me," I assured him.

"Well. If you are certain? Only meat, bread, and wine?"

"I am. Thank you."

He hurried off, and I saw him summon an underling. The servant gestured at me as he passed on my request to the man. The new servant met my glance and his eyes widened. He grinned, bowed obsequiously, and hurried off. I realized my hands were clenched at the edge of the table and folded them in my lap. Food. I was trembling with need for it. The intensity of my awareness of the smells and of my urgency frightened me. For the first time, I wondered if this was an unnatural appetite. Despite my fast, my clothing had become tighter. How could I not eat and become fatter? A frightening suspicion came to me. Magic. Was this the lingering effects of Tree Woman's intrusion on my life? I recalled my vision of my "other self" in her world. He had been heavy of belly and thick-legged. When I took him back into me, had I taken those attributes into my body as well?

It could not be. I didn't believe in magic. I didn't believe in magic desperately, in the same way that a badly wounded soldier did not believe in amputation. *Take it away, take it away,* I prayed to the good god. *If this be magic, put it out of my life and save me from it.*

The Dancing Spindle had moved for me. I had ridden it and I had witnessed it stopping. Did I not believe that had happened? I thought of my cinch that had not stayed tight on Sirlofty. But the modern rational man in me wondered if I deceived myself. Could not my saddle's cinch loosening be a result of my greater weight? If the halting of the Spindle meant that all Plains magic was failing, would not it affect every cavalla man's cinch?

I thought that I could ask Sergeant Duril about his recent cinch experiences. Then I sighed, thinking that right now I didn't have the courage to seek him out for anything. I'd disappointed him, and in some ways, disappointing my old teacher was a more personal failure than disappointing my father. And where was that food? The hunger boiled up in me again, driving all other thoughts from my mind.

Yet it was not food that came to my table next, but my father and mother. I had not noticed them enter the room, and yet there they were. My father took the chair next to me, and my mother seated herself just beyond him. A glance at their faces reassured me that, as yet, they had heard no gossip about my confrontation with Carsina. A servant followed them, carrying their prepared plates. As he set the food before them and the aroma of the rich foods floated toward me, I nearly swooned.

My father leaned over to hiss at me, "Don't take it to extremes, Nevare. You should eat at least something, to show your enjoyment of what was prepared for the wedding. To sit here at a wedding feast with nothing in front of you makes it seem you don't approve of the joining. It's an insult to our host. And may the good god save us, here he comes with his lady."

It could not have been worse timing. Lord and Lady Poronte had not entered the room to dine, but were merely strolling among their guests, greeting them and accepting congratulations and compliments on the gathering. They approached us, smiling, and there I sat, literally the starving man at the feast. I wanted to vanish.

Lady Poronte reached us, smiled at us, and then looked puzzled at the empty place before me. As if she were talking to a child, she wheedled in dismay, "Could not you find anything to tempt your appetite, Nevare? Is there something I could ask our cook to prepare for you?"

"Oh, no, but many thanks, Lady Poronte. Everything looked and smelled so wonderful, I did not trust myself to make a choice. I'm sure the serving man will be here directly."

Then came the final blow to my dignity and to my father's pride. The serving man arrived with my food. He carried a filled platter on each arm. Not two plates, but two platters, and each were laden to overflowing. Meat of every kind was heaped on one, slices of ham, half a smoked chicken, slices of beef cut so thin that they folded into ripples, tender lamb cutlets, each mounded with a spoonful of quivering mint jelly, and a spicy pâté ensconced on a special round of bread. On the other platter was the extreme opposite of my request for a simple roll of bread. There were two croissants, a scone, two muffins, rye bread in dark rounds nestled against its paler wheaten cousin, and dumplings in a ladling of rich brown gravy. Grinning as if he had accomplished some marvelous feat, the serving man placed both platters before me. He bowed, well pleased with himself. "Never fear, sir. I know how to properly serve a man like yourself. As you requested, only meat and only bread. I shall return immediately with your wine, sir." He turned with a flourish and left me surrounded by food.

I stared at the wealth of bread and meat before me. I knew

my father was aghast at my wanton display of gluttony. My shocked hostess was striving to look pleased. Worse, I knew that I could consume every bite of it with relish and pleasure. My mouth was running with so much saliva that I had to swallow before I could speak. "This is far too much food. I asked for a small portion of meat and bread."

But the serving man had already hastened away. I could not stop looking at the food, and I knew that no one at the table believed me.

"But it is a wedding!" Lady Poronte ventured at last. "And surely if there is a time to celebrate in plenty, it is at a wedding."

She meant well. She probably intended to put me at my ease over possessing such an undisciplined appetite and displaying such wanton greed at her table. But it put me in a very strange social situation. If I only sampled a tiny portion of the food now, would it appear that I had disdained her hospitality, or found her cook lacking in talent? I did not know what to do.

"It all looks absolutely wonderful to me, especially after the very plain food they serve us at the academy," I ventured. I did not pick up my fork. I wished they would all vanish. I could not eat with them watching me. Yet I also knew I could not refuse to eat, either.

As if he could read my thoughts, my father said in a chill voice, "Please, Nevare, don't let us inhibit you. Enjoy the wedding feast."

"Please do," my host echoed. I glanced at him but could not read his face.

"Your serving staff is far too generous," I ventured again. "He has brought me much more than I requested." Then, fearing that I would sound ungracious, I added, "But I am sure he meant well." I picked up my knife and fork. I glanced at my parents. My mother was attempting to smile as if nothing were amiss or unusual. She cut a tiny bite from her portion of meat and ate it.

I speared one of the dumplings swimming in gravy. I put it in my mouth. Ambrosia. The inner dumpling was fine-grained and tender, the outer layer softened with the savory broth. I could taste finely chopped celery, mellowed onion, and a careful measure of bay leaf simmered with the thick meatiness of the gravy. Never before had I been so aware of the sensations of eating. It wasn't just the aroma or flavor. It was the sweet briny ham versus the way the spicy pâté contrasted with the tender bread beneath it. The croissant had been made with butter, and the layers of the light pastry were as delicate as snowflakes on my tongue. The chicken had been grain-fed and well bled before it had been carefully roasted in a smoky fire to both flavor it and preserve the moistness of the flesh. The rye bread was delightfully chewy. I washed it down with wine, and a servant brought me more. I ate.

I ate as I had never eaten before. I lost awareness of the people beside me and of the festivity that swirled around me. I gave no thought to what my father might be thinking or my mother feeling. I did not worry that Carsina might chance by and be aghast at my appetite. I simply ate, and the intense pleasure of that exquisite meal after my long fast has never left me. I was a man caught up in a profoundly carnal pleasure. I felt a deep satisfaction at replenishing my reserves, and I gave no thought to anything else. I cannot even say how long it took me to consume both platters, or if there was any conversation around me. At some point, Lord and Lady Poronte passed some pleasantry with my parents and then drifted away to socialize with their other guests. I scarcely noticed. I was a soul consumed with the simple and absolute pleasure of eating.

Only when both platters were empty did I glide back into awareness of my surroundings. My father sat in stony silence. My mother was smiling and making vapid small talk in a hopeless effort to preserve the image of a couple having a conversation. My belly now strained against my belt. Embarrassment battled with a strong urge to rise and seek out the sweets table. Despite what I had consumed, I was still aware of the scent of warm vanilla sugar hanging in the air, and the fragrance of tart strawberries packed into sweet little pastries.

"Are you quite finished, Nevare?" My father asked the question so softly that someone else might have thought him a kind man.

"I don't know what came over me," I said contritely.

"It's called gluttony," he callously replied. He had excellent control over his features. As he spoke so quietly to me, his eyes roved around the room. He nodded to someone he saw there. He smiled as he said, "I have never been so ashamed of you. Do you hate your brother? Do you seek to humiliate me? What motivates you, Nevare? Do you think to avoid your military duty? You will not. One way or another, I'll see you do serve your fate." He turned his head, waved at another acquaintance. "I warn you. If you will not maintain your body and your dignity and earn a commission at the academy and win a noble lady as your wife, why, then, you can go as a common foot soldier. But go you shall, boy. Go you shall."

Only my mother and I could hear the venom in his questions. Her eyes were very wide and her face pale. I suddenly realized that she feared my father, and that right now her fear was extreme. He flicked a glance at her. "Excuse yourself, my lady, and flee this scene if it distresses you. I give you permission."

With an apologetic look to me, she did. Her eyes were anxious, but she put a bright smile on her face, rose, and gave us a tiny wave of farewell as if she regretted having to leave us for a time. Then she fled across the room and out of the hall.

I glued a smile on my lips and cursed my own creeping fear of him. "I spoke the truth to you, Father. I told the servant to bring me a small serving of meat and bread. Once that quantity had arrived and Lady Poronte had witnessed it, what was I to do? Waste the abundance they shared with us? Claim the food did not suit me and turn it away? The servant placed me in a bad position. I made the best of it that I could. Tell me. What should I have done?"

"If you had served yourself a simple meal, instead of waiting to be attended like an old noble's heir son, none of this would have happened."

"And if I had been born with prescience, that is precisely what I would have done," I retorted tightly. Where, I wondered in the shocked silence that followed my words, had that retort come from?

Astonishment that I would stand up to him jolted my father's smile off his face. I was tempted to believe that I had seen a brief flash of respect in his eyes before he narrowed them at me. He took a short sharp breath as if to speak, and then snorted it out in disdain. "This is not the place nor the time, but I promise you, I will have a reckoning with you over this. For the rest of the day, say little and eat nothing. That isn't a request, Nevare. It's an order. Do you understand me?"

I thought of a dozen things I could say. But that was after I had given him a tight nod, and he had pushed his chair back and left me. The two large empty platters on the table rebuked me. There was a swallow of wine left in my glass. I reflected bitterly that he had said nothing about drinking and drank it down.

By the time evening arrived and I again mounted to the top of the carriage for the journey home, I was more sodden with brandy than a well-soaked fruitcake. But that, of course, was civilized and acceptable behavior for a soldier son. No one ever rebuked me for that.

CHAPTER SIX

A DAY OF LETTERS

I did my best to be invisible during the following days of festivities at my home. It was not easy. I had to be present at the dinners, and with a house full of guests, it was difficult to avoid socializing completely. Most unpleasant of all for me was that the Grenalters had been invited to stay with us. Carsina and my sister Yaril snubbed me at every opportunity. If by chance I entered a room they were in, they would immediately sweep disdainfully from it. It maddened me with frustration, the more so in that never once did they enter a room and allow me the chance to vacate it as soon as I saw them. I told myself it was juvenile to long for the chance to show Carsina just how uninterested I was in her, but in my heart I burned to hurt her pride as she had injured mine. I contented myself with making savagely accurate accounts of all my interactions with her in my soldier son journal.

Rosse and Cecile had departed on their wedding trip. They intended to travel downriver to Old Thares, where my uncle would host a reception for them. Cecile had two aunts and three uncles in the capitol, so Rosse would be exhibited and inspected for several weeks before they returned home to settle into the rooms prepared for the new couple. I pitied them, having to begin a new life under my father's roof. My father, I was sure, would grant them little privacy and even less autonomy.

My father and I were at war now. He was courteous to me while houseguests were present, but once they all had departed, he made his displeasure clear. That evening, just as the house should have been peaceful, he verbally flogged me with all my shortcomings as a son, never giving me an opportunity to reply. After a time, from some depth I didn't know I possessed, I found an icy calm and refused to give him any response. When he angrily dismissed me, I went directly to my room and to bed and spent most of that night staring up at the darkened ceiling and seething. He sought to bring me to heel like a whipped puppy. He cared for nothing I might say in my defense. Fine. Then he would hear absolutely nothing from me.

After that, our conflict was conducted in silence. I avoided my father's company. When my mother sought conversation with me I spoke about the academy, my teachers and friends, and my uncle's family. Of my weight gain and my war with my father, I did not speak. When I was not with her, I rediscovered my boyhood haunts along the river. I went fishing. I counted the days until this "holiday" would be over and I could return to the academy.

My cold conflict with my father made him irritable with the entire family. Elisi retreated to her music and books. Yaril often appeared with her eyes red from weeping. My father had chastised her severely for her "shameless flirtation' with Kase Remwar. Plainly, there had been no marriage offer between the families. As an uncommitted first son, Kase had danced, dined, and chatted with any number of eligible young maidens at Rosse's wedding. I suspected it was simply his nature, but Yaril blamed me. I could have taken vengeance on her by telling my father that I'd seen her kiss Remwar before I'd even departed for the academy. But even in my anger and hurt, I knew that the consequences that would fall on her would be far heavier than her foolishness merited. And keeping that secret from my father was one more bit of damage I dealt him. He thought he knew so much about his household and how to run the lives of his children? He knew us not at all.

Vanze busied himself with visiting friends in the area before departing for the seminary. I found a quiet moment to bid him farewell privately, and told him that I wished him every success. We'd already spent so much of our lives apart that I had little else to say to my younger brother. We were strangers joined only by our bloodlines.

My mother had hoped I would spend at least another week at home, but by the third day after the wedding guests departed, I was eager to leave. She had found the leftover fabric from my original uniforms, and with great effort had managed to put eases into my trousers and jacket. Cleaned and brushed, my uniform looked nearly as good as it ever had. She carefully wrapped it up in heavy paper and tied it with string, cautioning me not to wear it on my journey back, but to keep it clean, so that I'd have clothing that fitted me on my first day back at my classes. Her concern touched me. As I took the package from her, I was bracing myself to tell her that I planned to leave the next morning when one of my father's men came up from the Landing with a larger than usual bundle of mail for him. My mother sorted through it as she always did. I watched her, waiting to have a quiet moment to speak with her.

"Here's something from the academy for your father. Probably another invitation to lecture. Oh. Here are two, no, three notes for you. Someone has scratched out the academy address and sent them on to you here instead of holding them for you. How peculiar. These will be invitations for Rosse and Cecile to visit when they return from their trip. Oh, and here's one for Yaril from Carsina. They've become quite the correspondents in the last few months."

I scarcely heard her words after she handed me my envelopes. The first one was in a dove-gray envelope, a very
heavy paper, but the return address was what shocked me.
Caulder Stiet was writing to me from Newton. So he had
gone to live with his scholar uncle after all. His proud father
had wanted nothing to do with his soldier son after the
plague had wasted him away to a shadow and broken his
spirit. The boy had been a nuisance and a pest to all the new
noble first-years at the academy, and to me in particular.
Still, I despised Colonel Stiet for what he had done. He'd
literally given his son to his younger brother, to raise as a
scholar instead of a soldier. Immoral. I shook my head and
looked at my other two letters.

One was from Epiny and the other from Spink. It seemed
odd that each would write to me. Usually Epiny penned me
a lengthy epistle and Spink just added a postscript. I studied
the envelopes. All three had been sent to my academy address, but forwarded to me at home. I scowled at that. What
was Rory thinking to send my mail trailing after me? I'd be
back soon.

Curiosity made me open the letter from Caulder first. His
penmanship had not improved. His very short and polite note
said that his uncle studied rocks and was very interested in
the one I had given Caulder. Would I be so kind as to send
them a detailed map that showed where I had found it? He
would be ever indebted to me if I could, and remained, my
friend, Caulder Stiet. I scowled over it and wondered what
sort of mischief or game this was. Although we had parted on
decent terms, I did not trust the little weasel and had little inclination to do him this favor. I would have set it aside, but it
contained a second note from his uncle, carefully penned
onto very expensive paper, noting that geology and the study
of minerals was his area of scholarship, and my rock was
quite an interesting mix. He would greatly appreciate my
time and effort to comply with Caulder's request. I set it aside
with a growl of irritation. I owed Caulder nothing and his
uncle even less. The only reason I did not discard it was that I
knew Caulder's father and my Aunt Daraleen were friends.
Any rudeness I committed might find its way back to my

Uncle Sefert's doorstep. And I did owe debts of courtesy to him. I would reply to this. Later.

Next I opened the letter from Spink. The first few lines made my breath catch.

> *The Speck plague has come to Bitter Springs. Epiny has become very ill and I fear for her life.*

The pages fluttered from my hand to the floor. Heart hammering, I snatched up the envelope from Epiny and opened it immediately. There was her familiar handwriting, perhaps a bit more scrawling than usual, and the first line read,

> *I do hope that Spink's letter did not overly alarm you. The spring water treatment proved nothing less than amazing.*

Heart still pounding, I gathered up the scattered pages of Spink's letter and took all of my mail into the parlor. I opened the curtains to let in more light, and sat down on a cushioned chair. I spread out my mail on a low table and pieced together the puzzle. Spink's letter had arrived at the Academy days before Epiny's had, but they had been sent on together. Relieved of the worst of my fears, I sat down to read the missives in order.

Spink's letter was wrenching, and not even Epiny's letter that proved her survival could eliminate all his bad news. He had no idea how the plague had come to their little settlement at Bitter Springs. No one had reported seeing any Specks, or even any ill persons. He himself had continued to make a slow but steady recovery from the illness, despite occasional bouts of night fever and sweats. He had thought he had left the dread disease far behind in Old Thares. A small group of Plainsmen who lived near Bitter Springs had succumbed to it first. It had devastated their little settlement, swiftly reducing it from seventeen families to seven. Before anyone had realized they were dealing with Speck plague, it had spread. Two of Spink's sisters had caught it. Epiny had insisted on nursing them, saying that as she survived the plague once, she was probably immune to it. She had been wrong. When Spink had mailed his letter to me, both his sisters and Epiny were severely ill and not expected to recover. His mother was struggling to care for them with Spink's help, but he feared that she would exhaust herself and also fall to the sickness. He strove to nurse Epiny just as faithfully as she had cared for him in his time of sickness.

It is a terrible irony that the disease that helped bring us together may now part us forever. It was so hard to write to her father and warn him of her decline. I tell you truthfully, Nevare, that if she dies, the better part of me will die with her. I do not think I will have the courage to go on. In a last effort to save them, we will resort to practices that my mother deems "little better than superstition." I will take her and my sisters to Bitter Springs and their supposedly healing waters. Pray for us.

So his letter ended.

I set his heartbroken letter aside and eagerly took up Epiny's missive. It was written in her usual rambling style, very frustrating to someone who simply wanted to know how everyone fared there. Nevertheless, I forced myself to read it slowly and carefully.

My dear cousin Nevare,

I do hope that Spink's letter did not overly alarm you. The spring water treatment proved nothing less than amazing. Having had the plague before, albeit in a much milder form, I was perhaps more aware than anyone else of how severely it had stricken me this time. My cousin, I did not expect to survive! I do not even remember the wagon journey to the springs, nor even the first time they immersed me. I am told that Spink carried me bodily into the water, and putting his hand over my nose and mouth, pinched them firmly shut, and then carried me under with him, where we remained for as long as he could hold his breath. When we emerged, he gave a similar treatment to each of his sisters. Others from the family settlement had journeyed with us and were similarly treated.

Then they set up a camp for us, unfolding cots under the wide blue sky and making of the meadow near the springs an open-air infirmary. On the first evening I awoke there, I already felt a lessening in my disease. Nonetheless, I was quite willful and difficult, and poor Spink was obliged to hold me down and force me to drink a large quantity of the spring water. Oh, it tasted foul and smelled worse! My fever was not entirely abated, and I called him names and scratched his poor dear face for his troubles with me. Then I fell again into a sleep, but it was a deeper, truer sleep, and when I awoke, feeling ever so much better, the first thing I demanded to know was who had scratched him so, that I could take revenge on her! I was so abashed to be told I had done it!

We remained encamped by the springs for almost a week, and every day we forced ourselves to drink that noxious water, and most of our food was cooked with it. When I realized how much I was recovering, and how swiftly, I demanded that Spink join me in this water cure. Nevare, you cannot imagine the change it has wrought in him! I will not say he is his old self, but he has begun to eat more heartily, to walk with more confidence, and most important to me, the light is back in his eyes and he laughs often. Already he speaks of returning to the academy and his studies and career. Oh, if only that dream can come true for him!

And now I must tell you—

"What is the meaning of this?" My father's roar of fury and anguish tore my attention from Epiny's letter. Loose pages in my hand, I looked up to find him glaring from the parlor door. He bore down on me like a cavalla charge. In one hand he held the large envelope from the academy. In the other were several sheets of paper. He shook them at me. His face was red, the veins standing out on his temples, and I would not have been surprised to see froth fly from his jaws, so wroth was he. "Explain this!" he roared again. "Account for this, you young scoundrel!"

"If you would let me see what it is, perhaps I could," I said to him. I did not mean to sound impertinent, but of course I did.

In fury, my father lifted his hand as to cuff me. I forced myself to stand up tall, meet his eyes and await his blow. Instead, with a snarl of frustration, he thrust a letter at me. I managed to catch it before it fluttered to the floor between us. It was on academy letterhead, but it was not from Colonel Rebin. Instead, I recognized Dr. Amicas's handwriting. In a bold hand at the top, centred on the line, he had written *Honorable Medical Discharge.* I gaped at it.

"What did you do? All the years I educated you, with the finest teachers I could procure! All the years of trying to instill values and honor into you! Why, Nevare? Why? Where did I fail with you?"

It was difficult to read while he ranted at me. My eyes skittered over the page, and phrases leapt out at me: *A postrecovery condition . . . unlikely to respond to any treatment . . . may worsen with time . . . impossible to carry out the normal duties of a cavalla officer . . . dismissed from King's Cavalla Academy . . . unlikely to be able to serve in a satisfactory manner in any branch of the military at any level . . .*

And at the bottom, the signature I knew so well, damning me to a useless life living on my brother's charity beneath the weight of my father's contempt. I slowly sank back into my seat, the page still clutched in my hands. There was a humming in my ears, and stupidly I thought of the Spindle and its endless dance. My mouth felt dry and I could not form any words. My father had no such problem. He continued castigating me for my irresponsible, self-indulgent, foolish, selfish, senseless ways. I finally found a breath and remembered how to move my mouth.

"I don't know what this is about, Father. Truly, I don't."

"It's about the end of your career, you fool. It's about no future for you, and shame for your family. A medical discharge for being too fat! That's what it's about! Damn you, boy. Damn you. You couldn't even fail with dignity. To lose your career because you couldn't refrain from stuffing food in your mouth. What have you done to us? What will my old comrades think of me, sending them such a soldier son?"

His voice ran down. His hands, still clutching additional papers, were shaking. He felt this as his personal failure. His shame. His dignity. The honor of his family. Never had he considered how this might feel to me. My father had gone to stand by the window. He read through his handful of papers with his back to me, the writing tilted toward the light. I heard him give a small grunt, as if he'd been struck. A moment later, I heard the gasp of an indrawn breath. He turned to look at me, the papers still held out before him. "Filth," he said with great feeling. "Of all the disgusting behaviors I might fear a son of mine might indulge in, this! This!"

"I don't know what you are talking about," I said again, stupidly. I wondered why the doctor hadn't spoken to me before I left. I knew a wild moment of hope in which I wondered if it were all a mistake, if this discharge had been written when I was still terribly ill. A glance at the date on the paper ended that dream. The good doctor had signed it several days after I'd left the academy. "I don't understand," I said, more to myself than my father.

"Don't you? It's here in black and white. Read it for yourself." He left the window and as he angrily strode from the room, he hurled the papers at me. It was not a satisfactory gesture. Not one even reached me. They fluttered out around him and settled on the floor. When he slammed the door behind him, that brief gust of wind stirred them again. I bent over to pick them up, grunting as I did so. My belly got in the way, and the waistband of my pants seemed too tight. I scowled as I painstakingly gathered up what proved to be my transcript and all my records, including my medical file.

I took them to the table and sorted them. Strange. All these papers were about me, and yet I'd never seen most of

them before. Here was a secretary's copy of the accusing
letter that Colonel Stiet had sent to my father over the incident with Cadet Lieutenant Tiber. Here was, surprisingly,
a letter of commendation from Captain Maw, saying that I
had shown extraordinary ability as an independent thinker
in his engineering and drafting class, and suggesting that I
might best serve the King's Cavalla as a scout on the frontier. Was that what had so upset my father? I sorted more
paper. There were tallies of my test scores for my various
classes. My grades were all exemplary. Surely they had
been up to his expectations, not that I'd ever expected him
to acknowledge it.

The medical file on me was thick. I had not realized that
Dr. Amicas had kept such complete records. There was a log
of my illness. It began with great detail, but by the fourth
day, when cadets were dropping like flies with the plague,
the entries were abbreviated to "Fever continues. Tried giving him mint in his water to cool his systems." Toward the
end of the file, I found notes on my recovery, and then more
notes that tracked my increasing weight and girth. He'd
graphed it. The continuing climb of the line was undeniable.
Had that angered my father? He now knew that I had lied
when I said the doctor had expected my weight gain to be
temporary. Looking at the evidence, I felt a sudden sinking
of heart. The line did not falter. It had risen every day since
my fever had subsided. Was that what the doctor expected
it to do? How long would it continue? How long *could* such
a trend continue?

Toward the bottom of the stack, I found what had damned
me in my father's eyes. This document was not in the doctor's handwriting. My name was marked on the top of the
sheet, and a date. Below it was a set of questions, questions
that rang oddly familiar in my mind. An aide's notes below
each one recorded my answer.

Did you go to Dark Evening in Old Thares?
Yes.
Did you eat or drink there?
Yes.

What did you eat? What did you drink?
Potatoes, chestnuts, meat skewer. Cadet denies drink-
*   ing anything.*
Did you encounter any Specks there?
Yes.
Cadet specifically mentions a female Speck. "Beauti-
*   ful."*
Did you have any contact with any Speck that eve-
*   ning?*
Cadet evasive.
Did your contact include sexual congress?
Cadet denied. Continued questioning. Cadet evasive.
*   Cadet eventually admitted sexual contact.*

I stared at the damning words. But I had not. I did not. I
hadn't had sexual contact with a Speck on Dark Evening,
and I certainly hadn't confessed that I had to the aide. I remembered him now, vaguely, as a dark shape silhouetted
against a window that was too bright with light. I remembered him badgering me for an answer when my mouth was
dry and sticky and my head pounded with pain.

"Yes or no, Cadet. Answer yes or no. Did you have sexual
contact with a Speck?"

I had told him something to make him go away. I didn't
remember what. But I'd never had sexual contact with a
Speck. At least, not in real life. Only in my fever dreams had
I lain with Tree Woman. And that had been only a dream.

Hadn't it?

I shook my head at myself. It was becoming more and
more difficult for me to draw a firm line between my real
life and the strange experiences that had befallen me ever
since the Kidona Dewara had exposed me to Plains magic.
In her medium's trance, Epiny had confirmed that I had indeed been split into two persons, and one of me had so-
journed in another world. I had been willing to accept that.
I'd been able to accept it because I thought it was over. I'd
recovered the lost part of my self and made it mine again.
I had believed that my Speck self would merge with my real
self, and the contradictions would cease troubling me.

Yet time after time, that strange other self intruded into my life, in ways that were becoming more and more destructive to me. I recognized him when I'd lain beside the farm girl, and he'd triumphed at Dancing Spindle. That Nevare, I felt, that "Soldier's Boy" had been the one to spout anger so drastically at Carsina. I'd known him by the anger pulsing in my blood. He'd had the courage to free the dove from the sacrificial hook. I'd felt him again whenever I'd found words to confront my father in the days since the wedding. He wasn't a wise influence on me. But he could rally my courage and foolhardiness and suddenly push me to assert myself. He relished confrontation in a way I did not. I shook my head. In that, he was a truer son to my father than this Nevare was. Yet I had to admit there had been times when I'd valued his insight. He had been with me the first time I glimpsed a true forest on my river journey to Old Thares, and it had been his anger I'd felt over the slain birds at Rosse's wedding. In quieter moments, his vision of the natural world replaced mine. I would see a tree sway or hear the call of a bird, and for the passing instant of his influence, those things would mesh with my being in a way my father's son would not understand. I no longer denied the existence of my Speck self, but I did all I could to prevent him controlling my day-to-day existence.

But this change to my body was something I could not ignore nor exclude from my daily reality. As part of my "real" life, it made no sense. The rigors of my journey home and my fast should have made me lose weight. Instead, I'd grown fatter. Had I caught the plague because I'd dreamed of congress with a Speck woman? Was my fat a consequence of the plague? If so, then I could no longer deny that the magic permeated every part of my life now. For a dizzying instant, I perceived that the magic was completely in control of my life now.

I snatched my thoughts back from that precipice. It was too terrifying to consider. Why had this befallen me? As logically as a mathematical proof, I perceived the beginning of these changes in me, the place where my path had diverged from the future I had been promised and into this nightmarish present. I knew when my life had been snatched out of my control. An instant later, I knew whom to blame for it.

My father.

At that thought, I felt the milling guilt in me stop just as the Dancing Spindle had ground to a halt. That single thought, that pinning of blame, made all events since my experience with Dewara fall into a new order. "It wasn't my fault," I said quietly, and the words were like cool balm on a burning wound. I looked at the door to the parlor. It was closed, my father no longer there. Childishly, I still addressed him. "It was never my fault. You did it. You put me on this path, Father."

My satisfaction in finding someone to blame was very short-lived. Blaming him solved nothing. Dejected, I leaned back in my chair. It didn't matter who had put me in this situation. Here I was. I looked down at my ungainly body. I filled the chair. The waistband of my trousers dug into me. With a grunt and a sigh, I shoved at it, easing it down under my belly. I'd seen fat old soldiers hang their beer guts out over their trouser tops this way. Now I understood why. It was more comfortable.

I sat up in my chair and gathered my papers together. When I tried to fit them all back into the envelope I discovered another letter among them. I tugged it out.

This last enclosure was addressed to me in the doctor's hand. I threw it on the floor in childish pique. What worse thing could he send to me than what he already had?

But after a few moments of looking at it there, I bent down laboriously, picked it up, and opened it.

"*Dear Nevare*," he had written. Not *Cadet Nevare*. Simply *Nevare*. I clenched my teeth for a moment and then read on.

> *With great regret, I have done what was necessary. Please remember that your discharge from the Academy is an honorable one, without stigma. Nonetheless, I imagine you hate me at this moment. Or perhaps, in the weeks since I have seen you, you have finally come to accept that something is terribly wrong with your*

body, and that it is a crippling flaw that you will have to learn to manage. It is, unfortunately, a flaw that renders you completely unfit for the military.

You were able to accept that those of your fellows whose health was broken by the plague had to give up their hopes of being active cavalla officers. I now ask you to see your own affliction in the same light. You are just as physically unfit for duty as Spinrek Kester.

You may feel that your life is over at this moment, or no longer worth living. I pray to the good god that you will have the strength to see that there are other worthwhile paths that you can tread. I have seen that you have a bright mind. The exercise of that intelligence does not always demand a fit body to support it. Turn your thoughts to how you can still lead a useful life, and focus your will toward it.

It has not been easy for me to reach this decision. I hope you appreciate that I delayed it as long as I possibly could, hoping against hope that I was wrong. My research and reading have led me to discover at least three other cases, which, although poorly documented, indicate that your reaction to the plague is a rare but not unique phenomenon.

Although I am sure you are little inclined to do so at this time, I urge you to remain in contact with me. You have the opportunity to turn your misfortune into a benefit for the medical profession. If you will continue to chart weekly your increases in weight and girth, while keeping a record of your consumption of food, and if you will send me that information every two months, it would be of great benefit to my study of the plague and its manifestations after the disease stage has passed. In this, you could serve your king and the military, for I am certain that every bit of information we gather about this pestilence will eventually become the ammunition we use to defeat it.

In the good god's light,
Dr. Jakib Amicas

I folded his letter carefully, though my strongest impulse was to rip it to pieces. The gall of the man, to dash my hopes and then suggest that I pass my idle time in helping him to further his ambitions by graphing and charting my misfortune! I moved very slowly as I put all the documents and letters back in meticulous order and slid them back in the envelope. When it was done, I looked at it. A coffin for my dreams.

I could not finish reading Epiny's letter. I tried, but it was all prattle about her new life with Spink. She liked taking care of the chickens and gathering the eggs warm from the nests. Good. I was glad for her. At least someone was still contemplating a future, even if it was one that involved chickens. I gathered my papers, left the parlor, and slowly climbed the stairs to my room.

In the days that followed, I moved like a ghost in my old home. I had entered an endless tunnel of black despair. This day-to-day existence of meaningless tasks was my future. I had nothing beyond this to anticipate. I hid from my father, and my sisters scrupulously aided me in avoiding them. Once, when I encountered Yaril in the hallway, an expression of disgust contorted her face and anger filled her eyes. Never before had she looked so much like my father. I stared at her, horrified. She made a great show of holding her skirts away from me as she hurried past me and into the music room. She closed the door loudly.

I considered cornering her and demanding to know when she had become such a foul little chit. Growing up, I had indulged her, and often shielded her from my father's wrath. Her betrayal stung me as no other. I took two strides after her.

"Nevare."

My mother's soft voice came from behind me. Surprised, I spun around.

"Let her go, Nevare," my mother suggested softly.

Irrationally, I turned my anger on her. "She behaves as if my weight is a personal insult to her, with no thought of how it affects my life or what I've lost as a consequence of what has befallen me. Does she think I did this deliberately? Do you think I want to look like this?"

My voice had risen to a shout. Nevertheless, my mother answered me softly. "No, Nevare. I don't think you do." Her gray eyes met mine steadily. She stood before me, small and arrow-straight, just as she stood when confronting my father. At that thought, my anger trickled out of me like liquid from a punctured water skin. I felt worse than emptied. Impotent. Humiliated by my show of temper. I hung my head and shame washed through me.

I think my mother knew it.

"Come, Nevare. Let us find a quiet place and talk for a bit."

I nodded heavily and followed her.

We avoided the music room, and the parlor where Elisi sat reading poetry. Instead, she led me down the hall to a small prayer room adjacent to the women's portion of our household chapel. I remembered the room well, though I had not entered it since I was a child and in my mother's daily care.

The room had not changed. A half-circle of stone bench faced the meditation wall. At one end of the bench a small, well-tended brazier burned smokelessly. At the other end, a stone bowl held a pool of placid water. A mural of the good god's blessings covered the meditation wall, with niches in the art where offerings of incense could be set. Two alcoves already held glowing bars of incense. A dark green mint-scented bar burned low in a niche painted like a harvest basket, an offering for good crops. A fat black wedge released the scent of anise into the air as it glimmered, nearly spent, in the niche for good health that hovered over a cherubic child's head.

With housewifely efficiency, my mother removed the anise incense with a pair of black tongs reserved for that task. She carried it to the small worship pool; it hissed as she dunked it in, and she stood a moment in reverent silence as the remains of the anise brick settled to the bottom. She took a clean white cloth from a stack of carefully folded linens and carefully wiped the alcove clean.

"Choose the next offering, Nevare," she invited me over her shoulder. She smiled as she said those words, and I almost smiled back. As a child, I had always vied with my sisters for the privilege of choosing. I had forgotten how important that had once been to me.

There was a special cabinet with one hundred small drawers, each holding a different scent of incense. I stood before the intricately carved front, considering all my choices, and then asked, "Why are you sacrificing for health? Who is ill?"

She looked surprised. "Why—I burn it for you, of course. That you may recover from what you have—what has befallen you."

I stared at her, torn between being touched by her concern and being annoyed that she thought her prayers and silly scented offerings could help me. An instant later I recognized that I did think her incense sacrifices were silly. They were playacting, religion by rote, an offering that cost us so little as to be insignificant. How, I suddenly wanted to know, did burning a brick of leaves and oil benefit the good god? What sort of a foolish merchant god did we worship, that he dispensed blessings in exchange for smoke? I felt suddenly that my life teetered on an eroded foundation. I did not even know when I had stopped having confidence in such things. I only knew it was gone. The protection of the good god had once stood between all darkness and me. I had thought it a fortress wall; it had been a lace curtain.

The elaborately carved, gilded, and lacquered cabinet before me had once seemed a gleaming casket of mystery. "It's just furniture," I said aloud. "A chest of drawers full of incense blocks. Mother, nothing in here is going to save me. I don't know what will. If I did, I wouldn't hesitate to do it. I'd even be willing to offer blood sacrifice to the old gods if I thought it would work. Cecile Poronte's family does." It was the first time I'd mentioned that to anyone. In the days since the wedding, I'd felt no inclination to share any conversation at all with my father.

My mother paled at my words. Then she carefully corrected me. "Cecile is a Burvelle now, Nevare. Cecile Burvelle." She stepped past me and opened the sage drawer of the cabinet. Sage for wisdom. She took out a fist-sized greenish brick of incense and carried it to the worship brazier. With gilded tongs, she held it to the slumbering coals, stooping to blow through pursed lips to wake their ashed red to glowing scarlet. A slender tendril of smoke rose to scent the room, and one corner of the sage brick caught the charcoal's red kiss. She did not look at me as she bore the sage incense to the alcove for health and tucked it safely inside.

She stood for a moment in silent prayer. Habit urged me to join her there and I suddenly wished I could. But my soul felt dry and bereft of faith. No words of praise or entreaty welled in me, only hopelessness. When my mother turned aside from the mural, I said, "You knew the Porontes worship the old gods, didn't you? Does Father know?"

She shook her head impatiently. I don't know if she was answering my question or dismissing it. "Cecile is a Burvelle now," she insisted. "It no longer matters what she did in the past. She will worship the good god alongside us every Six-day, and her children will be raised to do the same."

"Did you see the dead birds?" I asked her abruptly. "Did you see that ghastly little carousel in their garden?"

She pursed her lips as she came to take a seat on the bench. She patted a space beside her and I sat down reluctantly. She spoke softly. "They invited me to witness it. Cecile's mother sent an invitation to your sisters and me. The words were cloaked but I understood what it was about. We arrived too late. Deliberately." She paused for a moment and then advised me sincerely, "Nevare, let this go. I don't think that they truly worship the old gods. It is more a tradition, a form to be observed, rather than any true belief. The women of their family have always made such offerings. Cecile made the Bride's Gift to Orandula, the old god of balances. The slain birds are a gift to the carrion bird incarnation of Orandula. His own creatures are killed and then offered back to him to feed his own. It's a balance. The hope is that the woman offering the sacrifice will not lose any children to stillbirth or cradle death."

"Does trading dead birds for live children make any sense to you?" I demanded. And then, rudely, I added, "Do you really find any sense in burning a block of leaves to make the good god give us what we ask?"

She looked at me strangely. "That's an odd question to be

troubling a soldier son, Nevare. But perhaps it is because you were born to be a soldier that you ask it. You are applying the logic of man to a god. The good god is not bound by our human logic or measurements, son. On the contrary, we are bound by his. We are not gods, to know what pleases a god. We were given the Holy Writ so that we might worship the good god as will please him, rather than offering him things that might please a man. I, for one, am very grateful. Imagine a god who dealt as men do: what would he demand of a bride in exchange for future children? What might such a god ask of you as recompense to restore your lost beauty? Would you want to pay it?"

She was trying to make me think, but her last words stung me. "Beauty? Lost beauty? This is not a matter of vanity, Mother! I am trapped in this bulky body and nothing I do seems to change it. I cannot put on my boots or get out of bed without being bound by it. How can you assume you can even imagine what it is like for me to be a prisoner in my own flesh?"

She looked at me silently for a few moments. Than a small smile passed her lips. "You were too small to remember my pregnancies with Vanze and Yaril. Perhaps you cannot even remember what I looked like before my last two children were born." She lifted her arms as if inviting me to consider it. I glanced at her and away. Time and childbearing had thickened her body, but she was my mother. She was supposed to look that way. I could, vaguely, recall a younger, slender mother who had chased me laughing through the freshly planted garden in our early years at Widevale. And I did recall her last pregnancy with Yaril. I most recalled how she had lumbered through the rooms of the house on her painfully swollen feet.

"But that's not the same thing at all," I retorted. "The changes then and now, those are natural changes. What has befallen me is completely unnatural. I feel as if I am trapped in some Dark Evening costume that I cannot shed. You are so caught up in looking at my body that all of you, Father, Yaril, and even you, cannot perceive that within I am still Nevare! The only thing that has changed is my body. But I am treated as if I am these walls of fat rather than the person trapped behind them."

My mother allowed a small silence to settle between us before she observed, "You seem very angry at us, Nevare."

"Well, of course I am! Who would not be, in these circumstances?"

Again she made that quiet space before suggesting in a reasonable voice, "Perhaps you should direct that anger against your real enemy, to add greater strength to your will to change yourself."

"My will?" My anger surged again. "Mother, it has nothing to do with my will. My discipline has not failed. I work from dawn to dusk. I eat less than I did as a child. And still, I continue to grow heavier. Did not Father speak to you about Dr. Amicas's letter? The doctor thinks that this unnatural weight gain is a result of the plague. If it is, what can I do about it? If I had survived a pox, no one would fault me for a scarred face. If the Speck plague had left me trembling and thin, people would offer me sympathy. This is exactly the same, yet I am despised for it." It was horribly depressing to know that not even my mother understood what I was going through. I had hoped that my father would have explained my fat as a medical condition to my family and to Carsina's parents. But he had told no one. No wonder Yaril had no sympathy for me. If my mother, my oldest and staunchest ally, deserted me, I would be completely alone in facing my fate.

She pulled out the last block of support, speaking to me as if I were seven and caught in an obvious falsehood.

"Nevare. I watched you eat at Rosse's wedding. How can you say that you eat less than you did as a child? You devoured enough food to sustain a man for a week."

"But—" I felt as if she had knocked the breath from my lungs. Her calm eyes so gently pierced me as she met my gaze.

"I don't know what happened to you at the academy, my son. But you cannot hide from it behind a wall of fat. I know nothing of the doctor's letter to your father. But I do know that what I have seen of how you eat now would cause this change in any man."

"You can't believe I eat like that at every meal!"

She kept her calm. "Do not shout at me, Nevare. I am still your mother. And why else would you hide from your family at every meal if not because your gluttony shamed you? As it should. That shame is a positive sign. But instead of concealing your weakness, you must control it, my dear."

I rose abruptly. I towered over her, and for the first time in my life, I saw alarm cross my mother's face as she looked up at me. She knew that I could have crushed her.

I spoke carefully, biting off each word. "I am not a glutton, Mother. I did nothing to deserve this fate. It's a medical condition. You wrong me to think so poorly of me. I am insulted."

With what dignity I could muster, I turned and walked away from her.

"Nevare."

It had been years since I had heard her speak my name in that tone. It was to my anger as iron was to magic. Despite my inclination, I turned back to her. Her eyes were bright with both tears and anger.

"A moment ago, you said that nothing in this room could save you. You are wrong. You are my son, and *I* will save you. Whatever it is that has caused such a change in you, *I* will oppose it. I will not back down, I will not flee, and I will not give up on you. I am your mother, and for as long as we both live, that is so. Believe in me, son. I believe in you. And I will not let you ruin your life. No matter how often you turn away from me, I will still be here. I will not fail you. Believe that, son."

I looked at her. She held herself straight as a sword, and despite the tears that now tracked down her cheeks, her strength radiated from her. I wanted to believe that she could save me. So often when I was small, she had swept in and stood between my father's wrath and me. So often she had been the steadying influence, the true compass for me. There was only one answer I could give her. "I will try, Mother." I turned and left her there, with her incense and her smoke and her good god.

As I left the room, I knew I was as alone as I had ever been. Regardless of my mother's good intentions, my battle to regain my life would be a solitary one. She was my mother and she was strong, but the magic was like an infection in my blood. Oppose it however she might, she could not cure me. The magic had taken me, and I would have to battle it alone. I sought my room.

I found no solace there. The neglected letters still rested on the desk. I longed to sit down at my desk and immerse myself in them, but I had no heart to answer them just now. My bed complained as I lay down on it. I stared around at the bare walls and simple furnishings and the single window. It had always been a severe room, a place of minimal comfort, a room that would train a boy to embrace a soldier's life. Now it was a bare cell. In this room, I would live out the rest of my days. Every night I would lie down here alone to sleep. Every morning, I would rise to do my father's bidding, and when he was gone, I would have to accept Rosse's authority over me. What else was there for me? For a flashing moment, I thought of running away. I had a childish image of myself galloping away on Sirlofty, going east toward the end of the King's Road and the mountains beyond. The thought lifted me, and for an instant, I actually considered rising from my bed and leaving that night. My heart raced at the wild plan. Then I came to my senses and marveled at my foolish impulse. No. I was not going to give up my dream just yet. As long as I had my mother's belief to sustain me, I would stay here. I would resist the magic and try to reclaim my life. I closed my eyes to that thought and, without intending to, drifted off into a deep sleep.

I did not dream. The awareness that flowed through me was as unlike dreaming as waking is to sleeping. Magic worked in me, like yeast working in bread dough. I felt it quicken and grow, swelling in my veins. It gathered strength from my body, roiling through my flesh, drawing on the resources it had gathered against this necessity. With growing trepidation, I recognized that I had felt this sensation before. The magic had moved in me before, and it had acted. What had it done, without my knowledge or consent? I recalled the young man on the jankship, and how he had fallen after my angry words with him. That was one time, but there had been others.

The massed magic did something.

The languages I knew did not have words to express it. Could my flesh shout out a word, voicelessly, soundlessly? Could the magic, a thing that resided elsewhere than the physical world, speak a command through me, so that somewhere, something it desired happened? That was what it felt like. Dimly I sensed that something had begun. The first event that would trigger a chain reaction of responses had occurred. Finished, the magic pooled to stillness in me. Weariness washed through my body. I sank into an exhausted sleep.

When I awoke, the sun had gone down. I'd slept the rest of the day away. I got up quietly and crept down the stairs. At the bottom, I paused to listen. I heard my father's strident voice in his study. Rosse was gone; I wondered whom he was lecturing. After a moment, I heard my mother's soft response. Ah. I walked quickly past that door, and past the music room where Elisi drew a melancholy melody from her harp. The young fellow at Rosse's wedding had made no offer for her. Was that my fault? The house was a pool of unhappiness and I was the source of it. I reached the door and strode out into the night.

I wandered through the dark familiar garden and sat down on a bench. I tried to grasp that my future was gone. I could think of nowhere to go tonight and nothing to do. The ferry stopped at night, so I couldn't cross the river to Burvelle's Landing. I'd long ago read most of the books in our family library. I had no projects. I had no friends to visit. This was a foretaste of the rest of my life. I could do manual labor on the holdings and then wander aimlessly about at night. I'd be a shadow in my old home, a useless extra son and nothing more.

I gave myself a shake to rid my head of melancholy foolishness. I hitched up my trousers, left the garden, and walked over to the menservants' quarters. My father had built them as a structure separate from the house, and my mother still complained that it looked more like a military barracks than servants' quarters. She was right, and I was sure that it was deliberately so. One door led into a long open bunkroom for seasonal workers. At the other end of the structure, there were private apartments for married servants and rooms for our permanent help. I went to Sergeant Duril's door. Strange to say, in all the years he'd taught me, I'd only rapped on it half a dozen times.

For a moment I hesitated before it. For all I knew of the man who had taught me, there was much I didn't know. I wondered if he was even awake or if he was off at the Landing. At last I damned myself for a foolish coward, and knocked firmly on the door.

Silence from within. Then I heard the scrape of a chair and footsteps. The door opened to me, spilling lamplight into the night. Duril's eyebrows shot up at the sight of me. "Nevare, is it? What brings you here?"

He was in his undershirt and trousers, with no boots on. I'd caught him getting ready for bed. I realized that I'd grown taller than Sergeant Duril. I was so accustomed to him in his boots or on horseback. He had no hat on; the substantial bald spot on his pate surprised me. I tried not to stare at it while he tried not to stare at my stomach. I groped for something to say other than that I was horribly lonely and would never be able to go back to the academy.

"Has your saddle cinch been coming loose lately?" I asked him.

He squinted at me for a second, and then I saw his jaw loosen, as if he'd just realized something. "Come in, Nevare," he invited me, and stood back from the door.

His room revealed him. There was a potbellied stove in one corner of the room, but no fire at this time of year. A disassembled long gun dominated the table in the room. He had shelves, but instead of books they held the clutter of his life. Interesting rocks were mixed with cheap medical remedies for backache and sore feet, a good-luck carving of a frog jostled up against a large seashell and a stuffed owl, and a wadded shirt awaited mending next to a spool of thread. Through an open door, I glimpsed his neatly made-up bed in the next room. A bare room for a bare life, I thought to myself, and then grimaced as I realized that his room had more character than mine did. I imagined myself as Sergeant Duril years from now, no wife or children of my own, teaching a soldier son not mine, a solitary man.

The two of us filled the small room, and I felt more uncomfortable with my bulk than ever. "Sit down," he invited me, drawing out one of his chairs. I placed myself carefully on it, testing my weight against it. He pulled out the other chair and sat down. With no awkwardness at all, he launched into talk.

"My cinch has come loose three times in the last month. And yesterday, when I was helping the crew jerk some big rocks out, a line I knew I'd tied and made the 'hold fast' sign over came loose. Now, I can't remember that ever happening to me before. I'm getting old, and thought maybe I wasn't making the sign or maybe I was making it sloppy. Not a big thing to worry about, I told myself. But you seem to think it is. Why? Has your cinch been coming loose lately?"

I nodded. "Ever since the Dancing Spindle stopped dancing. I think the Plains magic is failing, Sergeant. But I also think that," and here I stopped, to slap my chest and then gestured at my belly, "that somehow this is a result of it."

He knit his brow. "You're fat because of magic." He enunciated the words as if to be sure that he hadn't mistaken what I'd said.

Stated baldly, it sounded worse than silly. It sounded like a child's feeble excuse, a cry of "look what you made me do!" when a stack of blocks toppled. I looked down at the edge of his table and wished I hadn't come and asked my foolish question. "Never mind," I said quickly, and stood to go.

"Sit down." He didn't speak the words as a command, but they were stronger than an invitation. His gaze met my eyes squarely. "Any explanation might be better than none, which is what I've got right now. And I'd like to know what you mean when you say the Spindle stopped dancing."

Slowly I took my seat again. That story was as good a place to begin as any. "Have you ever seen the Dancing Spindle?"

He shrugged as he took his seat across the table from me.

He picked up a rag and started cleaning gun parts. "Twice. It's impressive, isn't it?"

"Did you think it moved when you saw it?"

"Oh, yes. Well, no, I mean, I didn't believe it was moving when I saw it, but it sure looked like it was, from a distance."

"I got up close to it and it still seemed to me like it was moving. And then some idiot with a knife and a desire to carve his initials on something stopped it."

I expected him to snort in disbelief, or laugh. Instead he nodded. "Iron. Cold iron could stop it. But what's that got to do with my cinch coming undone?"

"I don't know, exactly. It seemed to me that . . . well, I guessed that maybe if iron stopped the Spindle, the Plains magic might all go away, too."

He took a little breath of dismay. After a moment, he wet his lips and then asked me carefully, "Nevare. What do you *know*?"

I sat for a time and didn't say anything. Then I said, "It started with Dewara."

He nodded to himself. "I'm not surprised. Go on." And so, for the first time, I told someone the whole tale of how I'd been captured by the Plains magic, and how it had affected me at the academy, and the plague, and how I thought I had freed myself, and then how the Spindle had swept me up and showed me the power it held before a boy's mischief and an other self I could not control had stopped the Spindle's dancing.

Duril was a good listener. He didn't ask questions, but he grunted in the right places and looked properly impressed when I told him about Epiny's séance. Most important to me, as I told my story, he never once looked as if he thought I was lying.

He only stopped me once in my telling, and that was when I spoke of the Dust Dance at the Dark Evening carnival. "Your hand lifted and gave the signal? You were the one who told them to start?"

I hung my head in shame, but I didn't lie. "Yes. I did. Or the Speck part of me did. It's hard to explain."

"Oh, Nevare. To be used against your own folk like that. This is bad, boy, much worse than I'd feared. If you've got the right of it at all, it has to be stopped. Or you *could* be the downfall of us all."

To hear him speak the true magnitude of what I'd done froze me. I sat, staring through him, to a horrible future in which everyone knew I'd betrayed Gernia. Wittingly or unwittingly didn't matter when one contemplated that sort of treachery.

Duril leaned forward and jabbed me lightly with his finger. "Finish the story, Nevare. Then we'll think what we can do."

When I had finished the whole telling, he nodded sagely and leaned back in his chair. "Actually, I've heard about those Speck wizards, the big fat ones. They call them Great Men. Or Great Women, I guess, though I never heard of a female one. Fellow that spent most of his soldiering days out at Gettys told me. He claimed he'd seen one, and to hear him tell it, the man was the size of a horse, and proud as could be of it. That soldier told me that a Great Man is supposed to be all filled up with magic, and that's why he's so big."

I thought that over. "The Fat Man in the freak show claimed he got so fat because he'd had Speck plague. And the doctor at the academy, Dr. Amicas, said that putting on weight like this is a very rare side effect from the plague, but not completely unknown. So how could that have anything to do with magic?"

Sergeant Duril shrugged. "What is magic anyway? Do you understand it? I don't. I know I've seen a few things that I can't explain in any way that makes sense or can be proved. And maybe that's why I say that they were magic. Look at the 'keep fast' charm. I don't know how it works or why it should work. All I know is that for a lot of years, it worked and it worked well. And lately it doesn't seem to work as well. So, maybe that magic is broken now. Maybe. Or maybe I'm not as strong as I used to be when I tighten a cinch, or maybe my cinch strap is getting old and worn. You could explain it away a thousand ways, Nevare. Or maybe you can just say, 'it was magic and it doesn't work anymore.' Or maybe you could go to someone who believes in magic and thinks he knows how it works and ask him."

That last seemed a real proposal from him. "Who?" I asked him.

He crossed his arms on the table. "It all started with Dewara, didn't it?"

"Ah, well." I leaned back in his chair; it creaked a warning at me. I sat up straight. "It's useless to try and find him. My father tried for months, right after he sent me home in shreds. Either none of his people knew where he was, or they weren't telling. My father offered rewards and made threats. No one told him anything."

"Maybe I know a different way of asking," Duril suggested. "Sometimes coin isn't the best way to buy something. Sometimes you have to offer more."

"Such as what?" I demanded, but he shook his head and grinned, enjoying that he knew more than I did. Looking back on it, I suspect the old soldier had enjoyed being my teacher. Supervising men clearing a field of rocks was no task for an old trooper like him. "Let me try a few things, Nevare. I'll let you know if I have any success."

I nodded, refusing to hope. "Thanks for listening to me, Sergeant Duril. I don't think anyone else would have believed me."

"Well, sometimes it's flattering to have someone want to tell you something. And you know, Nevare, I haven't said I believed a word of any of this. You have to admit it's pretty far-fetched."

"But—"

"And I haven't said I disbelieve any of it, either." He shook his head, smiling at my confusion. "Nevare, I'll tell you something. There's more than one way to look at the world. That's what I was getting at, about the magic. To us, it's magic. Maybe to someone else, it's as natural as rain falling from clouds. And maybe to them, some of what we do is magic because it doesn't make reasonable sense in their world. Do you get what I'm trying to tell you?"

"Not really. But I'm trying." I attempted a smile. "I'm

ready to try anything. My only other idea was to run away east on Sirlofty. To the mountains."

He snorted a laugh. "Run away to the mountains. And then what? Don't be a fool, Nevare. You stay here and you keep on trying. And let me try a few things, too. Meanwhile, I suggest you do things your da's way. Get out and move. Show him you're still Nevare, if you can. Don't make him angrier than he already is. In his own way, he's a fair man. Try it his way, and if it doesn't work, maybe he'll concede it's not your fault."

"I suppose you're right."

"You know I am."

I looked at him and nodded slowly. A spark had come back into his eyes. Purpose burned there. Perhaps I had done as much for him by coming to him as he had done for me by simply listening.

I thanked him, and there we left it for that night.

CHAPTER SEVEN

DEWARA

I knew when my father decided to inform everyone of my utter failure. When I descended the stairs the next morning and went to the kitchen for a quick bite of food, the servants already knew of my disgrace. Previously they had treated me with a puzzled deference. I was a son of the household, and if I chose to eat in the kitchen instead of with my family, it was my own business. Now I sensed my diminished status, as if they had been given permission to disdain me. I felt like a stray dog that had crept in and was hoping to snare a few bites of stolen food. No one offered to serve my meal to me; I was reduced to helping myself to whatever was there and ready, and all the while stepping back and out of the way of servants who suddenly found me invisible.

The gossip of the servants revealed that my brother and his new bride would be returning that evening. There would be a welcoming dinner tonight, and perhaps guests on the morrow. No one had bothered to tell me any of this. The exclusion from the family news was as sharp as a knife cut.

I left the house as soon as I could, taking a fishing pole from the shed and going down to the river. I baited for the big river carp, some the size of a hog, and each time I caught one, I battled it to the river's edge and then cut it free. I wasn't after fish that day, but after something I could physically challenge and defeat. After a time, even that ceased to occupy me. The heat of the sun beat down on me and I started to get hungry. I went back to my father's manor.

I tried to go in quietly. I'm sure my father was laying in wait for me. The moment I was through the entry, he appeared in the door of his study. "Nevare. A word with you," he said sternly.

I knew he expected me to follow him into the study. My Speck obstinacy surfaced. I stood where I was. "Yes, Father. What do you want of me?"

He tightened his lips and anger flared in his eyes "Very well, Nevare. It can as well be said here. Your mother shared with me the wild tale you told her." He shook his head. "Was that the best excuse you could manufacture? Mocking our god because you ruined your future? Now that you have destroyed all your prospects and cannot return to the academy, you think that we must support you for the rest of your days. I warn you, I will not shelter and feed a lazy leech. In the doctor's opinion, you are incapable of soldiering for the king in your present condition. But I intend to change your condition, while wringing some worthwhile work out of you, and eventually I intend to send you off to enlist as a foot soldier. You will never be an officer, but I will not support you in thwarting the good god's plan for you."

I held up my hand, palm toward him. I met his gaze in a forthright manner. "Simply tell me what tasks you want me to do. Spare me a lecture I've already heard from you."

His surprise only lasted for a moment. Then he gave me his list of dirty tasks. All involved heavy labor and most had something to do with dirt, excrement, or blood. A manor is like a farm, and tasks of those sort abounded, but always before, he had assigned them to hirelings. Now he chose them for me, and I was well aware it wasn't because he thought I could do them well but because he found them distasteful and therefore assumed that I would. I lost most of the remaining respect I had for him then. All the education he had poured into me, and in a fit of pique, he would waste it. I did not let my thoughts show. I nodded to him gravely and promised to begin my work. It involved a shovel and a lot of manure and a farm wagon. Actually, it was fine with me, and in accord with what Sergeant Duril had suggested, that was how I spent my afternoon. When I judged I'd put in a fair day's work, I left my task and walked down to a shoal water of the river. Thick brush guarded the riverbank, but there was a deer trail through it. The slower water in the shallows was sun-warmed. I stripped and waded out and washed away the sweat and grime of my work. I'd often swum here as a boy, but now it felt strange to stand naked under the sun, even in such an isolated place. I was ashamed of my body and afraid I'd be seen, I realized. The increased weight I carried brought more problems than simply ill-fitting clothes. My feet ached just from carrying my weight. I sweated more and smelled stronger after a day's labor. My clothing often chafed me. Nevertheless, after I'd sloshed water over myself, it was restful to lie in the shallows and feel the contrast between the warm sun on my skin and the cooler water flowing past me. When I finally came out, I sat on a large rock and let the sun dry me before dressing again. I'd regained a small measure of peace.

I stole an evening meal from the kitchen, much to the annoyance of the cooking staff. They were overtaxed that night, serving an elaborate meal to my family and the new daughter of the house. I wondered how my father would react if I walked into the room in my rough, ill-fitting clothes and took a seat at the table. There was probably no place set for me there. I ate a modest meal sitting in a corner of the kitchen, and left.

That became the pattern of my days. I arose, chose a task from my father's list, and worked all day at it. He intended such work to humiliate me, but I found it strangely satisfying. By my labor, I would either prove to my father that my fat was a magical result of the plague, or I would regain my former condition and perhaps be able to reclaim my place at the academy. I pushed myself each day, deliberately striving to tax my body even beyond the chores my father had given me. When frustration or humiliation gnawed at me, I shoved them resolutely aside. This, I told myself, was exactly what I needed to be doing. I ate frugally and worked my body steadily. And it responded, though not as I had hoped. Beneath the fat, my arms and legs bulked with new muscle. I gained stamina. I could lift more weight than I'd ever been able to lift in my life.

It was not easy. My heavy body was unwieldy for a man accustomed to being lithe and limber. I had to plan how I moved, and likewise plan my tasks. Strange to say, that, too, was satisfying. I applied what I'd learned in my engineering. When my father set me to building a stone wall to enclose a hog sty, I went at it as if I were establishing a fortification, laying it out to grade, leveling the first run of stone, making it wide at the base and less so at the top. I would have felt more satisfaction if it had won approval from anyone besides myself and the croaker bird that watched me all day. My father seldom bothered to view what I accomplished every day. He had written me off as a bad investment, like the peach trees that had gone to leaf curl and insects. Rosse made no effort to see me, and I responded in kind. I became invisible to my family. I still gave my mother "good day" if I saw her in passing. I did not bother speaking to my sisters, and they were likewise silent to me. I resolved that it did not bother me.

A simple life of arising, working, and going to bed held its own sort of peace. The physical labor of each day was not nearly as demanding as my studies at the academy. I wondered if other men lived this way, rising, working, eating, and sleeping with barely a thought beyond doing the same thing the next day. I'll confess that I felt a strange attraction to such a simple life.

When a week had passed by and I'd heard nothing from Sergeant Duril, I sought him out one afternoon. When he opened his door to my knock, the first words he said were, "You didn't tell me you'd been kicked out of the academy for being fat!" I couldn't tell if he was outraged on my behalf or angry with me for holding back information.

I spoke evenly, without anger. "That's because it isn't true."

He stared at me, waiting.

"Dr. Amicas gave me a medical discharge from the academy. I wasn't kicked out. He felt I couldn't serve as a cavalla officer as I am. If I manage to regain my old shape, I'll be able to continue my studies." I wasn't sure of that, but I had to hold onto the hope or sink into despair.

Duril stood back from his door and motioned me in. His apartments were stuffy after the sunny day, even with the door left ajar. I took a seat at his table.

Slowly he sat down across from me and admitted, "I took a lot of pride in your being at the academy. It meant a lot to me to think of you being there and being one of them, and knowing just as much as any of them fancy city boys, thanks to what I'd taught you."

That took me by surprise. I'd never paused to consider that my success might mean a personal triumph to Sergeant Duril. "I'm sorry," I said quietly. "I was doing well until this befell me. And once I've straightened it out and returned to the academy, I'll do you proud. I promise."

As if his first admission had opened a door, he suddenly added, "You never wrote to me. I had sort of hoped for a letter from you."

That surprised me even more. "I thought you couldn't read!" I said, and then flinched at how blunt my words were.

"I could have had someone read it to me," he retorted testily. After a pause he added, "I sent *you* a letter. When I heard you'd been sick and nearly died."

"I know. It reached me right before I came home. Thank you."

"You're welcome," he said stiffly. He looked away from me as he added, "I'm not an educated man, Nevare. I'm not even, as you well know, a proper soldier son, born to the career. What I know about soldiering, I taught myself or learned the hard way. And I did my best to pass it on to you. I wanted you to be an officer that, well, understood what it was to really be a soldier. Not the kind of man who sits in his tent and orders men to go out and do what he couldn't or wouldn't do himself. Someone who knew what it was like to have to go a couple of days with no water for yourself or your horse, someone who knew about the salt and sweat of soldiering for himself. So you could be a good officer."

And here was another man I'd failed. My heart sank, but I tried not to let it show. "You didn't waste your time, Sergeant Duril. I've no intention of giving up my career. Even if I have to enlist as a common soldier and rise as a ranker, I'm determined to do it." As I said those words, I was a bit surprised to find how deeply I meant them.

He cocked his head at me. "Well. I guess I can't ask more of you than that, Nevare." He smiled suddenly, pleased with himself. "And I think you can't ask more of me than what I have for you. Fancy an evening ride?"

"I'm not averse to it," I replied. "Where are we going?"

His smiled broadened. "You'll see." He went back into his apartments, and then emerged with a fat set of saddlebags slung over his shoulder. I wanted to ask what was in them, but I knew he was enjoying making his revelations as we went along. I held my tongue.

It had been some days since I'd ridden Sirlofty. Ever a willing mount, he reached for the bit, eager to go. Duril had the use of a clay-colored gelding. As we stood together in the paddock, saddling our mounts, we both glanced at each other. Then, as one, we made the "keep fast" sign over the cinches. I feared it would soon be an empty ritual, with no more true power than the acorns that some troopers carried for luck in finding shade at the day's end. We mounted, he took the lead, and I followed.

We struck the river road and traveled east for a short way before Duril turned his horse away from the river to follow a dusty, rutted trail. We topped a small rise, and in the distance I saw the Bejawi village. An upthrust of stone granted it some respite from the endless sweep of the prairie winds. Brush grew in the shelter of the stone barrier, and even a few trees. My father had chosen the location for it and laid out the original village for them. My father's men had built the dozen houses that stood in two neat rows. At least twice that number of traditional Bejawi tents surrounded the houses. "Is that where we're going? The Bejawi village?"

Duril gave a nod, silently watching me.

"Why?"

"Talk to some Kidona there."

"In the Bejawi village? What are they doing there? Kidona and Bejawi are traditional enemies. And the Kidona don't have villages. The only reason the Bejawi live here is that my father built it for them and they had nowhere else to go."

"And wasn't that a rousing success?" Duril asked with quiet sarcasm.

I knew what he meant, but I was still a bit shocked to hear him say something even mildly negative about my father.

In the era before the Gernian expansion the Plainspeople had been nomads. Different tribes followed different livelihoods. Some herded sheep or goats. Others followed the migrations of the herd deer that roamed the plains and plateaus, supplementing that meat with the seasonal gardens they planted in one season and harvested in another. Some of them built temporary mud huts along the river, little caring that they did not last long. The Plainspeople had few towns or what we Gernians would recognize as one. They built a few monuments, such as the Dancing Spindle. They kept rendezvous points where they came together each year to trade and negotiate marriages and truces, but for the most part they wandered. To a Gernian eye, it meant that the plains remained an empty place, unclaimed and scarcely used by the migratory folk who criss-crossed it in patterns that were generations old. Such land was ripe for settling, awaiting development of its full potential. The Plainsmen, I suspected, saw it differently.

Our "tame" Bejawi, as my father referred to them, were an experiment that had largely failed. He went into it with good intentions. When he set out to save them, the Bejawi had been reduced to mostly women, children, and old men. The Bejawi had been herders; killing their herds and a generation of their men had been the fastest way to subdue them. Deprived of their livelihood, the Bejawi were reduced to being thieves and beggars. My father took them in. Not all of them were willing to surrender their old ways in exchange for what he offered. My father bribed them with his promise that he would not let them starve. He had a village built for them, two rows of simple sturdy cottages. He gave them two teams of oxen, a plow, and seed for a crop.

Within two weeks, they had eaten the oxen and most of the seed grain. He then gave them goats, with far better success. Perhaps the goats reminded them of the woolly antelope they had once tended. Those creatures were extinct now, slaughtered during our running battles with the Bejawi. The boys took the goats to pasture each day and brought them back. The animals yielded meat, hides, and milk. When last I had discussed them with my father, he admitted that he still had to supplement their food supplies, but that some of the women were learning to make a cheese that he hoped they would be able to market. But in other areas, his success was more tarnished. A people who had no traditions of living in a settled village, they were used to moving on when a piece of land became tired of them.

The "village" stank. The smell of it hung on the still summer air. The tidy little cottages my father had erected with such pride were now derelict shacks. The Bejawi had no concept of how to maintain them. After several seasons of hard use had ruined the cottages, they had returned to their tents and set up a secondary settlement around the row of cottages. Offal and garbage, a problem that nomads left behind for the elements and scavengers to deal with, were heaped between the moldering cottages or piled into noxious waste pits. The children played in the garbage-strewn street, tanglehaired moppets with scabby faces and dirty hands. Few of the young men stayed once they became adults. Too many of the girls went to Franner's Bend to work as whores as soon as they were developed enough to pass themselves off as women. They returned to the village with their half-blood offspring when their brief blossoming of beauty had been eroded by the hard life of a post whore. The village my father had built never developed beyond houses to live in. There

was no store, no school, nothing that offered the people anything beyond eating and sleeping indoors. It was a place
where people waited, but did not know what they were waiting for.

Yet the Bejawi were not a foolish people, nor were they
stupid. They were not even a dirty people when they followed
their own ways. They had been dealt a hard blow by fate, and
had not, as yet, discovered how to recover. I wondered if they
ever would, or if they would vanish, leaving only a legend of
what they had once been. Once they had been a proud folk,
renowned for their beauty and handiwork.

I had read accounts of them written by Darsio, a merchant
trader who had bartered with the Plainspeople in the old days
before the Gernian expansion. His writing always made me
wish I had been alive then. The descriptions of the Bejawi
men in their flowing white robes mounted on their swift
horses leading their people, while the women, the children,
and the elderly followed, some shepherding the animals and
others on the sand sleds pulled by their sturdier draft animals,
were the stuff of epic poetry. The women manufactured beads
from a certain petrified tree stone, and this jewelry had been
the trade good that Darsio had sought from them. They made
delicate ornaments from bird bone and feathers, charmed to
bring good luck to the owner. Every woman of marriageable
age wore a veritable cloak of beads and ornaments and bells.
Some of the cloaks, Darsio wrote, were passed down for generations. The children, he wrote, were exceptionally beautiful, open-faced and bold, easily laughing, the treasure of their
people. The Bejawi flocks were a peculiar heavy-bodied antelope, prized for the thick undercoat they grew for the winter
and shed in spring. This lightweight, warm wool was the basis of Bejawi textiles at the time of Darsio's writings. The
first time I had visited the Bejawi village with my father, that
romantic image was what I had expected to see. I had come
away disappointed and oddly shamed. I had no wish to visit
the village again, but my curiosity was piqued by Sergeant
Duril's assertion that Kidona were there. I knew the Bejawi
hated the Kidona with a loathing that went back generations.

Every creature has a predator that preys on it. The Bejawi had the Kidona. The Kidona did not herd or harvest or hunt. They raided. They had always been raiders, descending on trading caravans or summer villages, or they stole, creeping up on herds, flocks, and tents to take whatever they needed. By their tradition, it was their right to do so. They traveled constantly on their potbellied striped-legged taldi, creatures that had little of a horse's beauty, but even less of a horse's weaknesses.

Dewara had been Kidona. I touched the double ridges on my ear, the healed scars from the notches he'd cut there when I'd disobeyed him. The man had starved and brutalized me, and then, in a turnabout that still baffled me, he had befriended me and attempted to induct me into his people's culture and religion. He'd drugged me into a shamanic trance, and in that trance I had first encountered Tree Woman. That spirit journey had changed my life and warped my concept of reality. All of it had been my father's doing. He hadn't really wanted me to be Dewara's student so much as he'd hoped Dewara's harsh treatment of me would finally force me to make my own decisions and stand on my own two feet.

Well, I supposed it had, but not in the way my father had hoped, nor in any way that had brought me confidence or satisfaction in my life.

I had come to a deep understanding of Kidona ways before Dewara and I had parted. Theirs was a strange morality, in which the clever thief was held in high esteem, and the clumsy one could claim no protection from anyone's vengeance. Dewara paid great respect to any man who could beat him, and disdained any fellow he could dominate. Prosperity was the equivalent of the blessing of his strange gods, and thus the opinion of a wealthy man was not to be disputed, while a poor man, no matter how experienced or kindly, was seen as a fool, unloved by the gods. Despite their skewed beliefs, or perhaps because of them, the Kidona were a tough, resourceful, and savagely efficient people. Even though Dewara had damaged my life, I grudgingly admired him, in the same way that one might admire any exceptionally competent predator, without any element of fondness or trust.

Sergeant Duril hadn't answered my most important question. I asked it again. "Why are Kidona in the Bejawi village?"

Sergeant Duril cleared his throat. "I suppose your father didn't write to you about it. It was an ugly incident, while you were away at school. Not too long after you'd left, farms around here began to lose stock. At first we thought it was wolves returning to this territory. Then someone pointed out that wolves leave carcasses, and we hadn't found any. The Bejawi were blamed at first, because of some trouble awhile back, but there was no sign of them having more meat than they should.

"Well, when the dust settled, it turned out that Kidona were up to their old tricks. A band of them camping mostly out of sight of settled places had been raiding flocks and herds and gardens. They got bold and took a dozen yearlings from a herd that belonged to the garrison at Franner's Bend. The commander there didn't take kindly to it and sent some of the fellows out to track down the raiders and teach them a lesson." Sergeant Duril's tone was light, but his face was grim. "The soldiers at Franner's Bend . . . well, you know how it is; you've seen the place. Those troopers never see any real action. It's a soft post. And in a way that makes the recruits antsy for it, and when they do have a reason to crack down on something, they get carried away, as if they have to prove they're as tough as real soldiers out on the border. Well, they got carried away with the Kidona raiding party they tracked down. Killed them all, and that was just about every male that wasn't still sucking on a titty. Well, that stirred up trouble with the other Kidona groups that were in the area. Especially when it come out that the group our troopers had slaughtered hadn't stolen the cows themselves. They'd traded for them with the thieves. So we had troopers slaughtering 'innocent' Kidonas, and the other Kidona in the area on the verge of an uprising."

"Why didn't they just buy them off? The Kidona feel no shame about taking blood money."

He nodded. "That's what we did. But that left the women

and tykes from the dead raiders to provide for. You know the Kidona. Practical and hard as stone. The survivors had nothing left in the way of resources. No taldi, no sheep, tents burned. The other groups of Kidona saw them as a liability. They didn't want to take them in, but they didn't want to see them starve, either. So this was the compromise. Your father said the Franner's Bend commander could settle them here, as long as he supplied shelters, food, and a pair of taldi for them to get started with again." He shook his head. "Putting Kidona in a village. That's like putting your foot in a hat."

I could easily distinguish the cottages and tents of the Bejawi from the shelters of the Kidona newcomers. There was not one village but two, forced into proximity. A line had literally been drawn, a row of stones and trash set as a boundary between the Bejawi area and the four military tents given to the Kidona survivors. As we approached, a Bejawi youth came to his feet. He appeared to be about fourteen and wore what looked like a dirty nightshirt and a drooping hat felted from goat hair. His pale eyes fixed on us accusingly as we approached. He leaned on a stave, watching us silently, no sign of welcome on his face. When Duril reined his horse toward the Kidona area, the young man sat back down and pointedly ignored us.

"Have they always kept a sentry like that?" I asked Duril.

"Doubt it. I think he's there to keep an eye on the Kidona, not us. But I could be wrong. I don't come here unless I have to. It's depressing."

It was. We rode past the wall of garbage that fenced the Kidona from the Bejawi settlement. The insult was obvious. Equally obvious was the misery of the Kidona tent village. The thin wailing of children was as pervasive as the ripe smell of the rubbish. The tents were pitched with military precision, so the troopers had at least set up the shelters for the widows and orphans. There were two cook fires, one burning and one a nest of banked coals. Sticks had been wedged against boulders to form a sort of drying rack, and two blankets festooned the ramshackle invention. About ten women, all middle-aged, sat on makeshift benches in front of the tent. One sat and rocked from side to side, droning a song under her breath. Three of them were employed in tearing old rags into long strips that one of them was braiding. I surmised they were making rag rugs to soften the tent floor. The others sat, empty-handed and still. Several taldi, one a pregnant mare, grazed on whatever they could find at the edge of the campsite.

A scatter of children idled in the area around the cook fires. Two were toddlers who sat bawling near a granny's feet. She did not appear to be paying any attention to their cries. Three girls of seven or eight years of age were playing a game with pebbles and lines drawn in the dirt. Their faces were dirty, and their braids looked like fuzzy blond ropes. A single boy of thirteen sat by himself and glared at us as we approached. I wondered how he had survived and what would become of him in this settlement of old women and children.

When we dismounted, all activity ceased. Duril took his saddlebags from his horse's back and slung them over his shoulder. "Follow me and be quiet," Sergeant Duril instructed me. "Don't look at anyone." I did as he told me. They stared at my body and a slow flush crept up my cheeks, but I didn't make eye contact with any of them. Duril walked up to the granny and her howling charges. He spoke Jindobe, the trade language of the plains. "I bring you fat meat." He lowered the saddlebags to the ground and opened them. He took out a side of bacon wrapped in cheesecloth and offered it to her. Her mouth twitched, carrying her chin with it. Then she lifted her old blue eyes to his and said, "I have nothing to cut it with."

He didn't pause. He unhooked his belt and slid both knife and sheath from it. He offered them to her. She stared long at the proffered gift, as if weighing what she lost by taking it against what she gained. The boy had drawn closer and was watching the exchange intently. He said something in rapid Kidona. In response, she made a quick flipping gesture with her hand, as if throwing something aside. His face set in an expression of anger, but he made not a sound as she took the knife and sheath from the sergeant. Turning, she handed it immediately to the woman next to her. "Cut meat to cook for the children," she said. Then she stood up, grunting with the effort. She stepped over the small children, who had never ceased their wailing, turned, and went into the tent behind her. We followed.

It was a gray canvas barracks tent, long and wide, with side walls. It was dim and stuffy inside the tent. To one side, there was a row of army blankets arranged as pallets. On the other side, there were several casks of hardtack, a tub of dried corn, and a wooden crate of withered and sprouted potatoes. Neatly arranged beside these donations were the remnants of their former lives. Tin and copper cooking pots were stacked beside a row of baked clay jars and plates next to folded bedding with the characteristic Kidona stripes.

They had cut a flap in the side wall of the tent. She unpegged the sewn strips that had fastened it shut, and sat down beside the small rectangle of light and fresh air it admitted. After a moment, Sergeant Duril sat down facing her and I took my place beside him. "Did you bring it?" she asked him.

I thought the bacon had been his bribe, but evidently that had only been for show. He reached into his shirt and took out his wallet. He opened it, and took out something I recognized from my childhood. I'd only seen it once before, but it was not a thing to forget. He held out the darkened and shriveled ear on his palm. Without hesitation, she took it.

She held it to the light, and then brought it close to her eyes, examining it closely. I was surprised when she sniffed it, but tried not to show my disgust. I knew the tale. In a moment of youthful rage, Sergeant Duril had taken the ear as a trophy from the body of a warrior he'd killed. In the same fracas, he'd gained the scar that had severed part of his own ear. He'd once told me that he was ashamed of cutting off the dead warrior's ear, and would have undone the deed if he could. But he couldn't return it to the body for decent burial, and he'd felt it would be wrong to discard it. Perhaps he'd finally found a way to be rid of it. She held it in her hand, looking down at it with a contemplative air. Then she nodded decisively. She rose and went to the tent door. She shouted something, a name, I guessed, and when the boy came, she spoke to him rapidly. He argued back, and she slapped him. That seemed to settle his disagreement. He looked past her at us.

"I'll take you now," he said in Jindobe. And that was all he said.

By the time we were mounted, he was on a taldi stallion and riding out of the camp. We had to hurry the horses to catch up with him. He didn't look back to see if we followed him, and never spoke another word to us. Instead he rode inland, away from the camp and toward the broken lands where the plains gave way to the plateaus. He kneed his taldi into a gallop. If he followed a trail or path, I could not see it, but he never hesitated as he led us on. As the shadows grew longer, I began to question the wisdom of what we were doing. "Where are we going?" I finally asked Sergeant Duril.

"To see Dewara," he said curtly.

It hit me like one of Duril's ambush rocks when I was a boy. "We can't be. My father did everything he could to find Dewara after he dragged me home. There was no sign of him, and the Kidona said they didn't know where he went or what became of him."

Sergeant Duril shrugged. "They lied. Back then, Dewara was something of a hero for what he'd done to your father's son. But petty glory is faded, and Dewara has fallen on hard times. That woman back there believed me when I said I'd give her brother's ear back to her if she'd give us Dewara."

I rode for a time in shocked silence. Then, "How did you know it was her brother's ear?"

"I don't. But it could have been. I left it up to her to decide."

We followed the boy into a narrow, steep-sided canyon. It was a perfect site for an ambush, and I rode with a chilly spot on my back. The boy's taldi still had a good lead on us. He started up a narrow path across a rock face and I had to rein Sirlofty back to follow Duril's horse up the treacherous way. I was becoming more and more dubious of our mission. If the boy was leading us to another Kidona encampment, I didn't like the odds. But Sergeant Duril appeared calm, if watchful. I tried to emulate him.

There was another switchback in the trail, very tight for

our horses, and then the ground suddenly leveled out. We had reached a long, narrow ledge that jutted out from the rock face. As soon as Duril and I were out of the way, the boy turned his taldi and silently started back down the path. Before us was a patched tent set up with a neat stack of firewood beside it. A blackened kettle hung from a tripod over a small smokeless fire. I smelled simmering rabbit. Dewara stood looking at us with no trace of surprise on his face. He had seen us coming. No one could approach this aerie without his being aware of it.

He was a changed man from the tough warrior I'd known. His clothing was worn and rumpled; dust stood in the ridges of the fabric. His dingy long-sleeved robe reached just past his hips and was belted with a plain strip of leather. The brown trousers he wore beneath it were faded to white at the knees and frayed at the cuffs. His swanneck hung at his hip, but the hair sheath looked dirty and frayed. The man himself had aged, and not well. Four years had passed since I had last seen him, but to look at him, it had been twenty. His gray eyes, once so keen, had begun to cloud with cataract. He had a stoop in his back. He had allowed his hair to grow, and it hung in a thin yellowish-white fringe to his shoulders. He licked his lips, giving us a brief glimpse of his filed teeth. No fear showed in his face as he greeted me. "Well. Soldier's son. You come back to me. You want a new notch in your ear, maybe?" His bravado did not fool me. Even his voice had aged, and the bitterness in it surprised me.

Sergeant Duril had not dismounted, and he did not speak. I sensed he deferred to me, but I didn't know what to say or do. The old Kidona warrior looked shriveled and small. I remembered belatedly that when I first met him, he had been shorter than I, and I had grown since then. But that was my "real-life" memory of him. In the far more vivid dream memory, he had been much taller than I, and had the head of a hawk and feathered arms. I struggled to reconcile those memories with the withered man who stood squinting up at me. I think that puzzle kept me from feeling any one emotion clearly.

I dismounted and walked up to him. Behind me, I heard

Sergeant Duril do the same. He stood behind my shoulder when I halted, allowing me this battle.

Dewara had to look up at me. Good. I stared down at him and spoke sternly. "I want to know what you did to me, Dewara. Tell me now, without riddles or mockery. What happened to me that night when you said you would make me Kidona?" My Jindobe had come back to me without hesitation. I felt as if I had leapfrogged back through the years to confront the man who had abused, befriended, and then nearly killed me.

He grinned, his pointed teeth shiny with saliva. "Oh, look at you, fat man. So brave now. So big. Still knowing nothing. Still wishing you were Kidona. Eh?"

I towered over him, dwarfing him in girth as well as height. Still he did not fear me. I summoned all my disdain. "If you are Kidona, then I do not wish to be Kidona." I drew on all my knowledge of his people to make my insults sting. "Look at you. You are poor! I see no women here, no taldi, no smoke rack of meat. The gods despise you."

I saw my words hit him like flung stones. Shame tried to stir in me, that I would attack someone in his situation, but I held it down. He was not beaten. If I wanted to wring answers from him, I must first dominate him. From some depth of courage in his soul, he summoned a grin and retorted, "Yet I am still Kidona. And you, you are still *her* plaything. Look at you, all swollen up with her magic like a sore toe full of pus. The fat old woman claimed you, and made you her puppet."

His words jabbed me and I retorted without thinking, "Her puppet? Her plaything? I think not. I did what you could not do. I crossed the bridge, and with the iron magic of my people, I laid her belly open. I defeated her, old man. What you could not do, even using me as your tool, I did alone." I struck a pose I remembered from our days together. I threw out my chest and lifted my head high, the same posture he had held whenever he wished to express how far above me he was. "I have always been stronger than you, Dewara. Even when I lay unconscious before you, you still dared not kill me."

I watched him, trying to gauge his weakness in this battle

of exchanged brags. To the west of us, the sun was dying in
a welter of reds and purples. It was hard to read his features in the fading light. Perhaps a shadow of doubt brushed
Dewara's eyes, but he brazened it out. "I could have killed
you if I wished," he said disdainfully. "It would have been
like crushing a hatchling in the nest. I thought of it. You
were useless to me. You claim to have killed her? Well,
where is your proof? You brag like a child. When I sent you
against her, you fell like a child. I witnessed that! The weakness of your people made you fail, not my Kidona magic.
You were not strong of heart; you did not have the will to do
what you should have done. If you had not spoken to the
guardian, if you had rushed forward and killed her as I commanded, then all of our lives would be better now. But no!
You are so wise, soldier's boy, you think you know more
than a Kidona warrior. You look, you think, *Oh, just an old
woman*, so you talk, talk, talk, and all the while her wormy
white roots sink into you. Look at you now, like a fat grub
from under a rotting log. You will never be a warrior. And
you will ever belong to her. She will puff you up full with
her magic, and when you are full, you will do whatever her
magic makes you do. Or maybe you have already done it.
Has the magic turned you against your own people?" He
laughed triumphantly and pointed a crooked finger at me.
"Look at you! I didn't need to kill you. Better to leave you
alive. Think. Is there a better revenge on your father? Fat
one! You belong to the Dappled People now. You'll never be
a soldier. Your father put iron in me to kill my magic. But I
had enough magic left in me to give his son to my other enemy. I had enough magic to make my enemies become the
enemies of each other. Long after I am dead, you will fight
and kill one another. The corpses you make will pile up at
my feet in whatever afterlife I am banished to."

I cannot describe how his words affected me. I had expected him to profess ignorance of everything I said. I hadn't
wanted him to admit that somehow we had shared that
dream, and that he recalled as clearly as I did what the Tree
Woman had done to me. He had just confirmed my worst
fears. A terrible cold welled up inside me. I crossed my arms

on my chest and held myself tightly, afraid I would start shivering. The last walls inside me were breaking; it felt as if cold blood were leaking inside my gut. I gritted my teeth to keep them from chattering. My heart thundered in my chest. Then, out of that turmoil, a terrible black calm emerged in me. I spoke in a soft voice I scarcely recognized.

"You still lost, Kidona. You lost to her and you lost to me. I went to your Dancing Spindle. I am the one who put the iron in the Spindle's path. I am the one who destroyed the Plains magic. You can no longer draw on its strength. I made you an old man. It is done, Kidona. Done forever. You cling to shreds and threads, but the fabric is gone. And I come here tonight to tell you, *I* am the one who tore it from your people and left you cold and shivering in the dark. I, Soldier's Boy of the People. Look at me, Dewara. Look at the end of your magic and your folk."

There paraded across his face such a progression of emotions that they were almost laughable. He did not comprehend what I said, and then suddenly he did. Disbelief dawned on his face, and then I saw him admit the truth of what I'd told him. I'd killed his magic, and the knowledge of that was killing him.

His face turned a terrible color and he made a strangling noise.

I never even saw him draw his swanneck. Foolish me, I had never thought it would come to blows. Aged he might be, but fury renewed his strength and speed. The curved blade swept through the air toward me, the bronze catching the red of the firelight and the sunset, as if it were already bloodied. I skipped back, feeling the wind of its passage in front of my face. As I drew my own sword, Dewara, his face purpling with effort, leapt forward. All the weight of his hatred was behind the sharpened blade. I had scarcely cleared my own sword of its scabbard before the tip of his swanneck sank into my belly. I felt the sharp bite of it, felt the ripping of my shirt as the fabric gave way to the metal and then, oddly, nothing. I grunted and my sword fell from my hands as I clutched at my gut as he pulled his weapon free of me. I stood there, my hands clutched over my wound, feeling blood seep out through my shirt and between my fingers. Shock stilled me. *What a stupid way to die*, I thought as he swept his blade back for the strike that would behead me. His lips were pulled back from his pointed teeth and his eyes bulged out of his head. I thought how disgusted my father would be with his soldier son for dying in such an ignominious fashion.

The explosion behind me jolted me with a shock of light and sound. The impact of multiple balls striking Dewara's chest stopped him in midlunge. For an instant, he hung suspended, caught between his momentum and the stopping power of the lead. Then he fell like a puppet with his strings cut, his swanneck bouncing free of his nerveless hand as he struck the earth. I knew he was dead before his body even fell to the ground.

There was a moment that seemed to last as long as a whole day. The sulfurous stench of black powder hung in the air. The magnitude of so many things happening at once paralyzed me. I stood, clutching my belly, knowing that a gut wound could fester and kill me as surely as being beheaded. I could not comprehend my injury, any more than I could grasp that Dewara sprawled dead at my feet. I'd never seen a man shot to death. Instantaneous death was shocking enough, but Dewara had been more than just a man to me. He'd figured in my most horrendous nightmares. He'd nearly killed me, but he had also taught me and shared food and water with me. He had been an important figure in my life, and when he died, a significant part of my experiences died with him. Of all that we had experienced together, I alone remained to recall it. And I might die. My own blood sang in my ears.

As if from the distance, I heard Sergeant Duril say, "Well, I didn't think much of this at first, but now I'm glad I bought it. The shopkeeper called it a pepperpot. Guess I peppered him, didn't I?"

He stepped past me to crouch over Dewara's body. Then he stood up with a grunt and came toward me. "He's dead. Are you all right, Nevare? He didn't get you, did he?"

Duril still held a small, multiple-barreled gun in his hand. I'd heard of them, but I'd never seen one before. They were good only at short range, but fired several balls at once, making it more likely that even without a chance to aim, you'd hit your target somewhere. My father had spoken of them as a coward's weapon, something that a high-priced whore or a table gambler might carry concealed in a sleeve. I was surprised that Sergeant Duril would carry such a weapon. Surprised, and very glad.

"I'm not sure," I said. There wasn't much pain. But I'd heard that the shock of a wound could keep a man from feeling pain at first. I turned away from Duril and staggered a few steps toward the fire, fumbling at the front of my shirt as I went. It seemed a private thing; I wanted to be alone when I discovered how bad it was. I managed to unbutton my shirt and pull it open just as he caught up with me.

"Good god, help us!" he muttered, and it was a prayer the way he said it. Before I could stop him, he leaned forward to probe the injury with his fingers. "Oh, thank all that's holy. It's just a jab, Nevare. You're hardly hurt at all. A flesh wound. And there was a lot of flesh there to wound, begging your pardon. Oh, thank the good god! What would I have said to your da before he killed me?"

His knees seemed to give out on him and he sank down to sit beside Dewara's fire. I turned a bit away from him, strangely embarrassed that I was not hurt more severely. I wiped my bloodied hands on my shirt and then gritted my teeth as I prodded at the cut on my belly. The sergeant was right. It was scarcely bleeding now. I felt humiliated that such a minor injury could have stopped me in my tracks and made me drop my own sword. A fine soldier son I was! The first time I actually faced an enemy in combat, the old man had disarmed me with a minor poke in the gut. The thought of my own proud sword lying in the dust shamed me. I went to retrieve it.

The light was going rapidly. I found my blade by touch, sheathed it, and then stooped to pick up Dewara's swanneck. For one boyish instant, I thought of keeping it as a trophy. In the next, I felt repulsed by such a vainglorious thought. I hadn't even killed the man who'd wielded it. I shifted it in the firelight, and watched as it illuminated the gleaming

bronze blade. Then I went queasy at what I saw. A full four
fingers of the blade's tip was bloodied. It had gone that deep.
With my free hand, I groped at my injury. No. There was
almost no pain.

It made no sense.

I carried the swanneck back to the fire where I could look
at it more clearly. Sergeant Duril was recovering from his
fright at my injury. He stood up as I approached the fire.
"Leave that!" he ordered me harshly. "Leave everything,
just as it is. We need to get down that trail before it gets any
darker."

He walked away from me. I stood alone in the firelight
and stared at my blood on the blade. I lied to myself, pretending that perhaps it had run there. I knew it hadn't. The
swanneck had pierced me, had gone right into my gut. And
my flesh had simply closed itself when he pulled it free. The
blade fell from my hand and landed in the flames. I turned
and walked away from it.

I didn't look at Dewara's body as I passed. When Duril
announced, "We're leading the horses down the trail, at
least as far as the switchback," I didn't argue with him.
Instead, I followed him just as trustingly as I had always
followed him when I was a boy.

I didn't dwell on what we left behind us. I doubted that
either the boy or the old woman would admit to anyone that
they had betrayed Dewara's hiding place. Even if they did,
even if we were connected to his death, he had attacked me,
and Duril had saved my life. It felt strange to leave him lying
where he had fallen, but it would have felt even more wrong
to take his body and bury it elsewhere.

Darkness filled the narrow canyon like water fills a
bucket. "Can you ride?" Sergeant Duril asked me gruffly.

"I'll be fine. It wasn't much more than a scratch." I hesitated, and then asked him, "Are you going to report this to
my father?"

"I'm not going to report this to anyone. Neither are you."

"Yes sir," I said, relieved to have that decision taken from
me so firmly. We mounted our horses and he led the way
back toward home.

We rode without speaking through the deeply shadowed canyon. When we emerged onto the plain, we came back out of night into evening. The last light of the setting sun still washed red across the flatlands. Duril stirred his mount to a faster pace and I pushed Sirlofty up alongside him. He didn't turn to look at me when he spoke.

"Well. You got what you were after?"

"I did and I didn't. Dewara's dead. I wasn't after that, not really. But I don't think he would have let it end any other way, once he knew what I'd done. But I don't think I solved anything tonight. I'm still fat. According to Dewara, I'm still in Tree Woman's power." I shook my head wildly. "And it all sounds like a strange old tale told by a fireside. How can I believe anything so bizarre?"

He didn't say anything. I kept my eyes straight ahead as I pondered everything that had happened. "He knew," I said at last. "Dewara knew what had happened in my dream. And he couldn't possibly know that unless he was there. And to him, it was just as real as our visit today. According to what he believed, the Tree Woman somehow enslaved me with her magic and doomed me to be, to be—this!" I could scarcely contain my disgust. "If I believe him, I'm doomed to be this for the rest of my life, and perhaps worse things will befall me. Maybe I *will* go on to betray all of Gernia!"

"Easy, boy. Don't give yourself too much importance," Duril warned me, a sour touch of humor in his voice. It jabbed me.

"But if I don't believe him, if I say magic doesn't exist or has no power over me, well, then, none of it makes sense. Then there's no reason for me being fat, and that makes it even harder for me to know what I'm going to do about it. How do I manage it, Sergeant? What do I do? Believe Dewara's truth, and give up because the magic will use me as it wills, or believe in my father's world, where I don't know why I got fat and nothing I do seems to change it?"

"Hold up a minute," he suggested. He reined his horse in and I pulled Sirlofty to a halt beside him. He dismounted and tightened his cinch. "Came loose coming down that trail," he observed. Then he looked up at me, squinting his eyes against the fading sunset. "Never used to do that, Nevare. The 'keep fast' charm held it tight. And now it doesn't. That's proof enough for me. The Plains magic is fading. Will you think me a fool if I say I'm sorry to see it go?"

"I'll never think you a fool, Sergeant Duril. But are you saying that you believe in magic? You believe I went somewhere with Dewara and that Tree Woman stole part of my soul, and that I took it back and killed her? And you believe that my being fat is not my fault but the magic affecting me?"

Duril mounted his horse again. He didn't say anything as he kicked him to a trot. I started Sirlofty after him, and in a few moments we were cantering. Before full night fell, we were back on the river road. We went more slowly in the dark, and finally he answered me.

"Nevare, I don't know how to tell you what to believe. On the Sixday, I worship the good god, same as you. But every time I saddled my horse for the past thirty years, I've made the 'keep fast' sign over my cinch. I've seen a wind wizard, and I've seen gunpowder send a bullet on its way. I don't really understand how either one worked. I guess what I believe in is whatever works best for me at that time. I think most men are like that."

"What am I going to do, Sergeant?" I didn't expect him to have an answer. I was shocked when he did. His voice was grim.

"We both have to pray to the good god that you can find a way to turn the magic against itself, I suppose."

CHAPTER EIGHT

JUDGMENT

I t was past full dark before Sergeant Duril and I reached home. We put our own horses up and said a subdued good night outside the stable. "Clean up that gash before you go to bed," he warned me, and I promised I would. A gash. I knew Dewara had thrust his swanneck into me. It still hurt, but less than my arse and back hurt from the long ride. I went in through the servants' entrance and stopped at the kitchen.

A single lamp was burning there, the wick turned low. The usually bustling room was deserted and quiet. The kneading table was wiped clean of flour and the food all stored away in crocks or covered with clean cloths. The room was still uncomfortably warm from the day's cooking. The week's baking of bread was set out in fragrant round-topped loaves on the counter. The smell was heavenly.

It was my father's pride that our home had water piped right into it. A large elevated cistern was regularly replenished from the river, and the gravity flow system supplied all our drinking and bathing water. The thick stone walls of the cistern kept the water cool even in summer. I drank three tall mugs of it, one after another, and then slowly drank a fourth. I damped a kitchen cloth and wiped the sweat and dust from my face and the back of my neck. It had been a very long day.

I wet the cloth well and gingerly opened my shirt. I had bled. I turned the wick for better light. Blood soaked the front of my shirt. The waistband of my trousers was stiff with it. Cautiously, I washed the blood from my gut, wiping it carefully away until a fine seam as long as my forefinger showed on my belly. I gritted my teeth against expected pain and prodded at it.

It didn't hurt. I couldn't even make it bleed. The blade of the swanneck had sunk into me, but this wound was no deeper than a bad cat scratch. Had I imagined it? No. There was too much blood. I traced the puckered seam with my finger. The scratch closed up behind my touch like magic. Like magic.

A wave of vertigo washed over me. I held on to the edge of the sink until it passed. Then, very carefully, I rinsed my blood out of the cloth and watched the dark water trickle down the drain. I wrung the water out and hung the rag to dry. My wound had healed. Like magic. Because it was magic. Magic inside me. I suddenly thought of Dewara's purpling face and bared teeth. Had Duril's lead shot killed the old man? Or had he been dying even as he attacked me? I recalled again the thundering of my heart and the seething of my blood. I poked at the idea that I had killed Dewara with magic. I didn't much like it. I took a deep and steadying breath.

The evening's ride and the weight of the revelations I had received had left me ravenous. I took a loaf of the still-warm bread and a small crock of butter to the table. I filled a mug with the cheap ale that my father kept for the servants. Then I pulled out a chair and sat down with a sigh. For a short time, I just sat in the dim stillness, trying to come to grips with what I had learned.

There was nothing new in what Dewara had told me. His words confirmed the fears that had grown in me for the last four years. I had not previously seen the truth because it was not a Gernian truth. To someone like my father, the things

I had experienced were simply not real. If I tried to explain them to him, he would think me a liar or a madman. What had I gained tonight? What had Dewara's death bought me? Duril had overheard what Dewara had said. Duril believed me. At least I had that.

I sliced off the crusty heel of the loaf, spread it with butter, and took a bite. The simple, familiar food was comfort to me in a time when my world seemed to be distorted beyond recognition. I chewed slowly. I swallowed and took a deep draught of the ale. The mug made a small, comfortable *thunk* as I set it back on the table in the dimly lit kitchen.

Magic was the province of the uncivilized world. It was the feeble and untrustworthy weapon of folk too primitive to create the technology to master the natural world with engineering and science. Magic, I had always believed, was suitable for trickery or small conveniences, but useless on a large scale. The little spells and charms I'd known about were handy but scarcely necessary. The "keep fast" charm was an example: it could save a man from having to stop and tighten his cinch. That was not to be confused with a true invention or real technology. Something as simple as a pulley or as sophisticated as a system of pipes that fed water into our house were genuine human innovation. Those were the things that lifted mankind from the squalor and sweat of daily toil.

Thoughtfully, I cut another slice from the loaf and buttered it slowly. Over and over, I'd seen technology defeat magic. Iron could destroy magic just by its presence. Iron pellets killed the wind wizard. Dewara blamed the weakness in his magic on having been shot by my father with an iron bullet. I'd witnessed a small steel blade bringing the Dancing Spindle to a sudden halt.

So how could magic do this to me?

I touched iron every day of my life. Magic should have no power over me. I was a Gernian, a follower of the good god, and a damn good engineer. Magic was for ignorant tent-dwelling nomads. I picked up the bread knife and studied the blade. Then I set it, flat-sided, against my arm. I felt nothing. No burn, no freezing cold, no antipathy to the metal at all. Disgusted with myself for even trying the experiment, I put the blade to its proper use, carving off another slice of bread. My ale mug was empty. I refilled it.

For the first time in my life, I wanted to sit down and talk with a priest. Most of them, I knew, dismissed magic entirely. It was not one of the gifts the good god extended to his followers, and therefore not the province of just men. They didn't deny it existed. It just wasn't allotted to me. I knew that from the Holy Writ. But what about what was happening to me? I didn't desire it, so how could magic reach out and take hold of me this way?

In the next instant, I admitted to myself that perhaps I *had* desired it. What else had I intended that long-ago night when I had followed Dewara over the cliff? He had made me want to be Kidona, enough that I had been blindly willing to risk my life. Had that been an offense to the good god? Had that been when I had literally fallen into the powers of magic? Unbidden, the image of the sacrificed birds came to my mind. The old gods had been willing to grant magic to those willing to make such offerings, or so the old tales said. I shivered, and the warm and friendly kitchen suddenly seemed darker and more ominous. As a child, I'd been taught that followers of the good god were immune to the horrors and brutality of the old gods. Had I lost that protection when I stepped over the cliff's edge? An image of a croaker bird came to my mind, wings extended and neck shot out as it cawed at me. I'd interfered with the sacrifice to Orandula, the old god of balances. He controlled death and life, fortune and misfortune. Had I offended him? Was I vulnerable to him now? Superstition stood all the hair up on my arms, and I nearly leapt out of my skin when a harsh voice spoke suddenly behind me.

"What are you doing?"

I jumped guiltily and turned. "Just having a quick bite to eat, sir. I came in late and didn't want to wake anyone."

My father crossed the kitchen with quick strides. I suddenly saw myself as he must see me: a fat boor, hunched over food in the dark, gobbling it down out of sight of others. The half loaf of bread, the greasy knife, the plundered crock of butter, and the ale mug all spoke of furtive gluttony.

"You pig. You *lying* pig. You avoid your family and refuse to eat with us so you can do what? Creep down here in the dark and stuff yourself with food?"

"I didn't eat that much, sir." I came to my feet. I stepped in front of the crumb-strewn table like a guilty child concealing a broken vase. "I ate only a few slices of bread and butter. Sergeant Duril and I went out for a ride and were out much longer than we intended. I came in hungry."

"You're supposed to be hungry, you fat idiot! That's the purpose of the work I gave you, to whittle the fat from your lazy back. I can't believe what I'm seeing, Nevare! I can't understand when or why your changed into this . . . greedy, gluttonous liar! Oh, you had me fooled these last few days. You made such a show of staying away from the family table. I've talked to the cooks. They say you eat only one plate of food and then leave. I thought, 'Well, the boy is trying, he's recovered some of his self-discipline and he's saving us having to watch him eat. He's working hard and eating little and soon enough he'll put himself right.' I could not understand why the weight was not falling away from you, but I thought perhaps I was being impatient. I was even, may the good god help me, thinking of using my influence to get you back into the academy once you'd shown you had the backbone to change yourself. But what do I find tonight? The truth! You put on a show for us, with your hard work and small meals, but in the dark of night, you creep down here and stuff yourself! Why? Didn't you think I'd work it out eventually? Do you think I'm a fool, Nevare?"

I was standing at attention now. I reined in~my~ anger. "No, sir. Never, sir."

"Then what, Nevare? What? Have you heard the reports of fresh skirmishes with the Landsingers and renewed clashes with some of the Plainsmen? They're blaming us for the damn Speck plague and rising up. In times like these, a good officer can make his career. But you seem to be running away from all your opportunities! Are you a coward? Are you too afraid to serve your king as a soldier? You're not lazy; I've had reports, you do your work each day. What? What is it?" His bafflement was driving him to rage. "Why do you want to bring shame on us all this way?" My father advanced on me, his eyes never leaving mine as he came on. He reminded me of a stiff-legged circling dog, selecting his position before he attacked. My thoughts ran in tiny circles. He was my father. He was being unjust. Most of this was his fault, not mine. I was transfixed by a question I could not answer: if he struck me, did I accept it, or did I strike back?

Perhaps he saw that uncertainty in my eyes, or sensed that I held fury in check. Whatever the reason, he stopped where he was. I heard his teeth grind, and then he spoke. "Discipline should come from within a man. You should have learned it by now. But as you have not, I will impose it upon you, as if you were a spoiled child. You will go to your room tonight, Nevare, and you will stay there. You will not leave it again until I give you permission to do so. I will regulate what you eat. Before the good god, I vow I will take that fat off of you."

"We can try that," I agreed, my voice flat. "But I don't think it will work, Father."

He snorted in disdain. "It will work. You've never seen a prisoner kept on bread and water for two months. You'd be amazed how fast a man can dwindle away."

"Probably I would, Father. And if this fat were because I'd been greedy or slothful, such a cure would probably work. But it isn't." The truth was all I had to offer him. With no forethought, I went on, "I've explained this to Mother. I know she told you. I know you believe I lied to her. I didn't. I've put on this weight because of a curse from a Speck wizard-woman. Or a goddess. I don't know exactly what she was. But she is the one who has done this to me, by claiming me for her magic. And she was able to claim me because you put me in harm's way when you fostered me out to Dewara the Kidona for training when I was fifteen. He 'trained' me, all right. He starved and abused me, and eventually he convinced me that the only way to be a true warrior was to become as Kidona as he was." My voice rang with accusation. My father stared at me, his mouth slightly ajar.

"I was drugged with something he put on our campfire one night. The smoke was sweet and very thick. And when he told me to follow him, I did. I jumped off a cliff after him, and I found myself in a different world. We traveled in that world for days, perhaps weeks. We reached a dangerous bridge and he commanded me to do battle with its guardian. And that was where I encountered the Tree Woman. But I could not bring myself to fight a woman; I underestimated the sort of enemy she could be. And so I fell to her, and came under her control. And this, this body that looks so fat, this is what she did to me. Inside this body, I'm the same person I've always been, with the same dreams and ambitions. I've never stopped wanting to be a soldier. I'm trying to undo what happened to me. Tonight, I went to a Kidona encampment, to try to find a way to break free of her magic. But there isn't, or at least that's what—"

"Silence!" My father roared the word. His face had grown starker and whiter with every detail of my story. I had thought it filled him with horror for what he had unwittingly done to me. For an instant, his mouth trembled, and then he demanded, "Are you mad? Is that what ails you? Insanity? What is all this talk of magic and Dewara? You are going to blame your gluttony on something that happened years ago, and make it my fault? Nevare! Look at yourself! Look at your belly, look at the mess you've left on that table, and then tell me you haven't done this to yourself! Magic! What idiocy! Or have you somehow gulled yourself into believing it has power over you and thus it does? I've heard of such things, men convinced they were under a curse and dying from it because they believed in it. Is that your problem, Nevare? Truly, you think *magic* did this to you?" He laded the word with scorn.

I took a deep breath and clenched my hands, but my voice still shook. "Magic is real, Father. We've both seen it; we've both used it! The 'keep fast' charm over our saddle cinches, and the wind wizard flying his boat upstream despite the river's current, and—"

"Nevare! Shut up! 'Keep fast' is just a soldier's superstition, one of the sillier bits of our traditions. You've believed it, all these days, even when you are a man grown? And that wind wizard was a Plainsman, so, yes, he could work his pathetic little magic. In the end, it couldn't save him, could it? Because what we have, our technology and our faith in the good god, is much stronger. Son. Listen to me. Magic didn't make you fat. *It has no power over you.* You listen to me and do as I say, and I'll prove it to you."

His voice had gone gentler, ever since he had said the word "son." I so wanted to simply agree with him, to put him back in charge of my life and let there be some sort of peace between us, even if it was a peace born of deception.

I couldn't do it. Was I finally finding what he had once sent me out with Dewara to seek, the courage to make my own decisions when I knew my commander was less informed than I was?

"I'll do as you say, Father. I'll confine myself to my room and subsist on whatever you judge is right for me. If that is what it takes to prove to you that I am correct and you are wrong, I will do it. But in the end, I think we will both have to admit that when you entrusted me to Dewara, you began the chain of events that did this to me. If anyone bears the fault for what I have become, Father, it is you, not me."

He slapped me. He didn't hit me with his fist. I think if he had, I would have struck him back. He slapped me as if I were an upstart child, and I knew I was not that, and so I let him. I felt it as a small triumph when he shakily told me, "Yes. We will prove which one of us is right. Go to your room and stay there, Nevare, until I myself come to your door. And that is an order."

I went, but not in obedience. I went with defiance, determined to let him regulate me as he wished and so prove to him that I was correct. I went to my room and shut the door firmly behind me. I seethed as I stripped off my bloodied clothes. *I should have shown them to him*, I thought furiously, and then realized that the dried blood on the dark fabrics could have been nearly any dark liquid. I lifted the side of my belly and pulled hard at where the wound had been, halfway hoping that it would suddenly open and gush blood that I could present to him as evidence of the night's adventures. It didn't. There wasn't even a mark there. I prodded it with my fingers and woke only a vague pain inside me. My body told me that nothing had happened tonight. I thought of getting up and going to Duril, but suspected that if I stirred out of my room, my wakeful father would descend, accusing me of more deceptions. The only thing that would possibly convince my father was allowing him to control my life and seeing that not even he could take the fat from me. I was not resigned to it. I was eager for it, in the way a warlike man is hungry for a confrontation.

I lay down to sleep on my bed. As I closed my eyes, I told myself that only the outside of my body had changed, that within I was still Nevare, and if my father could not see that, then he was both blind and stupid. But before I drifted off to sleep, I finally admitted that I had changed. My body had healed itself tonight of a potentially fatal wound. The fat and the shape of my body were an external change, but internally, I had changed also. The Nevare he had sent away to the academy would never have stood up to him as I had tonight. It was ironic that my father had finally got what he wanted out of me. He was not enjoying it very much.

And so began our battle of wills. The next morning, I awoke early, as I always did, and dressed and sat down on my bed wondering what the day would bring. Several hours later, my father entered my room, a very burly man at his heels. He didn't address me, but spoke to the servant. "He's to chop wood all day. He can have three water breaks. No food. At the end of the day, you're to bring him back up here. That's all."

The man knit his brows. "That's all I'm supposed to do? Watch him and make sure he chops wood and only drinks three times and doesn't eat anything?"

My father spoke in a flat voice. "If you don't think that will tax your abilities too much, Narl."

The servant scowled. "I can do that. Just seems like you'd want me to do more."

"No. That's all." My father turned on his heel and left the room.

I pulled on my boots and stood up: "Let's go chop wood," I suggested.

The man scowled so that his forehead stood up on ridges. "You want to go? I don't have to force you or nothing?"

"I assure you, I'm as eager to do this as my father is. Let's go."

"He's your father?"

I gave up trying to converse with Narl. "I'm going downstairs and outside to chop wood now," I told him. I started out the door and he followed me like an obedient dog.

I chopped wood all that day. No one spoke to me or paid me much attention. Once, Sergeant Duril wandered casually by and then walked away again. I suspected he had some thought or news he wanted to share with me, but I wouldn't acknowledge him in front of my guard. Blisters came up and broke on my hands and were torn away. Knowing that I could only ask for water three times, I schooled myself to wait until my body demanded it. Then I drank deeply. Evidently my father had not given the man any limit for how much water I could have.

It must have been boring duty for Narl. He sat on a section of log and watched me. He wore a floppy brimmed hat, and as the shade of the woodshed moved, he scooted his log section along to stay within it. Most of our wood was either skinny pole wood that I could chop with almost one blow or long heavy logs of spond wood salvaged from the river.

At the end of the day, Narl escorted me back to my room. As I entered, I noticed that a large, new hasp had been fitted to the outside of my door. So I was to be locked in at night, to prevent any midnight kitchen visits. *Thank you, Father.* My room was stuffy when I entered it. The window was shut, and a quick glance showed me that it, too, had been fastened closed from outside. My father wasn't taking any chances, not even that I would risk a drop from my upstairs window to the gardens below. I could vividly imagine what that would do to my knees and ankles.

My guard shut the door behind me, and I sat down on my bed. I waited to hear the hasp secured in some way, but all I heard was the guard's departing footfalls. The maid had refilled my water ewer. I noticed with distaste that a chamber pot had been added to my room. The wash water was welcome, though I would have preferred a bath or even a dip in the river shallows.

I did not wait long until I heard a different step on the stair. There was a tap on my door, and when I opened it, my father himself entered with a covered tray. He didn't look at me. I think even he was somewhat embarrassed by what he was doing to me. "This is your food," he announced, as if I could have mistaken it for something else. I could smell meat, and instantly my mouth began to water. My hunger, which I could somewhat ignore in the absence of food, became an obsession the moment I could smell or see anything edible. I was glad that he set the tray down without uncovering it. I feared that if he had shown me what he carried, I could not have focused on his words.

He spoke stiffly. "I hope you realize that I'm doing this for your own good, Nevare. Trust me, and I promise you that by the end of the week, those clothes will be hanging on you. I will prove to you that your fat is a result of your greed, not some 'magic spell.'"

"Sir," I said, confirming that I'd heard his words but offering no comment on what I thought of them. He decided that was rude, and left my room. He shut the door smartly and this time I did hear him fasten the hasp shut. Fine. I wasted no time in sitting down to my meal.

In a way, he was fair. I suppose he could have fed me bread and water. Instead, there was a meager portion of everything that my family was enjoying downstairs, even half a glass of wine. The cloth that had covered the tray became my napkin. I did not allow myself a morsel until I had divided every food on my plate into meticulously carved small bites. Then I began, eating each bite as if it were my last and trying to savor the taste in an attempt to make the small quantity satisfying. I had cut the meat so fine that I had reduced it to tiny bundles of fibers. I ground them between my back teeth and let them linger in my mouth until the flavor faded. I ate the peas individually, squeezing the tender insides out of their tiny jackets and savoring the difference in texture. I chewed the bread endlessly, delighted to discover that each tiny square somehow became sweet when it lingered on my tongue.

My father, perhaps from some sense of fairness, had even provided me with a tiny portion of a sweet pudding with three tart cherries in it. This I ate in bits that scarcely covered the tips of the fork's tines. Had I ever before been so aware of the sharp contrast between sweet and sour, ever mapped so clearly what portions of my tongue responded to each? My deprivation became an exercise in sensory exploration.

And when the last trace of stickiness had been scraped from the dish, I savored the half glass of wine. I wet my lips with it and then ran my tongue over them. I breathed the taste and then, drop by drop, consumed the rest of the glass. A meal I would have devoured in a few minutes at the academy lasted more than an hour in the privacy of my room.

Do not mistake me. I was not satisfied. Hunger opened its maw and roared within me, demanding more. If there had been anything remotely edible in my room, I would have eaten it. I longed for bulk, for large mouthfuls of food that I could masticate and swallow in huge gulps. If I had allowed myself to dwell on my hunger, I would have gone mad. Instead, I reminded myself that I had gone for days on far less in the time when I had traveled with Dewara. I was deprived but not starving. I set each dish back on the tray and covered it with my napkin. I took out my neglected schoolbooks.

I set myself a lesson from each text and doggedly completed it. I read and took notes from Gernia's military history. I studied a chapter of math, working each exercise and diligently checking my answers. I translated several pages of Varnian from Bellock's *Warfare*.

And when I was finished, I took out my soldier's journal and made a complete and unvarnished entry about the entire day. Afterward, I put out my lamp and went to bed in my stuffy little room.

The next morning I was awake and dressed when my guard unlocked my door. That day I worked on whitewashing several outbuildings. The work was not heavy, but it was constant. My shoulders ached and my raw hands could scarcely close around the brush. Nevertheless, I set my teeth and toiled on. I saw my mother once. She came out and stood silently at a distance, watching my toil. When she saw she had caught my eye, she lifted her hand, as if she pleaded with me to understand there was nothing she could do. I nodded to her and turned away. I did not wish her to interfere. This was between my father and me.

My guard allowed me to bathe that day before returning me to my cell. My room was stuffier than ever, for all the smells of my occupation of it were trapped inside it. My evening was a repetition of the previous one. My father himself brought me a small meal that I savored obsessively, and I set myself another night of lessons. If, against all my expectations, my father's plan worked and I managed to return to the academy, I did not intend to be behind my classmates. My hopes were torn. I desperately wanted to return to my old life. But I was equally obsessed with finally proving to my father that he was wrong and I was right. I tried to tell myself that either outcome would have its reward, but I found I longed for the former rather than the latter.

I don't recall how many days I passed with that routine. Every Sixday, I had a small reprieve. My father released me to attend his prayers with my elder brother, and then returned me to my solitude for an afternoon of meditation. But every other day followed the pattern of the first. I rose, I worked all day, I returned to my confinement and my meal and my lessons. My father shifted me from task to task. I gained muscle in my arms, so that my shirt strained more than ever at my shoulders. If my belt notch was any indication, I lost no girth. My guard was a man of few words, and I had even less to say to him.

There were few events of any note during those days of my life. One evening I asked my father for more paper and ink. I think he was shocked to discover that I was continuing my education. He brought me paper and ink, and, as a reward I think, a letter that had come from Epiny and Spink.

It was a welcome distraction. In her letter, my cousin told me that she and Spink were both recovered well from their most recent bout with the plague. Spink in particular showed marked improvement from when they had last seen me. He was much more like his old self, full of energy and ideas. Unfortunately, she wrote, it made him restless and more prone to being dissatisfied with living as a dependent on his brother's goodwill. He had too many ideas about how the family holding could be improved, and how tasks should be done. He and his older brother often quarreled, which made everyone miserable. Epiny wished there was some way Spink could return to the academy, but the expense was presently too great, especially since she would also need to be housed in the city while Spink was at school.

She thanked me belatedly for sharing her letters to me with her father. After a dearth of communication for several months, they were now corresponding regularly. Without stating it plainly, she implied that perhaps her mother had somehow blocked earlier letters between them. Lady Burvelle seemed to have lost all interest in Epiny and was focusing her efforts on grooming Purissa to be a consort fit for the very young prince. Epiny thought it disgraceful and heartless. But she also believed that her father was now far less disappointed in her than she had feared. I sensed a great relief in her penned words.

I wrote her a long reply in which I told her all that had befallen me, including my meeting with Dewara. Then, as I decided it was extremely likely my father would read all my mail before he posted it, I tore that letter up. The next one was very circumspect. I said only that my return to the academy was delayed due to some health difficulties that I hoped to resolve soon. I filled up the rest of two pages with generalities about life at home and best wishes for her and Spink.

Having started writing letters, I decided I would also answer the missive from Caulder and his uncle. I tried to describe the area in which I'd "found" the stone that Caulder had stolen from me. I recalled only too well how I'd come by that rock. It had dug its way into my flesh when Dewara had dragged me home. I even made a rough sketch that didn't merit being dignified with the name "map" and sent it with my letter. With that final, grudging courtesy, I resolved that I was now finished with Caulder and all his kin forever.

My days continued to be full of menial and backbreaking tasks, which didn't bother me. It left my mind free to ponder other things. I thought through, from beginning to end, my "love affair" with Carsina. I thought of how abruptly it had begun: I'd become infatuated with her the night my father told me that she was going to be given to me. And since the day when I had seen her at Rosse's wedding and she had so completely disdained me, I could think of her only with anger.

I am human. I had my boyish revenge fantasies about her. I would regain my formerly trim body, and then I would disdain her. I would do some magnificent and heroic act for her family, perhaps saving her mother from certain death when she was attacked by a prairie cat, and then when her father offered me anything that I could desire as a reward for my heroism, I would coldly ask only that he release me from my promise to marry his heartless and shallow daughter.

I played such scenarios over and over in my mind, until I was forced to admit that they would not have given me such pleasure if I were not still fixed on possessing Carsina. It was not, I realized one day between shovels of manure, that I loved her. It was simply that she had been part of the perfect future I'd envisioned for myself. In that golden fancy, I completed the academy, gained a good post as a young lieutenant, moved up in rank quickly, and then claimed the young woman of good family who had been promised to me. Any modification to that future somehow lessened it. I could no more imagine substituting another woman for Carsina than I could imagine following a different profession than soldiering. And anytime I imagined that Carsina's father might cancel his understanding with my father and bestow Carsina on Remwar instead, my blood seethed. I could not tolerate the idea that they might speak of me with laughter, or that Carsina might thank Remwar for rescuing her from the dismal fate of being my wife. The blow to my pride had quenched any love or affection I might have had for Carsina, but it had only sharpened my sense of possession of her. Sometimes I wondered what my Cousin Epiny would have said to me about such an attitude.

It bothered me that my mother and siblings never sought me out at all. I supposed that my father had forbidden the contact lest they be moved to bring me food. I don't know how many days I was into my ordeal when my guard asked me, "So your Pa is trying to make you lose some weight, right?"

"So it seems," I grunted. Narl was watching me load rocks onto a wagon, to be hauled off to build a stone wall.

"You don't look any thinner since you started."

I heaved a particularly large rock onto the wagon. I caught my breath. My mouth was dry, but I didn't want to use up one of my precious water breaks yet. "Yes," I agreed. I walked back to the pile to pick up another rock.

"So, you can tell me. Where and when do you get the food?"

"My father gives me one meal a day." I wondered if my father had directed him to ask me that question. Did he set a spy upon me now? I squatted down and maneuvered another rock up onto its side and then into my arms. I grunted as I stood up, crab-walked with it to the back of the wagon, and heaved it in. "That's a load," I gasped.

"Reckon it is. Follow 'long, now." In his wisdom, the guard had decided that I would benefit more from staggering along behind the wagon than riding on it to our unloading site. I hadn't argued. Perhaps some part of me now hated my body as much as my father did, and desired to punish it as severely as possible.

"Then why aren't you getting skinny?"

He stood with one leg up on the wagon, ready to mount to the seat. On a whim, I told him the truth. "I'm under a curse. It's magic. I'm doomed to be fat forever."

"Huh," he said. And that was all. Narl didn't talk to me much more that day, but almost every day after that, he ventured some conversational gambit. I learned that he was an orphan and abandoned and had no idea whose son he was or what he was supposed to be. So he'd come east, looking for a life, and found Burvelle's Landing and a job with my father. He'd been a pig tender before my father chose him for this task. He chuckled as he said it, and I suppose to him there was some humor in it. He had a girl across the river. She was a shopkeeper's daughter, and he hoped that when he got enough money, her father would let him marry her. Her father had no sons, so maybe any sons they had could be shopkeepers and have a real place in the world. He envied sons who knew what they were born to be.

He was good for bits and pieces of news from time to time. From him, I learned that the Kidona had simply vanished from the Bejawi village. One day they'd been there; the next time someone had visited the village to deliver supplies, they were gone. They hadn't even taken the tents or supplies that the troops at Franner's Bend had given them. Ungrateful savages. He told me, too, that the reinforcements for the fort at Gettys were due to pass the Landing any day now. For a moment my heart leapt as I recalled how I'd used to sit Sirlofty on the hill overlooking the road and watch the passing of the regiments on their way to assignments in the wild east. The rows of horse, the marching men, the wagons decked out with their regimental colors were as much pomp and heraldry as our part of the world ever witnessed. But I wouldn't even get to see Cayton's Horse and Doril's Foot as they passed, let alone have dinner with the officers if they paused at the Landing. It was likely my father would do all he could to keep me out of their sight.

And from Narl, I learned that there was sickness in Franner's Bend. Some poor families, half-breeds most likely, had come down with it first. Rumor was that they'd recently arrived at Franner's Bend. Dirty folk, was what he'd heard. And they'd brought a sickness to Franner's Bend, and rumor had it that those who caught it were dropping like flies from it. Fever, he told me, and vomiting. Diarrhea, too. That's what came of living dirty like that.

A chill went up my spine. "Does my father know about it? That there's disease in Franner's Bend?"

My guard shrugged. Narl hadn't supposed that my father took an interest in such things.

That night, when I was returned to my room, I paced it until my father arrived at my door with dinner. When he finally opened the lock and came in, I greeted him with, "Speck plague is spreading through Franner's Bend. I fear Burvelle Landing will be next."

"What?" He set my dinner tray down with an angry clack. He never received bad news graciously.

Tersely, I told him what I knew.

He shook his head at me. "That could be any of a dozen maladies, Nevare. When did you become such a nervous Nellie? Those people could have drunk bad water, or eaten spoiled meat. You'd do better to be focusing on what we're trying to accomplish here instead of imagining death and disaster on your doorstep. Speck plague. How would Speck plague come here?"

Then he added, coldly, "Stand straight. I want to look at you."

I made no verbal response. I stood as if at attention while he walked a slow circle around me. When he came back to face me, the color in his face was higher. "You haven't lost a pound that I can see. You've corrupted your guard, haven't you? He's bringing you food. That's the only possibility. What are you bribing him with, Nevare? Promises of money to be given to him later? Or do you have resources that I don't know about?"

Rage roared up in me, stronger than the hunger that still clawed at my inner ribs. "I've done no such thing! I've held myself exactly to our bargain. I've worked each day as you commanded me, and eaten only what you've brought to me with your own hands, Father. It's as I've tried to tell you; my weight has nothing to do with greed or lack of self-discipline. It's magic. What will it take to convince you of that? Or is it impossible for you to ever admit that not only are you wrong, but that your actions are responsible for how I look?"

His face contorted with rage. "You superstitious ignoramus!" He snatched up my food tray so hastily that the wine glass fell over. I smelled the sharp scent of the spilled wine. Against my will, my hands flew out to clutch at the tray and keep him from dumping the precious food. With a roar of fury, he snatched it away from me. It tipped and he deliberately swung the tray to dash the contents against the wall. I stared in horror at the splattered food and broken crockery. A large piece of the wine glass had stuck in the thick gravy of the meat pie. As I stared, its weight pulled it free and it fell to the floor with the rest of the mess. I turned my aghast gaze on my father.

His face twitched. For a moment, he struggled for control and then he released his temper. "There's your dinner, Nevare! Enjoy it! It's the last morsel of food you'll see for a time." He drew in a sharp breath through his nose. "I thought

I could trust you to adhere to our agreement! Will I never learn? You haven't a scrap of honor left, have you? You'll lie, you'll cheat, and you'll steal in whatever way you must in some idiotic effort to prove your ridiculous claims! And why? Because you are so desperate to make your failure my fault! Because you can't accept responsibility for your own mistakes. You always have wanted someone else to be in charge of you and I fear you always will! You will never lead, Nevare, because you cannot command yourself!

"But I will show you what it is a true officer does, and that is, he does what must be done to keep his troops prepared. There will be no more trust between us. You will stay here in this room, and I will supervise your fast. You will see that no magic is at work here, only your own sloth and greed."

He'd run out of breath. I remained standing and staring at him. May the good god help me as I recall that it was all I could do not to fling myself on my knees and snatch at the spilled food that was seeping across the floor. As if he knew the true focus of my attention, he pointed at it and snarled, "And clean that up!"

He turned on his heel and left me, shutting the door sharply. I heard him snap the lock into place. And the moment I knew it was latched and he could not surprise me, I dropped down to right the remainder of the glass that still cradled a mouthful of wine. The plate had not broken and part of my meal had sheltered beneath it. I cut my finger on the broken wine glass as I snatched up the spoon and carefully scooped as much of the meat pie as I could back onto the plate. Luckily, the flaky crust had kept most of its shape. I was able to gently slip my hand under it and lever it back onto the plate. The crusty seed roll was not damaged at all. The dish that had held my small serving of fruit compote had broken. I studied it, weighing the dangers of eating broken glass against the fragrance and flavor of the lush pieces of plump fruit gleaming with spiced syrup. Trembling with self-restraint, for the tantalizing aromas of the spilled food were all around me now, I forced myself to very carefully inspect each piece of fruit before I salvaged it. I placed my rescued meal back onto the tray and took it to my desk. The sight of the spilled and ruined food on the floor was almost more than I could stand. I draped the soiled napkin over it, and then hurried to my broken meal. When, an hour later, I had finished the last tiny morsel of bread, I sighed and set myself to the task of cleaning up the spilled mess.

It was only as I knelt like a penitent before the glass-strewn remnants of what should have been my meal that I forced myself to admit that my increased weight was not the only way the magic had changed me. Once I would have been too proud to salvage a meal that had fallen on the floor. Now the importance of food went far beyond its ability to nourish me. Even the pleasure I felt in the sensation of eating was secondary to another, deeper change in me.

I built my new body to house my magic.

The moment I framed the thought, I felt the rightness of it. Yes, I was fat. But I was strong now, stronger than I had ever been. And over the days of forced privation and heavy labor, I had noticed changes in myself. My body produced very little waste now. The despised chamber pot had gone largely unused. I noticed a stillness to my body that seemed new to me, in that when I sat still and studied, I felt my body sink into a greater state of rest. It reminded me of being suspended in water, or of awareness hovering in that nether place between sleep and wakefulness. I suspected that my internal workings had become terribly, terribly efficient, and that whenever I was not using my arm or my leg, it went into a suspension beyond simple rest.

I used what was left of the wash water in my basin to wet the napkin and clean my floor. I put the wet napkin and dishes and broken crockery on the tray and set it aside.

It took every bit of self-discipline I had to follow my routine that evening. I studied the lessons I'd set for myself, and faithfully entered the whole incident into my journal. I did not write there the questions that swarmed through my brain. How far would my father go in his quest to prove himself right? Would he let me die of starvation? I did not think so, but I was no longer certain.

CHAPTER NINE

PLAGUE

I came to awareness the next morning when the early summer sunlight reached through the window and touched my skin. It was simple comfort, one blessing that never changed. I closed my eyes and steeped my soul in it.

I arose at my usual time. As always, I washed and dressed and made up my bed. Then I sat down on the edge of it to await what the day might bring.

Is there anything so tedious as waiting? I tried to occupy my mind, first with my history book, and then by placing my chair near the window and watching the activities in the courtyard below.

At first, there was little to distract me. I saw a man ride in, a messenger from the town council in Burvelle's Landing by the armband he wore. He hurried up the steps, but his horse was not led away.

A short time later, my father and brother emerged with the messenger. My father was still putting on his coat. Two more horses were brought and they all rode away at a gallop. That effectively dashed my hopes of seeing my father that morning. I sat for a time longer, wondering if my keeper would come for me, even though the hour for that was some time past. But no one came.

After a time, suspense gave way to boredom. Hunger, my ever-present companion, tormented me. The intensity of the pangs always seemed greatest when I had nothing else to occupy my mind. I lay on my bed and tried to read the next chapter in Bellock's *Warfare*. The Varnian tangled in my mind, Bellock's prose seeming stilted and pompous, and after a time I lowered my book to my chest and closed my eyes.

I tried to think my situation through. Was there an alternative to this futile pissing match? I was virtually my father's prisoner. I could break down the door now, while he was gone, and then I could run away. Not only did the cowardice of that act repel me, but also the thought that it would confirm my father's poor opinion of me and dash even my tiny hope of returning to the academy and the future that I had always expected.

I took a deep breath, and as I sighed it out, I felt a sharp resolution form in me. Keen and hard as a sword's edge it was. I would persevere. I would not be the one to blink first. I slowly sighed out the air in my lungs, relaxing as I did so, and sank into a stillness deeper than sleep. I would escape hunger there. For a time, I hovered in a place that was quiet, dark, and empty.

For a time, I waited, feeling a slow peace seep into me. I felt that other me, quiescent for weeks, stir in me again. He was unalarmed by all that had befallen me. He accepted the changes, the thickening flesh that enfolded me, not placidly but with a lucid joy. As I took in another slow breath, I felt him unfold himself like a shadow filling my body. He stretched out into my arms and settled into my legs. He mourned my empty belly but joined me in my resolve. We would wait.

I felt a shiver of unease at his contentment, and then I accepted him as a passive part of myself. What harm could he do me? I sighed and again sank into his stillness. I dreamed of a forest, peaceful under the summer sunlight.

When next I became aware of myself, the sun had moved past my window. It was not dark by any means, but the golden square of sunlight that had soaked me had moved. I opened my eyes, blinking slowly. No one had come to my room. My nose told me there was no food to be had, only water. I rose and drank all that was left in my pitcher. Then, moved by an impulse I did not understand, I pushed my bed across the room into the slowly moving rectangle of sunlight from my window. I took off my shirt and lay down again, basking in the warm light on my skin. I breathed out again and once more sank my consciousness to the dim and comfortable place where my other self reigned. He took me in and sheltered me with dreams of deep-reaching roots questing for water. I dreamed of flowers turning toward the sun and of leaves absorbing light, their stoma shut tight to conserve moisture. The forest waited for me. It called me to become one with it. My breathing became an occasional wind that barely stirred the reaching leaves. My heartbeat was a distant, random drumbeat.

I awoke to darkness and the rattling of the hasp that secured my door. I sat up immediately, swinging my feet to the floor, and then felt a sudden wave of vertigo. Before it could pass, a kitchen servant entered bearing a tray. He lifted the branch of candles he bore, scowling round my dark room. He set down his candles and his tray on my desk. "Your dinner, sir." The simple words could barely contain the contempt he filled them with.

"Thank you. Where is my father?"

He stooped, full of disapproval, to lift the tray of soiled and broken dishes that I had left by the door on the floor. He was a tall fellow, pale as a mushroom, an unmuscled house servant. He sniffed loudly as if the smell of the stale food scraps disgusted him.

"Lord Burvelle has a guest this evening. He directed me to deliver this tray to you." He turned away, dismissing me as beneath his notice.

I stepped between him and the door. He recoiled from me

as if I were a threatening bear. At least my bulk was good for something, if only intimidating servants. "Who is my father's guest?" I asked him.

"Well, I scarcely think—"

"Who is my father's guest?" I repeated, taking a step closer to him. He backed away, now holding the tray of broken dishes as if it were a shield.

"Dr. Reynolds from the Landing has come to call today," he said hastily.

The mention of the doctor and my recall of the messenger I had glimpsed early in the day mingled and awoke an urgent fear in me. "Is there sickness in the Landing? Is that why the doctor is here?"

"Why, I'm sure I don't know! It's hardly my business to question why Lord Burvelle has a guest at his table."

"What did they talk about?"

"I do not eavesdrop on my betters!" He seemed incensed that I had even suggested such a thing and poked the tray toward me as if he were trying to intimidate a dog. "Out of my way. I have my work to do."

I stared at him, slowly realizing that he spoke to me as if I were nobody, an underling, a beggar. Not as if I were a son of the household. Would a time come when everyone treated me with such disregard?

"Say, 'please, sir,'" I instructed him softly.

He glared at me and then I think that something in my face persuaded him that was an error. He licked his narrow lips nervously and then fled back to formality. He spoke stiffly. "If you would please to step out of my way, sir, I'll be about my proper work."

I nodded to him. "You may go." I stepped aside. He hurried to the door and scuttled through it like a fleeing rat. An instant later, he slammed it behind him and I heard him clack the lock shut on the hasp.

"Tell my father I need to speak with him tonight!" I shouted through the door.

The only response I received was the sound of his footsteps retreating. I ground my teeth, almost certain that my message would not be delivered. Was I imagining a danger?

It could all be coincidence, my guard mentioning sickness in Franner's Bend, the messenger this morning, the visit from the Landing's only doctor. I tried to dismiss my worry, but could not.

But before my frustration could become anger, I was distracted from it. My nose had picked up a scent, and like a dog on a trail, I followed it to the tray on my desk. I lifted the napkin that covered my plate.

Bread. A single rounded loaf, a cross scored in the top of it, the size of my two fists put together. And next to it, a carafe of water. For a moment, I felt dismayed, but then my senses seized on what was there rather than on what I lacked. The loaf was a golden-topped mound. When I lifted it, I felt the slight grease on the bottom of it where it had kissed the hot pan. I broke it in my hands and tore it apart. The top was crusty, the inside slightly stretchy and tender. I smelled the summer wheat.

I filled my mouth with a bite. The flavor overwhelmed any other thought I might have framed. I tasted every element of the bread, the grain that had grown tall in our Widevale sunshine, the hint of salt, the yeast that had leavened it, the richness of the butter that had gentled the crust. I savored it all and it filled my senses. I ate without haste, taking bite after bite, only pausing to drink the cool, clear water. I felt the food enter my body—I swear I could feel it becoming part of me.

Plain bread and cold water. My father had threatened me with this as a hardship, but while I consumed my loaf and the flagon of water that accompanied it, I felt I truly had all that any man could need. When I drank the last of my water and set my mug down, I felt a wave of contentment come over me.

I tidied away my tray and set out my journal and my schoolbooks, resolved to follow my now too-familiar routine. My father, I decided, would or would not come to me, as he was inclined. There was nothing I could do about it.

It was harder than usual to keep my mind on my work. Doggedly, I forced myself to complete the lessons I'd set. Despite my day's rest, sleepiness kept creeping up on me.

Only the strictest self-discipline kept me to my routine. I followed my book work with an honest entry in my journal, confiding to that page my fear that disease might be threatening Widevale. When I closed my journal, I gave in to sleepiness and immediately went to my bed. I knelt and more by rote than by faith said my evening prayers. I prayed for Burvelle's Landing rather than myself, no longer certain that I believed in the strength and power of the good god so much as hoped that he existed and would hear my pleas for mercy. As I pulled up my blanket and closed my eyes, I wondered what I truly believed now. I thought of the Poronte family and their ghastly chandelier of dead and dying birds. Could their older gods have protected me from this fate? At what price would such protection come? Despite these thoughts, sleep reached up and pulled me swiftly under its waves. I did not dream.

When light first crept in my window, I came to awareness of it. I did not bother to dress. If anyone came to my door, that would be soon enough to rise. Instead, I got up only long enough to push my bed across the room to where the first rays of light illuminated it. Then I lay down again and once more plunged into something that was not sleep. I could feel how my body now conserved all things—water, food, and even the energy I used to breathe or move. I was like a mighty tree, standing silent and bare of leaf, life seemingly suspended until spring might come again.

That day, I arose only at intervals to move my bed to keep it always centred under the light. When the light finally faded from the sky and darkness poured into my room, the same servant once more tapped at my door, opened it, and brought me my loaf and water. "What tidings from the Landing?" I demanded of him as I sat up on my bed.

"Sickness," he said brusquely. Before I could rise, he was out the door, shutting it firmly behind him. For a moment, dread paralyzed me. Were my worst fears coming to pass? Or, as my father had said, was it merely some lesser illness that would pass like a summer squall? I rose, I ate, and I returned to my bed. I slept again.

The next day was identical, save for one thing. The

evening passed with no servant and no food. The hour for it passed, and then another. At last, I swallowed my dignity and pounded on my door and shouted. After some time had passed, I heard a maidservant's voice outside my door. "Sir, please! People are trying to take their rest."

"I've had no food or water today! Bring me something, and I'll be quiet."

Silence. Then, "I'll try to find someone who has the key, sir. Your father was away all the day and gave no orders about you. And your mother is ill, so I cannot ask her. I'll go tap on your father's study door, to see what he says. Be patient, please, and quiet. I'll see what I can do."

"Thank you. My mother is ill?"

There was no reply. I shouted "Miss!" but got no response. I sat down and waited as the night deepened. She did not return. I tried to imagine what might be happening in the rest of the house. If my mother were ill and resting in the other wing, the majority of the servants would be tending to her and her needs. I wondered where Rosse was, and Elisi and Yaril. Were they also ill? Worry for my mother replaced my concern about food and water. My hunger became a still emptiness inside me. With no other recourse, I returned to my bed and slept again. That deeper stillness reached up and claimed me.

Another day passed slowly. No one came to my door. I moved my bed to keep the sunlight on it. Several times, I pounded on the door and shouted, but no one came. I felt a curious lack of energy. It was hard to rouse myself, and harder still to force myself to take action. Rest seemed my wisest course.

On my fourth day without sustenance of any kind, I roused myself. A dull alarm motivated me; would my father truly allow me to starve to death? I shouted through the door. I did not hear even a footstep. I lay down and pressed my ear to the floor by the door. I heard faint voices from somewhere in the house. I put my mouth to the crack under the door. "Mother? Rosse? Anyone?" There was no response. I pounded on my floor, first with my fists and then with my chair. Nothing. Three times I slammed my still considerable bulk against the door. It did not give. Even that minor activity after days without food exhausted me. I drank what had been my washing water and slept again.

On the fifth day, I tried first my fists and shoulder against the door, and then broke my chair against it. It did not budge. It was made from a good slab of spond wood, the heraldic symbol of the Burvelles of the East, and it proved true to what it symbolized. It was hard and impervious to my blows and shouts. With a leg from my shattered chair, I broke a pane out of my window. I shouted again, but no one stirred in the courtyard below. It was a clear summer day out there; the lack of activity made the hair stand up on the back of my neck. What had become of everyone?

My mind conjured up all sorts of possibilities. My father was sick and no one had thought to check on me. Or my family had left on a visit and abandoned me to the servants, who had forgotten me. A darker thought kept pressing against my mind: every soul in the household was dead of the plague. It was terrifyingly possible. I thought of breaking out the remaining panes of glass and the framework of my window and jumping out, but it was a sheer drop to the paving stones below. If it did not kill me outright, I suspected I would die a lingering death from broken legs or back. I was trapped, like a rat in a box. I wondered how long it would take me to die.

The morning breeze through my broken window carried a bit of moisture. I opened my shirt to it and felt my skin take it in. I sat down and in a wavering hand made what I feared would be among the final entries in my soldier's journal. Then I lay back down on my bed and closed my eyes to my fate.

At least two more days passed. Time lost much of its meaning for me. My Speck self had merged more deeply with my being than ever before, and I paid more attention to the cycling of daylight to dusk than I did to the passing hours. The pangs of hunger had become such a constant that it seemed a normal state. I ignored them. My skin seemed thicker when I touched it, more like the rind of a tough fruit than the skin of a man. There was little moisture in my mouth and less in my nose and eyes. It was easier not to open them. I became slowly aware of the sound of someone rattling the lock on my door. Had I heard my name called? Was that what had roused me? By the time I rallied my consciousness enough to turn my head, whoever had been in the hall had gone away. I thought of shouting, but my throat and mouth were too dry. I could scarcely pry my sticky lips apart. My body forbade me wasting energy on an effort that might prove futile.

A time passed. Then I heard slow footfalls that stopped outside my door. Something scraped on wood, and then there was a creak followed by the sounds of wood rending. I heard the hasp and lock fall to the floor outside my door. I stared at the door passively. It seemed a miracle when it opened inward. Framed in the entry was a thin and haggard Sergeant Duril. He held a pry bar in one hand. "Nevare?" he asked me hoarsely. "Is it possible you are still alive?"

Ponderously, I raised myself up in my bed. Duril's eyes widened. I mouthed the word "water," feeling my lips crack as I did so. He nodded his understanding. "Let's go to the kitchen," he suggested. I rose and followed him stiffly, walking like a wooden man. As I stalked through the hall behind him, I began to smell the stench of illness. A terrible premonition welled up in me.

Neither of us spoke. Duril tottered along as if at the end of his stamina. I forced my knees to remember how to bend. My feet felt stiff as roots and even my hips worked grudgingly. When we reached the kitchen, I went directly to the sink, scarcely noting the untidy clutter that littered the tables. Dirty cups and plates filled the washing tubs. I ignored them and drank directly from the spigot, stooping and turning my head to suck in the cool water as it flowed. When I could drink no more, I filled my hands with water and splashed it over my face. I ducked my head under it and let it run over my neck and through my hair. I scrubbed my hands together in the water and rubbed it over my forearms. Dry skin sloughed off in the water as if I were a snake shedding an old skin. I cupped my hands and rubbed water into my eyes, only now realizing how crusted my eyelids had been.

When I had finally had enough moisture, I shut off the spigot and turned to Sergeant Duril.

"It was the plague, wasn't it?"

He nodded, staring at me in amazement. "I never saw a man drink like that. But then, I never expected you to be alive. Been sick as a dog myself, Nevare, or I'd have come for you sooner. When I dragged myself up to the main house to check on your da, I asked about you right away. He just stared at me. I'm afraid grief has turned his mind, lad."

"Where is he?" I rummaged through the pantry as we spoke. Anything fresh had been consumed or gone bad. The bread cupboard was empty. For the first time in my life, the big baking ovens were cold. Only the stale smells of cooking lingered in the air. I desperately wanted and needed food. Ever since my father had built this house, the kitchen had been full of food. There had always been bread, always been a simmering stockpot on the back of the stove, its steamy aroma mingling with the smells of hot coffee and sizzling meat. Quiet had replaced the chatter of the kitchen staff, the crisp chopping of their knives against the block, the rhythmic thudding of busy hands pushing and turning pale bread dough.

I did not know where anything was. Always, the food had been prepared for me and brought to the table, or I had discovered it cooling on the racks and shelves there. I opened drawers and cupboards randomly, finding cutlery and mixing bowls and folded towels. A terrible frustration began to build in me. Where was the food?

I found the barrels of flour, meal, and cut oats. They infuriated me, for I could not eat them as they were, and I did not have the time to cook. My body demanded sustenance now. At last I found some turnips in one of the root bins. They had withered, but I was not fussy. I bit into the purple and white root. As I bit into the tough vegetable, Duril spoke.

"I found your da sitting outside your brother's door. Rosse is dead, Nevare. So is your mother and your elder sister."

I stood before him, chewing, hearing his words, and sensations tore at me. In my heart, the sudden gulf of grief that opened was beyond anything I'd ever felt. I'd lost comrades when the plague swept through the academy, and teachers I had respected. Those deaths had shocked and hurt me. But the news that my mother, Rosse, and Elisi were all vanished from my life, seemingly in one instant, paralyzed my mind. I had expected to share the rest of my life with them. When I was old and unfit to serve my king any longer, I had expected to return to Rosse's estate and make my home with him. I had anticipated helping him raise his own soldier son, as well as seeing Elisi become a mother and wife. Gone was my own gentle mother, always a force in my life, always my advocate with my father. Gone, all gone.

Yet the food I chewed flooded my mouth with keen pleasure. The starchiness of the core became a mild sweetness in contrast to the peppery skin. There were two textures—the fibrous skin and the crisper inner vegetable. The sensation of swallowing a bulky mouthful of food after my long deprivation was an ecstasy in itself. The taking in of food, I suddenly knew, was not only my consumption of life but a victory of the continuation of life. I had once more survived, and my physical body rejoiced in that even as tears filled my eyes at my loss.

Duril was staring at me. "Aren't you going to go to him?" he asked me at last.

I shook my head slowly. My voice creaked when I spoke. "Give me some time, Sergeant. I've been days with no food or water. Let me eat and regain some strength before I have to face him."

A shadow of disapproval passed across his face, but he did not argue with me. Instead he waited as I ate all the turnips. I offered him some, but he shook his head wordlessly. When the turnips were gone, I found a crock of raisins and sat down to devour them one sticky, chewy handful after another. They tasted wonderful. Yet the more food filled me, the keener became my awareness of my loss.

That sensation of duality flooded me again. There was the Speck me who gloried in survival, and there was Nevare who had just lost most of his world. I looked up at Duril. "Please tell me all you know. I've been isolated for days. No food or water, no news."

"So I see," he said gravely. "It's soon told, for all that has happened. The sickness came from Franner's Bend. So I think, anyway. It happened so fast. Your da and brother went to investigate when Doc Reynolds first sent them a message about a dying family. It alarmed your da enough that he and Rosse came back here to plan the quarantine. But by the next morning, it was too late." He shook his head. "It spread through the Landing like a wildfire. Somehow it jumped the river. Your brother Rosse came down with it the next day. Your mother caught it nursing him. By then, anyone who could still move was running away from it. I done the best I could, Nevare. I turned out the stock to graze and put the stable beasts out in the fields. It was the most I could do for them. I got sick right after your mother did, so I don't know too much else until today. I finally decided I was going to live and crawled out of bed and staggered up here. I saw four covered corpses in the yard outside—I don't know whose, or even how long they've been there. Stink is something terrible. Most everyone seems to be gone; at least, I hope they are, and not dead in their beds or something. I haven't gone room to room—I came to find you first. Had no idea your da had locked you up like that, lad. It's a miracle you survived. A miracle. What did you eat or drink up there?"

"Nothing."

He looked at me skeptically.

"*Nothing.* I've had nothing to eat or drink for days!" I shook my head at his doubts and gave it up. "I've no time to convince you of it, Duril. But it's true. Whatever magic Dewara exposed me to is strong. I slept a lot. And deeply, like a bear hibernating, I suppose. And I still feel hungry enough to eat a horse. But—"

"But you haven't got any thinner. Your skin's strange, though. Dusky. Dusky as a dead man's."

"I know." I hadn't, but I'd suspected it. I rubbed at my forearm. It felt odd to my touch, thick and rubbery. I shook my head, pushing the strangeness away. "I have to go to my father, Duril. Then I have to do what you said—go room to room and see what I find."

I still cringe when I recall my father's first words on seeing me. He was sitting on a straight-backed chair outside Rosse's door. He turned his head at the sound of my footsteps.

"You," he said. "Still alive. Still fat as a hog. And my son Rosse dead. Why? Why would the good god spare you and take Rosse? Why would he serve me so?"

I had no answer for him then or now. He looked terrible, thin, haggard, and unkempt. I set his words aside.

"Have you had the sickness?" I asked him stiffly. He slowly shook his head.

"What should I do now, Father?"

He bit his lower lip. Then as he stood, his mouth worked suddenly, his lower lip trembling like a frightened baby's. "They're all dead! All of them!" He suddenly wailed. He staggered forward a few steps, but it was Duril he sought for comfort, not me. The old sergeant caught him and held him as he sobbed. I stood alone, excluded even from his grief.

"Yaril?" I asked him when he took a breath and seemed to be easing.

"I don't know!" He cried out the words as if I had inflicted a fresh wound on him. "When Elisi sickened, I feared I would lose all my children. I sent Yaril and Cecile away. I told them to ride to Poronte's holdings. I sent my little girl away, all but alone. There were no servants left who would come to the bell. I had to send them off alone. The good god alone knows what has become of her. All sorts of folk are on the road. I pray she reached there safely, I pray the Porontes took them in." He burst into open sobs, and then, to my horror, he sank slowly to the floor and collapsed there.

When I first tried to raise him up, he slapped at me feebly as if he could not abide my loathsome touch. I exchanged glances with Duril, and gave my father time to keen and moan. When he had exhausted his hoarded strength, I again stooped to take him up. I had to go down awkwardly on one knee, and my own belly was a barrier to picking him up. I was surprised to find myself strong enough to lift him easily.

Duril followed me as I carried him to the parlor. I put him on a cushioned settee there, and told the sergeant, "Go to the kitchen. Get the cook fire started and put on a big pot of porridge. My father needs food, as do you, and simple food will do him best at first, if my own experience of the plague is any guide."

"What are you going to do?" Duril asked me. My father had closed his eyes and sunk into stillness. I think Duril already knew the answer.

"I have to go to my mother's chamber. And Elisi's."

Duril looked guiltily relieved. We parted there.

The rest of that day comes back to me sometimes in my nightmares. That house had always been my home, a refuge to me. The large pleasant rooms, decorated to my mother's tastes, had always seemed an oasis of calm and respite from the larger world. Now it was filled with death.

My family had been dead for days. Rosse was stiff in his bed, and I suspected he had been the last to die. My father had tried to tend him. A heap of soiled linens was at the foot of his bed. A clean blanket had been tucked around his body, and a napkin covered his face. My elder brother who had always gone before me in life had also gone before me into death. My father's heir son was dead. I refused to consider the full magnitude of that loss. I left his room quietly.

Someone, probably Elisi, had sewn a hasty shroud for my mother. I had thought to bid her farewell with a last kiss, but the smell was so thick in the stuffy room that I could barely force myself to enter. Fat flies were bumping and buzzing against the window glass. I resolved to leave her covered and keep my last memory of her strong beauty intact. I thought of how I had nodded to her and then turned away, as if she were already a ghost. I regretted it as I regret few things in my life. I left her swaddled body without touching it and went on to Elisi's bedchamber.

She and I had never been close. When I was born, I was not only the new baby in the family, but a son and a soldier son. I had displaced her in many ways, and that had always colored our relationship. Now she was gone, and that gap would never be mended. The last time I had been in her room, it had been a little girl's room, with dolls on shelves next to expensive picture books with tinted illustrations.

The years had changed it. Some of Elisi's own watercolors of wildflowers were framed on the walls. The dolls were long gone. The fresh flowers had rotted in their graceful vases, and Elisi herself was a contorted corpse on the bed. A lovely comforter embroidered with birds was rucked all around her as if she had struggled free of it. She lay on her side, mouth gaping horribly, her clawlike hands reaching toward an empty pitcher on her nightstand. The fragments of a broken cup crunched under my feet. I left her room, unable at that moment to deal with her horrid death.

I forced myself to check every other bedchamber in the house. In the newly redone servants' wing, I found two more bodies, and one thin, frail maidservant. "They all ran off," she told me in a shaky voice. "The master ordered them to stay, but they crept away in the dark. I stayed, and I did my best, sir. I helped Mistress Elisi tend her mother to the end. We were sewing her shroud when the fever come over me. Mistress Elisi told me to get to bed, she'd finish it herself and then come to me. She said to just take care of myself. So I did. And she never came."

"It's all right," I said dully. "You couldn't have saved her. You did all you could, and the family is grateful to you. You will be rewarded for your faithfulness. Go to the kitchen. Sergeant Duril is cooking food there. Eat something, and then do whatever you can to restore the household." I hesitated and then added, "Care for Lord Burvelle as best you can. He is overcome by grief."

"Yes, sir. Thank you, sir." She seemed pathetically relieved that I had not condemned her as she shuffled off to the task I had given her. The rest of the bedchambers showed the signs of hasty departure. I wondered if those who had fled had saved their lives or only spread the plague further.

My father himself had laid out our mansion and estate. He had forgotten nothing in plotting out a home that he intended would serve the family for generations. Thus there was even a stone-walled cemetery with an adjacent chapel with shade trees, and beds of flowers. Niches in the stone wall held symbols of the good god: the pomegranate tree, the ever-pouring pitcher, and the ring of keys. I had seen them so often that

I no longer noticed them. The walled cemetery was a very pleasant place, really, as carefully maintained as my mother's garden. There, my father had once told me, "All of our bones will someday rest."

He had never expected that day to come so soon, nor that his children would die before him. For most of my life, there had been only five graves in it, simply marked with stone, markers for the retainers who had followed my father, serving him first as soldiers and later as servants, and finally dying in his employ.

All the rest of that day, I dug graves. Nine graves. Four for the poor souls who'd been left in the courtyard. Two for the bodies I'd found in the servants' quarters. Three for my family.

It was not easy work. I was surprised I could do it, given the privation I had endured. The top layer of soil was cultivated turf, but only a few inches below it I struck the rocky soil that was more characteristic of our lands. I set aside my spade and took up a pickax to break through that layer, and eventually into the claylike soil beneath it. It was a relief to focus my mind on this simple task. I made the sides of each grave straight, and threw the soil where it could not slide back onto me. The holes were wider, perhaps, than another digger would have made; I had to accommodate my own girth. My arms and back were stiff at first, but soon warmed to my work. My body complained far less than I had expected. It was good to be out in the fresh air and sunlight again. After a time, I stripped off my shirt and worked more freely, though not without some worry that someone might see me.

The hard physical labor kept my thoughts at bay. I toiled like the muddy-boots engineer I had once planned to be. I aligned my graves precisely, leaving uniform walking spaces between them. When my mind began to work again, I walked the edges of my grief, pushing away the full realization of what had befallen me. I did not think of my dead, but wondered where the servants had fled to and if they would return, or if they had carried their own deaths with them and perished alongside the road. From there, I had to wonder how Burvelle's Landing had fared. That small community on the other side of the road was my father's pride and joy. He had laid out the streets and persuaded an innkeeper and a smith and a mercantile owner to come there long before anyone else had seen potential for a settlement there. His men operated the ferry to it, and the little town council reported directly to my father for his final say on all their decisions. The existence of that town and our comfortable life in the manor house were tightly linked. I wondered if the streets of Burvelle's Landing were still and quiet, if the dead lay rotting in their homes.

I shied away from that image, but then found myself thinking about our landed neighbors and how they had fared. Some lived in relative isolation. I hoped that our folk fleeing the plague had not visited it upon them.

Then, like a willful horse on a lunge line, I came round at last to wondering if Cecile and Yaril had safely reached the Poronte manor, and if they had escaped the plague or borne it thither.

I had been so angered with and distanced from my little sister. Now, when I thought of her, I could only recall how wide and trusting her eyes had always seemed when she was a child. I discovered an odd thing. I had only been able to be so angry with her because I had believed that one day we would apologize to one another and resume our close relationship. It had felt safe to be furious with her, because in my deepest soul, I had been utterly confident that she still loved me, as I did her. Now I wondered with a terrible lurch of sorrow if she had gone to her death neither forgiving me nor knowing that I would forgive her. And with that last terrible thought in my mind, I flung the final shovel full of earth out of the ninth grave. Alone, I carried the bodies of the servants, one by one, to their resting places, setting them beside the holes where they would lie. I put my shirt on over my dirty body, and went quietly to the kitchens. The wonderful smell of simmering porridge and baking bread filled the air. I found Sergeant Duril and the maidservant there, talking quietly. Her name, I discovered, was Nita. Nita had set out salt and molasses on the table alongside a slab of butter from a cold cellar I'd been unaware existed. She had put several loaves of bread to bake in the reawakened ovens. She told me that they had given my father food and several very strong drinks before steering him into a clean bed in one of the guest rooms. They'd left him there, sleeping the sleep of exhaustion.

At my request, they went out to the four bodies I'd moved, to look on them a last time and to tell me what their names had been. The moment they left the kitchen, I could restrain myself no longer. I dished myself an immense tureen of porridge. I put several hunks of butter to melt in it, and then poured molasses over the top of it. I sat down and devoured it in huge spoonfuls. It was hot to the point of scalding, but that did not discourage me. I stirred it to cool it, melting the glorious yellow butter into the oaty porridge and mingling the rich brown threads of molasses in swirls. As fast as it cooled, I ate it, savoring the subtle flavors and the sensation of swallowing large bites of nourishing food. I served myself another bowlful from the pot, scraping it clean. I was generous with both butter and molasses. I devoured it.

They'd left a pot of tea on the table. I poured myself a cup, sweetened it to soupiness with more of the molasses, and drank it down. I could feel life and strength resurging in me with the consumption of the sweet stuff. I poured another cup, draining the pot. I put more water in the kettle and set it to boil again. The smell of the baking bread almost made me wild.

I was startled when Duril and Nita came back. In glorying in the food, I'd almost forgotten them and my grisly task. I hastily drained off the last of my cup of tea. Duril was looking at me in a sort of frozen dismay. I suddenly realized how I must appear, my face and shirt smudged with dirt and sweat, my nails and hands filthy, and supporting it all, my immense body. The sticky tureen was still on the table before me, the ewer of molasses almost empty beside it. I bowed my shoulders reflexively, trying to seem smaller.

"I have their names, if you want to write them down," Duril said heavily.

"Yes. Thank you. I do. We will have to have stones carved for them later, but for now, well, it is best that I put them in the earth."

Duril nodded solemnly. I went to my father's study for paper and a pencil. When I returned, Nita was washing up the porridge pot. "I'll go with you," Duril announced, and followed me out of the kitchen.

He said little, but I could feel his disapproval hovering over me. When we reached the bodies, he listed their names for me and I wrote them down carefully, along with whatever he knew about each of them. Then, as if I were planting tulip bulbs, I set one man and three women into the earth. Duril helped me as much as he could, but his strength was gone, and I fear we were not as gentle with those mortal remains as we would have been in better times. When they were in their graves, we returned to the house, and one at a time, I carried out the two dead servants I had discovered in their rooms. Their soiled bedding became their shrouds. Flies had found the one, and the hatching maggots worked in his nostrils and at the corners of his mouth. Even hardened old Sergeant Duril turned aside from that sight, and I repressed a gag as I covered the dead man with his bedding and wrapped it firmly around him. As I carried him out of the house, I wondered if we would ever get the stench of death out of the place.

Duril had known them both. I noted down their names and set them each in a grave. Then we covered them, with me doing the lion's share of the work, and Duril manning a shovel more for the sake of his self-respect than for any real help he could give me. The long summer day had found dusk before we were through. We stood by the six mounds of pale soil, and Duril, who had buried many a comrade, offered a simple soldier's prayer to the good god.

When we were finished, he looked askance at me.

"Tomorrow is soon enough," I said quietly. "They've lain in their rooms this long. One more day will not hurt. And perhaps by tomorrow my father will be recovered enough to help me give them a more formal burial." I sighed. "I'm going down to the river to wash."

He nodded, and I left him there.

But the next morning, my father was little better than he had been. He made no response when I tried to speak to him. Unshaven, his hair wild, dressed in his nightshirt, he would not even sit up in his bed. Several times I told him that I had to bury Mother, Rosse, and Elisi, that it was not fitting to leave them dead in their beds. He did not even turn his eyes to look at me, and at last I despaired of his help, and took on the mournful task myself. Duril helped me, but still it was a sad and messy duty. I found rope in the stable, and at least we were able to lower them into their graves with a bit more dignity. I wished for fine caskets or even simple boxes, but the stench and the rot persuaded me that it was best to act quickly instead. The trees surrounding our little graveyard were full of hopeful croaker birds before I was through. They sat watching me, jaunty in their black-and-white feathers, the wattles around their greedy beaks red as blood. I knew that the smell of carrion had attracted them. They were only animals, and they did not care whether it was beast flesh or human that they scented. Even so, I could not look at them without recalling the Porontes' wedding sacrifice to Orandula, the old god of balances. I wondered grimly what all these deaths balanced, and if it pleased him.

I put my family in the earth, and covered them, and said the prayers that I could summon to my mind. They were the childish prayers of comfort that my mother had taught me when I was just a boy. Sergeant Duril came out to stand beside me and witness that feeble ceremony. Afterward, I took my shovel and pickax back to the toolshed and hung them on the wall before I went to wash the grave dirt from my hands.

And that was how my old life ended forever.

CHAPTER TEN

FLIGHT

My father's recovery was agonizingly slow. In the first week that followed the burials, he was almost completely unresponsive to me. I went daily to his bedside, to speak to him and report what was going on, but he looked away from me. After several experiences of moving to try to meet his gaze and having him simply turn his head away, I gave up. I stood at the foot of his bed each morning and each evening and gave him a report of all I'd done, as well as presenting the problems that awaited me on the morrow. Each time, I stood quietly when I finished speaking and waited for a response. Silence was always his reply. I tried to take it in stride and keep on functioning. The terrible tragedy that had befallen our family had ended, I felt, our battle of wills. There were more immediate things to worry about than why I was fat or if I would ever be a soldier.

Nita fared better with my father than I did. She took his meals to him, persuaded him to shave and bathe, and eventually moved him back into his own chambers. In retrospect, I believe he was suffering not just from his grief but also from a mild form of the plague. In later years, I would come to find that most people seldom fell victim to severe bouts of the plague twice, but that some sufferers would catch a milder form and then endure recurrent bouts in the years that followed.

Whatever the cause, my father was incapacitated for a month, and despite my own burden of grief, the tasks of running the estate fell upon me. What a whirlwind of work that time was. Everything demanded my attention at once, and I had few resources at first to apply to them. The servants had not fled far. Some had gone to neighboring landowners, who had either taken them in or afforded them refuge in rudimentary shelters on the outskirts of their holdings. Others had been living rough. They trickled back, shamefaced, a few each day, until we had about three-quarters of our former staff. What had become of the rest of them, death or simply that they had abandoned us, I was never to know.

I wrote to Dr. Amicas about my experience, for I knew he was still gathering all information he could on the disease. I speculated that the people scattering had perhaps cut down on the spread of the disease, but also that the swifter deaths we had experienced were due to the sick being left without caretakers. I could not tell if that had led to a lower percentage of deaths, and added that I did not suggest it as a routine response to the disease, as it seemed likely to me that if the servants had had other towns to flee to the chance of spreading the plague to large population centers would have been much greater.

It was not just people that I had to care for. At the same time, there were cattle, sheep, pigs, and chickens to be thought of. Most of our livestock had done well enough foraging, thanks to Sergeant Duril's foresight in turning them loose, but some of our crops had suffered from their attentions. Every creature had to be gathered up and restored to its proper pen or paddock.

Yaril was foremost in my thoughts in those harried days. I longed to ride to Lord Poronte's manor myself to see what had become of Cecile and my dear little sister, but I dared not leave my father. In the end, I dispatched Sergeant Duril as soon as he could ride. He took a messenger bird with him, and before the day was out, it returned with a green band on its leg to let me know my sister was alive.

The worst news came from beyond Franner's Bend. Cayton's Horse and Doril's Foot were dead to a man. Two days past the Bend, they had begun to sicken. The officers had ordered a halt and set up an encampment. It became their graveyard. Franner's Bend had been too deep in its own troubles to lend them any aid, and other travelers fled when they saw the yellow banners that warned of sickness in the camp. By the time anyone came to their aid, there was no one left to save. The commander had died at his field desk, a neat tally of his men's death in his soldier son journal under his elbow. They'd managed to bury some of their dead; the rest of the bodies were burned in a funeral pyre. "If Gettys was hoping for more manpower this summer, well, they'll have to do without it," Duril observed grimly. "It looks like the King's Road won't be pushed forward much this year."

I pitied them, but my heart was more beset with my own problems. True to my worries, the Landing had been devastated by the plague. As soon as I could, I ventured a visit there, and found a state of chaos. Many had died, and the town council had let the rabble take it over. There had been looting, and violence against the people suspected of bringing the plague to town. Entire families had perished, and in that dire situation, even good men had resorted to pilfering food, blankets, and valuables from the houses of the dead. I was at first at a loss as to what to do to restore order.

Sergeant Duril, who had become my de facto adviser, shrugged and suggested, "In hard times, folks are comforted by what they're used to. Doesn't matter if it's porridge for breakfast or the same prayer each night. More than half that town was soldiers at one time or another. Put them back under military command until they remember how to run their own lives."

I decided he was right. I told him to choose his men. That afternoon, we crossed to the Landing with Duril at my side and his men behind him. We rode our horses into the center of town. There, in as commanding a manner as I could muster, I called what was left of the town council to order in front of me in the street. In no uncertain terms, I told them my father had empowered Duril to select a dozen men he judged trustworthy to represent order. I told them that under my father's authority, he would be using that patrol to impose martial law on the town, setting a curfew, boarding up unoccupied houses, commandeering and rationing supplies, and pressing a number of the more troublesome young men into service as gravediggers. Duril supplied the muscle; I kept the records, for I promised them that when the dust settled, people who cooperated would be reimbursed for whatever necessary supplies were seized. Despite my ungainly body, I did my best to strike a martial posture and suggest an authority that was mostly imaginary. I was a presence. I implied that Duril would report to me, and I would report to my father. This was true. What they didn't know was that my father continued to stare at the wall silently while I made my reports.

It worked. It took only ten days of such tactics before the townspeople recovered their sense of lawfulness, and proved ready to resume running their own affairs. I let the surviving members of the town council know that they could report to me, and that if necessary, I would have Sergeant Duril and his patrol enforce whatever rules they thought needed for the town's recovery. I took a great deal of satisfaction from that. I knew that the idea had been Duril's and that he had supplied most of the discipline at the lowest level. But I had conducted myself as an officer and a gentleman, and it had worked. I was proud of myself, and imagined that when my father came back to himself, he would share that pride and sense of accomplishment.

That was but one of the tasks that busied me from morning to night, and every day there were dozens of others that scarcely seem worth mentioning, but demanded my immediate attention and a solution. I had thought I knew a great deal about the running of the manor. Only when the cistern went dry did I recall that keeping it full required several men, a wagon, a team of horses, and water casks filled from the river to replenish it on a weekly basis. Dozens of young fruit trees in the orchard had gone unwatered during the plague, but I swiftly restored boys to that task, and was able to save more than half of what my father had planted that year. Fences the cattle had broken down had to be mended.

To me fell the grim task of notifying friends and family of our losses. I wrote to my uncle, to Epiny and Spink, and to other relatives, and sent messages also to neighboring farms and holdings. I wrote to the head of Vanze's order, telling him what had befallen our family and enclosing a personal letter to Vanze. I received in response a starchy response that Vanze was in meditation and isolation for a month, and that the news would be given to him when he returned. I sighed for my little brother, and then the other demands on my time claimed me. A brief letter from Dr. Amicas arrived, offering his condolences and suggesting strongly that I have any bedding and hangings in plague chambers burned, for fear that they might hold contagion. After I had carried out his order, I looked at my mother's stripped room and my heart misgave me. The smell of death lingered elsewhere in the house, so I ordered a thorough cleaning of every room.

Although most of our servants and hired folk had wandered back to us, certain key people had disappeared, and it fell to me to decide who would take on those tasks. Some of our people had suffered through the plague, and though they were recovering, they were scarcely ready to take up the full burdens of their usual chores. Impulsively, I moved Nita up to be the head of our housekeeping, and quickly discovered that although she was loyal and intelligent, it did not make her adept at making everything function smoothly. But I did not know how to demote her without insulting her, nor who I could put in her place if I did. So we limped along under her haphazard supervision.

I found my father's ledger books and his keys and did the best that I could to keep records up to date and to spend only what we needed. It was not easy, and I often wondered how he, a soldier, had so effortlessly managed all this business of being a noble. I had never imagined that it required so much accounting, let alone such a plethora of managing people.

Daily I prayed to the good god that my father would recover and take these burdens from my shoulders.

Two weeks after I had buried my dead, I decided that the household was close enough to normalcy that I would fetch my sister Yaril home from the Poronte manor. I ordered up the carriage, and made the same trip that only a few months ago had taken us to my brother's wedding. Now I went to visit his widow. I wore my best clothing, the suit that my mother had made for me for Rosse's wedding. It was now uncomfortably tight on me.

The plague had passed the Poronte estates by. It was strange to see an aspect of normality when I arrived. Men were working in the fields, cattle grazed peacefully, and the liveried servant who opened the door smiled a gracious welcome. Even so, when I entered the chambers that had been so full of flowers and music at my last visit, I found them decked for mourning. Cecile's parents came to meet me in their parlor. I formally thanked Lord and Lady Poronte for taking in my sister. They replied awkwardly that it was the least they could do for Yaril at such a dreadful time.

I had expected to bring both Cecile and Yaril home with me. But Cecile's mother begged me to allow her daughter to stay until the greatest blackness of her grief had passed. She said that the shock of passing from the joys of being newly wed to the horrors of disease and widowhood had been too much for Cecile's gentle spirit. She had been bedridden for days after she arrived there, and even now only rose for a few hours each day. She needed time, her mother said, time to recover and find her way into her sad new life. I wondered uneasily if they intended to let Cecile return at all. It was Cecile's duty to return to her husband's home and take up the management of it, but I did not have the heart to demand that. Instead I said that when my father was better, they could all take counsel together to decide what was best.

I was disappointed that Yaril had not come to greet me, but Cecile's mother told me they had asked her to wait in the garden until "things were settled." With the matter of Cecile decided, they released me to find her. When I saw Yaril walking alone on the sandy path between the meticulously tended herb knots, my heart went out to her. She looked so small and so young in her deep blue mourning dress. "Yaril?" I said softly, prepared to discover that she was still disgusted with me.

At my voice, she whirled about. There were dark circles under her eyes and she had lost flesh, but even so her face lit up and she ran toward me. I wanted to catch her up and whirl her about as I used to do when she was much younger. Instead she crashed into me and then clung to the front of my shirt with both hands, rather like a little squirrel trying to climb the trunk of a massive tree. I hugged her awkwardly, and for a moment we didn't speak at all. I stroked her hair and patted her back, and after a moment, she lifted a tearstained face to me. "Elisi didn't die, did she? That was a mistake, wasn't it?"

"Oh, Yaril," I said, and that was all I needed to say. She put her face against my chest again, her fists tightened on my shirt, and her shoulders heaved. After an endless time, she said, "We're all alone now, Nevare. Just you and me."

"We still have father," I pointed out to her. "And Vanze."

Her voice was full of bitterness. "Vanze belongs to the priests now. Our family gave him away. I never had Father. You did, for a time, while you were a good little soldier boy. But now you are worthless to him. You have even less value than I do. No, Nevare. We are alone. And I'm sorry for how I treated you. I'm sorry. It just seemed that Carsina and Remwar would not like me if I sided with you. And so I abandoned you, my own brother. And then, at home, if anyone said one good thing about you, Father became furious. He and Mother fought so much about that . . . she's gone. They'll never fight about anything again."

I wanted to tell her that somehow we would find a way through the difficulties we now faced. I knew that someday we would again have a life that seemed normal and routine, even boring. Boredom sounded so attractive to me now. I tried to imagine a day when a dozen problems didn't confront me and sorrow did not weight my every breath. I could not conceive of it.

"Come," I finally said with a sigh. "Let's go home." I took

her small hand in mine and led her to say our farewells to the
Porontes.

Our lives did resume. Young as she was, Yaril still knew
more about the internal workings of the household than I did,
and proved to be effective at undertaking dire reforms when
needed. She removed Nita as head of housekeeping by deftly
putting her in sole charge of my father's well-being, and replaced her with a woman who had been a maid with the family for years and knew what was required to run the household.
I suspected that she also took the private opportunity to reward those servants who had befriended her over the years
and rebuke those who had treated her as insignificant within
the family. I let her do as she saw fit. I was only too happy to
allow Yaril to assume responsibility for the household, for
not only did she make things run more smoothly, but also it
kept her from dwelling on all we had lost.

Yaril grasped that a return to schedules would be best for
us. She immediately reinstated regular meals served at the
table, and assumed the role of leading Sixday worship for the
women. I followed her example guiltily; I had not even considered assuming that responsibility, and our worship had
become a very slipshod observation of the forms. I realized
how important it was for us to offer thanks to the good god
for our survival when I heard the women and men of our
household let loose the tears they had restrained until then.
Ceremony and form, I reminded myself, gave shape and
meaning to our lives. I resolved never to forget that again.

As for the meals, Yaril's insistence on a return to normality there was a delight to me. It seemed like years since I'd
had the pleasure of sitting down to a carefully planned meal
in which the flavors and textures complemented each other.
My deprivation had schooled me to a far more sophisticated
appreciation of food than I'd ever had before. Having realized that even foods as simple as bread and water could be
enjoyed, well-prepared food now nearly paralyzed me with
delight. A sauce could send shivers up my spine. A contrast
in flavors in a simple salad could plunge me into a sudden,
rapt reverie. Unless I concentrated on keeping pace with
Yaril, a meal could take me three times as long to consume

as it did her. Sometimes I would look up from my soup to find her regarding me with a mixture of amusement and worry. At such moments, I felt ashamed of letting my senses carry me into a world of my own. Yaril and I were in this predicament together, and it was up to us to create an ongoing life for ourselves.

There were times when it felt like an elaborate pretense. Each evening, I escorted her into dinner. I would seat Yaril at the table and then move to my accustomed place. Around us, the empty chairs gaped at us. I felt as if we had returned to our days of tea parties in the garden, when Yaril and Elisi had always pretended to be great ladies and welcomed me solemnly to their gatherings. Could this really be all that was left of my family? After dinner, when we would seek refuge in the music room, Elisi's harp stood silent and watching us. In the parlor, my mother's chair was empty. There seemed no room where the absent did not outnumber the living people.

Then, one evening, Yaril instituted a change. I was shocked when our soup was a cream one, a type my father had always despised. Yaril eliminated the fish course, something she had always dreaded. When we rose from our meal, she announced calmly that we would be having our coffee in the garden. When I followed her there, I noted with approval that she had had a net pavilion erected to frustrate the mosquitoes that the little glass lamps would attract. Within the pavilion was a table with only two chairs. A flower arrangement and a deck of cards and a pot of markers were already set out for us. As I stared, a servant brought the coffee service out to us on a small side table. Yaril smiled at my astonishment. "Shall we play?" she asked me.

And for the first time since the plague had passed us, we shared a pastime, and made wagers and even laughed a bit.

And so the days passed, one after another. I controlled the estate and Yaril ran the household. I realized how completely Yaril had stepped into my mother's position when she informed me one night over dinner that she had sent for a seamstress and that tomorrow I was to be measured for new clothing. I didn't know what to say for a moment. I blushed hot. Every garment I had was stretched and strained at the seams. It was not a trivial matter for me; in some places I was chafed raw, and yet it had happened so gradually that I had not taken any steps to correct it.

She shook her head at my humiliation. "Nevare, you have no idea how uncomfortable you look. Just looking at how your clothing binds you distresses me. You can't walk around looking like that in front of the hired men, let alone when company comes. We have to do something about it. That's all there is to it."

I looked at my plate in front of me. I had just eaten a large meal, but not outrageously large. Still, stupidly, I said, "I've been putting it off. New clothing, I mean. I keep hoping I'll regain my shape and be able to fit into my old garments again." And the words that I had intended as an excuse were, I suddenly recognized, the absolute truth. I was still waiting for something that would restore me to the way I had been. A miracle was required, and I suddenly knew I was not going to get one.

"I am glad that you intend that," my sister said quietly. "And if you would try harder to do so, I'd be ever so proud of you. Not that I think you, well, not that I think you eat like a pig. I see you each day, Nevare. You work hard. And I don't see you eating gluttonously. Well . . . that is, your meals are generous, but Mother always said that you boys would eat more than we women did, and even more so when you were working. But, of course, you should strive to regain your physique.

"But in the meantime," she went on very seriously, "you must look presentable. So. Please come to the sewing room tomorrow at ten o'clock."

And that was that. My new suits were all in the deep blues and blacks of mourning, but that was only fitting. It was such a relief to put on a shirt that didn't strain at the collar and would reach around my belly to button. Of my own volition, I sent for the cobbler from the Landing, and had myself fitted for new shoes and a pair of boots. Having clothing that fit made me look much better. The fabric straining across my ample flesh had made me look fatter.

I did not enjoy the work of running the manor, but there

was satisfaction in doing it well. I sketched out the plans for new ferry landings and entrusted them to men capable of following them. I worked hard, ate well, and slept deeply at night. There was meaning in my life once more, and the companionship of my sister. For a time, I was content, and did not think beyond having the hay cut and stacked, and deciding how many pigs should be slaughtered for the winter's bacon.

When the ferry landings were completed, I made a trip across, to be sure they functioned as I had intended. I was well pleased, for my design had eliminated the muddy track that had once led down to the boats and my new floating dock facilitated the loading and unloading of the vessels. Once on the town side, I decided to visit the council. I found the Landing running smoothly and beginning to recover its prosperity and hope for the future. The keenest pleasure of that evening came when the council members thanked me for my intervention and commended Sergeant Duril for doing an excellent job in a difficult situation. The old sergeant, who often accompanied me on my rounds, blushed like a boy. The impromptu meeting turned into a meal together at the largest inn in Burvelle Landing, simply called the Landing Inn. The meal stretched into an evening of drinking, at which a number of townsfolk and several of Duril's patrol joined us as the night progressed.

We drank too much, of course. For me it was the first time to unleash my restraint and talk, as a man among men, about all that had befallen both manor and town. As the hours trickled by, both jackets and tongues were loosened. It was not the first time I had ever been drunk, but it certainly became the drunkest I had ever been. Perhaps the company of relative strangers was what made it so easy. The talk wandered from the plague and the aftermath to talk of beautiful women, and drinking, and easy women, and my academy experience and gambling and fickle women and true women. My rotundity was the object of not only curiosity but also jesting, some of it pointed but most of it good-natured. I had had enough to drink that none of it seemed too important. To the ones who seemed intent on needling me, I responded with what seemed at the time acid wit and endless good nature. Everyone laughed with me. For that night my fate did not seem so hard. It almost seemed that I received double credit for having stepped in and restored order to the town, for not only had I done it while being young but I'd done it while being fat. We drank until long past midnight, and I only set down my mug when Sergeant Duril was tipsily insisting that we had to return to the manor for the night. Arms about each other, we left the last tavern, and grandly commandeered the ferry for an unscheduled crossing to our side of the river. We had a long walk home from the ferry landing, and by the time we reached the manor, I felt nearly sober. Such was not the case for Duril, and I actually put the good sergeant into his bed before retiring to my own. He awoke the next morning with a terrible hangover, but to my amazement, I slept well, and when I rose I seemed none the worse for wear.

After that, at least once a week I would go into town to speak with the council and to have a few beers at one of the taverns afterward. It was very pleasant to socialize, and though I didn't patronize the tavern whores, it was flattering to be the subject of their flirtatious attentions. I might have been more tempted to indulge myself except that Sergeant Duril inevitably accompanied me, and the habit of behaving myself in his presence was still strong.

At the manor, things were much quieter. Yaril refused all invitations sent to us. Looking back on it, I realize now that we isolated ourselves, retreating into a world we could control. Eventually, there was a letter from Vanze, but his grief seemed almost abstract, as he saw it through the focus of religion and philosophy. Yaril was angry and hurt when she read it, but I think I understood his reaction. He'd been born to be a priest, and a priest's business was to find the good god's will and wisdom in everything. If he could apply it to what had befallen our family and take comfort from it, then I would not begrudge it to him.

The most annoying piece of correspondence I received was an arrogant note from Caulder Stiet's uncle, addressed to my father, blithely informing us that he and Caulder would be visiting us in the spring. He was confident that we would be glad to welcome them as houseguests and looked forward

to studying the geology of Widevale. As he did not think
their blooded saddle horses would be appropriate for cross-
country terrain, he would be obliged to borrow some rougher
mounts for their expedition. The man's assumptions grated
on me, and I fired off a letter that mentioned our family
losses and implied that plague was rampant in our area. I
suggested he should find another location for his holiday.
My missive was courteous, but barely so.

My father received letters from my Uncle Sefert. I longed
to read them, but they were addressed only to my father and
I had them taken directly up to him. If he replied, I never
saw the outgoing posts.

There was another long letter from Spink and Epiny, written in her hand. Her condolences on my losses were heartfelt.
The rest of her note was full of news, incredibly good news
that filled me with jealousy and frustration. My uncle had
decided that Spink deserved a second chance at his career as
a soldier son. Epiny did not write that her father was trying to
buy a better life for her, but I was certain that was the case.
My uncle had been impressed with the devotion Spink had
shown in nursing Epiny through her illness and so he had purchased a commission for Spink. It was not an excellent one;
it was with the Farleyton regiment, currently stationed on the
border at Gettys. Spink and Epiny would travel there by
wagon, and once there, Spink would become Second Lieutenant Kester. They had been warned that he would most likely
be assigned to Supply, but Epiny was already certain that his
commander would immediately recognize Spink's potential
and soon transfer him to interesting tasks.

Her letter was one long dither about packing, what to
take, what to leave, how she must learn to behave as an officer's wife, how overjoyed Spink was, and yet he felt humbly
indebted to her father, and her worry that in his drive to impress his superiors Spink might jeopardize his recovered
health. She confided to me that she was convinced now of
the healing properties of Bitter Springs, and had spent a
good portion of their savings on blue glass bottles and stoppers, for she intended to take a gross of dosages of spring
water with her. The folk of Gettys suffered much from the

plague and she was most anxious to see if the bottled water could relieve or perhaps prevent the disease. She went on for pages on what she hoped their quarters would be like and whether there would be other young wives to socialize with, and perhaps families so that when the good god finally blessed her with pregnancy she would be around women experienced in births and babies.

I tried to smile over her pages, but all I could think was that Spink had been given a second chance, one that I would have given my eyeteeth for. For the very first time, it occurred to me that I could take money from my father's account and do the same for myself. The dishonorable temptation lasted only for one sharp moment, and yet envy would nag at me for days afterward.

Spink's part of the letter was more restrained than Epiny's. Farleyton had once been a crack regiment, renowned for their valor in numerous campaigns. Since they'd been posted to Gettys, their star had dimmed substantially. Rumor said that numerous desertions and dereliction of duty had tarnished the regiment's reputation. Still, he was glad to accept his commission there. "Beggars can't be choosers," he wrote me. "I always dreamed that I'd join a regiment where I could rise swiftly. Farleyton's Horse may well be it. Wish me luck and say a prayer for me."

I did both, and tried to do them without an envious heart.

Every evening, Yaril had a place set for my father at the dinner table, always in the hope (or dread) that he might deign to join us. As the harvest progressed, my father improved but still kept to his room. When I tapped at his door each day and then entered, I usually found him sitting in a chair by the window, staring out over his lands. He still refused to look at me, and I still persisted in giving him my daily reports. Once he had confined me to my room to try to break me; now he confined himself to his room, but I felt his intention was the same. I felt that his grief over his losses had been consumed by his anger at his fate.

He did not treat Yaril so coldly. Her lot was harder. When she first returned to Widevale, she had gone to see him, and he had burst into tears at the sight of her, safe and healthy.

But his tears of joy at receiving the daughter who was left to him soon turned to tears of anguish over all he had lost. She sat with him daily, and daily he would recount his misery and despair. All he had striven for his entire life had been snatched away from him. She would emerge from her sessions with him pale and drained. Sometimes, she told me, he would rant against fate; at other times, he bade her pray with him, that the good god might show him a path through his misfortune.

My father's life had come to a dead end. His heir was gone, his soldier son a failure, his wife dead, his elder daughter gone. His game board had been swept clean of all powerful pieces, leaving him only pawns to manipulate. He agonized over who would inherit his estate, and endlessly dreaded a lonely dotage. He considered petitioning the king to allow him to move Vanze up from priest son to heir. But he was too much of a traditionalist to relish that idea. The next day would find him declaring that he would look among my cousins for a likely heir, a young man he could bring to Widevale and raise as a fit heir.

In between such ranting, he would fashion various fates for Yaril. His only daughter was precious to him now, he told her, for whoever wed her would be his sole ally. He would find an heir son for her, perhaps even an old noble's son. Then the next night he would tearfully say she was all he had left, and that he could never allow her to wed for she must look after him in his failing years.

One evening after a late game of cards she confided to me that she was weary to death of those discussions. I shrugged my shoulders. "Well, in all rightness, Cecile still has a duty to our family. She should come back here, and take the burden of running the household off your shoulders."

Yaril looked at me as if I were mad. "You aren't serious?"

"She is Rosse's widow. We made a bride-gift to her family. She is a Burvelle now."

"Well, she can just be a Burvelle in her mother's house! Prissy, primpy Cecile in charge of my life and our home? Afraid-of-her-shadow Cecile, always wanting to chop off some poor bird's head so her scary old gods won't do something awful to her? It was bad enough when Mother was alive to keep her in check. But to have her put over me, in my own home? No. No, Nevare. Leave her where she is, and good riddance."

I'd had no idea that Yaril had felt such animosity toward Cecile. I'm afraid it amused me. I grinned as I said, "So. I see now why Carsina was chosen for me; she was someone you are already friends with. Less potential for fireworks in the family."

I had meant it as a jest, but it was the first time Carsina's name had been mentioned between us. Yaril narrowed her eyes at me. "That bitch!" she said with great feeling.

I was shocked. "Carsina? I thought you were friends."

She scowled. "As did I. I thought keeping her friendship was the most important thing in the world, more important than my brother, even. I turned my back on you, to commiserate with her about how you had embarrassed her at Rosse's wedding. I supported her in insisting that your marriage agreement be dissolved. I was so shallow, Nevare. But she served me as I deserved. No sooner was her family free of their commitment to you than she set her sights on Remwar! She knew how I felt about him! She knew that he had promised me that he'd ask his father to talk to our father as soon as he could get him into a good mood! But the last I heard, he was finding every excuse to visit her family as often as he could."

My mind had snagged on her earlier words. I scarcely noticed what she said about Remwar. "Our marriage agreement is dissolved? How long ago did that happen?"

She looked at me with sudden pity. "Didn't Father speak to you about it? He told the family at dinner one night, soon after Rosse's wedding. He was stiff with fury, but said he could not blame them. He'd said you'd eaten yourself out of a career and a marriage . . . Oh, Nevare, I'm sorry. I didn't mean to speak of it that way. I just wish that, well, that you'd never let yourself go this way. Why did you do it? The cavalla was what you wanted more than anything else."

"I didn't do it." I looked at her. We sat in the netted darkness of our pavilion. The oil lamp on the table made a small orb of light around us. A light breeze carried the scent of the night-blooming flowers in the garden and the greener smell of the pond. It suddenly seemed that we two were alone in the whole wide world, and perhaps we were. I began talking, and found myself telling my little sister the entire tale. She listened in rapt wonder, her eyes wide, and when I reached the moment where I stepped off the cliff's edge at Dewara's urging, she shivered and reached across the table to take my hand.

By the time I finished the account, she had moved to sit close beside me as if I were telling ghost stories. She heard of my dual days at the academy, about Epiny's séance and her concerns for me, and of Dark Evening and the Specks' Dust Dance. I told her of my final battle with Tree Woman, and how the Spindle had stopped dancing and even how I had found Dewara and how he had died. She listened with rapt attention. In the silence that followed, as frogs and crickets creaked and peeped, she took a breath. "Are you making this up, Nevare?" she asked me. "Are you teasing me?"

"Yaril, I swear I am not," I said with great feeling. "As I have said, so it has been. The changes in my body are not my fault, and I do not believe there is anything I can do to change myself back, unless I resort to seeking out a magic user. And so far, that has availed me little."

Her reaction completely surprised me. "I must meet our Cousin Epiny! She sounds amazing. May I write to her?"

"I'm sure she'd be delighted to hear from you," I said weakly. "I'll give you her address tonight."

Yaril seemed much more entranced with Epiny's role and adventurous spirit than with what had befallen me. Yet it comforted me that she had completely become my ally again. I think that Yaril and I could have gone on like that indefinitely. I could have immersed myself in the running of the estate and forgotten my military ambitions. Yaril was both competent and content in her position. We had not forgotten our sorrows and loss, but we were healing, we two.

But one night, without warning, my father descended to join us at dinner. He came alone, pushing open the heavy wooden door to the dining room and clinging to it as he tottered in. For all the weakness that showed in his bearing, he had still prepared for this moment. He was immaculately dressed and shaved, with his hair carefully combed. Strange that it was only when he entered the dining room, properly attired for the evening meal, that I suddenly saw that the plague had aged him. He was thinner than he had been and his hair had gone grayer. As he approached the table, Yaril and I were as guiltily silent as children caught in mischief. He dragged out his chair at the head of the table, scraping it across the polished floor with obvious effort, and then seated himself at the place that Yaril had always had set for him.

Yaril was the first to recover. She took up the small bell beside her plate. "Father! I'm so glad to see you well enough to join us. Shall I ring for soup for you?"

He had been staring at me in a flat, ominous way. Now he turned his gaze on her. "That is what one usually does when one comes to table. One eats. Yes, dear daughter, by all means, send for some soup for the old, useless man."

Yaril's mouth hung open. The color drained from her face. Then she took an audible breath and rang her bell. When the servant came in, she said calmly, "My father has come down to dinner. Please find him a soup to begin with; he will not enjoy the cream one."

The man bobbed a bow to her. "I have a beef stock simmering."

"That would be fine. Thank you."

My father was silent through this interchange, and held his peace until the door had swung shut behind the serving man. Then he glared at us. "Well. Isn't this a pretty picture? Playing lord and lady of the manor, are we?"

I kept my cowardly mouth shut. Yaril didn't. Color came back to her face as two spots of pink on her cheeks. "We have done our best to go on, Father, yes. Does that offend you? We thought that you would be pleased that we had kept the estate operating and the household functioning during your convalescence."

"While the cat's away, the mice will play," he replied heavily. As if he had said something of great import, he nodded around the table, surveying us and then each of the empty chairs in turn. Then he pierced me with a stare. "I know more than you think I do, Nevare, you great fat slug. Do you think I've lain idle in my bed up there, day after day, while you trotted about playing the great man, giving orders, writing notes on my money, and changing things without my permission? No. I have not! I've been out and about, in the wee hours of the dawn when sleep runs away from an old man such as I. A few of the servants retain their loyalty to me. They've told me all your mischief. I've seen your fancy ferry docks. And I've marked how you put your mother and my heir and your older sister in the ground, right next to the common servants! I've seen your little party tent in the garden. I know what you've been up to, and I see the path that you're trying to lead Yaril down.

"The city corrupted you. I sent them an honest soldier son, well schooled and ready to serve the king. And what do they send back to me? A swine, bursting out of his uniform, corrupt to the spine! I had the bad conduct reports from Colonel Stiet. He saw you as a coward and a sneak. Fool that I was, I was outraged that he could suggest such a thing." He shook his head. "Colonel Stiet was right. The city tempted you and you fell. Stuffing your body with food. Fornicating with savages. Eschewing the role that the good god had given you. And why? I could not fathom why. I had raised you well. I had believed that you'd set your heart on the same lofty goals I had for you. But now I know. I've had plenty of time to puzzle it out, lying in my bed and staring at the wall. The corruption runs deep, doesn't it, Nevare? Corruption, greed, and jealousy.

"You saw those desperate nobles flaunt the will of the good god. When their heirs died, they raised their soldier sons to that position. You became jealous of Rosse, jealous of your brother and his place. You wanted to be the heir! So you made yourself unfit to soldier, came home, and waited, hoping for just such a disaster as befell us. And now you think you will dump his body in the ground and rise up to take his place. Don't you? Don't you?"

His diatribe took my breath away. I looked at Yaril to see

what she thought. Her face was white with shock. Another mistake.

"See how deep the corruption runs! Your father asks you a question, and instead of replying honestly, you secretly confer with each other. How long have you plotted against me, Nevare? For months? Or for years? How deep have you pulled Yaril into your schemes?"

"He's mad," I said softly. I honestly believed that he was. Yaril's eyes widened and she shook her head, a wordless warning. I should have bowed my head and apologized to my father. Instead, I met his eyes. They were fairly bulging from his head with outrage.

"I loved Rosse, Father. I have never plotted against you. I have never wanted any future save the one that the good god decreed, to be your soldier son. All I have done since Rosse's death, I have done as a placeholder, a steward of estates that will never belong to me. Is that not the duty of a soldier son, Father, as you taught it to me? That in times of disaster, he comes home from serving the king to protect his father's or his brother's holdings? I have made no claim of ownership or authority. All that I ordered, I did in your name. If you review the ledgers and speak to your overseers, you will find that I have run the estate exactly according to the example you set me."

A servant, silent as a ghost, flowed into the room, set a bowl of steaming soup before my father, and drifted out again. The silence held until the door swung shut behind him. Then I spoke again before my father could.

"As for the graves of Mother and Rosse and Elisi . . . yes. It is as you say. If you had given me other orders, I would have done differently, according to your will. I did seek you out, I did speak to you, but you did not reply. And so I buried them simply. I did not think to separate them from the humble folk who had served them so well in life. That I buried them quickly was not lack of respect but necessity. Their bodies were . . . Father, I had to bury them immediately. By the time Duril freed me from my locked room, they were . . . well, you were there. You know." I glanced at Yaril, implor-

ing her silence. I had kept from her that her mother's body
had lain unburied for days, decomposing into her bedding.
She did not need to hear that Elisi had died reaching for
water, unattended by family or servant. It was hard enough
for me to know those things. I would not inflict them on my
sister. I looked at him evenly, waiting for him to admit that
what I said was true.

He stared flatly back at me. "I was ill. You didn't say a
word to me about the graves. I trusted you, Nevare. I trusted
you to do what was right."

"I did my best, Father! The servants had fled. Those who
remained were weak or still sick. I did my best to step up
and take command of the situation."

"You wrapped them in blankets and tumbled them into
their graves. You didn't even trouble with coffins. You gave
your mother's body to the worms, as if she were some pau-
per found in the gutter. You held no prayers, you made no
offerings. They don't even have stones to mark them!

"You shoved them in the earth to be forgotten. And then
you and your sister proceeded to enjoy yourselves, to take
for yourselves what had belonged to your betters."

I glanced at Yaril. I had heard her gasp for breath several
times as my father painted his ugly images into her mind. She
was shaking. Anger flooded me at what he was doing to her.
"Trusted me? Trusted me? You left me locked in my room to
starve! I went days without food or water, and no one gave a
thought to me. If Sergeant Duril hadn't come looking for my
body, I'd be dead, too. Would that have pleased you?"

He looked back at me, his eyes as flat as a fish's. Then he
turned to Yaril and said, "He's lying. He's obviously lying.
Does he look to you as if he has been starved? He's trying to
turn you against me, Yaril. He wants you to agree with him,
to say I'm mad. Then he could petition the king to take control of the estate. And then he'd find a way to have himself
declared heir."

Yaril had bunched her napkin up in her hands. With both
hands, she held it up before her mouth. She was shaking as if
we'd doused her with cold water. I could barely understand

her words. "Stop this. Stop!" She sounded as if she couldn't catch her breath. "I don't know anything. I don't want anything except for this to stop. Stop fighting!" She leapt up from her chair, took two steps toward the door, and then collapsed, weeping, on the floor. I was shocked. She had seemed so strong, so recovered of late. I had not guessed how close she was to breaking. She tried to rise as I stood up. When she could not stand, she tried futilely to escape by crawling toward the door.

I hurried to her. Awkwardly, I went down on one knee and then, with an effort, raised us both. She trembled in my grasp, and sobs shook her with each breath she took. Her eyes were closed. Her hands still gripped her napkin convulsively. My arm around her shoulders held her upright. I spoke flatly. "I am taking my sister to her room. She is overcome. You have judged me wrongly, Father, and judged Yaril even more unjustly. We have been nothing but loyal and devoted to our family throughout the hardship. We are all you have left. Why do you want to turn us against each other?"

We were nearly at the dining room door when he let fly his last volley of barbed words.

"I know why you want her good favor, Nevare. I know why you coddle the sister you earlier ignored. You know that the man she marries may very well be your last refuge when you are old and need a shelter for your fat and doddering years. You know you won't find it with me, don't you? Because I disown you. I know everything you've done, every disgraceful deed: posturing about my Landing, pretending to be a proper soldier, giving orders, and swaggering about. Do you think I haven't heard of your drunken carousing in my Landing? I know how you shamed my name there, drinking with peasants and whores! You ruined my dreams for you! You are nothing to me. Nothing! Nothing!"

At his words, Yaril broke free from my grasp. She fled from the room. I turned to face him. I drew myself up tall and straight and met his gaze. "As you command me, sir," I said coldly. Deliberately, I saluted him.

It threw him into frenzy. "You great sack of blubber! How dare you salute me! You'll never be a soldier. You'll never be anything. You're nothing! Nothing! I take back my name from you! I take back from you your right to say you're my son."

His words should have horrified me and frozen me with terror. Instead I was flooded with a sensation that was now becoming too familiar. The magic roiled in my blood and rejoiced as it spoke. "Take it all back and welcome to it, old man. It has been years since I belonged to you. Take care of yourself. I won't be around to do that anymore. I've a destiny to fulfill, and it isn't here."

I cannot explain the sense of destiny I felt when I said those words. I felt power shimmer all around me. No task was beyond my ability to do. There was no anger in my voice. I stated my thoughts calmly, and when I looked at the gaunt old man at the head of the table, he was suddenly no longer my father. He was thin and querulous and entirely bereft of authority over me. All this time, I'd thought I'd needed him. But the opposite was true. He'd needed me to fulfill his dreams, and when I had grown fat, I'd taken that from him. I didn't need him. I had a life of my own, and it called to me.

As I turned to leave the room, he lifted his soup bowl and banged it on the table at me, like a thwarted child. "Get out of my house! Get out! Get out!"

He was still shouting those words, over and over, when I let the door close behind me. Yaril was standing frozen outside the dining room, her hands knotted into fists and curled against her chest. She looked as if she could not breathe. "Come with me," I said, and when she did not move, I stooped and lifted her bodily. She whimpered like a baby and curled up in my arms. It was awkward to carry her because of my own bulk, but at least I did not lack for strength. Her weight was nothing to me as I bore her up the stairs and to her room. I managed to get the door open, and only bumped her head lightly on the door frame as I carried her in. I set her down on her bed. She curled into a tighter ball there, and sobbed harder than ever.

I looked around the room. I pulled her dainty white-painted chair out from her secretary, and then knew it would never hold my weight. Gingerly, I sat down on the foot of her bed. It creaked in response. "Yaril. Yaril? Listen to me. You and I know what is true. We have done nothing shameful. We have both done the best we could, while that hateful old man huddled in his bed and did nothing. He has no right to rebuke us. None at all."

She only sobbed harder. I didn't know what to do. Just an hour ago, she had been a strong young woman defying disaster with spirit and courage. Had that all been a show for me? It horrified me that my father could so quickly reduce her to a shambles. It was a double horror that he *would* do so. I recalled my earlier skepticism when my Cousin Epiny had told me that a woman's life was very different from my own, that in many ways she was a valuable asset to be bartered off to the highest bidder. I had scoffed at her, but tonight, witnessing the horrible power my father had over Yaril, I had a glimmer of understanding. I sighed and helplessly patted my sister's shoulder until she had sobbed herself out.

Eventually, she quieted. My belly betrayed me by growling softly. For an instant I thought of the lovely dinner we had abandoned: prairie fowl with an onion stuffing was to have been the main course. Vindictively, I hoped my father would choke on it. My belly growled again, more loudly, and to my surprise, Yaril gave a stifled laugh. Her shoulder muscles relaxed, she gave a great sigh, and sat up on the bed next to me. "He's a vile man." She spoke the accusation hopelessly.

"He's our father," I said reflexively. I wondered if he was that to me anymore. Probably not.

"He's our father," she said, accepting the correction. "And he's a vile man and still I love him, and long to have his regard and approval. Can you understand that, Nevare?"

"I can. Because I feel much the same way about him."

"Oh, I don't think so. Not like I have." She pushed her hair back from her wet face. I offered her my handkerchief. She took it and matter-of-factly dried her face. As she gave it back to me, she shook her head wearily. "I've always been the 'extra' daughter, Nevare. Always striving for any crumb of approval I could win from him. When he turned on you, I joined him. Some part of me even felt glad that you had finally done something disgraceful and fallen out of his favor.

Because your failure gave me a better chance with Father. There. Now you know what a coward and a weakling I am."

A year ago, her words would have shocked me. Now I understood them. "I always took his favor for granted," I admitted. "Not that I didn't work hard to be exactly what he expected me to be. I did. And I worried, often, that he was secretly disappointed in me. But for all that, I still always believed he loved me. I never thought that he would—" And to my horror, my throat closed up on my words. Yaril's distress had distracted me. Now the impact of my father disowning me hit me like a musket ball. I wanted to run back down the stairs, fall on my knees before him, and implore him to change his mind.

Yaril looked at me as if she heard my thoughts. "He'll never change his mind. He's too proud. He'll stand by what he's said, even when he knows it's stupid and wrong. He's broken it all, for all of us. What are we going to do, Nevare? Whatever are we going to do?"

The words came to me slowly and fell from my lips like stones. "I'll have to leave. There is nothing else I can do." I swallowed past a sudden lump in my throat. Other words came out before I even thought to say them. "I should have left a long time ago, and then none of this would have happened. When I first found out I was dismissed from the academy, I should have run away east. To the forest, where I belong."

"What?" Yaril demanded, distraught.

"I meant the frontier. Where I could make a new life for myself." But that wasn't what I had meant at all. Like a shadow unfurling, for a moment my Speck self had seized my tongue and spoken to her. I could not imagine a worse time for him to assert his presence. A fresh wave of misery washed over me as I tried to comprehend the full disaster of my father turning me out.

Yaril made it worse. "I have to go with you, Nevare. No matter where you go. You can't leave me here. You can't. I'll die."

"Don't say that! You know I can't take you with me. I don't even know where I'm going or what I'm going to do.

I can't take you into a situation like that." As I said the words, I knew what I had to do. I must obey the good god's will. I had to enlist as a soldier. Franner's Bend was the closest military post. I could start there, and build a new life. I instantly rejected that idea. I would go as far away from my father as I could and build a new life where if I failed or disgraced myself, only I would bear the shame.

"If you leave me, I'll die, Nevare. Or I'll go mad. Don't go off and leave me alone with that crazy, vile man."

The first thought that came to me was that she had to stay, because otherwise our father would be left all alone. Despite all, I thought that too cruel to consider. "He isn't himself," I said instead. "Grief has turned his mind. In time, he may recover. And when he does, he will need you."

"Perhaps after he has driven me as mad as he is? Nevare, try to imagine what my life will be here. I will have no one to turn to. No one."

I sought my mind for something to offer her, some shelter or friendship that could sustain her. Carsina came to mind, and then I remembered their falling-out over Remwar. Our family had other friends and neighbors. True, ever since the plague, there had been little socializing. The news we had received from other households was sparse and often somber. But once the rains of fall and the snows of winter were past and the roads were good again, surely people would resume their old patterns of visits and invitations. In the meantime . . . well, at least she would be safe. I said as much.

"Safe. Safe to be belittled and ordered about every day. Safe to be married off to some man Father chooses, who will belittle and order me about in his home. You have a peculiar idea of safe, Nevare. The safest I've ever been has been since you brought me home from the Porontes and put me in charge of the household. Nevare, other than my grief, these have been the best days of my life. Oh, I know how shallow that sounds!" she cried out before I could reply to her strange remark. "But please, try to understand. For once I felt like I could relax and be myself. I could request meals of food that I enjoyed, and move the furniture as suited me and not be required each evening to give an accounting of what I had accomplished each day. And as a result, I actually did things that I thought needed doing, without fearing that they would not be approved. My life became more than matching buttons on my frock or learning a new piece of music."

I didn't know what to say to her. Words came out of my mouth. "This is a journey I must make. Whatever I need to make this journey will be provided to me." I felt my blood roil in me as I spoke. I shook it off. This was between my sister and me. It had nothing to do with the Tree Woman's curse. I tried to think of some way to comfort Yaril. I said the worst possible thing I could have said. "I'll send for you. When I've made a place for myself, I'll send for you. I promise."

"Will it be long?" she instantly demanded, and then, in the next breath, "I won't be able to stand it here alone. What if he marries me off before you send for me? Then I'll be trapped forever. Where are you going? How are you going to manage on your own? Where are we going to live?"

My heart sank. "I don't know. I don't have answers to any of your questions. But I promise that I'll send for you as soon as I have any sort of a situation. And if you are unhappy with where you are, no matter where you are, you'll still come to me. I promise. Keep in touch with Epiny. I'll be able to find you through her, when the time comes. I'll send for you, Yaril."

Yaril followed me to my room. She looked around it, at the bare walls, the simple desk, and my scant possessions. Her eyes lingered on the broken hasp that dangled still from my ripped door. "He did keep you here and starve you," she said quietly.

"Yes. He did." And our admission of that suddenly made it easier for me to leave.

I had little to pack. The only clothes that still fit me were the ones Yaril had had made for me. I took my cadet cloak, for I knew the autumn rains and winds were not far away.

I packed a basic medical kit of bandages, healing salts, and salve, and a fine needle and silk thread for stitching wounds. I hoped I'd never have to use it. I took my beautiful soldier son journal because I could not bear to leave it. It was hard to leave my schoolbooks behind and admit that a fine education was no longer part of my future.

I did not sleep that night. At dawn, I rose. I washed myself, shaved, and combed my hair. I dressed in the clothing that fitted me best, and made sure my boots were well blacked. When I went to get my sword and pistol, I discovered my father's final blow against me. They were gone. I stood a moment, staring at the empty spot on the wall where they were usually racked with the other weapons of the household. Very briefly, I considered taking Rosse's weapons. Then I hardened myself against such a base temptation. I would give my father no excuse to label me thief as well as failure. He was driving me out of the family unarmed. Very well.

I walked quietly down the hallway and entered my mother's room. I had intended to make a sort of final farewell. The stripped bed and bare windows made the room skeletal and cold. Little remained of the woman who had raised me. There were a few pots of her cosmetics at her dressing station, and her heavy silver-backed brush with its matching comb beside it. I walked to her dressing table, thinking to find a few strands of her hair to take with me. Instead, I caught my reflection in her mirror. I froze, staring at a man I didn't recognize.

I'd been carrying my mental image of who I'd always been. I'd been remembering that I had a sculpted face, high cheekbones, and short blond hair. I remembered a tall man who stood erect, with delineated muscles in his arms and chest. When I thought of myself, despite knowing I'd gotten fat, I still pictured myself that way. That man was gone.

My cheekbones and jaw were lost in the softness of my rounded face. I'd begun a double chin. I stood as straight as I could and vainly attempted to suck in my gut. It availed me nothing. My belly was a bulging sack. My shoulders were rounded with fat, my neck lost in them. My arms looked

shorter, pushed away from my sides. My longer hair looked
lank and greasy. I had dressed in my best, hoping to look like
a cavalla trooper as I rode away. Instead, I finally saw myself
as others did. I was fatter than ever. The extra flesh was like
a badly fitting garment that I'd slung on over my real body.
I could grab handfuls of flesh on my ribs, on my thighs, and
even on my chest. The features of my face were sinking in
doughy flesh. I turned from that nightmare image and walked
sharply from my mother's room, closing the door firmly behind me.

I was not surprised to find Yaril waiting for me at the bottom of the stairs. I managed a smile for her. She had packed
food for me, a generous packet. I thanked her and hugged
her one last time. She leaned against my belly to reach me
for a kiss on my cheek. I felt my body as a wall around me
that held my loved ones at a distance. Fort Nevare.

"Don't you forget your promise!" she hissed fiercely in
my ear. "Don't abandon me here, thinking that I'll be safe.
Send for me as soon as you are settled anywhere, no matter
how rough. I'll come."

I bade her farewell at the door, and turned away from the
house where I had grown up.

In the stables, I saddled Sirlofty and loaded my possessions into my saddle panniers. When I led him out of the
stables, Sergeant Duril was waiting to say good-bye. The old
soldier looked grim and tired. He already knew that I'd been
disowned. Very little of what happened in any noble family
remained private for long. I shook his hand.

He wished me well. "Write to me," he said, his voice going husky. "I know, I can't read, but if you write to me, I'll
find someone who can read it to me. Let me know what happens to you, lad. Don't leave me wondering."

I promised him I would. I mounted, levering my weight
up onto my saddle with difficulty. Sirlofty shifted under me
as if startled by the load. My buttocks settled onto my saddle
in a new and disconcerting way. I took a breath. I hadn't ridden in quite a while, but I'd soon be back in condition. The
next few days would be uncomfortable, but I'd survive. As I

rode away, I glanced back at the windows of my former home. Yaril was framed in hers, watching me ride away. She lifted her hand in farewell. I waved in response.

There was a twitch of the curtains in my father's room. That was all. When I reached the end of the drive and looked back a final time, I saw a croaker bird lift from the chimney pot. He circled my old home once, and then flew off ahead of me. He seemed an ill omen to follow, but follow I did.

CHAPTER ELEVEN

FRANNER'S BEND

It was midmorning before I felt I had truly left my home behind. I knew the lands around my father's holding so well and he made such extensive use of them for running cattle and sheep that they felt as if they, too, belonged to him. I rode in a daze, my mind occupied with my own inner turmoil.

My father had disowned me. I was free. Those two thoughts seesawed in my mind. Free to wander, to give a different name when people asked me. No one would rebuke me if I abandoned the destiny the good god had set upon me and became something other than a soldier. I was also free to starve, to fall victim to robbers, to suffer the misfortunes that befell those who challenged the good god's will. Free to struggle to find a place for myself in a world that largely disdained or ignored me because of my size.

The day was warm, but I already saw the early signs of the season's change. The tall grasses were turning gold and nodded, their heads heavy with seed. The cooler nights meant that more moisture condensed on the ground, and I could see the green fronds unfurling at the base of the winter-growing prairie fern. The tiny purplish flowers of the ground-hugging birdbrush on the gentle hills were giving way to the little black berries that birds and rabbits so loved. The land would give forth one final burst of generosity to all the life that teemed over it before it subsided into the cold hostility of winter.

I had not ridden Sirlofty for any great distance since I'd returned from my useless visit to Dewara. He was restive and willful, and I soon felt all the aches of a man who has been out of a saddle for too long. I gritted my teeth, knowing it would pass in the next few days. Until then, it simply had to be endured. My greater weight amplified every twinge and ache, and by midafternoon my lower back throbbed with every step my mount took. Sirlofty had become lazy as well. His pace was not what it should have been. Toward noon, I noticed a slight hitch in his stride.

I began to watch anxiously for the silhouette of the Franner's Bend stockade wall against the horizon. I had not made good time, I realized. I kicked Sirlofty up into a trot, but he soon lapsed back into a walk, and I let him. When he trotted, my body shook all around me as if I were encased in a pudding. It was a horrid feeling.

My world had changed. I remembered the long ride to Franner's Bend as a journey through wild lands, with nowhere to stop for refreshment, and no scenery other than the natural vegetation on the rolling plains. That was no longer so. The Midlands were becoming settled. There was sporadic traffic on the King's Road that paralleled the river, wagons and people on horseback and families traveling on foot or with donkeys heaped high with possessions. There was habitation, too. I passed several cotton fields, fringed with cottages for the workers. Just beyond them, I came to a long, low building immediately alongside the road. The outside of it was freshly plastered and painted a pale blue that was a shocking contrast to the sere land around it. The new signboard that swung from its post proclaimed it was The Last Bale, and it offered beer, food, and rooms for travelers. I marvelled at the thought of a real inn along this road. Farther along my way, a Plainsman herder in a conical hat and his two dogs shepherded a flock of flat-tailed sheep past me. I passed a little landing on the river with a cluster of buildings around it, the seed of an as-yet-nameless town. Just past it, a boy on a donkey watched over a grazing flock of goats. He watched me pass as if I were the intruder.

I had always thought of my family as living on the edge of the wild lands. Clearly, that was no longer so. Civilization had crept up and flowed around to encompass us. The land was becoming settled. I didn't like it. I had taken pride in growing up on the far reaches of the civilized world, tough and schooled in survival in a land that offered no refuge to the weak. All that was changing now.

I reached the outskirts of Franner's Bend as the sun was venturing toward the horizon. The Bend had changed even more than the countryside. When I'd visited it as a boy, the old fort had crouched in the bend of the river amid a hodgepodge of huts and a rudimentary market. Now ranks of baked-brick houses clustered on either side of the road as I approached the fort. The mud swallows that yearly invaded our barns and plastered their homes into the eaves were more competent builders. The roofs were roughly thatched with broom from the surrounding prairie.

Handcarts and foot traffic meandered along the road and down the alleys. Busy people still stopped and stared at me. One small boy shouted into the open door of a house, "Come see the fat man on a horse!" and a gaggle of children rushed to the threshold to watch me pass. The boy trotted along behind me for some way, gawking at me in amazement. I tried to ignore him. I'd have skirted this warren if I could, but the King's Road went right through the mongrel settlement.

The road passed a roughly paved square centered on a well and bustling with commerce. The buildings that fronted it were painted ochre and white and yellow-brown, with roofs of baked tile. In an open-fronted building, workers were lifting long swathes of fabric from dyeing vats. Men were unloading sacks of grain from a heavy wagon and carrying them into the warehouse like a trail of ants. I dismounted to allow Sirlofty to water at the animal trough by the well. Almost immediately, I drew attention. Two women who had been filling their water jugs giggled and stared at me, whispering like girls. One gangly old man from the grain warehouse was even ruder.

"How many?" he shouted at me as he approached. I suspected he shouted because he himself was deaf.

"How many what?" I asked him as Sirlofty lifted his muzzle from the water.

"How many stone, my man? How many stone do you weigh?"

"I'm sure I don't know," I replied stiffly. I tugged at Sirlofty's bridle, intending to lead him away. But the old man seized my sleeve.

"Come to my warehouse. I've a grain scale there. Come on. This way. This way."

I tugged my arm free of him. "Leave me alone."

He laughed loudly, pleased at my reaction. Workers gawked at us. "Look at him!" he invited them loudly. "Don't you think he ought to come to my grain scales for a weigh?" One woman grinned and nodded widely. Another looked away, embarrassed for me, while two young men laughed heartlessly. I could feel the heat rising in my cheeks. As I set my foot in Sirlofty's stirrup, it felt higher than it had that morning, and every aching muscle in my body screamed at the prospect of remounting.

One of the young men guffawed. "Look! His horse doesn't even want to stand for being mounted by him."

And it was true. The ever-mannered and deeply trained Sirlofty shifted away from me. He was clearly favoring one leg now.

"Ye're goina lame him!" the other young man warned me in a sneering, city accent I recognized from Old Thares. "Pity the poor beast. You should carry *him* for a ways, gutbag."

His warning was a true one. The only reason that Sirlofty would behave in such a way was if he were in pain. I stubbornly mounted him anyway. I rode away from the well and the square, ignoring the catcalls that followed me. As soon as I was out of sight, I dismounted and led my horse. He was not limping yet, but he was moving gingerly. My horse, my fine cavalla steed, could no longer bear my weight for a full day's ride. If I rode him again tomorrow, he'd be lame before the day was out. And then what would I do? What was I going to do now? I was scarcely a day's ride from my father's estate and already into problems. The hopelessness of my situation suddenly crashed in on me. I was pretending that all would be well, that I could provide for myself away from my father's largesse. Yet in reality, I'd never done that.

What were my options? Enlist in the military? I no longer had a horse that could bear me, one of the requirements to join the cavalla as an enlisted man. No foot regiment would consider me. I'd always thought that, if need be, I could live as the Plainsmen once had, taking what they needed from the land. In the last day, I'd discovered what the Plainsmen already knew: the open wild lands were vanishing. I doubted a cotton farmer would appreciate me camping in his field, and I knew that wild game retreated from areas where people kept cattle and sheep. It suddenly seemed that there was no place left in the world for me. I recalled Yaril's wailed words from the night before: "What are we going to do?" The answer seemed more elusive now than it had then.

The growing town had all but obscured the stockade of the old fort. The cannons were still outside the gate but could not have been fired. Flimsy market stalls selling warm grain beer and pepperpot soups and bread were set up all around them. I had to look twice to see the sentries. Two stood to each side of the open gates. The rubbish heaped up around the gates proved that they had been closed for months. Two of the sentries were talking and laughing together as a stream of people wandered past them into the fort. The other two were bartering with a half-breed woman over a tray of sweet-blossom pastries. I stood watching them for a time, wondering why I had even come to the gates of the fort. Habit, I supposed. My father and I had always stopped to pay our respects to the commander of the keep whenever we passed this way.

I led Sirlofty away from the gates, down a side street, ignoring the stares we attracted.

"You stole him, right? Want to sell him? I can get you the best price, I know all the horse dealers." A ragamuffin girl hurried up to trot alongside me. Her hair hung in two tattered braids down her back, and her dress was made from dyed sacking. Her feet were bare. It took me a moment to understand she'd insulted me.

"I didn't steal him. I am not a horse thief. This is my horse. Go away."

"No, he's not. Don't take *me* for a fool. That's a cavalla horse. Anybody could tell that. And you aren't a soldier, that's plain. That tack, that's cavalla tack. Good panniers. I know a man who will buy it all from you, and give you the best price. Come on. I'll help you sell him. Keep him too long, someone will track you down, and you know what happens to horse thieves in this town!" She rolled her brown eyes expressively as she hoisted tight an imaginary noose around her neck.

"Go away. No. Wait." She'd spun aside from me, but halted at my call. "You know so much, missy. Where's a cheap inn?"

"Cheap? You want cheap? I can show you cheap, but first it will cost you. Not much, not much at all, and what you pay me will be far less than what you'll save by letting me show you the cheapest inn I know." She instantly shifted her tactic, grinning up at me. One of her front teeth was missing. She was younger than I had thought.

I did not have much money. My father had not given me any since I reached home, and though tempted, I had not taken any cash when I departed. So my funds were limited to what I'd had left from the money he'd sent me to travel from Old Thares to home. I had seven hectors, fifteen talleys, and six pewters. I took two pewt from my pocket and rattled them in my hand. She looked interested.

"It can't be some dump with moldy hay for my horse and a fleabag for me to sleep in. It has to be decent."

She feigned astonishment. "I thought you said cheap."

"Cheap but decent."

She rolled her eyes as if I were asking for the moon, and

then held out her hand. I put one coin into her palm. She cocked her head at me and frowned.

"The other if I like the place you show me."

She sighed theatrically. "Follow me," she said in an exasperated voice. She led me around a corner and down a side street toward the river. As we passed through a narrow alley, she asked without malice, "How did you get to be so fat?"

"It's a curse," I said.

"Oh." She nodded sagely. "My mother gets that, too. But when she gets fat, she has a baby."

"I'm not going to have a baby." I discovered it was possible to feel offended and amused at the same time.

"I *know* that. I'm not stupid. Here. This is the place." She'd stopped outside a large house that fronted onto the river. The fenced yard and several outbuildings within its enclosure looked maintained but not well tended.

"This isn't an inn."

"I *know* that, too. That's why it will be cheaper and not have fleas. Guff! I've brought you a paying guest!"

She sang it out before I could say anything. In response, an old man stuck his head out the window. "Who's there?"

"Farvi. And I've brought you a man who needs a bed for himself and a stall for his horse tonight. He wants cheap with no fleas. I thought of you immediately."

"Did you? Well, aren't I lucky?" He looked at me skeptically for a moment, and then his glance fell on Sirlofty. "I'll be right out."

He popped out the door seconds later. He reached eagerly for Sirlofty's reins. "I'll put him in back where he won't be seen. Isn't he a fine one!"

"Leave off, sir! He's battle-trained." Sirlofty had instantly reacted to a stranger trying to seize his headstall. I put a hand on my horse to calm him, and then said coldly, "I've no need to hide what is mine. All I need is a place to sleep for the night, and a stall for my horse."

The man looked at me, glanced back at the child, and then looked at me again.

"Very well. But the only place I can put him is around the back. I've a paddock there. Shall I take him there?"

"I'll bring him." I was already feeling dubious about the man. But he led and I followed to a shed and small paddock behind his home. Two milk goats were the only occupants; there was plenty of room for Sirlofty. It was relatively clean, and the hay looked decent. I nodded my approval and put my horse up. The man fetched a bucket of clean water for him and I gave him a good feed of hay. While he was eating, I went down on one knee to check his hooves and legs. His left foreleg was warmer than the others but not badly swollen. I grunted my dismay, and hauled myself to my feet.

"Are you going to stay here?" the girl asked pointedly, holding out her palm.

I flipped her other pewter into the air. She snatched it and was gone.

"Precocious little wench," I observed to the man.

He shrugged. "Most convicts' get are. Or they don't survive."

"Her father's in prison?"

"He was. Then he came out here, working off his sentence on the King's Road. When his stint was done, he got his land allotment. And like a lot of the convicts, he had no idea what to do with it. They send thieves and rapists out here from Old Thares and say, 'Here you go, be a farmer.' They don't know how to milk a goat or plant a seed in the ground. Farvi's father wasn't a bad fellow, but stealing was the only way he knew to make a living. So someone killed him. Franner's Bend is full of men like him, and their half-wild children. Farvi's a smart little girl, but when she's old enough to turn to picking pockets or whoring, she will. There isn't much else for girls like her. Now. You wanted a room?"

The bluntness of his words took my breath away. I just nodded. I followed him through the yard where a young woman gaped at me, and then quickly resumed sweeping the flagstones. My host showed me to the back door of his house, and then to a very small room, not much bigger than the cot it held. I nodded it would do. "How much?" I asked warily.

"Six talleys."

At the look on my face, he added, "And I'll throw in your horse's food and a meal tonight and breakfast tomorrow for you." He cleared his throat. "Not large meals, mind, but enough to keep you going."

It was still more than I wanted to pay, but I nodded sourly. "I'm going out to walk about town a bit. Franner's Bend has changed a lot since I was last here."

"Oh, I'll wager that's true. It's changed since the beginning of summer, and not just from the plague sweeping through here. Keep your hand on your purse, that's my advice. Half the whores in this town will rob you blind. The other half have friends who will kill you and strip your body of everything you've got."

I wondered if he'd known I'd had a stray thought about that possibility. I shook my head at both of us. "Where would I find the horse dealers in town?"

The man squinted his eyes at me. "You want to sell that horse, I'll give you a fair price for him. Like I said before, you won't get far with him. It's too obvious that he's not yours."

"But he is." I spoke each word deliberately. "And I'm not interested in selling him. I want to buy a horse for my journey. A large sturdy one. Where would I look?" I knew what I had to do and was already steeling myself for the task.

"Big horses? Down near the Rivergate. There's usually a good selection there, because of the canal boats. Look for a man named Jirry and tell him Guff sent you."

"And he'll give me a better bargain."

Guff grinned. "No. But he'll know that he owes me a favor if you do buy an animal from him. And he's a competitive trader. He isn't the cheapest down there, but that's because he doesn't deal in worked-out animals. Try him, at least."

I promised I would and set out on foot for the Rivergate. Franner's Bend had become a sprawling warren of little mud-brick houses. The huts and cottages contrasted sharply with one another. Some were plain and others had been slapped with a lime whitewash. Minuscule gardens grew vegetables and a few flowers. Dogs and children ran loose in the streets. A few people looked prosperous, but a far greater proportion of the residents were ragged and scrawny folk.

The streets wound and wandered and abruptly ended or became so narrow that a single horseman could barely pass. In a few places, folk had dug shallow wells. With no planning for rainwater runoff or for foul water, I suspected that this was a miserable, fetid place during the rainy season. I thought of what I'd learned in the academy about engineering a sanitary, defendable fortification and wondered why the commander of Franner's Bend had allowed this slum to develop around the fort. If the Plainspeople did rise up against us, only a fraction of these folk could take refuge behind the stockade walls.

I stepped over a shallow, foul ditch and then found that my path would follow it down to the river. The reek from it was obscene and the objects in it were very recognizable. I walked as far to one side of it as I could, subduing my gag reflex. The passersby seemed immune to the stench.

My path led me through a section of Franner's Bend that seemed populated mostly by Plainspeople or half-breeds. The difference, oddly enough, was that the bricks of their houses were better formed, and their mud-plastered outer walls were decorated with images of deer, flowers, and fish. One structure with open sides sheltered several large ovens and brick cook stoves surrounding a large central table. In this community kitchen, people kneaded bread, stirred pots, and talked. The smells that wafted out reminded me of my childhood visits to the marketplace outside Franner's Bend. My stomach rumbled lovingly.

I hastened my steps, detouring down an alley that I thought would lead to the riverbank. That was a mistake. I ducked under twine strung between the cottages that supported fillets of fish or twists of meat or laundry hanging to dry. Milk goats hobbled with string pulled forage down from dried bundles tied to the cottage eaves.

Gernians obviously did not belong in this part of the Bend. Plainswomen, their hair bundled into bright scarves, sat on benches outside their huts, smoking long pipes as they worked their odd one-handed looms. As I passed, one stopped, nudged the woman next to her, and then turned to call something in her own language through the open window behind her. In an instant, two men crowded one another in the narrow door frame and stared at me as I passed. I kept my eyes straight ahead and strode on. One called out something to me, but I ignored it. I turned a corner at random to escape their lingering gazes and finally emerged onto a wider road paralleling the river. Rivergate was merely the gate in the stockade wall that was closest to the docks. Beyond a district of warehouses and wharves, I found the stockyard. Corrals full of dray horses belonged to one of the canal boat companies. Past them, some horse traders had staked out their wares along the riverbank, their asking prices chalked onto their horses' haunches. As Guff had warned me, I saw plenty of worn-out nags. Pulling laden barges against the river's current was heavy work for a beast. The freight companies worked their animals to the last shred of strength. Some of the poor creatures on display had obviously been treated with drugs to make them look livelier. Others were unapologetically labeled as meat animals.

After several queries, I found Jirry. To give Guff credit, his animals were in better condition than most I'd seen, but they were also priced accordingly. Jirry was not what I'd expected, either. He was a large man, yet not so when he stood next to me. His loose white shirt was soiled at the cuffs and collar, and he wore an ornately embroidered purple vest that only emphasized the swell of his belly. He wore the waistband of his trousers under his gut. His blond hair was almost to his shoulders, and elaborately curled. Looking at him was like looking at a mockery of myself. I didn't want to do business with him, but he had the best stock. Jirry appraised my purse while I looked over his horses.

When I asked him if any of them had ever been ridden, he nodded sagely to himself. He had a booming voice that made my business known to everyone in the street. "I thought you might be looking for a mount. Well, that narrows it down fast, doesn't it, my friend? Men like us, we need more than a pony! Let me show you the two I'd recommend. Clove there, he's carried a man before. And Sassy I bought from a farmer. She knows how to do just about anything you could ask of a horse. Gentle as a kitten, too."

His idea of a gentle kitten and mine were at odds. I narrowly missed having the dull imprints of Sassy's teeth in my forearm. I do not think she was placid so much as disinclined to move any part of her body to please anyone else. I settled on Clove. The dark brown horse was larger and heavier than Sirlofty, probably a cross between a draft horse and a riding horse. He was too small to be harnessed with other dray animals, and too heavy to keep up with a good saddle horse. But for me, he might be perfect. I inspected him as carefully as I knew how. I was horribly aware of how little cash I had and that I'd never bought a horse before. Always my father and brother had done the inspection, the selection, and the decision-making. I had no idea what the customs were, or even how much such an animal should cost. I did know Clove was sound, and better suited to my present weight than Sirlofty was. "Does he come with any tack?" I asked him.

"I'll toss in the halter he's wearing. That's about it."

"How much do you want for him?"

"Ten hectors."

My jaw dropped. I shrugged. "Sorry to have wasted your time." Good horses were a lot more expensive than I'd thought, but the plugs up the street looked like they'd die in the next fortnight.

A dire thought came to me. Perhaps I'd have to stay in Franner's Bend and take whatever work I could find. Perhaps this was my journey's end.

I clenched my jaw, shocked at how my whole soul revolted at the idea. I didn't want to stay anyplace where I might be recognized as Nevare Burvelle. I had to go on, I had to go east to the new life I would build. But I couldn't without a horse. My blood bubbled with frustration, and something more. I spoke my thought aloud. "I cannot pay that much. But I must have this horse to go on. Can't you make me a better price?"

The man's jaw dropped at my bold words. He literally goggled at me, as if I'd hit him with a club rather than baldly stated my need. Plainly I'd insulted him by speaking the truth. Before he could rant at me, I turned away.

"Hey!"

I turned back to Jirry's shout. He looked upset. I braced myself for a tirade, but he looked more confused than angry. "I thought we were striking a bargain here. Don't walk away from me."

I lifted my hands and let them fall. "You're asking far more than I can pay."

"So. What would you pay for him?" He had his fists on his hips, leaning toward me as if I'd already insulted him. "What's he worth to you?"

I spoke carefully. "I won't presume to tell you the value of your stock. You've named your price, sir. Frankly, I don't have it. Even if I did, I couldn't afford to spend that much on a horse without tack. I've a long way to go."

He got that addled look again, and then said reluctantly. "I might have a Plains saddle that would fit him."

"It's still more than I can afford. I'm sorry." I turned again.

The man actually stepped in front of me. His face was reddened. "Make me an offer, before you walk away," he growled.

It offended me to the roots of my soul. I'd been raised as the son of a nobleman. I was not a traveling tinker, to stand in the street and haggle price. A flush of shame spread up my cheeks. Was this what I had come to? Nevertheless, I steeled myself and revealed the extent of my finances. "The most I could give for any horse right now is five hectors."

"Oh! You're robbing me! You can't imagine I'd sell that animal for half what he's worth!" The volume of his outraged shout turned heads toward us.

I spoke stiffly. "Of course I don't expect you to sell him for half your asking price. But five hectors is the most I can offer. Good day." Before I could turn away, he'd seized the sleeve of my shirt.

"Surely you've got something else you could throw in to sweeten the pot? Come on, man, in the spirit of the trade, at least offer me something, to salve my pride if nothing else."

Mentally, I squirmed. I thought through my paltry possessions. Was there anything I was willing to part with? I had so

little. I could feel him watching me. "I have nothing else," I
said at last. "I'm sure he's worth more than five hectors, but
that's the best I can do."

"May the good god witness that you are robbing me!" he
shouted. We'd acquired an audience. I was sure they stared
at the fat man. I resented Jirry making me into a spectacle.

"Have done, sir," I said with what dignity I could muster.
"I must go."

"Give me the money, then, for I've a family to feed! And
when people ask you where you got such a fine beast, be
sure to tell them you stole him from poor Jirry!"

I took the coins carefully from my pouch, striving that he
should not see how many more I actually had. I felt shamed
at having driven his price down so far. I felt worse when he
dragged out a very worn but serviceable Plains saddle. It was
a rudimentary thing, a cross between a real saddle and the
dab of padding used by the nomads. The tree was not a good
fit for Clove's back, but it would have to do for now. Jirry
helpfully offered a small cask as a mounting block. It gave
way under me when I attempted it. I thanked him stiffly and
led my new purchase away from the grinning bystanders. I
glanced back as I left, still puzzled at how easy it had been to
bargain the man down. Jirry was looking after me incredulously. I saw him glance down at the coins in his hand and
then back at me as if he, too, wondered at the deal.

Out of sight of my circle of gawkers, I climbed a low stone
wall to get on top of my new horse. Clove seemed startled to
find that such a load could be a living thing. I kicked him
several times before he understood I wanted him to move.
Then he went forward at his own pace, turning his head from
side to side at every distraction, and once craning his head
back at me as if he couldn't quite believe I was riding him. I
suspected that he hadn't truly been ridden but perhaps had
tolerated people sitting on his back. I rebuked myself for not
trying to ride him before buying him, for I now saw that a
rein against his neck meant little to him. I literally had to pull
his head in the direction I meant him to go.

By the time we reached Guff's house, Clove was reacting
reasonably well to my kicks and knee presses. He was not

anyone's ideal mount, but he was not stupid and seemed like a willing beast. My dismount was more of a slide from his back. It was not graceful, and I was disgruntled to hear someone muffle a laugh. I turned, but Guff's daughter was already retreating into the house. Red-faced, I led Clove to the water trough and then put him in with Sirlofty. Then I stood looking at the two animals in the paddock. Sirlofty was tall and rangy, straight-legged, and black as coal from his nose to the tip of his tail. He wasn't young, but he had many good years left in him. He lifted his head and looked over at me, his small ears flicking forward as if asking why my attention was so intent. There was no doubting the intelligence in his eyes, or the years of schooling that my father had put into him. The horse had taught me almost everything I knew about riding like a cavalla man. He was the best and most valuable possession I'd ever owned.

Next to him, Clove was a clod. He was big. Everywhere. His head was big, his neck was thick, and his haunches were wide and round. His hooves looked the size of dinner plates next to Sirlofty's trim feet. At some time, his tail had been bobbed, badly. The hair that dangled from the shortened stub looked stringy. He was a clownish-looking horse, a fit mount for a fat man like me.

My horse came over to me, to sniff my chest and then push his head against me. I finally voiced the decision that I had already made. "I can't keep you, Sirlofty. If I do, I'll ruin you. You'll end up lamed in the middle of nowhere. You deserve better than that."

With many regrets, I separated my panniers from my saddle. It was a cavalla saddle, a relic of a lost dream, and my father's spond tree crest was embossed into the leather. I didn't want to carry that forward into my new life. I kept the bridle. It was well made and I thought I could adapt it to my new mount. I set the saddle onto Sirlofty's back. As I made the "keep fast" sign over the cinch, tears gathered in my eyes and then spilled down my cheeks. I wiped them away with the back of my hand. Useless, senseless things.

Evening was deepening into night. It seemed a fit time for my last hours with Sirlofty. I led him through the wandering streets of Franner's Bend. The cool night was moister than the day had been, enriching the smells of that rancid city. Sirlofty's sore leg had stiffened, and he now walked with a marked hitch to his gait. I didn't hurry him. As we walked, I told myself that he was only a horse, and that a cavalla man changed mounts any number of times in his career. The best I could offer Sirlofty was constant travel on an injured leg and short rations. Besides, I looked ridiculous on him. Better to part with him while he had some value, before I had ruined him. Clove would serve me well enough. When I got to wherever I was going, then I could see about getting a better mount, if my life demanded it. That wasn't likely. If I managed to enlist, it would probably be as a foot soldier, not cavalla. Likely I'd be relegated to cooking or totting up numbers or some similar task.

Outside the gates of the fortifications, I stopped for a moment. I dried my face of the tears that had run unashamedly as we walked together in the darkness. Then, like a boy, I leaned against my horse's shoulder and tried to hug him good-bye. Sirlofty put up with it.

I held to my purpose. I led Sirlofty through the gates. Even this late in the evening, the so-called sentries allowed us to pass unchallenged. I went directly to the commander's headquarters. I was fortunate to arrive before the commander had left. I passed myself off as a servant, and lied to his adjutant to see him. I told him that Nevare Burvelle's horse had come up lame, and he'd had to find a fresh one to continue his travels. I said that both Nevare and his father, Lord Burvelle, would be indebted to the commander if he would have the regimental veterinarian look at the animal, and then arrange for him to be taken back to Widevale as soon as he could make the journey without further injury. As I had expected, the man was happy to oblige. "Anything for Lord Burvelle," he assured me, and I bowed gravely and said that when I caught up with my master, I'd be sure to let Nevare know that his mount was in capable hands and would be awaiting him when he returned home.

On the way back to my rented room, I stopped at a tavern, got drunk, and paid a yellow-haired whore three times her usual rate to bed her. If I had thought to make myself feel better, I failed. I spent money I could ill afford to discover that intercourse had become a challenge. When the jut of a man's belly exceeds the length of his member, coupling with a woman requires imaginative positioning and a cooperative partner. The whore was barely that, and only did what she must to earn her coins.

"You see," she said righteously as I stepped away from the edge of the bed where I had knelt, "why I had to charge you more. That wasn't easy for me. You fair disjointed my hips!" She lay as I had left her on the edge of the bed, skirts dragged up to her waist and her legs spraddled wide to accommodate me. I recall thinking that it was the least alluring posture that I could have imagined a woman assuming.

"I'm finished," I told her abruptly.

"That's obvious," she drawled sarcastically.

I dressed and left.

My knees were sore as I walked back to my rented room. Pleasure was a word that didn't apply to what I'd done. The physical release I had experienced was inextricably mixed with the humiliation she had dealt me. Rather than taking comfort in the woman, I had completely proven to myself how much my life had changed in a few short months.

CHAPTER TWELVE

THE KING'S ROAD

T he good god never intended for people to live here."

The woman's words were to stay long in my mind. Her house was one of six inhabited structures in a ramshackle settlement near the second rise of the foothills before the mountains. There was little there save misery. Stumps dotted the sloping fields behind the town. The constant wind, heavy with wet chill, warned of winter. Dead Town was a "road town," a temporary settlement thrown together to house the penal workers and their families as the King's Road was pushed ever eastward.

Once I had believed in King Troven's dream of a wide road that led across the plains, over the mountains, and to the sea beyond, a road that would restore Gernia's power as a seagoing and trading nation. The farther east I went, the harder it was to sustain that vision.

Calling the structure she lived in a "house" was charity on my part. It was built of large stones and roughly skinned logs. The badly warped logs were smaller in diameter than anything I would have used for a structure. The gaps between the corkscrewed logs were chinked with wadded reeds and moss, with plastered mud over it. I judged the coming rains of winter would soon melt that chinking away. She had three small children, but if she had a husband, he was not to be seen.

My food had run out and I'd stopped to see what I could buy. The inhabitants of two other houses had already turned me away. They had little enough for themselves and no use for my coins. The irony was that I'd discovered, too late, that I was not as poor as I'd thought. When I repacked my panniers as I left Franner's Bend, I discovered a little yellow purse tucked in among my shirts. When Yaril had slipped it in, I didn't know. It contained fifteen hectors, a very substantial sum coming from a young woman. I resolved to use it well, and to pay it back to her when we were reunited. The extra money could not restore my battered self-respect, but it did shore up my sagging confidence. I invested some of my windfall in a battered draft saddle with a tree that fit Clove's back and a seat that didn't insult my own. After several fruitless efforts, I admitted that Sirlofty's bridle and bit would never adjust to Clove. I traded them away for a bridle that fit my plug horse, some straps to adapt my cavalla panniers, and a couple of heavy blankets in case I had to sleep outside. In the market, I stocked my panniers with hard bread, smoked meat, raisins, tea, and charily, a Plains food of meat and fruit ground together into a sort of sausage bound with sweetened suet. I bought tools for rough travel: a small hatchet, sulfur matches dipped in wax, and some strips of leather to make a sling. I wanted a firearm, but that was beyond the reach of my coins. The sword I bought was not well balanced and the blade was pitted from poor care. It was better than nothing. When I rode away from Franner's Bend, I felt I was as well supplied for the road as a man of my means could be.

In return, the road offered me next to nothing. Water was not a problem while my trail followed the river. Heat, flies, and boredom were my chief irritations by day, cold and mosquitoes by night. Clove ambled along.

For my first day's travel from Franner's Bend, the road was good. I passed several small villages huddled on the riverbank. They seemed prosperous, feeding off both the river and the road trade. They were older than the explosive growth of town around Franner's Bend, but in some ways they still exuded the rough, raw aspect of a frontier settlement. All the buildings were constructed from river offerings: stone rounded by the passage of water, mortar speckled with the tiny pebbles one always found in the river sand, and an occasional embellishment of wood. There was little real timber on the plains or plateaus, but rafts of immense spond logs from the wilderness passed by on the river. Spond timber was far too dear for these townspeople to afford; the wooden parts of their houses came from river driftwood largesse or salvage from broken log rafts.

Despite their humble roots, these settlements were growing into organized towns. The road between the towns was better maintained, as were the way stations for the king's couriers. Between the towns, fields had been cleared and the discarded stones used for rough fences. The brush that had sprouted among those stones had grown into hedgerows. Most of the outbuildings were still of mud brick, but the farmhouses were of worked stone. Gernian settlers were making their tenuous grip on the land more certain. Those households would stay.

On the evening of the second night, I came to a well-maintained farm with a signboard that showed a dangling cup and a handful of feathers, the old symbols for board and lodging. I stopped there for the night, and discovered that it meant a cold meal and a blanket spread over straw in the barn. Still, I'd slept in worse places, and I rose the next day better rested than if I'd slept by the side of the road.

The draft horse was not a bad mount, for what he was. Clove was big-boned and ponderous. I put him through his paces on our third day of travel. By then, he was answering the bridle and my heels, though not sharply. He didn't seem to mind being ridden, but he was not my partner in it as Sirlofty had been. He made no effort to stay under me. His trot rattled my teeth. His canter was actually rather smooth, once I finally persuaded him to that pace, but he could not sustain it for long, and I had no fixed destination or schedule. I followed the road, hoping that one of the fortifications along the way would take in a stray recruit.

My body was more at fault than my horse's for the discomforts of that journey. As an engineer, I could see that I was like an overburdened suspension bridge. Too much flesh was heaped around my bones and dependent on my muscles. My body no longer worked as it had been designed to do. Flexibility had been lost. Strength had been gained in my major muscles, but my back complained constantly. Clove's bone-shaking trot was also a fat-wobbling quake for me. My cheeks shook, my belly jounced, and the flesh along my arms and legs jostled in syncopation to his hooves. At the end of each day's ride, my ass hurt more than it had the day before. My expectation that I would soon toughen up and regain my ability to ride a full day without soreness was a vain hope. There was simply too much of me pressing my buttocks against the saddle, with the predictable consequences of developing sores. I tried to be grateful that they were on my flesh rather than my horse's, but that was grim comfort. I steeled my will and went on, wondering how long my determination would last.

Three days past Franner's Bend, I passed the site where Cayton's Horse and Doril's Foot had met their end. Someone had put up a wooden sign. The crude letters read "SITE OF THE SPECK PLAGUE BATTLE." If it was meant to be humor, it left me cold. Beyond it, row upon row of shallow depressions in the earth showed where the ground had sunk on the hastily buried bodies. Beyond them, a large ominous scorch mark on the earth was gradually giving way to encroaching grasses. I fancied that a smell of death lingered there; Clove and I hastened past it.

The first time the sun began to set with no shelter of any sort in sight, I turned Clove from the road and followed a

tiny trickle of a stream up a gentle hill and into the brush.
The faint trail I followed and a blackened ring of fire stones
at the end showed I was not the first traveler to camp here.
Hopeful, I lifted my eyes and soon found the sign that Sergeant Duril had taught me to look for so many years ago.
Carved into a tree trunk was the outline of two crossed sa-
bres. Wedged into a crotch of branches well above it was a
bundle of dry firewood. Farther out on the branch dangled
the bag that would hold kindling and emergency food. The
courtesy among scouts and cavalla troopers was to take
what one needed from such caches and replace it with whatever one could spare. The smoked fish I could smell was far
more appetizing than the travel bread in my pack.

Hunger was a constant companion that rode heavily in the
pit of my belly. It hurt, but less than my saddle sores. I could,
by an act of will and intellect, ignore it. Despite its pangs, I
knew I was not starving, and for the most part, I pitted my
will against the magic's outrageous demands for food with
determination. I knew that my rations were sufficient to my
needs, and by that logic I could ignore my hunger pangs until
I saw or smelled food. Then my appetite awoke, a ravening
bear roused out of hibernation and commanding all my attention.

The smell of the savory smoked fish overpowered me. To
scent it was to taste it, smoke, salt, and oil rich flesh upon
my tongue. I had to have it. My body demanded it.

I was too fat to climb the tree. I broke branches and scraped
my knees and belly trying. I threw stones at the food, trying
to knock it free. I stood and shook the tree like a bear, hoping
to make it fall. I even tried, futilely, the edge of my small firewood hatchet against the tree's thick trunk. In short, I exhausted myself trying to get at a bit of smoked fish.

It was full dark before I came to my senses. It was like
waking from a dream. I suddenly decided that the food in
my pannier would have to suffice. With a startling abrupt-
ness, my obsession with the fish departed. I used some of
the branches I'd broken to start a small fire.

I made a very rudimentary camp beside my little fire, ate
cold food with hot tea, and rolled myself in a blanket to

sleep. The ground was hard and I was cold. Toward dawn, the mosquitoes came out and discovered me. Even pulling my blanket up over my head did not discourage them, and I rose earlier than I was inclined to and traveled on my way. My only act of virtue was to cut the broken branches into firewood and leave them at the base of the supply tree.

As I traveled on, towns became less frequent and houses more scattered. Traffic dwindled. Every day, two couriers would ride past me, one headed east and one headed west, usually at a canter or a gallop. They carried the king's dispatches and, if there was room in their pouches, high-ranking officers' letters home. They did not acknowledge me at all as they passed. Some credited Gernia's expansion to the king's dedication to regular communication with even his most distant forts. Daily reports were sent on their way to Old Thares. Some of the courier stations rented space for profit-making messenger services as well. They were becoming more popular as Gernia's boundary and far-flung population expanded, but they were still an expensive service, patronized only by the wealthy. I did not see their riders as often.

One windy morning, I passed a place where a spring freshet had washed the road out. It had been repaired, but badly, with a stream still trickling through a wide dip in the road. I could see the remains of the stone culvert; the mortar had failed, I judged, and I suspected that next spring would see the road cut through when the waters ran high again.

It was not a real challenge for Clove and I, but the deep muddy wagon wheel ruts testified that it was an unpleasant passage for any wheeled vehicle. I saw few other travelers that day, and began to understand why some of the king's nobles in the west mocked this project and called it the King's Road to Nowhere.

Early in the day, I passed a relay station for the king's couriers. As there were no towns nearby, a small contingent of soldiers were stationed there to protect and maintain the station. There was little there except a stable for the post horses, a small storehouse, and a barracks. The buildings were set up in a defensible square with a stockade wall closing the gaps. The tall gates stood open, and coarse grasses grew along the bottoms of them. Months had passed since they'd last been closed. The surly soldier on watch eyed me unenthusiastically. Not an exciting post, I surmised. I wondered if being stationed here was regarded as punishment.

I rode Clove in and dismounted. As I let him water from the horse trough alongside their well, I looked around. The barracks and mess were painted in Gernia's standard green and white. I estimated their strength at about a dozen men. There was a watchtower at one corner of the fortification; a uniformed soldier ostensibly kept watch there for approaching messengers. A couple of men leaned in the open door of the barracks, smoking. Only one courier was currently in residence, lounging on a tipped-back chair on the long porch that ran across the front barracks. The young, skinny rider seemed very full of himself, openly rolling his eyes at my girth and making faces and gestures when he thought I wouldn't see him. I took some satisfaction in seeing that the men who kept up the station seemed to regard him as a jackanapes. When I mounted the steps to the barracks' porch, an older man in shirtsleeves came out to meet me.

"Do you need something?" he asked me brusquely.

"News of the road ahead would be welcome. And I thought I'd report that there's a culvert washed out, about an hour's ride back." Military regulations stated that the courier stations were to aid travelers, monitor the road, and report conditions to the proper authority. I considered it my duty, still, to apprise them of the road's condition.

The man scowled at me. It had been at least three days since he'd shaved. The only clean spot on his cheek was an old knife scar. Even without his jacket and stripes, I could tell he was in charge here. "I've been reporting that for two months. They keep saying they'll send a road crew, but the plague hit everybody hard. They don't have the men to spare. Nothing happens."

"And the road east of here?" I pressed him.

"It's no better. It was built fast with unskilled men, and the need for maintenance was underestimated. It's passable for a man on horseback, and there are only a few places that would give a wagon serious trouble. But once the rains start again, that story will change quickly." He spoke as if it were my fault.

Intending it more as a pleasantry than as a true query, I asked where their command was, and if their regiment had any openings for recruits. The old veteran looked me up and down and gave a contemptuous snort. "No. We've plenty of our own youngsters to sign up when we need more men. No need for outsiders."

I took that rebuff in stride. "Well. Any chance I can replenish my supplies here? Any food you could sell me?"

The courier had been listening in on our exchange. He interrupted mockingly with "You need to buy food? It doesn't look to me as if you've been going without! Or are you fattening up before you hibernate for the winter?"

It was a feeble jest, but the other man laughed at it. I forced myself to smile. "I've a way to travel. I'd buy whatever you could spare—flour, grain, travel bread, bacon?" I could smell stew simmering and longed to beg for a hot bowl. As always, any aroma of food roused a ravenous hunger in me.

"We've nothing to spare," the sergeant decided abruptly. "This is a way station for couriers, not an inn. The supply wagons haven't been as regular as they should. I'm saving what I've got for my own men here."

"Of course. But could I at least buy some oats for my horse?" Clove was not the forager that Sirlofty was. The constant travel and sparse grazing were starting to show on him. Because my father was responsible for the king's courier station closest to Widevale, I knew they were required to keep well stocked with feed for the horses.

The men exchanged glances with each other. Then the sergeant spoke again. "No. I've told you. We've nothing to spare. Best you be on your way."

"I see," I said, though I didn't. Plainly he was lying. I could not discern why, but I suspected it was simply because I was fat. I think he perceived me as self-indulgent and felt justified, even righteous, in denying me food. I looked at the circle of faces around me. Every one of them evinced some level of satisfaction in my disappointment. They put me in mind of how Trist had rejected Gord from the first moment he'd met the fat cadet. Gord hadn't had to say or do anything. Just being fat had made Trist despise him and seek to thwart him at every opportunity.

I needed supplies. My horse needed something more than grass. My experience with Jirry flashed back through my mind. On some level, I'd already accepted that the magic that had so cursed me could also work in my favor. I tried it. "I really need fresh supplies to continue on my journey." It was my first effort to bend the magic to my will. I pushed insistence through my words and deliberately sought to bend their wills to mine.

A few of the idle men got the same poleaxed look that Jirry had worn. But the old sergeant was made of sterner stuff. His eyes widened, and then, as if he sensed what I was trying to do, his face reddened with anger. "I said no!" he barked. He came to his feet and pointed commandingly at my mount. I'd failed. I turned away from him, trying to keep my dignity. But anger at their self-satisfaction seethed through me. I mounted Clove and then looked back at them. My own anger suddenly rose to meet the sergeant's, as if they were two swords clashing.

"As you have seen to the needs of the stranger, so may your own wants be met in your time of need." It was a verse from the Holy Writ, and I'd heard it most often used as a formal thanks at dinner parties. I'd never said it with such vehemence, nor had I ever moved my hand in such a strong gesture of dismissal as I said it. I had deliberately sought the magic's intervention, but now as I felt it rattle through my blood like pebbles tumbled in a torrent, I feared it. The gesture meant something, and the words I had uttered in a mockery of thanks now bristled like a curse. I saw one man startle, as if I'd dashed him with cold water, and the rider's chair tipped over under him, dumping him to the porch with a crash. The sergeant was transfixed for a moment, and then he charged at me with an angry shout. I kicked Clove hard, and for once he surged immediately into a canter that carried us away from their stronghold and back out onto the road.

I leaned forward on my big horse and urged him to run until his sides were heaving and sweat runneled the sides of his neck. When I pulled him in and let him walk, the courier's station was lost behind us. No riders swarmed out to pursue me, as I had half-feared they might. I knotted my fists and shivered suddenly. I'd done magic. I had felt the power surge through me and pass out of me. But exactly what I had done, I did not know. I passed a patch of brush by the riverbank, and a flock of black-and-white croaker birds flew up screaming, angry that I had frightened them off whatever carrion they had found. They seemed an ill omen, a sign from an elder god that he would take my blackened soul if the good god would no longer have me. I rode grimly on.

My meals for the next few days consisted of whatever game I could bring down with my sling. It wasn't much. In the short time between stopping for the night and falling asleep, I hunted what I could, and if I got a rabbit or a bird every other day, I thought myself fortunate. I still had a good supply of tea, sugar, salt, and oil, but a man cannot make a meal from those things alone. The lean meat of hares did not satisfy me, and if my clothes hung a bit looser on me for a few days, I attributed it to my diet.

For several long days, the scenery did not change. It seemed as if Clove and I followed an endless circular path, with the river always to the right of us, wide and gray between its brushy, gravelly banks, and to the left of us, the gentle rise of the rolling prairie. The hills were ahead of us. Their flanks were gray-green or purplish with gorse, and in the higher regions, clumps of buckbrush and nettleme grew. Regularly spaced towns and real inns were left far behind me.

The next courier station I passed was larger and better fortified. They sold me oats and journey bread, but other than that, they seemed as unfriendly as the last station had been. A full troop of foot soldiers was stationed there, with a score of cavalla. A small village of former penal laborers flanked the station, and were engaged in making more formidable the wall and ditch defenses that surrounded both station and village. If any engineering had been applied to the enterprise, it was well concealed from my eyes.

I gathered my courage and then asked for a meeting with the commander, and was shown into the offices of a very young captain. When I told him I was a second son and interested in becoming a soldier, he looked incredulous. I'll give him credit for attempting to be tactful. He leaned back in his chair, looked at me, and then said in measured tones, "Sir, despite your birth order, I do not think the life of a military man in our region would suit you. Here, we endeavor to recruit our men at an early age, the better to shape them to the lives they will lead. Perhaps you would fare better in the west."

"I am still short of my twentieth birthday, sir. And I know I do not look fit or able, yet if you will try me, I'm sure you'll find me more capable than you might think." Those words consumed all of my humility. My cheeks burned with shame.

"I see. Well. You look older than your years." He cleared his throat. "Our resources here are limited, and right now our supplies must stretch to support the road workers the king has lent us for the fortification of this place. Much as I would like to take your oath and find you a place where you could serve both your king and the good god, I must turn you away. I do think you would fare better applying to one of the regiments in the west. In the more settled areas, a man may still serve his king and obey the will of the good god in less strenuous ways than the borderlands demand of a soldier."

I heard the finality in his words. I knew he was attempting to let me leave with my pride and dignity intact. It was more than most folks had done for me on my journey. So I thanked him, and Clove and I went on. But as always, we rode toward the east and the mountains.

I came to a decision point when we reached the fork where the Mendes River joins the Tefa. I rode north for half a day, following both the road and the river. When I came to a new town with the ambitious name of Kingsbridge, I crossed the Mendes on the town's namesake, and then halted, considering my options. If I followed the Mendy trail north, I'd have several options for enlistment. There was Mendy itself, a substantial bastion and one of our earliest strongholds on the plains. In its earliest incarnations, before we had come to open strife with them, Mendy had been a place for Gernian merchants to enjoy commerce with the Plainspeople. Traditionally, the Third, Seventh, and Eighth Regiment of foot called Mendy home, as well as Hoskin's Horse. There was opportunity for me there.

My most sensible choice would have been to follow the river to Trade Post, or cross it and try to enlist at Lakegard or Laston. North offered me more opportunities. And yet, when Clove tossed his head and tugged at his bit in annoyance at standing so long, I did not follow the Mendy Trail. Gettys was the only Gernian outpost in our new direction. With the loss of Cayton's Horse and Doril's Foot, Gettys would be severely undermanned. Their misfortune might be to my benefit.

I did not allow myself to think that Gettys was in the foothills before the Barrier Mountains, the home territory of the Specks.

As each day passed, the land slowly changed. Trees began to appear, as scattered thickets and then as a solid forest that covered the hillsides. The quality of the road declined as it climbed higher into the foothills. The Tefa River was to my left now, and half the size it would be when it passed my old home in Widevale. I became resigned to sleeping outside each night and supplementing my rations with wild plants and whatever small game I could hunt as I traveled. The road was an anomaly here, a man-made thing that ran through a land that didn't seem to recognize humanity's reign. My journey seemed endless. At intervals I would see derelict wagons and other broken and abandoned equipment at the side of the road, the detritus of the road's continuing growth. Several times I passed large cleared areas, where rags of canvas and other garbage spoke of a large encampment of men, probably for the penal crews building the road. The few other travelers I encountered were brusque, hurrying past me as if I were a threat. I encountered a train of supply wagons, returning empty from the farthermost road construction camp. The dust they raised was swept away by the endless wind. The quiet that flowed back after their passage seemed final. Winter and the snows it would bring had slowed all trade by road or water to a trickle.

I could scarcely believe my eyes when I topped a rise one afternoon and saw a small town in the distance. The land had been cleared around the settlement; it crouched on a steep hillside dotted with stumps. My heart lifted at the thought of an inn, an opportunity to resupply, to eat a hot meal, to sleep under a roof. But the closer we came, the more my hopes sagged. Chimney smoke rose in only a few places. The first structure I passed might once have been a house. It had slipped to one side and then collapsed. Beyond it there was a rail-fenced area. A double row of depressions in the earth were the only indications that it was a graveyard.

I rode on, passing other empty houses. The houses, both fallen and standing, had been built of logs rather than plank. The town was abandoned, or nearly so. When I finally sighted a house with a trickle of smoke rising from its chimney, I halted and dismounted. I approached the door cautiously, knocked, and then stood back from it. Some moments passed, then a very old man opened the door slowly. Before I could offer any greeting or even ask to buy food and a night's lodging, a woman's voice shrieked from inside. "Close it! Close that door, you old fool! Why do you think I barred it? He's here to murder us and rob us. Shut the door!"

"I've money to pay for a meal!" I shouted hastily, but the old man only looked at me with pale, rheumy eyes and then obediently but gently shut the door in my face. "I can pay!" I shouted at the closed door. There was no response. I shook my head in frustration and walked on, leading Clove.

I passed five shells of houses and then stopped outside a fenced area where a man was digging potatoes. His cottage looked well-tended, as did the little garden that surrounded him. At sight of me, he stopped his digging. He switched his grip on the shovel, holding it as if it were a pike.

"Good day, sir," I offered him.

"Keep on your way," he advised me gruffly.

"I'd like to buy a meal and a night's lodging from you. I can pay. I can show you the coin."

He shook his head. "I've no use for coins. What would I do with them? Make soup?" He looked at me more sharply, and then, perhaps deciding a fat man was not much of a threat, asked shrewdly, "Got anything to barter?"

I shook my head slowly. I had nothing I could afford to

part with, nothing I could give up that would not leave me in worse need.

"Well, we've nothing to spare for beggars. Be on your way."

I opened my mouth to say that I had not begged. I could feel my resentment rising in me. I thought of the soldiers and how the magic had boiled with my anger. No. I would not do that again. I would not loose that which I did not understand. I turned away from him and led Clove on.

I was hungry, cold, and weary. Thick clouds had been gathering all day and were starting to darken, promising rain by nightfall. If it had been otherwise, I think I would have mounted up and ridden off. The rising wind tugged at my cloak. If all I could buy myself was a dry night's sleep, I was resolved to have it. At the next cottage with chimney smoke rising from its stack, I gathered up my courage and knocked at a rough wooden door.

It was slow to open. I stood still before it, smiling, for I suspected that someone was peering out at me through one of the numerous chinks in the wall. The small woman who finally opened the door held a large pistol in both her hands. I stepped back. The muzzle of it pointed squarely at my mid-section. She could not possibly miss me at this range. I lifted my hands to show they were empty. "I'd just like to buy a night's lodging and food, ma'am," I said with great respect.

A small towheaded boy suddenly shoved his head out past his mother's skirts. "Who's that?" he demanded. And then, almost with admiration, "He's really fat!"

"Hush, Sem. Get back inside." She looked at me speculatively. I could almost see her decide that I wasn't much of a threat. She was small but stocky. She had to use both hands to steady the pistol. She lowered the heavy gun, but now the barrel menaced my legs. "I don't have much to spare."

"I'd be content with anything hot, and a dry place to spend the night," I said humbly. "I can pay."

She laughed in a sour way. "And where would I spend it? I've got no use for money. Can't eat it. Can't burn it." Her blue eyes were hard. I didn't doubt the truth of her words. She looked as worn as her clothing. Her dark hair was knotted back in a no-nonsense way that spoke only of practicality, not attractiveness or even neatness. The skin of her hands was rough. The boy's eyes looked too large in his thin face.

I could think of nothing else to offer. "Please," I begged.

She tightened her mouth and narrowed her eyes. It made her look like a thoughtful cat. I stood humbly before her, hoping. Two more children peeped out around the door frame. One was an older girl of about five, the other a curly-headed toddler. The woman shooed them back, then looked me up and down skeptically. "Can you work?" she asked me coldly.

"That I can," I promised her. "What do you need done?"

Her smile was tight. "What don't I need done? Winter's coming. Look at this place! I'll be lucky if it stands through the first storm." She sighed and then said, "You can put your horse in that house over there. We use it for a shed. The roof doesn't leak much."

"Thank you, ma'am."

She almost winced. "I'm not ma'am. I'm not that old. I'm Amzil."

I spent the rest of the afternoon and early evening chopping wood. She had an old ax with a splintery handle. I put an edge on it with a stone. She had been turning the adjacent buildings into firewood, but the ax was big for her and the house timbers too heavy. She'd been limited by the size of log she could chop through. "The little ones burn up too fast. I can't build a fire that lasts the night," she told me.

I worked steadily in the chill wind. I selected a small house that was mostly collapsed, and worked at turning it into firewood, cutting the timbers into chunks and then splitting them. One at a time, her scattered neighbors made excuses to drop by. I felt their eyes on me, but as none of them spoke to me, I ignored them and labored on. Their attempts at conversation with Amzil were brief. I heard one man say to her, "I only come to see if he had something to trade. It's nothing to do with you at all, woman!" I sensed no community there, only a sour rivalry for the diminishing resources of the failed settlement. The old woman did not come to Amzil's door but grimly eyed me from a distance, scowling as I pulled logs free and then chopped them into firewood.

I had been aware of Amzil's children spying on me all day. The muffled giggles of the older two had betrayed them as they hid around the corner of her house and took turns peeking at me. Only the smallest child, a tiny girl, was honest in her complete curiosity. She stood squarely in the open doorway to gawk at me. I had not thought I remembered much of Yaril's babyhood. But looking at the child, I found I did. Yaril had stood like that, her babyish tummy thrust out before her. Yaril had turned her head and smiled shyly like that. When I stopped to wipe sweat from my neck, I smiled back at her. She squeaked and darted out of sight around the door. A moment later, she emerged again. I waved at her, winning a high-pitched giggle. As the sun was setting, the first threatened drops of rain came pelting down. Amzil emerged suddenly from her house, scooping the baby up in passing. She called out stiffly to me, "The food is ready."

It was the first time I'd been inside her home. There wasn't much to it. It was a single room, with log walls and a dirt floor. The hearth was rock plastered together with river clay. Their bed was a shelf across one side of the room. Other than the door, there was a single window with a crude wooden shutter. No glass. The only freestanding furniture was a bench by the hearth. The only table was a shelf in the corner with a washbasin on top of it and a water pitcher beside it. Clothing hung from pegs in the wall. Sacks on hooks and a few rough shelves held the food stores. There wasn't much.

I ate standing. The children sat on the floor, and Amzil sat on the bench. She ladled thin soup from a kettle hung over the fire. She served me first, the thin broth off the top and a single scoop of vegetables from the depths of the pot. She served herself the same, and then measured out a scoop for each child that left the ladle scraping the bottom of the kettle. The children got most of the bits of food; I didn't complain. She had a single mound of hearth bread. She broke it into five equal pieces and handed me one. We ate.

I savored the first spoonful of the warm broth. I tasted potatoes, cabbage, onion, and little else. As I had schooled myself to do, I ate slowly and enjoyed what I had. The bread was coarse, but good, for the flavor of the badly ground grain was stronger than if it had been made from fine flour. The texture was a good contrast to the thin soup. I saved the last bit of bread to wipe the final trace of soup from my bowl. Empty. I sighed and looked up to find Amzil regarding me curiously.

"Is something wrong?" I asked her. I was not unaware that her pistol rested on the bench beside her hip.

Her brow furrowed. "You're smiling."

I gave a small shrug. "Good food."

She scowled at me as if I were mocking her. "It wasn't good soup before I added enough water to stretch it for five." Little spots of anger danced in her brown eyes.

"Any food is better than none. And any food tastes good after a time of privation."

"Privation?"

"Hard times," I clarified.

Her eyes narrowed again. "You don't look like you've ever known 'privation.'"

"You'd be surprised," I said gently.

"Maybe. Here, we've eaten the same thing for so long, I don't even taste it anymore." She rose abruptly, picking up the pistol as she did so. "Children, stack your bowls. You, you can sleep in the shed with your horse. The roof doesn't leak much." It was a clear request that I now leave her house.

I cast my thoughts desperately for an excuse to stay a bit longer in the light and warmth of the small home. "I've no real food to share. But I still have tea left in my panniers."

"Tea?" Her eyes were distant. "I haven't tasted tea since . . . well, since we left Old Thares to follow Rig's coffle."

"I'll get it," I offered instantly. I rose, moving my bulk carefully through the flimsy furnishings of the small room and out the rattly door into the chill night.

I'd left Clove picketed in an alley to get whatever graze he could on the coarse grass and weeds there. Now I moved him into what had once been someone's home. He barely fit through the door, but he seemed grateful to be out of the wind and rain. I'd stowed my panniers and tack there earlier. Now, considering the desperate poverty of Amzil's neighbors, I decided to take my panniers with me into the house.

I set them on the floor in the middle of her room, and knelt down beside them. Her children crowded close as I opened them and rummaged inside. Amzil stood back but looked no less curious. I found the block of black tea. As I opened its wrapper, Amzil caught her breath as if I were unveiling treasure. She had already put a kettle of water to heat, and it seemed a year before the water bubbled to a boil. She had no teapot, so we used my own small kettle to brew the tea. The children huddled around it as if they were worshipping it as Amzil poured the boiling water over the shriveled leaves. The delightful aroma of brewing tea blossomed with the steam. "The leaves are unrolling!" her son, Sem, exclaimed in wonder. We waited in silent anticipation for the tea to brew. Then Amzil ladled out bowls for each of us. I lowered myself carefully to the dirt floor, to join the children in their half-circle around the fire. I cupped the bowl in my hands, feeling the warmth of the liquid through the rough pottery.

Even the baby, Dia, had a small bowl of tea. She sampled it, scowled at its dark taste, and then watched the rest of us sipping. She sipped again, pursing pink baby lips over its bitterness. I smiled at her solemn expression as she imitated us. The child wore a simple robe, obviously sewn from the remnants of an adult's garment. It was well made, but the rough cloth looked more suited to a man's trousers than a little girl's robe. Amzil cleared her throat. I looked away from her baby to find Amzil frowning at me warily.

"So. You came here from Old Thares," I said, when the silence began to feel awkward.

"That we did." She didn't sound inclined to talk.

"You're a long way from home, then. It must be very different for you here." I prodded her with words, trying to start a conversation. She turned the tactic against me.

"Have you ever been to Old Thares?"

"I have. I went to school there for a season." I would not

mention the academy. I had no desire to tell the long tale of why I was no longer there.

"School. Ah. Never been myself. And if you were in a school, you never saw my city." She was adamant.

"I didn't?" I asked cautiously.

"Do you know the part of town down by the river docks? Some folk call it the Rats' Nests?"

I shook my head, inviting her to go on.

"Well, that's where I come from. I lived all my life there, until I come here. My father was a ragpicker. My mother sewed. She could take old rags my father gathered, wash and press them, and turn them into the best things you ever saw. She taught me. A lot of folks throw away stuff that just needs a good washing and a bit of mending to be fine again. Some will throw out a whole shirt for a stain down the sleeve, as if you couldn't make something nice out of the part that was good. Rich people waste a lot of things." She said it self-righteously, as if challenging me to disagree. I said nothing.

She sipped from her tea, then admitted, "My husband was a thief." Her mouth twisted on the word. "He was a thief like his father and grandfather before him. He used to laugh and say that it was the good god's will that he follow in his father's footsteps. When our boy was born, he even talked about how he would teach him to cut purses when he was older. But then Rig was caught and the choice was put to him—lose his hand or come east to work on the King's Road."

She sighed. "It's my fault we're here. I talked him into coming east. They made it sound so good. Hard work for my husband for two years, but then our own home in the town that they'd build along the King's Road. They made it sound so good. We'd have own little house and garden in town, and land of our own outside of town. They told us any man could learn to hunt and that made meat free, and with what we'd grow in our garden, we'd never be short of food again. And they said the King's Road would flow golden with travelers and trade, right past our door. I imagined that we would have a wonderful new life."

She pursed her lips and stared into the fire. For a moment, caught in that old dream, she looked much younger, and with a jolt I realized she probably wasn't much older than I was. Her musing look changed to a scowl. "It's getting late," she warned me without looking at me.

It wasn't just that I feared she would send me away from the fireside. I truly wanted to hear the rest of her tale. I steeled myself to the loss and then said, "I've a tiny bit of sugar left in my panniers. Shall we have one last cup of sweet tea to end the night?"

"Sugar!" the elder girl said in wonder. The other two children looked puzzled.

Thus I bought myself a longer stay by the fire. Amzil pulled her chair closer to the hearth and told out her sad tale: the long miserable journey east, camping each night by the road, the callousness of the guards who forced them on each day, the primitive conditions in the camps. I'd seen the shackled lines of prisoners moved past our home in Widevale. Summer after summer, the coffles of convict workers and their military guards had passed my home. I'd always suspected it was a miserable journey, but Amzil's tale of hardship made it real. As she spoke, her elder daughter's face grew grave, obviously reliving those memories with her mother.

"We traveled to the end of the road. There was just a work camp here, with other men working off their crimes. There was no town with little houses and gardens for us! Just canvas stretched over boards and rough huts and dirt and work. Tents to sleep in, ditches to piss in, and the river for hauling water. Some new life! But they told us we were 'home' now, that it was up to us to make it into a town. They gave each household some canvas and some basic food and tools, and my husband and I put up what shelter we could. And the next morning, they put the men to work on the King's Road, and left the families to cope as best we could."

By day, the men left their families to go to work on the road. By night, they returned, too tired to do anything more than sleep. "Or curse," Amzil said wearily. "My husband often cursed the liars who'd brought us here. Toward the end, Rig cursed me, too, for believing their lies and wanting to come. It was all my fault, he said. He said that even with one hand, he could have provided better for us in Old Thares.

"While they were building this stretch of road, it wasn't too bad. It was noisy and dusty, of course. Heavy wagons and big horses everywhere. They dug and scraped and leveled and measured the land over and over. It seemed silly to me, the way they dug down into the earth to set down big stones, and then filled up between them with smaller stuff. And the amount of time they spent tamping it down! Why the road couldn't just be a wide path, I don't know. But they built it up in what everyone started calling an agger, with a lot of gravel, and all sorts of men with measuring sticks, always worrying about leveling things and making drains. I never knew what all went into a road before then." Amzil's dark hair had pulled free of the string she used to tie it back. It was feathering around her face, blending her features with the shadows behind her.

"But at least there were lots of folks here then. There was a big kitchen set up to feed everyone, and we could all go there for a meal once a day. The food was plain and not very good, but as you said, any food is better than none. And there were more people here, families as well as the other workers and the guards. There were other women to talk to while I did the wash at the river, and other women to help me when my baby came. The women who were already here when we arrived had learned a bit of how to manage, and they taught us. But most of us didn't know a thing about how to live outside a city. We tried. Most of the houses you see around here, women built. And some fell down faster than we put them up, but we had each other to help." She shook her head and closed her eyes for a moment. "Then it all went bad at once."

Without asking her I added the last of the hot water to the uncoiled tea leaves in the bottom of the pot. It made a final pale tea. I divided what remained of my sugar equally among the five bowls and carefully dippered the weak tea over it. The children watched me as if I were stirring molten gold.

"What happened?" I asked as I put Amzil's cup into her hands.

"Rig had an accident. A heavy stone fell off a wagon and crushed his foot. He couldn't work anymore. So even though his time wasn't up, they let him stay at home here with us all day. I was glad to have him here at first. I thought he could help me a bit, could mind the children while I tried to make things better for us. But he didn't know how to do anything around a house and his foot wouldn't heal. It only got more painful, and he had a fever that came and went. The pain made him mean, and not just with me." She glanced at her elder daughter and old anger flashed in her eyes. She shook her head. "I didn't know what to do for him. And he hated me by then anyway." Her eyes went past me to the fire and all feeling emptied out of them.

"Two days before he died, the guards said it was time to move camp. The prisoners who had worked off their time and their families could stay here and build a new life, they said. A lot of them decided to move on with the work crew anyway. But those who stayed got a shovel, an ax, a saw, and six bags of different kinds of seed. And they gave us what they said was two months of flour, oil, and oats. But it didn't last our family more than twenty days." She shook her head again.

"I did my best. I dug holes and planted those seeds. But maybe it was the wrong time or maybe the seed was bad or maybe I did something wrong. Not many plants came up, and a lot of the ones that grew got eaten by rabbits or just died off. I wasn't the only one who didn't know how to grow vegetables. Before too long, people just started to leave. Nothing here to hold them, I guess. Some of them lasted the first winter. Others didn't, and we buried them. When spring came, pretty much everyone who could got up and left, heading back west, trying to get back to a place where they knew how to live. Some of us couldn't go. Kara might be able to walk a full day, but Sem and Dia are too small to walk that far, and I couldn't carry them both. I knew that if I started walking, at least one of them would die on the way. But maybe that would have been better than staying here. Here we are, winter's closing in again, and we have even less this time than we had last year."

A long silence fell and then she said, "I fear we're going to die here. And my biggest dread is that I'll die before my children do. And there will be no one left to protect them from whatever comes next."

I had never heard such black despair. Worse was to see in the children's eyes that they fully understood what their mother said. My heart spoke. "I'll stay a day or two, if you want. I can at least help you make this place tight for the winter."

She looked at me flatly and then asked with acid sweetness, "And what will you want from me in exchange?" Her eyes traveled over me disdainfully. I knew what she thought I would ask of her, and that it disgusted her. I also read in her eyes that if that were what I demanded, she'd give it to me, for the sake of her children. She made me feel like a monster.

I spoke slowly. "I'd like to sleep in here, near the fire instead of out in the shed. And I'd like a day or two of rest and grazing for my horse, and some time out of the saddle. That's all."

"Is it?" She was skeptical. Her mouth pinched again, bringing out the cat in her again. "If that's all, I'll say yes to that, then."

"That's all," I said quietly, and she nodded sharply to the deal we had struck.

· She and her children slept in the only bed, across the room from the fire. She put herself between me and her children, and her pistol between her and me. I slept on the floor by the fire.

The next day, I built a wood crib for the firewood, so I could stack it so it would stay dry. It was crudely built from salvaged wood and nails, but it worked. I put a roof over it to keep the snow off the firewood. Amzil and Kara stacked the wood between the supports as I showed them while the other children played nearby. I found good thick logs and cut them into stout chunks. "These will burn a long time, once you've got a bed of coals going," I told her. "Save them for the worst nights, when the snow is deep and the cold hard. Until then, use up the small stuff, and whatever else you can forage for yourself."

"I've had one winter here. I think I know how to manage," Amzil said stiffly.

"Probably better than I do," I conceded grumpily. I'd worked all morning. My shirt was stuck to me with sweat despite a chill wind blowing off the rain-soaked hills. Hunger gnawed at my guts. I couldn't stand it anymore. I rolled my shoulders and stretched. I leaned the ax up against my chopping block.

"Where are you going?" Amzil demanded suspiciously.

"Hunting," I decided abruptly.

"With what?" she asked. "For what?"

"With a sling, for whatever I can get," I replied. "Rabbits, birds, small game."

She shook her head and folded her lips, obviously thinking I was wasting time when I could be cutting more wood. But the morning's work had already convinced me that I'd need a more substantial meal than watery soup. I'd begun thinking of food, against my will, and had suddenly become aware of the birds calling to one another.

"Can you do that?" she asked me suddenly. "Kill birds with a sling?"

"We'll see," I said. "I used to be able to."

I was fatter than I'd been as a boy, and out of my territory. Dawn and dusk were the best times to hunt, and this was neither. I tried the woods first, where tree trunks that spoiled my swing and tiny branches that deflected my missiles frustrated me. From there, I moved to the logged-off hillside behind the town, and there I did better, braining a rabbit that foolishly stood up on its hind legs to see what I was.

It wasn't much of a hunter's bag, but Amzil seemed delighted with it. She and the children gathered round me as I gutted and skinned it and cut it up for the pot. While she took it inside to start it cooking, I scraped the skin and stretched it as tightly as I could before tacking it, skin side up, on a board to dry. "You'll need to keep this out of the weather," I told her. "Once it's dried, it will be hard and stiff. You'll have to work it, rolling it slowly until it softens up again. But it will give you a rabbitskin with the fur on. Four or five of these sewn together would make a blanket for the little one."

I'd kept back the sinew from the rabbit's hind legs. I showed it to her. "This makes the best snares. There was a lot of rabbit sign out there. If you set two or three snares each evening, you'd have a fair chance of having some meat in your diet on a regular basis."

She shook her head. "They're too smart. I've seen rabbits out there, at dawn and in the evening. But I've never been able to catch one, and the traps I've made don't hold them."

"What kind of traps?"

"I dug holes for them to fall into. I caught a couple of babies like that in the spring. But the others soon learned to go around them."

My amused smile offended her. I quickly wiped it from my face. *She knows nothing of rabbits, or of hunting,* I thought to myself. Her skills from her life in the city were useless here. That wasn't her fault, and I shouldn't look down on her for trying. At the same time, I could not help feeling a bit superior. "We'll make the snare lines very fine, so they're almost invisible. And I'll show you how to know where the rabbit will lift its head as it comes down the trail and out of the brush. That's the best place to hang a snare, to make sure you get a quick, clean kill."

"The young ones I caught were alive. I wanted to try to cage them and breed them, like people do pigeons and doves in the city. But . . ." She glanced at the children. "Sometimes meat today is more important than saving for a tomorrow."

I found myself nodding. She was right. With the right kind of trap, live rabbits would provide her with a ready source of meat. "I might be able to come up with a pit trap that would work, then," I offered.

"We'll set some of both," she decided firmly.

I was feeling rather satisfied with myself as I followed her and the children into the little house. The rabbit was simmering with onion and potato in a pot near the edge of the fire. The aroma of the cooking meat assaulted my senses. I almost lost myself in it. Then I saw my panniers open on the floor. All my possessions were stacked around them. I could not keep the chill from my voice as I asked her, "Did you find what you were looking for?"

She met my gaze, and her cheeks went a bit pink. But she did not look guilty. Instead, her chin came up. "Yes. Your washing and mending. That seemed a fair trade to me for the work you've done with the wood and the hunting. And when I found you had salt in there, I took some for cooking the meat. As you were going to be eating it alongside us, I thought nothing of it. Do you find fault with it?"

I didn't like it. Everything I had in the world was in those panniers, including my journal and what money I had. A sneaking part of me resolved that at my earliest opportunity, I'd make certain it was still there. She was meeting my eyes in a very direct way. I took a breath. She'd meant well and she was honest about it. Traveling can make a person suspicious. "It took me aback, yes."

"It was something I was *willing* to do for you." From the emphasis she put on the words, she made it clear that there were other things she'd be unwilling to do for me. "My mother was a good seamstress and she taught me well. She sewed for some of the best families in Old Thares. She knew how to make clothing fit a . . . portly man. And I learned it at her knee. I can make your garments more comfortable on you. So you can chop wood without straining the seams."

Why was it so hard to say, "Thank you. I'd welcome that"? I suppose it was because I wished she could see me as something other than a fat stranger who wanted to lie with her. I had to admit that in many ways, it was a fair appraisal of me. It wasn't that I was infatuated with her or wished her to like me. She was pretty enough, in a weary way, and she was a woman, and the first woman other than my sister I'd spent any appreciable time with in weeks. That was all, I told myself. It was simple proximity and honest lust. A man didn't have to be ashamed of that, as long as he didn't force himself on a woman. It was just the way a man was made.

That evening was both more comfortable and less easy. The food was more substantial, and once again we had tea to finish with, even if there was no sugar. But she had told me her story the night before, and I had no wish to tell her mine, so talk was scarce. Firelight was the only light in the room. We sought our beds early. I lay on the floor, rolled in my blanket. I tried not to think of her, soft and warm and only a few steps away. For all my harsh training to be a soldier, I thought to myself, this family lived in harder circumstances than anything I'd ever experienced. There were no evening pastimes for the children, no storybooks or music, no toys save what they had invented for themselves. Amzil had little education; I doubted she could read. Whatever culture she had absorbed growing up in the grand city of Old Thares would be denied to her children, growing up in poverty in this wilderness. It was grim to speculate on their future, not just during the harshness of the coming winter but for all the years after that.

I closed my eyes, but I couldn't shut down my thoughts. She'd as much as admitted that she'd whored for passing travelers last winter to get food for herself and the children. With such an example before them, what would Kara and little Dia expect of life? What sort of a man would Sem grow to be, watching his mother sell herself to support him? It was tawdry and disgusting. Yet when she looked at her children, her gaze was familiar, for it was the same way my mother had always looked at us. In the last year, I'd had my eyes opened to my mother's place in our world, and had come to realize that in many ways she had sacrificed her own interests to ours. The seeds of thought that Epiny had sown in my mind were growing in uncomfortable ways. My mother had always been my mother and my father's wife. I don't think I'd ever stopped to wonder who else she might have wanted to be, outside of those roles. Now I'd glimpsed, several times, how she had had to bow her head to my father's decisions for her children, and witnessed more clearly how she had battled him for a say in our lives. She'd never expected to be a nobleman's wife; she'd been married off to the soldier son of a good family, with no higher expectation than that he would advance in his career as an officer. When she'd left her father's house, she would have believed that eventually, when my father retired from the military, she would return to Old Thares, to live at the Burvelle mansion there, to visit her childhood friends, to go to the theater and enjoy the cultural and social events of her home city. Instead, my father's elevated status had meant that she lived far from the capital city and that her social friendships were limited to women similarly uplifted. She had traveled to visit her family in the city perhaps once every five years, and only after we children had become mostly self-sufficient.

Until then, she had not left us for a single day. Was that what it meant to be a mother?

I shifted uncomfortably on the packed earth floor. The cold from it seeped up through my blankets and made me ache. I tried to fall asleep, but my eyes kept opening, to stare around the dismal little room. I didn't want to think about my mother and how life had trapped her in a similar way to how life had trapped Amzil. That led to wondering how deep of a trap I had fallen into myself. Here I lay, the son of a nobleman, a soldier son destined to be an officer, and I'd begged shelter and food from an ignorant seamstress, the widow of a thief. And I'd been grateful for what I'd received.

Clove had had a couple of days' rest and some grazing. The days were getting cold and the nights even colder. It was stupid to linger here. The sooner I reached my journey's end at Gettys, the sooner I would know what awaited me there. There was a danger to waiting too long. If the commander there didn't accept me for enlistment, I'd probably have to winter there, and then ride out in spring to try my luck at other citadels and forts. There was no guarantee that any regiment would have me. My thoughts spiraled into darker speculation. If no regiment would have me, what then? What if I had to face being a soldier son who could not be a soldier, a noble's son who had been disowned? A brother who had not kept his word to send for his sister? A fat man who begged shelter and food of strangers? A man who looked at a woman with interest, only to have her turn away in disgust?

I didn't much like any of my possible new identities. I made an abrupt decision. I would leave at first light tomorrow.

CHAPTER THIRTEEN

BUEL
HITCH

I stayed with Amzil nearly a month. I think that almost every night I made a resolution to leave in the morning. But every morning brought some small task that I thought I could do before I left. And somehow each of those tasks led to others. It was always the task of the day that I stayed for; I never allowed myself to think how pleasant it was to have the company of this woman, how enjoyable I found it to be the one who could provide. My father had rubbed my nose in my failures for so long that even I was astonished at how much I could do for this orphaned and destitute family. It felt good.

It began with keeping my promise to show her how to snare rabbits. I convinced myself that I had to stay an extra day to be sure that the snares were working and that she knew how to reset them. I spent the afternoon of that day cutting more wood and mending the roof of the shed that Clove had been using as a stable. Midway through that task, the man who had turned me away from his door only a few days before came to ask if he could barter with us for a few days of Clove's labor. The man had devised a sort of plow and hoped that with the use of Clove's strength, he could plow a much larger garden area for the next spring. I pointed out to him that it was the wrong season for plowing. He retorted that he was not stupid, but that breaking the soil now might make it easier for him to plant a larger area next spring.

Fabricating a harness for Clove proved to be the trickiest part of the project. Yet by evening's end, and with a lot of sweat, Merkus and I had managed to break the sod on a quarter-acre of land. It was rocky soil, threaded through with old roots. A good part of our toil went to chopping side roots so that Clove could jerk old stumps free of the earth. Merkus traded us a sack of potatoes and half a day of his labor the next day.

So I had little choice but to decide to stay for another day. Our evening repast seemed very rich, for in a surge of optimism, Amzil had used the meat from two rabbits and five whole potatoes to make the meal. We had caught a total of three rabbits, so I showed her how to hang the extra meat in the chimney to smoke it and preserve it. The three rabbitskins joined the first one to dry.

The extra food seemed to give the children more energy. They were not as willing to go to bed that night, so we sat up for some time by the fire. Amzil surprised me by telling the children several stories to pass the time. Then, after she had settled them into bed, we sat up a short time longer talking about what projects were most crucial for the coming winter.

When Merkus arrived the next morning to work off his debt, he and I tightened the roof and door of Amzil's house before moving on to make the roof of the shed sound. Long before noon, I had earned his grudging respect. Over the next few days, Clove's great strength made short work of tugging down several ramshackle structures so that we could reduce them to usable timbers. Once I had stockpiled the lumber that I thought I could use for Amzil's dwelling and the adjacent shed, I put Merkus in our debt once more by using Clove to haul a number of heavy timbers down to where he wished to use them.

All this activity roused the curiosity of the other scattered dwellers. The old man and his nagging wife came to the door of their hut to watch Clove pass. I discovered there was one other family in the otherwise deserted town, a man and a woman of middle years with two half-grown children and a baby. They watched us from afar, but did not speak to us that day.

Amzil and I checked the snares together that evening. We had only caught one rabbit, but she still seemed very pleased with it. Under my guidance, she moved the snares to fresh locations on some of the many rabbit trails throughout the stump field.

"If the game becomes scarce here, then you can always set snares along the river, especially in the wintertime." I told her. "Watch for the paths where animals go to water. Set them there."

"The river freezes along its bank in winter," she told me.

"There will still be tracks to it. You'll see."

Kara had tagged along with us, and to my surprise Amzil had the child set the final snare. She seemed very young to me to be doing such a task. Nonetheless, I held my tongue, suspecting that in this, Amzil probably knew best. Small as she was, the sooner Kara stepped up to help provide for her family, the better they would do.

The cottage became a snugger place as each day passed. We mixed grass, moss, and mud, and chinked the gaps between the logs. With our salvaged wood, we put a floor in the cabin. I hunted each morning with my sling. My best day was when a lucky shot brought down a goose that I'd startled off the river. It was fat. Grease had never tasted so good to me. Amzil caught every drop of it before it could drip into the fire and saved it to flavor the lean rabbit that made up most of our meals.

Our days began to have a pattern. Each morning I hunted. I brought my kills home to Amzil, and she cooked them. In the afternoons, I did whatever I thought best to improve her cottage. It was rough, crude work for the most part, but even so, it made a difference. A slab of wood and three stick legs made a stool. I longed for an awl, but managed to bore and whittle the leg holes with my knife. I made a low table so that the children could sit on the floor in front of the fire and have their meals more comfortably. Every day, Amzil set aside a part of my catch to either smoke or dry as jerked meat. It pleased me to watch her little larder grow full. I built her another shelf.

Three times in that period, I saw travelers pass. The couriers who served the king passed every day, but other than them there was little traffic on the road this time of year. Once it was a train of wagons pulled by oxen, heading toward Gettys. The men driving them were hard-eyed, and both the first and the last wagon had guards perched on the wagon seats, long guns slung across their knees. Plainly they wanted nothing to do with anyone. We stared at one another, but no one called out a greeting. Another day, it was a man riding a horse and leading two mules laden with furs. He was headed west on the road. He nodded to my "Good day" but kept on his way. And the other traveler I saw was a tinker with a wagon pulled by a mismatched team. The wagon was painted with pictures of his wares, but the bright panels were thick with dust and the tall yellow wheels of his wagon were crusted with mud. I was on the edge of the stump field. I waved my arms at him, hoping he'd stop. I wanted to see what tools he had for sale. He waved back at me, but then stirred up his team to a trot, plainly disinclined to pause. I shouted after him, but he was gone, leaving only dust hanging over the road in his wake.

Often the children would come out to watch me at my tasks. I began to teach them the nursery rhymes I knew, the counting songs and memory games. They liked the one about the farmer calling his five goats. Kara wanted to learn how my sling worked. I made her a smaller one, and set her targets. She became a fair shot, but Amzil seemed reluctant to let me take her out to hunt. I could not decide if she did not trust me alone with the child or did not think it a proper task for her.

I cut firewood every day. It became a wall between Amzil's cottage and the hut where the old man lived. At night, our fire was more generous and it filled the small space with both warmth and light. One night I took it upon myself to be the storyteller, and it flattered me that Amzil listened as attentively as her three small children. I told them two tales that my mother had told me when I was a boy, and then I found myself telling a story that I did not remember hearing, yet I knew I was not making up. It was the tale of a young man who sought to avoid doing a task that his mother had given him, and of all the misfortunes that befell him as a result of his attempt to ignore his duty. The ending was, in a way, quite comical, for when the boy finally surrendered and went to do his task, he found that his mother had already done it. The children seemed to enjoy the story, but after Amzil had put them to bed she said to me, "That was a rather strange story." Her tone made it clear that she did not quite approve of it.

"It's a story that the Speck tell to their children," I said, and then wondered how I had come by such knowledge. "I think it's to teach them that some tasks are so important, they cannot be ignored. Someone will do them."

Amzil raised her eyebrows at me. "And your telling it makes it all the stranger," she said with even greater disapproval. A short time later, she sought her bed with the children, and I rolled myself in my blankets to sleep before the fire.

That night I dreamed of the Tree Woman's forest. I walked alone down paths where once we had walked as a couple. It was autumn in the forest and the leaves on the deciduous trees were turning. I had never seen such a spectacle. In the area of the plains where I had grown up, there were groves of trees along the river or following the streambeds. In autumn, their leaves turned a soggy brown and hung on the branches until the frost and falls of snow took them down. Never before had I experienced walking in a forest where the leaves had gone yellow and gold and scarlet. When I lifted my eyes, the brilliance of their color against the bright blue autumn sky was shocking. The leaves had already begun to forsake the trees; there were drifts of them across the path, and as I waded through them they rustled around my feet. There was an incredible smell in the air, a rich odor of decomposing leaves and fresh rain and the promise of a sharp frost in the night to come. I felt alive, and in the strange clarity of that dream I felt that this life was larger and brighter and sharper-edged than in my waking world. I was going somewhere. I could not have said where, and yet I was hurrying to get there, eager to arrive. I went down a hillside through a forest of white-trunked birches with golden leaves fluttering in the autumn breeze. At the bottom, I came to a swampy place where high-bush cranberries dandled their translucent scarlet fruit below palm-sized leaves that had gone red with the frost. Willows grew there, and their long narrow leaves had gone a different shade of red. I cupped a scant handful of the fruit and tasted it. The berries burst in my mouth with the sweet of summer ending and the sharp tang of winter yet to come. I chewed the seeds as I walked on, deeper into her world.

Her world it was. I came to her at last, supine on the earth. My sword had bitten deep into her trunk, and she had fallen, just as a tree would have crashed to earth if most of the trunk had been severed. The stump of her body stood and her torso had fallen beside it, but that torso was still connected to the stump by a thick bend of bark. By that, she lived. She was somehow a great tree and she was an immense woman, with all the attributes of both. She had stretched her length out on the forest floor when she fell, a glorious statue toppled from its pedestal. Her torso and head melded with the fallen portion of the tree. The mass of her hair ranged from glossy curls around her face to flowing tresses that merged with the rough bark of the trunk beyond her head. Like a nursery log, a sapling was sprouting from her, a slender tree growing up from between her breasts. The felling of her tree had created a clearing in the forest canopy. Light spilled from above to warm the earth. A host of plant life had sprung up around her. I knelt beside her, knees cushioned by moss and leaves. I took her hand. "So I didn't kill you. You didn't die," I said with gladness.

She smiled up at me. "I told you. Such as I do not die in that way. We go on."

Cautiously, I set a hand to the smooth bark of the slender sapling. "This is you?" I asked her.

She put her hand over mine, closing my fingers around the growing trunk. "It is me."

Wonder caught me. Life pulsed in the sapling. Skin to bark, I could feel her magic at work as she transferred her power into the new life springing up from her bosom. Even in that place, a shiver of awe ran over me.

She had shifted her gaze to speak to me. Now she looked up at the infinite blue sky above us. Her long hair coiled and looped around her head like a corona. "Soldier's Boy, you know you have a task. It was given to you by the magic. I know what the task is. You are to save us. But only you know how you are to accomplish that. That was why the magic was given to you. Not so that you might amuse yourself, but because you are the one who would know what you must do to accomplish your task. With power comes responsibility. You understand this." Her voice was gentle but her words were absolute.

"Of course I do," I said readily, though until that moment, I do not think that I had.

"You must come to where the destruction is. See it for yourself. Then tell me how you will defeat it. It is my weakness that I hunger to know these things. When I walked in the world that you now tread, I was a curious woman. Even here, even now, that curiosity remains. I know the magic, I trust the magic, and still I want to know. Will not you tell me?"

"When I know for myself what it is that I must do to defeat the end of our world, then I will tell you. I promise you that."

She relaxed more deeply into her mossy couch. Ferns had sprouted around her where she had fallen. The fallen leaves of autumn had drifted around her supine form, cushioning her curves with their gold. I cannot describe how glorious she was. When I looked on her, I saw her as a Speck would. She was not fleshy, but lush; her rounded belly, her voluptuous breasts, the softness of her face all spoke of a time of plenty, of fruition and harvest. "I hold you to your promise, Soldier's Boy. Do not tarry. There are others, less patient than I, who think that a swifter solution must be reached. I have told them of you, in dreams and visions. Nonetheless, they will soon take steps of their own to rid our lands of the invaders. They say that the dance has failed. They say it is time to use the intruders' own ways against them."

A deep foreboding rose in me, tainting my dream. I smelled smoke, and the fallen leaves suddenly became sodden and black and rotting. I sank into them. All around me, the forest became a cemetery of snaggled stumps and bare, oozing earth. The tree woman sagged into a rotting corpse. Her lips, mottled with mold, tore as she spoke her last words to me. "The magic was not given to you to use for yourself. Be wary of that temptation. Tarry no longer, but come to us. Our need is great."

And then she was gone, flesh and bones sinking into a swamp of rot that was not the healthy compost of a living forest but the stink of too many dead things left heaped in a pile. I tried to get away, but my feet and legs sank into the muck. I struggled wildly, wallowing deeper. It reached my thighs, and with infinite loathing I felt it close around my loins and lap against my belly. I tried to open my eyes, knowing that I dreamed, but no matter how I contorted my face, I could not waken myself. I gave a sudden wild cry of absolute despair.

I think my own shout awakened me. It was small comfort at first, for I was sprawled in mud and leaves and surrounded by ghostly stumps. Rain was falling all around me. I was wet, cold, and completely disoriented. How had I got here? The moon glided briefly from the shelter of the clouds and granted me a gray wash of light. I staggered to my feet and wrapped my arms around myself, shivering. I was barefoot, and my clothes were coated with mud and dead leaves. My hair, long grown out of a soldier's cut, dangled wet on my brow and dripped into my eyes. When I pushed it back from my face, I smeared my forehead with muck from my wet, gritty hands. I cursed myself for an idiot for making it worse. I stumbled back through the storm and the treacherous stump field to Amzil's door. It was closed tight, with the latch string pulled inside; I wondered if I'd shut it behind me when I went sleep walking, or if Amzil had wakened to a draft and closed it.

I wanted to pound on it and gain swift admission to the dry fireside. The thought of waking not only Amzil but also her children dissuaded me. Reluctantly, I sought the shed. I was glad we'd tightened up the roof. It was dry inside, and Clove's huge body radiated warmth into the small space. In the darkness, I found the saddle blanket and made a rough bed for myself until dawn. Then I rose, cold and stiff. I took Clove out and hobbled him in deep grass near the river's edge so he could graze. I went for a walk along the riverbank until I was sure that Amzil would be awake. Then I returned to her cottage.

"You're up early," she observed softly. The children were still sleeping.

"Fish are jumping after mosquitoes in the shallows of the river. If we had fishing tackle, you could have a nice breakfast on mornings like this."

She smiled sourly. "If I had fishing tackle. If I had a net. If I had seed, or a loom, or yarn, or fabric. There are so many ways I could better our lot, if I had even the most basic tools to begin. But I don't, and I've nothing to trade or sell, and even if I had something to trade, it would take me days to walk to a marketplace, and I'd have to take the children with me. I've had months to think my situation through, over and over. There's no reason for a town to be here. There's nothing to make people come here. It's just a place to pass by on your way to somewhere else. I have no way to acquire even the most basic things I'd need to make a life here. Perhaps if my husband had lived, we could have managed, for one of us could make the long trip to Gettys while the other stayed here with the children. But I cannot take them so far alone. Sometimes I think that was what the king intended. He took all the poor folk who broke the laws to live, and sent us out here to die."

Her words nudged my dormant loyalty to the king. "I don't think that was his intent. I believe he truly thought you could make a new beginning here. He spoke of the road becoming a great river of trade between west and east, and of

towns springing up along it and becoming centers of commerce. When more people begin to travel the road, there
will be trade opportunities. Even as it is now, any sort of an
inn here would be welcome by travelers, I'm sure."

"An inn." She looked at me with tried patience. "That's an
old idea. There *was* an inn here, for a very short time. You'll
find the burned timbers at the east end of town."

"What happened to it?"

She sighed with exasperation. "It was burned down by
angry patrons who claimed they had been robbed while they
slept."

"Were they?"

She shrugged one shoulder and looked almost guilty. "I
don't know. Perhaps. Probably." She poked at the fire angrily, stirring the coals to flame as she added a small piece
of wood. "Do you forget who we are here? Do you forget
why the king chased us out of Old Thares? When you make
a town of pickpockets, thieves, murderers, and rapists, what
do you think will happen? What happens when a family of
thieves opens an inn?"

That silenced me for a time. I had not stopped to think
about what it would be like to settle in a town where the entire population consisted of criminals and their families. Unwillingly I asked, "Your neighbors. Were they . . . ?"

"Of course. Why do you think I live apart from them? That
old man Reeves? He was sent from the city for raping young
girls. His wife will tell you they all tempted him, if you let her
speak to you for more than five minutes. He strangled the last
one; that was how they caught him. Merkus, who you plowed
for? He murdered a man in a tavern fight. Teme and Roya, up
the hill with their youngsters? They were both in the jail. He
stole from the old woman he worked for, and Roya helped
him sell her furs and jewelry."

"But you are not a criminal. And travelers do pass this
way. Merchants, new recruits for Gettys, the soldiers, and
the prisoner workers they escort. Even if there is not yet
much traffic, there are enough people going by for you to
make something from their passage."

She glanced at me. "Pretend, for a moment, that you are a

woman alone with three small children. Some travelers might be glad of a clean bed and a warm room, even if I have no food to sell them. Some would pay for it, with coin or barter. But others would simply take whatever they wanted from me and be on their way. If I was lucky. Don't you see that I'd be tempting danger by opening my door to strangers? When the soldiers and the long prisoner trains pass, do you know what we do? We run down to the river and hide there until they have gone by. The soldiers who guard the prisoners know that this was a town made for criminals. They don't trust anyone who lives here, and they don't respect the lives of anyone who lives here."

"You have a gun," I pointed out.

She hesitated, opened her mouth to speak, closed it, and then said abruptly, "And they have many guns, and far more ammunition than I do. How do you imagine they would treat us if I killed one of them trying to defend what we have from them? Would any of my children survive? I doubt I would, and I don't like to think what their suffering would be after I'd died."

I had no reply to the grim picture she painted. She seemed to take angry satisfaction in my silence. She mixed two handfuls of coarse meal into a pot of cold water and set it over the wakened fire. Breakfast would be the same thin porridge she had cooked every morning since I arrived. I'd been intending to tell her that I'd be leaving that day. Suddenly, it seemed that I couldn't just yet, that there had to be something I could do for them before I went. I went out to check the snares.

We had one rabbit. But one of the other snares looked odd to me. A moment of considering it proved all Amzil's suspicions of her neighbors' were correct. The thrashed ground around the snare showed me that a rabbit had been caught there. Someone had come, taken it, and awkwardly reset the snare. Anger flamed through me. I wondered who would stoop so low as to steal from a woman and three small children. The answer came to me: anyone who was hungry enough. I moved the snare, and took our catch back to Amzil's cottage.

As I skinned it, my mind was spinning with thoughts.

There was so much I could do if I stayed here. I could teach her to use a sling. That would work on birds as well as rabbits. I could make a fish spear and show her how to use that. I was far from the wide plains where I had grown up, and I did not know as many of the plants here as I would have at home. But there were still some I knew. The roots of the cattails along the river; did she know she could dig them and grind them into a sort of meal? And the cottage next to her shed was not in terrible shape; I could patch the roof of it and tighten the walls. It would not be an inn, but it would be shelter she could rent to travelers in need, without bringing them under her own roof.

I suddenly understood my friend Spink's restlessness when he watched his elder brother run the family holdings and suspected that he could make a better job of it. I looked at Amzil and her children and her situation, and knew that with time and the strength of my hands, I could better things for all of them. I wanted to do that, in the same way that one wants to right a crooked picture on a wall, or smooth the upturned corner of a rug. To me, the tasks were relatively simple, and the benefits to Amzil and her children might be the difference between starvation and well, not prosperity, but at least less want.

For the first time in my life, I felt I might be free of the fate that the good god had decreed for me. I felt sinful even to consider that idea, and yet there it was. If, through no fault of my own, I could not find a place for myself in military service, then what was I to do? Become a beggar on the streets? Or make a place for myself somewhere, a place where I could be useful to others and take some satisfaction in my own achievements? The children were awake. Kara came out and squealed gleefully at the sight of the skinned rabbit. I gave it to her to take to her mother. Little Sem stood under my elbow and nearly got nicked by my knife as I scraped the hide clean and then added it to the other skins. He followed me as I walked past the shed to the next cottage. It was as poorly built as Amzil's, and had a decided lean to it. I walked all the way around it, the little boy at my heels. There was another cottage built just off the corner of the first one; it would be fairly simple to build a room to connect them into one, larger structure. The idea of an inn had taken hold in my mind, and it now seemed the inevitable answer to Amzil's situation. It was easy to dismiss her naysaying. She was a woman alone, and thus it had all appeared impossible to her. But if I stayed on, I could show her how it could be done. And with a man in charge, other men would be less prone to attempt to take advantage of her. I could do it. I could become her protector.

I pushed away the thought that tried to creep to the forefront of my mind: that once she had seen that I could both provide and protect, she might look on me with a more favorable glance.

I looked at the cottages with an engineer's eye, and shook my head. They were pathetic. Yet they could be made to serve, at least for now. With timbers and logs from the nearby abandoned huts, I could shore them up to make them last the winter. Surely winter travelers on this road would welcome any sort of a shelter for the night. And the room I would build to connect them would be level and strong, the heart of a new structure that would eventually rise in place of the old. Sem was at my heels as I entered the second cottage. I was pleased to find it had a very functional-looking fireplace and chimney. Like Amzil's home, the floor was of earth. A table with two broken legs leaned against a bed frame full of rotting straw and bugs. The table was beyond repair, but the bedframe was salvageable. I checked the inside walls of the cabin, testing the wood with my knife. Some rot, but not much. This structure was in much better condition than the first cottage, and I immediately decided I would begin my renovation here.

"Sem! Sem, where are you?" There was a frantic note to Amzil's cry.

"He's here with me! We're coming!" I called back to her, and Sem piped up, "We're coming!" in such an obvious imitation of me that I had to laugh. As we made our way through the weedy space between the huts, a very familiar smell suddenly rose to my nostrils. Looking down, I found that I was standing on the crushed remains of a small cabbage. I blinked, and recognized the top of a carrot, and there the rounded purple shoulders of a turnip pushing up from the weedy earth. We were standing in the remains of a badly choked vegetable garden. It looked as if the seeds had been randomly thrown on the soil and had sprouted haphazardly. I found another cabbage, not much bigger than my fist but sound. I gave it to Sem to carry, and pulled up both the turnip and the carrot. The carrot was a long, dark-orange root, gone woody in its second year of growth, and root maggots had left a trail on the turnip, but for all that, the good parts could be cut off and stewed down. I felt I had discovered treasure rather than some old and wormy vegetables.

I looked up from my knees to find an angry-looking Amzil bearing down on us. "What are you doing out here with my son?" she demanded.

"Seeing how sound this building is. Watch where you step! There's a vegetable garden gone wild here."

"You have no right . . . what?"

"We're standing in a grown-over vegetable patch. I stepped on one cabbage before I realized it. But Sem has another, and I found a carrot and a turnip, too."

Her eyes darted from her son holding the cabbage to me and back again. Conflicting emotions flashed across her face. "This is wonderful—but never again take my boy out of my sight without my permission."

The vehemence in her voice shocked me, and I realized that however comfortable I had become here, she still regarded me as a stranger. And dangerous.

"Sem followed me," I said quietly. I knew it was unreasonable to feel hurt or angry, yet in truth, I felt both.

"I'm . . . I'm sure he did. But I don't like any of my children to wander out of my sight. There are many dangers here in the wild country." It sounded like an excuse, not an apology.

"And you think I'm one of those dangers." I spoke flatly.

"You might be," she replied frankly.

"I'm not. Not to you or to your children. I thought I'd been helping you."

"You have. You did." She looked down at the small boy. He was frowning as he tried to follow our conversation, looking back and forth between us. "Sem, go home. There's porridge on the table for you. Eat it up."

The mention of food was enough to send the boy flying. He scampered off, still clutching the cabbage in his arms. When he was out of earshot, she looked back at me. Her expression was not unfriendly, but neither was it kindly. She spoke bluntly. "You have helped us. And in return, I've sewn your clothes for you, and allowed you to share our roof and fire, and whatever food we had. And I admit that it's thanks to you that we've had more food in the last few weeks than we've had for some time. But—well, but I don't wish to be in your debt. I don't want you to start thinking that because you've done things for us, we owe you something. Well, I mean, I know that I do, but I won't . . . that is—"

"I don't think you're a whore, Amzil. I won't try to buy you with coin or food. Nor would I do any harm to any of your children. You seem to think me some sort of a monster, capable of anything!" Then the hurt did break into my voice, despite my best efforts. She looked startled. I felt embarrassed. I looked away from her. I tried desperately to think of something to say that would change the topic. I cleared my throat. "Someone stole from us last night. They took a rabbit from one of our snares. They reset it, but poorly. I could tell what had been done."

"I'm not surprised." She spoke quickly, as if glad to talk of something new. "It was bound to happen." Then anger flared again in her voice. "But what can I do? If I stay up all night to watch the snares in the stump field, the rabbits won't come. And I'll be too tired to take care of the children by day. It's hopeless."

"Have you ever thought of trying to form an alliance with some of your neighbors?"

She gave me an incredulous glance. She began to walk back to her cottage and I followed her. "I told you what they are. Murderers, thieves, and rapists. I don't trust them."

"But your husband was a thief." I tried to speak the words gently, but they still sounded like an accusation. "Oh, look there," I added before she could reply. "Lettuce."

"It doesn't look like lettuce. It's tall with little leaves."

"It's gone to seed." I went down heavily on one knee in the sodden weeds. I broke the top off the plant and lifted it carefully, my hand cupped under the seed head. "You can save these and plant them next spring. Or you can dig up the ground and plant them now. The plants here either wintered over or reseeded themselves, so it didn't get cold enough here to kill them completely. Actually, if you plant some now, you might get an early crop in spring. And then plant the rest of the seed after that, for more lettuce later. But always leave a few plants in the garden to go to seed, so you'll have seed for the next season."

"Oh," she said faintly. She stopped walking and looked back at the overgrown garden. "I feel so stupid. It makes sense now."

"What?"

"That they gave us seed, and told us it should be enough to last us. I had nothing to plant this spring. I was lucky enough to find some onions and potatoes growing where I'd planted them last year. I thought I'd just missed them when I harvested them."

"It was a cruel thing they did, putting you out here without teaching you first how to grow a garden or catch a rabbit."

"They did give us some chickens. For a short time, we had eggs. Then someone stole them and ate them, I suppose. That happened soon after we first arrived, when more people lived here." She gave me a very uncomfortable glance. "Thank you. What's your name?"

I realized she'd never asked me and I hadn't told her. "Nevare Bur—" I stopped short. My father no longer claimed me. Did I wish to claim his name?

"Nevare Burr. Thank you, Nevare."

She said my name, and for a moment I felt an odd thrill, similar to the first time that Carsina had touched my hand. She was walking in front of me and could not see my cynical smile. Of course, Nevare. Fall in love with the first woman you befriend, simply because she is willing to say your name. Ignore how she looks at you; ignore how frightened she was just a few moments ago when she thought you had lured her child away. I forced myself to confront how desperately lonely I'd become. I was so alone. As alone, I reminded myself, as Yaril. I did not need to fall to a wild schoolboy infatuation with Amzil. I had my sister and her affection to sustain me. Instead of thinking how I could change Amzil's life if she allowed me to, I knew I should focus my efforts on creating a life for myself, one that would eventually allow me to send for Yaril.

Amzil hurried ahead of me; I walked more slowly. I stopped. I turned to look back at the two cottages that had, for a few moments, been in my imagination an inn. Yet, why not here? I asked myself. Why should I not build the inn, just as I had imagined it, but for myself and eventually for Yaril? And if my efforts here produced benefits for Amzil and her children as well, that would simply be an additional good. "I could stay here and build a life for myself," I said softly.

At my words, lightning flashed through me. I remembered my dream, all in that instant. In the next moment, I stood trembling in full daylight, possessed of a knowledge I did not want. I could not stay here. I couldn't build an inn or make a place for Yaril. I was supposed to go on, to the land of the Specks. If I did not, evil would befall me. No. Not just me. Evil would befall any who held me back from that quest.

The corollary to that axiom fell into place for me. Misfortune had befallen my home and family in Widevale because they had sought to keep me there. The plague had come to Widevale, and scoured me of my family because I had defied the magic. The magic had cut me free of my old life. I shook my head. It could not be true. It was a stupid uncivilized superstition, something an ignorant man or a savage might believe.

My gut cramped with guilt and pain.

I bent over, clasping my great wobbly belly in my hands, sickened with the knowledge that filled me as much as by the emptiness of the hunger that suddenly assailed me. It was not a hunger for simple sustenance. I needed to eat to feed the magic that dwelt in me. It demanded food, and it demanded that I continue on my way to Gettys, to the territory of the Specks.

"You. You! Help me! In the name of the king. Help me."

The voice was faint, both from distance and weakness in the man who called. I looked around me, and then lifted my eyes to look up the hillside, past the stump field to where the uncut trees began. A man stood there, leaning heavily on a tough little horse beside him. He was bearded and without a hat, dressed in rough, ragged clothing. His head wobbled on his shoulders. When he saw me looking at him, he took two steps toward me, and then collapsed. He rolled a short way and then lay still.

I ran toward him. For a very short way. Then I stopped, caught my breath, and hurried on as best I could, through the crooked lanes between the ramshackle houses and across the stump field and then up the steep rise of the hill. In all that time, the man did not move. When I reached him and knelt beside him, I saw he was a larger man than I'd thought. He'd finished his tumble flat on his back. His eyes were closed. His clothing was not ragged from long use, but hung in tatters where something had attacked him and torn his garments with its claws. His cavalla trousers were stained with blood and dirt. He'd bound rags from his shirt across his chest and his upper right arm. Lesser gashes scored his belly, and showed on his legs through his torn trousers. The cuts were crusted dark with scabs and soiled with leaves and dirt. It was hard to guess his age through his whiskers and shaggy hair, but I thought him a man of middle years. "Sir! Wake up!"

He groaned, his chest rising and falling with it. His eyes fluttered a bit and then opened. "Big cat got me," he said, as if I'd asked him. "I'd just downed a fat grouse. I was plucking it. Cat decided that me and the bird would make a nice meal for him."

"Let's get you down the hill and into the house."

"I got to get to Gettys. I was due there today. Supposed to report in."

I took his shoulders and raised him to a sitting position. He silently snarled his pain as I did so. "You're a scout?"

He caught a ragged breath. "Lieutenant Buel Hitch." He grunted with pain, and then found breath to speak again. "And by the king's authority, I can order you to help me. I got to get to Gettys."

"You don't have to order me. I'd help you anyway."

"I'm sure you would," he replied with tight sarcasm. "You just love the king and his soldiers, don't you?"

"I am loyal to my king. And as a second son, it is my fate to be a soldier. Not that I've had much success at it. But if you have finished insulting me, I'll take you down to where your injuries can be cleaned and properly tended."

He looked at me for a few moments. His hoarse breath sawed in and out of him. Then he said, "You're no convict. What are you doing in Dead Town?"

"I was passing through on my way to Gettys. I ran out of supplies. So I stopped for a few days, to barter work for food."

"This town, I'm surprised you got anything at all for your trouble, other than a rock behind the ear. Stoop down and let me get my arm across your shoulders. You're a big one, aren't you?"

There seemed little need to reply to that observation. I did as he asked, and once he had his grip, I grasped his belt and raised him to his feet. He swayed against me. I carried most of his weight, but he tried to walk. He gasped and groaned as we tottered along. It was slow progress down the hill. I glanced back to see his horse following us.

Halfway across the stump field, I shouted for Amzil to put water on to boil. I called twice before she came to the door of the cottage. Her eyes widened, and she darted back inside. When we approached the door, I was shocked to see her standing in it, her huge gun once more leveled at my midsection. "What?" I asked her.

"You're not bringing him in here." She spoke the words flatly.

"But he's hurt."

"This is my home. I've my children to protect. You're not bringing that stranger in here."

I just shook my head at her. Then I turned and started limping him toward the other hut I'd inspected that morning. "Put my panniers outside your door, then," I said, and did not bother to hide the disgust in my voice. Behind me, I heard the door of her cottage slam shut.

I took Lieutenant Hitch into the cottage that had the sound fireplace. I eased him down, and then went to the shed for Clove's saddle blanket. I made it into a flat pallet and then

fetched kindling and firewood from the pile I'd made for
Amzil. My panniers were outside her closed door, along
with a tumble of my other possessions I'd left inside her
home. The message was plain. I carried them all back to the
hut where the soldier waited.

"Looks like you pissed her off right good," he observed. I
couldn't tell if he was grinning or gritting his teeth with
pain.

"It's a talent I have with women," I told him.

He hissed through his teeth and then fell silent.

I made a fire, and then fetched water and set my small pan
over the flames. When the fire had warmed the room a little
and the water was hot, I helped him undress.

I tended the minor wounds first, washing the ragged
scratches as best I could. Every one of them was warm to
the touch and suppurating. He hissed and swore as I washed
them clean. The deeper ones bled a bit.

When I reached to undo the bandage on his chest, he
stopped my hand with his. "Got anything to eat or drink?"
he asked me shakily. "I could do with a bit of fortifying
before we take this on."

"I think I have a little bit of tea left. That's about it out of
what I can call mine."

"That would be good, then. There's some dried meat in
my saddlebags. Could you bring them in?"

I took the saddlebags from his horse's back, and then slipped
his bit so he could graze easily on the weeds between the huts,
carefully moving him away from the half-choked vegetable
garden. As I passed the garden again, I found two overgrown
carrots and tugged them from the ground. When I carried them
into the cabin, the lieutenant looked at me curiously. "Soup," I
explained. "They're too tough to eat any other way. With the
dried meat tossed in, they ought to stew up fine."

That was easier said then done. They were so woody I had
to chop them up with my hatchet. I cut them fine and tossed
them in a pot of hot water. I then went into Hitch's saddlebag.
He watched me, and as I took out a large packet tightly
wrapped in several layers of oilcloth, he said, "No. Not that
one. Put that one back." The second packet, wrapped in greasy

brown paper, proved to be the smoked meat. I took a slab of it
the size of my hand, chopped it fine, and added it to my carrots. By then my kettle was boiling. I made the lieutenant a cup
of hot tea and waited while he drank it. When he set down the
empty mug, he nodded to me. "Let's get at it," he said grimly.

I took out my untouched medical kit. Hitch's eyes widened at the sight of it. He clenched his teeth as he watched
me dissolve the healing salts in the hot water; he knew how
they would burn and sting, but also knew they were necessary. The bandaged claw slash across his chest was a nasty
one. The cat's claws had gone deep and the wound, unban-
daged, gaped open. It, too, was festering. I washed it out
with the warm salted water, an operation that left Hitch
hammering his fist against the dirt floor. He swore, but did
not cry out with the pain. "It should have been stitched," I
said. "I think it's too late to do it now."

"I know that. Do you think I'm an idiot? Or that I could
have stitched myself up one-handed out there in the dark?"

I bit my tongue and made no reply. Instead I smeared the
edges with salve and rebandaged it more firmly, strapping
the flesh back in place and hoping it would find a way to heal
together. The gash on his arm was similar, deep and gaping
and oozing pus. The smell was foul; my gorge rose. Breathing through my mouth didn't help. I gritted my teeth against
my nausea and treated the arm wound as I had his chest. It
used up the last of my bandaging and salve from home.

"You're a well-prepared traveler," Hitch said tightly.
Sweat beaded on his face from the pain he'd endured.

"I was," I said with scant humor.

"Don't worry. When we get to Gettys, I'll see that everything you used for me is replaced."

"When we get to Gettys?"

"You said you'd help me. Even if I didn't demand it of you.
Well, I've got to get to Gettys. And I know damn well that I
won't get there on my own. You'll have to go with me."

The soup was beginning to bubble. I could smell the dried
smoked meat and the carrots simmering. I stirred it a bit. I
looked around the room. I could still see the possibilities
there. I knew they didn't belong to me. "I'll take you."

He gave a short nod. "I want to rest for the rest of the day and the night. And then we'll start at dawn. You've done a good job on me, but I know these things will pus up again in no time. There's a doctor at the fort. He's my best chance. Is that soup done yet?"

"How good are your teeth?"

"Good enough. I'm famished."

I gave him my bowl. I ate from the pot. The carrots were hard and stringy, but they still tasted good to me. I ate as my habit prompted me, carefully, savoring every bit. I drank the hot broth slowly, closing my eyes as it passed over my tongue and down my throat. I felt the warmth of it reach my belly. I opened my eyes and saw the bottom of the pot. I lowered it to find Hitch staring at me. I wiped my mouth on the back of my hand.

"Where did you come from?" he asked me, and it seemed like more than a request for my hometown.

"Back west," I told him, and found I didn't want to tell him even that much. I used my favorite trick to shift his thoughts away from me. "What happened to the cat that attacked you?"

He grinned humorlessly. "It won. I broke free of it and ran. Luckily, it let me go. I suppose it decided the dead bird was enough. When I got back to my camp and my horse, I fixed myself up as best as I could, and then headed back toward the road. That was four days ago. No, five. Four? Four, I think."

He pursed his lips for a moment and continued to regard me steadily. I stood up. He asked, "Can you get my sleeping roll for me? I'm going to rest now."

"Good plan. I'll build up the fire for you."

"Thanks."

I got him settled, built up the fire, and then left, shutting the door behind me. Outside the cabin, I wiped my hands down the front of my trousers and heaved a huge sigh. My feet had carried me to Amzil's door. I didn't knock on it or try to open it. I stood outside and announced, "I'm leaving tomorrow morning. I have to get that man to Gettys so his wounds can be treated by a doctor."

She didn't reply. I could hear the children inside, their

higher voices raised querulously. I turned to walk away. Behind me, I heard the door open a crack. "You think I'm a terrible person," she accused me.

I thought and then replied, "I think you're very afraid. And that makes you hard."

"Hard is better than dead, or raped and left for dead."

"That man was injured. He was no threat to you."

"He was a soldier, a scout. I've seen him before. And I know that where one soldier is, others follow. If I'd let him in and he died, I'd have been blamed. Better to have nothing to do with him."

"He's a human being in need, Amzil. How can you just turn your back on that?"

"Just like they done it to me. That's how. How many times have soldiers ridden through here? At first, when my husband was dying, I asked for help. They told me I'd brought my own troubles on myself, marrying a convict and having his babies. Well, that's what I say to that soldier now. Whatever happened to him, he brought it on himself, by riding about being a soldier."

It was true, so I couldn't argue with her. I no longer saw the point of arguing with her at all. "I'll be taking him on to Gettys tomorrow morning," I said.

Her mouth went sullen. Almost angrily, she asked, "And what about all your fine talk of building an inn here, and taking trade from the road and all that? What about that?"

I was startled. "You told me it wouldn't work. You gave me a dozen reasons why it was a stupid idea."

"If I was trying to do it alone, then, yes. But if a man were running it, even a man like you, travelers might respect it. It might work then."

Even a man like me. A fat man like me, that was what she meant. Scarcely a man at all in her eyes, but big enough to be scary. I looked away from her. "I have to take him to Gettys. If I don't, he'll die from infection. He might still die."

"Then why bother?"

"Because he's a soldier. And I'm a second son. I'm meant to be a soldier."

"You never told me that." She spoke as if I had lied to her.

I felt her eyes run over me, and knew how unlikely she thought it that I'd ever be anything of the kind. I admitted it. "Well, I'm not exactly what any commander wants when he thinks of a recruit. Nonetheless, the good god made me a second son. My plan was always to go to Gettys, to see if they'd accept me as a recruit. If I can serve as a soldier, I will."

"So you'll just ride off and leave tomorrow."

I wanted her to ask me to stay. Or at least, invite me to come back. I stood straight before her, meeting her eyes as I looked down at her, and wondered if she even guessed at what I hoped. "I have to take him to Gettys."

She looked away from me, as if there were something important on the hillside behind me. I knew there wasn't. "You've helped me a lot in the time you've been here." She paused, wet her lips, and then said, "The children will miss you."

"I'll miss them," I said sadly, and found it was not just a nicety. I *would* miss them. But Amzil would not say she would miss me, nor ask me to stay or if I might come back. "Thank you," she called to my back when I had gone a dozen steps. "For the meat, you know. And the firewood."

"You're welcome." I shifted one shoulder in a shrug. "Thanks for the roof and the fireplace. And for sewing my clothes."

"They look much better on you now." She called the words after me.

"Thanks," I said, not calling the word out, but loud enough that she would know I had said it. I walked back to the cottage that might have made a good common room for an inn. Hitch was still sleeping. His face was slack, his mouth ajar. I put water within easy reach of him, took my sling, and went out and up the hill.

I hunted until dusk. "I owe her," I said aloud to the magic. "If she hadn't let me rest here, do you think my horse would have lasted? If I hadn't taken the time here to rest myself, and eat decently, do you think I'd be on my way to Gettys now? No. I'd be dead by the road somewhere. I owe her and I want to pay her."

I waited to feel something, that tingling stir of my blood

that came when the magic moved through me. Nothing happened. I hunted anyway. I missed the first rabbit I saw, and a tree trunk deflected my missile from the second. It was not the right time of day for hunting. And I'd been a fool to think I could wield the magic. An hour later, I decided I'd been a fool to believe in it at all. There had been coincidences and I'd had nightmares. My faith and my rationality chased one another in circles until I was certain that I was a fool to attempt to know the truth of anything.

When I saw the deer, I cursed the fate that had made my father withhold my weapons from me. He was not a large animal; probably he was a yearling. I looked away from him, recalling that Dewara had told me that any prey could feel the stare of a hunter's eyes. I mouthed my new words silently. "I need food for my journey to the territory of the Specks."

There was a rock in my sling, smooth and hefty. It would easily have stunned a rabbit or a bird. It would not kill a deer. When I moved my arm to wind up momentum for the sling, the deer would startle and be gone. I knew there was no magic in me, no magic anywhere. I was merely a fat man, my body the freakishly rare result of my exposure to Speck plague. My heart thundered in my chest as I let the stone fly.

It hit the young buck just above his left eye. I heard the crack of stone against bone. The animal started, and a tremor ran through him. He took two steps. His front legs folded under him as if he were going to bed down for the night. He sank down. With a heavier crash, his hind legs teetered under him and he fell. His entire body gave a jerk.

I did not wait. I rushed forward, running down the hill at him, drawing my sheath knife as I ran. I turned one ankle slightly, hit a sapling with my shoulder, and plunged on. When I finally reached him, he was trying to get up. I fell on him. Using every bit of my strength, I punched my knife into his throat just behind the curve of his jawbone. He gave a wild leap and an inhuman cry of pain. I threw my weight on him then, and held him down as I sawed with my knife, groping for some vital artery. He tossed his head wildly, crashing his skull into mine. I shouted wordlessly and worked the knife in him. A leap of bright red blood rewarded me. Still, his hind legs kicked and it was some moments before he subsided into death.

Panting, I rolled off him, feeling shaken and bruised. For a time, I lay on my back next to the dead yearling, staring up at a blue sky through yellow leaves. I tried to decide if I'd been lucky, or if magic had prevailed. I decided that as long as it came down to having meat, I didn't care.

Dragging the dead deer through the forest was a trial that I shall never forget. It would have been a task even if I'd been my old fit self. It had no antlers to drag it by, only nubby spikes. I tried hauling it by the hind feet, but the grain of its hair created more drag than I would have thought possible. I ended up gripping the front feet and dragging it that way, with the head flopping about and snagging on every imaginable obstacle. As soon as I had it to the edge of the stump field, I left it and went back to the door of Amzil's house.

"I've killed a deer," I said to the closed door. "If you help me butcher it, I'll leave you a goodly share. But some I've got to take with me, to travel on."

"A deer?" The door all but flew open. "How did you kill a deer?"

"With a rock," I replied.

"That's impossible," she said.

"I used my magic to help me," I answered, and she took that for a joke.

I gutted the deer and cut its head off. I gave the liver, heart, kidneys, and tongue over to Amzil, since they were best used fresh. With the hide still on to keep flies off it, I hung the animal, head down, in the shed to bleed. Even with a small deer, it was a lot of work. I left it with the dark blood dripping onto the earth floor. I got my extra set of clothing from my panniers. Hitch slept on. I went down to the river to wash.

I was sweating and sticky with blood. I gritted my teeth against the chill, stripped, and waded out into the river to wash myself. It was an unpleasant experience. I realized that it had been some time since I'd washed myself, not because I enjoyed being dirty but because I'd been avoiding my own body. I used sand from the riverbank to scrub myself. In some places, I had to lift my flesh to wash in the deep fold beneath it. There were sweat scalds under my arms and starting between my thighs, the result of the afternoon's endeavors. My navel had retreated into a deep dent in my belly. A second pouch of fat beneath my belly had formed over my genitals. My buttocks sagged, and my chest was fleshy with breast fat. The experience of washing my own body shamed away any triumph I might have felt in taking the deer. If this sagging fleshy body was the price of having magic, I didn't want it. It was small good to me. It only answered at its own fickle will, and then only if what I was attempting benefited its command for me. This magic offered me no power, only a tether to people and forces that I did not understand.

And tomorrow morning, I would leave Amzil and her children and go on to Gettys. The part of me that persisted in being my father's son said that I would once again attempt to enlist. If the commander at the stronghold there took me, then I could write to Yaril and tell her that soon I'd have a place for her. I wondered what the magic would think of that.

On the heels of that thought, I wondered what I would do if the commander turned me away. I could come back here. I wasn't sure that I should, but I could.

I waded out to the bank and dashed the water from my body. I dried myself on my dirty shirt, dressed, and then spent some time scrubbing the worst of the dirt from the clothing I'd been wearing. I wrung out my laundry and carried it back to the cabin where Lieutenant Hitch slept. I built up the fire and then stretched my wet clothes over the broken table. I hoped they'd be dry by morning.

With the next day's journey in mind, I emptied out my panniers and repacked them. When I came to the pouch of my remaining coin, I smiled, thinking how little good it had done me. I stowed it carefully. There was very little to pack in the way of food. I glanced at the scout. Hitch must have wakened at some point, for the water I'd left him was gone. I wondered how well supplied he was; in his condition, I judged it best that we push for Gettys with all possible speed. Stopping each evening early enough to hunt was not going to be an option. Sheepishly, I wondered if Amzil would let me take some of the smoked rabbit with me. I could take a day or two of venison, but the uncured meat would not travel as well as dried or smoked would.

I was just marshaling my courage to go back to her cabin when the door opened. Amzil was preceded by an amazing smell: fresh deer liver sizzled in goose grease and flavored with onions. My body came to alertness like a hunting dog pointing out a bird. She halted just inside the door; she was carrying the hot pan in her heavily padded hands. Her gaze didn't quite meet mine. "I thought you might be hungry."

"I'm ravenous, and that smells wonderful."

"There should be enough for the hurt fellow. My mother always said that liver was wondrously healing food."

The smell alone seemed to be working wonders. Lieutenant Hitch stirred in his pallet and then opened his eyes. "What's that?" he asked groggily.

"Fresh deer liver cooked in goose fat with onion," I told him.

"Help me sit up. Please." The eagerness in his voice even woke a smile from Amzil.

She set the pan down near our fire. "I have to get back to my children," she said awkwardly to me.

"I know. Thank you."

"It was the least I could do. Nevare, I'm . . . I'm sorry I can't be more . . . welcoming to strangers. But I have my children to protect. You know that."

"I do know that. And you do a good job of it. Before you go, I've another favor to ask. Can I beg some of the smoked rabbit from you? We've a way to go, and fresh venison won't travel as well."

"Of course. It's your meat. You killed it and smoked it." Despite her words, her voice was stiff with dismay.

"And I gave it to you. Do you mind if we take some? I'll be leaving almost all the venison."

"Of course it's fine. I'll be grateful for whatever you leave me. My children have eaten well in the time you've been here, hunting for us. I'm grateful for that."

"The venison. You should let it hang for a few days before you skin it out. Let it bleed well. It will be more tender that way. You can use it fresh, but you'll want to smoke or dry most of it." It suddenly seemed to me that I was leaving her an immense task.

"I have to get back to my children," she said again, and I realized how uncomfortable she felt without quite understanding why.

"Of course," I said. "I'll bring your pan back to you tonight."

"Thank you." And with that she was gone as abruptly as she'd come.

Buel Hitch had levered himself up onto his elbows. He looked toward the pan longingly. "Coffee and some of that meat, and I'll feel like I'm alive again," he said.

"No coffee, I'm afraid. But we have water and fresh-cooked liver, and that's not bad at all, really."

"That's true. But there should be some coffee in my saddlebags, if you want to brew some up for us. It would go a long way toward putting me on my feet again."

The mere thought of coffee set my mouth watering. I put water to boil and then served up the meat for us. Hitch's mess kit was of battered tin, a pan and bowl and an enameled mug. The precious horde of coffee was packed inside it. The aroma of the beans dizzied me.

We ate in silence. I gave my complete attention to my meal, only pausing to add the coffee to the water when it boiled and then set the pot where it would stay hot while it steeped. The smell of the brewing coffee enhanced my appreciation for the meat.

She'd cooked the liver perfectly. It was moist and tender still; I could cut it with the side of my fork. She hadn't used much onion, but what she'd used was evident in tender translucent pieces of the vegetable and its affable flavor throughout the goose grease. The meat was the most alive thing I'd eaten in a long time. I can think of no other way to express it. Liver is always rich and flavorful, but that evening I was suddenly aware that I had transferred life from the deer's body to my own. There was something so essential in that meat; I had no name for it, and yet I felt it replenishing me as I chewed and swallowed. The taste was so thick and strong, the goose grease so satisfying that when I scraped the last sheen of it from my plate, I felt more satisfied than I had in days. I looked up to find Hitch staring at me.

As I returned his stare, he grinned honestly at me. "Can't say that I've ever seen a man enjoy his meal as much as you do. That coffee done yet?"

He had wolfed down his portion of the meat. I doubt that he'd even tasted it, and somehow that seemed a shame, that he did not realize as I did that the life I'd taken from the deer had passed into us with this meal. It diminished what I'd done in taking the deer's life. I felt oddly disgruntled, as if his gobbling of the meat were disrespectful of something. But I said nothing of that, only poured coffee for both of us. He gulped his down and had a second mugfull. I drank mine in long, lingering sips, and then put more water onto the grounds to try to get a second brew out of them. While it simmered, I took Amzil's pan outside, cleaned it, and then returned it to her. When I tapped on her door, she opened it a crack. She took the pan from me with a quiet "thank you." She didn't invite me in and I didn't try to intrude.

When I returned to Hitch, he was pouring some of the re-brewed coffee into his mug. He hunched near the fire on his blanket, looking miserable but alive. "Well, that was quick," he said.

"I was just returning her pan."

He smiled knowingly. "She's a difficult one, isn't she? Sometimes she will, sometimes she won't."

Dismay mingled with anger and churned in me. I tried to keep anything from showing on my face. "Meaning?" I asked him.

He shifted slightly, his brow furrowing deeper. Obviously the move hadn't eased his pain. He rubbed at his face. "Meaning only that, for a whore, she's an odd one. Sometimes a man can buy a night inside and a bit of comfort from her. Other times, she's either boarded the door up tight or there's no one there. She's moody. But good when you can get her, is what I heard."

"Then you've never had her?"

A small smile crooked his mouth. "Old son, I *never* pay for it. Not Buel. I don't have to." He drank the last of the coffee in his mug and tossed the dregs into the fire. He grinned. "Guess that means you ain't had much luck with her."

"I didn't try," I said. "Didn't think she was that sort of a woman, with three children around her and all."

He gave a choked laugh. "What? You think whores don't have kids? Well, I suppose they don't, if they can help it, but most can't. That woman there, she's been there, oh, a year I guess. Used to have a husband, but he's gone now. Probably up and left. But it's known a man can buy her. Not for coin; she's got no use for that. No, she only barters it for food, and only when she's in the mood for it."

I could not begin to sort the emotions running through me. I felt stupid and used; Amzil was only a whore, and even though I'd paid her fee in food, day after day, she'd never allowed me to so much as touch her hand. That wasn't a fair judgment and I knew it. She'd as much as told me that she'd sold herself for food when she'd had to. Doing what she must to feed her children; did that make her a whore? I didn't know. I only knew that hearing another man talk of it so bluntly made me intensely unhappy. I'd known what she was, I admitted. But until Buel Hitch had come here, I hadn't had to face that a lot of other men knew it, too, and far more intimately than I did. I had pretended she was something else, and pretended all sorts of other things about her as well. That she had a heart I could win. That she would be worth winning. That my protecting her and hunting food for her might make her something other than what she really was.

"You still up to traveling tomorrow?" I asked Hitch.

"You bet," he replied.

CHAPTER FOURTEEN

JOURNEY TO GETTYS

I did one final task before I left the next morning. I got up at dawn and slipped out of the house before Buel was stirring. I needn't have been so quiet. His cheeks were red, and he slept the slumber of an ill man. But I went like a creeping mouse, for I wanted no witnesses.

I went to the abandoned vegetable patch. I stooped down and set my hands on the earth. I closed my eyes. I pressed my palms firmly against the wet and matted vegetation and the soil beneath it. I spoke aloud, more to focus myself than because I thought it necessary. "I will travel better and more swiftly if I know that Amzil and her children are provided for. Grow."

After a time, I opened my eyes. A fine misty rain was falling all around me. It beaded in tiny droplets on my shirtsleeves

and clung to my eyelashes. My gut was in my way. It was
hard to crouch low and touch the ground. I felt like I was
folding myself. I couldn't take a full breath. And nothing
had happened.

But I hadn't really expected anything to happen, had I?

Revelation. How could anyone do a magic that he didn't
believe in? I gave up my crouch. I knelt on the wet earth. I
pressed my hands firmly to the soil. I took a deep breath,
and discarded both my disbelief and my deep-seated fear
that the magic was real and I could do this. I made myself
recall the sense of power I'd felt when I'd clasped the sapling growing from Tree Woman's breast. That power. That
flowing transference of being. That was what I wanted. I
took a deep breath. Then I clenched my fingers in the gritty
soil and breathed out, breathed out until there was no air
left in my lungs, and still I forced *something* out of myself,
not from my hands but from my gut and through my arms
and down and out of my fingers. Colors danced at the
edges of my vision. Something was happening. I watched
it. The ragged grasses and jagged leaved weeds dwindled,
sinking back into the earth. The vegetables I blessed
swelled and grew. Turnips shouldered purple tops above
the soil. A yellowing stalk of a potato plant went green,
lifted from the ground, and thrust up buds that opened to
small white flowers. The fronds of carrots lifted above the
brown soil, stood tall and dark green. I held the flex of
whatever it was I strained, held it until spots danced before
my eyes.

I opened my eyes, lost my balance as the world spun
around me, and rolled over on my side in the soil. I breathed
deep gasping breaths. My arms and legs tingled as if they'd
fallen asleep. I worked my aching hands, flexing them, trying to get the blood flowing through my numbed limbs.
When I could, I sat up.

I had expected the vision to pass. It had not. All around
me, in a perfect circle, the weeds had vanished. My chosen
vegetables remained, crisp and tall, ready for harvest. There
were round heads of cabbage set in wide-leafed cups of foliage and the tall feather fronds of carrots, there were turnip

leaves and red-stemmed beet tops and a patch of potatoes gone to bloom.

It took me three efforts to push away from the ground and stand up. Then I teetered on my legs like a new colt. I was giddy, not just with what I had achieved, but from the effort I'd spent achieving it. It took me a few moments to realize another, even more amazing change.

My clothing hung almost loose on me.

It was a minor change, or would have been to anyone else but me. The uncomfortable binding of my trouser waist-band, the way my shirt cut into me under my arms, the tight-ness of my collar—in short, in every place where a moment ago my garments had been uncomfortably tight, they now rode looser. To prove it to myself, I seized the waistband of my trousers and shifted them around my waist. They moved freely. I was still a fat man. But I was marginally less fat than I'd been a few moments before.

And I was ravenously hungry.

With that realization, my senses woke to the bounty all around me. An overpowering drive to replenish what I had lost drove all awe from my mind. I tugged a carrot from the earth. It was long and a deep orange-red. The end of it broke off in the soil. I forced my fingers through the packed earth, seized the broken piece, and pulled it up. I wiped the loose damp soil from the pieces and then crunched into the carrot. The grit on it ground between my back teeth as I chewed it, adding its own earthy note to the flavor. I ground the orange root to juicy sweetness in my mouth. Never had I tasted such a remarkable vegetable. The innermost core of it was sweet, and the whole of it was crisp, not tough at all. I chewed on the thick end of the green, curiously tasting the feathery tops of the carrot. My glance fell on a turnip. The leafy top came off in my hand when I tried to pull it. No matter. I stuffed the greens into my mouth and chewed them as I dug my fingers into the earth around the purple-and-white root. I pulled it up in one try. Smaller roots like seeking tendrils hung from it, crusted with dirt. I shook it and then wiped it on my trouser leg.

The skin was fibrous and peppery. I peeled it away in a

layer and ate it before I went on to the shiny inside of it. My
fingers left muddy prints. No matter. I finished it and then
stood tall, looking for what I wanted to devour next. I wiped
my mouth on the back of my hand. My lips left a mucky
smear. I frowned at it, trying to recall something.

And in that moment, Nevare the soldier son came to
the fore again. I scrabbled backward from the now thriv-
ing vegetable garden into the dank weeds that ringed it.
Despite the haphazard placement of the plants, it looked
as if someone had tended it, watering and weeding it, and
now, at full peak, it awaited harvest. I had been the center
of the circle of tended earth. Heart pounding, I stepped
away from the garden and back into the real world. Almost, I expected it to have vanished when I glanced back,
but no, it remained, as real as the misting rain falling all
around me.

I fled. I brought in both horses that I had picketed for the
night, for neither had wanted to enter the shed with the
hanging deer in it. Feverishly, I readied everything for our
journey. I moved like a hunted man, darting in and out of
the cabin with my arms full of Hitch's gear and my own. I
went to the hanging deer and peeled back enough hide to cut
strips of journey meat for Hitch and me, packing as much as
my cooking pot would hold.

When all else was loaded on the two animals, I went and
tapped on Amzil's door. She opened it, her hair still tousled
from sleep. "Is something wrong?" she asked me anxiously.
I suppose my shock at the proof of my magic still showed in
my face.

"No," I lied. "I just have to make an early start to use the
daylight as best we may. I've come to ask if I can take some
of the smoked meat away with me. I took some of the venison already, but I left all the rest of it for you."

"Of course," she said distantly. She turned from me, and I
left her door to go back to the other cottage and awaken
Hitch.

He jerked awake at my touch, and then slowly sat up,
shivering. "Is it time to go?" he asked me miserably, knowing full well it was.

"Yes. If we leave now, we can put a good distance behind us. How far do you think it is to Gettys from here?"

He knew I did not mean in miles. "If it were just Renegade and I, and I were myself, we could cover it in four days. But that isn't the case, is it?"

"No. But I think we'll still make good time." I tried to be reassuring. The cockiness the man had exhibited yesterday was gone. I wondered if it were because the infection was gaining on him, or if he could simply let his guard down now, knowing there was someone to offer him aid.

"Well, then. Let's go." He wobbled to his feet and walked the few steps to the hearth. He leaned there, taking in the fire's warmth, while I packed the few items that remained. When it was time to leave, I avoided the garden patch. He leaned on his horse for a few moments before he mounted, but he did that on his own. "I'll just be a moment," I told him, and turned to go back to Amzil's cabin for the meat she'd said we could have. But as I looked up, she was coming toward me. She chose to walk down the road in front of the houses. I breathed a sigh of relief. She wouldn't yet have seen the change in the garden. I didn't want to answer any questions. She carried a canvas sack in her arms. As I took it from her, she said, "You've got two rabbits in there."

"Thank you. That should get us there."

"And you've got my best sack."

I frantically racked my brains for something else I could put the rabbits in. They'd have to be packed loose in my panniers. But when I started to open the bag, she said quietly, "No. You can use it. But I expect to get it back."

"I'll make sure you do." I was a bit startled by her demand.

"I'll hold you to that," she said. She was standing very straight. She looked almost angry. I didn't know what to say to her. She had very few possessions. To trust me with this simple sack was evidently difficult for her.

"Good-bye, Amzil. Tell the children I said good-bye."

"I will." She kept looking at me, as if she were waiting for something.

"Will you be all right on your own?"

Then the anger did glint plain in her eyes. "I've been so before. Why wouldn't I be again?" she asked me tartly. She turned away from us and walked back toward her house.

I wanted to just let her go, but I also wanted to be sure that she was the one who had the advantage of what I had done that morning. "Harvest those vegetables as soon as you can," I called after her. "Before someone else discovers them and takes them." She didn't turn. "Good-bye," I said more quietly.

Lieutenant Hitch coughed and then spat to one side. "You sure stepped on that cat's tail," he observed mildly.

"Let's go," I responded. I mounted Clove. From the draft horse's back, I towered over my companion. I felt foolish. We followed the road and it took us out of the dilapidated ruins of the failed town. I glanced back once at the rising chimney smoke thinking, *Almost.* Back there I'd almost taken control of my own life. Now I was back to duty.

The misty rain lasted all day. I'll say this of Buel Hitch: he wasn't a whiner. He rode beside me and didn't say much. Now and then he coughed and spat. He drank frequently from his water skin. When we came to the river, I halted and refilled both our water bottles. Before we went on, we ate half of one of the rabbits. It wasn't enough for me, but Hitch looked as if he had to force down every bite.

"Are you ready to go on?" I asked him when he cast the last of his bones aside.

"Do I have a choice? I know what's happening to me. Cat claws are dirty. The infection will spread." He touched his chest gingerly. "I can feel it. The heat. Let's go."

So on we went that day. Early in the afternoon, a couple of traders' wagons passed us going west. The men were crouched on their seats, hats pulled low and shoulders hunched against the rain. I called a greeting, but received only a sullen nod from one of them. I decided there was no point in asking them for help. I glanced at Hitch. He made a scornful face, evidently sharing my opinion.

As we continued on our own way, I found myself wondering if the carters would stop in the abandoned town, and then tormented myself with wondering if Amzil would make them welcome. It was stupid. I had no claim on her and she had made it clear she had no interest in me. I should not care what she did, if she whored herself out to strange men or not. She was out of my life, merely a woman I'd met as I stopped on my way east. I'd forget her. I'd find someone to take her stupid canvas sack back to her, and I'd put her out of my mind. I wouldn't think about her anymore.

The wet penetrated our clothes and soaked the horses' coats into runnels. I began looking for a likely place to camp before dark. I saw the stacks of rocks, three and then two on top of each other, and turned our horses off the road and into the brush. The trail was narrow, winding uphill through the trees, but as the scout's sign had promised, it led me to a cleared campsite with a covered supply of firewood.

I dismounted. Hitch sat his horse a few moments longer. "So," he observed gruffly as he swung himself stiffly down, "maybe you are a soldier son. What branch was your da?"

"Cavalla," I said briefly. I had no wish to discuss my father or family with him. I took firewood from the stack and dug in my panniers for my hatchet to reduce some of it to kindling. The wind gusted and the trees released a shower of raindrops and wet leaves on us. It was going to be a nasty night. "Let me get a fire started, and then I'll rig a shelter for us."

He nodded, grimly silent. I could only guess at his level of pain. He stood stiffly, his arms crossed as if to hold something in. He didn't offer me any help; I hadn't expected any. His roll of canvas was designed to shelter one man, not two, but I managed to rig it to the tree trunks in such a way that it cut most of the wind and shed rain. It was not perfect. Errant gusts still drove rain and wet leaves in at us, but it was far better than simply sitting in the storm. The half-naked trees provided little shelter from the incessant rain. I picketed our horses, got water from a nearby streamlet, and brought it back to the fire, putting it on to heat while I took out the venison. I cut it in strips, poked holes in the strips, and then threaded the meat onto some skinny branches. I toasted them over the fire, and we didn't much care that the meat stayed bloody in the middle. We made coffee from Hitch's supply and ate the hot dripping meat from the skewers.

I'd spent far worse nights on the road, but not as a fat man. My weight and size made every small task of sharing a camp more difficult. The shelter belonged to Hitch and he was injured. It was only fair that he get the most benefit from it, but my bulk meant that part of me was always out in the storm. Rising to bring more firewood, bending over the fire to set the coffee in the coals, cleaning the pot and cups afterward: every small task was made more onerous by the weight of flesh I carried. Even just rising and then sitting down on the ground again was more of a chore than it had been when I was fit. I told myself that it was my imagination that Lieutenant Hitch watched every move I made. I angrily decided it was what I must expect. People had paid to see the Fat Man in the carnival at Old Thares. I was not as large as he had been, but a man of my bulk was still a noteworthy sight anywhere. Once I arrived at Gettys, people would stare. I'd best get used to it.

"You ain't always been fat," Hitch said suddenly.

I gave a snort of amusement. "How would you know?"

"The way you move. You act like a packhorse who's carrying more than his fair share, or one that's been badly loaded. If you'd carried that fat all your life, you'd be used to it by now. But I been watching you, and how you set your feet before you try to sit down, and how it takes you two tries to get up."

I shrugged. "You're right. This time last year, I was leaner than you."

"What happened?"

Hitch's eyes were a bit too bright. Fever burned in him. "If you want, I could go back to those willows and shave off some bark. Willow bark tea is supposed to lower a fever."

"It's supposed to, yes. It tastes awful. But actually, I'd rather you answered my question. What happened to you?"

I tried to find a comfortable way to sit. My arse was sore from a day in the saddle, and there was nothing to lean back against except an uneven tree trunk. "I got Speck fever. Everyone else either died or came out of it like a rack of bones. But I got better. Then I started to gain weight. The doctor at the academy knew what was coming. He said that this is a rare side effect of the plague. And they gave me a medical discharge."

"Academy boy. Should have known," Hitch muttered. He smiled derisively. "So that makes you Lord Grand Somebody's son, right?"

"No. I'm nobody's son anymore. My father disowned me. I failed him. I disgraced myself. I didn't get through the academy to be a cavalla officer, and he reckoned that I'd never be a soldier of any kind."

"Probably reckoned right. Most regiments won't take you in like that, not even as a foot soldier." He tossed his empty toasting stick into the fire. "But if you wanted, I could put in a word with Colonel Rabbit for you."

"Colonel Rabbit? Does he command Gettys?"

He laughed out loud. "Yes, he does. But his real name is Colonel Haren. The other name is a bit more apt. He spends all his time hiding in his hole. But you probably shouldn't call him that if you're trying to get on with him." His voice was wandering.

"I think your fever's coming up. I'm going after some willow bark while I still have light to see by."

"Suit yourself." He leaned his head back against a tree trunk. I took my kettle with me, and went back to the streamlet. I knew little other than that willow bark tea was supposed to be good for a fever. I scraped some from the trunk of the tree there, and some from the more supple branches. I filled the kettle half-full of tree shavings and then topped it off with water. I took it back to the campfire, added a few more bits of the dry wood, and left it to heat.

The light was fading. As much to warm myself as to be a good soldier, I took my hatchet and went looking for more wood. Most of what I found was soaked by the rain, but I cut it into lengths and stacked it for the next traveler who might come this way and read the sign. By the time the willow bark tea was steaming, Hitch was shivering. The tea didn't smell appetizing, but it was hot and he drank two full mugs of it. Then he abruptly closed his eyes and slumped down in his blankets. I dashed the dregs from his mug and made myself as comfortable as I could.

It was a long night. Hitch moaned and twitched his way through it. The wind finally blew the clouds on their way, but as the night cleared, it got colder. I was awake and waiting for the dawn when it came, my body tight with chill. Hitch was the opposite. He burned with fever.

I woke the fire and warmed the willow bark tea for him. I had to help him sit up. He drank the first few sips while I held the mug for him. Then he took it in both hands and nodded at me that he could manage on his own. While he drank, I brought the horses up and saddled them. He had a hard time standing up, but once he was on his feet, he moved around a bit while I loaded our gear. I had to pack the blankets wet. I grimaced to myself, thinking of how unpleasant it would be to sleep in them that night. Before we mounted up, Hitch had me bind his injured arm across his chest. "It'll joggle less," was all he said. I did as he asked, trying not to wrinkle my nose at the smell.

"Maybe we should wash it out again," I suggested.

"With no clean bandages, there's no point to that," he replied.

I helped him into his saddle and we set off again. He was quieter, giving all his attention to sitting his horse. The day was a repetition of our first day together, save that we left the river behind and began a steeper climb into the foothills. About midday, the quality of the road sharply declined. A few hours later, it had degenerated to a rutted wagon track, deeply muddy and very unpleasant for the horses. Riding to one side of it was nearly as bad.

"Shouldn't there be a crew at work along here, extending the road?" I asked Hitch.

He lifted his head suddenly, as if I'd awakened him. "What?"

"Where are the road crews, the prisoners building the King's Road?"

"Oh." He looked vaguely around him. "They'll have taken them on to the prisoner camp outside Gettys. The weather is starting to turn. They won't get any more miles of road until spring comes again. Not that they got many while the weather was good. Can we stop for food and water?"

I wasn't sure that stopping was a good idea. I was afraid that if he got off his horse, I wouldn't get him back on it. But I'd underestimated his toughness. He dismounted and stood by Renegade, holding onto his saddle while he drank deeply from his water skin. I took out the other half of the smoked rabbit, and we made short work of it standing there. Lieutenant Hitch sucked a stubborn bit of meat from a bone and then gestured at the low hills to our left. "If we left the road and cut across those hills, we could save half a day's travel time."

I looked at him and then spoke frankly. "I think I should stay to the road. It's plainly marked and takes the easiest path there. If I get you up in those hills and you reach a point where you can't tell me where I'm going, we're both going to be lost. And you'll pay for it with your life."

He set his hand briefly to his chest, winced, and then said, "We're racing against time now. Half a day might mean I live. I'm willing to gamble it. Are you?"

I thought for a few moments. "It's your life," I said reluctantly. I didn't want to take a relative stranger into unknown territory and have him die on me. But it did seem to me that he had the right to make the decision.

"That's right. It is," he said.

When we were mounted again, he turned Renegade's head away from the road. I followed him. He cleared his throat. "Renegade knows the way home. If I die, you sling me across his saddle, and let him lead. Don't you leave me in the woods to rot."

"Of course not. One way or the other, I'll take you to Gettys."

"Good. Now talk to me, Never. Keep me awake."

"My name's Nevare, not Never. What do you want me to talk about?"

"Anything. Women. Talk to me about women you've had."

I thought back. "Only one worth mentioning," I said, thinking of the warm-hearted farm maid.

"Only one? You poor bastard! Well, tell me about her."

So I did, and then he told me a rambling and feverish tale of a Speck maiden who chose him as her own and fought two other women over him, and how she had ridden him "like a lord riding to the hunt" for fifteen nights in a row. It seemed wildly improbable to me, and yet parts of his tale rang true with some hidden truth within me. Somehow I knew it was the custom of Speck women to be the instigators of such a relationship, and that they jealously possessed the men they chose. He talked until his mouth was dry, and then drank all the water that remained in his bottle, and most of what I had. All the while, he, or perhaps Renegade, led us further and further from the road, up into rolling hills. The lower slopes were thick with bracken and buckbrush, but as we went higher, we entered an open forest of deciduous trees. We crested the first row of hills, descended into a shallow valley, and then began a second, steeper ascent. The vistas were astonishing. Some of the bracken had gone scarlet with early frost. The buckbrush was thick with its seasonal white berries, while the leaves of the alders and birch of the open forest were scarlet and gold. The day had stayed clear but the air was moist, and the smell of the forest was rich and gentle. Something inside me relaxed and felt a sense of homecoming. I said as much to Hitch.

He was swaying in his saddle as he rode now, holding unabashedly to the horn with his one good hand. A smile crossed his pained face. "Some men feel it. Others don't. Me, once I got away from houses and streets and bricks and noise, I suddenly knew that I'd never belonged there in the first place. There's men that need that, you know. They need the shouting and the crowds. They get two nights away from an alehouse, and think they'll die of boredom. They need other people to make them think they're alive. They only feel like they're important if someone else tells them they are." He snorted out a laugh. "You can always tell who they are. They aren't happy just living their own lives. They want to control yours, too. You know the men I mean . . ."

I smiled stiffly. "My father."

"Your father. You don't even have to tell me, Never. He's still got his boot on your neck. I can just about see it if I squint."

"Explain yourself." I spoke abruptly, stung by his words. He laughed at me.

"I don't have to, Never. You feel it yourself, don't you?"

"I left my father's home. And when I did, I left him behind as well."

"Sure you did." His tone was mocking.

I reminded myself that he was a very sick man. But in the depths of my soul, I suspected that Hitch had always been a needler and a digger, always a man who took pleasure in provoking others. I made no response.

The silence lasted a bit. Then he laughed oddly, long and low. In a reedy, childish voice he said, "I know you. I see you, Never. You can't hide from Buel Hitch. He's been too long in the forest. You can't hide behind the trees."

"I think your mind is wandering from the fever," I said reasonably.

"No. I can see a part of you that ain't no soldier son. I see something stronger than your pa's boot on your neck. You're going to the Specks, ain't you? You got the call to be a Great Man."

I knew it was a sick man's rambling thoughts. Nonetheless, it stood the hair up on the back of my neck and on my arms. "We'd best start looking for a place to camp tonight," I said uneasily.

"Very well," Hitch replied agreeably. For a time we rode in almost companionable silence. Renegade moved steadily along, and the horse truly seemed to know where he was going. There was no true trail; instead we had followed a deer track up a hill, diverged to follow a stream as it wound down the next slope, traversed a valley beside it, and then climbed the next hill on a game trail. We had been following a ridge as the sun moved ever closer to the horizon. Now, as we descended again, the shadow of the hill falling across us made evening seem much closer.

"You don't much like it, do you?" he asked me. Then, before I could ask him what he meant, he gestured at a stand of mixed trees. "There's a good place. There's a spring down in those rocks beyond the trees. You don't much like the magic telling you what to do."

"We'll camp there, then," I said, ignoring the words I didn't want to hear from this stranger.

"It's a good spot. The evergreen trees break the wind. You don't need to be ashamed. I don't like it, either. It was a poor bargain. Not that I had much say in the terms of the bargain. You decide you want to live, and then it's got you. One way or another. I was sent to fetch you. I said no. But you don't say no to the magic, do you?"

"You're raving, Hitch. Ride quiet. Save your strength."

He coughed, and it was too weak a sound for a grown man. "I don't have any strength left, Never. Save what the magic gives me. I said, 'No, I don't have time.' And the magic sent me the cat, and I knew that if I wanted to live, I had to do what it wanted. And I always want to live. Looks like you do, too. But I think you got a dirtier shake of it than I did. Them Specks and their diseases. You know, they don't call them diseases. Or even sicknesses. No. To them, they're magic spells. Well, that's not quite the way they'd call them. The word doesn't translate. But it means like a gate or a funnel. The magic sends it, and the people go through it, and they come out dead or changed. Even fevers from wounds, like I got. Even this fever now, they'd say it's a melting. A burning to purify the body and the spirit. If a Speck does something really bad, they'll put a fever in him to cure him. Scratch him with something that makes him sick, or put him in a hut with a fire in the middle and build fires all around, to fever the wickedness out of him. You got any more water, Never? I've talked myself dry."

We'd reached the campsite. The ring of fire-blackened stones said the place had been used before, and the grass growing against the stone said that it had been at least a season since it had last seen use. There was no ready-cut supply of firewood, but the trees around the spring had shed dead branches. I gathered what I needed and soon had a fire going. Hitch just sat on the ground, his blanket around his shoulders, staring at the fire. I was pretty sure I was looking at a dead man, and he knew it.

My mind had been sifting his ravings and finding far too much that made sense, if the crooked logic of Speck magic could be said to make sense. I felt caught in the middle of a bridge. On one side was the insanity of believing that magic had made me fat, and that the magic had a plan for me. On the other side was my faith in the good god, my destiny of being a soldier son, and all the logic and science of Gernia. Somehow it seemed that neither one worked for me, but that trying to weave them together in the middle worked worst of all. I could disregard Lieutenant Buel Hitch and his wild talk. I could put it down to a fever and ignore it. Or I could encourage him to talk and try to find some sort of handle on whatever I was battling.

I did my camp chores while I pondered it. I fetched water and set it to heat, and cut toasting sticks for the venison. I was filling our water skins at the spring when I noticed a water plant I didn't recognize. Its leaves were wide and a few were green, but most had gone spotty and pale with the threat of winter. I stared at them. I was sure I'd never seen it before, but it was uncannily familiar. I gave in to the impulse and reached into the water to pull one up. It came up reluctantly, a thick white root sucking out of the mud as I dragged on it. I rinsed it off and took it with me when I went back to our campsite.

Hitch had made an effort to be useful. He'd scraped together a couple of mounds of fallen leaves and pine needles. One-handed, he was trying to put my blanket on mine.

"In the good god's name, Hitch, just rest. I can take care of that in a moment."

He turned his whole head to look at me. "I hate being useless." Nonetheless, he sank down to sit on his own leafy bed. "I hate owing anybody anything."

"You don't owe me anything. Stop worrying about it." I handed him his water bottle.

"What's that you've got there?"

"These? Some kind of water plant. It looked vaguely familiar. You know it?"

He leaned closer, peering at it, and nearly fell over. He swayed back into place, chuckling grimly. "Yes. I do. The Specks use it. They call it drawroot."

"How do you cook it?"

"You don't. It's medicinal. For a fouled wound." With his good hand, he fumbled at the buttons of his shirt. "You cut the fresh root and put it, cut side down, on the wound. It sucks the foulness out." He gave an exclamation of disgust as his opened shirt permitted a wave of stench to waft from his chest injury. "Damn magic seems to be working again. At least this time it's to my good."

I helped him get his shirt open, tugging it gently free from his injured arm. He gritted his teeth so hard I heard them grind. He directed me as I cut the root and placed it. I had to go back to the spring for more of it. Luckily, it seemed plentiful, so I harvested a good supply. He lay back on his bed near the fire, sections of cut root arranged over his pus-oozing wounds. I had small faith in their efficacy. He closed his eyes and dozed as I finished the camp chores and arranged our venison to cook over the fire. The fresh meat was starting to sour, so I decided I'd cook it all. It made a fine, toothsome smell as it sizzled over the fire. I looked up at the deep blue of the evening sky. Scudding clouds obscured the early stars. I hoped we'd have no more rain.

"Food's done," I announced, and he opened his eyes. He didn't sit up at first. Instead, one by one, he peeled the slices of root off his arm and chest. They came free stickily, with sucking noises. He shied each one off into the woods as he loosened it. Where the roots had rested, the angry wounds had calmed from red to pink, and the swelling was substantially reduced.

"That's amazing," I said.

"That's why they call it magic," he replied.

I handed him a stick laden with dripping meat and took one for myself from the fire's edge. "How did you get caught by it?" I asked him quietly.

He smiled slightly in the firelight. "A woman. Of course."

I was quiet, waiting.

He took a bite of the venison, holding the meat on the stick to rip it free. The meat was good, juicy and flavorful, but not very tender. I was chewing a mouthful myself when he added, "I wanted her. Not that it would have mattered if I didn't. She'd made up her mind to have me and with a Speck woman, what she wants is what she gets. But there was a sort of initiation she put me through. The first time it was a holy smoke she made on a fire inside a small hut. We sat there, breathing it. And the second time, it was a tree resin that she made me chew. I . . . traveled. I saw things and I was tested." He stopped speaking for a few moments and then said, "I don't really want to talk about that part of it. Does any man want to admit he found the limits of his courage? When they asked me if I wanted to live, I said yes. And they let me. As a servant of the magic."

I swallowed my meat and took another skewer from the fire.

"You know how it is," he said, and it wasn't a question.

We talked that night. At first, we feinted and dodged, but slowly our two stories were spilled to one another. They were in some ways similar and in others wildly different. I told him how my father had given me to Dewara, and how the Plainsman had sent me up against the Tree Woman. I spoke of my other self, the one who lived and learned in a dream world. There were two places where I faltered and nearly lied to him. I didn't want to admit that I had loved the Tree Woman. That I still did love her. And I didn't want to confess that I was the one who had given the signal to the dancers she had sent to Old Thares. With a motion of my hand, I had bid them do their Dust Dance, and in that motion, I had betrayed all of Old Thares. Hundreds of people had died because of me. I confessed that guilt to Lieutenant Hitch. He shrugged his shoulders to it.

"It wasn't you, Never. It was the magic. You can't hold yourself responsible for what it makes you do."

I winced. He had confided much to me. He had done things that shamed him, though nothing so foul as what I had done. Nevertheless, although I did not utter the thought aloud, I thought his sentiment a cowardly one. "I think I have a duty to my own people to resist it," was all I said.

"Do you?" he asked me quietly. "Do you believe that Gernians are the most important people in the world? Or do you think so only because you were born one? If you'd been born anywhere else, would you still think that you had a duty to protect the interest of Gernia, no matter what it cost other people?"

"I don't see anything wrong with being a patriot. I love my country and I respect my king. As soldiers, should we do less?" I felt pushed by his words.

"As soldiers, that is very admirable. It's only when we are being more than soldiers that it comes into question."

I let a silence fall. I considered all he had said. Realization dawned on me. "You pretend to be common-bred. But you're not."

"I never said I was."

"But you talk like it. Sometimes you sound like an ill-bred, ignorant man, but I think you do that on purpose. There are moments when your thoughts are too exact, too concisely phrased. I believe you were nobly born."

"And?"

"So why do you deceive people?"

He lifted one shoulder. He didn't look at me. "Isn't that what we scouts are supposed to do? We blend. We cross borders. We live in the space between peoples."

"Did you want to be a scout? It doesn't sound as if you admire what you do."

"Did you want to be a soldier? Pass me more meat, please."

I did as he asked. "I had no choice in being a soldier. I'm a second son. It's what I am destined to be." I took another skewer of meat off the fire for myself. "But that doesn't mean I'm opposed to being a soldier. On the contrary. It's what I always dreamed of doing."

"You took your father's ambition for you and made it your own."

"No. I think that my father's ambition for me and my ambition for myself happened to be the same thing." I said the words firmly, perhaps to cover that I suddenly wondered if they were true.

"So you did consider other careers. Poet, engineer, potter?"

"Nothing else appealed to me," I replied staunchly.

"Of course it didn't," he replied agreeably.

Stung, I demanded, "What do you want of me, Hitch?"

"Me? Nothing at all. But I'm not what you have to worry

about." He shifted, grunting as he did so. His injuries were improved, but they still pained him. "I don't know why I'm even badgering you about it. Listen, Never. I know a bit about this, but not everything. And maybe all I'm trying to do is offer you my knowledge in exchange for yours. So I'll go first, and you tell me if anything I say goes counter to what you know."

I nodded tersely, and tossed my toasting stick into the fire. "Very well, then." He cleared his throat, paused, and then laughed. It was the first honest laugh I'd heard from him. "Damn. I still feel like a boy, telling ghost stories by the fire. There's a part of me that can't let go of everything I learned growing up, a part of me that just can't believe this is real, let alone happening to me."

I suddenly felt a loosening in my shoulders. Quietly I said, "That lines up exactly with what has bothered me the most about this. When I try to talk about it, people think I'm crazy. My father was furious with me. He just about starved me to death, trying to prove I was lying about it."

"I'm surprised you even tried to tell him. Did anyone believe you?"

"My cousin. And Sergeant Duril, an old fellow who was my tutor. And Dewara. He believed me."

He squinted his eyes at me. "I'm not sure you should have told him. It seems dangerous to me."

"How?" I hadn't told him Dewara was dead.

"I'm not certain. It just does." He smiled grimly. "The magic has had me for a long time, Never. A good ten years. I've grown accustomed to it, just as a horse learns to wear his harness, no matter how much he might resent it at first. And I've come to have a feel for it. I know a little of what it can do for me. But I know a lot of what it can make me do. It's ruthless. Always remember that. Always remember that you are just a tool to it."

His words put a chill in me. "I've used it," I admitted. "At first I didn't know what I was doing. But in the last few days, I've used it twice, knowing that I did so. Yet each time I was shocked when it worked."

He raised an eyebrow. "What did you do?"

I told him first about the deer. He nodded slowly. "But that could have been sheer dumb luck. You know how it is. You believe you can do a thing, and then you actually do it."

I nodded. "That's what I thought. So I decided to prove to myself I wasn't imagining things." And I told him about the vegetables.

He whistled low and shook his head. "That's more than I've ever done. More than I've ever seen done, even by the Speck village mages. I think you'd best tread more carefully, my man. What you did was like flinging down a challenge to the magic. You may think you mastered it and made it do as you wished. But I think that sooner or later, it will demand payment of you for that."

"What can it ask of me?" I demanded with a bravado I didn't feel.

"Anything, brother. Anything at all."

CHAPTER FIFTEEN

GETTYS

Three days later, we finally rode into Gettys. We made an odd sight, I'm sure. I sat on big Clove while Hitch rode hunched beside me on Renegade. The drawroot had doubtless saved his life by sucking much of the toxic infection from his flesh, but that did not mean he was a well man. His fever had not abated. By night, it rose and tormented him. It had burned the flesh from his bones. I took him straight to his regiment's doctor.

That morning we had descended from the hills into a wide, shallow valley. As we finally broke clear of the cover of the trees, I reined in, startled at what I saw.

I'd always had a clear image of Gettys in my mind. I'd pictured it like the great stone citadels of the west. It would have watchtowers on its high walls, and secondary earthworks surrounding it. There would be banners flying from its ramparts, and it would bristle with soldiers and artillery. The flags would snap smartly in the breeze on that last fortification of the Gernian kingdom. Savage wilderness would surround it.

What I saw was a cruel joke on my boyhood vision. On the hillside on the other side of the valley, commanding a view of the valley, was a wooden palisade that boasted a mere four watchtowers, one at each corner. In the valley below us, we could see the King's Road, cutting a straight line toward the stronghold and continuing past it up the hills and toward the mountains. Behind the fort, the land rose abruptly in steep foothills that were the final line of defense before the Barrier Mountains. The mountains, which loomed above them, were steep and tall and thickly forested.

On the north side of the fortress, there was a compound with several long, low buildings that reminded me of barracks surrounded by a lower palisade, with two watchtowers looking over them. On the opposite side, a neat town had been laid out, with straight wide streets and sturdy structures. But outside that tidy heart a hodgepodge of makeshift cottages and houses scabbed the valley floor. Smoke from several hundred chimneys smudged the clear autumn air. The streets straggled and wandered among the houses like a child's scribble on rough paper. The valley trapped the smoke, the smells, and the distant sounds of the disorderly settlement below us. What struck me the most about the sprawling community was that so much of it was made of wood. Old Thares had been brick and stone, and Franner's Bend had been constructed of mud brick. I had grown up on the plains, where lumber was used to decorate stone buildings. Never before had I seen so many structures in one place all built entirely of wood. On the valley floor, between the settlement and us, farms had been claimed. Few looked prosperous. Rail fences had fallen, and in some fields the weeds stood tall and brown. In others, the stumps of trees still stood where some ambitious settler had logged off a pasture but gone no further with it. The whole panorama of fortress, town, and surrounding farmlands spoke of an endeavor begun with energy and order that had wavered and fallen into disrepair and despair.

"There it is," Lieutenant Hitch said without enthusiasm. "Gettys. Your new home. My old home."

"It's bigger than I expected," I said when I had recovered somewhat.

"Regiment's about six hundred strong. It was almost a thousand in our peak days, but with plague and desertion, it's all the colonel can do to keep us above five hundred men. We were supposed to get reinforcements this summer, but the plague got them first.

"Thanks for getting me here. Let's go down and see if one of the Gettys doctors can mend me. And if they can't mend me, let's hope they'll have enough laudanum that I won't care."

We rode across the brushy plateau to the King's Road, and followed it down toward the city.

I've come to the conclusion that the only thing dirtier than a very old city is a rather new one. In an old city, people have established where the garbage and waste of all kinds will go. It's not that there is less of it, but that it has been channeled to one place, preferably in a less desirable area of the town. Gettys had no such protocol. Nor had it grown naturally, with farms supporting a growing population and a pleasant setting that attracted more settlers that in turn stimulated more commerce. Instead, there had been a military occupation inside a fortification, followed by a population of deportees that had scant skills for settling a wilderness. Their failed efforts were manifest. Fields had been plowed and perhaps planted once, but now were a rumpled tapestry of stones, broken earth, and weeds. Drunken fences wandered across the land. Feral chickens scratched in the earth and fled at our approach. We passed open waste pits just off the side of the road. A flock of croaker birds hopped and squabbled on one fresh rubbish heap. They did not flee us, but opened their black-and-white wings and squawked menacingly to warn us off their feast. I could not repress a shiver as we passed them. Always, they reminded me of that dreadful wedding offering. We saw some scattered cattle and one small flock of eight sheep with a little boy watching over them. But for every sign we saw of industry and effort, a dozen failures flanked them.

The outer town around the fort was a mixture of old

shacks and hasty new construction, interspersed with collapsed remnants of earlier efforts at housing. The smells and
sounds of dense human population surrounded us. Cart and
foot traffic vied with one another at the intersections of the
rutted, mucky roads. A bony woman in a faded dress and a
tattered shawl gripped two small children by the hands as
she hurried along the windy street. The children wore no
shoes. One was bawling loudly. Hitch nodded his head at
them. "Prisoner's family. Free workers live in this part of
town. Poorer than dirt, for the most part."

At the next corner, I was shocked to see two Speck men
sitting cross-legged. They wore wide brimmed hats of woven bark and castoff rags. The begging hands they reached
out to passersby were disfigured with peeling blisters. "Tobacco addicts," Hitch told me. "That's about the only thing
that makes a Speck leave the forest. They can't take direct
sunlight, you know. Used to be a lot more of them, but a lot
of them caught a cough and died last winter. We're not supposed to sell or trade tobacco to Specks, but everyone does.
You can get just about any Speck-made thing you want for
tobacco."

"This place is even worse of a slum than Franner's Bend,"
I observed. "All of this will need to be razed if Gettys is ever
to become a proper city."

"Gettys will never be a city. None of this will last," Hitch
pronounced. "The Specks resist it with every bit of magic
they can muster. That's why it can't prosper. The Specks
dance to make it fail. For five years now, they have danced.
No town can stand against that. It will wither and die and
go back to the earth. Wait a day or two. You'll start to feel
it, too."

His words were no stranger than many of the things he
had told me over the last couple of days. I only wished I
knew how many to give credence to. The tales and admoni-
tions he offered me were sometimes so far-fetched, it seemed
it must be the fever talking rather than a rational man. I now
felt that he knew more of me than I'd ever shared with anyone, and that I knew far more of him than I was comfortable
with. Even so, he remained a stranger to me, for I wondered

who he would be if I removed the fever that both clouded and colored his thoughts.

We drew curious glances from the people in the streets. Their attention lingered on Hitch slouching in his saddle as much as they did the fat man on the big horse. I soon discovered one advantage to Clove and that was that people gave way to him. Even in the crowded marketplace, the gathered folk parted to let us pass. Renegade and his burden followed in our wake.

We came to the older, more prosperous section of Gettys. The main street was lined with stores and warehouses. Their proprietors had smelled a profit to be made off this ragtag town, and come east to take advantage of it. Their dwellings were neatly maintained and tightly roofed, with glass windows and rain gutters and sheltered porches. The side streets were straight, and I glimpsed well-built if poorly maintained houses. "The cavalla families live here," Hitch told me. "This part of town was built a long time ago. Before the Specks turned against us." Outside a tavern four men in cavalla uniforms sat on a bench, smoking and talking. They were all thin and hollow-eyed. I stared at them for a moment, and then grasped the reality of something I'd known for years. Plague regularly swept through this town. Most of the regiment would be plague survivors. We rode past a bake house, the clay ovens bulging from the side of the structure out into the street. For a few moments we were warmer as we passed. The aroma of fresh bread assailed me so strongly I nearly tumbled from Clove's back. I imagined it so strongly that I could feel the chewy texture on my tongue, taste the golden butter that would melt as I troweled it onto the bread, even the rasp of the crust against my teeth. I gritted my teeth and rode on. *Later*, I promised my rumbling gut. *Later.*

We reached the wooden palisade. The skinned logs had been set vertically in the ground. Weathering had silvered them, and bits of moss and tiny plants had found purchase in the cracks. In a few places, ivylike vines were twining up the logs as if they were a trellis. The plants, I thought to myself, would devour those walls. Whoever had let them get started near the fort was a fool. The gates stood open, but the sentries on duty there possessed a military bearing that those at Franner's Bend had lacked. I pulled in Clove, but Hitch lifted his head and rode around me. "Let us through," he said gruffly. "I'm in a bad way and I need the doctor. And he's with me."

To my surprise, that was all that was needed. They did not salute the lieutenant or ask him any questions, but mutely nodded and let us pass. Renegade and Hitch had taken the lead and we followed. A few heads turned to mark our passage, but no one impeded us. They seemed unsurprised to see Lieutenant Hitch in such dismal condition. I merited longer stares than he got.

The inner Gettys disappointed me as much as the outside had. Instead of crack soldiers, I saw men who wore their uniforms with days of dust settled in the wrinkles, and frayed cuffs and stained shirtfronts. Some of them wore their hair longer than mine. I saw no one walking with purposefulness, no troops drilling, and felt no sense of military preparedness. The men on the streets looked listless and unhealthy. I had expected to endure the avid curiosity of their stares. Instead they regarded me with an almost bovine acceptance.

Lieutenant Hitch kept up his façade until we reached the doors of the infirmary. This structure appeared to be better maintained than the rest of the buildings inside the fort. I dismounted, exchanging the discomfort of riding for the new aches of standing on my own feet, and went to help Hitch.

"I can do it myself," he said, and then fell off his horse. With difficulty, I kept him from hitting the street. He gave a soft caw of pain as I hauled his good arm over my shoulder and walked him into the infirmary. The front room was whitewashed with a single desk in it and a bench along the wall. A pale young soldier looked up at me in surprise. His uniform was badly fitted; his jacket, cut for a man with broad shoulders, drooped oddly over his concave chest. He did not look competent to be left in charge, but there was no one else there.

"Lieutenant Buel Hitch has been mauled by a wild cat. The wounds are badly infected. He needs a doctor's skills right away."

The boy's eyes grew very wide. He looked down at the logbook and the two pens and inkwell carefully arranged on the bare desktop as if hoping to find some advice there. After a moment, he seemed to make a decision. "Follow me," he said. He opened a door opposite the one I had entered by, and I found myself in a wardroom. There was a long row of beds along one wall. Only two were occupied. In one, a man was sleeping. In another, a man with his jaw bandaged stared disconsolately at the wall. "Put him on an empty bed," my guide instructed me. "I'll go fetch the doctor."

Hitch roused himself slightly. "Get me Dowder. I'd rather have a drunk who knows what he's doing than old Poker-up-his-ass, I'm-a-doctor-because-I-read-a-book Frye."

"Yes, sir," the boy replied, unsurprised, and hurried off to do as he was bid.

I sat him down on a tautly made bed. "You seem very familiar with this place."

Hitch began fumbling with the buttons of his shirt. "Too familiar," he agreed, but did not elaborate. As he worked his slow way down the row of buttons, he asked me, "Do you have a pen and paper?"

"Do I have what?"

He ignored my incredulous question. "Go borrow some from the desk. I'll give you a note to the colonel. There's no sense you waiting on me. They'll be keeping me here a few days, I imagine."

"Longer than that, I'm guessing."

"Go get the paper and pen. I'm hanging on by my teeth, Never. Wait too long, and I'll be no good for you."

"Nevare," I said, and went out to the boy's desk to borrow the requested items. He was not there, and after a moment's indecision, I simply took what I needed. I carried them back to Hitch.

He took them with a sigh. There was a small table by each bed in the ward. He grunted as he leaned over it to write.

"What shall I do with your horse and gear?"

"Oh. Bring my saddlebags in here. Tell the boy to make sure Renegade is cared for properly. He'll call someone to take care of it."

By the time I returned with his saddlebags, which he had me put under the bed, the note was finished. He blew on it carefully and then handed it to me, unfolded, so that I might read what he had written. "Take it to the colonel."

"Are you sure you don't want me to stay here with you until the doctor comes?"

"There's no point to it. The boy will find Dowder, they'll sober him up with a cup of coffee or two, and then he'll do what he can for me. You got me here alive, Never. That was more than I thought anyone could do."

"It was the magic, not me," I replied jokingly.

A ghost of a smile touched his mouth. "You only laugh because you don't know how true that is. Get out of here. I'm going to sleep until Dowder comes. Pull my boots off for me."

I performed that service for him, and then helped him swing his feet up onto the bed. He hissed out a stream of quiet curses as he eased himself back onto the bed. In contrast to the clean blanket and muslin-covered pillow, his filthiness was shocking. He closed his eyes and his breathing deepened. "I'll come by and see you later," I told his still form.

I put the pen and ink back as I had found them. I walked outdoors into the sunlight before I allowed myself to look at what he had written. The letters straggled over the page, the scrawl of a very ill man. It wasn't the kindest letter of recommendation I'd ever seen.

"This is Never. He doesn't look like much, but you should let him enlist. He's got a spine, and he sees things through. If he hadn't come willing and helped me, I'd be dead now, and you know how much that would annoy my dear father, not to mention inconvenience you."

That was it. No date, no greeting the colonel by title, not even Hitch's own signature. I stood staring at it, wondering if it were some sort of a terrible joke on me. If I dared show this to the colonel commanding Gettys, would I immediately be thrown out of his office? I was reading it over again when I saw the boy soldier hurrying back. A tall, dapper man with a captain's insignia on his collar followed him.

The boy stopped at the sight of me. "What did you do with the scout?" he asked me worriedly.

"I left him on a bed in the ward, as you suggested. He asked me to ask you to look after his horse."

The boy scratched his nose. "I'll get someone to do it."

I turned to the captain. "Do I have the pleasure of addressing Captain Dowder?"

"I'm Captain Frye. Doctor Frye to almost everyone. Who are you?"

His question was both brusque and rude. I kept my temper. I knew I did not present a respectable appearance. No doubt I was nearly as filthy as Buel Hitch. "I'm Nevare Burv—" I fell over my own surname. I let it go. "I brought Lieutenant Hitch in. A wildcat has mauled him badly. He asked that Dr. Dowder be fetched for him. I'm sorry you were bothered."

"So am I. But I'm sober enough to walk, and Dowder, as usual, is not. Nor does Lieutenant Hitch command this entire post, though he seems to think he does. Good day, sir."

"Sir? If I might ask a favor?"

He turned back to me irritably. The young soldier had already vanished inside.

"Could you tell me where I might find the commanding officer? And where, prior to that, I might find a bathhouse?"

He looked even more annoyed. "There's a barber just outside the gate. I think he has a bath in the back."

"And the commanding officer's headquarters?" I felt stubborn now, determined to wring the requested information from him.

"You'll find Colonel Haren in that building over there. The writing over the door says, 'Headquarters.'" He stabbed a finger in the direction of a tall structure just down the street from us, and then turned on his heel and went into the infirmary.

I took a breath and blew it out. Well. I'd asked for that, I supposed. The faded lettering was almost legible from where I stood. I simply hadn't noticed it. With a sigh, I led Clove away.

I found the barber with little difficulty. It was a bit harder to get him to take me seriously when I requested a bath, a shave, and a haircut. He demanded my money first, and took it before he would even heat the water. He had several tubs in the back room of his shop. I was glad to find them all empty. It was not modesty, but shame that made me relieved no one would witness my ablutions. None of his tubs were large enough for me to bathe comfortably, and he was remarkably chary with the hot water and soap. Nevertheless, I managed to get cleaner than I'd been in many a day, and even to soak away some of my aches. I emerged from the lukewarm water feeling more like myself than I had in a long time. When I was dry, I dressed in my cleanest clothing and went out for my shave.

He was good at his trade, I'll give him that. His tools were sharp and shining. He gave me a soldier's haircut. As he shaved me, he handled my face familiarly, pulling skin tight as he worked and pushing my nose to one side. "How many of these chins would you like me to shave?" he asked me once, and I forced myself to laugh at his jest and told him, "All of them."

Like most men in his trade, he was garrulous, asking questions of me when it would have been very hazardous for me to attempt to speak, and telling me all the gossip of the fort as he worked. I soon knew that he'd been there six years, and that he'd come east with his soldier cousin, reasoning that wherever there were soldiers, a good barber could find work. Brede Regiment had been holding Gettys then. Brede had been a good regiment before it came to Gettys. But everyone said that about Farleyton Regiment, too, and look at it now. He hated Gettys, but would never have the money to move back west, so he tried to make the best of it. Everyone hated Gettys. He'd had a wife once; she'd run off with a soldier, and when he left her, she'd turned to whoring. I could probably buy her for less than what I'd paid for my bath and haircut, if I fancied heartless sluts. I'd soon discover that I hated Gettys, too, he predicted. He asked me where I was from and accepted a mumbled answer from me as he scraped busily at my throat. While he was cleaning his blade, I told him that I'd brought Lieutenant Hitch back to Gettys after he'd had a run-in with a wildcat.

"Hitch, eh? I'd probably have helped the cat myself," he told me, and then went on with a long tale of a very complicated brawl in a tavern in which Hitch had distinguished himself by ending up fighting both of the men who had originally been combatants. He seemed to find it very amusing.

"So. You'll be heading back home now," he asked me when he'd finished and offered me a towel to wipe my face on.

"Actually, I thought I'd try to see Colonel Haren and enlist," I told him.

He took that as a knee-slapping joke. He was still roaring with laughter when I handed his towel back to him and took my leave.

The sentries on the gate likewise found it amusing. Getting entry to the fort was not as easy without Hitch, I discovered. After they had dismissed my first request as a joke, I reminded them that they had admitted me in Hitch's company only a couple of hours ago. "Oh, yes. Now that you mention it, I remember your great big . . . horse!" one exclaimed. After several more jests of that subtlety, they consented to let me pass. I reentered Gettys and went directly to Colonel Haren's headquarters.

Colonel Haren's headquarters were constructed entirely of sawn lumber and once had been painted. Flakes of green paint clung to the weathered timber. The splintery planks that made up its porch were uneven and warping away from one another.

The slum that had sprung up around the fort, the lethargic air of the sickly soldiery, and this final evidence of a commander without ambition filled me with trepidation. Did I want to enlist with such a regiment, under such a command? The rumors I had heard about Farleyton Regiment came back to haunt me: once a top outfit, now fallen on hard times. Desertion and dereliction of duty were rampant here.

What other regiment would take someone like me?

I ascended the two steps, crossed the rough porch, and entered. A sergeant in a faded uniform sat behind the desk.

The walls of the room were lined with wooden shelves jumbled with books and stacks of paper at all angles. A gun rack in the corner held two long guns and an empty stock. An unsheathed sword kept them company. The sergeant had taken a saber cut down the face in some distant past. It had healed into a fine seam that pulled down at his left eye and the corner of his mouth. His eyes were a very pale blue, so pale that at first I wondered if he were blinded by cataracts. Gray hair in a wild fringe stuck out around his bald pate. As I entered, he looked up from some bit of sewing. When he set it aside on the corner of his desk to greet me, I saw he was darning a black sock with white yarn.

"Good morning, Sergeant," I greeted him when he just stared at me.

"You want something?"

I controled my disdain of his sloppy manners. "Yes, Sergeant. I'd like to meet with Colonel Haren."

"Oh. He's in there." He tilted his head toward the single door behind him.

"I see. May I go in?"

"Maybe. Try knocking. If he's not busy, he'll answer."

"Very well. Thank you, Sergeant."

"Yeah."

He took up his sock and bent over his work again. I tugged my shirt as straight as it would go, crossed the room, and rapped sharply at the door.

"Come in. Is my sock mended yet?"

I opened the door to a dim room, lit by the fire in an open hearth in the corner. A wave of heat rolled out to greet me as I opened the door. I stood a moment, letting my eyes adjust.

"Well, come in, man! Don't stand there letting the cold get in. Sergeant! Is my sock mended yet?"

The sergeant called the answer over his shoulder. "I'm working on it!"

"Very well." He answered as if the delay were anything but "very well." Then he transferred his gaze to me and said irritably, "Come in, I said, and close the door."

I did as he bade me. The room confounded me. It was dimly lit and stuffy with heat. I felt as if in one stride, I'd

covered hundreds of miles and was back west in Old Thares.
Fine carpets covered the floors, and tapestries hid the planks
of the wall. An immense desk of polished wood dominated
the center of the room. Oak bookcases filled with leather-
bound volumes lined one entire wall, floor to ceiling. A
marble pedestal supported a statue of a maiden with a basket of flowers. Even the ceiling had been covered with plates
of hammered tin. The shock of contrast between this inner
sanctuary and the rough building that housed it nearly made
me forget why I was there.

The reason for his query about the sock was abundantly
clear. One of his feet was bare. The other wore a dark sock
and a lambskin slipper. I could see the cuffs of his cavalla
trousers. Over them he wore an elaborate silk smoking jacket,
belted with a tasseled length of the same fabric. The silk
skullcap on his head also had a tassel. He was a pale, bony
man, taller than me, with long feet and hands. What hair he
had was blond, but his magnificent mustache looked rusty.
The ends of it were waxed to points. He looked like a carica-
ture of a country gentlemen rather than the commander of
the king's last outpost.

There was a well-cushioned chair with a footstool before
the fire. Colonel Haren ensconced himself there and then
demanded of me, "What do you want, then?"

"I wished to speak to you, sir." I kept my tone extremely
civil despite his brusqueness.

"Well, you are. State your master's business and be quick
about it. I've other things to do today."

Two ideas fought to be first out of my mouth. At my realization that he thought I was a servant, I longed to tell him
in no uncertain words that I had no master. The second was
that I doubted he had anything else to do today. I closed my
teeth against expressing either and then replied tightly, "I do
not come as a servant with a message from his master. I
come as a soldier son, hoping to enlist with your regiment."

"Then what's that in your hand, man?" he demanded,
pointing to Hitch's roughly worded letter of recommendation. I understood now, I thought, why Hitch had phrased it
so crudely. Even so, I did not want to present it, lest he think

the rough sentiments were my own. I kept a firm grip on it, despite his open and waiting palm.

"It's a recommendation from Lieutenant Buel Hitch. But before I present it, I'd like to tell you a bit about myself and my—"

"Hitch!" He sat up straight in his chair, letting his unshod feet fly off the footstool and slap onto the floor. "He was due back days ago. I could not imagine what detained him! But he's back at the fort now?"

"Yes, sir, he is. He was badly injured when a big cat attacked him. When I met up with him, he was feverish and weak from blood loss. I've been traveling with him for the last five days or so, to be sure that he arrived here safely. I took him straight to the doctors when we arrived."

He looked agitated at my news. "But . . . he was carrying a package for me. Did he say nothing of it?"

I instantly recalled the oilskin-wrapped package in Hitch's saddlebags. "He said nothing of it to me, sir. But his saddlebags are intact. I put them under his bunk in the infirmary. When I came away, Dr. Frye was going in to see him. I have high hopes for his full recovery."

I could have saved my breath. As soon as Colonel Haren heard that Hitch was in the infirmary, he strode to the door of his office and flung it open. "Sergeant. Stop whatever you're doing. Go directly to the infirmary. Scout Hitch is there. His saddlebags are under his bed. Bring them directly here."

The sergeant moved with surprising alacrity to his command. Shutting the door, the commander turned back to me. "Well done, man. Thank you for letting me know Hitch had returned. You have my gratitude."

The way he spoke and the way he returned to his chair before the fire indicated that our interview was at an end. When I continued to stand there, he glanced back at me, nodded emphatically, and repeated, "Thank you."

"Sir, letting you know that Lieutenant Hitch had returned to Gettys was not my sole reason for coming here. As I was telling you, I'm a soldier son. I'm interested in enlisting in your regiment."

He raised one eyebrow. I noticed it had a sort of a tufty twirl. "Impossible, man. Don't deceive yourself. You're not fit to be a soldier." He spoke the words bluntly.

I advanced to him, desperately holding out Hitch's recommendation. "Sir, you're my last hope," I said bluntly. "If you will not take me, I do not know how I will fulfill the good god's destiny for me. I beg you to consider me. Use me in any capacity. I will take the humblest assignment. All I wish to be able to say is that I serve my king as a soldier."

He seemed surprised at my vehemence. He took the piece of paper I offered him, and while he read it, either slowly or several times, I considered the offer I'd just made him. Did I mean it? Could I humble myself to serve in any capacity? Was it still so essential to my pride that I be able to call myself a soldier? A few short days ago, I'd been willing to put all that behind me and begin a new life as an innkeeper in a ghost town. Yet here I stood with my pride abandoned and my heart beating like a drum as I hoped by all I held holy that the eccentric man before me would accept me into his dispirited, sloppy regiment.

He looked up at last from the piece of paper. Then he leaned forward carefully and set it on the flames of the fire. My heart sank. As he straightened up, he said, "You seem to have made a good impression on my scout. Few people manage to do that. Myself included."

"Sir," I said, neither agreeing nor disagreeing.

He leaned back in his chair and breathed out through his nose. His wriggled his feet, one slippered and one bare, on the hassock before him. "It's not easy to keep men at this post. A lot of them die of the plague. Those that survive are sickly, and often die of something else. Some desert. Others prove unsatisfactory in an extreme enough way that I am forced to dismiss them. Even so, I try to hold to a certain standard for choosing those who will serve under me. Under ordinary circumstances, I would not choose you. I'm sure I don't need to elaborate on why."

"Sir," I managed to say again, keeping my tone even. He did not look at me, but only at his own feet. He touched their toes together.

"But the circumstances are not ordinary." He cleared his throat. "My scout makes few requests of me. I make many of him. Most of them, he fulfills for me. I am inclined to grant him this request." As I caught my breath in hope, he finally turned his head to look at me. "How do you feel about cemeteries?" he asked me.

He asked in a pleasant and engaging way, as if he had asked a little girl her favorite color at a tea party.

"Cemeteries, sir?"

"We have one here at Gettys. Two, actually. The old one is just outside the walls of the fort. That one doesn't concern me. It's the new one, an hour's ride from here, that is the problem. When plague first struck here, several years ago, my predecessor had a new cemetery established some distance from the fort. Because of the smell of all the dead bodies, don't you know? He's buried there himself, as a matter of fact. That's why I'm the commander now. It passed me by." He paused a moment and smiled a tight and toothy smile, as if very pleased with his own cleverness at not dying of the plague. I wasn't sure what response to make, and when I was silent, he spoke on.

"The cemetery is rather large considering the size of our living population, and that it is only recently established. And Colonel Lope gave no thought, when they started burying people there, that it might be a hard location to defend. Four times now I have requested a budget and artisans so that our cemetery might be properly protected with a stout stone wall, and perhaps a watchtower. Four times now, I have been ignored. The road is all our king can think of. His road. And when I ask for supplies and funding to wall the cemetery, he always responds by asking me how many miles of road I've built in the last season. As if the two were connected!"

He paused for my reaction. When it became clear that I didn't have one, he harrumphed and continued. "I've assigned men to guard the cemetery. They don't last long at the duty. Cowards. And as a consequence, the depredations against our beloved dead continue."

"Depredations, sir?"

"Yes. Depredations. Insults. Ignominy. Blasphemous dis-respect. Call it what you will. They continue. Can you stop them?" He gravely tugged at the ends of his moustache as he spoke.

I had no clear idea what he was asking of me. But I did comprehend that it was my sole opportunity. I rose to the occasion. "Sir. If I cannot, I will die trying."

"Oh, please don't. It would just be another grave to dig. Well. That's settled then. And just in time, it appears!"

He spoke the last words as he leapt from his seat, for there had been a knock on the door. Even before he reached it, the sergeant had opened it. He entered, bearing Hitch's saddle-bags. The colonel seized them greedily and dug though them to resurrect the same oilskin-wrapped packet that Hitch had guarded so assiduously. "Oh, thank the good god, it's not been harmed or stolen!" he exclaimed. He carried it directly to a small table near the fire's light. I stood, feeling awkward, unsure if he intended me to witness this act or not. I felt I should go, but feared that if I left, no one else would recog-nize that I'd been accepted into the regiment. I needed to know where to go to sign my papers and assume my duties. So I quietly remained. The sergeant departed as quickly as he had entered.

Colonel Haren carefully untied the string that had bound the packet shut. When the last fold of oilskin was carefully laid back to reveal the contents, he gave a huge sigh of con-tentment. "Oh. Beautiful," he exclaimed.

My nose had already told me what he had unwrapped. Smoked fish. I could smell it, and my day's hunger clawed at me with frantic desire. My mouth watered, but my brain wondered how smoked fish could be so important.

"Alder-smoked river salmon. It's glazed with honey. There is only one small group of tribesmen who still pre-pare their fish this way. And they will only trade with Scout Hitch. Now, I suppose, you see why a word from him is held in such high esteem by me. Only he could obtain this for me, and only at this time of year. Ah."

As I watched in consternation, he pinched off a tiny mor-sel of shining, dark red fish and lifted it to his lips. He set it on his tongue and then, without closing his mouth, breathed in past it. Eyes closed, he finally closed his mouth. I could have sworn that his mustache quivered with delight. He moved the food about on his tongue like a wine connoisseur savoring a vintage. His throat moved very slowly as he swallowed. When he opened his eyes and looked at me, his face held a look of dazed satiation. "Are you still here?" he asked me vaguely.

"You didn't dismiss me, sir. And I have not yet signed my papers."

"Oh. Well. Dismissed! The man at the desk out there will help you with your papers. Just make your mark where he shows you. You can trust him." And with that, he turned back to his fish. As I opened the door, he added, "Take Hitch's saddlebags back to him, would you? Nothing else in there for me, I'm sure."

I picked up the worn leather bags and slung them over my shoulder. I shut the door quietly as I left, wondering if the man was completely mad or just so eccentric that I couldn't tell the difference. Then I decided that it didn't matter. I wouldn't question my luck in finding someone who had allowed me to enlist.

The sergeant put his darning aside with a sigh when I stood in front of his desk. "What is it?"

"Colonel Haren said I should see you about my enlistment papers."

"What?" He grinned, certain I was joking.

"My enlistment papers," I said flatly.

The smile faded slowly from his face. "I'll draw them up for you," he said with obvious reluctance. "It may take a little while."

"I'll wait," I told him, and did so.

CHAPTER SIXTEEN

THE CEMETERY

T he sergeant took some time to draw up my papers. On purpose, I thought. I signed promptly, as Nevare Burve, and then annoyed him further by insisting that I would wait there until Colonel Haren had signed my copy. When he came out of the colonel's office, I asked him to whom I should report. He vanished back into the office and reappeared quickly. "You'll be loosely attached. Rather like a scout. If you have any difficulties, come here, and I should be able to get them sorted out for you."

"Isn't that rather irregular?"

He laughed. "The whole regiment is rather irregular just at present. None of us expected to be here for another winter. We thought we'd be replaced and sent off in disgrace by mid-summer. Given that we are here and have one more chance, as it were, to prove ourselves while we are more under-manned than we have ever been before, irregular is about the best we can do. Don't worry; you'll become accustomed to it. I know I have." He paused, then asked almost paternally, "Has anyone told you that you should ride out to the end of the road, first thing? We recommend it to all our new recruits. It helps them understand our mission here."

"Thank you, Sergeant. I'll make a point of it."

"You do that, trooper. You do. You're one of us now."

His words warmed me, and he actually stepped around his desk to shake my hand. Once that was settled, he sent me off to a supply sergeant. A note from the colonel's desk sergeant informed him of my "cemetery guard" assignment. He laughed at me, and then diffidently gave me a kit that included no uniform parts that fit me save a hat. "Best I can do for you," he dismissed that issue. The long gun they gave me had seen hard use and little care. The outside of the barrel was badly pitted, and the stock had cracked, but been repaired with brass tacks and string wound tightly around it and coated with varnish. The butt plate was missing entirely, and the saddle scabbard needed restitching. "Probably wouldn't be much good to you anyway," the supply sergeant answered my scowl. "Out where you are, if the Speck ever got serious, one rifle wouldn't hold them back. But chances are you'll never see one doing any mischief to take a shot at him. Don't worry about it, sojer." I accepted my "weapon" with a frown, resolving to inspect it thoroughly for myself before firing it.

"You riding out to the end of the road today?" he asked me as I turned to go.

I turned back to him. "Sergeant Gafney in Colonel Haren's office did recommend it to me."

He nodded sagely. "He's wise to do so. 'Twill give you a much better grasp of what we're all about. Good luck, trooper."

I had not been assigned to any patrol. I had no corporal, no sergeant, no officer at all to report to. Like the scouts I had once disdained, I was loosely connected to the regiment, given a task, and would be, I suspected, ignored unless I failed. When I went to the infirmary to return Hitch's saddlebags, he gave me a dazed smile when I outlined my enlistment. The laudanum the doctor had given him for his pain had made him very genial. "So you're off to the cemetery, are you, then? Better and better, Never. You'll have one of the more lively commands around here. It's the best I could have hoped for, for you and for me. Rest in peace!" He lolled his head on his pillow. "Laudanum. Ever had laudanum, Nevare? It makes getting hurt worth it." He sighed, and his eyes started to sag shut. Then they abruptly flew open, and he said with sudden command, "Before you go to the cemetery, ride to the end of the King's Road. It won't take you more than a couple of hours. Do it today. Very educational." He flung himself back onto his pillows as if he had told me something of great import. And on such a note, I left him there, glassy-eyed and slack-jawed.

I made a final stop at a general store to buy food with some of my hoarded coins. I was not sure how regular the pay would be in such a remote location. I'd been told that I could ride into town each day to eat in the mess, but thought it would be nice if I had food available at my lodgings at the cemetery. No one escorted me to my new assignment, or even gave me a list of expectations. The sentry at the east gate of the fort pointed out my road to me. "Just ride that way, toward the mountains. You'll see it." And that was that.

The cemetery was more than an hour's ride from the gates of Gettys. The road got progressively worse the further Clove and I went, while houses and other signs of settlement dwindled almost immediately. Soon I had left all signs of successful settlement behind. Occasionally I would see an overgrown cart track that led to an aborted farm, but no one lived out this way. It seemed very peculiar to me that every single farm east of the fort had been abandoned. As the road became steeper, winding ever upward into the foothills, all attempts at settlement vanished. The forest drew closer to both sides of the road, dark and menacing. I caught myself riding as warily as if I knew I were being stalked, but saw no one.

I came finally to a rough sign by the side of the road. "GETTYS CEMETERY," it read, and an arrow pointed to a narrower road that led up a bare hill. The hill had been logged off; in some places, stumps still dotted it, while beyond the cleared zone, the ranked trees of a deciduous forest stood in a straight row where the logging had stopped. I started to turn Clove's head toward it, and then recalled Hitch's words. "*Ride to the end of the King's Road.*" I glanced back at the sun, wondered how far it was, and then decided that I'd find out. If I didn't come to it by nightfall, I'd simply turn back.

I soon began to doubt that decision. The road led ever uphill. It was poorly engineered; there were washouts down the center of it, and in one place a stream had eaten a gully across it. It had been repaired badly with coarse stone. I wondered at how shoddily the King's Road was being built. Was not this the king's great work, the project on which he pinned so many hopes? What ailed the men overseeing its construction? I could understand that common criminals were not the best workers for such a project, but surely competent engineers oversaw them?

The road narrowed, and the forest grew ever closer. Twice I startled at motion, just at the corner of my peripheral vision. In each case, I turned my head and saw nothing. Later, I caught a glimpse of the largest croaker bird I had ever seen. It perched in a tree that was half dead, on a bare branch that almost overhung the road. I marveled at the size of it, for it looked like a black-and-white man perched up there. Then, just as I rode alongside it, it suddenly separated into three birds that took flight. I watched them go, wondering how I could have mistaken three for a single entity, and wondering, too, what a scavenger such as a croaker bird was watching for beside the road.

I began to see signs of ongoing work. An empty wagon rattled down the hill toward me. Clove and I gave way and allowed the team to pass. The driver did not so much as turn his head or nod at me. His gaze was set, and he hurried his team at a dangerous pace for such a heavy vehicle going downhill. I began to hear sounds in the distance and soon passed a rough work camp by the side of the road. In a small clearing there were five crude shelters, a corral holding a dozen horses, and an open-sided barn. Two wagons sagged on broken axles beside the barn. It looked desolate and, except for the penned horses, deserted. I had never seen a drearier place. Hopelessness wafted from it like a bad smell.

I suddenly did not want to go any further. I'd seen enough. It was all adding up to something I didn't want to admit. The old nobles had been right. This was a futile, senseless project. It would never be completed, no matter how long we worked on it or how much the king spent. It was wasteful, stupid, and cruel to the men dragged from their city lives to toil in a foreign wilderness. I wanted to turn Clove around and go back. But in the distance, I could hear men's voices raised in command and the creak of heavy wagons. Hitch had told me to see the end, and I resolved that I would, if only to satisfy my curiosity as to why he would give me such a strange command. It did not take me much longer to come to the work site.

I'd seen my father's much smaller road crew at work and knew how it was supposed to operate. There was a rhythm and order to good road building. The best route should have been marked out, the trees taken down, and the ground surveyed to grade. In some places, earth would have to be scraped away and in others, wagons would dump the excess to build up the roadbed. Rock and gravel would be brought in, to lift the roadbed above the lie of the land. Done right, the operation was almost like a dance as some men prepared the way and other workers followed.

The operation before me was chaos. The overseers were either ineffectual or did not care. I saw a wagon driver shouting at men who were digging in the path that his laden wagon must traverse. Further on, two groups of workers had paused to watch their foremen come to blows. The men were fighting doggedly, trading heavy blows in a sullen, mindless way. No one tried to stop them. The convicts in their ragged shirts and trousers leaned on their shovels and picks and watched the fistfight with dull satisfaction. The workers wore leg irons that limited them to a short stride. It struck me as barbaric.

Discord and disorder surrounded me. Weeds and brush grew on heaped fill dirt beside the road. An overturned wagon, its load spilled beside it, had simply been abandoned

where it fell. I came at last to where the road was only a raw
scar in the earth, with stumps of trees sticking up to show
where it was supposed to go. The stumps were silvery, and
on some moss had started to grow. These trees had been
logged at least a year ago and more likely three. It made no
sense to me. The road should have been growing much more
swiftly than that.

A uniformed guard oversaw a coffle of convicts inef-
fectually grubbing up the stumps. He waved an arm at me
as I rode through. He wore a corporal's stripe on his
sleeve. "Hey! Hold up! Where do you think you're going?"
he demanded of me.

I reined Clove in. "Just to the end of the road."

"The end?" He gave a great haw of laughter, and around
him his fettered prison crew joined in. It took him several
moments to get his merriment under control.

"Is there a problem?" I asked him. I cringed as I realized
that I'd addressed him as a noble son would address a common worker like himself. That was a reflex I'd best learn to
control. Once I'd donned the uniform of a common trooper, I
doubted it would be tolerated. But he didn't appear to notice.

"A problem? Oh, no, none at all. You just go your merry
way. Usually we only get new recruits visiting it, but for myself, I think every visitor to Gettys should go out to the end of
the road. It really takes you to the heart of our mission." He
grinned broadly as he looked around at his work crew, and I
saw his dispirited workforce nodding and smirking sourly
among themselves, doubtless over my fat. I nudged Clove,
and we passed through the midst of their work. Beyond them,
all work seemed to have come to a complete halt.

The road ended in a tangle of three fallen trees. I had never
seen logs so large, nor stumps so wide. They must have been
cut years before. The dead bare limbs and the stumps of the
trees had gone gray. Their giant bodies were a barricade of
death against the road's progress. The standing trees beyond
them were even bigger. No wonder the logging crews had
given up. No one could cut a road through trees that size. It
was an insane task. This was the king's great vision? Anger
was growing in me beside a sudden self-loathing. It suddenly

seemed that everything I had been taught, all my pride in being a soldier son, was a part of this fallen ambition. Stupid. I was stupid, the king was stupid, and the road was a folly.

I sat on Clove's broad back, disillusioned and discouraged, staring up into the ancient forest. Then I dismounted and walked forward, trying to see beyond the fallen giants. The ground was uneven, and underbrush of thistles and thorns had grown up swiftly when the ground was granted sunlight. The bushes were so dense and evenly spaced, they almost seemed a deliberately planted hedge against intruders. These brambles had sharp-tipped leaves as well as thorns all down their flexible canes. I made a halfhearted attempt to push into the thicket, but soon tangled in their barbed branches like an insect in a spider's web. Withdrawing cost me snags in my trousers and long bleeding scratches on my arms. I'd wakened a horde of tiny stinging gnats and they swarmed about me. I waved at them wildly and retreated to the road.

The gnats continued to hum about me, trying to settle and sting as I climbed up onto one of the huge stumps. I could have hosted a dinner party for twelve on top of it. The additional height gave me just enough of a vantage to see into the forest beyond the barrier of brambles.

Only in my dreams had I seen such a place. The trees on the hill above me made the stump I stood on seem a sapling. The trunks of some of the trees were as big around as watchtowers, and like watchtowers, they soared toward the sky. Their lower trunks were straight and limbless, and the bark was rumpled and fissured. High over my head, the bark looked smoother, and that was where the branches began. The smoother bark was not rough and brown, but a softly mottled blend of greens, hazels, and red-brown splotches. The leaves were immense, at least the size of dinner platters. The branches of each tree interlaced and meshed with others, forming a dense mat of foliage overhead. Beneath those trees, there was little underbrush, only deep carpets of leaf mold and a silence that seemed part of the permanent twilight under those behemoths.

Never in my life had I seen such trees.

Yet I had.

Not in this flesh, but as my other self. I knew it, and then the knowledge flickered away from me. I reached after it, knowing it was immensely important, but again it was concealed. I took a deep breath and sat very still. I closed my eyes for a moment, focusing my concentration. He was part of me; we were one. What he knew, I could know. What was the significance of the trees?

My eyes flew open.

The trees were alive. They loomed over me. There were faces in their rumpled bark, not faces such as men had, but the faces of the trees themselves. They looked down upon me, and I cowered. They were so full of knowing. They knew everything about me. Everything. Every despicable thought or deed I'd ever committed, they knew. And it was within their power to judge me and punish me. And they would. Now.

I literally felt terror flow up inside me. Like an engulfing flood, it rose through my body. My feet and legs felt nerveless. I sagged and staggered where I stood. When I was a boy, I had experienced nightmares in which my legs turned to jelly and I could not stand. Now, as I collapsed, I discovered that it could happen in real life. The fear that washed through me loosened every joint in my body. I barely managed to crawl to the edge of the stump, dragging my useless legs after me. I fell from the stump to the thorn-choked earth. The thorns tore the flesh of my hands; their tiny teeth snagged in my clothes and tried to hold me back. I sobbed and wallowed toward Clove. My horse stood regarding me with distrust, his ears folded back at my odd behavior.

More than anything, I feared my horse would abandon me here. "Clove. Good boy. Good horse. Stand, Clove. Stand." My words came out in a hoarse, shaky whisper. I wanted to weep with terror; it was all I could do to control myself. I managed to get to my knees. Then, with a huge effort, I surged to my feet. My quaking legs would not take my weight, but I was close enough that I fell forward against Clove's side. My nerveless hands gripped feebly at my saddle. "Oh, good god, please help me!" I moaned, and somehow found the strength to drag myself upright. I got a foot in a stirrup and, while I was only half in the saddle, urged Clove to move. He did, meandering confusedly while I clung, shaking and sobbing, to his saddle. I was inexpressibly grateful that he moved in the correct direction, away from the end of the road and the hideous, crouching forest that waited there. Waves of blackness threatened my consciousness. I was ashamed of what a coward I was, but could not help it. I focused all my thoughts, all my efforts, on getting my leg the rest of the way over the saddle, and when I did and hauled my weight up onto Clove's back, the first thing I did was urge him to a gallop, heedless of the uneven surface and how my panniers jolted behind me. Up ahead of me, standing across the road like a barrier, I suddenly saw a group of road workers gathered in mass. They stood like a wall, whooping and laughing. Clove's good sense more than my direction made him slow his pace and then halt before we overran them. It was all I could do to hold onto the horn of my saddle. My breath still rattled in and out of me. Tears of terror had left tracks down my cheeks. I opened my mouth to shout a warning to them, and then could not think what to warn them about. The fellow who had spoken to me earlier asked with false solicitude, "So, did you find the end of our road? Did you like it?"

I had the barest edge of control of myself. Shame warred with the last fading shreds of panic. What had frightened me so badly? Why had I fled? I suddenly had no idea. I only knew that my throat was parched and that my shirt stuck to my back with fear sweat. I looked around at them, confused by what I had felt and done and deeply insulted by their grinning faces. One of the guards took pity on me.

"Hey, big man, don't you know we've all felt it? That's what the 'end of the road' means here. Sheer shit-your-pants terror. Hey, don't feel bad, trooper. It gets done to all of us. Initiation, you might say. And now you're one of us. Gettys-sweated. That's what we call it. You got a proper Gettys sweat worked up."

A roar of laughter went up as he approached me and offered me his own canteen. I reached down, drank from it, and as I handed it back, I managed a completely insincere smile and a weak laugh. "It happens to everyone that way?" I managed to ask. "The terror?"

"Oh, yeah, that it do. Count yourself a tough nut. There's no piss running into your boot. Most of us here can't brag about that." The fellow slapped me companionably on the leg, and strange to say, I felt better.

"Does the king know about this?" I blurted out, and then felt a fool when my words woke another general laugh.

"If it hadn't happened to you, would you have believed it?" drawled the fellow who had befriended me.

I shook my head slowly. "No. Like as not, I wouldn't." I paused, then asked, "What is it?"

"Nobody believes it until it happens to him," he agreed with me. "And nobody can say exactly what it is. Only that it happens. And that we can't think of a way to get past it."

"Can't we go around it?"

He smiled tolerantly, and I almost blushed. Of course not. If they could have, they would have. He gave me a nod and a smile. "Go on back to Gettys. If you go into Rollo's Tavern and tell them that a Gettys sweat requires a Gettys beer to quench it, he'll give you a free one. It's a tradition for new recruits, but I think they'll extend it to you."

"I am a new recruit," I told him. "Colonel Haren just signed me on. Loosely attached me, that is. I'm the new cemetery guard."

He looked up at me, and the smile faded from his face. Around him, the other men were exchanging glances. "You poor bastard," he said with feeling. And then they opened their ranks and motioned me to ride back to Gettys.

The notion of a free beer at a friendly tavern was a powerful draw. I considered it carefully as I rode back toward Gettys. I still couldn't decide if I felt insulted or hurt by the prank that had been played on me, or relieved that they'd all seen fit to initiate me. In the end, I decided that Hitch's remark had been the most accurate one. It had been very educational. And I was in no position to resent it, I reminded myself. I wasn't a junior officer and the son of a battle lord. I was a new recruit, at the very bottom of the social order. I should probably have thanked my stars that my initiation was no rougher than it had been.

Now that I was well away from the end of the road, I could ponder what had overcome me. I didn't want to try to remember that fear too clearly, nor to dwell on it. A comforting thought came to me suddenly. It wasn't really my problem. I wasn't building the road. All I had to do, simple soldier that I was, was guard the cemetery. I heaved a sigh of relief at that thought and rode on.

But when I reached the sign that pointed the way to the cemetery, I decided that my visit to the tavern could wait for tomorrow. Evening was coming on, and I wanted to see what my new billet looked like.

A cart track wound up the hillside. Clove and I followed it. I soon reached the first rows of rough headboards, for such they were, grave markers made of wood, not stone. To come on such a sprawling cemetery so far from any domiciles, was a very strange sensation. The graveyard was in an open meadow on a gentle roll of hilltop. Tall grass surrounded it, and the inevitable tree stumps. After the immense trees I had seen that afternoon, these seemed quite small and ordinary. I reined in Clove and sat on his back, enjoying that vantage of height. The only sound was the sweep of wind across the grasses, and the calls of the birds in the nearby forest. The cemetery told its own sad tale. There was a row of individual markers, and then what I could only describe as a filled-in trench. The hummock of earth over it showed that the dead had not been buried deeply. Beyond it, the individual graves resumed, but soon enough, those tidy rows were again interrupted by a long hummock of grass-grown earth. The farther I went, the newer the grave markers became.

It was an efficient cemetery, without thought for sentiment or beauty. The grass growing in it had been scythed, but not recently. There were no plantings, no walkways wandering among the graves, and not even a fence to indicate the boundaries of it. I rode Clove along a narrow track through the graves until I reached my destination: three wooden structures on the far eastern edge of the graveyard. As I approached the buildings, I found them better constructed than I had dared hope. They were tidy and tight, built of squared-off logs and well-caulked with clay. Grass had crept into the walkway along with weeds. It had been weeks, at least, since anyone had trodden them on a regular basis.

I dismounted, slipped Clove's bit so he could graze, and set out to tour my new domain. The first shed held the tools of my new profession. Shovels, rakes, a pickax, and several axes were neatly hung on one wall. Four plank coffins, plain as dirt, were stacked ready in the back for whoever might die next in Gettys. A supply of planks for making markers leaned beside them. The very small building between the other two was a necessary. A small paper-wasp nest on the eave by the door showed it had not been used in some time. The other structure proved to be my new home.

The single room held a bed built into a corner, a table likewise attached to the wall under the sole window, and a hearth that would both supply my warmth for the winter and cook my food. Three pots of various sizes hung on hooks above it. A cupboard fastened to the wall would be my pantry. There was a chair, but a single glance told me it would not hold my weight. There was little else of note there. An enameled washbasin on a shelf next to the hearth held a motley assortment of dishes and utensils. I felt vaguely grateful that the previous occupant had at least washed them before he left.

Dust and spiderwebs coated every surface. It did not look as if the cottage had been occupied for months. Well, I'd have some washing and dusting to do before I settled into my new abode. I went outside to see to Clove first. I picketed him where he could graze the deep grass, and took his tack to my tool shed before I returned to my cabin.

The straw tick on the bed was musty. I opened a seam and shook out the old straw onto the earth. Tomorrow, I would cut fresh grass with my scythe and put it to dry before I stuffed the mattress again. For tonight, the bare bed would serve me.

There was a tidy rick of firewood outside the door. I started a fire in the hearth and was pleased to find that the chimney drew well. I had to free the broom from its cobwebs in the corner before I could put it to use. I propped the door open and swept a cloud of dust, dirt, and spiders outside.

The work wakened my suppressed appetite to new fury. I found a wooden bucket in the corner, and took it with me while I followed a faint track from the door to the edge of the woods. There I found a sullen spring seeping water up into a greenish pond. I scowled at the thought of using such water for drinking or cooking. When I knelt down to fill my bucket, I saw a wooden box peeping from the nearby reeds. I pulled off the clinging grasses that had overgrown it, to find that someone had carefully set a box into the spring and filled the bottom with sand and gravel. The water standing in it was much clearer than the rest of the pond. As I sank my bucket into it to fill it, a movement in the woods across the pond startled me. I lifted my eyes, but saw nothing. My heart began to beat fast. The fear the end of the road had wakened in me was still fresh in my mind.

A game trail led from the forest's edge to the water. Doubtless the motion had been a deer, or even the flicker of a bird's wings. I seized the handle of the bucket and heaved myself to my feet. As I did so, I heard a gasp, and then the unmistakable sound of someone fleeing on two legs. I had a glimpse of a bush shaking, but did not see the intruder. For a moment longer I stood frightened. Then I sighed and shook my head at myself and my fears; I had thought I was far enough away from the town that I would be spared people peering at me. Perhaps with time they would become accustomed to me, and the stares would stop.

I took my bucket of water back to my new home. As I returned to my cottage, I considered how squarely and snugly it was built. Whoever had built it had put time and thought into it. I suspected that Gettys had not always been the haphazard place it was now. Once a real officer had commanded it; I judged that the caretaker's cottage had been built during his time.

I was fairly occupied for the next few hours. The simple work calmed me, and I was able to set the last of my fears aside. I put water to boil on my freshly swept hearth, and proceeded to put my food supplies away on the pantry shelves. As I opened my panniers to do so, I rediscovered Amzil's bag. I'd promised to return it to her. I decided to ask Hitch when next

I saw him if he knew of anyone heading in that direction. A pleasing fancy came to me, that I would put in a few things for her and her children. In the next moment, I wondered if she would think me fatuous for doing so. She had made her lack of interest in me plain. Even so, imagining the surprise and delight of the three youngsters made me smile, and I decided that I didn't care if Amzil thought me foolish. I hung the bag on one of the hooks on the wall so that I would not forget.

When I opened the pantry doors, a pleasant surprise awaited me. The previous inhabitant had departed but left a goodly store of dried lentils and beans in two fat crocks with heavy stoppers. Neither damp nor insects had reached them. I immediately put some to soak for cooking. I had spent some of my remaining coin on coffee, tea, sugar, and salt, along with four measures of meal and a rasher of bacon. My biggest indulgence had been a loaf of freshly baked bread.

My days of travel had taught me a great deal about my new body. Limiting my food intake did not dwindle me, but I did become more lethargic, and in extreme cases very irritable. I had continued my habit of savoring food, and I fancied that I better understood now how my body had changed. Almost all that I took in as sustenance, my body retained. I produced very little waste, a fact that had been rather disconcerting to me at first. When I could not find as much food as I wished, I began to crave quantities of water, which, thankfully, had been plentiful through most of my journey.

My hunger was a constant. I had come to accept it as a companion to my life, just as some men had to deal with poor eyesight or deafness. The cramp in my gut was always there, but I had learned to master it. There were still moments when my hunger could seize my attention, as it had near the bakery that morning, and in severe cases, it could distract me until nothing would do until I had found something to put in my mouth. I had learned to set aside a bit of food against moments such as that, for when such hunger overtook me, I became almost irrational. It was a terrible thing to fear that I might slip into such a frame of mind, almost like dreading a bout of madness.

But tonight I had no such fears. I allowed myself a very

hearty meal of coffee, bread, and bacon. The drippings from the bacon made a wonderful spread for the fresh bread. By the time I was finished eating, I felt more satisfied than I had in weeks. I tidied up my pan and plate; checked on my horse, which seemed as contented with his lush grazing as I had been with my meal; and then resolved to walk the perimeter of my new domain.

I returned from that walk a sobered man. Grass grew past my knees throughout most of the cemetery. The trench graves I had noted earlier betrayed the regular waves of plague that had swept through Gettys. The markers for individual graves, mostly made from slabs of wood, were rapidly losing the painted or carved epitaphs they had once held, but they retained enough information to be heart-rending. The cemetery had begun in an orderly fashion. In the oldest section, officers and their family members were grouped together, as were enlisted men. But after the first trench grave, the burying ground had become a much more egalitarian place. Infants reposed alongside captains, and humble nameless privates rested next to colonels. I had thought every grave untended. That was not so. True, wild grasses dominated the area, but here and there I would literally stumble across a marker standing sentinel above a groomed grave site. On a few, flowers grew. On one, perhaps a child's, a simple string of wooden beads, their paint fading in the weather, festooned the marker.

When I came to the most recent section of the graveyard, the change was remarkable. Here, only a season had passed since the last wave of interments. The last mass grave was a weed-covered hummock crawling across the hillside. A row of individual graves marked the first rank of those who had fallen to the plague. A second row after the trench grave marked, perhaps, those who had lingered before they succumbed, or the natural deaths that had occurred since the last wave of plague. The markers were newer and easier to read.

To my horror, I discovered that some kind of animal had burrowed into one of the most recent graves. A mostly decomposed hand had been brought to the surface and feasted upon. It was a man's hand by the size of it, shriveled and dark. The animal had gnawed at the fleshy palm and mostly ignored the curled fingers with their yellowed nails. I looked away from it firmly. The size of the burrow made me think the scavenger was a fairly small creature. I wondered if these were the depredations that Colonel Haren had been lamenting. If they were, then a good watchdog might be my best assistant. Jaw traps might also help me find a solution. But surely a sturdy coffin would have been the best preventive of such incursions.

I performed my first act of duty, though I will admit that it made me feel not just edgy but queasy. There were no sticks close at hand. With the toe of my boot, I nudged the hand back into the creature's excavation wishing I had a stick to poke it farther in. Again with my boot, I scraped and kicked soil back into the hole, and finished up by firmly plugging it with several rocks of the right diameter. It did not seem a very respectful way for me to deal with it, but I judged that in this case, promptness exceeded the need for reverence. I patrolled the rest of the line of recent graves, and found three other places where wildlife was intruding on the resting places of the dead. I repeated my rock- and earth-scuffing at each site, resolving that after this, I'd always take a shovel with me when I made my daily circuit of the graveyard.

The high clouds and fresh wind of the day had thickened to dark overcast and bluster. The first heavy drops began to fall. The moisture in the air made it hard to continue ignoring the clinging smell of the place. Nothing smells quite like rotting human flesh, and my experience at Widevale had forever associated that terrible stench with my own stunning losses. It horrified me that such a foul smell carried my mind immediately to thoughts of my mother. Worse were the mental images of Elisi that came with it. Try as I might, I could not recall my elder sister at her harp or sewing, but only as that perpetually sprawled and futilely grasping corpse. The thought ambushed me that I had done no better by my family with their hasty burials than Gettys had done with theirs. It both shamed me and woke kinship in me.

This duty that had been given to me, however lowly anyone else might regard it, was a trust. In life, these men had served their king as best they might. They and their families deserved respectful rest. I saw now the wisdom of the stored coffins in the shed. There were not enough of them. I wondered if I could persuade my commander that we needed a warehouse full. I grimaced as I imagined how that would affect morale at the fort. Planning to be decimated by disease was scarcely optimistic. But I thought I could convince him it was better than being overwhelmed with dead bodies when the annual onslaught of Speck plague began.

I thought of the anonymous trench graves. Well, that was within my power to correct or at least lessen. I'd proven myself as a gravedigger. If I dug a grave daily and left it open and waiting, would I stay ahead of the plague victims when the hot dusty days of summer brought the sickness again? I was not sure, but it was worth trying.

The rain began to fall in earnest, a driving curtain of water. As I cut short my tour of the graves and cut across their lines in my trek back to my cottage, I resolved that I would remember that every body buried here had been beloved by somebody. I passed Clove, hobbled in the tall standing grass. He'd turned his big rump to the wind and had his head down. He was already drenched, and I pitied him. I led him to the lee of the shed. If winters here were as harsh as I'd heard, I'd need to put up some sort of shelter for him. I'd forgotten to request his corn and oats; a cavalla man's horse received his own rations from the regiment. Tomorrow, I promised myself. Winter was just around the corner, and I still had much to do to make myself ready for it.

The downpour firmed my decision that I would not return to town this evening. I found I rather looked forward to my first night in my own residence. Once inside my cottage, I shut the door firmly behind me. I was pleased to find that the roof was tight, and that the hearth was sufficient to warm the room to a comfortable temperature. I took off my wet cloak and hung it on a peg by the door, and pulled off my boots and stood them under it. And there I stood, suddenly safe within doors in my own little place, with more comforts than I'd enjoyed in weeks and with remarkably little to do.

I busied myself as best I could. The beans had begun to

swell in the water. I added more liquid to them and set the kettle at the edge of the hearth. By tomorrow they would be softened. I would add salt and the last of the bacon to them, and let them cook all day. Contemplating that gave me so much satisfaction that I was rather shocked at myself. Surely I wanted more out of life than to simply have my next meal secured and a tight roof over my head.

But did I?

It was strange to look around my little cottage and realize that I'd fulfilled my ambition for myself. I was, technically, a soldier. I had a post and a task. If I saved enough of my pay to afford it, I could have a uniform made that would fit me and I could wear it. I doubted that my father would ever be proud of me, but at some point I was sure that I'd let him know that despite his lack of faith in me, I'd achieved what the good god had decreed for me.

And did I want no more than that out of life?

I was irritated with myself. I took the spindly chair and set it by the hearth and cautiously perched in it. I'd come all this way to do this, and now that I'd done it, the first thing I did was question the value of it. Could not I take even one night of satisfaction in my accomplishment? What was wrong with me?

I added a bit more wood to the fire and stared at it for a time.

Yaril came to mind. I had said that I would provide for her, that I would send for her as soon as I was able. In the next few days, I should write to her and tell her where I was and that I was, indeed, a soldier. I looked around my snug little cabin. Then I tried to picture my sister there. My heart sank. Yaril had said that she would manage anywhere I did, but I could not imagine my pretty pampered sister coping here. She had always lived in privilege and comfort. Could she adapt to life here? I would have to add another room onto the cabin. How long would she be content, sleeping on a sack of straw, cooking on an open hearth, fetching her own water to bathe in a pan? Gettys would offer her little in the way of amusement or company. How soon would she become bored and bitter? How could I offer this to Yaril as an escape?

I sat down with my journal. I took paper from my extra leaves, and wrote Yaril a letter telling her briefly of my adventures on the road and that I was now at Gettys and an enlisted man. It was hard to tell her that my situation was such that I could not welcome her yet. I tried to make the words gentle and affectionate, but feared that no matter what or how I wrote, she would feel abandoned. I sealed the note, resolving to send it the next day.

My thoughts had spiraled downward. I suddenly saw that all my life, I'd been shallow and without ambition, content to take my birth order destiny and make it the sole focus of my life. I made my nightly entry in my journal. I recounted how I'd finally enlisted, but also included my terror at nothing and my final image of myself at the end of the day, a lowly soldier unable to keep his promise to his sister. It was a savage denunciation of myself. The tidy little cabin I had so enjoyed earlier in the day now seemed an empty little shell that I had moved myself into, something that would permit me no growth, nothing but existence.

My hearth fire was the only light in the cabin. I banked it, undressed, and lay down on my hard bunk. I listened to the wind howl, pitied poor Clove standing in it, and then fell into a deep sleep.

I dreamed of a smell, rich and spicy. It took me some time to identify it, and then I recalled it. It was the smell of magic, the same aroma I'd inhaled when I stood on the pinnacle of the spire and plunged my hands into the magic of the Dancing Spindle. But in my dream, the scent of magic became instead the perfume of a woman's body. She stood naked before me, perfectly comfortable in her speckled skin. Her nakedness revealed the pattern of her markings. They were much like a tabby cat's stippling, suggestive of stripes. Like a curious cat, she moved soft-footed and wary around my cabin.

I watched her. The palest parts of her skin were lighter than mine, the darkest a smooth velvet black. She explored my cabin and my possessions. She lifted my shirt, fingering the fabric, and then raised it to her face, where she sniffed it with flared nostrils and half-open mouth. I caught a glimpse

of her white teeth and dark tongue as she tasted my scent.
When she set down my shirt and moved again, I could see
the darker streak that ran down her spine. The speckles that
were almost stripes radiated out from that streak. The nails
of her hands and feet were dark. Once she stopped her
prowling and stared long at me. I looked back at her frankly.
Her belly was paler than the rest of her, but still speckled.
The nipples of her breasts were dark. Her hair was long and
coarse and as streaked as the rest of her. The rain had
washed her, and her hair clung flat to her skull and was a
soaked veil down her back. Streaks of rain glistened on her
skin and small jewels of it sparkled in her pubic hair.

She was not the first Speck I'd seen, nor even the first
Speck woman. But this time there were no cage bars between
her and me, and I felt her feral grace as a muted threat. Her
body was strong, her legs muscled, her thighs and haunches
powerful. She was easily as tall as I was. Her breasts were
heavy, swaying with her walk, and her belly curved frankly
above the furred mound between her legs. There was nothing delicate about her. She was as unlike a Gernian woman
as a wolf is unlike a lapdog. I watched her scoop two fingers
full of beans from my pot and taste them, frowning. She
pulled her fingers from her mouth and shook them disdainfully. Then she moved again, and came to stand over me in
my bed. She leaned down close to me, so close I could feel
her breath on my cheek. I smelled her. Arousal shocked
through me with an insistence I'd never felt before. I lunged
for her.

I awoke on the floor with skinned knees. I was shivering
with cold, and still desperately kindled. But there was no
woman, not a scent or sight of her. The cold wind and driving rain were coming in through the open door. There were
wet leaves tracked across my floor. I wanted most to believe
that there had been a woman there, but knew the more logical explanation was that I had been sleepwalking again. The
rain had chilled me and a few wet leaves were still plastered
to my feet and calves. I stumbled across to the door, shut it
firmly, and made sure of the latch. I added wood to my fire
and then crawled back into my bed.

I tried to find sleep again, but could only skim the surface of it for moments, like a thrown stone skipping across a river. I listened to the storm rant and rave outside, and toward dawn I heard it finally give up, more from weariness than satisfaction.

I arose to a world washed clean, to blue skies and a fresh, cold wind sweeping the world. Such mornings usually energized me, but today I felt old and stiff and hampered by my weight. I was hungry, yet too bleak to want to prepare food for myself. The swollen beans had burst their wrinkled skins; they looked disgusting. I nudged them closer to the coals and covered them to continue their slow cooking. I hated myself for being too stupid and greedy to save some of yesterday's loaf to break my fast. I toasted the remaining bacon on a skewer over the fire, ate some, and dropped the rest into the bean pot

When I went for water, the tall standing grass soaked me to the knees. When I stood up from dipping up a bucketful, I looked up at the forest on the hillside above me. I felt an echo of the wonder I'd felt once before at such a sight. But in the next instant, a wash of fear swept through me. I imagined slogging through wet leaves while water dripped down on me and tangled roots tripped me. Buzzing insects would sting me, to say nothing of the threat of poisonous snakes and the larger predators of the forestlands. No. I wanted nothing to do with the forest. I turned away from that gloomy, dangerous place, wishing my cabin were not so close to it. I hurried away with my bucket.

I made a morning of heating water, washing my clothes and myself, and stringing a clothesline inside my cabin to dry my clothing. I put on my cavalla hat, a jacket that would not button, and a shirt and a pair of trousers still damp from washing. I built up the fire in the vain hope that the rest of my clothing would be dry when I returned, saddled up a disgruntled Clove, and rode back to Gettys.

My cavalla hat was my admission though the gates. I went back to Colonel Haren's office. I had no success in getting in to see him. When I told his desk sergeant that I wanted to request supplies to build a shelter for my horse, he seemed shocked that I'd have the ambition for such a task. He filled out a requisition form for me, acquiescing to everything I asked him for, but taking such a long time to do it that I felt I'd spent half my life in the office before he gave it to me. I told him that I wished to speak to the colonel about creating a supply of coffins against the projected need in plague time, and that I wished to discuss the wisdom of digging graves beforehand.

His smile might have been a grimace. "Well, aren't you the ambitious one? Do what you think needs doing, soldier. Either no one will notice it, or someone will complain about it." He smiled at his own jest and sent me on my way.

The supply sergeant took the requisition form from me, glanced at it, and then told me to help myself to what I needed in the warehouse. When I asked for the use of a wagon to haul it, he shrugged and told me again to take what I needed. The warehouse was worse. I finally found the men on duty behind the warehouse, leaning against the back wall and smoking. Three of the four were bony plague survivors. I doubted they had the muscle to lift a hammer. I showed them my form, and they told me, as the sergeant had, that I might take what I needed. In the end, that was what I did. I found a cart and a heavy harness, stiff with disuse. I put patient Clove between the traces. The lumber was of poor quality, the nail kegs were jumbled together, and there was no order to any of it. I took what I wanted, including corn, oats, a sack of hay, and a currying brush for Clove, and loaded it all myself. When I was finished, I found the warehouse sergeant out at the back with his men. I asked him if he'd like to inventory what I'd taken. "I'll trust you," he replied, and did not even walk around to look at the laden wagon. It seemed to tax his ambition to walk as far as his untidy office, where he put a sloppy signature on my form and thrust it back at me. I left there feeling vaguely insulted by the whole procedure.

Before I left town, I took my letter to the dispatch office and paid a breathtaking fee to have it delivered. Then I went to the infirmary to visit Hitch again. He was much as he had been the day before. When I complained about how slack discipline seemed at Gettys and the apathetic warehouse

men, he grinned lazily. He motioned me closer to his bedside, as if to tell me a secret, and then said softly, "They
danced it out of us, lad. You went to the end of the road,
didn't you?"

"Yes, I did. I didn't find it humorous, Hitch."

"That's Lieutenant Hitch, soldier!" he said sharply, and
when I flinched, he laughed softly. "You should see what
happens every time they try to send a road work crew into
the forest. Half of them can't remember their own names by
the day's end, and in a week, you might get a day's worth of
work done. Try it sometime yourself. Go walking into the
forest. You'll feel it. You feel it already, I'll wager. I'm surprised you had the sand to get this far."

He lay back in his bed and let his eyes droop closed.
"Don't fight it, Never. There's no point in fighting it. Your
pay's the same whether you work or slack. Relax, trooper."

I put it down to the laudanum. As I stood up to leave, he reminded me, "Hey. You didn't salute me when you came in."

I could not tell if his words were a rebuke or a jest. I stood
and gave him my best salute. He rewarded me with a faint
laugh and a feeble wave of his hand.

I pulled my coat tighter around me as I emerged onto the
windswept street. If this were a foretaste of winter, I'd soon
need to do something about my wardrobe. The bleakness of
Gettys struck me all over again. Everywhere I looked, neglect met my eyes. Weeds straggled along the sides of the
street. The paint was peeling from the fronts of the buildings, and shutters hung crookedly. Although people moved
on the streets, there was no bustle. A young soldier, his shirt
stained with old gravy, walked past me, his eyes on the
ground. I wondered if morale was always so low at this post,
or if the stormy weather were to blame.

The lone exception was a young woman in a blue gown
with voluminous skirts. The wind had pressed her skirts
against her legs, effectively hobbling her. She wore a heavy
black cloak as well, and this the wind whipped wildly. She
was struggling with it and a market basket she carried, and
did not notice my scrutiny. "Drat!" she exclaimed sharply
when the wind wrenched the garment free of her. It took

flight down the street like a crippled blackbird, and she raced
after it and captured it by making a wild leap and landing on
it with both feet. As she picked up the flapping cloak from
the muddy ground, I suddenly recognized her. Epiny. My
cousin was older than when I had last seen her. A moment
later, I revised that. No. She was dressing as a woman now,
but if she had matured in any way, it did not show.

As I stared at her, a sergeant hurrying out the door of the
store bumped into me. "Stop blocking the door," he barked
at me. Then as he caught sight of Epiny in the street, he
glared at me. "Oaf. You'd rather stand and leer at a woman
than offer her help. Get out of my way."

He hurried across the street to offer his aid. She thrust
the heavy basket at him and then spun in a circle, letting the
wind lift the muddied cloak wide, before she sort of danced
herself into it, finally trapping it around her. There was a
large dirty patch on the back of it now. I blushed for how
foolish she looked as I heard her thanking the man for his
help.

I think she felt my stare. They both glanced toward me,
and I found myself lowering my head and turning to one
side. She did not know me. The brim of my cavalla hat hid
my face, and there was nothing about my body that she
could possibly recognize. I walked quickly around the
wagon and climbed up onto the seat. I could not find a clear
thought for why I was avoiding her. "I'm not ready," I muttered to myself. "Not yet. Let me get settled, and then I'll
make myself known to them." I took the wheel brake off
and shook the reins, and Clove leaned into his harness. I
think he was grateful to be back to pulling rather than being ridden. The ride home took longer than when I'd ridden
horseback. The road had been soaked by the rain, leaving
the ruts full of standing water. As I let Clove pick his way, I
tried to sort out my thoughts and feelings on seeing Epiny.
I'd felt that lift of anticipation at the sight of a familiar face,
followed by my surprise that she and undoubtedly Spink
were here and settled in already. For some reason, I thought
it would take them far longer to transfer their home. I
thought of how pleasant it would be to call on them, to sit

down to a meal and talk of people we knew. And then I laid
my own dread bare to myself: that would never happen
now. Cousin or not, Epiny was an officer's wife. Spink was
no longer Spink to me: he was Lieutenant Kester. By now
they probably had their own circle of friends among the
other young officers stationed at Gettys. What could I be to
them, save an embarrassment? Yet even as such a thought
came to me, I knew that Epiny and Spink would both stand
by me, whatever my rank or physical condition.

Yet it was not their reaction but my own that concerned
me. Could I salute my best friend and stand before him and
wish him well, without spoiling it with the greenest of envy?
Could either Spink or I make Epiny understand that no matter what had gone before, Spink was now an officer and I
merely an enlisted man, and thus could not fraternize with
any comfort? All I could see would be discomfort, embarrassment, and shame on my part. I felt the greatest wave of
revulsion that I had ever felt for my body at that moment. It
surrounded and engulfed me in a wall of yielding flesh. I felt
it with every jounce of the cart, how my thighs met and my
elbows rested against the roll of fat that masked my ribs. I felt
the heaviness of my jowls and cheeks. It was even in how my
hat sat upon my head. My soldier's hat, the sole symbol that
I was a soldier son.

When I reached home, I turned to what I always could
rely on to empty my mind. I worked. The sack of hay became stuffing for my mattress. It was clean and fragrant,
and Clove would not miss it. I unloaded my building supplies, and put the harness in my storage shed. I'd take the
cart back to Gettys tomorrow, I decided. I doubted anyone
would miss it.

It was a chill day, but I was soon sweating. I'd decided
that Clove's shelter would be attached to the toolshed, to
save myself constructing one wall. I worked with shovel and
pickax to level an area next to it that would make a generous
box stall for the big horse. Setting the two uprights made me
wish I had another set of hands and eyes to help me. I felt it
even more keenly when putting up the supports for the roof.
The carpentry was a different sort of work than I'd done in

months, and I lost myself in the simple pleasure of working steadily and watching what I had imagined take shape. The smell of the sawdust, the rhythm and sound of a nail squarely driven, the satisfaction that comes when the final plank fits snug and true in a wall: there is a lot to be said for honest work and the ease that it can bring to a troubled heart.

The dimness of the early night had crept up on me before I was finished. I felt more satisfaction over that stall than I had over signing my enlistment papers. When I poured the corn into the grain box, Clove came gratefully into his new shelter. I went into my little cabin, taking my mucky boots off by the door. I built up the fire again and lifted the lid off my bean pot. Fragrant steam rose gratifyingly. I hung up my cloak, and then dismantled my makeshift clothesline and folded or hung my extra clothing. As I put it all neatly away, I tried to retain the sense of satisfaction I'd felt earlier. I set my little table with my cutlery and bowl, and ladled myself a generous helping of the baked beans. I had tea to go with it, and sugar. I ate my meal with pleasure, perched carefully on my rickety chair. Tomorrow, I resolved, I'd remedy that. I'd make myself something that not only could accept my weight but would be comfortable to sit on.

As night lowered outside and the world grew chill and black, I was safe and warm within my shelter. I had much to be grateful for, and very little to complain about, I told myself. Nevertheless, when I sought my now-softened bed that night, a bleakness of heart settled on me once more.

CHAPTER SEVENTEEN

ROUTINE DUTY

I began each day with a patrol of the cemetery, shovel in hand. Diligently I repaired animal damage to any grave. I made notes of headboards that would soon need replacing, jotting down information that might otherwise be lost. I maintained the paths and improved them, evening out the ruts and adding drainage. And every day, I dug a fresh grave. I measured them precisely, and dug them deep and straight-edged. I mounded the soil so it would not fall back into my excavations. I did this past the time when the frosts came and froze the ground. I stopped only when the snows began. My diligence was the only reason that when Narina Geddo died from pleurisy at six years, three months, and five days, an open grave was waiting.

I knew Narina Geddo's age to the day because I was

informed that one of my duties as cemetery guard was to carve the grave markers. I did hers in my cabin one long evening. I put the plank on my table and puzzled out how to engrave the letters and numbers into the wood with the few tools I had. I'd never been a whittler, but I fancy that I did well enough. I threw the chips and shavings into my fire as I worked, and when I was finished, for good measure, I heated the poker and burned black each letter and number in the hopes they would remain legible a bit longer.

The next day I drove to town with a coffin in the back of my cart. Clove snorted and steamed as the cart jolted along over the frozen ruts of the road. When I stopped outside the small house that belonged to Corporal Geddo, his older daughter opened the door, looked out, and gave a wild shriek of fear. "It's a croaker-bird man, come for little Narrie! Papa, don't let him eat her!"

I heard later that the tale of her words scampered through the town and brought laughter to those untouched by the tragedy. But that day, no one laughed at her words. I bowed my head and held my tongue. I suppose that with my cold-reddened face and flapping black cloak, I did look like one of Orandula's carrion birds. The little girl's solemn father came to my cart and wordlessly took the coffin from it. I sat and waited in the biting wind. A time passed, and then he and another man carried it back and loaded it. It weighed very little. I wondered if I'd been thoughtless, bringing such a large box for such a small body. I wondered if a man so gripped by grief could care about such things. Clove and I led, and the small funeral procession of men and women on foot and horseback followed.

I had cleared the grave cavity of fallen snow the night before, so there was a trodden path for the mourners to follow. I did not stand with the attendees. Instead, I watched from a distance as the family lowered their child into the frozen earth, and Gettys' sole priest, a thin, pale plague survivor, said words over her. When they were gone, I went back with my pickax and shovel to break the frozen mound of snowy soil into lumps that thundered down on her coffin as I shoveled them in. It seemed a harsh and cruel sound, and heartless somehow to bury a little girl beneath frozen clods of earth. Yet, in a way, I was proud of myself. Without my foresight to dig a grave, I was told, her little body would have been stored in the coffin and toolshed until spring softened the earth and she could be decently buried. So they had done in years past.

Putting such a young child to rest put me in mind of Amzil and her brood. I had not thought of her in weeks, and her carry sack that I had borrowed still hung on my wall. That day I resolved I would make good on my promise to myself, and also attempt again to win an audience with the colonel. I saddled Clove in the dim afternoon, and rode to town.

I was less of a spectacle than I had been when I first arrived. I still heard the occasional sniggering remark as I passed, but fewer folks stopped and stared. They'd probably had their fill of doing it. Now that I lived among them, I'd lost my novelty. I came to town several times a week to take a meal in the mess hall with the other troopers. I'd found Rollo's Tavern and claimed my beer and admitted my Gettys sweat. People knew me as Nevare the cemetery guard, and some I called friend. It did not mean, however, that everyone regarded me kindly or even neutrally. It still unnerved me to find that my size stirred feelings of extreme dislike in people, even when I had given them no other cause to take offense.

My pay as a common soldier was not generous, but I had relatively few wants, and I'd been very stingy with the money that Yaril had slipped into my pack, so I still had a small cache of funds. I took my saved money to town and tried to be wise in the gifts I bought for Amzil and her children. In the mercantile, I bought red woolen fabric, four loaves of barley sugar shaped like flowers, a box of tea, and a small round cheese. I'd already spent more than I'd intended when I saw the book of nursery tales with hand-colored pictures in it. It would be a foolish gift, I told myself. None of them could read it, and the price was very dear. Nonetheless, I found myself giving over the money for it and sliding it into the worn rucksack with the other items. "That's more than I meant to spend," I observed innocuously as I counted out the scrip on the counter.

"What you want it for, anyway? Going to read stories to the dead?" The young son of the storeowner had been waiting on me. He looked as if he were about twelve, or perhaps a very unhealthy fourteen. Since I'd walked in, he'd regarded me with the same disdain he exhibited to me every time I came in for supplies. I was weary of him, but his father's store had the best supplies in Gettys. Nowhere else could I have found a picture book, let alone barley sugar shaped like flowers.

"It's a present," I said gruffly.

"For who?" he demanded, as if he had the right.

"Some children I know. Good day." I turned to leave.

"A bit early for Dark Eve gifts," he observed to my back.

I shrugged one shoulder by way of response. I was nearly out the door when another voice spoke behind me. "Nevare?"

Despite myself, I turned to my name. A young man in a lieutenant's uniform had stepped out from behind a tall rack of tools. The moment I recognized Spink, I turned away again. I headed for the door as if I'd never paused.

"Wait!" I heard Spink exclaim. I didn't.

I was out the door and mounting Clove before he caught up with me.

"Nevare! It *is* you! It's me, Spink! Don't you know me?"

"Excuse me, sir. I believe you're mistaken, sir." I was shocked he knew me. I scarcely would have recognized myself as the trim academy cadet I'd once been. I avoided looking at him.

Spink looked up at me incredulously. "Are you saying that I don't know who I am, or that I don't recognize you?"

"Sir, I don't think you know me. Sir."

"Nevare, this is ridiculous! I can't believe you're going to insist on this bizarre charade."

"Yes, sir, I am. May I be dismissed, sir?"

"Huh." He breathed out in a harsh sound of disbelief. "Yes. Dismissed, soldier. Whatever is the matter with you? What's become of you?"

If he expected an answer, he didn't get one. I rode away from him. The afternoon was already dark, the yellow lights of Gettys leaking out from the small houses and businesses. The streets were all dirty churned snow over hard ice ruts. Clove's big round hooves threw up chunks of frozen muck as I urged him into a ponderous trot. I rode him toward the gates, but when I judged that Spink would no longer be staring after me, I turned him aside to go to Colonel Haren's headquarters

I resolved that I would not let my encounter with Spink rattle me from my course. I told myself that I'd done what was best for both of us. Spink was a lowly lieutenant, still new to Gettys, an officer with no years of experience behind him nor good social connections. It would not do him any good to admit that he was related by marriage to the fat gravedigger.

No. It was best to leave everything as it was. My life served a useful purpose. Actually, I was more than useful. I was succeeding at a task where all others had failed. Perhaps I was not serving my king as an illustrious officer; perhaps I would never lead a battle charge or win the day for Gernia. But then, neither would Spink, in his role overseeing food supplies and deliveries for the fort. In reality, how many soldiers ever did win a burst of glory? Even if I'd completed the academy, like as not I'd have ended up doing some mindless task, much as Spink had. It was not so bad, what I did. It was necessary.

Even Colonel Haren said as much. That day, I finally managed to get in to see him. I think it was more his sergeant's decision than his. I'd been coming in every third day, and each day been turned away. When I'd tried to voice my concerns to his sergeant, he'd gravely informed me that as I was outside the chain of command, reporting directly to the colonel, he could not help me. That afternoon when I walked into his room, the sergeant had sighed heavily, flipped a hand at the door, and suggested sourly, "Go ahead. Try your luck. Don't blame me if it's all bad."

"Thank you." I'd immediately crossed to the door and knocked briskly. When the colonel barked irritably, "What is it?" I'd taken advantage of the query to enter and present myself.

Colonel Haren did not look surprised to see me. He was

exactly as I'd seen him weeks before, as if he hadn't moved the whole time. He still wore his smoking jacket and cavalla trousers. This time, at least, he had two slippers on his feet. As before, the warmth in his room was overpowering. After a glance at me, he went back to staring at his roaring fire. "Well. I knew you'd be back, trying to go back on your word. 'I'll do anything,' you said, didn't you? Now I know what you'll say. Can't cut it, can you? Did you come to me to beg me to reassign you, or threaten to desert? Or will you say you're ill? I've seen better men than you fail at this assignment. 'He won't last,' I told myself when I gave it to you. And here you are."

I was startled. "Sir?"

"Now you're going to tell me all the same stories I've heard before. Haunts and ghosties wafting out of the trees at night. Loneliness that cuts to the bone. Strange chill winds when you walk through the cemetery, even on a sunny day. Odd scratching sounds at night, and an utter discouragement with your life that you cannot shake. Thoughts of suicide. I'm right, aren't I?"

Although all of those things sounded somewhat familiar, I shook my head. "No, sir. I'm here to discuss gravedigging, coffins, and what I am allowed to do about renewing the markers on the old graves. Some are scarcely legible anymore. Were any written records kept of who was buried where?"

His eyes widened at me. "Well, what would be the sense in that?"

"For their relatives, sir. So they might know where their sons are buried. In case they came to Gettys to visit the grave."

He shrugged that off. "The ones that really care about such things pay to have them carted home. The others . . . well. If you've the time and it gives you comfort, repair the markers as best you can. Dismissed."

"Sir, that isn't the only reason I came."

He compressed his lips and knotted his fists. Then he swung his feet off his hassock and sat up straight to face me. "Do your duty, soldier! If graves are being desecrated, then it's your own fault for not guarding them well enough! If a body is taken, it's up to you to track it down, untangle it from the tree, bring it back, and rebury it. Quietly. And I for one do not care how many times you have to do it! So do it and don't complain."

I was shocked, stunned to silence. I finally had a complete description of what my job was to entail. "No bodies have been stolen, sir," I managed to say. "But I would like to talk to you about coffins, sir. I think a ready supply of sturdy coffins might be good planning. To prevent the very sort of desecration you've spoken about."

He seemed very relieved that I was neither trying to quit nor reporting stolen bodies. "What do you want, man?"

"I've looked at the cemetery and how it has been filled. It's obvious to me that at regular intervals, such as every summer, we are overwhelmed with Speck plague victims. Bodies are buried in one communal trench, without coffins. I'd like to remedy that, sir. I've begun by digging surplus graves. Now I'd like to suggest that we warehouse coffins. If we built them now and set them by, any man who died would at least be assured of the dignity of a proper burial."

"Oh, and that would be a real morale booster, wouldn't it, trooper? I could address the whole regiment, 'Well, fellows, seeing as how the foul weather and utter lack of anything cultural significance in this godforsaken posting has left you idle, I propose that you each build at least one coffin each, so that when summer arrives with the heat, dust, and plague to end your miserable existence here, you'll be assured of a nice burial.'"

I was aghast. "I didn't mean it like that, sir. Only that, well, prudence dictates that recognizing that a problem exists and taking measures against it is . . ." I faltered to a halt. That bit of wisdom had come from an engineering instructor at the academy.

"Quite so. But a warehouse full of coffins might not create the best impression on visiting dignitaries the next time . . . if there is a next time . . ." Now his voice dwindled away. I read in his silence thwarted ambition and dreams gone awry. "This is a dreadful post," he said quietly. "I was an ambitious man when I arrived here. Now look at me. I can't get out of my own path. Something about this place sucks the heart out of a man, trooper. The rate of desertion, suicide, and plain dereliction of duty defies all common sense." He stopped, and suddenly seemed to realize that he was talking to someone so far his subordinate that we could have nothing in common. He sighed.

"Very well. You are correct. We would be prudent to take measures against the inevitable. But I shall not order the building of coffins. I shall authorize the men to acquire a supply of wood, saw it into lumber, and keep a supply of the needed dimensions to build coffins. Acquiring the wood will be a difficult enough task. Are you satisfied? I'll issue the orders that will ready planks for our yearly devastation."

"I'm sorry that it was necessary for me to ask, sir," I said quietly. "And I thank you for granting my request." I longed to know more about the other things he had mentioned, but there was no acceptable way for me to ask those questions.

I turned to go.

"Burvelle."

I turned back to him. "Yes, sir?"

"You're not very good at deception, are you?"

I stared at him, flummoxed. He said nothing. I think it took over a minute for me to comprehend what I'd done. He'd called me by my proper name and I'd responded. I looked down at the floor. "No, sir. I suppose I'm not."

He sighed. "Neither am I. Your father would prefer that you not know he's aware you are here. But I'm in command of this fort, not him. And I'm not going to play cat-and-mouse with any of my troopers." He turned and looked back at the fire. "He must have sent the dispatches out the same day you left. I suspect he sent them to every place he thought it likely you'd try to enlist. He stated, quite coldly, that you had no right to call yourself his son or to use his name anymore."

I felt like someone had fisted me in the gut and driven all the air from my lungs. I hadn't thought my father's ire would push him so far. "That's my father," I said quietly. "Always smoothing the path for me."

"Indeed," Colonel Haren replied grimly. "But I should let

you know that he also wrote that you were a soldier son, destined by the good god to serve as a soldier, and that if any of us saw fit to sign you on, wretchedly unfit as you were, we had his blessing to do whatever we thought best, no matter how harsh, to hammer some sort of a soldier out of you. Even so, when I first set eyes on you, I didn't want to take you in. He'd made you sound like a whining spoiled rich man's son, hiding from his duty. You impressed me when you said you'd take any post, no matter how dirty. So I signed you on. Today you've surprised me. In a good way, I'll add. I don't regret letting you enlist with my regiment."

There was an awkward pause between us. Then I said quietly, "Thank you, sir."

"Don't thank me. It's not a favor to you. It's a matter of my own ethics." A hint of steel was shining through the rust on the officer. Truth to tell, I was glad to see it. I remained at attention, looking straight ahead at the dim tapestry on the wall. I wondered if he'd report back to my father. Did I want him to? I kept my mouth shut. He'd tell me what he wanted me to know.

He took a breath and then let it out rapidly, as if he'd decided something. He changed the topic abruptly. "Burvelle, I deplore the 'initiation' that most of our recruits are put through. But I assume you endured it. What did you think of it? Speak freely."

"It was horrible, sir. But it did do what everyone told me it would do. I now understand our mission. And how hopeless it is."

"I was afraid you'd come to that conclusion. Far too many of my officers and men have. I sit here, day after day, and ponder my dilemma. I've a road to build. But no one can get close enough to the end of it to push it any further. We can't even seem to finish the approach to it. You're academy-trained, in leadership as well as engineering, I assume. So with all that fancy schooling, I hoped that you'd have an insight for me, perhaps."

I didn't, but I didn't want to state it that baldly. "I only went for a year, sir. And it was interrupted by the plague."

"Nonetheless, you come from a good bloodline. New

noble's son or not, the blood of the old Burvelle line runs through you. Continue as you've begun, and I'll see that you get a chance to rise through the ranks. You'll have to earn it, but I want you to know that I'll not hold you down because of your father's ire. Nor raise you because of your name."

"Thank you, sir." His words kindled something in me, a hope that I'd thought had died. I suddenly burned with the need to distinguish myself before this man, as more than just a cemetery guard. "Sir, I see three ways to approach the dilemma of the road."

"Well. Let's have them."

"The first is obvious and I'm sure it has been tried. Go around whatever it is."

He shook his head. "The road's development follows the old trading trails that go up and eventually through the mountains. There is one good pass fit for the King's Road. Unless we intend to level hills and fill in valleys for miles, this is the best and only approach. What are your other two thoughts, trooper?"

I'd heard as much from the other men. There was seldom a night that the dilemma of the road was not discussed in every tavern. Farleyton Regiment had fallen on hard times, but they still had their pride. If there was a way to succeed at this damnable mission, they wanted to find it.

"Find a way to shield the men from the terror."

He furrowed his brow. "Do you have any practical suggestions for doing that? Are you saying you think armor would stop it?"

"No, sir. But it's well known that sometimes drink will make a cautious man foolishly bold. Can a man be numbed to the terror, yet still alert enough to carry on his work?"

"You're suggesting liquor. Or a drug?"

"Laudanum seemed to set Scout Hitch's mind at ease over his injuries."

He gave a short sharp nod to himself. "That's a new suggestion. I'll speak to the post doctors and see if there's any value in it. And your third thought?"

"Find what causes the terror, sir, and stop it. From the talk I've heard, the old trading trail was used for generations.

Now no one can pass that way, and the Specks have to come down to trade. So I speculate that something caused that fear to, well, to start. It wasn't always there. And if something can be made to start, perhaps it can be made to stop."

He pursed his lips and then sucked them in as if he'd forgotten his mouth wasn't holding a pipe. "That's an . . . unusual way to see it. But sometimes that's how you get around a problem. Looking it at from a new angle." He nodded to himself and for a short time stared at the lampshade. I hoped he was pondering some new thought rather than completely forgetting that I was still standing there. I summoned up all my nerve. "Sir. May I ask a question?"

"You may."

"Does the king know what we face here? Does General Brodg?"

"Attempts have been made to explain it to the king. He did not accept the explanation. As for General Brodg, he has, as have the rest of us, experienced a Gettys sweat. Often, when I hear him criticized as having too much sympathy for the common soldier, I think that perhaps that is at the base of it. He has come to Gettys; he has seen what we face here, not just the terror, but the plague." He suddenly cleared his throat, perhaps feeling he'd said too much to a common soldier. "You're dismissed, trooper. Back to your duties. Tell the sergeant to write up the orders to have the carpentry shop turn out planks of a proper length for fifty coffins, but not to phrase it that way. I'm sure he can deal with that. And be assured that I'll be watching you, Burvelle. Burve. Dismissed."

I about-faced smartly and left the room. After a brief conference with the sergeant, during which I wondered if he were also aware of my secret, I left the headquarters and went back out in the street.

I'd left the colonel's office with more questions than I'd come with. I couldn't decide if our commander were mildly insane or a damn good officer. The chance that he might be both was particularly unsettling.

The colonel's unpredictable mood and my chance encounter with Spink had disturbed me. I decided that rather than go back to my cabin and dwell on those things, I'd take my meal at the mess with the other enlisted men. It was something I did occasionally, when I was in a mood to endure gibes and mockery for the sake of some socializing. Some of the men were almost my friends.

The mess was in a long, two-storey building. The lower room was for the enlisted men; the officers always went up the stairs to a more genteel atmosphere. At one end of the big open room, there was a kitchen, with three large hearths for cooking and big ovens built above them for turning out enough bread to feed everyone. It was probably hellishly hot in summer, but in winter the heat from the cooking and the smells of the food made it a welcome oasis. The ceiling was low and darkened with smoke. In the enlisted men's mess, the floor was made of rough timber and permanently filthy. The tables were battered wood, and the long benches were uncomfortable and awkward for me, but I'd come to like the noisiness of the place. I missed the sounds of people talking, laughing, and eating almost as much as I missed my books and lessons. My glimpse of Spink had brought all those memories back afresh.

Ebrooks and Kesey were seated when I came in. I picked up a large bowl of steaming mutton stew and four fresh rolls of bread and went to join them. They were not the brightest of fellows. Their summer duty was to keep the grass in the cemetery mowed down. In winter, they shoveled snow or cleared ice from the walkways. In the plague season, they dug graves.

"Hey, Fats," Ebrooks greeted me without malice. He called Kesey "Curly." The man was nearly bald. "How's the gravedigging business these days?"

"Cold," I told him, and he laughed as if it were funny. Then Ebrooks lowered his face to his soup bowl to spoon up more food. He always ate like that. His spoon never had to travel more than a couple of inches. I sampled mine. It tasted like wet sheep smelled. "What brings you to town?" Kesey asked. He was an older man and had lost several teeth in the front of his mouth, but I didn't know if it were to fighting or rot. He made a lot of sucking noises at meals as he freed the food trapped in his mouth.

"I had some questions for the colonel. And I wanted to do some shopping. Do either of you know anyone who's headed west on the road soon? I've got a package I'd like delivered." I stirred the stew in my bowl. A quarter of an onion, three carrots, and some crumbling lumps of potato. There were two gristly lumps of meat coiled defensively in the bottom of the bowl and little slivers of meat in the flour-thickened broth. And pepper. Lots of pepper. I think it was the only spice they used. I chose the carrot first. It had been cooked too long; its texture was gone. But the flavor had lingered and I savored it.

"Delivered where?" Kesey demanded, breaking into my food reverie.

"Dead Town. There's a woman named Amzil there, with three kids. She put me up for a while and loaned me a rucksack. It's time to send it back to her."

"Oooooh, Amzil. Yessir. That's a nice bit, when you can get it. I'm surprised you don't want to 'deliver' that yourself." Ebrooks waggled his tongue appreciatively.

"It's nothing like that. Just a return for hospitality." I tried not to let my annoyance show.

"You're out of luck, Fats. All the carters have stopped for the winter. If a winter storm catches you on the road this time of year, you're a dead man. Snow comes down, wind blows it smooth, and whoops, where did that road go? Most of them won't chance it. There won't be much traffic until spring. You might find a scout heading out that way, but good luck getting a favor from any of them. You might have to make the trip yourself if you want it delivered. Just go. Who's to know?"

"I might," I lied. My feelings about Amzil were decidedly mixed. I wanted to send her the gifts, not just for the children's joy but to make her think well of me. At the same time, I wasn't sure I wanted to see her again. I'd heard too many men casually refer to her as the Dead Town whore. I wasn't sure I could visit her without her seeing that in my eyes.

"I think that one of the scouts might take it for you. Hitch, or that new fellow, Tibber, Tiber, whatever his name is."

"Lieutenant Tiber? He's here?"

"You know him?" Ebrooks looked surprised.

"Not really. I've heard of him."

"What did you hear?"

"Oh, just rumors. He's a noble's son, isn't he? Didn't he go to the academy?"

"Who cares? Jumped-up bastards." Kesey sounded disgusted that I'd even give it a thought. As far as they knew, I was a common soldier's son, as they were. They expected me to share their disdain for officers who were born to that calling. That stung, but I nodded and went back to my food. The potatoes were as overcooked as the carrots. The bread was good, though. I tore the bread and used the pieces to mop up the peppery broth. I thought about the food, not about Tiber and the ambitions we had once shared. The jealousy of the old nobles' sons had dashed his hopes. My brush with Speck magic had stolen mine.

Ebrooks broke into my thoughts again. "What'd you ask the colonel?"

"I asked him if we could stockpile more coffins. We know the plague is going to come again. It comes every summer. And from what I can see, every summer, we run out of graves and coffins and the time to make more, and end up burying our dead in a trench. I just thought we could admit what happens, and have coffins ready. I've been doing my part. I dig a new grave every day."

"Aye. See. I told you he wasn't going to go off like Rheims did." Ebrooks addressed this to Kesey.

"Who's Rheims?" I demanded.

"Last fellow who had your job." Kesey paused to suck noisily at the gaps in his teeth. "He come to town three times, begging the colonel to put someone else out there. Then he killed himself. Or so some say. Some fellows said they saw him dead over his gun, then come to town to report it. When they sent us out there to see, there wasn't anything there. No gun, no body."

"No blood?" I asked them.

They looked at one another and shrugged. They didn't know. They probably hadn't looked for it. I suspected they'd felt only relief at not having a body to bury. They weren't curious in that way, I suppose. I'd met them the second time I'd come to the mess hall to eat. They'd sat down beside me and introduced themselves as gravediggers and caretakers of the cemetery in summer. The graveyard was the common bond that made us friends.

"Was his body ever found?" I asked. I expected that to be a negative.

Again, they exchanged a glance. "We found it. Finally. And we brought him back and buried him."

"Where did you find it?" I felt resigned to having to pull the story from them a bit at a time.

Kesey ran his tongue over his teeth, then opened his mouth with a popping sound. "The usual place. In a tree."

"Someone stole his body and left it in a tree?"

"'Course in a tree. Where else?"

I was bewildered. "Why a tree? Did an animal drag him up there?"

"You might say that," Kesey snickered.

But Ebrooks was incredulous. "You don't know about the bodies in the trees? I thought sure they would have told you that when you took the job."

I shook my head. "All I know is that I'm a soldier son, I needed to enlist, and after I helped Scout Hitch, Colonel Haren said he'd have me. And he assigned me to guard the cemetery." I knew a bit more, but I thought feigning ignorance might encourage them to talk.

Again, they shared a look. "And you said he had to be some kind of brave to take the job." Ebrooks scoffed at Kesey. "Damn fool didn't know a thing about what he was getting into!"

Their grins were wide but also uneasy when I said, "So why don't you tell me, then? What about the fellows who have guarded the cemetery before me? What about the stolen bodies?"

"Well, ain't all that much to tell," Kesey said cheerily. "Sometimes it happens, sometimes it doesn't. You bury somebody, and poof, the next day the grave's dug up and the body's gone. Then you got to go into the forest and look till you find it. And that's damn hard, you know, cause one day the forest will be full of spooky noises and the next you'll go in there and under the trees it's so thick with weariness and discouragement, a man can't hardly keep his eyes open. But anyway, you find the body, tear it free, and bring it back and bury it again. Sometimes, if you're lucky, it stays buried. Sometimes you got to go get it again the next day. Easier the second time, because it will be in the same tree. But it will be worse for dragging it around, because the bodies go bad so fast, after a tree has been at it, you know."

They spoke so calmly, and I found myself nodding. A long-ago memory surfaced, of words overheard in the night outside my father's study. "The Specks do it?" I asked.

"Well, sure. Who else?"

"Why?"

"Because they're savages, with no proper respect for the dead. They do it to mock us!" Ebrooks was adamant.

"I don't know about that," Kesey said. "Some folks think they do it like it's a sacrifice to their gods."

"No. It's to make fun of us, to force us to go into their damned forest. That place is enough to drive a man mad. But we know we've got to go in there, to get our own dead back."

"Why is it so difficult to go into the forest?" I asked. "I live right near the edge of it. It's not like the end of the road is."

They looked at one another again, sharing their conviction of my idiocy. I decided if they did it one more time, I might try knocking their heads together. "Don't you talk to anyone?" Ebrooks demanded. "Don't you know anything about the Specks?"

I fancied I knew a great deal more about the Specks than they did. Before I could phrase a more tactful thought, Kesey grinned and challenged me, "Why don't you just try going into the forest, Nevare? Find out for yourself."

"I probably will, but I'd like to know—" My request was cut short by a sergeant bellowing their names. They both rose hastily and followed him. The sergeant gave me a disdainful glare before he turned and led them away. I knew the man slightly. His name was Hoster, and he was the man who had helped Epiny with her cloak that windy day. He'd formed a bad opinion of me that day and had never troubled to change it. He seemed to find my fat a personal affront. Today his harassment was veiled, limited to sending away my dining companions on some trivial task.

I sat by myself, finishing my cooling stew and savoring the fresh bread. I let myself focus on the bread, how it tore between my fingers, on the difference between the brown crust and the softer interior. I felt my teeth break it down with my chewing, the satisfaction of swallowing. This, I could always rely on. Food never failed me.

I cleared my place at the table. Most of the men were dispersing. As I was leaving, Lieutenant Tiber entered. He let the door bang shut behind him and stepped to one side to unwind a long muffler from around his face and throat before taking off the heavy woolen cloak he wore.

I had not seen him since he'd left the academy to become a scout. I still could not look at him without feeling a measure of guilt. If I had spoken up sooner about what I'd seen the night he was beaten and left for dead, perhaps scandal would not have stained him. Winter aged him as it does some men: he looked bitter, and the lines in his face were deepened by the redness of his cheeks. The mud-spattered edge of his cloak seemed to attest to a journey just completed. He glanced at me, grimaced with distaste at my portliness, and then his eyes slid away, dismissing me as being of no consequence.

I watched him strip the gloves from his hands; despite their protection, his hands were red with chilblains. I challenged myself to approach him and ask if he could carry my gifts to Amzil on his next mission in that direction. But he was an officer, and obviously tired, cold, and in a hurry to get to hot food. I halted and he strode past me without a glance. I left the mess hall.

The ride home in the dark seemed longer than usual. The rucksack hung at my saddle, a bag full of good intentions. I idly wondered if Colonel Haren would grant me leave to deliver my gifts myself. He'd probably think I was trying to desert. Then I wondered if anyone would notice if I took half a dozen days to ride out to Dead Town and back. Would Amzil be glad to see me? Or would she think that I'd heard of her reputation and come to try my luck with gifts? I clenched my teeth. I had no time for a schoolboy's infatuation based on a woman being civil to me.

The year was coming to an end and the night seemed darker and the stars closer. Moonlight made the road a dirty streak between the snow-mounded fields. I trusted Clove to find his way home. The thoughts I'd been avoiding all evening occupied me. Was this duty my destiny, the summit of my life's ambition? Did my father know I was here? Did I hate him more for how he'd sought to be sure I couldn't use his name to gain favor? I shook my head to clear it of thoughts of him. Almost immediately, Spink came to mind. How long could I avoid him and my Cousin Epiny? If Spink told Epiny he had seen me, I doubted it would be long. And then what? She'd want to know every detail of my life and I didn't think I could stomach a long confession, let alone her misguided good intentions to help me. Better for all of us if she never knew I was in Gettys. I offered a vain prayer to the good god I had once so trusted that Spink would have the common sense to hold his tongue and say nothing to Epiny.

My spirits sank deeper when I perceived that the single window of my little cabin leaked yellow light into the night. I had left the fire banked on the hearth. For light to spill out from the closed shutters meant that someone had lit the lamp. I dismounted from Clove and dropped his reins, creeping toward my dwelling cautiously. Who had intruded and what did they intend? Strangely, I did not fear robbers so much as I dreaded that Spink might have tracked me down.

Then I recognized Renegade standing outside my door. I advanced, relieved it was not Spink, but puzzled as to why Hitch would visit me. I'd called on him several times while he was recovering from his cat attack, but each time, the differences in our ranks had become more awkward. It had been some weeks since I'd last seen him. As I set my hand to the latch, I wondered how I should greet him. I was annoyed that he would so freely enter my dwelling place; on the other hand, on a night such as this, I could scarcely have expected him to wait outside for me. Curiosity finally overwhelmed all else and I opened the door.

My cabin had undergone several changes since I'd first moved in. I'd built myself an ample chair, uglier but much sturdier than the original. I'd also reinforced the table and widened and strengthened the bed. Hitch sat in the original spindly chair by the hearth. He didn't startle when I opened the door, but merely turned his face toward me with a slow grin. The aroma of fresh coffee filled my cabin.

"Put the wood in the hole, boy. It's cold out there."

I shut the door as he bade me. Hitch had shed his wet outer garments in an untidy heap on the floor.

"It's pleasant to see you, sir," I said stiffly. The smell of the hot coffee beckoned me.

"I left my 'sir' on the other side of your door. Pardon me if I don't get up to fetch it." He nodded at my pot full of his coffee. "Hope you don't mind that I extended your hospitality to myself. It's a black, cold night out there, and a man has to take comfort where he can." He looked around my small home. "So. It looks like you've done well for yourself."

I wasn't sure if he meant to be sarcastic or not. "It's better than some places I've been," I said guardedly.

He laughed at my cautious tone. "Never, come on in and get comfortable. Pull up a chair, have a cup of coffee. After all, it's your house. Your life."

"That's true," I said pointedly. "Back in a moment, after I put up my horse."

When I returned from seeing to Clove, Hitch had poured me a mug of coffee. Several apples sat on the table next to the mug. As I hung up my cloak and muffler, I asked him, "How on earth did you get apples at this time of year?"

"I'm an officer. We have access to the better supplies." He laughed at the expression on my face. "You're torn between 'It's not fair' and 'I should have been an officer, too, so I could have those unfair apples more often.'"

"I think both statements are true," I said with mangled dignity.

"True has nothing to do with what is," he said blithely. "Sit down, Never. Drink your coffee and eat an apple. Let us discuss our lives with one another."

"Let's not," I said succinctly, but I took an apple and the mug from the table and moved my chair to join him by the stove. "What really brings you to visit me?" I asked after my first sip.

"Renegade," he said, and laughed at his own feeble joke. Then he cleared his throat. "I don't know, Never. I just had an impulse. Do you ever get impulses like that? You suddenly feel like you ought to do a thing without knowing why?"

"Not really," I said.

"Really?" he asked conversationally. "Let me rephrase that. Have you ever done something impulsively, and suddenly felt that your careless words or passing touch would have far greater significance than you'd intended?"

A creeping dread invaded my bones. "No, I don't think so."

"I see. So you never attempted to enlist at a small courier station? And as you left, you never departed with a quote from the Holy Writ? Something like, 'As you have seen to the needs of the stranger, so may your own wants be met in your time of need?' "

I sat very still, looking at him. He smiled mirthlessly. "I range a bit. Sometimes I go a bit beyond the scouting missions I'm sent on. Sometimes I've a mission of my own. Such as when I'm sent out to set something to rights after someone else has unbalanced it."

"Do you do that often?" I managed to ask. The apple sat round, smooth-skinned, and untasted in my hand. I could smell its end-of-summer fragrance. It spoke of sweet juice and tart flesh just under the red-streaked skin.

"Not before you came along." He shifted in his chair, stretching his stockinged feet closer to the fire. "Things are pretty strange at that courier station, Never, my lad. Think about it. I'm guessing you wanted food and they sent you away empty-handed. They remember you quite well, by the way. It was the day after you passed through that the first supply wagon arrived empty. No one had any explanation.

The wagon pulled in, the troopies came out to unload, and the crates were empty."

"Bizarre," I managed to say. A stillness was growing inside me.

"Once would be bizarre. The second supply wagon never arrived. Nor the third. Well, let me make the tale short. In an incredible string of bad luck and odd mishaps and inexplicable events, that particular courier stop has gone unsupplied since you—or someone very like you—passed through and cursed it. At least, that's how the tale is being told." He paused for a moment and then added, "They're not starving, exactly. They can go out and hunt for themselves. But it's been very disruptive. A lot of people have heard about it and are paying attention to it. That could be bad for you, Never."

He was no longer asking if I'd done it, and I saw no point in denying it. "The words just came out of my mouth," I said. "I just meant to be sarcastic. Not to curse them."

He sank a bit deeper into his chair. "Speck magic has a life of its own, Never. You might think you're using it, but it's always using you. Always. I warned you to be careful of it."

"That happened before I ever met you," I retorted, and then felt childish for needing to make the excuse. I took a bite out of the apple. The taste of it overwhelmed me for a few moments. My head reeled with sweet and sour, with the crisp texture of the flesh and the sturdy flap of apple skin that I ground between my teeth.

"There he goes again," Hitch muttered to himself. "You don't listen to a word I say. The more you use it, the more power it has over you. There. Is that plain enough for you? The magic isn't yours, Nevare. You belong to it. And the more you use it, the more hold it has on you."

"Like the 'keep fast' charm," I said slowly. "Only it doesn't seem to work anymore."

He shot me a look. "Yes. I was coming to that. You do seem to get around, and to do a lot of damage in the process."

Uneasiness ran over me with cold, wet little feet. "I don't believe that you've gone as far as the Dancing Spindle on a scouting expedition."

"Me personally? No. But there were witnesses. And information like that travels. If a person wants to hear about it, he only has to listen. And some people very much wanted to hear what had suddenly impacted the whole system of Plains magic. You're fair on your way to being a legend in your own time, Never."

"Just who do you 'scout' for, Hitch? The information you're gathering doesn't sound like something Colonel Haren sent you after." I was beginning to feel angry, the kind of anger that comes when fear threatens and one doesn't know the exact source.

"Damn you, Never. You sit there and I talk to you and you hear the words, but it's like you don't listen to what they mean. It's Speck magic, old son. It's got you. I told you before, it's got me, too. It uses me. It uses you. The scary part is that you seem to be using it and I don't think you have any concept of what you are doing. Or how heavily in debt you are to it. When it demands to be paid back, you're going to have to give it more than just yourself. You're going to have to give it things that don't belong to you, things I care about. I'm here to tell you that you have to draw a line with it and fight. Be a Gernian, man, at least a little."

"It seems to me that a few weeks back, you didn't think so highly of my patriotism. If I recall correctly, you mocked me for it."

"I mock anyone who does things without thinking for himself why he does them. And that is what you're doing with your magic. You took out the Dancing Spindle. And when you did, I think that what the Plains magic lost, Speck magic gained. And certainly you seemed to have gained. You do things I've never seen anyone do, and I've seen quite a bit of Speck magic in my wandering. Last time I went through Dead Town, I saw your little vegetable garden. You told it to grow. It's still growing. Just as the people at the courier station are still not receiving supplies, just as they denied them to you. You're setting things in motion, Never, with no heed as to the ultimate consequences. You stopped the Spindle turning, but you've set all sorts of little things spinning for you."

"Look," I said bluntly. "I did those things. Well, I guess I did them. You say so, and I'm going to believe you. But I don't know how I did them. And I don't know how to undo them. If anyone is at fault here, it's the damn magic, not me. It came into my life and took it over. I never sought it out. It's ruined everything for me. It's taken my body, my career, my fiancée, my family, even my name. I've lost everything to it. And I still don't know how it works or why it works or what it wants of me. But with all the things it has done to me, why can't I use it to do a little good? Amzil and her children were starving. Was it so bad, what I did?"

He huffed out his breath in a blast of disbelief. "Damn me. You *did* do it. You really did!" He took a breath as if to restore his steadiness. "Was it so bad? You ask that as if you think I know the full answer. All I can tell you is that this magic gets into you, like ivy putting roots into a tree trunk. And it climbs up you and it steals your light and sucks out your sustenance. It uses you, Never. And every time you use it, you give more of yourself to it. Do you understand me? Tell me that you know what I'm talking about."

"I don't! That is, I do and I don't. How do you know so much about it, anyway?"

"I told you. There was a woman, a Speck woman. She wanted me, and what a Speck woman wants, she takes. And a Speck woman is just like their magic. She makes you her own, and that's it." He stood up so suddenly his chair nearly fell over. With lightninglike reflexes, he caught it and then stepped clear of it. He walked a turn around my small house, staring at the walls as if he could see through them. "Never met a woman like her before. Once you start going among them, you'll see what I mean. They got a whole different way of seeing the world, a whole different idea of how life works. And once they take you in, suddenly it seems that it's the only way to see things. They just accept the magic. They don't go around thinking that they're going to decide how their lives go. They laugh at us for that. Once, that woman showed me a little plant growing by a stream. She said, 'You see that little plant, all by itself, having its own life?' And I said, 'Yes, I see it.' And she said, 'That's you. And you see that other little plant over there, on the other side of the stream? You see it, all by itself over there? That's me.'

"So I thought she was trying to tell me something, about how the stream separated us, about how different we were. But then she went over and grabbed the plant that was me and she pulled it up out of the ground. But its tough little roots came with it. And she started following that root, lifting it up out of the ground, and that root went from my plant to another to another and to another and finally it went right under the stream and come up on the other side and she pulled it up and it went to the plant she said was her. And she stood there, holding up all this network of roots, and she said, 'See. There isn't one little plant growing alone. It's all of us.' "

He fell silent, palm up and empty, reached out toward me, waiting for a response. He seemed terribly moved by what he had told me. "It's a nice story," I said at last. "But I don't see how it helps me understand whatever it is you're trying to say."

He shook his head at me in disgust and went back to sit in his chair. "For her, it's not a metaphor. It's reality. She truly believes that we are connected to one another and that in some way we are all part of one big . . . something."

"Some big what?"

"We don't have a word for it. She's told me about it a hundred times, but her truth is in a place where our words don't reach. It's like disease. Our children get sick, we try to find out why, and we try to make them better. We cover them up with blankets to try to sweat the fever out or we give them willow bark tea. Because we think sickness means something is wrong with a child."

"And Specks don't think something is wrong when a child gets sick?"

"No. Do you think something is wrong when a boy's voice changes or he sprouts whiskers out of his face? They think children are supposed to get sick. Some get better and live, and that's fine with them. And some die, and that's fine with them in a different way."

"Do you see her often?"

"Who?

"Your Speck woman!"

"Yes. In a way."

"I'd like to meet her," I said quietly.

He seemed to think about that for a long time. "Maybe you can, if she wants. In spring."

"Why not sooner?"

"Because it's winter. No one sees Specks in the winter."

"Why not?"

"Are you playing with me, Never? You are so damn frustrating. How can you have Speck magic all through you and not know a thing about them? Specks don't come around in winter. They just don't."

"Why not?"

"Well—I don't know. They just don't. They're gone in winter."

"Where? Do they migrate? Do they hibernate?" I was getting as impatient with Hitch as he was with me. He'd come here, full of mystical hints and warnings, and told me next to nothing.

"I just told you, I don't know. They keep to themselves in winter. No one will see a Speck around here until spring."

"I saw a Speck woman here, but it was only a dream." I think I threw the words out just to see what he would say.

He gave a huff of displeasure. "I like how you say 'only,' Never. Are you that comfortable with it? Speck comes walking around in my dreams, it still puts the wind up my back. Of course, to them it's nothing; they go journeying by dream all the time. Noselaca, she can't understand why I make such a fuss about it."

"So you dream of your woman—Noselaca?"

"She's not my woman, Never." He spoke quietly, as if sharing a dangerous secret with me. "Never talk about a Speck woman that way. She could put you in a bad way over something like that. And I don't dream about her. She comes into my dreams."

"What's the difference?"

"In the world you and I grew up in, nothing at all. In her world, well, in her world she walks into a dream like you walk into a different room."

I'd almost forgotten the apple in my hand. I took another bite of it and chewed it slowly, thinking. "She believes that she can visit you in your dreams."

"She not only believes it, she does it."

"How?"

"Are you asking how I experience what she does, or how she does it? The answer to the first is that I fall asleep, and I think I'm having an ordinary dream, and then Noselaca comes into it. As to how she does it, I've no idea. Maybe you should be telling me. You seem to be the one using a lot of magic."

The apple was down to a stem and the core. I looked at it for a few moments, then put the core in my mouth and chewed it up. I tossed the stem in the fire. "A year ago, I would have thought this whole conversation was utter nonsense. Now half the time I don't know what I think. A dream is just something that happens in your mind at night. Except when a Speck woman walks into it and starts teaching you things. Hitch, I can't make sense of my life anymore. Once, it was all laid out for me so clearly. I'd go to the academy, graduate with honors, and I'd get a good commission with a top-notch regiment. I'd move up fast as an officer, I'd marry Carsina, the girl my father had chosen for me, and we'd have children, and eventually, when I was old, I'd retire from the military and go back to Widevale and live under my brother's roof until I died."

"Well, who wouldn't dream of such a life?" Hitch asked with false enthusiasm.

"You can mock me if you like," I replied grumpily. "It wasn't a bad dream. If I'd been posted to the right regiment, I'd have had a chance for adventure and glory. And I don't see anything wrong with looking forward to a well-bred wife, and quiet waters and a snug home at the end of one's days. What do I have to look forward to now? If I get really good at burying bodies, perhaps I'll earn a corporal's stripes. And when I'm too old to dig graves, what then? What then?"

"You can't really believe that you're stuck here the rest of your life?"

"Well, I don't really see what else there is for me!" I retorted. Saying it aloud made it more real. Maybe I'd be promoted. Maybe I'd get a few stripes on my sleeve, but I'd still

be fat and alone and digging graves. And when I couldn't do
that anymore, when my body gave out under the strain of
carrying all this extra flesh, then I'd be one of those ex-
soldier beggars in some dingy town. I sat back in my chair. I
couldn't catch my breath.

"Take it easy, Never. You've got all this magic running
through you. And you're worried that you'll have a boring
life. Actually, you should be praying for that. Boredom is
vastly underrated. Boredom means that nothing is trying to
kill you every day." He smiled grimly at his own wit.

"I almost wish—" I began, but stopped at a sharp motion
from Hitch.

"You, of all people, should be very careful what you wish
for. If you haven't heard a word I've said all evening, then
listen to me now. Your wishes have an uncanny habit of
coming true. Be careful where you bend your will. Magic
seems to go with it."

"Perhaps once or twice," I began, but again he cut me off
impatiently.

"You wished to enlist here. And because it served the
magic's purpose, you were allowed to. This duty you've
been given—do you think this was a random choice by our
colonel? I venture to say there is Speckish benefit somewhere here."

"How could my guarding the cemetery be of any benefit
to the Specks?"

"I don't know," he finally retorted in a low voice. "But it's
something *you'd* best think about, Never. Why would they
want you here? What do they want you to do?"

"I don't know. But whatever it is, I won't do it. I won't
betray my people." I thought I knew what he feared. "I won't
be lax at my guardianship. I won't allow them to mock and
desecrate our dead."

"Mocking the dead would be very un-Speck-like." Hitch
said quietly. "They show their own dead vast respect. They
claim that wisdom gained never passes away, not even with
death. Did you know that?"

I shook my head. "This part of me that is here and
speaks to you knows very little about the Specks. But there

is another part of me that I fear knows too much and too well."

He allowed himself a smile. "That you know that part exists and that you admit it to me shows me that you are gaining wisdom, Never." He heaved a sudden sigh and stood up. "It's late. I'm going back to town. There's a new whore at Sarla Moggam's brothel. I plan to sample her before she's worn out."

"But you said you had a Speck woman."

He lifted one shoulder and gave a smile both sheepish and defiant. "Once in a while, a man likes to be in charge of things. Speck women don't give you much chance of that. They do things their own way and expect you to follow meekly along."

For some reason, that put me in mind of Amzil. "You've reminded me. I've still got Amzil's carry sack. Next time you go by Dead Town, would you take it back for me?"

"I could," he conceded. "If you think you must. Nevare, it's just a rucksack. Don't put too much importance on it."

"I promised her that I'd return it. My promise is worth more to me than the rucksack. Besides, I've put in a few gifts. For the children."

He shook his head at me. "I've warned you, old son. Amzil's a hard nut to crack. I don't think you'll get to her through the children. Save your time and effort. Come to Sarla Moggam's with me."

The invitation was more tempting that I wanted to admit. "Another time," I said regretfully. "When I've got more money. Will you take the carry sack to Amzil?"

"I said I would," he agreed. "And will you be more careful in how you spend your magic?"

"I would if I knew how. I wish I could undo what I did to the men at the courier station. It was only their sergeant who was so hard-hearted to me. I'd no wish to curse them all."

"All the more reason for you to be careful. If that's what you do when you don't mean to harm anyone, what would happen if you really intended it?"

It was a sobering thought. "I'd undo it if I could. I don't know how."

He was standing by the door, the laden rucksack in his hand. "That's a feeble excuse, Never, and you know it. You said you did it without knowing how. If I were you, I'd be trying to undo it." He shook his head at my expression. "Don't be stubborn. This isn't something you want connected to you. You're a dangerous man, Never. The fewer people who know that, the safer you are. Good night."

And so he left me to what was not a good night at all. I didn't like that he thought I was "dangerous," and I liked it even less that, on consideration, I concluded that I was. I was like a foolish boy with a loaded gun. It didn't matter if I knew how the gun worked; I'd fired it, and someone had suffered the consequences. Was I so different from the two young fools on the riverboat who had felled a wind wizard with iron shot? They'd probably had no real notion of the harm iron could do him. I'd despised them for it. But here I was, spraying magic out just as carelessly. According to Hitch.

I lay in my bed and stared up at my shadowed ceiling. I wanted so desperately to be able to go back to where magic was the stuff of tales, not something that affected my life every day. I didn't want it to be a power I had, with no concept of how it worked or was controlled. The light danced with the flames in my hearth and I decided I should try to undo whatever I had done to the courier station. It wasn't easy. In the moment I'd said those words, I'd wholeheartedly desired that they suffer exactly as I did from their lack of charity. There was still a hard part of me that thought they deserved what had happened. I discovered that I would need to forgive them before I could truly wish to undo what I had done to them. That forgiveness was an easy thing to say, but a harder thing to feel in my heart.

I groped toward an understanding of the magic I had done. It had gone beyond what I'd said to what I'd felt toward them. Feelings, I discovered, did not yield to logic or even to ethics. Why should everyone at the relay station suffer because their sergeant had been so stiff-necked? Why should any of them suffer at all, at my say-so? Who was I to judge them?

I chased my morality in circles that night, trying to find it. When it came to actually living as an upright man, I discovered that I was no more truly tolerant and forgiving than any worshipper of the old gods.

The moment that I realized I was no better than the men who had turned me away when I begged their help, I was able to forgive. I felt something move through me, a prickling in my blood, followed by a stillness and a sense of effort expended. Had I worked magic? I couldn't tell. I had no way of knowing, no way of proving that I had or had not. Perhaps all of this was a silly illusion, a game that Hitch and I played, pretending to powers that didn't exist.

My refusal to surrender and completely believe in magic was my final defense that enabled me to live in a world that made sense to me. The early morning was a pearly darkness of falling snow. I burrowed deeper into my blankets and finally slept.

CHAPTER EIGHTEEN

VISITOR

I tried to find the rhythm of my days again, but it was broken. The snow was too deep and the ground too frozen for me to dig graves, and there was very little else for me to do. I missed my schoolbooks. Writing in my journal almost made things worse. I had far too much time to think. Magic, my father's opinion of me, Spink's knowledge that I was in Gettys, Colonel Haren asking my opinion on the road dilemma: I had too much to ponder.

I tempted myself to go into town, thinking that any sort of company might be a welcome distraction, but I felt an almost irrational fear that I would encounter someone who knew me from my academy days. I isolated myself at the graveyard until a rider came out one day to fetch me. An old man had died. I hitched Clove to the wagon and went to town for the coffin and corpse. The old man had been an ex-soldier and a drunk who had died in debt to everyone who had tried to

befriend him. The poor fellow had no mourners to follow me
out to the grave site.

Once I had him loaded, I steeled my heart to my own callousness and completed my own necessary errands. I picked
up hay and grain for Clove and some basic food supplies for
myself. I forced myself to take my noon meal in the mess
hall. Ebrooks was at table, shoveling his food into his mouth
as if it were a competitive sport. From him I learned that
Kesey was sick in bed with a toothache, but hadn't the courage to have the molar pulled.

"That side of his face is swollen like a melon, and so tender he can't eat a bite. Even drinking water hurts him. I told
him, go have it pulled and be done with it. How could the
pain be any worse? He still hopes it will go down by itself.
But he almost counts himself lucky to have been sick in bed
last night after what happened in the streets."

"Why? What happened?"

He shook his head and then lowered his face to his plate
to shovel in another large spoonful of beans. He spoke
around them, muffled. "Ain't sposed to talk about it. Gonna
be hushed up and smoothed over, like they allus do."

"What?"

He swallowed noisily and gulped coffee to be sure the
food had gone down. He glanced around the mess and then
leaned closer to me. "Murder last night. I heard something
'bout a whore, an officer, and some soldiers. What I heard
was the officer fancied the bit and got mad when the soldiers
had her first. He shot one of the boys. Something like that."

"That's ugly," I said, leaning away from his breath.

"Life's ugly," he agreed, and went back to his food.

I turned my attention to my own plate, and a short time
after that, Ebrooks pushed back from the table and left. My
meal was four rashers of bacon and a steaming sea of brown
beans with biscuits. I enjoyed it more than the food merited,
until I noticed Sergeant Hoster at a nearby table with a couple of his cronies. His friends were grinning broadly as they
watched me eat, but Hoster was regarding me with a stare of
flat dislike. One of Hoster's friends rolled his eyes and muttered something to Hoster. The other man snorted wildly

into his cup of coffee, spattering liquid all over their table while the first one leaned back, choking with juvenile laughter. Hoster's expression didn't change. He rose slowly and approached my table. I kept my eyes on my plate, pretending I didn't know he was coming. I refused to look up until he addressed me directly.

"You look tired, Burv. Keeping some late hours?"

I had to swallow before I could reply. "No, Sergeant."

"You sure about that? You didn't come to town last night for a bit of fun?"

"No, Sergeant. I stayed home last night."

"Did you?" He didn't wait for a response. "Must get lonely out there. A man lives alone all the time, he can get real hungry for the company of a woman. Isn't that so?"

"I suppose." I suspected he was setting me up for mockery. I was trying not to rise to the bait.

He leaned very close to me and spoke softly. "Did you hear the news, Burv? She didn't die. In a few days, the doctors think she'll feel well enough to talk. She'll be able to describe who attacked her. And I'd say you're a hard man to mistake."

He was accusing me of being one of the rapists. Outrage vied with shock. I kept calm with difficulty. "I was at my cabin all last night, Sergeant. I've heard about the attack on the woman. It's a terrible thing. But I had nothing to do with it."

He straightened up. "Well. We'll see, won't we? Don't think about running off. You wouldn't get far."

All around the mess hall, men had stopped eating to stare at us. They continued to stare even when Hoster sauntered away to rejoin his friends. I glanced around at the speculation on their faces and then back at my food.

All pleasure in my meal vanished. I kept my eyes on my plate as I finished eating, ignoring the sergeant and his friends even when they walked out right behind my seat. The company of others, I reflected hotly to myself, had done little to distract me from my own dark thoughts. I left the mess and walked out into what was left of the cold day,

I buried the old soldier as the last of the day's light fled, and I'm afraid the only words I said over his body were a

feeble prayer to the good god that I would not end up just like
him. The day was unpleasantly cold, the kind of cold that
cracks lips and numbs fingers even when a man is working
hard. The hair inside my nose froze and prickled me, while
the muffler over my mouth grew frosty from my breath. The
soil that I threw down on the coffin was as much ice and
snow as earth. I mounded it well over the grave and then
trampled it down as tightly as I could. By the time I sought
my fireside, afternoon was darkening into evening.

I divested myself of my chilled garments, built up my fire,
and swung the pot on its hook over the awakening flames.
This week's stock was a good one, with barley and a meaty
beef bone as the base for it. I had taught myself, via trial and
error, to make hearth cakes using saleratus as leavening.
They were not bread, but my recent efforts had been palat-
able. I stirred up some to go with my soup. Bending over my
belly to crouch down by the hearth to watch them and then
turn them was uncomfortable. Some days, I scarcely noticed
the inconvenience and simply accepted my body. At times
like tonight, I felt as if I were bound up in someone else's
garments. I could recall so clearly how my body used to
work. I felt I should still be able to crouch low and jump high,
to chin myself or reach down and tie my shoe without holding my breath. But every time I forgot the flesh that enclosed
me and attempted such a movement, I paid with a twinge or
a cramp or failure.

When all my hearth cakes were browned, I stacked them
on my plate and with a grunt heaved myself to my feet. I set
them on my table and then ladled a generous helping of soup
into my bowl. By virtue of great self-control, I still had one
of Hitch's apples left to accompany my meal. I sat down to
my repast with anticipation. Food always worked. No matter
how distressing the rest of my life might become, food and
the sensations of eating it were always pleasant. Food had
become my comforter and my companion. I refused to dwell
on what Hoster had implied. As he had said, we would see.
When the woman recovered enough to describe her attackers, my name would be cleared of the sergeant's foul accusation. I was an innocent man with nothing to fear.

Just as I sat down, I heard a sound outside. I froze, listening. There were the small sounds of a man dismounting from a horse, and then the *squeak-crush* of boots on packed snow. I expected a knock at the door. Instead I heard a voice say firmly, "Nevare, let me in."

I had an almost overwhelming urge to sit silently where I was. I didn't answer. But after a moment I went to the door and lifted the latch. Spink stood on my doorstep. The cold had pinched his face white, save for his red nose and the tops of his cheeks. Steam came out of his muffled mouth as he asked, "Can I put my horse in with yours? It's cold out here and getting colder."

"If you want," I said, for there seemed nothing else to say.

"I'll be right back," he told me, and turned to lead his horse off to Clove's lean-to. I shut the door to hold both the cold and my past at bay. And then I did something that was probably childish. I went to my table and drank down my hot soup as fast as I could, and gobbled down as many of my hearth cakes as I could manage, listening always for the sound of Spink's boots outside. It was not greed. I was hungry, and I did not want to be thinking about food while Spink was there, nor did I want to watch him watching me eat. It was going to be hard enough to sit across from him and try to ignore how his eyes would wander from mine to the rest of my body, wondering and speculating on how I could have changed so much.

When I heard his footsteps outside, I went to the door and opened it. "Thanks!" he exclaimed and came quickly in, immediately opening his coat and moving closer to the fire. "That's the coldest I've ever been in my life, and I'm afraid the ride back to town will be worse. It's absolutely clear outside; the stars seem like you could reach up and pick them out of the sky." He drew off a set of heavy mittens, and then awkwardly peeled off his gloves before thrusting his hands toward my fire. His fingers were nearly white. His breath came in shuddering sighs.

"Spink, why did you come out here tonight?" I asked him sadly. I dreaded the confrontation that I knew must follow this meeting. Why couldn't he just have let things alone?

He mistook my meaning. "Tonight was the first chance I've had to slip away without Epiny demanding to know where I was going and why. She's having some kind of meeting at our house tonight, with women from all over Gettys. All sorts of talk about bettering their lot and providing more opportunities for soldiers' widows and daughters. We don't have a large house; in fact it's quite small, even by Gettys standards. Fill it full of women who all seem to be talking at once and it gets even smaller. When I told Epiny quietly that I simply must leave for a time, she scowled at me, but let me go. And here I am." He smiled sheepishly, as if loath to admit that Epiny had so much management of his time.

I had to smile back. I'd never imagined it would be any other way.

The moment I smiled, Spink burst into a grin like a sunrise. He came quickly to me and seized my right hand in both his icy ones and shook it, saying, "Nevare, I'm so glad to see you alive! Everyone thought you were dead!" He let go my hand and flung himself into my spindly chair by the fire.

"Even Yaril has given you up for dead," he went on, "for she said you had promised to write to her, and that it was a promise you would not break. Your father told her your horse came home riderless. That made her nearly certain. Epiny has shed buckets of tears over you. When I saw you in the mercantile, I could not believe my eyes. Then, when you refused to admit it was you, it was so . . . peculiar! I didn't know what to think. I nearly told Epiny but then I decided that before I allowed her to leap blindly into this, I'd find out exactly what was going on. It's just so hard to get a few hours away without having to explain to her where I've been every moment that I'm gone. But here I am, blathering on, when what I really want to hear is, what has happened to you?"

I tried to consider my response. As I took a breath to speak, Spink broke forth again. I stared at him, somewhat astounded. I supposed that living with Epiny, he had had to learn to speak all his thoughts whenever he had the chance, or forever give up the opportunity. "We had your letters from Widevale, of course. Then they just stopped, but after a time, we began to receive letters from Yaril. Then they stopped. That really worried us, but finally we had a stern letter from your father, returning a letter that Epiny had sent to Yaril and telling her that he would not brook anyone interfering with his daughter's proper upbringing. Epiny had only said that we'd welcome a long visit from Yaril if she felt she needed some time away from home. Well . . . I'm making it much milder than what Epiny actually wrote, to be honest.

"She actually wrote that if Yaril felt she could no longer tolerate living under your father's roof, she could come and live with us." Spink sighed abruptly and then drew a breath. He shook his head. "My dear wife is sometimes a bit too frank, I suppose. Not that I'm telling you anything you don't already know. Her exhortations to Yaril to think for herself offended your father. He wrote that Epiny's letters were unwelcome, that Yaril would not receive them, and that he was going to be sure his brother knew how far his daughter had strayed from her upbringing." The lines around his mouth deepened as added. "You can imagine the sort of storm that provoked in our home."

"Yes, I can," I said quietly. My father was still a good soldier. He unerringly aimed for the weakest point in the enemy's defences. Diverting Epiny's attack on him to make it a battle between her and her own father was a brilliant tactic. I could imagine how he would sit, pipe lit, eyes narrowed, smiling and nodding to himself over it. Telling Yaril that Sirlofty had come back without me was the perfect way to end her hopes.

"I did write to Yaril," I told Spink. "Several times. The news wouldn't be what she hoped for, for I told her of my situation here and pointed out that it was impossible for her to come and stay with me as we'd discussed. I assumed she didn't write back because she was angry or disappointed. Obviously, she never received them. Since my father has disowned me, he will not feel I deserve the courtesy of a reply from him. Very neatly done. I imagine he's letting Yaril expend a lot of energy writing letters to Epiny, which he then diverts. If Yaril thinks that I am dead and that Epiny no longer replies to her letters, she will become very discouraged. And probably much more tractable."

"So what are you going to do about it?" Spink asked me.

I looked at him in surprise. "Do? What can I do? Nothing."

His manner toward me stiffened slightly. "You didn't give up so easily when you were a cadet. I recall how you stood up to the old noble second-years when they persecuted us. And how you solved the bridge problem in engineering."

I shook my head at him. "Those were schoolboy solutions to schoolboy problems. And all of that happened before I was the size of a barn door, and when I still had the prospect of a good commission and a real life before me." All my bleakness came flowing back. "You shouldn't be here, Spink. You'll only damage your career by associating with me. I'm a fat cemetery soldier, an enlisted man with no prospects save grinding toward a stripe or two. The last thing I want is for people to know that we are related, even if it's only by marriage."

He looked at me for a time in utter discouragement. Then he shook his head and said quietly, "I should have known it would get to you, too. It weighs us all down, but I thought *you* would see through it. The discouragement you feel isn't natural, Nevare. I'm not sure that I agree entirely with Epiny's analysis of it, but one can't argue at all with the end product."

I sat like a sack of oats, refusing to be prodded by my curiosity. Spink gave in before I did.

"Morale here is terrible. It isn't just the prisoner-workers or the soldiers who guard them, though they have the worst problems. Did you know, in the last two years, there has been no substantial progress made on pushing the road up into the Barrier Mountains?"

I looked at him. "I was initiated," I said. "I've broken a Gettys sweat. I know about the terror at the end of the road. I'm not surprised that we've made no progress. But what does that have to do with me?"

"The discouragement you feel, the horrible depression, it's not just you. It's every man who is assigned here. How much of Gettys history do you know?"

I smiled sourly. "We didn't get that far before I was pushed out of the academy."

"It's not funny, Nevare, not when you know it. Gettys was a trade outpost a long time before it was a Gernian fort. There was good fur trade with the Minda folk, but none of them live around here these days. Traders came in the summer to go up into the mountains and trade with the Specks.

"Then came the plains wars and the push east. King Troven decided that this would be the eastern boundary and his soldiers made it so. The fortress was built and the basic buildings, and the town was laid out around it. You can tell just by looking at it what was done back then. It's all sound. And after the skirmishing was over, things pretty much went on as they always had, with traders coming and going. But then came the king's idea for a road going up into the mountains, through the pass and down to the sea on the other side. Survey crews came and marked out the likeliest path. The Specks didn't seem to care. Then the road started getting built. Progress was rapid at first. Mostly it involved making improvements to established trails. Then it reached the foothills and started snaking up toward the mountains. And the pass. Right through the forest."

He paused in his telling and looked at me significantly.

I lifted a hand for him to proceed. I didn't know what he was getting at.

"Nevare, the summer the road crews began clearing for the road to venture up into the forest was the first summer that we ever had a bloody clash with the Specks. They didn't do well against our firearms, of course. They retreated to the mountain forests for a time, and we pushed the road on. We began to have trouble with morale at Gettys that year, and with the prisoner-workers. They became lethargic; some would fall asleep standing. Or there would be days when all the crews felt frightened of their own shadows. It came and went, and it was put down to laziness or cowardice.

"Eventually the Specks returned, and even came out of their forest to trade. That had never happened before. It was hailed as progress, and there were hopes that the road construction could proceed without any more bloodshed. But that same summer, those three trees were felled at the end of the road, the fear came, and work stopped. Before summer's end, we had the first outbreak of Speck plague. The fear has been at the end of the road ever since then."

Spink's voice had spelled me like a fireside storyteller's. I hung on his words.

"Morale here plummeted. It got so bad that General Brodg decided to do a complete changeover in the troops here. The fellows here had lost all heart. They blamed it on the plague coming, year after year, with no relief and heavy losses. Desertion and suicide were taking as many soldiers as the plague was. Brede and his crack regiment came in here to take things over and put Gettys back on the map.

"They got here just in time for the plague season. They dropped like flies. After that, everything went to the dogs. Desertion, dereliction of duty, suicide, rapes, and murders. Good solid officers turned into drunkards. The worst was a captain who came home and strangled his wife and then drowned their two children before shooting himself. It was hushed up here and the tale never went west, but there isn't an officer in Gettys who doesn't know what happened." He paused, his eyes looking far.

"That sounds awful," I said faintly. I couldn't even imagine it.

Spink nodded vaguely. "Everyone thought so. That was two years ago. General Brodg reassigned Brede to the Fort in disgrace. The Fort is the only outpost more desolate than Gettys. He rebuked them for slovenliness, dereliction of duty, and even cowardice because other officers had known the captain was losing his mind and did nothing. General Brodg even confiscated their colors. Then he assigned the Farleyton Regiment to replace them. Can you believe our regiment were the golden boys at the time, the soldiers General Brodg would send into any desperate situation when he needed real action? Farleyton was a great regiment three years ago. We put down the uprising at Hotchkiss Springs and lost only three of our own men in the process. Two years before that, when some Plains warriors formed an alliance and tried to overrun Mendy, Brodg sent Farleyton in and we not only broke their siege, we ran them off completely." He shook his head sadly. "I've heard all the old glory tales from the senior officers, usually when they're drunk. It's all about what used to be. None of them can really say what happened. The regiment was assigned to Gettys, and ever since then, it's gone downhill.

"This meeting that Epiny is holding tonight, for the women? She said she had to do it. Wives are fleeing back west and taking their children with them. Married men are turning to whores for comfort here, and the honest women who do remain are often treated like whores. There was a rape last night, rape of an honest woman; she was Lieutenant Garver's sister, come to take care of his children because his wife died of the plague. Some enlisted men caught her on the streets and, well, they left her for dead afterward. Garver hunted one down and killed him, and wants to kill the others when he finds them. They'll hang, most likely, but killing them won't repair the insult to his family or the injuries to his sister. Or the damage to our regiment's reputation. None of the women feel safe anymore. Not even Epiny. The very men who should be willing to die to protect them are preying on them."

I almost told him that Hoster had accused me of being one of the rapists. I decided it would serve no purpose. Spink's face had gone pale with his telling. His fists were clenched with his anger. Slowly it came to me that this wasn't just his regiment he was talking about. It was mine, too. I'd enlisted with Farleyton when I signed with Colonel Haren. Funny. I'd never have said "my regiment" as Spink did when he was speaking of their past glories. They were just the outfit that had finally let me sign papers. I thought of how my father had always puffed up with pride when he spoke of his old regiment. He lionized them as heroes, one and all. And what were mine? Drunks, murderers, and layabouts. I still made excuses for them. "We're isolated out here, Spink. Everyone knows that's bad for morale. Maybe Brodg should rotate his troops more often."

"That's not it," Spink said gruffly. "And you know it. There's a feel to this place, Nevare. You come in through those gates, and you can smell the despair. Everything is grimy and shoddy. The only people who stay in Gettys are the ones who have to." He met my eyes suddenly and said in a challenging voice, "Epiny says the place is under a curse. Or a spell. She claims there's an aura to the whole town, a darkness that eyes can't see. It hangs in the air. We breathe it in, and it drowns all happiness. She says it comes from the Speck. She said it's the same sort of magic that held you when first she met you."

I plastered a cynical smile on my face. I felt queasy. "So Epiny is still playing the medium, is she? I had hoped that being a married woman would settle her down a bit."

Spink didn't smile back at me. "She's not playing, as you very well know, Nevare. I was there, remember? Why do you do that? Why do you pretend not to believe things you've actually experienced?"

I'd made him angry. I looked away from him and tried to formulate a reply when I scarcely knew the answer myself. "Sometimes, Spink, when all the things in my life seem to collide and contradict each other, I pick one set of facts and believe those, no matter what." I lifted my eyes and met his as I asked him, "Do you blame me?"

"I suppose not," he said in a lowered voice. "But," and here his voice rose again, "don't mock Epiny. She may be your cousin, but she is my wife. Give her credit where it is due, Nevare. She saved both of our lives, I believe, when she took care of us during the plague days. She defied her family and society to make herself my wife. Her life since then has not been easy, nor has it been at all what she supposed it would be. But she hasn't left me. A lot of the married men here in Gettys wish they could say the same. They were soldier sons and they married women they thought could be good cavalla wives. But the women couldn't take what Gettys served them, and they've left. Epiny looks it in the face for what it is, and stays on."

"And Epiny believes it's Speck magic that is undermining morale at Gettys."

Spink didn't flinch at my blunt assertion. "That's right," he said levelly. "She does."

I leaned back in my big chair. It creaked slightly as it gave to my weight. "Tell me what she says," I requested softly. I knew I wasn't going to like it. I knew I already believed Epiny.

"She's very sensitive. You know that. The night before we reached Gettys, when we were traveling here, she had her first nightmare. She woke wailing, but couldn't say what had scared her. Her dream was full of macabre images with no sense to them. Jaws with rotting teeth. Babies covered with mud, sitting alone in a swamp, endlessly crying. A dog with a broken back dragging itself in circles. She couldn't go back to sleep that night, and the next day she was nervous and distraught. I thought she was exhausted from travel. When we reached Gettys, I thought our problems were over. Epiny could get some rest, have hot food, and sleep in a real bed. We were both dismayed by the quarters we were assigned. They were dirty. No, not just dirty, filthy, as if whoever lived there before us had never cleaned at all. Everything was in bad repair, and I had to leave her to it, for Colonel Haren put me to my new duties immediately. She was left to cope while I was put to inventorying a warehouse full of dusty supplies. The men they gave me were surly and lazy and incompetent." He practically spat out the last words and rose abruptly from his chair by the fire. "But I don't think they were always that way. I think it's the haze that overhangs Gettys. I believe it's the Speck magic, Nevare. Ask yourself how you've felt about your life since you came here. Do you feel drained of hope and ambition? Does all of it seem pointless and drab? When was the last time you awoke in the morning and actually wanted to get out of bed?"

He'd come closer to me as he asked each question, as if the answers might prove something. I gestured at my swollen body. "If you were trapped inside this, would you feel hope or ambition, or look forward to hauling it out of bed each day?" A sudden thought came to me. "You haven't even asked what happened to me. You don't seem shocked to see me this way."

He tilted his head and smiled sourly. "Did you forget that Epiny and Yaril have exchanged letters? If there is anything you told your sister, be sure it has been shared." He shook his head. "And I'm sorry about all of it, Nevare. Losing your mother. Carsina's faithlessness. And what the Tree Woman's magic has done to you. Unlike you, I don't regard any of that tale with any skepticism. I've seen the power of Speck magic too close." His voice had become very dark.

"What do you mean?" I asked softly.

"Epiny tried to take her life a couple of weeks after we arrived here."

"What?"

"She tried to hang herself in the middle of our bedroom. If I hadn't forgotten my penknife and come back to get it, she would have succeeded. I was barely in time, Nevare. I cut her down and pried the rope out of its groove around her neck. I wasn't gentle; I didn't have time to be. But I think the shaking around actually brought her back to the world of the living.

"I was so angry with her, so furious that she could even think of leaving me that way. She said she didn't even recall it as something she decided to do. She only remembers odd bits of it, going to the stables to get the rope, and then standing on a chair to get it over the rafter. And tying the knot. She told me she particularly remembered tying the knot because she had the most peculiar sensation of doing something she hadn't done before, but knew how to do."

Ice was creeping through my heart. My mind raced and I asked the only question that came to me. "How do you dare to leave her alone? Couldn't she be overcome again, at any time?"

Pride and trepidation warred in his expression. "She told me, 'Fool me once, shame on you. Fool me twice, shame on me! I won't let the magic creep over me like that again. Never.' And she battles it. As do I. As does every officer and soldier in Gettys who's worth anything. You can tell which ones fight daily to go on being who they once were, and which ones have given up and sunk down to the lowest level."

When he said that, I wondered which he thought I was. But he did not pause nor look at me accusingly. He continued, "We do all we can to shore each other up, Epiny and I. Your sister's letters were a great source of strength to her, until they stopped coming. So now you can see that the loss of that cor-

respondence and your father's threat to tell Lord Burvelle of
her waywardness were heavier blows than you might have
imagined. Oh!" He darted back to his chair and thrust his
hand into the pocket of his heavy cloak he'd slung over the
back of it.

"Your sister's letters. I brought them with me. I came here
thinking you a heartless wretch to leave her in such cruel
suspense. I thought if you read how she has suffered, wondering what has become of you, that you would be moved to
write to her. Now, knowing that your letters have no better
chance of reaching her than ours do, perhaps it is cruel of
me to let you read these. Still, I think it is your right to know
what goes on at Widevale in your absence."

He tugged a substantial packet of letters, bound together
with a ribbon, from his pocket. I recognized Yaril's sprawling handwriting with a sharp pang. When I'd seen that penmanship on letters sent to me at the academy, it had always
sent a thrill through me, for I knew she would have found a
way to smuggle me a note from Carsina. Now it was my own
little sister whom I missed with sudden and heartbreaking
strength. I reached for them.

Spink handed them to me, but with a warning. "I cannot
let you keep them long. Epiny will surely miss them."

I lifted my eyes to his. "Then you haven't told my cousin
that I'm here."

"I wanted to offer you the chance to do that yourself."

I shook my head. "I cannot, Spink. I've told you why."

"And if you've listened to me, then you know why it is
more important that she does know you are alive and well.
We three, we can be a strength for each other, as we were
before. Please, Nevare. I'll let you think about it, but not for
long. I've held your secret from Epiny, and already that
shames and disturbs me. We do not keep secrets from one
another, nor deceive each other. Don't put me in that position. It's a shameful thing for one friend to do to another."

"Spink, I can't truly be anything to you, or Epiny. I'm an
enlisted man and a fat gravedigger. We cannot socialize with
one another. You know that. And you know full well that
Epiny will not recognize that, and it will make difficulties

for both of us. Do you wish to be mocked as the gravedigger's cousin? To have people sneer at your wife because of our relationship? How can we be a strength for one another when I can only be a source of shame to you?" I softened my tone at the look on his face. "I am humbled and grateful that you'd want to continue being my friend under the circumstances. And I am doubly grateful that you have offered to share Yaril's letters with me. As things stand, they are likely to be the last news from home that I'll have for a long time. If you don't mind, I will keep them, just for a night or so, to read them. I'll find a way to quietly return them to you."

Sparks of anger lit in his eyes. "That's the dulling magic of this place talking, not the Nevare I knew."

"Spink. Please. Just let me borrow my sister's letters."

He appeared to relent. "Do you think you can get them back to me with no one the wiser?"

I thought. "If we decide on a place and meet by night, it should be possible."

He grinned. "So it should be equally possible for us to meet in such a way for friendship, as well as the passing of letters between us."

He was incorrigible. I had to smile, but I did not share his optimism. "So it might seem, for a time. But sooner or later, we'd be noticed. And then it would all come unraveled. We are not talking about a pretence that must be kept for weeks or even months, Spink. We are talking about years. For as long as we both belong to the same regiment. To my death, most likely."

"Well, aren't you a cheerful, optimistic soul? The Nevare I knew had a lot more spine! What happened to you, Nevare? Where did you go?"

"This isn't school anymore, Spink. This is life. As to where I went, well, behind this wall of fat. And I can't get out."

"Are you sure of that?" The way he asked it made it a genuine question.

"I've tried everything. Working hard, fasting . . . my father took me to the edge of starvation, Spink."

"I know," he broke in quietly. "Yaril told us, in her letters.

It's still hard for me to imagine that any man could treat his own son like that."

"It's true," I said defensively.

"I believe it. But I think you're overlooking the obvious."

"Which is?"

"That magic brought this on. You have defeated that magic before, with Epiny's help. *We* have. Don't you think Epiny would come to your aid again? She's already immersed herself in studying Speck magic, not just to discover what is behind the miasma of depression that afflicts Gettys, but also to research your condition. It's not unique, Nevare. You must know that."

"I'd guessed it," I replied grudgingly. "Dr. Amicas said as much." I almost feared to let him see how much he piqued my interest.

"Epiny has researched it as much as our rather paltry resources have allowed. Most of what she knows is hearsay. There isn't much written about the Specks. They are a people who prefer to keep to themselves. One of the doctors here in Gettys has quite an interest in the native people. Unfortunately, he has quite an interest in drinking, also. Trying to get information from him is like trying to squeeze it out of a wet sponge; you get as much of the liquor as you do the facts. But according to him, the Speck wise folk or holy folk are referred to as Great Ones and not just because of their wisdom. According to Dr. Dowder, the Great Ones are immense in size, so big that they hardly ever leave their homes high up in the mountain forests. Their size reflects their power and their magic; the bigger the man, the more important he is, and the more dominant."

"And the women," I said quietly.

He took it as a question. "Well . . . possibly. I'd never considered that possibility. Oh. Of course. The Tree Woman. Well, she's dead. What I'm trying to say, Nevare, is that if this, er, fat is a consequence of Speck magic, then perhaps it can be undone. The three of us, perhaps, could break it, and loosen the gloom and fear of this place. We'd begin by getting you back to who you were."

I wanted so badly to hope and didn't dare. "I don't think

so. I've felt the changes, Spink. My body works differently than it did before. That's an inadequate way to express it, but it's the best I can do. I don't think I can go back to what I was."

"But you don't *know* that," he said triumphantly. "We should let Epiny know you are here, and then see what can be done. And of course, a way must be found to let your sister know that you are alive, and that if she wishes to defy your father, she is welcome to join us here."

I nearly told him that was not his task. She was my sister; I wanted to be the one to protect her. Instead I said simply, "I'll find a way to get a letter to Yaril. Never fear."

"I shall leave that in your hands, then. Well. It's late. It's been good to see you, Nevare, but if I'm to keep your confidence for now, I'll have to get back to town before all Epiny's company leaves and she starts to wonder where I've been. I'll find a way to come back this way next Sixday. Captain Oford's wife has invited all the officers' wives to join her for a late lunch and some inspirational readings. Epiny dreads it, but she knows that a junior officer's wife cannot shun her social duties. I'll ride out this way again, shall I?"

"If you can without anyone noticing you. If not?"

"If not, I'll find an excuse for another late-night visit. I trust I'll find you in?"

"Small danger that I'd be elsewhere."

"Until then. Nevare, you have no idea how pleasant it has been to talk to someone simply as a friend, not as a fellow officer or a superior or as someone under my command. I've missed you sorely. Epiny must know you are here. Then we three shall find some better way to gather for conversation than this!"

"Let me think about it, Spink, I beg you. And in the meantime, do be cautious."

"Oh, I shall be." He'd already risen from his chair. He picked up his outer clothes with distaste. "Brrr. I dread going back out into the cold. It bites down to my very bones."

As he was drawing them on, I noted something that had escaped me before. "You've recovered well from the plague, Spink. In fact, I don't think I've ever seen any plague survivor who looked so much like his former self as you do."

He grinned unexpectedly. "I wrote to you about it, but I suppose you didn't credit it any more than I did at first. The water from Bitter Springs cured me, Nevare. And Epiny. She's as feisty as ever. The plague victims who were able to get to the spring promptly survived, and many recovered completely. It's not a complete cure for everyone, perhaps, but it is better than anything I've heard of yet."

"They *all* survived? But that's miraculous. Spink, you haven't kept this knowledge to yourself, have you?"

"Of course not! But it's difficult to make anyone believe me who hasn't seen it for himself. Epiny brought a number of small bottles of Bitter Springs water with us. I warned her that it might be less than useful; we've no idea how much it takes to effect a cure such as we've enjoyed. We used complete submersion and drank only that water for days. Nonetheless, she told me she could not come to such a plague-ridden place as Gettys without bringing the water in hopes of saving some poor souls when next the plague strikes. I hope it does not make me sound cruel to say that I almost look forward to the next outbreak so that our water can be tested against it."

A chill ran through me. "Don't even say such things," I begged him. "I know the next plague season must come. And I dread it. I've made such preparations as I can, but—"

"Your pardon, Nevare. I had not paused to think how gruesome your tasks would be at that time. But if the good god wills it, our water may prove effective, and it may be less horrendous than you fear."

He was dressed again for the outside by the time he finished speaking. "May the good god will it," I agreed with him, with small faith that such a thing would be. I'd come to wonder just how much power the good god had against magic as old as the Specks'. "Spink. You recall Dr. Amicas from the academy. Have you written to him about this water cure? Dare I ask if you could send him a sample of your water?"

"Getting it to him would be a fair trick. Have you any idea what it costs to send a simple letter? But you are right, we can at least write to him, and tell him about the Bitter Springs cure."

I hastily donned my own cloak and boots, and carried my lantern to walk Spink out to his horse. The gelding was a sorry mount for any cavalla man, let alone a lieutenant. I said not a word of that, but only waited until he mounted the shaggy beast and then bade him farewell. I watched him ride off into the cold night and then hurried back to my cabin. I read all of Yaril's letters that night. There were only six of them, and in truth there was not much of real news in them. Mostly she recounted, in excruciating detail, all she and I had gone through when the plague struck our home, and afterward. Spink had warned me, but I was still shocked at how intimately she had written of my problem to Epiny. And Spink had read these letters as well! Yaril's description of the weight I had gained and how it hindered me were far more accurate than flattering. When I'd set down the last page, I tried to be grateful that my friends completely understood my situation, without my having to explain it all. It was a very thin comfort.

There were a few other items of interest in there. Carsina had attempted to renew her friendship with Yaril, but my sister had repulsed her. Remwar's family had engaged him to the eldest daughter of an old noble family in Old Thares. Carsina's father had found a promising young captain for her, and she would be traveling east in the spring to meet her future husband. Odd how such news could still pierce me.

My father had received a letter from Vanze's monastery. It commiserated with him on his recent losses, and proposed that Vanze could be partially released from his priesthood if my father wished to name him as his heir son. Gar Sunwer, Vanze's superior, recognized that it was a very unusual offer for them to make, but said that in such times, it was only sensible to be sure that the noble names of the king's lords were carried on. Yaril's tone was cynical as she wrote of it.

Father had received a note of sympathy from Caulder Stiet and his uncle. They had taken my advice not to visit while the family was in the first throes of grief, but would be pleased to come in the spring. The uncle had been almost "obseequious" in his phrasing (here I paused, and wondered how Yaril would know that. Was she sneaking into our father's study and reading his letters?), and Yaril feared that my father had fallen victim to his fawning style. He had written back to say that they would be welcome and that he would find a man to interpret the map I had sent them and help them to find the locations where the interesting mineral sampling had come from. Yaril had heard of Caulder from me and did not look forward to the visit. Yaril's final letter revealed that the estate was not prospering. My father had dismissed many of the men I had put in positions of authority, including Sergeant Duril, and his health was not good enough that he could teach his new foremen their duties, let alone check on them properly. She thought that some of them were dishonest, and said that if her father did not soon take them in hand, she might do so herself. Such a thought shocked me.

In that same letter she mentioned twice that she feared I was dead because she had not heard from me, and my horse had come back riderless. That mention, along with the news that Duril had been cast out for "conspiring" with me, were what cut me most deeply. I'd treasured a brief hope that perhaps I could send a note to Duril and he could have someone read it to him and then share the news with Yaril. To hear that my old mentor had been so harshly rewarded for his years of loyalty to the family sickened me. Where would he go and what would he do? I could not find a way to get a letter to Yaril; I would have to beg leave of Colonel Haren and return myself to rescue her and find out what had become of Sergeant Duril.

As I refolded the last letter into its envelope, I felt both lonely and yet comforted. I was alone, and yet there were still people in this world who cared deeply about me. That night I did as I had not in some time, and that was to go down on my knees by my bed and pray to the good god to protect those I loved.

CHAPTER NINETEEN

WINTER

Spink and I met twice more during that long winter. The first time was only a handful of days after the first meeting, when I returned the letters to him. He could not stay long, and I scarcely had time to do more than thank him and beg him not to betray me to Epiny just yet.

I am sure he intended to get out to see me again, but fate intervened. We were given the news that the king was severely disappointed in us, and that a contingent of highly ranked officers and several nobles were scheduled to visit Gettys to inspect our regiment and review us before offering their advice regarding us to the king. Depending on how we showed, General Brodg might be replaced as commander of the eastern divisions. This news did nothing to lift our morale, and everything to panic our officers into an irrational frenzy of discipline and inspections. I could guess at the pressure Spink was under, as a junior officer, to whip his men into line. The higher officers would be counting on him to make them look competent. I did not envy him his task.

Even I, isolated as I was, was not completely immune to the sudden rush to bring all of Gettys up to a spit-and-polish standard. Sergeant Hoster made a trip out one afternoon, for a "surprise" inspection of my quarters. I could tell he was quite disappointed that I was not living in squalor. He still managed to find a substantial list of things he wished corrected, one that included everything from cutting my firewood to more uniform lengths before racking it to acquiring a proper uniform for myself. His mockery was very insulting as he stated that last requirement. I applied myself to meeting his expectations, cursing him for every wasted moment of my time, but when the day for his promised second visit passed, I decided that his first inspection had simply been opportunistic harassment. I kept my quarters tidy, in case he decided to descend on me again, but refused to dread him.

I buried four more soldiers that winter. One had cut his foot with an ax while chopping firewood and bled to death. Two others died of pneumonia, and a fourth had got drunk, passed out in the street, and frozen to death in the dark. The last one was one of Spink's men, and Spink accompanied the five other mourners to the graveyard to see him laid to rest. He lingered for a short time afterward, but could not stay long. I begged him to let me borrow any books he might have, for my mind was atrophying from boredom. He promised he'd do his best, and again asked if he could not let Epiny know I was there. Once more, I held him off, but he told me sternly that if I did not soon capitulate, he would have to tell her anyway, for he could not bear how she would look at him if she knew how long he had deceived her.

I promised myself I would think about it, and then procrastinated.

The long dark days of winter dragged on. Dark Evening came and was celebrated by the enlisted men with an orgy of drunkenness, fights, and the arson of one officer's house. I had avoided the town that night, and only heard of the ruckus the next day. The general misbehavior of the troops brought more reprisals. Morale was no longer low; it was

lost completely in a simmering hostility toward the officers.
I feared the regiment was on the edge of general insubordination and avoided Gettys as much as I could. I went only
for essentials and stayed as short a time as possible.

Despite that, I was in one of the mercantiles, buying some
thread to mend my trousers, when I caught a glimpse of Epiny
just as she came in the door. I stepped away from the counter
and immersed myself in studying a row of axes behind a tall
stack of blankets. Hidden there, I listened to her ask the man
for her whistles. He told her that he had none in stock. She then
complained that she had requested he order fifty brass whistles
for her two months ago, and she considered it unreasonable
that they had not yet arrived. He explained rather impatiently
that Gettys did not enjoy regular delivery service from anywhere, and that doubtless her order would arrive when spring
made travel less arduous. She pointed out that the whistles
would make only a small packet, something a king's courier
could easily bring, and asked him if he did not care about the
safety of the women and girls of Gettys. I wanted to step out of
the corner and hit him when he told her that their safety was up
to their husbands and brothers, and if she hadn't noticed, he
wasn't the king and did not have the king's couriers at his dis-
posal. His words were sensible enough; it was his sneering
tone that angered me. She departed in high dudgeon, observ-
ing as she left that perhaps she would make her concerns and
efforts known to Colonel Haren, and perhaps he could arrange
a swifter delivery of such essential items. Despite my irritation
with the shop owner, I rather pitied Colonel Haren at that moment. I wondered what on earth she wanted so many whistles
for and what they had to do with the safety of the female population of Gettys, but had no one to ask. I paid for my thread
and left town.

Day after drab winter day dripped by, slow as cold molasses. The generous firewood stack that had come with my
home began to dwindle. One clear winter day, I took an ax,
some rope, and Clove and headed for the forest behind the
cemetery. I wanted to find dead wood, either standing or
fallen. I'd cut the log to a manageable length, have Clove
drag it home for me, and then chop it into firewood.

Clove and I followed my footpath to the spring and then broke a snowy trail into the woods beyond. Here I found giant cedars, towering and stout, their needled branches heavy with snow. Most of them were scarred veterans of a fire many years ago. Around and between those survivors, the younger forest was deciduous, birches and cottonwood and alder, and most of these no bigger around than a child's embrace. Their bare limbs supported wandering walls of snow. Frozen drops of water hung from the tips of their branches. It was a beautiful snowy scene, yet ethereally foreign to a Plains-bred man like myself.

A dozen steps into the shelter of the trees, I began to feel uneasy. I stopped and stood very still, listening. A good soldier develops a sixth sense for when he is being watched. I listened, I looked carefully around, and I even flared my nostrils and took a deep breath of the air. Carrion eaters like bears have a distinctive stench. But my physical senses detected nothing that I should fear. Small birds flitted through the trees. Occasionally the weight of one would dislodge a pouf of snow that would fall in a crystalline shower of tiny flakes. Other than that, I detected nothing, not even a winter breeze moving in the upper branches.

Clove was waiting passively for me to decide what it was I wanted to do here. His calmness decided me; if his senses gave him no cause for alarm or interest, then mine were probably at fault. I tugged at his lead rope and we walked deeper into the forest.

All seemed peaceful. The snow was uneven around us, pocked with falls from overhead, crossed with rabbit trails or smoothly hummocked over the forest floor. Clove and I forged uphill, wading through snow that varied from knee- to thigh-deep. Other than birds overhead, I saw no creatures moving in the woods, but I could not shake the feeling that I was being watched. More than once I halted and looked back the way we had come. I wished I had a better weapon than the ancient gun that had been issued to me. I'd cleaned it, the rod waking clouds of rust from inside it, but I still had no confidence that it would either fire well or hit accurately.

I finally spotted a standing snag. It was uphill from us, and more massive than I'd sought, but I resolved I would have it down and drag at least half of it home with me. The tree was obviously dead. It looked as if a random lightning strike had blackened one side of it. Great scabs of bark had fallen away to reveal silvery-gray wood beneath. It was more than enough to replenish my firewood supply, and dry wood would burn well with little fouling of my chimney. I pushed aside my feelings of unease and labored up the hill toward it. Clove docilely followed me.

When I finally reached my dead tree, I paused to breathe, leaning against it. My heart hammered in my chest, and despite the chill of the day, sweat coursed down my back. I scooped up a handful of clean snow and ate it from my mittened hand to ease my thirst. But all the while, I kept scanning the woods around me for any sign of an intruder. I moved Clove well out of the way of my operation and took up a stance where I could fell the tree downhill of us.

The first blow brought down an icy shower of dry snow on me. It fell again on the second and third chops, and then the branches had lost their loads. I'd sharpened my ax that morning, and it bit deep into the dry wood. I tugged the blade loose, set my feet firmly, and swung again. The blade struck at an angle to the first cut. Tug, swing. The first chips flew out onto the trampled snow. I poised my axe for the next blow and clearly felt the presence of someone behind me. My peripheral vision caught motion, and I felt the air of his passage. I turned quickly. No one was there. I spun the other way. There was nothing, no bird on the wing, no random fall of snow load from a tree. Nothing. Clove stood, wearily patient, betraying no interest in anything. I'd imagined it.

Imagination or not, my heart still thudded in my chest. I took several calming breaths and took up my ax again. I put the energy from my fright into my swing, and the ax bit so deeply I had to wrench it loose. A half-dozen blows later, chips littered the snow and my own sweat warmed me. I labored on, trying to ignore my growing conviction that someone was watching me. "Trust your gut," Sergeant Duril had always told me. It was getting harder and harder to ignore my instincts. A dozen ax swings later, I straightened up and spun around, my ax at the defensive. "I know you're there!" I roared at the surrounding woods. "Show yourself!"

Clove lifted his head and gave a startled snort. I stood, chest heaving, staring wildly all around me. My blood was thundering in my ears. I saw absolutely nothing that could be considered threatening. My horse regarded me with mild concern. I glared at the tree. I was not even halfway through the trunk.

I set my teeth, steeled my mind, and put myself to chopping. I threw my not inconsiderable weight behind each blow. The sound of my ax rang defiantly through the woods. "I refuse to be afraid," I said to myself, and then on my next blows, I began my grunting chant.

"I'm."

"Not."

"Running."

"Away!"

The ax bit deep and the chips flew. On my next four strokes, I said the words louder, and soon I was shouting with every blow, putting all my strength into each strike of the blade. The tree shuddered. I struck again, and again, and then as it groaned, I jumped back out of range, for the trunk seemed to literally jump from the stump as if fell with an explosive crack that echoed through the frozen woods. It came down with a crash, falling through the frozen branches of the adjacent living trees, injuring them as it fell, shattering the stiff branches or leaving them to dangle brokenly. For a brief moment, the falling snag jammed against the trunk of a live tree, and then it fell with a resounding crash to the snowy forest floor. I stood blinking in the hanging mist of crystalline flakes that the falling snag had released. They stung my face like a cold rebuking slap from the forest.

I had underestimated the task I'd taken on. After the tree had fallen, I had to divest the trunk of all its branches. This included the ones that lay underneath the fallen snag. The early evening of winter was threatening me before I finally had a section of trunk cut that I thought Clove could manage. I put a rope on it and fastened it to Clove's harness.

I had never been so glad to put a place behind me. I

wanted to hurry, but dragging the log downhill through the snowy forest was not as simple as it had seemed it would be. I put a rope on it so I could guide it to keep it from running up on Clove or snagging on trees. I could not focus on the task. The sensation of being watched blazed up in my mind, and I kept glancing back over my shoulder at nearly every step. The sweat that soaked and then chilled me was as much from fear as exertion. I could just glimpse the open area beyond the outskirts of the forest's edge by the spring as the bluish shadows of the trees on the snow were turning to black.

In Widevale, evening and night had always fallen slowly, with twilight a long process of losing the sun to the flat horizon. Here on the edge of the mountains, night came like the drawing of a curtain as rumpled hills swiftly devoured the pallid sun. I felt the darkness coming on, and suddenly I could no longer control my terror. I ran forward, floundering heavily through the deepening snow, startling Clove by seizing his headstall and tugging him along, urging him to haste.

We must have made a comical sight, the fat man and his heavy horse, floundering through deep snow, encumbered by the tree trunk that Clove dragged. I was making small sounds of terror, my panting becoming higher-pitched. I tried to swallow my fear and could not; the more I gave in to it, the greater it became, like the boy who gives way to shrieks of hysteria when night terrors convince him that he cannot escape into the safe world of day. There were no sounds in that darkening world save the ones we made: the *thud-crunch* of Clove's hooves through the dry, crusty snow, my terrified panting, and the slow *whoosh* of the timber as it cut a trough through the snow behind us. No sound at all, save a single peal of laughter, clear and pure as any birdsong that rang out in the forest as we left it behind us.

It was the final spur to my fear. Dignity abandoned, I ran, outstripping my placid horse. I ran all the way to my own front door and burst into my tiny cabin as if all the nightshades of the old gods were in pursuit of me. I slammed the door behind me and stood panting and shaking. My heart hammered in my chest, and my ears rang with it. The fire was blazing in the hearth and the kettle singing next to it. I smelled hot coffee. Scout Hitch was ensconced in my big chair by the fire. He looked up at me and smiled.

"I see the forest is breathing terror today." He rose slowly from my chair, and sauntered to the door I had slammed shut behind myself as I entered. He opened it and looked out over the dimming landscape. He whistled softly, as if in admiration, while I stood burning with shame. But when he glanced back at me over his shoulder, the wonder on his face seemed genuine. "It's later than I thought. I must have taken a nap while I was waiting for you. Have you been in the forest all this time?"

I gave a stiff nod. My terror had fled, cast out by my embarrassment, but my heart still pounded and my throat was parched too dry to speak. I began to peel off my outer garments. Opening my coat released the stench of my own fear-sweat. Never had I been so ashamed.

Hitch had continued to stare out of the door. "And you plundered a log for yourself as well. Damn. Nevare, you never cease to amaze me. No, you take your things off and get settled. I'll put your horse up. I want to talk with you."

By the time Hitch came back from seeing to Clove, I'd changed into a dry shirt and felt a bit more like myself. He'd made free with my hospitality but also contributed, I saw. He'd brought the coffee, and there were another three apples on my pantry shelf. The crowning gift was a loaf of bread that had been kneaded full of raisins and cinnamon. A dusting of sparkling sugar crowned the round loaf. It sat amid its wrappings like a king on a throne. I didn't touch any of it. Instead, I drank three dippers full of water from my water cask, and then washed my face and combed my unruly hair back into order. I was mortified by my terror and humiliated that he had seen it. And try as I might, I could not forget that clear peal of mocking laughter.

Hitch opened my door, stamped the loose snow off his feet, and came in, shutting the door firmly behind him. It was full dark outside now. "Ain't you cut up that bread yet? It's best toasted," he greeted me, as if he had not seen me quaking like a coward.

I was grateful that he'd turned the subject aside and yet shamed even more that he did. "I'll do it now," I said humbly.

I cut thick slices of the fragrant bread, and we improvised toasting forks to warm it by my fire. The heat released the scent and flavor into the room. We both ate it greedily, dunking the slices in the hot coffee and then devouring the dripping edges. As I ate, I could almost feel my courage coming back to me, as if I sated something more than hunger. Hitch watched me knowingly, and after a time, I could not stand it.

"So. What brings you to visit me?" I asked him.

He grinned. "Told you before. Renegade." He snorted a laugh at his tired joke, and then said, "You were probably asking me why I come here, right?"

I nodded and tried not to scowl. It irritated me when he used language that made him sound like an ignorant fool. I knew it was a masquerade. Why did he continue to mask himself before me?

A second smile flitted across his face, and I suddenly knew why he did it. To needle me. To remind me that I, too, pretended that I was not the soldier son of a noble family.

"I come to let you know that I delivered your little present bag to Amzil."

My interest leapt. "Did she like it?"

"Can't say. She made me leave it on her doorstep; said she'd take it in after I rode away." He shook his head. "She's cut a new hole by her door. A horizontal slot that she can poke that old gun out of and threaten people without opening the door."

Unease replaced my anticipation of pleasure. "That doesn't sound good."

"No, it doesn't. And it isn't good." He watched my face as he said, "Probably the only thing more unlucky than being the poorest family in a poor town is being the richest family in a poor town."

"What do you mean? I didn't send her that much; certainly nothing that could be considered riches."

"Well, it doesn't take much to be the richest family in a poor town. A few bulging sacks of potatoes, a cold bin full of cabbages and carrots, and the like . . . that might wake the avarice in your neighbors. Folk have been known to kill over a lot less than food."

If he had hit me in the belly, the spreading pain could not have been worse. I felt my heart lurch and then thud on unevenly. "What have I done?" I asked myself softly. The vegetable garden intended to tide her over through a harsh winter had made her a target among her neighbors. Why could I not foresee that would happen?

"You used the magic for your own ends, and it hit back at you. I warned you about that. 'Course, I warned you about that after you'd done it, so I can't really say, 'I told you so.' Only, learn from it, old son, and don't let it happen again."

"How bad is it for her? Is she all right?"

"All I saw of her was the business end of her gun, and it seemed just fine to me. Ever noticed how much bigger the muzzle of a gun looks when it's pointed at you? I swear, she stuck that thing out the hole, and it looked just like a cannon to me. She's smart. She cut that hole at gut level. Biggest target on a man, and the worst way to die that I know."

My question had gone unanswered, but my imagination was glad to supply a hundred dark possibilities. I wondered if my good deed had had the worst possible consequences for her and her children. Did she sleep always with one eye open, afraid to leave her children for even a few moments? The cynical side of my mind asked me if she had not always done that.

I couldn't bear to think about it anymore. My mind leapt sideways and I found myself asking, "What did you mean when you said the forest breathed terror today?"

He looked at me curiously. "How is it possible you don't know? You live right on the edge of it here, where most men can't stand to be for long. Except for people like us, of course." He suddenly dropped his voice a note and looked at me with sadness in his eyes. "The magic owns us, Nevare. I can warn you not to do foolish things with it. But nothing I can say will save you from the things it can make you do. I can't even save myself from that."

I couldn't decide if he was being dramatic or deeply

sincere. I leaned back in my chair and balanced my coffee cup on top of the swell of my belly. "Hitch, I'm not going to drag it out of you. Either you explain it or you don't."

He leaned forward for the pot, poured himself more coffee, and then settled back in his chair with a groan. "Spoil all my fun," he complained. "Oh, very well. I know you've been to the end of the road, so you know the terror that's there. It's worst there, and always there. The rest of the forest isn't so bad. Sometimes the forest breathes terror. Other times, it's utter weariness. And over all, always there is discouragement and despair. That flows over all the land surrounding the King's Road. You have to ride for at least two days before you get away from it. Three if you're following the road itself. Some people are more vulnerable to it than others, but no one, not even us, is completely immune."

I tried Epiny's theory on him. "That's what is wrong with the morale at Gettys. That's why top regiments come here and within a year become slovenly and prey to desertion."

He opened his hands wide, as if acknowledging the obvious. "Prey to desertion is an understatement," he added quietly. "And things will only get worse after our 'visiting dignitaries' see how we've lost our shine."

"Do you think they'll rotate us out of Gettys?" I asked him, and felt a vague stirring of hope.

He looked at me flatly. "Never, never, Nevare." He smiled at his own words. "They may rotate the regiment out, but you and I, we shall never leave this place. The magic lives here, and the magic owns us."

"Speak for yourself," I told him irritably. I was getting more than a bit tired of being told I was a puppet plaything. "Where my regiment goes, I follow. I'm at least that much of a soldier still."

He smiled a different kind of smile. "Well. I'm sure there's no arguing with you. When the time comes, we'll see who stays or goes. Right now, I'm the one to go. I've a dark cold ride ahead of me, and a warmer one after that."

"What do you mean?"

"I'm off to the whorehouse, man." He looked at me consideringly. "Why don't you join me? Probably do you good."

"Thought you said you never paid for it."

"You know any man who admits that he does? Why don't you come with me, and you can pay for both of us?"

"Another time," I said reflexively.

"Pining away for Amzil? Put her out of your mind, man. No one rides that mare, save that she want to carry him."

"I'm not pining for Amzil. I just owed her a favor in return for her hospitality. That was all."

"I'm sure it was. So. The whores, then?"

It was a cold dark ride to town, and all the way there, I questioned my own wisdom. But there are times in the heart of winter when a man doesn't want to be wise, only satiated. If Hitch hadn't brought up the idea to me, I doubt that I'd have gone. But once it was presented, I couldn't think of any good reason to turn it down. I was tired of being alone and cold, and I needed something to scrub the shame of cowardice from my soul. So I went.

We rode up to a long low building on the edge of Gettys Town. The snow was well trampled outside it, and six saddled horses waited sullenly in the cold. There were no windows.

I suggested that we enter separately. Hitch told me he didn't particularly care who knew that we knew one another, but he gave way to my request. So, some moments after he had thumped on the rough wooden door and been admitted, I knocked. They let me stand outside in the dark for a few more moments. The man who opened the door was a big, burly fellow. He wore a white shirt, a bit grimy at the collars and cuffs, and made-over cavalla trousers. He was thick-necked and solidly muscled and scowling. Yet as he ran his eyes over me, his scowl gave way to a delighted grin. "Hey, Glory-girl!" he shouted over his shoulder. "I got a fellow here who'll match you pound for pound. Here's finally a man you'll notice when he's between your thighs."

"Clamp your jaws, Stiddick. You know I'm not working tonight. My Auntie Flo's come calling. Less that's something you prefer, big man?" A large, heavy woman in a very tight pink gown loomed up from the dimness behind the man. Tall as he was, she looked over his shoulder easily; I'd never seen

a woman so tall. She raised the corner of her upper lip at me
in a crooked cat smile. "Well. Look at you. Let him by, Stiddick. Mama Moggam, come take a look at this one!"

Sarla Moggam stepped up, seized my wrist, and dragged
me past both of them. With both Stiddick and Glory no longer blocking my view, I was finally free to peruse the room.

Erotic tapestries draped the walls. Several scantily clad
women lounged on chairs scattered throughout the room.
The lamps on the low tables had their wicks turned down,
and their glass shades were pink or violet. As my eyes adjusted to the dimness and my nose took in the smells of the
place, my expectations dropped. I was still in Gettys. The
trappings of the brothel were tired and worn. Smoke had
dimmed the florid pink flesh of the preposterous nude in the
painting over the fireplace. The dingy carpet that floored the
room needed beating. A huge fire roared in the big hearth at
the end of the room, but its warmth was feeble where I stood.
There were three tables with chairs around them, mostly unoccupied. At one a man sprawled, facedown on the table. His
lax hands still clutched at an emptied bottle. Hitch was nowhere to be seen.

There were four other women in the room besides Glory.
Sarla Moggam was the one who commanded my attention.
She was a small woman, well past her middle years, with unlikely yellow hair that fell in loose ringlets to her bare shoulders. I don't know what to call the garment she wore. It had a
black lace skirt that barely brushed the tops of her knees and
a beribboned top that held her breasts up as if they were in
goblets. The brazenness of it would have been shocking on
any woman; on someone of her years, it was appalling. The
flesh of her throat was lined with wrinkles. Even in the dim
light, I could see how her rouge was caught deeper in the lines
of her face. She held me firmly by the wrist, as if I were a
petty thief she'd caught and cackled as she turned to her girls.
"Look at this one, sweeties! Who'll have him?"

"Don't even look at me," a raven-haired woman warned
me in a faked Landsing accent. She rolled her eyes in disgust that I'd even consider her, and I felt a tingle of both anger and desire at how she disdained me, for in truth she had

been the first to catch my eye. I considered the other woman. She was either drunk or exceptionally tired. She couldn't seem to make her eyes focus on me. One sleeve of her green dress was torn free of the bodice and dangled at her side, unnoticed. She gave a few blinks and then forced a sloppy smile onto her face. She muttered some sort of greeting, but it was so slurred I couldn't make out what she said.

"I'll take him, Mama."

I turned my head to see who had spoken.

I saw a woman about my own age, but only a third of my size. Her brown hair hung loose to her shoulders in waves. Despite the chill of the room, she was barefoot. She wore a simple blue shift, and I realized that I had seen her, but had immediately classified her as a maidservant rather than one of the prostitutes. She walked toward me with the assured arrogance of a house cat. "I'll take him," she repeated.

Sarla Moggam had never relinquished her grip on my wrist. "Fala, you greedy girl!" she rebuked her with a smile. Now she put my hand out to the girl as if I had absolutely no say in the matter, and at that moment, I didn't. Fala smiled at me as she took my hand in hers; the simple warmth of her touch inflamed me, and the light in her eyes grew knowing, as if she sensed my immediate response to her. "Come with me, big man," she said, and led me away from the hearth, toward a long hallway that ran down the center of the building. I followed her, docile as a lamb.

The brothel's doorman stepped suddenly between us. "Pay first," he growled at me. Then, grinning at Fala, he asked her, "Aren't you afraid of biting off more than you can chew?" This provoked a round of general laughter from the room.

His manner was offensive and I felt a flash of anger. But the girl ignored him, smiling at me so beguilingly that I handed over to Stiddick more than twice what Hitch had told me a whore cost here. I didn't even quibble, and Fala laughed delightedly as Stiddick stepped out of my way and I lumbered down the hallway behind her. He leered after us, and chuckled knowingly. I ignored him.

Doors opened off the dim hall at regular intervals. Grunts and rhythmic thudding left no room for doubt about what went on in the rooms. I heard a muffled yell from one, of anger or ecstasy, I could not tell. My guide had taken my hand again and she tugged me on. "The last door," she told me breathlessly, "is mine."

She halted outside it and turned to face me. I could not help myself. I pressed close to her. She set her small hands against my chest and laughed up at me. "You like me already, don't you, big man?"

"That I do," I breathed down at her. I reached past her for the doorknob. Her hand was there first, stopping mine.

"I'm going to do you special," she said quietly. "Trust me. I know what you'll like."

She turned from me to face the door, and as she did, she let her breasts, free beneath her simple shift, brush against me. Was it deliberate that her buttocks rested lightly against my thighs before she opened the door and drew me into the small room?

A single candle, a tall fresh taper, burned in a clay holder beside a rumpled bed. The room smelled of sex and other men, and at any other time, I think I would have found it a repulsive odor. Tonight, it was an aphrodisiac. I followed her in, shutting the door behind me. "Sit down," she bade me, and when I started for the bed, she caught at me and said, "No, not there. In my chair. Sit down. Lean back. Be comfortable. I want to show you something."

It had begun to seem to me that she was much more like the friendly little kitchenmaid of my first experience than the whores I'd known since then. I could not take the foolish smile from my face. I sat down in a chair in the corner of the room. "Watch me!" she bade me, as if I could have stopped myself from doing so. She reached down and took the hem of her shift in both her hands, and then, in one smooth movement, she lifted it up and over her head and then tossed it to one side. She shook her tousled hair free, and her breasts moved with the gesture. She was completely, smoothly naked. She danced toward me. "Let's not hurry. Touch me first. However you want. Then I'll touch you." She halted before me, feet a little apart and eyes closed, inviting me.

I leaned forward in my chair and ran my hands over her warm, soft flesh. I touched as I pleased, hefting the weight of her soft breasts, discovering the warmth between her thighs. She gave a sudden shiver as I did so. I tried to pull her to me, but she jumped back and then said suddenly, "My turn. Lean back. Shut your eyes."

I did as she bade me, lost in delight at her playfulness. I felt her tug at my belt, and then the bliss of buttons giving way to her nimble fingers. For one instant, I was free, and then, to my shock, I felt her clamp her mouth on me. I opened my eyes, jolted to my core at such wild and strange behavior. I knew it was not what I wanted. I tried to pull free of her, but she held me fast, and in another moment, I suddenly knew it was what I wanted beyond all else. I gave a groan of protest and delight and then surrendered to her. It was happening far more quickly than I intended, and with an intensity that left me mindless. I had read of such an act, in one of Caleb's more depraved journals, but I'd certainly never expected to take part in such perversity. I felt unmanned that she had taken such control of me, and yet completely dominant as she knelt before me with my fingers tangled in her hair. Her small hands pressed against the overflow of my belly, holding it back. I clasped her head between my hands and feared my own strength, for her skull felt fragile as a child's. Sensations I'd never even imagined coursed through me. In the moment before her skillful tongue freed me from all thought, I knew that I wanted, more than anything, to grant her such bliss as she worked upon me.

And even in the midst of sexual release, I felt the telltale tingling of the magic moving in my blood. Her mouth came suddenly free of me and she gave a wild cry, a sound as elemental as a doe calling for a mate. She fell bonelessly to the floor in front of my feet, her wet mouth ajar and moaning. "Are you all right?" I asked her in alarm. I clutched my clothing around me and knelt next to her. Her eyes were rolled back in her head. She took a shuddering breath, coughed it out, and then gasped in another one.

"I'll get help," I told her, and tried to rise. She grasped at me with vague hands.

"No. No, please. I'm all right. I think." She tried to sit up, and then collapsed back to the floor. "That's never happened to me before," she said in faint wonder. "That was . . . oh. I don't know what that was . . ." Her voice trailed off into incoherence.

"Isn't that how it's supposed to be?" I asked her. "Mutual?"

"I . . . don't know, I suppose. I didn't know." She caught a ragged breath. "I didn't know," she said, almost defensively. "I didn't know it was supposed to be like that."

Her comment stunned me. It had never dawned on me to wonder if whores enjoyed their work. I had assumed they did, for the most part, or why had they become whores? Then I recognized the cruelty of that thought. Had I ever imagined that Amzil enjoyed the whoring she did to keep her children alive? "I'm sorry," I said quietly, not quite sure what I apologized for.

"Don't be," she said, slowly sitting up. She peeked up at me shyly, her face full of confusion touched with awe. "You didn't even touch me," she said. "I don't understand what happened."

Her hair had fallen across her face and clung to her sweaty brow. With one finger, I lifted a sheaf of it so I could see her eyes. She continued to look up at me. "It is supposed to be like that," I assured her. "It's always supposed to be this good."

I helped her crawl up on her bed and tenderly tucked a blanket around her. I knew she was a whore and I'd had the time I'd paid her for. She owed me nothing more than what she had already given me. Reluctantly, I started to leave her there, but with a cry, she caught at my hand and drew me down beside her. "Stay a little while," she said quietly. "I don't want Mama Moggam to make me bring another man back here. Not just yet." She gave a sudden shiver. "It's like it's echoing in me," she said.

I lay down beside her. "You're warm," she said, and moved closer to me. She put her head on my chest. "I feel like I could fall asleep."

"If you want, you can," I told her. For a time, I held her close in a warmth that I suspect neither of us had felt in a long time. In its own way, it was better than the sex had been.

The candle had long since guttered away to leave us in blessed darkness when I heard a heavy pounding on the door. Stiddick's voice rousted us. "You! In there! You're done now. Leave!"

I startled awake, for I'd dozed off for the second time. Even so, I would have lingered for another go-round, but she pushed at me lightly. "No. Enough. Good-bye, big man."

As I walked out, Stiddick was waiting in the hall. He pushed past me to get inside. As the door swung shut, I heard him ask her, "Did he hurt you? I never known you to let a man stay so long."

When I walked down the long hall to the entry room, I found it deserted and the fire burning low. Hitch was long gone, I was certain. I rode a surly Clove home in the cold and dark of early morning. Several days later when I came to town again and dined in the mess hall with Ebrooks and Kesey, I heard that rumors about me had circulated through the lower folk of the town. Ebrooks muttered that some were saying I was strangely endowed or unnaturally skilled. Fala had told the other whores that she'd never had such a man. The next night, she'd refused to work. Within the week, she'd abruptly left the brothel's employ. No one knew where she'd gone, and Kesey warned me to stay away from Sarla Moggam's, for the brothel owner blamed me personally for the ruination of one of her most profitable whores. My brief spark of fame among the enlisted men was poor compensation for the loss of a welcome at the brothel, nor did Hitch's evident enjoyment and mockery of me about it make it any easier to bear.

But I held tight to the moment of true tenderness that I'd shared with Fala, and wished her well, wherever she had gone. It was the one warm night I enjoyed that winter.

CHAPTER TWENTY

SPRING

E very season must eventually give way to the next. There were times, during that winter in Gettys, when I doubted the truth of this. It was the darkest, coldest time I'd ever passed in my life. Now that Spink had enlightened me as to the nature of the magic that seeped through Gettys' streets like a fog and Hitch had confirmed it, I was more attuned to it. I could feel the ebb and flow of the bleakness that afflicted the town. I could sense, without entering the woods, the days on which terror and panic emanated from them, and the days in which weariness and discouragement lurked there. None of that, however, put me any closer to bettering my own state of mind, let alone to breaking the magic's hold on me.

There were even times when I allowed myself to wonder if that was what I truly desired. As the days slowly lengthened and spring softened the snows by day, I had time to ponder Hitch's warnings. I could see, now, the danger of using the magic I'd been given. I'd intended good for Amzil, and perhaps exposed her to danger. Had I cheated the man who had owned Clove? But there were times when I'd felt the magic's tingle, and no evil had come of it that I had seen. Perhaps it was not as Hitch saw it, a dangerous balancing act between my will and that of the magic, but only the much older idea that the more power one has, the more carefully it must be wielded. If I was trapped in this fat body, and if the magic was to have a hold on me, might I not learn to use it wisely and perhaps even well? Such were my thoughts in the evenings, at least, when I lay alone in my bed. I will confess that, a time or two, I tried to summon the magic so that I could use it in small and harmless ways. Could I kindle a fire with it? Command water to freeze or turn a stone to bread as magicians did in the old Varnian tales of magic? Those were feats I attempted and failed at. Afterward, I laughed at myself for such foolish fancies. But late at night, I would again wonder if such magic was that different from commanding vegetables to grow, or waking a whore to true passion's reward.

Summoning the magic, I decided at last, demanded not will or intellect, but emotion. I could not raise such emotions in myself simply by thinking of them, any more than a man can truly make himself laugh heartily when nothing has amused him. Recognizing that the magic raced in my blood only when strong emotion summoned it was a solid warning to me that it was unlikely to be something I could ever rationally control. Wisely, I decided to leave it be.

During the day, I did my best to keep myself busy. I missed books desperately, so much so that I often resorted to rereading my own journal entries and adding notes in the margin from my older and wiser perspective. I'd lost a strap from Clove's harness somehow. It took me most of a day in town to get another one from supply. I saw Spink there, but we gave no sign of knowing one another. I came home feeling angry and depressed.

I cut and stacked the wood that I'd brought from the forest. When that log had been reduced, I forced myself to once more take Clove and reenter the woods. I chose a day when only fatigue threatened, and forced my way through the glum discouragement that tried to overwhelm me. My trophy was another section of the trunk from the dead snag. Resisting the urge to lie down even in the snow and take a rest demanded all my willpower. Even after I reached my cottage, weariness debilitated me, and there I did surrender to a long afternoon nap.

Having to battle magic just to have firewood awoke me to what the road workers had to endure daily. Hitch had said that my connection to the magic gave me a slight immunity. I wondered what Spink and Epiny battled each day.

When I was a boy, my father had kept me continuously occupied with lessons and chores. At the academy, the first-year schedule was deliberately designed to be both demanding and exhausting, the better to keep young men from finding mischief when they had free time. That winter was the first time in my life that I'd had dragging hours with nothing to fill them. There were dozens of ways I could have improved my cabin, of course, but the most I did was devise elaborate plans. The dull seep of magic from the forest drained my will.

As the snows melted and the sap ran in the trees, the tiny leaf buds swelled on their branches. The forest beckoned, with game trails to follow and hunting that could fill my dinner pot with meat, but the prospect of battling either terror or fatigue dimmed my enthusiasm and kept me close to home. Every morning, I'd stand by the spring with my water bucket and gaze up into the forest depths. Birds flitted there, and new green leaves bedecked both trees and bushes. I longed to enter, and knew it was a foolish wish. It was a relief when the thawing ground allowed me to resume my gravedigging. It gave me a physical task to occupy my body if not my mind.

One welcome aspect of spring was that the supply wagons began to once more make the long eastern journey to us. The dusty windows of the mercantile stores were uncluttered and wiped clean. Fresh wares were displayed in them: shining tin washtubs, woollen and cotton goods, a gleaming long gun with a curly maple stock that no man could pass by without ogling. Within the store, new casks of pickled herring from the far coast had arrived, along with fresh stocks of sweet fruit preserves and bright packets of garden seeds.

All these and much more were bait for hearts and eyes jaded by all the oldness of winter. Yet I had come to the store that day not for anything so gleaming and grand but only in the hope of looking through some of the newspapers that had finally reached us. The articles in them might be weeks or months old, but they were a link to Old Thares and the cities of the west that gave us an inkling of the changes going on in the greater world.

Ostensibly, they were for sale, not casual perusing, but they were displayed in a rack on the wall, and I was not the only fellow standing and reading the front pages.

The papers were expensive, and I could spare money only for one. After I'd read it, I might be able to trade it to some fellow reader for his purchase, but I wished to make the wisest choice. At length I chose one with a front-page story concerning a vote in the Council of Lords about taxation. A side column was an editorial on the number of noble sons who had been shifted into roles other than that prescribed by birth order following the previous winter's plague deaths. Evidently, some cousins who had hoped to inherit titles were seeking legal redress against "heirs who were not truly heir sons." I took the paper from the rack and then waited, holding a few packets of vegetable seeds and gripping a fistful of coins, for the clerk to deign to notice me. He was the same supercilious youth who always scorned to wait on me. Today he took my money and passed over the journal with the comment, "Are you sure this is what you want? You can't eat it, you know. And we've a stock of plain paper for wrapping things."

"Just sell me the seeds and the newspaper, please. I'd like to read it," I replied quietly.

"Ah, he reads! Will wonders never cease? There you go."

I ignored his mockery, took my paper and my garden seeds, and turned to leave. As I did so, two women entered the shop. One was a woman of middle years whom I'd frequently seen around Gettys. I was puzzled to notice that she now wore a large brass whistle on a fine chain around her neck. But a greater shock to me was to recognize the finely dressed young lady who accompanied her. My erstwhile fiancée looked lovely. Carsina Grenalter was wearing the latest style from

Old Thares, I was sure. Her green bonnet could not contain the flaxen curls that bounced about her shoulders. The cut of her forest-green dress flattered her buxom figure. Little gold earrings gleamed in her earlobes. The fresh air of spring had pinked her cheeks and the tip of her nose. She glanced about the mercantile and gave a strangled laugh. "Oh, my dear Clara! This is dreadful! Is this what they deem a dry goods store in Gettys? My dear, I'm afraid we shall have to send away for the proper buttons and lace if we are to retrim your dresses in the new styles!"

By the time Carsina had finished speaking, her companion was flushed a bright pink. I did not know if it were shame for Gettys' poor quality of stores, or Carsina's forthright announcement that Clara would be retrimming her dresses rather than purchasing new frocks. It didn't matter. I looked at Carsina, and delightful as she appeared, I wondered how I had ever believed I could be happily partnered with such a thoughtless woman.

If I had thought to take vengeance on her, I got it without making any effort at all. Carsina's eyes had found me; it would have been difficult to miss a man of my size in any setting, let alone amid the crowded shelves of the mercantile. There I stood, unlovely and immense in my well-worn "uniform," looking back at her. Our eyes met. She recognized me. I knew that from how her eyes widened and her silent gasp. She instantly turned away from me and fled toward the door, exclaiming, "Come, Clara, there must be other stores in Gettys. Let us see what they have to offer us."

"But—but, Carsina, I've told you, this store is the best of them. Carsina!"

The door shut behind her. I hadn't moved. "Can't blame her for taking fright," the youth behind the counter smirked. "And what can I do for you today, Mistress Gorling?"

Clara Gorling was a lady. I'll give her that. She cast me an apologetic glance before telling the lad, "Well, I thought we were going to look at buttons and lace, but my husband's cousin seems to have fled. I do beg your pardon. She's only newly arrived in Gettys. It's been arranged for her to meet Captain Thayer. Their families are discussing a betrothal.

My cousin spent the best part of the winter in Old Thares. You can imagine the shock she feels, coming straight to Gettys from the society and culture of the capital. Well. As I'm here, Yandy, would you please put up two pounds of herring for me, and two measures of corn meal? At least I'll get the day's shopping out of the way."

She glanced out of the window as she spoke, and I followed her gaze. Carsina lingered outside the mercantile with her back to the store. Did she think I would pursue her? Why would she imagine I would want to, after she had treated me so badly and tried to turn my own sister against me? Yet that random thought of Yaril suddenly made me realize why I had to speak to Carsina. I hurried out of the store.

The streets were muddy and rutted from the rains of spring. Carsina lingered on a cobbled walk, trying to hold her skirts away from the mud without flashing her ankles into view. The spring wind from the mountains tugged at the scarf that she held close to her throat with her free hand. There was no one near to overhear me. I walked softly up to her and spoke in a low voice. "Such a surprise to see you in Gettys, Carsina. I understand you're here to meet your new fiancé. Congratulations. I'm sure he'll be as charmed as I once was."

I had intended my words as a compliment, to calm her and make her regard me with gratitude before I asked my favor of her. Instead, she seemed to regard them as either insult or threat. She turned her head to look at me, eyes flashing, and then jerked her gaze away. "Leave me alone, sirrah. We have not been introduced, and I'm not accustomed to conversing with common strangers." She took several hasty steps away from me and then paused, staring anxiously at the mercantile door. I knew that as soon as Clara came out, she would flee. I only had a moment to convey my need to her. A soldier who was riding past stared at us curiously.

I approached her again. "Carsina, please. There is just one thing I need from you, a small and simple favor. Won't you help me out, please, for old time's sake? For Yaril?"

Her face had gone white and she stood stiff as a stick. She looked all around us, as if fearing someone would see me speaking to her. "Sir, I do not know you!" she said quite loudly. "If you don't stop bothering me, I shall scream for assistance." Two ladies had just turned the corner near Gettys' only teashop. They halted at the sight of us, staring.

"Don't do that!" I whispered hoarsely. "You don't need to do that. Carsina, it's about Yaril, not me. Once you were the very best of friends. Please, for her sake, help me. She thinks I am dead. I don't have any way to—"

"Leave me alone!" She all but shrieked the words as she took several more tottering steps away from me.

"Excuse me, ma'am. Is he bothering you?" The voice came from behind me, and I turned, dread in my heart. Sergeant Hoster, puffed up with hostility, looked absolutely gratified to have an excuse to humiliate me. He didn't wait for Carsina to speak before he barked at me, "Step away from the lady, Gutbag! I seen you whispering at her. She warned you off twice. Now get on your way and leave her alone. Better yet, get back to the cemetery where you belong."

Carsina stood with her back to me, trembling as if with terror, her handkerchief clutched to her mouth. I knew what she feared, and it wasn't that I'd harm her. It was that somehow the folk of Gettys would connect her with me.

I spoke deliberately to her back. "I meant no harm, ma'am. Obviously, I mistook you for someone else." A vengeful demon inside me wanted to call her by name, wanted to announce to every fool on the street who had stopped to gawk that I had once been engaged to her. Coldly I clamped down on the impulse. I must not antagonize her. She was my best hope of getting a letter through to my sister. If I could catch her alone, I could if necessary threaten her with exposure to get her to write to Yaril. But that ruse would have to wait. For now, I lowered my head and stepped back apologetically.

Clara Gorling had emerged from the shop at last. She gave an exclamation of dismay at Carsina's distress and hurried to her side. I turned and walked quickly away. Behind me, I heard Sergeant Hoster apologizing to her for "the lady's bad experience. No woman should walk the streets of Gettys alone, more's the pity. Some of the enlisted men have no more manners than savages. She's not harmed, ma'am, merely shaken. A walk home and a hot cup of tea will likely put her right." He turned and shook his fist at me. "I'd give you the thrashing you deserve, if it weren't for all these ladies watching. Count yourself lucky!"

Clara Gorling was no shrinking violet. She called out loudly after me, "You should be ashamed of yourself, trooper! Ashamed! Animals like you are why the ladies of this town must carry whistles and walk in pairs just to be safe in broad daylight! I'll be speaking to Colonel Haren about you! Don't think I shan't! You're a hard man to mistake! My husband will see that you get what you have coming to you!"

And all I could do was hunch my shoulders to her words and slink away like a chicken-killing dog. I almost expected the onlookers to stoop and fling stones after me to make me run. For a terrifying moment, I wished death on all of them. Yet the moment I felt my blood begin to seethe with magic, a horror seized me and I quenched the emotion and the evil thought it had spurred. I felt physically ill and more of a monster than even the gawking folk believed I was. As quickly as I could, I turned down an alley and escaped from their sight. I had not intended to take Sergeant Hoster's suggestion that I hurry back to the cemetery, but that was what I did. For the rest of the afternoon, my mind seethed, not just with plans of how I could persuade Carsina to help me clandestinely contact my sister, but also with genuine fear of the emotions she had stirred in me. Eventually I took out my dearly bought newspaper and tried to absorb myself in the news from Old Thares and the civilized world.

But the news that had been of such pressing interest to me but a few hours earlier now seemed irrelevant to me. I tried to care about the old nobles and the new nobles and questions of birth order and life roles and could not. None of it, I told myself, would ever touch me again. I was no longer a new noble's soldier son, but only an enlisted man who wasn't even truly a cavalla trooper, but only a cemetery soldier, a guardian of graves. The storekeeper had been right, I told myself in disgust. Just because I could read the newspaper did not mean that any of it applied to me.

No. I was a creature of this border world now, a man infected with magic. A monstrous power slept inside me, and unless I could rid myself of it, I would have to live in fear of my honest emotions. I had to find a way to rid myself of the magic. I had starved my body of sustenance to no avail. I had thought that if I could regain my former body, I could take back my former life. Now I saw that I had been starting at the wrong end of the problem. If I wanted to take back my old life or any semblance of it, the first thing I had to do was be rid of the magic that lurked inside me. It was the true change that had befallen me, not the layer of fat that covered me. My fat was only an outward sign of the real transformation.

Spink had offered to help me. I suddenly longed to be able to seek him and Epiny out and have someone I trusted on my side in this battle. Perhaps I could find a way to contact Spink, and I tempted myself with the thought of revealing myself to Epiny. I banished the hope by recalling how the folk in town had looked at me today. Did I want to bring that kind of disgust and shame to Spink's doorstep? Did I want tales of whores and insults to women on the street to attach themselves to my real name, as they surely must if Epiny acknowledged me as her cousin? I imagined such gossip reaching my father's ears, and Yaril's, and I cringed. No. Isolation was better than shame. I would continue on my own. This was my fight and no one else's.

I stayed away from town for over a week. I was well settled in my cabin now. I dug myself a garden patch, well away from the grave sites, and planted a small vegetable garden. I tended the graves of the folk I had buried over the winter; the frozen earth I had tossed down on their coffins had settled unevenly. I leveled it now, and whenever I noticed wild flowers sprouting near my path, I dug them up and moved them to the new graves.

Rabbits and birds were attracted to the spring grass on the open hillside of the graveyard, and I began employing my sling to obtain fresh meat for myself. I began to wonder how independently I could live. Eventually I must return to town for fresh supplies and to fulfill my duties, but each time I thought of going, I found an excuse to stay home.

I was hoeing in my little garden one morning when I heard hoofbeats. I hurried around the front of my cabin and then stood and watched as a lone horseman followed by a mule and cart came up the rough road to the cemetery. It took some time before I recognized Ebrooks and Kesey. Even then, I was reluctant to go and meet them. I stood silently until they pulled in their animals. Ebrooks dismounted and Kesey clambered down from his cart. The cart held a coffin.

"No mourners?" I asked as I approached them.

Kesey shrugged. "New recruit. He managed to get himself killed the first day he was here. The corporal that did it is locked up now. I expect that before the week is out, you'll be burying him, too."

I shook my head at the sad tidings. "You could have just sent a messenger out here. Clove and I would have come for him."

"Yeah, well, it's that time of year. You'll be seeing me and Ebrooks regular now. Colonel doesn't like the grass to get more than ankle-deep here. We'll be cutting some each day; it's the only way to keep it down."

It was strange to have company. They helped me lower the coffin into the waiting grave, and then watched me fill it in. It annoyed me that neither one appreciated that a dug grave was already waiting, nor did they help to fill it. At least they bowed their heads with me as I said a simple prayer over the grave.

"Used to be every soldier from our outfit had a real funeral," Kesey observed. "But I guess funerals are like birthdays. Once you reach a certain number of them, they don't seem so special anymore."

"As long as I'm here, I'll do my best to see every man buried with dignity," I replied.

"Suit yourself," Kesey said. "But Ebrooks and I won't always have time to help you, you know."

His callousness angered me. I took a petty revenge. I professed ignorance as to how to put an edge on a scythe. I watched them do all the tool sharpening, and then feigned that I did not know how to use one and spent the rest of the day "learning" by watching them. I discovered they were actually very competent at their tasks. We began at the oldest section of the cemetery, and worked row by row to take down the grass that had grown too tall. As we raked it into piles and collected it, they complained that once simply putting a couple of sheep out to graze had accomplished this task. It had been stopped not out of exaggerated respect for the dead, but because three times in a row, the sheep had been stolen. When I expressed surprise, they laughed at me. Had I forgotten that most of the population of the town around the fort were criminals?

As the afternoon shadows lengthened, we returned to my cabin. To my surprise, they'd thought to bring food with them, and we made a meal together. They were not companions I would have chosen for myself, yet it was still good to eat and talk and laugh without regard to anything else.

After our meal, they headed back to town. They invited me to come with them and join them in a beer, but I'd spent my money on the Old Thares newspaper, and told them so politely. And so they departed, with the promise or warning that they'd return to work again tomorrow. As they waved at me, they laughed, and told me to keep good watch tonight, lest the Specks come to steal my latest resident. I waved them off and went back into my cabin.

I'd worked longer hours than I had in some days, and I went to bed early, actually anticipating the morrow with some pleasure. After all my days alone, it would be good to have company each day. I tried not to wonder if I would soon weary of the twosome. I slept well and deeply.

Dawn woke me, and I rose and followed my routine. When I went to fetch water, I received again the strong impression that someone was watching me from the forest. I steeled myself to the magic's insidious creeping and shook my fist at the forest before I carried my bucket of water home. While I waited for the icy spring water to boil for tea and porridge, I took my sling and went out across the grave sites looking for rabbits or birds. I'd resolved to make a nice meat soup for all of us for supper, and suspected that the scent of newly shorn grass might have lured in a few fat spring rabbits, or perhaps some birds come in quest of gravel or worms.

What I found instead shocked and horrified me. Somehow, the tales of body-snatching had seemed only that: tales to frighten a man new to his task as a cemetery guard. To see the gaping grave and the plundered coffin crookedly perched upon the heaped soil raised the hair on the back of my neck and sent a shiver down my spine. I approached it cautiously, as if it were somehow dangerous to me. It was empty. Only a smudge of caked blood from the dead man's wound remained to show that a body had been in there. In the loose soil beside the grave, I found two sets of barefoot prints. I lifted my eyes to the forest that crouched on the hillside above the cemetery.

The Specks had come and taken the body into those woods. Somewhere in there, I'd find him. All I had to do was muster the courage to go and look for the corpse.

Ebrooks and Kesey found me gathering what I thought I'd need. I'd found a piece of old canvas in the tool shed, possibly left over from crude shroud-making for plague victims. I had the canvas and a good length of rope. I'd slung those onto the back of Clove's saddle. My long gun was in the scabbard. I hoped I wouldn't have to use it, and not just because I didn't want to face a difficult situation. I had no faith in the battered weapon. I had expected them to share my horror at the body snatching. Instead, simpletons that they were, they roared with laughter at my predicament and wished me "good hunting" but declined to make any effort to help me. Kesey offered me the only helpful bit of information. "Sometimes they puts them right at the end of the road, where the workers would find them. I think they do it to frighten them. But other times, well, there's just no saying. That feller could be anywhere in the woods, from here to the other side of the Barrier Mountains."

"Why do they do it?" I demanded furiously, not expecting an answer.

"Most likely because it bothers us so much. For a while there, Rheims, the fellow who dug graves before you, he kept a list of the ones that were stolen, and which ones he brought back and buried and which ones he never found. Colonel Haren got angry about that."

"That he never found some of the bodies? I don't blame him! That's awful. Think of the families."

"No, not that. He got mad that Rheims kept a list. Sergeant Hoster told us a new rule for it, after Rheim disappeared. You got to go look for the body at least three times. If you don't find it after that, you can just fill in the grave and keep your mouth shut about it. Now, Ebrooks and me, we asked him, 'What do you mean?' Do we only have to go looking for the corpse three times all told, or that we got to try to find it three times each time it gets stole, no matter what?"

The horror I felt was only getting deeper. "What did Hoster say?" I asked faintly.

Ebrooks laughed sourly. "Not much. He just shoved Kesey down and called him an old fool and then stomped off. And over his shoulder he shouts at us, 'Work it out for yourselves.' So we did. And we decided three times was the maximum we'd go into the woods for any body. And that's how we've been doing it."

I felt queasy. "And how many bodies have been lost that way?"

They exchanged a look. It was an agreement to lie. "Oh, not many," Ebrooks said airily. "But we don't really know the count, because Colonel Haren forbade keeping track of it. And neither of us are much good at writing anyway."

"I see."

They went off to their grass-cutting after that, and I took Clove and my corpse-packaging materials and went back to the empty grave. I resolved that I would start there and see if I couldn't discover any sort of trail. I also decided that I would approach Colonel Haren about acquiring a dog, to both help me guard the cemetery and to help track down stolen bodies when the occasion demanded it. This time, however, I knew I was on my own.

From the tracks in the disturbed soil around the grave, I decided there had been two intruders, one smaller than the other. They had walked through the uncut grass burdened with a corpse. I mounted Clove to enjoy a better vantage point. There had been a heavy dew the night before. As I had hoped, the passage of the grave robbers had disturbed enough of the moisture on the tall grass that I could see where they had gone. Even better, it indicated they had left after most of the dew had formed. I kicked Clove, and we followed their trail through the grave markers. It made straight for the woods.

The forest looked beautiful in the morning light. The new leaves were at their brightest, and the contrast between the shades of green shown by the different kinds of trees made a springtime palette. The sky was a pale blue, with wispy clouds. In the near distance, the mountains shouldered up above the hills, still mantled with snow. It looked as if clouds had snagged on their rugged tops and flew there like banners. The woods should have looked welcoming, but the closer I got to them, the more they breathed dullness and fatigue and deep dark despair.

At the edge of the meadow, I dismounted. From here, I'd have to walk if I was to keep my eyes open for sign. And walking would force me to stay awake. Already sleepiness buzzed in my ears and my eyelids were heavy. I rubbed my eyes, scratched my head briskly to try to rouse myself, and entered the woods. Clove came behind me.

The packed litter of the forest floor looked deep and undisturbed. I tried to imagine myself as two men, burdened with a corpse. Where would I choose to walk, what would I avoid? I picked my way up the hillside, avoiding the denser thickets of underbrush. I struck a deer trail, and was rewarded by a fresh scuff mark on the bark of a tree beside it. I yawned prodigiously, shook my head, and forced myself to go on. The forest smelled lovely, both lush and rotting in the rising warmth of the spring day. It reminded me of something . . . no, of someone. Of her. Tree Woman. It was the smell of her breath and body. In a sort of daze, I drifted into a walking dream of lying beside her, in warmth and ease. My discouragement turned to a shameful longing for a past that I didn't even remember.

Can a man fall asleep walking? I'm not sure, but it is possible to waken by jolting into a tree. I shook my head, and for a moment I could not remember where I was or what I was doing there. Then Clove nudged me from behind, and I recalled my task. We had not strayed far from the deer trail. I went back to it, and trudged on. I used every trick I knew to keep myself alert. I bit my lip. I scratched the back of my

neck. I forced myself to walk with my eyes open very wide.
Such antics kept me awake and moving, but it was devilishly
hard to focus on trying to find marks of a trail. I saw nothing
for a long time, and cursed my luck, wondering if in my
sleepiness I'd missed some key clue. Then I saw the unmistakable mark of three muddy fingers on a tree trunk. Someone had paused there and steadied himself. I tottered on,
yawning. That hand mark meant something more than the
fact they had passed this way. My mind chewed the thought
slowly. I decided it meant they were getting tired.

The nature of the forest was changing. The woods right
above the cemetery were of fairly young trees interspersed
with large charred stumps and fire-scarred giants. Clove and
I came now to the edge of that old burn, and in a dozen
paces the open, airy forest of deciduous trees abruptly gave
way to something darker and more ancient. The underbrush
dwindled and gave way. The crowded trees that competed
for space and survival had no place in this cathedral of giants. The forest floor became a deep carpet of moss. A few
broad-leaved plants and ferns broke the floor, and occasionally the long, crookedly sprawling and fiercely thorned canes
of demon's club sprouted like strange forest cacti.

Previously, Clove had had to shoulder his way along the
narrow path. Now we were dwarfed. The trunks of the trees
were columns that held up a distant sky. The giants were
widely spaced, and I could not reach the lowest branch on
any of them. Their leafy limbs began far overhead and
reached out to mingle in a canopy that, when their leaves
were fully developed, would completely block the light. I
had never walked in such a forest, and the magic's sleepy
spell was abruptly dispersed by a jolt of genuine and deeply
felt fear. I'd recognized these giants of trees. They were the
same as those at the end of the road. I halted where I stood
and stared all around me. The vista of thick columnar trunks
extended in all directions. I had no name for the trees; I'd
never seen them anywhere else. The upper reaches of their
trunks were mottled in color, from green to reddish-brown.
But down here, at my height, the surface of their bark was
ropy, as if the trunks were braided tendrils rather than a

single stem. The roots that radiated out from the trees raised hummocks in the forest floor. Their fallen leaves from last autumn made deep leafy beds of humus among the tangling roots. The rich smell of healthy rot filled my nostrils.

The silence in that place was a pressure I felt in my ears, and between one heartbeat and the next, I suddenly acknowledged a thing I had always known but never fully realized. Trees were alive. The colossi that surrounded me were not the work of man or the earth's bones of stone. They were living creatures, each one begun from a tiny seed, and older, far older than anything I could imagine. The thought sent a sudden shiver up my spine, and suddenly I needed to see the sky and feel moving air on my face. But the trees hemmed me round and closed me in. I glimpsed an area that seemed more light and open and made directly for it, heedless of leaving the deer trail that was now only a winding indentation through the mossy earth.

My area of light marked where one of the giants had half fallen. It leaned at an angle, its roots torn from the earth, and its bare branches pushing half a dozen fellow trees aside. Its falling had opened a window to the sky; spring sunlight reached the mossy forest floor. In that irregular patch of light, several young trees had sprung up. I would have said they were large, old trees if I had seen them growing in Old Thares. Among these giants, they seemed like saplings. And fastened to one of the saplings I found the corpse I had been pursuing.

I had seen only his coffin when we buried him. It was a shock to find him such a young man, little more than a boy, really. He sat with his back to the tree, his head fallen forward on his chest and his face covered by a sheaf of yellow hair. But for the discoloration of his skin, he might have simply fallen asleep there. His hands, darkened by death, lay in his lap. He looked at peace.

I stared at him, and wondered what I had feared I would find. The Specks had not stripped his body. They had not cut his limbs away or in any way dishonored him that I could see. They had simply carried him all this way, only to set him down against a tree.

The shafts of spring sunlight falling from far above illuminated him as if he were god-touched. Tiny insects danced above him in a flickering cloud of gossamer wings. Behind me, Clove snorted impatiently. I glanced back at my horse, and at the roll of soiled canvas and old rope he carried. Suddenly it seemed that I would be the one disturbing the rest of the dead. A man spoke beside me. "Please, sir. Don't bother him. He is peaceful now."

I leapt sideways and landed in a defensive posture. Clove turned his big head to look at me curiously. The Speck man did not flinch or move. He didn't shift his eyes toward me, but stood with his hands clasped loosely below his belly and his head bent as if praying. For a long instant, we were frozen in that tableau. The Speck was a man of middle years, naked as the sky. His long streaked hair was held back with a tie of bark twine. He carried no weapons; his body was unadorned by jewelry of any kind. As natural as an animal, he stood in submission before me. I felt foolish in my wrestler's crouch, with my fists held up before me. I calmed my breath and warily straightened.

"Why have you done this?" I asked him severely.

He lifted his eyes to look at me. I was startled to see that his eyes matched the streaking pigment on his face. A brown eye looked at me from the dark blotch on the left side of his face, and a green eye peered from the tan area around his right eye. His gaze was mild. "I do not understand your words, Great One."

Clove and my scabbarded long gun were several steps away. I edged toward them as I tried to think of a different way to phrase my question. "Yesterday I buried this man in a coffin. Why have you disturbed his rest by stealing his body and bringing him here?"

He puffed his cheeks at me lightly, a gesture I would later learn indicated a sort of denial. "Oh, Great One, I cannot understand what you say."

"Speak the language, can't you?" The woman who suddenly stepped out from the shelter of a tree snapped these words with asperity. She had been leaning against the mottled trunk in a way that had allowed her to blend with it.

Now that she stood clear of it, I wondered how I had not seen her before, and wondered, too, why Clove showed no sign of alarm. He paid these Specks no more mind than if they were jaybirds hopping near him in his pasture. When, I wondered, had he become so accustomed to them? A paranoid fear that there were actually unseen Specks all around me suddenly seized me. I glanced about and then put my back to Clove's barrel body. My long gun was on the other side of my horse. I started to edge around him.

As I took that precaution, the woman walked toward me. She was as naked as the man, and completely comfortable in her bare skin. She reminded me of a large, heavy-bodied cat as she stalked me. She was lithe, but there was nothing slight about her. As she drew closer, I halted my flight. Her modest breasts hugged her body; muscle moved in her powerful thighs. I tried not to stare at her nakedness, but it was just as difficult to meet her eyes. They were the deepest green I had ever seen. A sooty streak ran down the center of her face, dividing her eyes and darkening her nose. She had more specks and larger ones than the man did; at some points, the dashes on her body almost became stripes. Her streaky hair fell in a mane down her back, and in color it reminded me of varnished oak.

If I felt uncouth staring at her body, she was not so inhibited about perusing mine. Her eyes ran over me familiarly, and she said to the man, "Look at him. He's huge. He could make two of you even now, and yet it is plain that no one cares for him. Think what such a man could look like with the proper care." She was only an arm's length away from me, and she lifted both her hands as if she would measure my girth with them.

"Keep your distance!" I warned her, unnerved by her casual attitude toward me.

"Speak the language, I said! Are you rude, or stupid?"

"Olikea! It is dangerous to speak so to a Great One!" The man offered his warning in a humble tone, as if he must defer to her. It made me wonder what her status was; I tried to gauge her age and decided she must be close to twenty. Her nakedness, I suddenly realized, confused me. I was accustomed to dress defining both a woman's status and her age.

She laughed, a clear peal that shattered the quiet of the woods. The sound woke a memory in me. I'd heard that laugh before. "There is no danger, Father. If he is so stupid that he cannot speak the language, then he will not be offended by what I said. And if he is so rude as to speak his own tongue to us when he can understand the language, well, then I have only returned that rudeness to him. Is it not so, Great One?"

"My name is not *Great One*," I replied testily. And then my tongue halted of its own accord. I had spoken Gernian to her, until I came to the words for *Great One*. That phrase I had returned to her in her own language. I knew then that I could speak the Speck language, and recalled when I had learned it and from whom. They were speaking Speck and I'd been replying in Gernian. I took a breath and tried again. "Please. Keep your distance from me."

"There!" she exclaimed to her father. "I knew it. He was just being rude. Because he thinks he can." She turned back to me. "Keep my distance. That I shall. This is *my* distance, Great One." She stepped closer to me and set both her hands on my chest. Shock paralyzed my body and my tongue. She ran one hand down my side, and slapped me firmly on the hip as if she were checking a horse or dog for soundness. Her other hand simultaneously traveled up my chest and up the side of my neck and stopped on my cheek. She ran her thumb lightly over my lips. Her bold gaze held my own. She leaned in closer until her breasts brushed my chest. Then the hand that had lingered on my hip suddenly groped my groin. Startled, I sprang back from her, but Clove's huge body blocked my escape. She squeezed me playfully and then stepped back, grinning broadly. She spoke over her shoulder to her father, who stood, his eyes cast down, as if he wished to avoid seeing her outrageous behavior. "Oh, you see, he regrets being rude already." She cocked her head at me and wet her lips. "Would you like to apologize to me?"

It was very hard to think. The sudden idea that I had succumbed to the spell of the forest and fallen into a deep sleep came to me. If this was a dream, I could do whatever I wanted, without repercussions. No. I recalled the last time I had lain with a Speck woman in a dream, and all that had followed. I made fists, digging my nails into the palms of my hands. I lifted my hands and scrubbed roughly at my face. Either the dream was a very strong one, or this was real. Either choice was frightening. I took a breath and spoke firmly to the man. It was hard to summon an authoritative voice when the woman still hemmed me in against my horse. "I have come to take the body back to our graveyard. Stand clear of me and let me do what I must."

The man lifted his eyes to mine. "I think he prefers to be where he is, Great One. Go to him. Speak to him. See if it is not so."

He spoke with such confidence that I looked toward the corpse. Was it possible that by some horrible error the man still clung to life? No. He was dead. Flies were walking on him. I could smell him. I decided to put my decision into words the savage could comprehend. "No. He wishes to be back in his coffin, buried in the ground. That is what I must do for him." As casually as I could, I turned back to Clove. I took my roll of canvas and length of line from his saddle and slung them over my shoulder. The woman had not moved. I had to edge past her to walk toward the corpse. She followed me.

The man clasped himself and rocked from side to side as I approached the body. "Great One, I fear you are wrong. Listen to him. He wishes to stay. He will make a fine tree. When the trees of your people fill our forest, the cutting will have to stop. Your own trees will stop you."

I understood each word that he said, but I could not take his meaning. "I will ask him what he wishes," I told the old man as I dropped the canvas next to the body. I knelt briefly by the body and pretended to listen. "Yes. He wishes to go back to the cemetery," I told them.

I pulled the rope free of the canvas and unrolled the cloth. I bent to seize the corpse by the shoulders. Insects buzzed over my head, and the distinctive smell of death surrounded me. I held my breath. Resolved to get it over with quickly, I

seized him by his shoulders, intending to pull him over onto
the canvas and then quickly roll him up in it.

The corpse didn't budge. I tugged at him several times,
and then had to step away to take a deep breath of untainted
air. The stench of death clung to my hands, and it took all
my will to keep from retching.

All this while, the Specks had watched me, the man solemnly and the woman with amusement. Their presence
bothered me; if I must do such a distasteful task, I would
rather have done it without an audience. Obviously, they had
fastened him to the tree somehow. I stood up straight, unsheathed my knife, took a deep breath of air, and once more
approached the corpse. I could not see any binding. When I
could hold my breath no longer, I took another gasp of air
through the sleeve of my jacket. Then I tried to slide my
hand down behind his back, between him and the tree. Immediately, I encountered a number of tiny rootlets project-
ing from the tree and into the corpse, thrusting right through
the fabric of his jacket and shirt and into his flesh.

I could scarcely credit it. I knew that the man's body had
not been here more than a few hours. That a tree could send
greedy, questing roots into him so quickly was macabre. I
tried the blade of my knife against those I could reach; it
was a hopeless task. They were pencil thick and as hard as
oak knots.

I do not like to recall the next half hour. The stench was
stronger because the rootlets had pierced his dead flesh in so
many places. Every atom of my nature rebelled against the
idea of manhandling the dead. Yet, in the end, that was what
it came down to. I jerked him loose. The rootlets that had
entered his body so quickly had fanned out inside him as a
network of tendrils. By the time I pried the body loose, it was
leaking foul fluids from dozens of gaping wounds. It smelled
far worse than it should have; I suspected something in the
roots was hastening the breakdown of the corpse. Pulling the
body free of the roots left the tangled root masses dangling
from the tree and dripping gore. Liquids and particles of
flesh and gut smeared my hands and arms before I finally
managed to lay him out on the canvas. I flung an end of it

over him and then dropped to my knees to roll him up in the coarse shroud. I bound the parcel with my rope.

I was tying the final knot when the Speck man spoke again. "I do not believe he wished to go. But in this I will defer to your wisdom, Great One." He sounded ineffably sad.

The woman spoke with more scorn. "You did not even try to listen to him." She puffed her cheeks at me several times, making her lips flutter. When I made no response, she said, "I will come to see you again. This time not as a dreamwalker, but in the flesh." She cocked her head and eyed me appraisingly before she added, "And I will bring you proper food."

I could think of no response. It was difficult to lift the swathed corpse to my shoulder and even harder to rise with it, but I would have died before I would have asked either of them for help. I lugged the dead trooper over to Clove, who snorted his distaste, but accepted the nasty burden. I could almost feel the Specks' eyes boring into me as I secured the body to my saddle. Both ends of my parcel stuck out awkwardly. The journey home would be a complicated one once we reached the narrow path through the younger forest. I spoke over my shoulder to the watching Specks as I tightened the rope that lashed the corpse to my saddle.

"The way of my people is to bury our dead. It is my duty to protect their graves. I do not wish to have problems with you or your people. You must leave our dead alone. You must never again do what you did last night. I do not want to bring harm down on either of you. But if you again take a corpse from our graveyard, I must. Do you understand?" I tugged the last knot tight and turned to look at them.

I was alone.

CHAPTER TWENTY-ONE

OLIKEA

Much later that afternoon, I presented myself at Colonel Haren's office. After I'd reburied the unfortunate trooper I'd hauled bucket after bucket of water and scrubbed myself raw, but the stink of death clung to me. I wanted to throw away the clothing I'd been wearing, but I did not have that luxury. Instead, I washed it and left it dripping on my newly strung clothesline. I avoided Ebrooks and Kesey entirely. I didn't want to speak to anyone about my encounter with the Specks, but thought that perhaps I must report it to Colonel Haren.

The sergeant kept me waiting. I had learned that the person I really had to wear down was his sergeant, not the colonel. So I stood before his desk and watched him shuffle his papers. "You could leave and come back later," he suggested to me sharply at one point.

"I've nothing more demanding to do. And I feel I should make my report to the colonel as soon as possible."

"You can simply give me your information to pass on."

"I could, Sergeant, of course. It's rather detailed. But if you wish to write it down for the colonel, I could come back tomorrow for his response."

I don't know why he didn't simply order me to leave. Perhaps because he knew I would come back. There were a few chairs along the wall of the office, but I had observed that my standing seemed to chafe his nerves more than if I withdrew quietly. He sorted his way through a stack of dispatches, assigning them to different piles. Then he looked up at me, sighed, and said, "I'll see if he can see you now."

Despite the spring weather, the colonel still lounged in his chair by the blazing hearth fire. No ray of daylight penetrated his chamber. I wondered if he ever left this room.

He turned his head as I entered and sighed. "Trooper Burve. You again! What is it now?"

"Specks stole a body out of the graveyard last night, sir. I had to enter the forest to recover it. I had contact there with a Speck man and woman."

"Did you? That's the only part of your story that is unusual. Did you antagonize them?"

I considered his question. "I took the body back. They didn't seem to approve, but I simply did it."

"Well done." He nodded sharply. "We've found that to be the best way to deal with them. Approach what must be done calmly, inform them of it, and then do it. They soon come to understand that we know what we're doing and it's for the best. For the most part, they're a passive people. The only time they've ever attacked us, we had shed Speck blood first. They became very distressed about the road construction and tried to interfere with it. Instead of talking to them, some fool lost his head and shot one. Instead of fleeing, the Specks charged at us. Well. We had no choice except to use our weapons then. A lot of Specks died. Such a one-sided battle was unfairly called a massacre. The papers in Old Thares published a very biased account, and all the officers involved were rebuked. What should they have told their men? 'Don't shoot until they've killed some of us?'"

His indignation had brought two bright spots of color to

his cheeks. He took a deep breath to calm himself. "So. We don't want a situation like that again. Do as you've been doing. Simply bring the bodies back. Don't make threats. Don't shoot at Specks. Just do your duty, but don't provoke them to bloodshed. Remember I assigned you to the cemetery to prevent this, not so you could come here and complain about it. You did recover the corpse and rebury it?"

"Yes, sir, I did. Sir, I thought I should report my contact with the Specks."

He lifted a wine glass from a table at his elbow and sipped from it. The liquid was a dark crimson. "It's of no consequence. It's spring, trooper. Spring always brings the Specks down to trade. Soon it will be summer. Then it will be high summer, and people will die of plague. Lots of them. And as fast as you bury them, the Specks will try to dig them up. By the end of summer, if you don't die of the plague, you'll be like all the rest of us. Praying for winter to come and cursing it when it gets here."

He spoke with absolute certainty. When he was finished, he resumed staring into this fire.

"Sir. It seems to me I might better serve in my post if I could find a way to prevent the Specks from stealing bodies before summer and the plague season hits."

I waited for a response from him. When he didn't give me one, I took it as permission to speak on. "I'd like to acquire a dog, sir, with your permission. He could serve in two capacities: he could keep watch in the graveyard by night and bark to warn me of intruders. And if a body was stolen, a hound could help me track the culprits and bring the corpse back sooner."

He made no response. I tried again. "I'd like to keep a dog, sir."

He gave a sudden harrumph of laughter. "So should we all, trooper. But tell me this. Where would you get one? Have you seen any dogs in Gettys since you arrived?"

It was such an obvious lack, I wondered how I had missed it before. "Perhaps dogs could be brought from the west?" I ventured, certain that this had already been tried.

"Dogs disappear from Gettys. Dogs do not seem to like

Specks and Specks certainly do not like dogs. Except in stew. So. You will not be getting a dog to help you fulfill your duties." He glanced away from the fire to look at me, and when I didn't move, he demanded testily, "Was there anything else, trooper?"

"May I attempt to build a wall around the cemetery, sir? Or at least along the side of it that is closest to the woods? It might not prevent all such incidents, but I should like to make stealing bodies as difficult as possible for them."

He shook his head. The neck of the bottle chinked against the lip of his wineglass as he poured. "Did you pay any attention when I let you sign on? I told you that I've requested a shipment of stone for a wall. I've asked for it several times now, and each time I've been put off." He took another sip from his wine. "Obviously, the King's Road is far more important than our troopers resting in dignity after they die in this forsaken place."

A silence fell between us. I made a final unwilling effort. "I could build a fence, sir."

He did not turn his head toward me but only shifted his eyes. "From wood, I assume."

"Yes, sir."

"And where do you plan to get it? Not from our supplies. Wood, ironically, is hard to come by. We can harvest it only from the edges of the forest because . . . because, well, you know how difficult it is for our crews to enter the actual forest. So how would you build a fence without wood?"

Some stubbornness I had thought long vanquished from me reared its head. I did not point out that he seemed overly generous with his own supply of firewood. "I'll get my own wood, sir."

He leaned deeper into his chair and considered me. "Taking wood from that forest is not as easy as it might appear. Have you attempted it, soldier?"

"I've been in the forest twice, sir. I know its challenges."

"Yet you'd willingly attempt such a thing"

Perhaps he weighed my courage against the appearance of my body. I felt as if he were seeing me for the first time rather than just the flesh that enclosed me. I spoke the truth.

"I'd rather try to take wood from that forest than have to hunt down stolen corpses in it, sir."

"I suppose you would. Very well, then. Feel free to attempt it. But don't neglect your other duties. I've had good reports of your predigging the graves. Continue with that effort. But in your spare time, you may attempt to build a fence as well."

"Thank you, sir." I felt anything but thankful as I left. I emerged into the dusky streets of Gettys. The colonel had kept me waiting for longer than I thought. Evening was coming on.

What had I been thinking, volunteering to fence in the cemetery? I had enough work to do, and with no dog to help me, I might have to start keeping a night watch over the fresh graves. I thought of the long boundary the cemetery shared with the forest, and tried to picture a fence. A tall fence of solid wood plank would be the most effective. A rail fence would do little more than slow the graverobbers. I considered a palisade of logs and rejected the notion. The idea of cutting that many substantial logs, digging the holes, and erecting them was beyond a lone man.

Clove awaited me patiently at the hitching rail. I stared at it, and at the weeds that grew vigorously at the base of its supports. It reminded me of my father's hedgerows, founded on lines of rough stones hauled from the surrounding fields. I'd encountered no sizable stones while digging graves. The largest ones were no bigger than my head. But even those, set in a row, could provide a demarcation. And if I planted thorny or densely growing bushes, I might make a barrier of the very stuff of the forest that so daunted me.

The moment the idea came to me, I recognized the rightness of it. It would take time to grow, of course. So I'd erect a rail fence to begin with, and any stones I encountered in my gravedigging could go along the bottom of it. The Specks went naked. I'd plant brambles and briers along it. Yes.

Clove's reins were loose in my hands. He tugged at them, reminding me that I'd been standing there, lost in thought, for some time. I realized abruptly that I appeared to be staring at two women approaching me on the sidewalk. In an effort to counteract that rudeness, I smiled affably and gave a friendly nod. One gave a squeak of fear and her hand darted to seize the brass whistle she wore on a chain around her neck. The other woman abruptly took her companion's elbow and steered her quickly out and across the street. They walked briskly and glanced back at me once, whispering together. My cheeks burned in embarrassment, but I also felt a tinge of anger. I knew, with absolute certainty, that if those women had so encountered me two years ago, they would have smiled and returned my greeting. I resented that the shape of my body made them judge me so hastily. Within, I was the same man I'd always been.

Almost. I realized I was still staring after the women, and mentally contrasting their figures to the naked Speck woman I'd glimpsed earlier. Walking about clad only in her flesh, she had still been less self-conscious and more confident than either of them. And she had been aggressive, as Hitch had warned me that all Speck women were. He'd said that his Speck woman had simply chosen him and that he'd had no say in it, then or since. I wondered what that would be like, and caught my breath at the idea. It didn't displease me.

I hadn't planned to go back to Sarla Moggam's. Yet I found myself there, and tying Clove to the railing. It was stupid of me, I thought. Did I really want to spend what little remained of my month's pay on this? Fala was gone, I reminded myself as I knocked at the door, and the other whores had appeared uninterested in my trade. I'd be wiser to go straight back to my cottage.

Stiddick opened the door to my knock. "You!" he exclaimed the moment he opened it. Over his shoulder, he said to someone, "The cemetery guard is back." He stood solidly in the door opening. I could not pass, nor even look inside.

Before I could say anything, he was thrust to one side and Sarla herself darted out. She wore a red dress with many little white bows on the skirt of it. A layer of lace inadequately concealed her shoulders and the top of her bosom. She fairly quivered with anger. "You've got a lot of nerve coming here!" she exclaimed. "After what you did to Fala!"

"I didn't do anything to Fala," I protested, but my voice

went soft and guilty on the last words. I had done something to Fala, I just couldn't explain what.

"Then where is she?" Sarla demanded angrily. "Where does a woman go in Gettys in the dead of winter? You come here, you spend the whole night with her, something Fala never did with anyone. Then you're gone, and she just isn't herself. Turns away every man who comes to her for two days, and then just disappears. Where?"

"I don't know!" I'd heard Sarla was angry with me over Fala's leaving her employ. I hadn't expected her angry questions.

Her harsh smile of vindictive triumph deepened the lines in her face and flaked the powder from the corners of her mouth. "You don't know? Then why didn't you ever come back to see her? Everyone saw how satisfied you were. You come to my establishment just once, spend the whole night with one of my girls, and then she vanishes. But you never come back looking for her. Because you knew she was gone, didn't you? And you knew she wasn't ever coming back. And how does a man know that unless he makes sure of it himself?"

I was dumbstruck for a moment. Then, with all the dignity I could muster in the face of her outrageous words, I said carefully, "Are you accusing me of something, madam? And if you are, would you state it plainly?"

If I had thought a blunt response would rattle her, I was wrong. She leaned forward from the waist toward me, her hands on her hips, thrusting her breasts at me like weapons. "I say Fala came to a bad end. That's what I say. And I think that you know just how. Is that plain enough for you?"

"It is." Cold anger was building in me. "I only knew Fala for a few hours. But, as you say, I was a satisfied man. I had no reason to wish her harm, and every reason to be grateful to her. If she has met with foul play, I will be very grieved to hear of it. But it will have been none of my doing. Good day, madam."

I turned, seething with anger, to depart from her door. When I turned my back, Stiddick struck. It was a doltish schoolboy attack. He punched me squarely in the back, between my shoulder blades. I don't know what he thought would happen. Perhaps he thought that because I was fat, I must also be weak or cowardly. I do know he wasn't expecting it when I spun around and gave him a straight-from-the-shoulder fist to the face.

His head snapped back on his neck. Then he dropped like a rock. Time seemed to observe a long silence while he lay there, flat on his back and still. For one aching instant, I thought I'd killed him. Then he made a terrible retching sound, rolled over on his side, and curled up in a ball. Blood was flooding from his face, through his cupped hands and curled fingers. He yelled wordlessly, and Sarla began shrieking. I turned and walked away. As I mounted Clove, my hands started to shake. I'd never struck a man that hard. Gravedigging builds up a man's back and shoulders and arms. I thought of my defense: "I didn't know my own strength." Oh, that sounded good. I rode away, knowing that what I'd done was justified, but also that I felt queasy about it.

All the way home, I wondered what consequences I might expect. An official rebuke was the least of my worries. I had no witnesses who'd take my part in telling the story. They could say anything. Sarla had already as much as accused me of killing Fala. Dropping her doorman scarcely made me look more innocent. I berated myself for rising to such a schoolboy goad. I could have walked away.

But by the time I reached my cottage, I knew the truth.

No. I couldn't have.

If I'd walked away once, those sorts of attacks would have become a constant in my life. I'd done nothing wrong. I hadn't killed Fala, and when Stiddick had struck me, I'd only struck him back.

The night was mild, the air calm. I put Clove up and went to my cottage, thinking only that I'd wake the fire, eat something, and go to bed. When I reached my doorstep, I was alarmed to see the door ajar and light issuing from within. I reached for the door handle and almost fell over the basket there. It was a curious sort of basket, with a frame and handle of hard wood, but the sides woven of fresh green creeper, with leaves and flowers still on it. It looked very pretty and yet it filled me with dread. It could have come from only one place. I looked over my shoulder, across the graves to the forest edge. But no lone figure waited there in the dim shadows for me to find her gift. At least, my eyes could not pick out anyone.

I looked at the door. But surely if she were inside, she would not have left the basket outside? Cautiously, I eased the door open. I could see no one. After a few moments of hesitation, I picked up the basket and entered my cottage.

The fire had burned down to coals. I did not have many possessions, and as a result, they were kept in precise locations. Someone had explored my home. My journal and writing supplies were undisturbed, but my clothing seemed to have been examined. One of my more frequently darned socks still lay in the middle of the floor.

Several items in my limited pantry had been sampled and rejected. I set the basket down on my table next to the remains. The basket of cold biscuits on the shelf was to have been part of my dinner. Those she had apparently enjoyed. The napkin that had enfolded them held only crumbs.

I filled my tea kettle and swung it over the fire on its hook. Then, as gingerly as if it were a basket of snakes, I opened the woven cover of the basket. Incredible smells, earthy and rich, wafted up from it.

I ate everything that was in the basket.

I didn't recognize any of it in a specific way. I knew that there were mushrooms, roots, fleshy leaves, and scarlet gobbets of fruit that were sweet as honey yet stung the tongue with tartness, too. Almost everything I devoured was exactly as it had been harvested, uncooked in any way. But wrapped in leaves were a stack of golden flat cakes. I could taste honey in them, but whatever else they were made from, I did not know. I only knew that they were particularly satisfying, as if this were food I'd been seeking for a long time.

The basket was the size of a book satchel. When I was finished, I sat back, almost moaning with satiation. The skin of my belly was stretched tight. I didn't remember loosening my belt, but I obviously had. My conscience fussed at me that I had been both greedy and foolish; the food could have been poisonous. In all my days of travel and at Gettys, my circumstances had protected me from gluttony. My low pay had not permitted me to indulge in huge meals on my own, and my pride kept me from excess when I was eating in the mess hall where others could see me. This was the first time that I'd had access to a quantity of food that did not have to be rationed out over weeks, food that I could devour in privacy. I'd thought I'd had self-control. I'd just proved I did not.

But louder than my conscience was the satisfaction of my body. I felt nourished as I had not in months. Waves of well-being washed through me. The rightness of consuming it overpowered all my doubts, as did my sudden urge to sleep, nay, almost hibernate. I walked from my table to my bed, pausing only to latch my door. I dropped clothing as I went, and by the time I reached my blankets had nothing more to do than crawl in and close my eyes. I slept the sort of sleep that one never gets as an adult, a deep, dreamless repose.

I awoke the same way, between one breath and the next, feeling alert and rested. For several long moments, I lay there, taking simple pleasure in the comfort of my bed and the cool gray light of dawn that found its way through my loosely closed shutters. No list of daily tasks pressed upon me. All the things that usually weighted my soul, that I was fat, alone, without prospects, that I had left my sister in terrible circumstances, uncertain of my survival, that my life was as completely different from how I imagined it as it could possibly be—in short, all of the things that always flavored my mornings with defeat and despair were absent.

I sat up, swinging my bare feet to the wooden floor. And then those things did come to me, but they came without teeth. So my life was different from what I'd planned. Or, I thought to myself, more accurately, what my father had planned for me. It was still a life. Even the thought that Yaril believed me dead did not rend me as it usually did. I might as well be dead to her, I thought, for I could not, in good conscience, ever bring her to a place like Gettys. My father would attempt to oppress her, but from her letters to Epiny, I had the feeling that she would stand up to him if she finally believed that she had no other choice. Perhaps she could now begin to govern her own life without hoping for rescue from someone else.

As for myself, I could now rise as I was, unencumbered by clothing or shackles of any kind, and walk away from this ridiculous life of regulations and expectations. I could go to the forest and live in freedom, learning to serve my magic and my people.

I stood up to leave.

And my real life engulfed me like a wave washing over me. The dread, the sadness, and the frustration rose like walls around me, cutting me off from the peace and optimism that I'd briefly enjoyed. I struggled against it. Was the bleakness that now enveloped me the miasma of magic that Epiny had claimed to sense, or was the bright beckoning dream an illusion that could not withstand the light of day? For a moment, I teetered on a fence between the two realities, almost as if I could choose which world I would step into. Almost.

Habit made me stoop and pick up my worn trousers from the floor. I put my familiar life on with them. I grunted as I stepped into them, and cursed myself for being greedy when they proved hard to fasten. By the time I had dressed myself, brewed my morning tea, and decided to punish myself by going without breakfast, I heard the sounds of Ebrooks and Kesey arriving. They would soon be at my door, expecting to be invited in. I couldn't face them. They were too sharp a contrast with the world I'd briefly visited and too much an affirmation of the world I now felt trapped in. I seized my jacket from its hook and hurried out of the door. By the time they arrived, I had strapped a selection of tools onto Clove and was leading him toward the forest.

"Where you going?" Ebrooks called after me. I could hear the disappointment in his voice. A hot cup of tea or coffee together before starting the day's work had just begun to be a habit among us.

"Forest!" I called back to them. "I'm going to start my fence today."

"Ya, sure you are!" Kesey mocked me. "We'll see you back before noon."

I made no reply. I half-suspected he was right. The forest exuded a dark mix of terror and discouragement today. I steeled myself to it, and led Clove into it.

We toiled up the wooded hillside through the young forest. Immediately the sensation of being watched by hostile eyes flooded me. I took a deep breath and tried to focus my mind on what I needed. I wanted a stout, straight tree to cut into lengths for a corner post and my first few fenceposts. I resolved that I'd set the uprights first, and then use smaller poles for the rails.

The deeper I went into the woods, the more futile my task seemed. It would take me ages to cut enough wood to fence even one side of the cemetery. The trees here were all softwood. My posts would rot through in no time at all. Why had I volunteered for such a senseless task? And none of the trees seemed suitable. This one was too skinny, that one too thick, this one forked, that one bent. In despair, I finally chose one at random, telling myself that once it was cut down and limbed, Clove would drag it out of the woods for me and I'd at least be away from the darkest part of the woods' magic.

I unpacked my ax from Clove and selected where I would begin my cut. I lifted my ax to begin my swing.

"What are you doing?"

The voice didn't startle me. I turned to look at the same Speck I'd seen the day before.

"I'm cutting this tree down. I'm going to build a *fence* around the cemetery, so that our dead can rest in peace."

"*Fence*." His tongue twisted the foreign word painfully.

"Pieces of trees all in a line. With limbs blocking the path. Other plants and bushes will grow along it." I searched the Speck language for words that would approximate what I was doing. I had no qualms at all about letting them know I was setting a boundary.

He frowned at me, slowly taking the meaning from my words. Then a great smile dawned on his face. "You will put trees for your dead? Trees will grow on the hill that was made bare." I heard him draw in a great breath before he exclaimed, "This is an excellent idea, Great One! It would take one such as you to see this resolution that could be made."

"I'm glad you approve," I said. I wondered if he could sense the sarcasm behind my words. I readied my ax again.

"But that is not the right kind of tree to take, Great One." His tone made it clear that he was very reluctant to point out my error.

I lowered my ax again. "What sort of tree do you think I should use, then?" I asked with cautious curiosity. I'd heard rumors that the Specks were very territorial of certain groves of trees. Perhaps the tree I'd chosen was precious to him. I was willing to take a different tree. I was going to have to cut a lot of trees before I had a fence. There was no sense in antagonizing the man any more than I must. Besides, that was Colonel Haren's order.

He turned his head at a slight angle and almost smiled. "You know! These trees will not bring the dead peace or hold them properly."

We were talking past one another again. I tried to find a clear question for him. "What trees should I use then?"

Again, he cocked his head at me. It was hard to read his expression. Perhaps it was only the colors that interrupted his face that made him look quizzical. "You know this. Only kaembra trees will enfold the dead."

"Guide me to the kaembra trees that I may take," I suggested to him.

"Guide you? Oh, Great One, I should not so presume. But I will accompany you."

He was as good as his word. I soon realized that in his presence, the power of the forest to sway my mood waned. I did not know if he distracted me from it, or if his presence neutralized the evil magic of the place. In either case, it was a great relief to me. Despite his words, he did take the lead. I followed him, with Clove lumbering along behind me, his heavy tread nearly silent in the deep turf of the forest. "Why do you call me Great One?" I asked when the silence had stretched too long.

He looked back at me over his shoulder. "You are filled

with the magic. Today you shine with it. You are a Great One, and so I address you."

I glanced down at the swell of my belly and experimented with the notion that I was not fat, but instead was filled with a power I did not completely understand. What if my size were not a weakness, not an indicator of lack of self-control or sloth, but a sign of strength? This Speck, at least, seemed to regard me with respect and treat me with deference. I shook my head. His reverence for me only made me uncomfortable, for I felt I deceived him. We walked on, going ever uphill. Clove's big hooves scored the forest floor; even if my guide abandoned me, I'd easily track my way back. Birds sang and darted overhead. A short distance away, a rabbit thumped an abrupt warning and then fled. My perception of the forest shifted; it was a pleasantly mild spring day. The young forest around me was leafy and sunlit and smelled wonderful. A sense of well-being smoothed away all my anxiety. I relaxed my shoulders even though I resolved to maintain my wariness. I became aware of the silence and said awkwardly, "My name is Nevare."

"I am called Kilikurra. Olikea is my daughter."

"She was with you yesterday."

"I was with her yesterday," he confirmed.

I glanced around at the surrounding forest. "And is she near today?"

"Perhaps," he said uncomfortably. "It is not for me to say where she is."

Ahead of us, the forest grew thicker and darker. We passed through an intermediate zone of mixed trees, some youngsters and others fire-scorched giants, before the morning sunlight gave way to the eternal dusk of old forest. Single shafts of sunshine intermittently penetrated the canopy. Insects and motes of dust danced in those beams, and where the light struck the forest floor, flowering plants or patches of brush grew. One bush was already bejeweled with hanging drupes of scarlet fruit. I recognized it as the same luscious fruit that had been in the basket the night before. The fast I had maintained since dawn suddenly seemed a hollow and foolish thing to do. Denying myself food would not change the shape of my body. All it did was torment me with hunger, and make me both irritable and sad. "Shall we stop and eat the berries?" I asked my guide.

He looked back at me with a smile. For the first time, I realized that one reason his face looked so strange was that his lips were as black as a cat's. "As you will, Great One," he said, but he spoke as if I'd honored him with a royal invitation.

The drupes hung heavy on the twigs. Perhaps it was the open air or the freshness of the fruit or simply the enhancement of greater hunger, but the flavor exceeded anything I'd ever tasted. The bush was not large, but it was laden with berries. They were a glowing scarlet in the sunlight, with thin skins, almost liquid flesh, and a single pip in each. We shared what was there, unhurrying, savoring the simple pleasure of absolutely ripe fruit. When the last berry was gone, I sighed. "I do not know why I find these so delicious and satisfying," I said. It was true. Two handfuls of the berries had been my sole meal that day, and yet my hunger was sated.

"They are a powerful food, Great One, and the rightful food of the mage. You feed your magic as well as your body when you eat them. Everything that comes from the forest is your rightful food, and all of it will nourish what you are. But some foods are especially yours and fuel for your growth. I am honored that you have allowed me to partake of these alongside you. Already I feel my awareness unfold. I hear the kaembra trees whispering even though we have not yet reached them."

"Food for a mage," I said. I wondered if I had eaten something that would give me hallucinations. I recalled my experience with Dewara and the gore frogs. Yet . . . had that been a hallucination brought on by poison, or a true journey? If it had not been a true journey, would I be here now? Again, I walked a thin line between realities. A disturbing thought came to me. I could not straddle this boundary forever. Soon I would have to choose one of these worlds and walk in it for the rest of my days.

If Kilikurra sensed my distraction, he did not show it. "Certainly, a mage food. Some, such as the reddrops, an ordinary man like me can enjoy when invited. Others, as you know, are food for mages alone. Certain mushrooms may be harvested only if they are to be taken to a Great One."

I had to smile at how carefully he spoke to me. "You are telling me many things that I have not known. Earlier you said that I must know these things. Now I think you realize that I do not, and therefore you instruct me."

His hands fluttered in a subservient gesture, one that shooed my words away, but respectfully. "Great One, I would never presume to think I knew anything that you did not. I am a talkative, foolish fellow. Anyone will tell you that I am known for saying that which needs no saying, and for repeating what all folk already know. It is a tiresome trait, I know. I beg that you will tolerate it in me."

The forms of another courtesy, unknown and yet known to me, niggled at my mind. The proper sort of response came to me. "I shall enjoy your conversation, I am sure. These many things are known to me, but it is helpful of you to recall them for me."

As I said it, I felt it was truer than I had intended it to be. That other self, taught by Tree Woman, rippled through my awareness, like a fish seen silver in the murky depths of a river. His knowledge was in me, and the longer I walked in this world, the clearer it would come to me. We reached the shoulder of the hill, went into a brief steep fold of valley, and then climbed again. "I do not wish to go much farther," I warned him. "I would rather find suitable trees at a lower level, so that I do not have to haul them so far."

He looked at me oddly. "But what you wish differs from what is, Great One. The trees you must use do not grow lower down. So you are jesting with me?"

I could not think of a reply. So I said only, "When we get to these trees, then I shall decide."

Whether it was the berries or Kilikurra's presence or simply that I was becoming accustomed to the forest, I began to enjoy my journey. I was not nearly as weary as I should have been. The light under the trees was gentle and restful to my eyes. No wind stirred there. The deep moss muted not just Clove's hoof-thuds but also seemed to absorb our voices and to cushion my footfalls gently. I was looking directly at a tall stump when Olikea stepped out from its shelter. She had not been behind it, but merged against it. She was naked except for several strands of red-and-black beads around her waist and a tight necklace of blue beads around her throat. She was so comfortable with her nudity that I felt no embarrassment for her. Rabbits and birds were naked in the same way she was. Kilikurra's nudity had not even registered with my mind as something important to notice. I was considering that as she came towards us. She smiled when she spoke. "You are looking much better today, Great Man. The food I brought replenished you."

"Thank you," I replied awkwardly. I was not accustomed to compliments from women. She approached me until she was standing less than an arm's length away. She was almost my height. When she lifted her chin to look me in the eyes, it was almost as if she were inviting me to kiss her. I noticed now that she had dressed her hair. She had bound it back from her eyes with a bark-cloth strip. Wooden beads secured several tiny thin braids that hung down just in front of her ears. She smelled wonderful. When she licked her lips, I noticed that her tongue was both dark and pink, as mottled as the rest of her. She smiled wider, and I knew she was enjoying my awareness of her, and my physical reaction to that awareness.

"I hope you enjoyed all of it."

"I beg your pardon?"

She shook her braids back from her face. "The basket of food I left for you. I hoped you would be in your shelter, but you were not, so I left it for you to find. I hope that you ate it all with great pleasure."

"That I did."

"Good." She lifted her arms and stretched like a cat. Her eyes never left my face.

My mouth went dry. I cleared my throat and then said, "Your father, Kilikurra, is helping me to find trees I can use to build a *fence* around the cemetery, so that our dead may rest in peace."

"Is he?" She glanced around, and when her gaze came

back to my face, her smile was secretive. "But he seems to be gone now. And you know there are no trees here that can be cut. So. Shall we occupy our time another way?"

While my attention had been focused on her, Kilikurra had vanished. I now wondered if everything he had said and done had been a ploy to lure me to his daughter. But why would any father conduct a stranger to his waiting daughter and then abandon her to him?

I tried to awaken a sense of wariness in myself, but all I could recall was how brazenly she had touched me on our first meeting. She reached a hand toward me now and fingered the fabric of my shirt. "These garments look uncomfortable. And ridiculous."

I stepped back from her. "They protect me . . . my skin. From scratches, and cold, and insect bites. Among my people, they are required. For courtesy."

She puffed her cheeks briefly, the Speck gesture for denial. "I am your people. I do not require them. How do these work?" She had stepped up as she spoke and seized the front of my shirt. The first button went flying. Her eyes followed its flight and she laughed delightedly. "They jump like frogs!" she exclaimed. Before I could react, a sharp tug had sent a second and third to join the first.

With every fiber of my being, I longed to tumble her immediately on the mossy forest floor. What held me back was not morality or modesty, or even a reluctance to couple with a Speck. Rather, it was simple shame at showing my body to her. This was different from seeking out a whore. A prostitute took money and had small right to quibble about her customer's appearance. The last thing I wanted to do was to have this young creature see me naked, and react with either horror or laughter.

And so I stepped back from her, catching at the flapping front of my shirt. "Stop!" I bade her. "This is unseemly. I scarcely know you." My embarrassment put a starch in my words that I did not intend.

I needn't have worried about offending her. She laughed merrily at my reluctance and advanced on me, unabashed. "You will scarcely come to know me by fleeing from me!

Why do you hesitate? Is the mossy floor of the forest not soft enough for you?" She cocked her head as she looked into my eyes. Her hands were on my chest again. "Or do you find me undesirable?"

"Oh, never that," I assured her, but one questing hand had already assured herself of just how desirable I did find her. I could scarcely get my breath. "But your father . . . will he not . . . object?"

She puffed her cheeks at me. "My father has gone about his business. Why should he care what I do? Am I not grown, and a woman? He will be pleased if his daughter should have a Great One at her hearth; all my wide family will take a share of this honor." My belt buckle gave way to her fingers. The buttons on my trousers were more stoutly sewn than my shirt buttons. One by tantalizing one she undid them. I scarcely heard what she said anymore. "But mind you that my sisters and cousins take no more from you than the honor of your presence. In all else, you will be mine. Oh. Yes. You are ready. Here. Give me your hand. Touch me."

I did. Her nipples were erect. She deliberately brushed them against me. I wanted to howl in frustration. My great bulging belly was a barrier between us. I pulled her close against me, but found the longed-for contact denied. Shame coursed through me, strong enough that I tried to pull away from her. She let me go, but then caught my hand and pulled me down on the moss beside her. "Sit," she bade me. "Let me free you from all this."

"Olikea, I am too fat. I don't know how—"

She hushed my mouth with her fingers. "Sshhh. I do." She stripped my clothing away from me. Shirt, boots, socks, trousers were all flung aside. Then, to my dismay, she leaned back and looked at me. I expected her to recoil, but to my amazement, she gazed on me greedily, as if she were a child contemplating a feast. She licked her dark lips with her dappled tongue. Then she put her hands on my shoulders and pushed me back to recline in the moss. "This is what you must do," she whispered. "Lie on your back. And resist me as long as you can."

"Resist you?" I was puzzled.

"Stay hard," she clarified.

In that long afternoon and early evening, I learned about women and sensuality. She was not to be rushed in her enjoyment. She spoke plainly of exactly what she desired of me, with blunt words and a frankness that went beyond anything I'd ever heard men say about sex. She found multiple ways to fit our bodies together and used me shamelessly for her own pleasure. It felt strange to be explored and exploited. At one point, as she was posting along on top of me while I stared at the blue sky through the branches overhead, it occurred to me to wonder if this was how women sometimes felt when men mounted them and took what they wished, as they wished it.

She was noisy in her enjoyment of me, and once even Clove came wandering over to see what the fuss was about. She pushed his muzzle away, laughing where another woman might have been horrified at his animal curiosity.

I lost all sense of time. The third time that we dozed off together, I awoke to find it so dark that I could not see my hand in front of my face. Overhead, only a few stars managed to show themselves in patches of sky. I was shivering. "Olikea," I whispered, and she drew a great sighing breath and moved against me. "Are you cold?" After all she had done for me, I suddenly wanted to shelter her from every discomfort.

"It's night. It's supposed to be cold," she told me. "Accept it. Or, if it pleases you, use your magic to change it." She plastered her body against mine once more. Where we touched, I was warm. She seemed to go back to sleep.

I thought about it. "I want to be warmer," I told the night. But it was my own body that answered me. I felt my skin slowly flush with warmth. Olikea murmured with satisfaction. We slept.

CHAPTER TWENTY-TWO

FENCEPOSTS

I opened my eyes to birdsong. I was on my back. There was a pattern before my eyes. After a time, I resolved it into tree branches against a dark gray sky. The air was cool and crisp as I breathed it, and very clean. I lay perfectly still, wanting for nothing, in deep satisfaction and harmony with all that existed. The sky above me lightened, and the frequency of birdcalls increased.

I don't know how long I would have remained in that state of awareness without connection if Clove had not come up and curiously nuzzled my foot. I looked at him and then lifted a hand and scratched my face. I felt as if I had returned from a very long journey, and now all that had once been familiar was strange and new. I sat up slowly, and then reached around to brush a few twigs and leaves from my naked back. A glistening black beetle was crawling on my thigh. I brushed him off and yawned hugely.

I was alone. "Olikea?" I called softly, but there was no

response. I came back more to the world, and noticed my scattered clothing on the nearby moss. I yawned again and got up slowly. I had expected to be aching or stiff. I was fine.

"Olikea?" I called more loudly. A bird cawed a raucous response to me, and then I heard it take flight from the upper branches. I had no more than a glimpse of black-and-white feathers. Other than that, my call brought no response. Either she had left me and gone back to wherever Specks came from, or she was close by but choosing to remain in concealment. It was unnerving to be uncertain.

"Olikea!" I shouted her name, and then felt almost angry with myself for calling for her like that. She knew where I was. If she chose not to be there, then I would not demean myself by bellowing for her like an abandoned child.

I gathered up my dew-damp garb. In the dim forest morning light, my clothes looked drab and shabby. I felt reluctant to put them on, yet I was not accustomed to walking about naked. It was difficult to dress. Pulling on damp, chilly clothing made the day seem cold. I put on my old life with my discomfort. I suddenly shivered, and became aware that my constant hunger was not only present but raging. I rubbed my whiskery face and felt as if I had only just wakened.

I went to Clove and leaned on him, taking comfort in his warmth and solidity. My experience with Olikea seemed like an excursion into an imaginary world, one that made no sense to me as the stronger light of day dissolved its mists. I felt a hundred years apart from yesterday.

"Let's go home, Clove," I told the big horse. I was troubled by the idea of returning to the cabin after an absence and empty-handed, but not so troubled as to linger to look for fenceposts. The urgency of my hunger was strong enough to make me tremble. Olikea's vanishing seemed a shoddy trick. I couldn't understand her behavior, and then I wondered why I was bothering to try. She was a Speck. What had I expected from her? It was time to go back to where I belonged.

As I had anticipated, Clove's big hooves had scored the forest moss heavily. It was easy enough to go back the same way we had come. I led and he followed willingly. There was

little in the shaded forest for him to graze on. He was probably as hungry as I was. We wended our way down through
the forested hills we had climbed the day before.

It came to me that the forest no longer breathed either terror or weariness at me. I wonder if the magic had stopped,
or if I'd been granted full immunity to it. In either case, it
was something of a relief. I could finally see the forest as it
truly was. Its beauty was breathtaking. The shifting shade
of the overhead branches mitigated the bright sunlight. It
was the perfect light for the eyes of a hunter. I stopped to
catch my breath and let my aching calves rest. The long
climb up the hill had become steep.

As I looked around me, two things struck me: this area
looked very familiar, and I did not recall going down such a
slope as this yesterday. But Clove's tracks were clearly im-
printed in the forest soil. I glanced up at the sky, but the trees
overhead obscured most of it. I could not tell if I traveled east
or north. An icy shiver ran up my spine. I knew this place, yet
I was suddenly certain it was not yesterday that I had walked
this way, but last year, and then I had walked as my Speck
self and Tree Woman's acolyte. I knew that if I followed
Clove's trail up the steep incline to the top of this ridge, I
could then follow the ridge until I came to the path to the
Tree Woman's waterfall.

My mouth was dry. I wanted to go back. Yet I knew trying to avoid this was futile. The forest had brought me to
this place, and the magic would not be satisfied until I had
followed it. Behind me, Clove snorted, irritated with halting
on such a steep slope. I resumed my steady climb. Now I
could see, ahead of me, a large opening in the forest's canopy. I knew who and what awaited me there.

I cannot describe my feelings when I came to that inter-
section of my worlds. I had heard of battle shock. I think I
experienced something akin to that. My ears rang and I
could not get a full breath. My face and lips flushed, tingled,
and then went numb. My ears felt blocked and I was uncertain of my balance. Yet I tottered forward, my shaking hand
outstretched.

The cold hilt of the cavalla sword rasped against my hand.

Its blade was deeply sunken in the partially severed giant stump of the fallen tree. Impossible that such a blade could have cleanly swept through the huge tree, but that was how it appeared. A single slash of a saber had felled a tree, yet the cut was wildly disproportionate to the length of the blade. I could have parked a wagon on the cleanly cut portion of the stump. I had swung this saber, not at a tree, but at Tree Woman. And it had swept through her belly and then stuck in her spine. I'd seen her entrails spill and seen the slow gush of her sap-thick blood. She had toppled backward, just as this tree had fallen, not cleanly split in two, but with part of her torso still intact and the saber wedged deep in her.

I had never been here before. The last time I had physically touched this saber, I had been standing on my father's lands in Widevale. Months later, I'd found its empty scabbard where Dewara had disdainfully discarded it. Now I stood gripping the cold hilt and shaking with discord. I had called this weapon from the real world into Dewara's dream world, and it had come to anchor one end of a spirit bridge. I had seized it and used it to slay Tree Woman, and then abandoned it in the other world. And now, impossibly, it was here.

Which world did I stand in today? Did Gettys even exist in this place?

I looked around me again. There was no Tree Woman that I could see. The fallen tree was of the same kind as the one that had gripped the corpse, the same as the trees at the end of the King's Road, though not their equal in size. It was still a giant compared to any of the trees of the Plains or Old Thares. The long trunk had measured its length on the forest sward, brushing aside lesser trees as it fell and opening a huge gap in the forest canopy. In the year that had passed since I'd felled it in a dream, moss had crept up the sides of the fallen log. Mushrooms sheltered beside it. What had been a branch on the top side of the trunk was metamorphosing into a sapling growing upward from the fallen tree. And as I looked at it, I thought of another thing Tree Woman had said to me. "Such as I do not die as you do." She had fallen to my sword, but her tree lived on.

I tugged on the saber. It did not budge. I set my teeth and

jerked on it as hard as I could. It remained where it was, as if it had become a part of the tree. I released it and looked around the clearing that Tree Woman's fall had created.

Other great trees surrounded hers, but none were as large as hers had been. I still felt a sense of antiquity that surpassed anything I'd felt from the buildings of Old Thares. These trees had stood for generations and unless something disturbed them, they would continue to stand.

But would they?

As if summoned, I left the uneven stump of her tree and followed what had once been our path. After a short walk, it emerged from the twilight of the forest onto the rocky end of the ridge. I toiled a little higher, to a jut of stone that had been our lookout, and suddenly I felt I was standing at the edge of the world. Below me was a billowing sea of green treetops in the cup of a shallow valley. I recalled it as full and green from my dreamtime. But when I looked down, I saw the King's Road trickling to a halt in the forest below me. It cut through the foliage like a worm's trail in an apple bound directly through the stand of ancient trees below me. I could make out the road crews at work; they looked like busy insects eating their way into the forest. That straight avenue of empty space was a gash of light and bared soil that pointed directly toward me.

The roadbed would follow the easiest path up into the hills. From here I could see what was not apparent from the road. All the trees along the road's edge had been weakened by the slash opened beside them. The leaves of some were a sickly green; the road had cut through their root systems. Some of the trees at the edge of the road gash were starting to lean out into the open space. The next snow load would bring them down, in turn weakening those who stood behind them. Those trees would die. I was saddened by the thought but knew they were ordinary trees. More could be grown. But the three trees that had been cut at the end of the road were kaembra trees, the same sort of tree that Tree Woman had been. They were irreplaceable. The loss of three of them was a cause for mourning. For more to fall would be disaster. If the road continued, it would cut a wide swath through an ancient grove of them. I turned and followed the trail back to my tree.

"I see why you are making a stand," I said. I stood beside the fallen trunk of her tree. "I see why you thought you had to strike back at the very core of my people. We had attacked the core of yours. But eventually, the road will be forced through and the kaembra trees will fall. It cannot be changed."

"Do you think so, still?" she asked me. Her voice reached my ears plainly. I did not turn to look at her or her stump. I did not want to look on what I had done.

"They will not stop, Tree Woman. You can send magic waves of fear or weariness or sorrow at us. But the convicts who do the work are little better than slaves, and live constantly in fear, sorrow, and weariness. Your magic will slow the work, perhaps by years, but it will not stop it. Eventually the King's Road will flow up these hills and through the mountains. People, trade, and settlers will follow. And the kaembra trees will be no more than a memory."

"Memories are what we are right now. I have not been bone and flesh for many hundreds of seasons. But age does not make me less powerful, Soldier's Boy. Rather, I grew in strength as I grew in girth. The wind through my leaves carried my thoughts across the forest. Not even you with your cold iron could fell me. You have brought me down, but I rise again, and there will be another me, containing the past and sinking roots and lifting branches into the future. Do you understand now?"

"I understand less now than I did before. Let me go, Tree Woman. I am not of your people. Set me free."

"And how shall I do that, when the magic binds me more tightly than it does you?"

I could almost see her from the corner of my eye. She was a fat old woman with graying streaky hair, or perhaps a willowy girl, her pigment-speckled face as engaging as that of a fierce and friendly kitten. She smiled at me fondly. "Flatterer!"

"Let me go," I begged her again, desperately.

She spoke softly. "I do not hold you, Soldier's Boy. I never did. The magic binds us both, and it will have of us what it wills. In the days of my walking the world I served it, and I serve it still. You, too, must serve. From the moment it seized you from the Kidona coward and turned you to its own end, you have served it. I have heard the whispers of what it has done through you. With your hand, it stopped the turning of the Plains Spindle, did it not? They will never threaten us again. That was the magic working in you, Soldier's Boy. It has quenched a mighty people who once spilled over all the flatlands and thought to creep up into our mountains. Do you think it will do less against those who encroach from the far sea? No. It will use you, Soldier's Boy. Some task of yours, some word, some gesture, some act will destroy your folk."

"I did not do that," I said faintly. "I did not destroy the magic of the Plains people." I spoke the lie as if by saying such words I could undo it. Her truth had struck and sunk into me, cutting and sticking just as my iron blade had done to her. I had been there when the Spindle stopped turning. I'd felt that magic falter and fail. If I had not been there, if I had not chased the boy from the Spindle's tip, would he have gone to work his mischief at the base of it? If not for me, would that wedge of cold iron have fallen to where it stilled forever the Spindle's dance?

And if I had done that, and by doing it, had begun the final end of the Plains people, did it have to mean that I would also be the demise of my own folk? "I cannot do this. I cannot be this."

"Oh, Soldier's Boy." The wind or the caress of a ghostly hand moved through my hair. "So I said, too. The magic is not kind. It makes nothing of what we would or would not do. It takes us as we are, small and simple folk for the most part, and makes us Great Ones. Great Ones! So others name us, thinking we have power. But you and I, we know what it is to be a reservoir of power for the magic. We are tools. The power is not for us to use. Others may think so, and they may think that by befriending us or claiming us, they will gain influence over our power."

"Are you warning me about Olikea?"

She was silent. I almost wondered if I had embarrassed her. Was it possible that she felt jealous? I think she heard more than I intended. She gave a soft laugh that held echoes of regret. "Olikea is a child. There is little to her; you have already experienced all she has to offer you. But you and I—"

"I have no memories of you and me," I interrupted hastily.

"You do," she asserted calmly. "They are deep in you, as deep as the magic. As real as the magic."

Her voice had grown warmer. I bowed my head, and my throat suddenly tightened with a sorrow that did and did not belong to me. Tears pricked my eyes. I groped out and my hand touched the rough bark of her stump.

"Do not grieve, Soldier's Boy." Fingertips of moving air caressed my cheek. "Some loves go beyond bodies and times. We met in the magic and there we knew one another. I schooled you for the magic; it was what the magic demanded of me. But I loved you for myself. And in the place and time where ages and shapes have no meaning, and there is only the comfort of kindred spirits touching, our love remains."

"I'm so sorry I killed you," I cried out. I fell to my knees and put my arms about the standing stump of the great tree. I could not embrace it; it was far too large. Still, I pressed my chest and face against her bark, but could not find her there. There was another man within me, one who was me but who had lived a separate life from the young man who had attended the academy. I had battled that self and won, but he resided in me still. The tearing grief I felt was his. It was and was not my sorrow.

"But you didn't kill me. You didn't," she comforted me. "I go on. And when the days of your mortal flesh are done, you will go on with me. Then we shall have a time together, and it will be a far longer time than humans can count."

"That's a cold promise for now," I heard myself say. And it was my own voice and it was me. The tree I leaned on was just a stump with moss creeping up it. I pressed hard against the stump, trying to recapture Tree Woman's presence, but she was gone, and with her my awareness of my Speck self.

I stood up, and smeared the tears from my face. I left that

place. I was only a little surprised to find that a single set of hoof tracks led me uphill to it. We had not come this way before. Neither Clove nor I had ever been here in the flesh before.

I came eventually to where I had diverged from the correct trail home. I plodded along it, hungry, tired, and confused. Was I a dutiful soldier son, a loyal trooper in my king's cavalla, or was I a disowned son masquerading as a soldier in a threadbare frontier existence? Was I the forest mage's student who had both loved and slain her? Had I shamed myself deeply last night by having relations with a Speck, or had I simply had a wonderful, extravagant sexual experience? Without success, I tried not to wonder what my encounter with Tree Woman and my other self meant. I had felt the echoes of their emotions and could not doubt the sincerity of what they had felt. It was all the stranger in that I had been a dumb and blind participant in their romance.

When I saw daylight breaking through the forest roof ahead of me, I knew it traced the demarcation between the ancient forest and the younger trees on the burned hillside. My steps slowed. I would soon be leaving one world for another, and as I approached the boundary, I was not entirely sure that I wished to do so. If I left the forest, I would be making a large decision, with consequences I didn't fully grasp. What did the magic want me to do? I didn't know, and I also didn't know if I wanted to fall in with the magic's plan for me, or fight it with every ounce of my strength. Tree Woman had said that if the magic had its way, I would be the downfall of my entire race. That seemed impossible. But I had been there when the Dancing Spindle stopped turning. It seemed that with my aid, the Speck magic had hastened the end of the Plains magic and all its people. Could I possibly bring a similar destruction down on my own kind?

As I led Clove from the old forest to the new, my eyes fell on a neatly stacked pile of cut poles beside the trail. There were about twenty of them, no bigger around than my wrist, and only about eight feet long. They had rough gray-green bark still on them. I had no doubt that Kilikurra had cut them and left them there for me. I was surprised that he had felt comfortable cutting trees in the forest when the Specks seemed to so oppose our tree cutting for our road. My second emotion was disappointment. He had misunderstood me completely. I had intended to harvest some hefty logs for stout corner posts that I could set deep in the earth. By the time I dug holes for these posts, my fence would be only five feet tall, and so spindly that the wood would likely rot through in just a couple of years.

I half expected Kilikurra to step out of the dappling shadows and claim the credit for his good deed. When he did not, I decided that I could not be sure he wasn't there, and that my best course was to appear grateful. I put a hitch line on the bundled poles, and then bowed gratefully to the forest.

Clove didn't like the strange contraption scraping and jolting along behind him, but eventually we managed to get down to the cemetery. I left the poles there, having decided I could use them as stakes to set out the straight lines for my barricade. I was freeing Clove from his unwanted load when I heard the heavy thunder of running feet. I straightened and turned to find Ebrooks coming at me at a dead run. Kesey, panting heavily, was some distance behind him. I looked behind me, saw no cause for the alarm on their faces, and turned back to them, shouting, "What is it? What's wrong?"

"You're . . . alive!" Ebrooks gasped out the word. He reached me, seized me in a sweaty hug, and then leaned on me, panting. Kesey had given it up. He stood, bent over, his hands on his knees, his mostly bald pate bobbing as he tried to catch his breath. After a time for breathing, Ebrooks panted, "When you didn't come back by nightfall, we waited for you. But when night shut down and fear was flowing out of the forest thick as tar, we went back to town and told the colonel you were dead. God's breath, Nevare, how did you survive? Are you sane still? No one knows how you can stand to live this close to the forest. And now you've gone and spent a night in there. Are you crazy, man?"

"Clove and I got turned around in there. We had to wait for dawn to find the way home. That's all. It wasn't pleasant, but I'm not hurt at all." The lies were nearly effortless. "Why did you tell the colonel I was dead?"

Kesey had staggered up to us by then. "Well. That seems to happen a lot to fellows that have this job."

"And the colonel was really upset to get the news. He said, 'That's all I need, with this review coming up! Another dead cemetery sentry.' And he tried to tell us we'd have to take on guarding the graves. But we said, 'No, sir, thanky kindly.'"

"I didn't think you could just say, 'No, thank you' to an order."

Kesey and Ebrooks exchanged a look. Ebrooks spoke. "It's been a long time since the colonel issued a real order. I expect he's afraid of what he'd have to do if he did and no one obeyed it. Easier not to test his authority than find out it's gone."

Kesey shook his head sadly. "It's a shame, really. That man used to be able to blow fire when he wanted things done. But since we come here, well. He ain't the officer he used to be, that's all."

"And we ain't the regiment we used to be, either," Ebrooks pointed out sourly. "It's one and the same. We've lost so many men to desertion and suicide or just plain bad ends that the colonel worries all the time about his numbers. They keep sending us scads of prisoners to work the road. Well, pretty soon they're going to have more prisoners than their guards can manage, even with soldiers to back them up. And if the prisoners don't turn on us and burn the place down, then the Specks will get us. Gettys is a bad post. I wish they'd send their high mucky-mucks to inspect us and have done. They'll turn us out of Gettys, probably send us somewhere worse. Though it's hard to imagine anywhere worse than this."

"Well. I suppose I'd best get cleaned up and go let the colonel know that I'm not quite as dead as he'd heard."

"That would be good," Ebrooks agreed. I think he was happy that I'd offered to do it myself, rather than suggesting that he should have to correct his own mistake. They went back to their groundskeeping while I went to my cabin. I was ravenously hungry, and I emptied most of my small larder. By the time I'd washed, shaved, and changed my clothing, it was late afternoon. I saddled Clove and headed for town.

Several surprises awaited me there. The first was that a contingent of Specks had set up a scattered tent village on the outskirts of Gettys. I would later learn that they always came by night to pitch their tents for the trading season. When it was over, they vanished just as swiftly. Within the tents' shelter, both male and female Specks were strangely but decently clad in a mix of Gernian garments and Speck versions of Gernian garments. Those I saw outside the tents' shade were veiled in head-to-toe shrouds woven from bark cloth supplemented with fresh leaves and flowers. The garments looked like fishnets that had been dragged through a garden but protected their sensitive skins from sunlight.

Their trade goods were furs, carvings, smoked venison, bark, and leaves for brewing what the Gettys folk called "forest tea," as well as mushrooms, berries, and a prickly fruit I didn't recognize. I looked, but did not see any of the fruits or mushrooms that Olikea had brought to me. Either Olikea and her father were not among them or they were veiled and unrecognizable. I thought it intriguing that despite our fear of the Speck the trading was brisk, with local merchants competing with traders from the west to buy the best furs.

The Speck trade gave an oddly festive air to Gettys. It was the liveliest I had ever seen that mournful place. The Specks were acquiring fabric and felted hats, mostly for novelty, I suspected. Glass beads and brightly painted tin toys were almost as popular as sugar, candy, and sweet cakes. One wily Old Thares trader was exchanging casks of honey for the best furs

When I walked into the colonel's offices, his sergeant jumped as if he had seen a ghost. He didn't make me wait to speak to the colonel, but ushered me right in. When he left, I noticed that the door didn't shut firmly, and I suspected he listened outside it. The colonel was extremely pleased to find me still alive. He actually offered to shake my hand before giving me a rambling lecture on not straying too far from my post and letting my superiors know when I thought I might be gone overnight. He claimed that he had just been putting together names for a search party to send after me, though I saw no signs of such activity. He was singularly uninterested in what had befallen me in the forest. Instead he actually patted me on the shoulder and gave me a silver piece from his own pocket, telling me that he was sure I could use a drink after my "jittery night."

I thanked him for it as humbly as I could manage. Sometimes his eccentric kindness toward me grated on my pride. He dismissed me, but spoke again when my hand was on the doorknob. "And do something about that uniform, soldier. You know we have a contingent of nobility and officers coming to inspect us at the end of this month. Since we arrived here, I've never had a man in my command look less like a soldier than you do."

"Sir. I'm sorry, sir. I've asked several times for a better uniform. Supply always tells me that they have nothing in my size."

"Then you may tell them I said they should issue you something that you could have altered. You should at least be somewhat presentable, though it would probably be best if you avoided town while the inspection was in progress. I don't intend to have our inspection team visit the cemetery, but the good god alone knows what they'll take it into their own heads to do."

"Yes, sir," I replied grimly. I tried to keep my face expressionless. I knew that he only spoke the truth, but it did not make it any easier to accept. I touched the doorknob.

"Trooper. Regardless of what others may think of me, I know what goes on in my command. Your efforts with the cemetery have not gone unnoticed. I'll add that although you look the least like a soldier of all my troops, in your efforts to protect our honored dead, you've behaved more like a soldier than most men in my command do at present. Now go have that drink."

His words smoothed my rumpled feathers a bit and I left in a better state of mind. The silver piece was a generous bonus, and I decided I'd take his advice and have a beer before I left town.

Gettys was a lively place today. In addition to the Specks coming to town, several western traders had arrived with merchandise to sell to the soldiery and trade goods to barter with the Specks. The streets were busy, so when I encountered Spink and he frantically signed to me that I should meet him in the alley behind the blacksmith's shop, I was not much worried that we'd be noticed together. Nonetheless, even in that noisy area, I resolved to maintain appearances.

"Nevare! I heard you'd gone missing. Thank the good god that you're alive and unharmed!"

That was how Spink greeted me, but as he moved to embrace me, I reminded him of our varying statuses with a brusque, "Thank you for your concern, Lieutenant Spinrek. I assure you, it was not much of an adventure, but mostly my own foolishness that delayed me." I hoped the look on my face conveyed that there was far more to tell, but that it would have to wait. Behind us, the smithy's harsh clanging of metal on metal screened our words.

He drew back and stood still for a moment. I could tell from his eyes that he took no offense from my caution. Instead, he said carefully, "A lot of mail has arrived from the west. A washed-out bridge on the road had caused a great bottleneck of wagons and travelers. Perhaps there is some for you. My own lady wife has been very pleased to hear from her young cousin in the Midlands."

Now it was my turn to practice restraint. I wanted to demand to see the letter from my sister immediately. Instead, I kept my voice steady as I said, "I trust all is well with her family, sir?"

"Oh, excellent," he replied, but his eyes said differently. "She wrote that they were enjoying a long visit with houseguests from Old Thares. Her father seems to think that the young man would be an excellent match for her, and his uncle is prone to agree."

I racked my brain for whom he could be describing. No one came to mind. At last I said, "Well, for her sake, sir, I hope the lad is of a good family."

The pleasant expression on his face looked forced and sick. "Oh, they are not of the first quality, but they are still well placed. His father was in charge of the King's Cavalla Academy for a time."

That shocked me out of my pose. "Caulder Stiet? Impossible."

Spink's smile grew wider, but there was nothing of pleasure in it. "There Yaril agrees with you. It's a desperate letter, Nevare. She still thinks you are dead. She risked her reputation to slip away from the house and go alone to a little town to post her letter to us."

"What am I to do? What can I do?" I felt frantic with worry. The thought of Yaril being given over to that shallow, trembling boy filled me with loathing. I hated the idea of him being near my sister, let alone claiming her as his wife. I wondered if my father was mad, if this was his vengeance on Yaril, or if he genuinely thought it was a good match for her. Caulder wasn't even a soldier son anymore. If Yaril married him, her sons would be "gatherers of knowledge" like Caulder's geologist uncle.

"Write to her. Tell her you're alive. Give her a refuge, or at least the strength to defy your father and refuse Caulder."

"How can I get a letter to her?"

"Write to your father. Demand that he tell her. Write to your priest-brother. Write to her friends. There must be some way, Nevare."

Were the fates listening? I looked past Spink's shoulder. Carsina was crossing the street. "You see that girl. That's Carsina, Spink. My erstwhile fiancée and once Yaril's best friend. She's the best chance I have of slipping a letter to Yaril past my father. Excuse me."

"We need to arrange a meeting later," Spink hissed after me, but I didn't pause. I strode hastily down the street, on a deliberate course to intercept Carsina. She hadn't seen me yet; I had to reach her before she did. I cringed as I thought of my appearance. My uncut hair hung shaggy around my ears. My boots were starting to crack at the sides. My trousers showed wear at the knees and seat, and I had to buckle my belt under my belly these days. Above my belt, my gut bloomed out in a swell that my shirt strained to cover. I didn't blame Carsina for recoiling in horror from the thought that she had once been betrothed to me. But I didn't desire any acknowledgment from her, only a small and simple favor. All I needed was an envelope addressed in her hand to my sister.

My hat was shapeless and dusty. Nevertheless, I removed it as I approached her. I'd give no one any reason to think I was being less than courteous to her. "Excuse me, ma'am," I addressed her respectfully. I kept my eyes lowered. "I've a favor to ask you, not for myself, but for my sister, once your friend. Grant me this, and I promise I'll never ask anything else of you again. I won't so much as nod at—"

I got no further in my humiliating plea for her aid. A sudden blast of sound assaulted my ears. I clapped my hands over them and lifted my eyes. Carsina had raised a brass whistle to her lips and was blowing blast after blast on it as if her life depended on it. Her cheeks were distended with the effort, her eyes almost bulging. If her action had not been so irrational, it might have seemed humorous. I stood transfixed, staring at her.

But elsewhere on the street, others had sprung into motion. My first warning was when a small woman in a white apron brought a broom down firmly on my back. It stung and raised dust. "What?" I asked in consternation as I dodged away from the enraged shopkeeper's wife. But that only brought me into range of a young woman with a furled parasol. She whacked me solidly with it on the back of my head, shrieking, "Get away from her! Leave her alone! Help! Help! Assault! Assault!"

All the while, Carsina continued to shrill on her whistle and women continued to converge on me, also blowing whistles. I gave ground hastily. "I've done nothing wrong!" I shouted at them. "I said nothing ill to her! Please! Listen to me! Please!"

Men were gathering as well, some to laugh and point at the sight of the big fat man beleaguered by a flock of angry women. Others were striding more purposefully toward the scene of the confrontation, anger on their faces. One tall, thin man was being dragged angrily toward me by his fussing, scolding wife. "You get in there, Horlo, and you teach that rude fellow what happens to men who say foul things on the streets to good women!"

"I'm leaving!" I shouted, not wishing to be attacked by the ineffectual-looking Horlo or anyone else. "I'm going. I'm sorry the lady took offense. None was intended. I apologize!"

I'm not sure that anyone heard my words over the shrill whistles and shriller voices that surrounded me, calling me names and raining abuse on me. I lifted my hands over my head to show that I was not returning any of the blows from the brooms, parasols, fans, and dainty fists. I felt both a coward and a buffoon, but what could I do, assaulted by a mob of angry women? I had broken clear of the circle and thought I'd escaped when I heard an angry voice shout a damning accusation. "He's the one they say raped and murdered that poor whore! He's the big fat scoundrel who killed that Fala woman and hid her body!"

I turned back in horror. "That's not true! I've never hurt anyone!"

The mob of women surged toward me. A flung stone struck me in the face. A larger one rebounded off my shoulder. I didn't know the man striding fearlessly toward me through the hail of rocks, but he was well muscled, fit, and grinning the snarl of a man who loves a good fight. A wash of cold rose through me. I could die here, I suddenly knew. Stoned, beaten, kicked to death by a mob of folk who didn't even know me. I caught a sudden glimpse of Sergeant Hoster. He stood to one side of the crowd. His arms were crossed on his chest and he was smiling grimly.

Spink had always had more guts than common sense. Even when I'd been a lean and fit cadet, Spink had looked small beside me. He charged into the fray, shouting, "Desist! This moment! Halt! That's an order!" He reminded me of a barking, snarling terrier protecting a mastiff as he spun to face the oncoming tide of roused people. "Halt, I said!"

They didn't exactly halt, but they stopped advancing. The crowd roiled, and another stone came winging from someone in the back and bounced off my chest. It didn't really hurt, but the fury it symbolized was frightening. The women were all talking, and several were pointing at me. I no longer saw Carsina anywhere. The large man I had glimpsed pushed his way to the front of the mob.

"Halt!" Spink barked again.

"Sir, are you going to let a filthy lout like that get away with insulting a decent woman? The least he merits is a good beating, and if the rumors are true, he ought to be hanged."

Spink's shoulders were very square. He kept his eyes on the crowd as he spoke in a stern voice. "I'd like the woman he insulted to come forward, please. I'll take her complaint right now."

My mouth went dry. I knew he had no choice, but once Carsina accused me in public, she'd be far too proud to back down. The least I'd get was a flogging.

"She's . . . she's not here, sir!" The young woman who spoke had a quavery voice, as if she were about to burst into tears. "She was overcome, sir, with what he said to her. Two other ladies have helped her home. I imagine her brother or her fiancé would be glad to speak on her behalf." This last she uttered with savage satisfaction. She glowered at me as if I were a rabid dog.

"Direct them to me. Lieutenant Spinrek Kester. I'll take down the details of any complaint they wish to lodge. As for the other, until a body or a witness is found, it remains a foul rumor and no more than that."

The man's brow furrowed and his face flushed an evil dark red. "So what are you going to do, sir? Just let him roam around loose until we find a body with him standing over it?"

Sergeant Hoster suddenly decided to act. He strode over to Spink, saluted him, and then said, "I'll be happy to escort him to the cells, sir."

Spink held his ground. I felt a fool standing silent behind him, as if I were a huge child cowering behind his diminutive mother's skirts. "I appreciate your offer of help, Sergeant Hoster. But we don't lock men up on the basis of rumor. If we did, likely not one of us would be walking free."

Hoster dared to question his decision. "Perhaps this is a time when we should choose to err on the side of safety, sir."

Spink reddened at the man's insubordination. But he kept his calm. "Do you have any hard evidence, Sergeant? A witness?"

"No, sir."

"Then there is no reason to hold this man prisoner." Spink turned suddenly on me, and the anger on his face was convincing. "You, soldier. Take yourself out of town. Innocent or guilty, tempers are hot over this, and I judge it best that you isolate yourself until these rumors are resolved. I'll speak to the mess hall, and have some supplies sent out to you. And I warn you, behave in an exemplary manner. I'll take it on myself to check up on you from time to time. You'd best be where I expect you to be. Now go. Now!"

I looked from Spink to the mob. It would only take one wrong word to ignite them. But I couldn't just slink away like a kicked cur. I came to attention and looked only at Spink. I spoke, trooper to lieutenant, but I made sure that my voice carried to the crowd. "Sir. I did not speak rudely or suggestively to the lady. And as to Fala's fate, I do not know what became of her. I am innocent of both these things."

An ugly muttering rose from the gathered folk. I feared I had pushed them too far, as did Spink from the expression on his face. He spoke sternly for their benefit. "I hope in the good god's name that you are speaking the truth, trooper, for I will be looking into this personally. And if you have lied to me, you will find the punishment I extract for a lie will be the equal of the other two offenses. Now go!"

I obeyed him, my cheeks burning and resentment simmering in my heart. I felt that all of Gettys stared at me as I walked to where I'd left Clove tethered. It took all my self-control not to look back over my shoulder to see if I would be followed. As I mounted up and rode out of town, I wondered if I'd chosen the wrong world.

CHAPTER TWENTY-THREE

TWO WOMEN

What are you doing here?"

It was not the kindest greeting I could have given her, nor the one I would have preferred if I'd had the luxury of thinking what I'd say to her. But the shock of seeing Amzil sitting at the table inside my cabin when I opened the door jolted the words out of me.

She took it better than I had a right to expect. "Mending your shirt," she pointed out, holding up the offending item. "Half the buttons are off this. These ones won't match, but at least you'll be able to button it. I took them off that old shirt there. It looks little better than a rag, so I thought you wouldn't mind."

Her literal answer to my question left me gaping. She seemed to find that amusing, for a smile twisted her mouth.

She looked gaunt and weary and more threadbare than the last time I'd seen her. Yet her hair was tidied and put up in a roll on the back of her head, and she wore a dress with a skirt made from the fabric I'd sent her, almost as if she were trying to put her best foot forward for me. I came cautiously into my own cabin, feeling oddly displaced by seeing her sitting at my table. All my clothing had been sorted into heaps around her. Her smile grew more anxious in my silence. "I've made myself a cup of tea. I hope you don't mind."

"Of course not. You're welcome. You're very welcome. Where are the children?"

"I left them in town. Another woman at the boarding-house said she'd watch them for me if I did her washing for her when I came back. It looks as if you've done well for yourself, Nevare."

"Yes. That is . . . yes. I was able to enlist, and the colonel gave me this post. I guard the cemetery. Dig the graves and whatnot. But what brings you to Gettys?"

She set the shirt she had finished mending on the table, and tucked the needle neatly into the thread on the spool. "Well. I had to leave my old house. Things got very ugly there this winter. I know you meant well when you left us plenty of meat. And I don't know how you weeded the vege-table patch like that; I had no idea there were that many plants there. But the problem was what it always is. The more you have, the more ruthless people will be in trying to take it from you. At first my neighbors come to my door begging. And I said no. Not to be cruel, but because I knew that what you left, while it seemed a lot at the time, was probably just enough to keep us all fed through the winter." She picked up the shirt she had mended, turned it over in her hands several times, and set it down again. She shook her head to herself, and the sunlight from the window moved on her dark hair, making it gleam. She tried to smile, but it came out more as a grimace.

"Then they came trying to trade, but I said no again, for the same reason. How could they blame me? I have the three little ones; my first duty is to keep them alive. And my old neighbors would have said the same to me had the shoe been on the other foot! Well, after that, they started stealing from me. I tried to defend what I had, but there was only one of me. They were getting to my snares before I ever did; resetting them was a waste of time, because I was just doing that work for them. But I thought, well, I've got the deer meat, and I'd brought in all the garden vegetables to the shed.

"I put as much as I could inside the cabin with us, but then I scarcely dared leave the place, for fear they'd come in and take it while I was gone. They stole every bit of the meat that I had to leave hanging in the shed, and dug all through the vegetable patch, looking for any small potatoes I'd missed, for anything at all. I scarcely dared go to sleep at night. It was like living in the middle of a pack of wolves."

Her voice had dropped down to a murmur. She fell silent, staring at the worn cuff of my shirt. When the silence stretched, I got up and put the kettle back on the fire. "Hitch said you wouldn't even let him inside the door. Did you get the things I sent in the carry sack?"

She looked startled. "Oh. The book. And the sweets. Yes. Yes, we got the gifts, the children loved them. I—thank you. I didn't say thank you, did I?" She suddenly smoothed the folds of her skirt and looked down, speaking awkwardly. "At the time, I was shocked. Just shocked. I'd hoped that you would come back, to return the sack if nothing else, but I didn't expect you just to send it with someone, full of gifts, for no reason." She suddenly pinched her lips together and her blue eyes flooded with tears. She took a little breath. "I can't remember the last time a man gave me a gift when he didn't expect something back for it." She lifted her face, and her eyes suddenly met mine. For a moment her vulnerability shone through her tough expression, and with it, her youthfulness. I suddenly wanted to fold her in my arms and protect her, for she seemed as small and defenseless as my little sister. But the instant passed, and she abruptly looked as stony as she ever had. I was glad I hadn't acted on my impulse; she probably would have scratched my eyes out. I sought for something to say.

"Well, you've saved me the trouble of mending my shirt. For that, I'm grateful."

She made a dismissive gesture at the garments on the table. "Your trousers need to be let out again. And what you are wearing now looks no better. You look more like a scarecrow than a soldier."

She said the words carelessly and probably didn't intend that they stung, but they did. "I know," I said tersely. "The men in charge of uniforms have not been very forthcoming. They simply say they've nothing that will fit me, and give up. Today the colonel said that I might say it was his order they be more helpful. But—" My words halted of themselves. I didn't want to tell her what had happened or why. "I didn't have time to stop there," I finished lamely.

An awkward silence fell between us. The kettle was boiling. I took it off the hob and added more hot water to the teapot and another pinch of leaves. Amzil was looking everywhere but at me. Her eyes roamed around the room and then she suddenly said, "I could come and live here and do for you. Me and my children, I mean. And I could keep your washing done and sew you up a decent uniform, if you got the cloth. I can cook and mind that little garden you've got going."

I was looking at her incredulously. I think she thought I wanted more from her, because she added, "And we can keep care of your horse, too. And all I'll be asking of you is a roof over our heads and what food you're willing to spare us. And, and, that would be all. Just those things."

My mind filled in what she hadn't named. She wasn't offering to share my bed. I had the feeling that if I pushed for that right now, she'd add it to the list, but I didn't want to have her. Not that way. I chewed on my lip, trying to think of what to say. How could I tell her that I wasn't sure I'd be staying in this world? With every step of my ride home, the forest had looked better to me.

Her eyes had been scanning my face anxiously. Now she looked away and spoke more gruffly. "I know what's going on, Nevare. What they're saying about you in town. In a way, that's why I came here." She folded up the shirt and set it very firmly on the table. Then she spoke to it. "My children aren't at a boardinghouse. They're at a . . . one of Sarla Moggam's girls is watching them for me. She can't work right now because, well, because she can't. But no one knows I came here. See this?"

She reached down the front of her dress. While I regarded her, dumbstruck, she fished up a brass whistle on a chain. "The girls at the house, they give this to me when I first got there yesterday. They told me some officer's wife in town, she started this thing where all the women wear them, and if they feel they're in danger, all they have to do is blow the whistle, and every woman what's wearing a whistle has to promise that no matter what, if she hears a whistle blow, she'll run toward the sound and help whoever is in danger. That's the deal. And when I said, 'Well, what kind of danger?' they told me about not just whores but decent women getting beaten up and raped, and that a girl from Sarla's own house had just vanished and everyone thought she was murdered and even though most people knew who did it, no one was stepping forward to protect the whores, so they'd decided they'd join the whistlers and protect each other. And when I asked who killed the girl, one of them said a big fat sonofabitch named Never that guarded the cemetery."

She stopped and took a deep breath. The words had spilled out of her like pus squirting out of an infected boil, and I felt much the same way about what she had told me. I wanted to cry. It wasn't a manly reaction, but it was my overwhelming response to what she'd said. Even after what had happened to me in town today, it was still shocking to hear that people were talking of me as a rapist and murderer, naming me as the man who had killed Fala. I wondered why they were so sure she was dead and why they blamed me. I had no way to clear myself of their suspicions. Unless Fala showed up somewhere, alive and well, I could not prove she hadn't been murdered and that I hadn't done it. I muttered as much to Amzil.

"Then you didn't do it." She spoke it as a statement but I heard it as a question.

I replied bluntly. "Good god, no. No! I had no reason to, and every reason not to. Why would a man kill the only whore in town who would service him willingly?" Anger and fear made my heart race. I got up and left the table and went to the door to stare out across the graveyard toward the forest.

"They said—" I heard her swallow, and then she went on, "They said that maybe she wasn't willing, that you kept her in the room a lot longer than any man ever had before. And that maybe you caught her alone, and maybe she said no, not for any money, and that maybe then you raped her anyway and killed her in anger."

I sighed. My throat was tight. I spoke softly. "I don't know what became of Fala, Amzil. I hope that she somehow got away from Gettys and is having a nice life somewhere. I didn't kill her. I never saw her again after that one night. And I didn't force her to keep to her room with me. As far-fetched as it sounds, she wanted to be there." Even as I said the words, I realized how unlikely they would sound to any-one else in the world.

"I didn't think you had, Nevare. I thought of all the nights we were alone in my house. If you were the kind of man who would force a woman, or kill her if she refused, well—" She paused, then pointed out, "If I'd believed what they said, would I have come all this way out here, alone, not tell-ing anyone where I was going and leaving my kids with strangers who'd toss them out on the streets if I never came back? I didn't believe it of you."

"Thank you," I replied gravely. I felt truly grateful. I thought about that. I was grateful because a woman didn't think I was a murderer. When I'd been tall and handsome and golden, everyone had thought well of me. Carsina had told me how brave I'd looked. Encase the same man in this slab of flesh and these worn clothes and women saw a rapist and murderer. I lifted my hands to my face and rubbed my temples.

"So. Nevare. What do you think?"

I dropped my hands and stared at her. "What?"

"I know it's not much time to think about it, but I have to have an answer. Last night they let me stay for free. They say that my little ones' can sleep in one of the empty rooms at night while I'm working. But that won't change that they'll be growing up as the children of a whore. And I know what will happen to my girls if they do. Don't know what would become of Sem. Truth to tell, I don't even want to wonder what happens to a boy growing up in a whorehouse. I got to get them out of there today, or I got to go to work there tonight. And I know that you know in the past, I've done whatever I had to do to get by, but Nevare, I never thought of myself as a whore. Just as a mother doing what she had to do, once in a while, to get stuff for her children. But if I start working there, night after night, well, I will be a whore. And no denying it."

"Why did you leave your cabin finally? What drove you out?"

She met my gaze squarely. "You remember that fellow up the hill? He tried to break in. I had my gun and I warned him, four, five times I shouted at him to get away from the door or I'd shoot. He shouted back that he'd never seen me fire that thing and he didn't think I knew how or that I had any bullets. And the way he was yelling, I knew that he wasn't just going to break in and take what he wanted. He was going to get rid of us, to be sure he could have all we had. So I shooed my kids behind me, and when he finally got the door chopped in, well, I fired. And I killed him. And then I packed up my children and what we could carry and we ran away from there." By the time she finished speaking, she was hunched over in her chair as if she expected me to strike her, wringing her hands together. She looked up at me from her cower. "So now you know," she said very softly. "I am what they accuse you of being. I murdered him. I'm telling you the truth, because I want you to know the truth before you decide if you'll help me or not."

I sat down heavily in my chair. "You can't stay here, Amzil. It . . . it wouldn't be safe for you or for the children. I'm not even sure if I can stay here anymore."

She was silent for a time. Then she said furiously, "It's because I killed him, isn't it? You think someone from Dead Town is going to come here and accuse me, and I'll hang and you'll be stuck with my children."

The way she said it told me far more than she'd planned.

She'd intended me to be her hedge against that possible disaster. She'd intended to bring her children to me in the desperate hope that if she was found out and executed, I'd protect them. I tried to speak in a calming voice. "I'm flattered. No, I'm honored that you would think of bringing your children here. And it means a great deal to me that you would hear such stories about me and disbelieve them. There are not many in town or in the fort that would be willing to stand by me as you would. But I'm serious when I say that it wouldn't be safe here for you. Feelings are running high. Today, when I was ordered to leave town, I worried that I would be followed. I have no confidence that I won't be attacked tonight or burned out of this house. That was the kind of hatred I saw today. I can't take you in, Amzil. I wish that I could."

"Of course you do," she said with hard skepticism, and stood to leave.

I blocked her exit. Sparks of anger came into her eyes, but I didn't move. I took the colonel's piece of silver from my pocket. "You take this," I began.

"You don't owe me anything," she hissed.

"I owe you what you offered me. The belief that I know you well enough to say that you didn't murder that man. You did what you had to do in defense of your children. Now you take this coin, for the little ones. It will at least feed them tonight. Get them out of Sarla Moggam's brothel. It's a foul place. Take them to—" For a moment I hesitated, then I plunged on, "Take them to Lieutenant Kester's house. Ask around. Someone will know where he lives. Lieutenant Spinrek Kester. Tell him the same thing you told me. That if he'll give you and the children a place to sleep, you'll help cook and clean and so on. Tell his lady that you used to be a seamstress, and you want to make an honest living for yourself. She'll help you. She's like that."

She looked at the money that I'd pushed into her hand. Then she looked up at me, confused. "Do I tell them that you sent me? Do I . . . do you want me to come back here sometimes? At night?"

"No," I said quickly, before I could be tempted by her offer. "No. You didn't offer me that, and I'm not asking for that.

And don't tell them I sent you. Tell them . . . No. Tell *him* that you wish your whistle were shaped like an otter, that you've heard that whistles shaped like otters are lucky enough to save a man's life. But you only say that to him if no one else is around. Do you understand me? It's important."

Bewilderment flickered over her face. "So, you want me to make him think I'm daft, so he'll give us shelter out of pity?"

"No. No, Amzil. It's just something he and I both know, something that will make him know it's important to help you as he was once helped."

"A whistle shaped like a beaver," she said carefully.

"No. An otter. A whistle shaped like an otter."

She closed her fist tight on the coin. Then she said suddenly, "Give me your trousers, at least."

"What?" It was my turn to be bewildered.

"Your dirty trousers there. Give them to me. I'll wash them, and I'll let them out and bring them back to you."

I was tempted. But, "No. Anyone who saw them would know to whom they belonged. Amzil, until I can clear my name, you must not be associated with me. Now. Thank you. Go and do as I said."

She looked down at the floor. "Nevare, I—" She stepped suddenly forward, and I thought she would hug me. At the last minute she extended her hand and patted me timidly on the arm, as if I were a dog with an uncertain temperament. "Thank you," she said again.

I moved away from the door, and she fled. I watched her go, a small woman hurrying down the dirt road, away from the cemetery and toward the town. I yielded to an impulse, bowed my head, and asked the good god to look after her.

I hadn't had an opportunity to buy food. Despite everything else that had happened, I was ravenous again. I drank my tea, trying to swallow my hunger with it. Then I methodically secured my house. I closed and latched the shutters of my window. I took my disreputable weapon down from its hooks on the wall and prepared five loads for it. Then, scowling, I prepared an additional five. I hoped against hope that I'd never have to use them. Perhaps, I thought sourly, I'd be lucky, and if a mob came to drag me from my house, this ancient derelict of a gun would blow up and kill me quickly.

Ebrooks and Kesey came to my door before they went back to Gettys for the night. They were sweaty and tired and looking for a few moments of talk and a cool drink before they began the walk back to town. I let them in, and watched them dip up water from my cask. The room was small, and while they were in it, they filled it with their noise. They talked about how much grass they'd cut and what they had to do tomorrow as if it all were of tremendous importance. It was trivial and meaningless to me. Dead soldiers and their wives and children were all rotting back into soil, and the soil grew the grass, and these two men would cut it to make the cemetery look tidy, and then more grass would grow and they would cut that, and more folk would die and we would bury them. I thought of the body that had been stolen and how outraged I'd been, and all the effort I'd put into recovering it. What if I'd left him there, a soldier whose name I didn't now recall, and the tree roots had penetrated his body and the beetles and ants had carried off his flesh? How was that any different from burying him in a hole and marking the spot by writing his name on a plank of wood? I thought about what I'd claimed as my life, that I would call myself a soldier and guard the place where bodies were buried. And I would do this because I was the second son my mother bore, and therefore I must wear the king's uniform on my back and, at least ostensibly, serve him.

It was all so meaningless when I looked at it that way. It was meaningless in the same way as when I stood up from a game and then looked down on the scatter of playing pieces, and realized that they all were just bits of polished stone on a wooden board marked with squares. All the meaning they'd had moments before when I'd been trying to win a game were meanings that I'd imbued them with. Of themselves, neither they nor the board had any significance.

I could not decide if I were just a playing piece, or if I'd finally stepped far enough away from the game someone else had made of my life to discover that I no longer wished to be a playing piece. I shook my head as if I could rattle my own brain, trying to find my way back to my own world where all these things were accepted and important and mattered.

"Something wrong, Nevare?" Ebrooks asked me abruptly. I realized that both he and Kesey were looking at me oddly. I'd been staring sightlessly out the window. Now I looked at them. Their faces were damp with sweat and smudged with dirt, but their eyes seemed genuinely concerned.

"You know what they're saying about me in town?" I asked them.

Ebrooks looked away and said nothing. Kesey looked stricken. It was enough.

"Why didn't you say something to me?" I demanded.

"Aw, Nevare," Kesey exclaimed, "We know that ain't true. You ain't got that kind of mean in you."

"I hope not," I said. "I just don't understand how a rumor like that could get started, or why so many people would be willing to believe it."

"Well, it's how you are, you know," Kesey said ponderously. "Living out here, all alone, near the forest. And being, you know, big like you are. And no one knowing much about you. It just, well, maybe it makes it easier for them to make up something about you. You ought to come to town more often, drink with the boys, let 'em see you aren't so strange."

"Good advice too late," I grumbled. "Not that I ever had the money to do much drinking with the boys. I'm all but banished now. I nearly got stoned to death today."

"What?" Ebrooks demanded, horrified.

They listened to my tale, nodding gravely. When I described the man who had come toward me out of the mob, Ebrooks nodded and said, "That'll be Dale Hardy. He's new. Give him a month in Gettys and he won't be so piss and vinegar. He'll get ground down like the rest of us."

We talked for some time longer, and then they left, promising to bring me supplies from the mess hall the next day. That was small comfort. I'd had next to nothing to eat all day, and the hunger inside me now was not to be ignored. An equation nudged into my awareness. I'd used the magic last night to keep myself warm. And today my hunger was proportionately strong. Magic, it seemed, demanded more food than physical effort. I wondered idly if I could work enough magic to shed the wall of fat from my body. I decided that the appetite it would create would probably drive me insane before I succeeded.

I went out into the gathering evening to see if I could find anything to eat. I carried my gun with me, even as I told myself I was worrying needlessly. If the mob were going to hunt me down and hang me, they'd have done it by now. Wouldn't they?

As yet, my vegetable garden wasn't yielding. I went to Clove's stall and abashedly took a measure of his grain. It was coarse and hard and none too clean, but I rinsed it and put it to soak in a pot near my fire. My water cask was nearly empty; I took my bucket and headed down to the spring.

As I had that very first day, I had the strong feeling that someone was watching me. I heard a shuffle of feathers overhead and looked up hastily to find that a croaker bird had just settled in a tree at the edge of the woods. The silhouette of the trees and the bird were black against the day's fading sky. He croaked suddenly. A shiver ran up my spine. I lurched to my feet, and my brimming bucket sloshed a little cold water down my leg.

"Nevare." A voice spoke softly from the woods. It seemed to come from the trees just below the bird's perch. Although it was a woman's voice and I recognized Olikea's tone, my first thought was that death had called my name. On the fleeting heels of that thought, however, was the heated flush of my memory of Olikea. All my senses came to sudden quivering attention. I stared into the shadowy woods and saw no one and nothing, until she moved. Then I could not understand how I had not seen her before. She stepped clear of the sheltering trees, but did not venture out of the forest.

Abruptly I became aware of the basket that she carried on one arm. She held out a hand toward me, beckoning me. I took a slow step toward her, trying to find logic in my mind. Did I wish to reenter her world? I saw her flex her fist, and the scent of fresh crushed fruit suddenly filled my nostrils. She had pulped something in her hand. "Nevare," she called again, softly, coaxingly. She took a step backward toward the forest. I dropped my bucket and lunged after her. She laughed and fled.

I followed her into the forest. She paused and ran, dodged, hid, and then revealed herself, and I pursued her mindlessly like a dog tracking a squirrel as it jumps from tree to tree. She had reduced me to my most elementary drives, food and sex. Dignity, intellect, rationality fell away from me as I hunted her through the dusky woods.

Night deepened under the interwoven branches. My eyes adjusted to the dimness and my nose became a keen ally. She did not seriously try to elude me, but only stayed just out of my reach, laughing when I got close to her, then fleeing with a sudden dash and vanishing again from my sight as she camouflaged herself in the tricky sunset light.

Before I knew it, we had reached the eaves of the true old forest. Then she ran in earnest, basket jouncing on her arm, and her buttocks bobbing. She made no attempt to hide from me now, and I ran, heavily, panting, but running like a dog on a scent, tirelessly and determined.

Did I catch her or did she turn and snare me in her arms? I could not say. I only knew that near a welling spring, the game suddenly ended in triumph for us both. She had splashed out ankle-deep into the water. I followed her, and there she came to me, suddenly willing and not coy at all. I kissed her, an act that seemed to surprise and intrigue her. She pulled back, laughing and saying, "You do not need to eat me, Great One. I have brought the right foods for you, the foods that will restore you, the foods that will reveal you. I have the dream traveler's berries and the bark of the flight-of-eyes. I have ever-heal and never-tire. All that a Great One needs, I bring to you."

She took both my hands and drew me to the riverbank. There she would not allow me to do anything for myself. She fed me from her hands, even to cupping cool water for me to drink. She took my clothing from me, and then offered me more food and herself. The tang of the soft, thin-skinned fruit was interspersed with the play of her warm, wet tongue as she mixed her kisses with feeding me. She had learned so quickly. She held mushrooms between her teeth and offered them to me, refusing to let go so that I had to bite them from her mouth. Her hands were sticky with the fruit she had crushed, and as she ran them over me, the smell of the fruit nectar mingled with the musk of our bodies to become one scent.

Later, I would think it depravity. At the time, it was lust and gluttony combined into one glorious, sense-engulfing indulgence. The moon was high before we had finished our consumption. I lay back on deep, soft moss, completely sati-ated in every way I could imagine. She leaned over me, breathing her wine breath into my face. "Are you happy, Great One?" she asked softly. She stroked the curve of my belly, following the line of hair that led downward. "Have I pleased you?"

I was far beyond being pleased with her. And yet it was her first question that clung to my mind. Was I happy? No. This was transitory. Tomorrow I would be back in my cabin, fearing to go into town, digging holes to bury men I'd never known, and planning a fence that would keep out this world that I now wallowed in. I answered neither of her questions.

"Olikea, you are a very kind woman."

She laughed at that and replied, "I am as kind to you as I hope you will be to me. Will you be kind enough to come to my village? I wish to show you to the people there."

"You wish to show me to your people?"

"Some there do not believe that one of your kind could become a Great One. They mock me and ask, 'Why would the magic choose as defender the one who has invaded us?'" She shrugged the question aside as if it were of no conse-quence to her. "So I wish to prove I speak true to them. Will you come with me to my village?"

I could suddenly think of no reason to refuse. "Yes. I will."

"Good." She stood up suddenly. "Let's go."

"Now? Tonight?"

"Why not?"

"I thought the Speck villages were far back in the forest. Days or even weeks from here."

She tossed her head and puffed her cheeks. "Some are.

All the winter villages are. But our summer village is not. Come. I'll show you."

She stooped and seized both my hands. I laughed at the thought of her being able to tug me to my feet. With a groan and a lurch, I rolled over, got my knees under me, and stood up. She took my hand. She led and I followed her, away from the spring and my discarded clothing. Away from everything. At the time, I didn't even think that I was leaving my old life behind, only that I was going somewhere with Olikea.

The night was velvet around us. Olikea occasionally swatted at the gnats that hummed about her head, but none came near me. If she followed a path, I could not detect it. We walked on banks of moss and waded through drifts of fallen leaves from decades past. Other animals moved in the forest, as softly as we did. Our way led us across the sides of steep hills at a slant, always ever higher. We came to a place where the trees were as big around as towers, their tops lost in leafy darkness. We topped a ridge and went down into the shallow valley beyond it, and never once left the shelter of the trees.

Night was still deep around us when we came to her summer village. I smelled first the soft smoke of small campfires. Then I heard something that was more akin to the humming of bees in a hive than music, but was pleasant all the same. I began to catch glimpses of subtle firelight pooling in the hollows of the sheltered valley. As we descended, I expected to see a humble village of rustic dwellings. Instead, I saw only forest. It was only when we reached the edges of a natural clearing that I could see shadowy folk passing in front of the several small fires that dotted the dell. I estimated the population at about sixty, but there could have been three or four times that many in the darkness.

I had almost forgotten my nudity. It had seemed completely natural to move unclad and unencumbered through the soft darkness of the forest night. Now that I faced the reality of walking into a community of Specks unclothed, I suddenly felt intensely uncomfortable. I halted and said softly to Olikea, "I need to go back for my clothing."

"Oh, do not embarrass me," she chided me and, seizing my hand, led me inexorably forward.

I followed her as if unable to exert my own will in the matter. I walked into a child's nursery tale. That is as close as I can describe it. The soft glow of the campfire was cupped gold in the mossy hollows that had formed around each hearth; they lit no more than the circles around them. Shadowy people moved intermittently as black silhouettes before it. The dappled folk who dozed or lounged and spoke quietly around the fires were, for that time, the legendary denizens of the forest, creatures forever beyond my ken. They were comfortable in their naked skins. Their adornments of feathers, beads, and flowers were aesthetic ornamentation only, and all the more potently beautiful for that. The summer village seemed a place where the forest had chosen to welcome the humans. The earth had shaped itself to receive humanity, rising as mossy couches around the fire circles. The curving roots of one immense tree cupped three small children curled and sleeping in its grasp. In the hollowed trunk of a still-living tree I glimpsed a couple indulging in unabashed passion in a privacy granted to them by their fellows and graced by a flowering vine that did not quite curtain them from the firelight. A hummock of earth sheltered a moss-floored cave. Glowing insects formed chains of light on the walls inside it, creating a mystical light for a group of women who were weaving baskets. Our destination was a central firepit where a group of people were singing. Olikea's fingers imprisoned mine in a firm grip. She led me on a winding path through the village. She did not pause as we circled down and down to the lowest central firepit in the dell where the song was continuing. I felt she deliberately led me past the smaller family fires, as if she were leading an especially fine livestock purchase home and wished to be sure that her neighbors admired it. If that were so, she was achieving her purpose, for as we passed, people were rising from their fires to follow us. At last we stopped on the outskirts of the musicians' circle. The men were humming a series of deep bass notes. The women were breathing out a sweet soprano counterpoint. A few shook bundles of dried seed pods that made a soft shushing sound. It was a gentle concert. At our approach, the music faltered, broke into pieces, and then died.

Olikea did not let go of my hand as she broke into the circle of gathered singers, and so I had to follow her. I hoped my high blush was invisible in the low light. She spoke not loudly, but in a clear, carrying voice. "Behold, I have found a Great One of the plain-skin folk. I have made him mine and brought him here. Behold."

In the hush that followed her words, I could hear my heart beating in my ears. I had expected only an introduction to her people, which had been a frightening enough prospect. To be announced as a Great One and presented like a prize bull filled me with uneasiness. As my eyes began to adjust more fully to the firelight, I recognized Olikea's father among the singers. He had a contraption of leather thongs strung on a wooden frame attached to something that was like a drum. He did not stare at me, but looked into the flames. Next to him, a woman a few years younger than Olikea suddenly stood. She pulled the man beside her to his feet. He was a stout fellow, more dappled than most of the men gathered there, and with a face made even odder by the dark mask of pigment around his blue eyes. His hair was long and uniformly black rather than streaked. He wore it in many plaits. At the end of each plait, the hair was knotted through a small, polished animal verte-brae. He stared at me in astonishment and dismay. The woman spoke angrily. "We have a mage already. We have no need of your plain-skin Great One, Olikea. Take him away."

"Olikea's Great One is bigger," someone said. The voice was not aggressive, but was clearly audible. Murmurs of agreement followed this announcement.

"Jodoli is still growing," Olikea's rival protested. "Already he has blessed us many times over. Continue to feast him, and he will continue to grow and fill with magic for you."

"Nevare has scarcely begun to grow!" Olikea countered. "Look at how big he is, and he has never been properly fed. Since I have taken him over, he has grown, and he will grow even more as he is correctly cared for. The magic favors him. Look at his belly! Look at his thighs, his calves. Even his feet are fattening. You cannot doubt he is the better one!"

"He is not of our people!" the other woman declared shrilly.

Olikea feigned amazement. "Firada, how you talk! He is a Great One. How can he not be of our people? Do you dispute one that the magic has chosen and sent to us?"

Firada was not persuaded. "I . . . I do not see how it can be so. Who has taught him the magic's way? He is fat, that is true, but who could have trained him? Why does he come to us?" She turned to address the gathered folk. "Is this wise, my family, to take in a Great One who does not come to us from our own? Jodoli we have seen since the day his mother birthed him. We all witnessed the fever, and we all saw him return to us, and when he began to fill with magic, we rejoiced. We know nothing of this plain-skin Great One! Shall we replace Jodoli with an untried stranger?"

I spoke, much to Olikea's quick disgust. "I did not come here to replace anyone. Olikea simply asked me to come and meet you all. I cannot stay."

"He cannot stay tonight!" Olikea hastily corrected me. Her hand gripped mine firmly. "But soon he will come to live among us, and the richness of the magic that swirls inside him will benefit all of us. All of you will be grateful for the mage I have brought you. Never before has our tribe-family been able to boast of such an immense mage loyal to our clan. Do not doubt him lest he be offended and, leaving us, choose another family for alliance. Tonight you must dance and sing a welcome to him, and bring him food so that we may feast the magic."

"Olikea, I cannot . . ." I began in a low voice.

She gripped my hand hard, digging her nails into me. She leaned close to speak by my ear. "Hush. You need food. Eat now. Then we will talk. See. They already scatter, to bring you food."

No other words could have driven all my concerns so completely from my brain. My hunger came back, a roaring beast. Like a returning tide, the People came back, bearing with them every imaginable sort of food. There were berries and drupes that I had no names for, but also the tender tips of leaves and flower buds, a bowlful of nectar-heavy blossoms, and finely shaved tree bark. They brought me dense, golden bread, made not from grain flour but from ground tubers. It was studded with dried fruit and spicy little nuts. I hesitated over a basket of smoked insects. The woman offering them to me took honeycomb in her fingers and pinched it to drizzle the honey over the gleaming black bodies. They were crunchy and smoky and strangely oily. Delicious. I washed them down with a forest wine served in wide clay bowls.

I ate, and as each dish was emptied, others were pushed forward to take their place. Eating had become an adventure in sensations, with no relationship to appetite or nourishing the body. I fed something larger than myself, something that took satisfaction in every morsel that entered my mouth.

There were moments when my true self broke through, moments when I realized the incongruity of my pale nakedness in the flame-lit velvet darkness, moments when Olikea's satisfied patting of my swelling belly reminded me that in the streets I had walked this morning, that distended paunch was a source of mockery and shame to me. My hidden self that Tree Woman had nourished and educated emerged into his own. He, at least, understood that this tribute was due to him and proper, and he showed his satisfaction in ways that would have made my aristocratic self shudder, had I taken time to consider it. He licked his fingers and moaned with pleasure at some tastes, smacking his lips over others, and licking bowls to obtain every last morsel of the best offered to him.

The People adored his praise of the food they brought him. As the night progressed, they built the fires higher, making the circle of light broader. They joined in the feasting, serving to themselves the lesser food unfit to offer me. When I was full nigh to bursting and had reduced my activity to sampling the best morsel from each dish presented to me, I became aware that the other mage had seated himself beside me. I turned to look at him. Jodoli gravely inclined his head to me.

"My people feast you well," he informed me. There was no warmth in his voice, only the statement of fact.

I suddenly felt awkward. The scattered fragments of my real self assembled and I found myself groping for manners. "They feast me better than I have ever been fed." I started to thank him and then hesitated. Was not I supplanting him?

Would thanking him be rude? Who should I be thanking for this amazing meal? I glanced toward Olikea for guidance, but she was temporarily absent, circulating among her people. I watched her for a moment, nearly forgetting Jodoli. Olikea walked like a queen bestowing favor. Her nakedness was always graceful, but now her swaying walk suggested a swagger that was both attractive and intimidating to me. She inclined an ear to the people who sat or reclined on mossy couches, eating and drinking. To some she nodded and smiled, to others she raised her brows or waved a hand indecisively.

"Great Man Nevare." Jodoli's low voice summoned my attention back to him. His gaze held mine. It was singularly uncomfortable to look at him. His eyes were unnaturally light in the patch of darkness that swathed them. "Have you come to take my place?" he asked me bluntly.

"Olikea said—" I began, but he cut my words off with a strange smile. He was rubbing the fingers of one hand together as if he were polishing a small coin. "These people of mine," he warned me. "They may not be as easy to win as you might think. You are bigger than me. And you know as well as I that the magic courses through you. But magic is like any other strength, Plain-skin. It must be trained to be useful. And I do not think you have been trained."

"And you have?" I asked him with a coolness that I did not really feel.

"My teachers stand all around you," he said. I felt him watching me as he spoke, and knew that I was being tested just as surely as I knew I was failing that test. I looked at the gathered people and wondered what I could set against them. Mentioning the academy would probably not impress him.

"My teacher is within me," I said impulsively, mostly for the sake of saying something different from what he had asserted. The words had no meaning for me, but I was pleased to see a flicker of uncertainty in his masked eyes.

"I propose a small competition," he said. "One that will allow my people to choose wisely between one who is better schooled and one who is greater in girth."

His eyes flickered away from me as he made this challenge. I followed the direction of his glance and saw the woman who had earlier championed him standing at the edge of the firelight's circle. I sensed how they conspired to unmask my ignorance. For one instant, I scrabbled for a strategy. Then I realized I simply didn't have one. My Speck self might have a working knowledge of magic, but I didn't have access to it. I leaned back lazily and smiled at him, wondering if I should bluff. What did Olikea expect of me? She seemed to have deliberately maneuvered me into this confrontation. My eyes roved the gathering, looking for her. The moment my gaze touched her, she lifted her face. Our eyes met. I saw Olikea become aware of my danger. She began trying to hurry back to me without betraying her haste. Her gaze warned me, but I looked away from her. The smile on my face was becoming fixed. I nodded at Jodoli as if I'd been carefully considering his challenge. "What sort of a competition did you have in mind?" I asked him.

"The simplest sort," he replied complacently. "As you know, in times of plenty, the People care for their mage. In hard times, we burn our magic and ourselves to care for the People. So. Shall we show which one of us is more capable of taking care of the folk in lean or dangerous times?"

I was not sure how to reply to him. A woman carrying a flat tray toward me blocked Olikea. Her eyes flashed desperately toward me, but I looked away from her at Jodoli. He'd judge me weak if he caught me looking at a woman for advice. If I were going to move among these people, I must make my own way. I sized up my rival carefully. If this fellow thought he could best me in a competition of strength, he was wrong. I was not only wider than he was, but at least a head taller. My daily labor meant that my muscles were hard under the fat that coated him. He looked soft to me. The food I'd eaten had charged my magic. I could feel it scintillating through my blood, heady and intoxicating as liquor. Power. I had power and I had it in greater quantity than he did. Hitch had said I'd worked wonders beyond anything he'd ever seen a Great One do. Perhaps I had a natural talent for magic. I knew I had the benefit of a military education. Everything I'd ever learned about strategy warned me that now was no time to appear indecisive or afraid. My only hope was to draw Jodoli out and try to find a weakness. "Set the terms of the challenge as you wish," I told him affably. Did he look surprised at my nonchalance? I hoped I was buying time.

He bowed his head. I thought for an instant that he smiled, but when he lifted his face to mine, his mouth was serious. "And when shall we begin?" he asked me softly.

"Whenever you like," I said magnanimously.

I opened my eyes to dim light filtering down through the forest canopy. A light rain of dew was sprinkling down from the leaves high above me as the morning breeze stirred them. The falling droplets sparkled in the random rays that broke through the canopy. They fell on my face, my bare chest and belly, for I lay flat on my back. I yawned and stretched. I could not recall a morning when I had awakened feeling better. My belly was still pleasantly full from the evening before, and I had slept as deeply as if I'd been snuggled into the finest featherbed. I sat up slowly and looked around.

I was alone on a forested hillside. The events of the evening before came back to me in a rush of sensation and detail. Try as I might, though, I could recall nothing after I'd accepted Jodoli's challenge. As if someone had blown out the lamp, darkness followed his words until I opened my eyes to this day.

Yet something must have happened, for there was absolutely no sign at all of the fires or the feast or the Speck encampment. The lay of the land did not match my recollection at all; the Specks had been settled in a little dell and I rested on a slant of hillside. I doubted I had been carried here, yet surely I would remember if I had come here under my own power? Most annoying of all was Olikea's absence. She might at least have stayed by me after luring me to visit her people. I stood up slowly, gradually realizing how peculiar my circumstances were. I was stark naked. I had no supplies, nor tools nor weapons of any kind. I was not sure where I was. Belatedly, I recalled that Spink had hinted he would be coming to see me today. He'd even given me a direct order to remain at my cabin so he would find me there. I needed to get back to my world.

I looked around me, trying to get my bearings and finding nothing familiar. The leaves and branches overhead screened the sun. The forest of ancient trees looked the same in every direction. I recalled that as I pursued Olikea, we had climbed higher and higher up the forested flanks of the mountain. Downhill seemed my best choice.

I walked the morning away. I could not see the passage of the sun, so I was uncertain of the passage of time. I cursed my own stupidity for following Olikea. I had been blinded by greed and lust, I told myself. And magic. I blamed the magic, and tried to convince myself that it and not my own poor judgment was responsible for my situation.

The immense trees towered over me. I walked on and on. Birds moved overhead, and twice I startled deer. When I came to a trickling stream at the bottom of a ravine, I stooped for a drink and then sat down with my back against an ancient tree while I soaked my aching feet in the cold water. When I heard someone whispering behind me, I sat up straight and looked all around, both hoping and dreading that Olikea had returned to aid me. I would have welcomed her guidance to return to my world, even as I dreaded her disappointment in me. I could not recall what had befallen me, but I was certain that I had lost to Jodoli's challenge. That would displease her. When I saw no sign of anyone, I forced myself to rise and go on.

My feet ached. My ankles and knees complained and my back hurt. Sweat streamed down me and myriads of insects came to dance around me, humming in my ears and getting tangled in my hair. The moss underfoot was mostly kind to my feet, but even small twigs and thorns are shocks to feet accustomed to boots. The underbrush was not thick, but there were places where I had to force my way through. By afternoon, I was sweaty, scraped, scratched, and insect-bitten. I did notice that the abrasions to my skin and the mosquito bites did not bother me as much as they once would have. At least my fat did me some good.

In late afternoon, I recognized a lightning-scarred tree. I knew my way now. I could not explain why it had taken me so many daylight hours to cover terrain that I had obviously crossed in just a few hours the night before. Dusk was thickening when I passed from the ancient forest into the burned zone of younger trees. It was full dark, and I was grateful that it was when I finally emerged, naked, scratched, and itching, from the forest onto the bare hill of my cemetery. I was home.

CHAPTER TWENTY-FOUR

AN ENVELOPE

I awoke the next morning feeling as if I had a wild and
drunken night to atone for. I lay in my narrow bed, looking
up at a cobweb in the corner, and tried to make sense of my
life. I failed. Then I tried to remember something that I
wanted above all else, and could not discover anything. That
was the lowest moment I'd had in a long time. Rescuing my
sister from my father's oppression and starting a new life
here seemed like a wild fantasy for an idealistic cadet in a
green jacket with bright brass buttons, not something for a
fat man covered with scratches and insect bites and infected
with a magic he could not master.

Spink *had* come out to see me yesterday. He'd left a note on
my table, a very formal note from Lieutenant Spinrek Kester,
saying that he was extremely disappointed not to find me at

my post, and that the next time he came out to the cemetery, he expected to find me at my duties. To anyone else, it would probably look stern. To me it sounded desperate and worried. I wished he hadn't come; I wished he were not involved in what looked to be the continuing disaster of my life.

When I eventually got out of bed, I was surprised to find that it was still very early in the day. I hauled water and washed myself, dressed in my second set of clothing (much regretting the loss of my other garments), picketed Clove in fresh grazing, and generally tried to behave as if I were starting a normal day. A normal day. That was something I could set my sights on and long for. Normality.

I cut and sharpened some stakes and with what simple means I could devise, I shot a straight line for my new fence. I threw myself into that engineering project as if I were constructing some life-saving rampart rather than building a simple barrier to protect a graveyard. I was digging my third posthole before I finally confronted the reason for my glum spirits.

I had run away to the Specks and found that even among a bunch of savages, I could not prevail. I had failed. I dropped one of Kilikurra's poles into the hole, shoved earth in around it, and held it upright as I stamped down the soil. My bruised feet protested. I missed my boots. The low shoes I wore today were broken at the sides and worn at the soles. This afternoon, I'd have to go back to the forest and find my discarded clothing and boots. I dreaded it. It seemed that now I dreaded almost everything, so it was simply one more task I had to face. I sighed, sighted down my line of stakes, and moved on to dig the next posthole.

I was digging when Ebrooks and Kesey arrived. They had walked out from town, and I did not hear them coming until they were right behind me. They both seemed subdued until Kesey blurted out, "Where were you yesterday, Nevare? Some lieutenant from supply came out here looking for you and was really upset when he couldn't find you. We didn't know what to tell him. At first we said you'd only been gone a little while, but he kept asking so many questions that finally we had to tell him that we hadn't seen you all day, but that we thought you'd only been gone a short time because you didn't often leave for very long. He went into your shack."

"I know. He left me a note."

"You in much trouble?" Ebrooks asked worriedly.

"Some, probably. But I'll tell him the truth. I went into the woods and I got turned around and it took me all day to find my way home."

A silence greeted my words. I'd expected them to accept my excuse. Instead, they exchanged glances. Ebrooks shook his head slightly and then, seeing me scowl, gestured toward the graves and said gruffly, "Kesey and me, we better get to cutting grass."

But Kesey stood his ground. Slowly he moved his shoulders back and his chin came up. His dark eyes had always looked mournful to me, and dispirited. But today he folded his arms on his chest and bored into me with his gaze. "Nevare, I got something to say. Lots of people in the regiment don't like you, but me, I think you're a decent fellow, just really fat, and that shouldn't count against you no more than me being bald or Gimper having only two toes left. It's just how you are. Now we got an inspection coming up, and if every man don't look good, it's going to come down hard on all of us. Maybe you think we aren't much of a regiment, and maybe we haven't been since you joined us, but once we were plenty proud and a damn crack outfit. Things aren't the best for you, I know, what with the rumors about you and that fancy woman making a big squawk that you said something dirty to her. You might think going native is a way out. You wouldn't be the first to just walk off into those woods and never come back again. But don't you do it, Nevare. You take some pride in what you are and who you are and you tough it out like a true-born soldier son. Nobody says it much anymore around here, but I'll tell you this. You owe it to this regiment to be the best soldier you can be. Not just when we're stepping smart and pretty, and we've got our banners flying and good days rolling along. Not just when there's gunpowder and smoke and blood. But during times like this, when no one thinks much of us, not even

ourselves, and we know we're going to get our comeup-
pance from that inspection team. Even in times like this,
we got to do what we can, and be soldiers like our fathers
was before us. You hear me?"

He took a deep breath after he'd spoken his piece. It was
the longest speech and the most sense I'd heard out of the
man since I'd met him. There he stood in a wrinkled uniform
jacket with one button dangling from a thread and the knees
of his trousers gone shiny with wear. His hat was dusty and
rain had speckled the dust. What hair he had stood out in
tufts above his ears. But he stood as straight as a ramrod, and
his words sank into me like rain falling on parched soil.
They moved me as I hadn't been moved in a long time. They
restored my true self just as absolutely as the forest food had
satiated my Speck self. Nothing could have stirred the dormant duty in my soul as plainly as the heartfelt call to arms
of that wizened old soldier.

I lifted my eyes to meet his. "You're right, Kesey. You're
right."

That was all I said to him, but he beamed as if I'd just
given him a commendation. He marched off to follow
Ebrooks and as they went, I heard him say, "I told you he
was a right fellow, Ebrooks, now didn't I? Just needed a bit
of reminding, that was all."

I did not hear Ebrooks's muttered response. I applied myself to my task with fresh energy. By early afternoon I'd
used up all of Kilikurra's poles. They looked pathetic: a
widely spaced fence of shovel handles sticking up out of the
earth. But when I stood at one end of the row and sighted
down them, they lined up perfectly. I took pleasure in what
I'd accomplished with only crude tools.

I carried my shovel and pick back to my tool shed, returned to my cabin for water, and was just thinking of going
to look for my clothing when I heard the snort of a horse
outside my open door. I rose from my chair, but before I even
reached my door, Spink rushed through it. He stopped short
when he saw me and exclaimed fervently, "Oh, thank the
good god that you have returned! Nevare, I feared I would
never see you again."

"I was lost in the forest overnight, sir, but as you can see, I've returned safely and taken up my duties again."

Spink whirled as neatly as a cat and slammed my door behind him. Then he turned back to me and I saw that the relief on his face had been replaced with something akin to anger. "We're talking plainly today, Nevare. No hedging. Where were you yesterday? And I warn you, I want the whole story."

It was not a tale I could imagine telling to Spink or anyone else. Not just yet. So I replied stiffly, "I told you. I went into the forest. It got dark faster than I thought it would, and I got turned around. Even when daylight came, I couldn't get my bearings. It took me a long time to find my way back home. I returned late last night."

"Why did you go into the forest in the evening, Nevare?"

I hesitated too long, trying to find a good answer for that. When I opened my mouth, Spink waved his hand at me. "No. Don't lie to me. If you aren't going to tell me, then just don't tell me, but please, Nevare, don't lie to me. You've changed enough as it is. When you start deliberately lying to me, then I'll know there's nothing left of our friendship to salvage."

His eyes bored into mine so honestly, and the hurt in them was so plain, that I was shamed dumb by it. I looked away from him. After a moment he said, "Well, let me tell you what has been transpiring in my home, and perhaps you can give me some answers to what you know of that."

"In your home?" I asked, startled.

He took a seat at my table as if he expected to be there for a time. I slowly sat down across from him. He nodded at me sternly, affirming that I should take this conversation seriously. He cleared his throat. "Yesterday morning, a woman came to my door. She told me that she had been told that my lady wife could use a servant, and that she was willing to do anything our household required in exchange for shelter and whatever food we could spare them."

"Amzil," I said reflexively. I had completely forgotten that I had sent her to Spink's door.

"Yes. Amzil. The Dead Town whore."

A small silence followed his words. I felt both angry that he called her such a name and abashed that I had thoughtlessly

sent a woman who merited such a name to his door. The awkwardness built between us as I tried desperately to think of
something that would take us back to a place where we were
friends who could talk to each other.

Spink cleared his throat and then added accusingly,
"Amzil AND her three children. Of course, Epiny was immediately entranced with all of them. Have you any idea
what a junior lieutenant's pay is, Nevare? And how much
noise three children make in a very small house? And how
much they eat, especially that little boy? It fascinates Epiny.
She just kept putting food in front of him, waiting for him to
stop. But he didn't, not until he suddenly put his head down
on the table and fell asleep."

A leaf turns in the wind, and you suddenly have a different
perception of what color it is. It stung that Spink could call
Amzil a whore, but he had no way of knowing that she was
someone I cared about. I wondered when she had become
"someone I cared about" rather than just Amzil the whore.
That realization was as jolting to me as the sudden knowledge
that I was the one throwing up barriers between Spink and
me. "I didn't stop to think about that," I admitted. "Amzil
came out here, wanting to live with me. She thought that was
her only option, other than raising her kids in a brothel."

"And you turned her away?" Spink sounded surprised.

I shifted in my chair and then said grudgingly, "It was right
after that incident in town. I didn't think they would be safe
here. And she wasn't offering me—I know they call her a
whore, Spink, but I don't think that's fair to her. She's done that
occasionally, out of necessity, to feed her children. And I suspect that sometimes she wasn't given the option of saying no,
that men went out there, used her, and left money or whatever
so they didn't have to think of themselves as rapists. Well. I
don't know. But yes, I sent her to you. Without thinking of what
a financial burden they might be. Did you let them stay?"

"Epiny answered the door." It was the only reply I needed.
He went on, "She's a strong woman, my Epiny. Not in the
flesh; I'll admit that her health has suffered since we came
here, and that like the rest of us, she is prey to the darkness
of spirit that flows out of the forest. But she fights it. She has

made the women of Gettys her special project. Having a woman come to the door and say that she'd rather scrub floors for us than be a whore was a validation of all that Epiny has been trying to accomplish with her whistles and meetings and night classes for women."

"Classes? Classes in what?"

Spink rolled his eyes. "In whatever they want to learn, I expect. By the good god, Nevare, you don't think I've attended, do you? I'm sure you recall how adamantly Epiny endorsed my mother's idea that women must be able to manage their own households in the event that one is widowed or abandoned by her husband. Epiny teaches them the basics of arithmetic, and gives them an understanding of banking and, well, I don't know. Whatever it is that she thinks women need to know when there are no men about."

I gave an involuntary snort of laughter. "Amzil might be a better teacher than a student in such a class."

"I suspect she might. She probably will be, if Epiny has her way. Despite their differences, Epiny is quite glad to have another woman around the house, because of her condition. She loves the children already. She has very much missed her younger sister, you know."

"Epiny's condition?" I feared the worst. It was well known that plague survivors often had impaired health and sometimes died young. "Is she ill?"

"Quite the contrary," Spink assured me. His cheeks had gone pink, but he was grinning. "Nevare." His voice suddenly deepened with emotion. "I'm going to be a father."

I leaned back in my chair, astonished. "You've got my cousin with child?"

His cheeks went redder. "Well, your cousin is also my wife. Had you forgotten that?"

I hadn't, but I'd never dwelt on exactly what that meant. I was suddenly jolted to my core. They would be a family. They *were* a family. It was silly that such a concept could shock me, but I hadn't really seen Spink and Epiny as a couple, let alone as the seed of a family. And now it was there. It was shameful, but I suddenly pitied myself, losing both of them to each other. I felt even more alone. I was glad for them, but my gladness was edged with envy. I kept that out of my voice as I offered him congratulations.

"With that the situation, you can see why Epiny feels that the good god himself sent Amzil to our door. She's had three children herself, and has assisted at other births, she told us. And she's a hard worker. She's already proven that. Epiny has tried to be a good housekeeper for us, but it is work she was never taught, and there are no decent servants to be hired in Gettys. So in some ways, it has been a relief for Amzil to come in and give the floor a proper scrubbing and put the kitchen to rights."

I breathed a sigh of relief. "Then it may work out well for all of you."

He gave me a flat look. "It may work out in ways you hadn't planned on, Nevare. Your Amzil did find a way to get your message to me, not that she needed to convince me to take her in. She already had Epiny's goodwill on her side. But it's only a matter of time before she notices that Epiny's whistle matches the one in her 'password' and then what will she make of it?"

I considered it for a moment. "I don't know."

"Nor do I. But I already suspect Amzil is not one to let a mystery rest in peace. How long before she asks Epiny what it means?"

"I specifically told her not to say anything about it to Epiny, only you."

He rolled his eyes at me. "Oh, well, that's such a relief. Nevare, don't you see that such a command would only add oil to the fire?"

He was right. I'd told Amzil that the otter whistle had saved a life, and when she saw Epiny's whistle shaped like an otter, she'd know it was the one I meant. Spink was right; Amzil couldn't leave such a mystery alone. I sighed. "Well, if she talks to Epiny, then she does, and I'll deal with it then."

"That's not good enough, Nevare!" He slapped the table at me and leaned forward earnestly. "I've kept your secret for you far longer than I should. When Epiny finds out, she will be murderous toward me. Since she became pregnant, she's been more emotional than usual. Learning that I've deceived her for months could destroy us. I came out here to ask you—no, I came out here to *tell* you that I'm going to tell her the truth. So you'd best be prepared for her."

"Spink, you can't! You mustn't! You know what my reputation has become in Gettys. You can't allow her to link her name to mine. It will ruin both of you. Which officers' wives will keep their friendships with her after they discover that her cousin is suspected of rape, murder, and propositioning virtuous women on the streets? She won't have a female friend left in Gettys. Think what that ostracism would do to her. Think what it could do to your child's future!"

He looked down at his feet and then up at me. "I have thought about it, Nevare. I'm not a saintly man, but I have my honor. I would lose more of it by denying you than claiming you, especially at this time of need in your life. Don't look at me like that! I can see what's happening to you." He stood up abruptly and paced around the room, halting by my window. He stared out of it as he spoke. "You grow fatter daily. I don't say that to rebuke you, but to tell you I notice. And I do believe it has some magical force behind it, for I don't see any of our other enlisted men growing as you do, and some of them spend far more time swilling beer and eating than you ever have. But it isn't just that. You go into the forest, Nevare, and you stay there, far beyond the amount of time than any of the rest of us could tolerate without going mad. You're drifting away from us. I can feel it when I talk to you. You remind me of that scout, Hitch. He gets that same look in his eyes sometimes."

He glanced back over his shoulder at me suddenly as he said this, almost as if he expected to catch something in my expression. But I controlled my face well. All the while I was weighing in my mind just how much of my experience I could share with Spink. I would be ashamed to tell how I had indulged myself with Olikea, or to admit how much contact I'd had with the Specks. He was uncomfortably close to the truth; I had thought of staying in the forest with them. I probably would have if I had not lost to Jodoli's challenge. I wondered again what had happened, then reined my mind violently back to the present as Spink suddenly slapped his forehead.

"What an imbecile I am! Here we've been talking away,

and I almost forgot the most important reason for my visit, the one that makes it absolutely necessary for Epiny to know that you are here. Look at this, Nevare, and tell me that it changes everything for you."

From inside the breast of his jacket he drew out a simple white envelope and set it on the table before me. My heart turned over in my chest. At one time, the sight of that handwriting had meant so much to me. The pen strokes in Carsina's hand spelled out my sister's name and my home address. I glanced at Spink, then opened the unsealed envelope and drew out two sheets of paper.

> *My dear Yaril,*
>
> *I regret that I could not find time to visit or write to you before my departure to the east. The oppertunity arose and my beloved parents judged it best that I act upon the invitation swiftly. I am staying with my cousin and his wife, Clara Gorling, so that I may have the time to become better acquainted with her cousin, Captain Thayer, my fiancé. Gettys is a rather wild place, it's true, but I think I will find true happyness here with such an ambitious young officer. He is the most dashing fellow you could imagine, with dark curly hair and the widest shoulders I've ever seen! Oh, I do wish you could meet him! He is far handsomer than Remwar ever was! I feel so silly when I think that I was jealous of your flirtation with him. What children we both were!*
>
> *Please write to me at your earliest convenience to say that you have missed me as much as I have missed you and that we can renew the friendship that sustained us through so many happy years.*
>
> *With affection,*
> *Carsina Grenalter, the future wife of Captain Thayer*

"What is this?" I demanded of Spink, though my mind was already putting the puzzle together.

"I went to Carsina. It was difficult for me to get in to see her, for it seemed a score of women had closed in to stand guard over her and commiserate with her on her terrifying experience. It was harder still to find a way to speak privately with her. I pretended I was there to get a detailed statement of exactly what you had said to her and how you had insulted her. She's a fine little actress, Nevare. She stuttered and wept and fanned herself until I sent her maid out of the room to fetch a glass of water for her. Then I told her, bluntly, that I knew who she was and who you were and that I'd even seen some of the letters that she had written to you while you were in the academy. I told her that you had saved them, and that if it came to a court-martial over your behavior, you could produce them to prove that your prior acquaintanceship gave you every right to speak to her on the street. I think she came close to really swooning then."

Spink was grinning as he spoke, and I found a rare smile stretching my face as well.

"I told her that if she wanted the whole matter quieted down, she could simply accede to your request and give me an envelope addressed to your sister in her hand. I assured her that was all you wanted and that you had no interest in her beyond that.

"By then her maid returned with her water. Carsina sent her immediately for paper and pen, and this was in my hands before I left the room. I suggested to her in the maid's hearing that it was all a mistake, that I had talked with you and you had said that you had only asked her name, for she resembled someone you had once known. She very faintly agreed with me. I am sure I left her with a dilemma, for she had been denouncing you so rabidly that it will be difficult for her to retract what she has said. But her fear of her own letters may keep her from taking her wicked lie any further than it has gone. I can't tell you that your good name has been restored, but I don't think Carsina will dare to blacken it further."

I looked up from the letter in my hands. While he had been speaking, I'd read it through again. I was sure that her references to her future husband were put in to needle me. I was surprised by how little it bothered me. "Truth to tell, I do have her old letters. They're shut in my soldier son journal, with all the rest of my papers." I heaved a huge sigh of relief. "Spink, I don't know how to thank you. You've boxed her in quite neatly. If I presented those letters, I'm sure it would be the end of her engagement to Captain Thayer. I doubt that she'll do or say anything that would damage her own reputation in such a way."

He glanced away. "I felt rather a bully at first, to tell you the truth. But once I had threatened her with exposure, I could not believe how her sweet little mouth stopped trembling; I swear she longed to spit at me. I know you once loved the girl, Nevare, but I think she did you a favor when she ended your engagement. I cannot imagine you harnessed to such a woman for the rest of your life."

"Nor I," I muttered. The last remnants of my old fondness for Carsina were long gone. I wondered if she had ever been the sweet and simple girl I had imagined her to be. Was it possible that both Yaril and I had been so mistaken about someone? Or had the harshness of fate changed all of us?

"Well, we have what we needed. You must write to Yaril at once, and I'll put it in the military post for you. Tell her that she is more than welcome to come and stay with Epiny and me; Epiny would be delighted."

Nothing would do for Spink but that I undertook that task immediately. He stood over me as I took my pen and ink from my soldier son journal. "You've filled pages and pages of that!" he exclaimed when he saw it. "I've scarcely touched mine. I've been waiting for something significant to occur in my career."

"My father taught me that I should write at least a few lines every night, for insight comes from detail, and often a man can look back and see that a problem or a solution had its roots in earlier actions." I glanced at the dwindling supply of blank paper. "I suppose that soon I shall have to stop keeping it. It wasn't really intended for an ordinary soldier anyway, and if my father ever read all that I've put into it, I think he would be horrified. But I suppose I shall keep it until I run out of paper."

"You won't send it home to him when it's finished, so he can replace it with a fresh one?"

I looked at Spink to see if he was making a bad joke. He was sincere.

"No, Spink," I said quietly. "I am dead to that man. He disowned me. He wouldn't want to see it."

"Then entrust it to me, when you are finished, for I am sure you have written many valuable pages. I'll take care of it. Or give it to Yaril, to pass on to her own soldier son."

"Perhaps. If she has one. Now I need to think before I write."

Silence reigned for a time. I'd dipped my pen, but that ink had dried before I thought of what to say and how to phrase it. I did not write a long letter; too fat an envelope might invite my father's scrutiny. I told Yaril only the bare facts, that I was alive and at Gettys, enlisted as a common trooper, but that Spink and Epiny were living in a situation better befitting Yaril's station and had offered to make her welcome. With every word I penned, I was painfully aware that my father might read my words and judge me on them. I hesitated long over mentioning Spink's invitation, for fear it would prompt my father to some radical maneuver to keep Yaril at home. At last I decided that I'd have to chance it. The sooner that Yaril knew she had a bolt-hole, the more opportunities she could find to use it.

"How can she reply to this? She may need money to make the journey, or she may need to let us know when she might arrive."

Spink grinned. "I've already arranged it. Tell her to write back to Carsina, but to enclose a second, sealed envelope addressed to me. That should work. Be sure to let her know that Epiny is most eager for her to join us."

I added the requested instructions. As I sanded and then sealed the letter, I asked him, "Just how large a household are you planning to support on a junior lieutenant's pay?"

His smile faded slightly as he took the envelope from my hand. "Well, I'm sure it will all work out some way," he replied. And then, more sternly he added, "And I don't expect to shoulder it alone, Nevare. You realize that once Yaril writes back to us, you will have to talk with Epiny. This deception you practice will end. You will have to step up to your responsibilities. Yaril will be coming here. You know that. Her only other recourse would be to stay under your father's roof and marry Caulder Stiet, and I can't imagine a woman of even rudimentary intelligence taking that path. Your sister will be here. Both she and Epiny will expect to see you living and working as a proper soldier son, even if you are not an officer. So I suggest you begin now.

"You need a proper uniform, and you need to maintain yourself as befits a soldier. That means shaving and keeping your hair cut and asking the colonel to position you in the regiment in the regular chain of command instead of reporting directly to him. Devote yourself to your duties, and you can earn some rank. The dice rolled against you and you aren't starting your career as a lieutenant, but that doesn't mean you have to surrender your ambitions. Many a man with less intelligence and fewer connections, I might add, has managed to work his way up through the ranks. For everyone's sake, you had best start conducting yourself as a soldier son. You're a part of this regiment, and it can only be as good as the worst soldier in it."

His voice had grown sterner and more officious as he spoke. I raised an eyebrow, and he flicked a sideways glance toward the window. I instantly divined that either Ebrooks or Kesey was within listening distance. I came to my feet as quietly as I could and quietly acceded, "Yes, sir. I'll do better, sir."

"Yes. You will. Because this is the last warning you'll be receiving from anyone. Whenever I choose to drop by here, I expect to find you at your duties, soldier, and looking like a proper trooper. Good day."

"Yes, sir."

Spink left immediately afterward. Outside, a light summer rain had begun to fall. I knew that Spink had admonished me for show, but as he rode off, I took his words to heart. I'd been teetering on the brink, but now I'd stepped back to safety in my life as a soldier son. I would do more than simply drudge along. I thought of Gord and how natty he had kept his academy uniform despite his girth. I could do that. It would take effort, but a soldier's lot was effort. And there was no real reason that I could not set my sights on making rank. I'd begun well with my cemetery duties. Colonel Haren had said so. I could earn my stripes and perhaps more.

I spotted Ebrooks slinking away behind Clove's stall. I hailed him as Spink rode off into the sprinkling rain. "Well, that wasn't quite as bad as I thought it would be," I told him, trying to sound like a man who had just been soundly rebuked by his superior. "In fact, he said pretty much the same things that Kesey did. Shape up for the good of the regiment and all that."

"Yah. I heard him. But you know, Nevare, he's right. Things have been hard for the regiment here, and there's some of us as would welcome being shipped off somewhere else, disgraced or not. But the rest of us remember the old days, and while we'd like to leave, we'd like to see the road get pushed through first. So that when we walk away, we can say, well, it was hard but we done it."

I looked at rough, plain-spoken Ebrooks and noted that although his uniform shirt was stained, it was as clean as it would come. He was clean-shaven and his hair was combed. He wasn't much of a cavalla trooper, but right now he stood in front of a nobly born, academy-trained soldier son and looked far more like a soldier than I did. I felt ashamed of myself and also envious.

"I wish I could have joined this regiment in better times, and know it as you do," I said humbly.

He gave me a sour grin. "Nevare, in better times, we wouldn't have had you. That's harsh, but it's true. So you come to Gettys and you got a chance to join us. Make it an opportunity. Live up to what we were rather than dragging us down any further. That inspection team won't arrive for another ten days. Get yourself together. I don't suppose we're going to win any citations from them while our primary objective goes undone, but at least we can try to avoid disgrace."

"You mean the King's Road? I thought it was up to the prisoners to build it."

"Well, the shovel-and-pick labor, yes. But our scouts and engineers were supposed to lay it all out for them, and map out the tasks and say what was needed to get it done and how fast it could be done."

"And didn't they?"

He gave me a look. "You go walking into that forest like it's nothing, Nevare. I don't know how you do it. But for the rest of us . . . well, whips and threats are all that keep the prisoners working, and even so, the progress is so slow it's like going backward. Colonel Haren thinks he's onto something. Rum. And laudanum. I don't know where he got an idea like that. Get a batch of prisoners drunk or doped up and give them axes—that's got to be a recipe for trouble." He gave a lopsided shrug. "But I hear that it's working. Drunks are too stupid to be afraid of anything. Some of them get gloomy or cranky, but a man with a whip or a gun can persuade you that you've got to work no matter how gloomy or cranky you are.

"They've started cutting into those monster logs and hauling chunks away. Like ants trying to carry off a loaf of bread crumb by crumb is what one guard told me, but it's better than no progress. Even liquored up, most prisoners can't stand to work there more than an hour, and the guards have to be almost as drunk as the workers are. Makes cutting grass here look like a real pleasure."

Stillness washed through me. The road might go through. And I'd given the colonel the idea of how to do it. Haren seemed a fair man. He might not credit me with the idea, but I suspected I'd have a stripe or even two on my sleeve by the end of summer. Crashing against that idea like two waves meeting was the terrible sick sense that I had betrayed the forest and Tree Woman. I'd given the intruders a way to defeat the magic. They would keep cutting and gouging, an hour at a time, one tree at a time, until they'd cut right through the heart of the forest and the People. I'd betrayed the Specks just as completely as I'd betrayed the Gernians when I'd signaled the Dust Dancers to spread their plague. I felt queasy with what I had done. "You look pale. Are you sick?" Ebrooks asked me.

"Maybe," I said.

"Well. I got work to do. I'll see you later." He walked hastily away. Not much was left of the day, but Ebrooks went back to his work and I went back to mine. Some of my posts were leaning. I tamped them in more heavily. I wished I could just stop thinking and do this simple work in front of me. Why couldn't my life be simple, like Ebrooks's? He had duties, he did them, he ate, had a beer, and went to sleep. Why couldn't I have that life? I knew the answer. Because I didn't. When I reached the end of my line of posts, I stood for a time looking up at the encroaching forest on the hillside above me. Then I walked up the hill and into it.

As I entered the young forest, I tried to recall how terrifying and depressing it had been for me the first time I'd walked here. It seemed like a strange dream. I tramped through it, trying to remember where Olikea had fled so I could retrace my path from last night. That seemed like an even stranger dream. Spink and the letter and the lectures from both Ebrooks and Kesey had recalled me to my duty and my life. What had I been thinking, to even consider abandoning Yaril to a forced marriage with Caulder Stiet? How could I have imagined that I could tear off my clothes and run off into the forest to live among the Specks?

Twilight was falling when I found my scattered clothing and boots. I gathered them up and as I did so, I noticed how worn and smelly they were. The cracked leather of my scuffed boots was gray; I could not remember the last time I'd blacked them or even cleaned them. When I held up my trousers, they wrinkled and sagged into a parody of my buttocks and legs. Tomorrow, regardless of consequences, I'd visit town and push hard for a proper uniform from supply, even if I had to simply beg for fabric and then hire Amzil to sew for me. The thought of going to Amzil for help made me recall that she was living at Spink's home now. Epiny was there, and Spink had said he was going to tell her that I was alive in Gettys. The thought of that filled me with both dread and anticipation. With my dirty clothes draped over one arm and my boots in my free hand, I turned and started back when suddenly a shape separated herself from a tree trunk. Olikea stood before me.

"Now I find you!" she exclaimed accusingly. "Where did you go?"

"Me?" I was affronted. "I woke up in a strange place alone. I don't even know how I got there or what happened." I halted my words. I was speaking Speck; I'd made the transition without thought, without effort. Again.

She made a sound between a hiss and spitting. "Jodoli! What did he say?"

"He challenged me to prove that my magic was stronger than his."

She furrowed her brow at me. "But you are bigger than he is. You hold more magic than he does. You should have won."

"I may be full of magic. Sometimes I feel that I am. But that does not mean that I know how to use it. Jodoli said as much."

She puffed out her cheeks at me and made her disparaging sound again. "Then he turned his power on you."

"His magic made me fall asleep and wake up somewhere else?"

"It could be. Or he made you think you were somewhere else and just awakening, and you wandered off. Or he made it so you could not see us, or I could not see you. I do not know how his magic was done. I only know that he did it. And my sister mocked me, and all the People had to bring tribute to Jodoli and to her today to make up for their doubts."

I felt a pang of defeat so immense that I could scarcely comprehend it. I'd lost. It was impossible and horribly unfair. I who had undone the power seat of the Plains people, I who had stopped their magic forever so that they could never again menace the People or threaten our lands, had been tricked and defeated by a mage scarcely worthy of the title. He was no Great Man. He barely had the belly of a pregnant girl! And then, as before, my perception shifted, and I was once more Nevare, the soldier son. I looked down at the rumpled and soiled uniform on my arm, at the dirty scuffed boots I still clutched. "I have to go back to my people," I told her. "I'm sorry I disappointed you. I have to go back. Others are depending on me."

She smiled at me. "You are right. I am glad that you have come to see it."

"No," I told her. She had come closer to me, and I could already sense the warmth and musk that radiated from her body. It was so hard to deny her. "Olikea, I have to go back to my own people. To the Gernians. I have to become a good soldier, I have to make a home for my sister."

She stood less than a hand's-breadth from me now, tilting her face to look up into my eyes. "No. You are wrong. You are not to be a soldier, but a Great One. That is how you will serve the magic. And no man should make a home for his sister. Women go out and make their own homes, and it is *not* with their brothers."

It was hard to find words when she stood so near. She put her hand on my chest and my heart leapt to meet it. "I have a duty to my people."

"Yes. You do. And the sooner you fulfil it, the less suffering there will be on both sides. You must use the magic to make the Jhernians go away." Her lips twisted the name of my folk, and made them foreigners to my ears. "The sooner the war ends, the sooner the suffering will stop for all."

"War? What war? We are not at war with the Specks."

"That is the most foolish thing I have ever heard you say. Of course we are at war. They must leave, or we must kill them all. There is no other way. We have tried and tried to make them go away. Soon there will be no choice for us. We will have to kill them all."

These dark words she breathed against my mouth as she carefully aligned her body to mine and pressed herself against me. "Only you can do it," she said quietly when she lifted her mouth from mine. "Only you can save all of us from that. That is your duty. You must stay and do it." She ran her hands down the sides of my belly, caressing it sensuously. The sensations she woke drove all thought and internal division from my mind. She made me hers again, and I fell to her willingly.

CHAPTER TWENTY-FIVE

THE ROAD

I became a pendulum, swinging between two lives, committed to neither.

By days I labored in the cemetery. I dug graves and worked on my cemetery wall. The third day after I had set the poles in the earth to mark my fence line, I noticed that the bud nodes on their bark were swollen. In the next few days, leaves unfurled. I decided I had nothing to lose by watering them, and hauled each one a bucket from my spring daily. I thought that the leaves were a last desperate bid at life, and expected them to curl, wither, and die. But they did not. Instead the "poles" began to thrive as swiftly as if they were carefully transplanted saplings rather than posts. The rate at which they put out new stubs for branches was astonishing. I devoted myself to moving rocks, flowering plants, and bushes into alignment with my poles. I hammered stakes and strung lines to mark where the other hedgerows would eventually be, and generally took care that if the inspection party chose to visit, they would find evidence of careful and daily industry.

Amzil surprised me with a visit, one that was all the more astonishing in that she brought tailor's tools and an assortment of worn cavalla uniforms that she had disassembled into fabric. I was both relieved and embarrassed to have her take on the task of making me presentable. She obviously regarded it as a debt she owed me, for she went at it with pinched-lipped determination. I made one effort at asking her how she did in her new position. She narrowed her eyes at me and said that she much admired the lieutenant's lady, for she seemed like a woman who deserved better than the hand that life had dealt her, but was nevertheless making the best of her fortunes.

"Such a small woman, and having such a hard time just now. She can't keep a bite of food down, and yet she said she could watch my three while I did a bit of sewing work." Somehow her words seemed accusing, and I let a silence fall that was broken only by her commands that I lift my arms, turn, and hold a paper of pins for her. It was more humiliating than being measured by my mother's seamstresses, for this was a woman, I reluctantly admitted to myself, for whom I had feelings, even if I was not exactly certain what they were.

Once I had been measured, she turned me out of my own house. Midway through the day, she called me back and left me to try on what she called "the basted pieces." Both the jacket and the trousers had more seams than any such garments I'd ever seen before, for she had had to "ease them," as she put it, to fit me. By the time I finished my work and returned to my cabin that evening, I found a jacket and trousers and a shirt that I could actually put on and button. I walked around my small home, marveling at how freely I could sit, stand, and even bend. Then, but with reluctance, I carefully hung them up, resolving that I would not wear them again until the inspection team arrived.

By day I appeared content to be a cog doing this humble

work for my king. I resumed the proper regimen of a soldier. I rose early, as I always had. I made an honest entry in my journal. I had resolved that no one but me would ever read it, and thus I did not mince words. Afterward, I washed and I shaved. Both Ebrooks and Kesey commented on my new demeanor, and they themselves began to look more clean and trim. They both had seniority over me, if not rank, but I began to notice that they deferred to me in how the cemetery was kept. I was their de facto corporal even if the sleeve of my uniform lacked stripes. By day, I was a good soldier.

By night, I belonged to the forest.

It was not always a conscious decision. I was coming to think of my other self as my Speck self. He was part of me and apart from me. Some nights, after darkness had fallen and Ebrooks and Kesey had left, I would enter the forest and seek Olikea. At other times, when I tried to resist the double sirens of food and sex and simply go to my own bed, I would awaken from a dream of walking in the forest to find that I was, indeed, walking in the forest, the dew-heavy hem of my well-worn nightshirt slapping against my calves. I thought of tethering my wrist to my bed, as the sergeant in my academy dormitory had once suggested to me, but I decided it would do little good. I was living two lives now, and with a bystander's neutrality, I watched and waited to see which one would come to dominate me.

Olikea I did not understand. She had come too suddenly and too completely into my life. Every night, she awaited me in the eaves of the forest. Every night, she lured me into its depths, and then, when I reached the ancient forest, she would claim me as her own. I could not look at her without becoming aroused, and the food she brought me was the food that a Great One should always eat in order to maximize the growth of the magic. I could not refuse it any more than I could resist her favors. And yet I was not sure that either one was good for me. I could almost feel myself growing fatter when I ate what she offered me; it was not that there was a vast quantity of it, only that it seemed always the perfect food and exactly what I had wanted that evening.

As for the woman herself, she, too, satisfied my body beyond anything I could have imagined. She was imaginative, daring, and completely shameless in how she joined her body to mine. She relished our congress beyond any expectations I'd ever had of a woman. Her response to me seemed almost masculine, she was so aggressive, and she felt no qualms in letting me know exactly what would give her the greatest pleasure. She was noisy in her appreciation of my efforts, and in return, she left me mindless with fulfilment.

Awkwardly, guiltily, I courted her. The small gifts I brought her delighted her far beyond their worth. Brightly colored boiled sweets, brass bangles, cinnamon sticks, and glass beads were treasured by her, but made me feel as if I bought her with trinkets.

By day, it grieved me that she loved me so. I knew that in the long term, nothing could come of it but sorrow. She could never join me as my wife in my world. One evening, she took me to a place where she had hung a sort of sling between two trees. It was low and very large, and before I knew it, she had shown me how it could facilitate an entirely new form of coupling for us. And afterward, as I reclined in it, she joined me, molding her body along mine. The night was balmy and windless, and her body was warm where it pressed against me. A wave of sentiment washed through me. She deserved better from me than this casual sexual play.

I steeled myself to explain it all to her. I had been a cad, using her, allowing her to become attached to me, when in reality I could offer her nothing. I tried to express my apology for letting her become involved with me. A better man, I was sure, would have refused her advances.

But my explanations only baffled her. I looked up at the black network of branches against the starry sky and found myself groping for words I did not know in her language. "I do not feel I am worthy of your love, Olikea," I spoke plainly at last. "I fear that you have plans and dreams for a future that cannot be."

"Any future can be!" she replied, laughing at me. "If it were not so, if it were fixed, it would be a past. You say a foolish thing. How can a future be impossible? Do you hold the gods' powers in your hands?"

"No. I do not. But I speak of things I cannot or will not do, Olikea." Now that I had become determined to have this talk with her, what I had to say sounded colder and crueler than ever. But cruelest of all, I decided, would be to let her labor on under a delusion of a bright future with me. "Olikea, my father has discarded me from his household. I doubt I can ever return there as a respected son, and I will not return there as anything less. But even if I could, I could not take you with me. He would not accept you. Do you understand what I am saying?"

"I do not understand why you think I would wish to go there." She was genuinely puzzled. "Or why I would allow you to *take* me there. Am I a sack that you would carry off with you?"

I perceived I had to be even blunter. "I can never marry you, Olikea. You can never stand beside me as my—" I searched for a Speck word and found I did not know one. I used the Gernian instead. "*Wife.* You can never be my *wife.*"

She leaned up on top of me to look down into my face. "What is that? *Wife*?"

I smiled sadly. "*Wife* is the woman who will live with me for the rest of my life. The woman who will share my home and fortunes. The woman who will have my children."

"Oh, I will have my children," she assured me calmly. She lay back beside me. "A daughter, it is hoped. But I do not like your home, out there in the bare lands. You may keep it. As for fortune, I have my own fortune, so I do not need yours. You may keep it."

Her calm assurance that she would have my child unnerved me. "I don't love you, Olikea," I burst out. "You are beautiful and you are seductive and you are kind to me. But I do not think we truly know one another. I do not think we share anything beyond this passion for the moment."

"I share food with you," she pointed out reasonably. She stretched and then settled more comfortably beside me. "Food. Mating." She sighed, pleased with herself. "If a woman gives these things to a man, then he is fortunate and he should not

ask for more from her. Because," she added in a tone between
teasing and warning, "more than those things, he will not get.
Though he may earn her displeasure by asking."

The last was plainly a warning. I let the conversation die
away. Her head was pillowed on my shoulder and her hair
smelled sweet yet musky. I decided that there were great differences between our people, greater than I had imagined.
There was still the one thing that I could not keep silent on.

"And if you have my baby, Olikea? What then?"

"Your baby? *Your* baby?" She laughed. "Men do not have
babies. Women do. Your baby." She chortled again. "When I
have my baby, if it is a daughter, then I will celebrate and
reward you. And if it is a boy," she puffed her cheeks briefly,
"I will try again."

Her words gave me plenty of food for thought for several
nights. I remembered a saying that my father had: "Don't
measure my wheat with your bushel." He'd used it whenever
our opinions differed so much that I could not predict what
he was likely to do next. It suddenly seemed that that was
what I'd been doing with Olikea. The Specks had a strange
set of values, and I decided that despite my continued contact with them, I knew very little of their ways.

Yet with each passing day, I knew that I was closer and
closer to having to make a decision. Things were happening,
and some of them were events I had set in motion. Sooner or
later, I would have to stop balancing on the wall between my
worlds and make a choice. Some days I dreaded the idea that
a letter from Yaril might arrive; at other times, I longed for
it. As the days passed with no word from her, I suspected
that my father had intercepted the letter and destroyed it.
Then I decided it was equally possible that Carsina had received a letter from Yaril for Spink and kept it. I tried to
decide what I must do next, but I could not think clearly.
Little sleep and long hours of work interspersed with frantic
coupling do not lead to clarity of mind.

Dr. Dowder, ever an advocate of alcohol as a means to
soothe his own nerves, seemed to have come up with a balanced dose of rum and laudanum that deadened both workers
and soldiers to the terror at the end of the road. Work was

proceeding, not at a pace that would have caused rejoicing
in any other circumstances, but with a steadiness that was
nothing short of astounding given the record of the last few
years.

It was, as Ebrooks had noted, a monumental task. Before
the road could progress, the three gargantuan trees they
had initially felled had to be cut to pieces and hauled away.
According to what I heard from Ebrooks and Kesey, it was
being carried out as if it were a military operation. The cutting crew, properly dosed with alcohol and laudanum,
worked an hourlong shift of cutting chunks of the logs and
hitching teams to them to haul the cut pieces away. Each
piece was hauled beyond the "fear zone" to where a sober
crew of prisoners would take it over. The forward men
worked for an hour, then fell back to be replaced by prisoners and guards who had been freshly fortified against the
fear. Slowly but steadily, the fallen trees were being diminished. A cutting crew had already been sent forward to
mark the next trees that should fall. Morale in Gettys was
improving, and not just because of the road progress. Colonel Haren, after consulting with Dr. Dowder, had decided
that a milder "Gettys dose" was to be available to any man
or woman who felt the need of fortification. According to
Ebrooks, the entire town was mildly intoxicated most of the
time. I had no way of confirming that, but did notice that
both he and Kesey smelled of rum.

I did not venture into town anymore. Just as I had hoped
the furor over Fala's disappearance would die away, her
body had been found. She had been strangled with a leather
strap and her body discarded in a pile of waste straw behind
the stables. Falling snow and subsequent piles of waste straw
mucked out from the horses' stalls had been heaped over
her, or she would have been found much sooner. As it was,
she was only discovered when the straw was being loaded
into a wagon to be hauled away for the general tidying-up
that Gettys was undergoing prior to our inspection.

I did not bury her, nor attend her funeral. Colonel Haren
proved that he was not unaware of the rumors and temperament of the town, for he ordered me to take myself to the

end of the road and lend a hand to the work crews there for that day. I wished I could have paid my final respects to a woman who had, although very briefly, been a comfort to me. Later, I would learn from Kesey that the funeral had been "a regular tea social" as he put it, for all of the Whistle Ladies of the town turned out to follow Fala's coffin to the cemetery and watch her lowered into the ground. I think this display of sympathy was intended to inform the men of Gettys that the women would not tolerate the mistreatment of any woman, no matter how common. I wondered, but dared not ask, if Epiny had been part of that delegation.

For me, the day was a peculiar one. Clove and I appeared, as ordered, at the road's end, just beyond the fear zone. Once we were there, however, no one was quite sure whom I was to report to or what we were to do. I passed the day as an object of curiosity to the prisoners and their keepers. It was the first time I had observed the lot of the penal workers at such close range. I still cannot decide which appalled me more, the brutal treatment they received from their guards or the brutish nature of the louts that made them seem almost deserving of such abuse. By the end of the day, my only clear judgment of the whole operation was that it dehumanized the keepers just as much as those who were kept. I resolved to never belong to either group.

When I returned to my cemetery that evening, I went to Fala's grave and paused there for a moment of prayer. It pleased me to see that her grave had been strewn thickly with flowers from those who had attended her funeral. I fervently hoped that whoever had ended her life in such a brutal fashion suffered similarly at his own end. What sort of a man could murder such a slight woman so cruelly and then so heartlessly dispose of her body under a heap of soiled straw? Her fate weighed on my mind as I cooked my simple meal, and it was probably why I sought my bed that night rather than seeking Olikea on the edges of the forest.

I had hoped to spend a night asleep if not at peace in my own bed. Yet sleep eluded me, and when finally I wrestled my way into it, I dreamed not of Olikea or of Fala, but rather of Orandula, the old god of balances. I stood beside him, helping him to balance scales that were fixed, not with two bowls, but half a dozen in a circle, very similar to the carrion carousel I had seen at Rosse's wedding. The cruel hooks impaled not doves, but people, and worse, they were folk I knew. Dewara was gaffed on one, Tree Woman on another, poor Fala on yet a third, and my mother on a fourth. Around me in a circle, dully awaiting my choice, were Epiny and Spink, Colonel Haren and Olikea, my sister Yaril and even Carsina.

"Choose," the old god insisted in a caw as hoarse as a croaker bird's, and indeed he wore the head of a great croaker bird on his man's body. His red wattles wobbled when he spoke. "You unbalanced it. Now you must make it balance again, Never. You owe me a death. Choose who next feels the talons of death. Or shall it be you?"

It was not an idle question. When I tried to protest that I could not possibly choose, he swung a tool like a hay hook as if he would gather them all. I leaped forward to try to stop him, and felt the cold iron sink into my sternum.

I came awake with a gasp and a jerk. I was trembling all over, with cold as well as fright, and I took a second shock at finding myself standing on the rocky ridge near Tree Woman's stump. I was facing the edge, gazing down on the violation of the road visible to me as a streak of darkness in the silver-leafed bowl of trees that the full moon showed me.

Of late, I had almost become accustomed to sleepwalking. I took several deep breaths and had almost calmed myself to the point of wondering how I would find my way home through the deeply shadowed forest when a man's voice spoke beside me. "So. Which would you choose?"

I gave an involuntary cry and sprang back from the dark figure that suddenly stood beside me. It was too accurate an echo of my nightmare. "I cannot choose!" I cried out, and it was my answer to Orandula that I gave him.

I blinked, and my eyes adjusted to the dimness of the moonlit night. It was not the old god who stood beside me, but Jodoli, the Great Man who had bested me in the Speck village. His eyes shone oddly in the mask of pigment that barred his face. He grinned, and I caught a glimpse of his white teeth. "That is the first sensible thing I have heard you say, Plain-skin. You are right. You cannot choose, because the choice has already been made for you. Yet you swing from side to side, delaying and dawdling, careless of the hurt that you do to everyone. Look down there. Tell me what you see."

I didn't have to look. "I see the road pushing deeper into the forest."

"Yes. I walked down there tonight. I found many sticks driven into the earth, marked with bright cloths. And I found the marks where cold iron has bitten into the trees of our ancestors. The last time I saw such marks, it meant those trees were marked for death. As I walked among them tonight, they cried out to me, 'Save us! Save us!' But I do not think I can. I think that magic is for you to do, if anyone is to work it. Why do you delay? Is it because, as Kinrove has said, that the Endless Dance has failed, and only bloodshed will save us now?"

"Jodoli, you speak of things I do not understand. I do not know this Kinrove, nor of the Endless Dance. Over and over, I have been told that the magic has claimed me, and that something I have done or will do will doom my people and save yours. The idea that I will be the bane of the Gernians gives me great pain. Why must there be this conflict? What do you fear? Our people have come together in trade. I see that the People bring furs down to us, and I see you enjoy honey and fabric and ornaments that you otherwise would not have. What is evil in this? Why must our people be set against one another?"

Jodoli did an odd thing. He reached out a cautious hand and patted my belly firmly. When I lifted my fists, affronted, he stepped back quickly. "I meant no offense. I do not know how you can be so much larger than I am, so filled with the magic, and profess not to know anything. When last we met, I could not grasp how easily I defeated you. I pondered it for many days afterward, and finally I thought that you had mocked me, or used me for your own ends. All these days, I have waited for your vengeance to fall upon me, and it has filled me with anxiety. I thought of running away, but Firada threatened to disgrace me if I fled. Firada said that you were a false Great One and that you had chosen to go back to your own kind. I knew that was not so. I felt the magic running through you when last we met. I dreaded you. Then tonight I was called by the magic, and when I saw that you, too, had been summoned, I dared to speak to you."

I was distracted from his words, for I felt another subtle presence. Tree Woman was not far from where we stood. Someone else's sorrow washed through me and I suddenly longed to visit the stump of her tree, to feel for a time her presence, dwindled as it was.

"Walk down with me," he said, and I flinched as if awakening from a dream. "Ask your question of the eldest ones."

"Down where?"

"There." In the dimness, he pointed at the valley and the road arrowing into it. Without waiting for my answer, he started out, and I found myself following him.

At first there was no path and the going was steep, but Jodoli soon struck a game trail that led us at a slant across the face of the steep hill and down into the valley. I followed him into the deeper darkness under the trees. The moon became a silver memory, and I was surprised at how my eyes adjusted to the darkness. As I followed Jodoli, I noticed a strange thing. For a large fellow, he moved swiftly and was very light on his feet. There was no ponderous sway or heavy tread to his progress. I could hear him breathing through his nose as he hurried along, and I was impressed with how fleetly he moved without tiring.

Then it came to me that I was keeping pace with him. It occurred to me to wonder at how quickly I had moved in my sleep to pass from my cabin to the Tree Woman's ridge in the dark of night. I wondered briefly if we were truly there at all, or if I was walking, not in my sleep, but through a dream of this place.

My impression of unreality was heightened as I became aware of whispers in the stillness. Voices were quietly conversing in the distance. I would have put it down to the soft rustling of leaves, except that there was no breeze and the sounds followed the cadence of speech. I strained to hear what they were saying, but could not pick out individual words, only a tone of worry and anger. As we reached the valley floor and began to move in the darkness of the true forest giants, the whispers grew louder. I suspected that Jodoli was taking me toward a gathering of Specks at the end of the road. I wondered what he intended. I did not wish to be the sole Gernian in a mob of angry Specks. I slowed my steps. "Where are they?" I demanded of him. "I hear them whispering. How many of them are there?"

He halted and looked back at me, puzzled. "They are, as you see, all around us. I have never thought to try to count them." He took a step or two back toward me, and now I could see envy plain on his face. "You can hear them already? Without touching them?"

"I hear whispers. I can't make out the words, but I can hear them whispering."

For a moment he was silent. Then I heard him sigh. "Olikea was right. You are full of the magic, and will always be a more powerful mage than I could ever hope to become. I hear nothing yet. And it has always taken all of my concentration and used up much of my magic to listen for long. Sometimes Firada rebukes me for this, for twice I have used so much magic that I have fainted, and she has had to come searching for me, to find me with my skin lying loose around me. Then she must feed me for days to restore my strength. She says I do no good for my people just by listening and that I waste the magic she labors to build in me. But I think that first I must listen if I am to learn the wisdom of my elders."

"Then you could use up so much magic that you wouldn't be fat anymore?" I asked him, and held my breath to hear his answer. He turned and started walking again. I followed. He spoke over his shoulder.

"There are tales of it happening to Great Ones in the old days of war with the Plains people. You can die from loss of magic, just as you can die from loss of blood. But it seldom happens to us without the mage knowing exactly what he is doing. It takes a great deal of will to burn every bit of magic out of yourself. A mage would have to push past pain and

exhaustion to do it. Ordinarily the mage would lose consciousness before he was completely dead. Then his feeder
could revive him if she were nearby. If not, the Great One
might still perish. That was why Firada was angry with me.
She has invested much of her time in me. I have not managed to give her a daughter. She says that if I die of my own
foolishness, she will not even bother to haul my body to a
tree. That is how angry she becomes. Even when I tell her
that I think this is what the magic wishes of me, she remains
angry. She says that I should be content to do only what the
magic forces me to do rather than seeking out its will. Sometimes," and here he turned to flash me a liar's grin, "I wonder if I would not have been better off with the younger
sister? But of course, I do not ask Firada this! There is
enough rivalry between those two to start a war. Some even
say that Olikea would not even have taken you on except
that she so longed to say that her Great One was larger than
her sister's."

"They say that, do they?" I muttered, and instantly wondered if it were true. It would explain so much. I suddenly felt
disheartened, and was surprised at how bolstered I had felt
at the idea that Olikea was genuinely fond of me. Only a few
days ago I had thought I should tell her that I could never
truly love her. To hear that she did not love me, either, should
not have wounded me. But it did. I felt my pride bleeding.

"There. See how the light breaks through the wounds in the
world's roof, even from the moon. During the day, it is hard
for me to come here. My eyes hurt and I grow dizzy. Now,
those of us who can hear the elders can only come by night to
listen to them. It is hard. We know that even if the Gernians
are turned back, it will be generations before the light is banished from this part of the forest and the People can walk
freely here again."

Ahead of us, the trees had become pillars of darkness
against faint moonlight. We were coming close to where the
King's Road ended. The whispering had grown louder.

"See this?" Jodoli asked me, and with his toe, he scuffed
at a flagged surveyor's stake driven into the earth. "This is
their sign that they mean to cut deeper into the forest. Once

before they came into the forest and drove many of these into the earth, in a line that went far up into the mountains. We pulled them all up. But this one, new planted, means that they intend to try again."

"Yes. It does." I raised my voice to make myself heard above the muttering of a hundred angry voices. Then my own words sounded strangely loud to me. I looked around in the darkness. "Take me to the elders you spoke of. Let me talk to them, and hear from them how they think this can be resolved."

"They think there are only two ways. The Gernians must go away. Or the Gernians must die."

A chill went up my back at his words, but I replied, "Let me speak to them. There must be another way. I know my people well. They will not leave."

"Then they will die. I take no joy in telling you that," Jodoli replied. "This way," he added before I could speak again and led me forward to the very edge of the cut. Jodoli stopped when he was still in the shelter of the woods, but I walked forward as if pulled by a magnet. I stepped out of the forest onto the torn bare earth and looked around me in awe. Behind me, I heard Jodoli's frantic call of, "Come back! Come back!" I ignored it. I had to see for myself what my king's ambition had done.

The huge fallen trees were not completely gone, but the pieces that had blocked the progress of the road had been cut to pieces and hauled away. The ground under my feet was yellow with fragrant fresh sawdust that had been churned and mixed with forest soil by the passage of heavy hooves. The stumps had been removed by a combination of digging, chopping, and burning. Nothing remained of them save a sunken spot in the earth. With my back to the forest, the road stretched out before me, a wide avenue of light. I could see that the repairs to the eroded parts of the road had proceeded well. When the inspection team arrived in a few days, they would be shown a stretch of well-constructed road with fresh progress into the forest. Colonel Haren would be proud.

Then I turned my back on the road and looked into the forest. Squarely in the path of the road stood another immense tree. The preliminary bite of the ax showed pale against the dark bark. As yet, it was a small chip out of such a great trunk, less than a mosquito bite on a man's ankle. And yet that bit of whiteness caught the moonlight and winked back at me, as if sharing an evil joke. Jodoli leaned up against the tree, and the uneven shadows made his dappled body difficult to distinguish from the mottled bark. He had pillowed one cheek against the tree and his eyes were closed, his brow furrowed. Slowly I left the Gernian world of the road and walked back into the Specks' forest.

"Jodoli," I said to him when I stood by him, but he appeared lost in thought. Or asleep. I touched his shoulder.

The whispers rose to a roar and then thinned out to a single voice, a man's voice raised in anguish and outrage: "—and the fear no longer prevails against them. They drug their senses and do not feel it. I have watched them, pale little grubs, burrowing and chewing away at the others. They are gone. Tomorrow I shall begin to die. It will take days for them to kill me. This I know from what happened before. It is too late, perhaps, for you to save me. So I do not ask this for myself, but for those who stand in ranks behind me. Discouragement has not worked. Not even the purification of the fever has awakened them. They dismiss the vision sent to them; they ignore the messengers sent back to them. Only death will stop them."

"What of the plain-skin Great One? He is large with magic. Is not this what he was supposed to do, to turn back the Gernians?"

I felt the wave of disdain that emanated from the trees. The scorn burned me. "Lisana made him. Wise she is, but not the wisest. She said that the magic commanded it, that the magic brought him to her and bade her claim him. We doubted, and many said that she was too young and should not have been set to guard the way. I was one of them. And look what has befallen her. He turned on her, and set her plan awry. He turned our own magic against us. She herself fell to him; now her trunk lies prone. It will be many turns of seasons before she has regained the girth to speak loudly and well again. Does this speak well for Lisana's wisdom?"

Lisana. My heart knew that name. "Tree Woman," I whispered. Bits of knowledge tumbled through my mind and fell into a pattern. These great trees were literally the elders of the Speck people. When we cut them, we were killing their ancient advisers, the ones who preserved the wisdom of centuries past. These were sacred trees to the People. We were at war with them, without intending to be.

"I know what I have to do," I said. My spoken words rang strangely loud in the forest night. "I must return to the Gernians. I will go to my leader tomorrow and tell him that the road must not go through here. Surely there is another path that we can follow over the mountains and to the sea? Lisana was wise." Convincing them of that suddenly seemed very important to me. "She made me to be a bridge between our peoples. I cannot send them all away. But I can speak for you and make them see that cutting these trees is a great affront to the Speck people. I promise, I will do my best to save you, old one."

"Can it be so easy?" Jodoli asked me.

"No!" The spirit of the tree was contemptuous of my offer. "Do not trust him, Jodoli of the People. He is a man of two hearts. He can be true to neither."

I shook my head. "I can be true to both. You will see."

It sounded so simple, there in the moonlit night.

CHAPTER TWENTY-SIX

DANCERS

I ran home as quickly as I could. I could feel the magic burning in my blood with my need to be swift, and I was. It was as if the ground itself hastened me to my destination. I followed a path that was impossibly short, and arrived home before dawn had grayed the skies.

And when I arrived home, I sat up in my bed. I swung my feet over the edge of the bed to the floor, my heart pumping urgency. Then I caught my breath.

For a long time, I sat still. Realities fought in me. I had just run home through the forest. My bare feet were dry and clean. I could not remember opening my cabin door, nor shutting it behind me, nor lying down in my bed again.

One of two things was real. I had dreamed it all, and none of it was real.

Or I had used magic to travel in my dream, and it was entirely real.

I began to breathe as if I had truly run that distance. Sweat broke out on my back and brow. A trembling ran through me. It became a shudder, and suddenly I was clutching myself, teeth chattering and quivering like a leaf. Waves of trembling passed through me as if I would tear myself apart. I felt hot and then cold, and then as suddenly as it had all come on, it ebbed away. My breathing slowed. I accepted it, whatever "it" was. I decided that however the knowledge had come to me, it was real. I would act on it.

I bathed, I shaved, and I dressed in my best uniform. I knew I had consumed magic to make that swift journey home. I knew the signs of it now, not just the ravenous hunger that bread could not assuage, but also that my trousers were almost loose on me. Almost. I still decided that I would not risk their multiple seams by straddling Clove's broad back. I hitched my big horse to the cart and drove into town just as the sun was coming up, feeling fired with purpose and even hope. If I could convince the colonel that rerouting the road, difficult as it might be, would put an end to our differences with the Speck and stop the evil magic pouring out of the forest, then it was quite possible that I would have saved us all. I'd be a hero. My smile twisted as I thought the word. A fat hero, and no one would ever know of my heroics. But that wouldn't mean I hadn't done it.

It had been days since I'd last dared go into town. I was surprised by the changes I saw. The Speck trade village was still set up on the outskirts of Gettys, but it was Gettys itself that amazed me. A change had come over the town. It was more than fresh paint and gravel in the worst ruts and potholes, though those were changes enough. Cavalla-green bunting festooned the doors and windows of shops and taverns. Windows had been washed. But even those changes were not what impressed me. Even this early in the day, the people moving on the street had lost the tension and weariness that I'd come to accept as a normal part of Gettys. If anything, the citizenry seemed relaxed, even lethargic. Two women, their best bonnets lavishly decorated with green ribbons, strolled slowly arm-in-arm down the street. I slowed

Clove to a walk, for they seemed scarcely aware of our approach, smiling and nodding to one another as they talked. I guided Clove around them, and we continued on our way.

I had to divert from my normal route to the colonel's office. The street in front of headquarters had been roped off. A dais had been erected in the middle of the street, and a squad of men were setting benches out in rows around it. On the arch erected above the dais, a sign welcomed General Brodg and General Prode, as well as a list of lords. I was surprised to see Prode's name there. He had been the king's commander in the east before General Brodg had taken over. I wondered if the presence of that old general was intended to honor Brodg, or as a subtle rebuke that more progress had been made in Gettys and on the King's Road in the days before Brodg had taken over.

I left Clove and the cart on a side street and walked to the headquarters door. The paint on the building was so fresh I could smell it. The brass doorknob was slick with polish. I had to grip it firmly to turn it. Stepping inside the door, I received another surprise. The sergeant's domain had been completely refurbished. The walls were newly painted, the wood of the desk gleamed with linseed oil, and there were plump cushions on the waiting chairs. The shelves were dust-free and lined with books and manuals. At the sergeant's desk sat a lieutenant I'd never seen: he looked as freshly renovated as the rest of the room. His buttons shone, and his shirt was so starched it looked painful. His pale scalp contrasted strangely with his tanned face: it was obvious his hair had been cut very recently.

I drew myself up straight at the sight of him, expecting to be rebuked for entering so casually. Instead he gave me a level look and asked solemnly, "Do you have an appointment, soldier?"

"No, sir, I do not. In the past, the colonel has been so kind as to allow me to report without an appointment. I've brought information that I think might be useful to him, sir."

"I see," he replied absently. He looked down at a paper on his desk, blinked at it, and then back up at me. He gave me a vague smile. I kept my soldier's demeanor and waited. He picked up the pen from his desk, fiddled with it for a bit, and then asked me gently, "You want to talk with Colonel Haren, then?"

There was a faint waft of rum on his breath. That widened my eyes. Drinking on duty? No. Probably the Gettys dose that Ebrooks had told me about. I found myself wondering about the two placid women I'd see strolling down the street earlier. I cleared my throat. "Yes sir, if that's possible. I'd like to speak with Colonel Haren."

He leaned back suddenly in his chair and out flung a generous arm at the colonel's door. "Be my guest, then, soldier. Be my guest."

Feeling furtive as a mouse under a cat's stare, I walked to the colonel's door and tapped on it, expecting that at any moment the lieutenant would change his mind. But he seemed to have forgotten about me entirely, and was giving his full attention to wiping the tip of his pen. At my second tap, I heard the colonel's muffled invitation to enter. I opened the door and walked in.

I was almost relieved to find the room largely unchanged. There were the same layered carpets on the floor, the same tapestry-covered walls. The fire burned smaller, but there seemed to be more light in the room because all the lamp chimneys had been freshly cleaned. All the horizontal surfaces had been cleared of clutter. Colonel Haren himself, nattily attired in his uniform and a gleaming pair of black boots, sat bolt upright in a chair beside a small table. At the sight of me, he exclaimed, "Oh, for the good god's sake, what are you doing here?"

I came to attention. "Sir, I've come to request a few moments of your time. I have information about our problems with the road building and the Specks. I think it may lead to a resolution of our difficulties with pushing the road through."

He lifted one eyebrow at me. "Where have you been, man? The problem with pushing the road through was solved several weeks ago. Dr. Dowder's research has finally yielded fruit. Properly fortified, our road crews have made more progress in the last few weeks than they previously had in the last two years. That problem is solved!

"You, however, present an entirely different problem. Look at your uniform, man! Why is there a seam up the front of each trouser leg? That is not regulation. And your general physical conformation leaves more to be desired than I could possibly list at this moment." He shook his head at me and made a decision. "Back to the cemetery, trooper. The inspection team is scheduled for a two-week visit here, with a possible extension to a month if they feel they need more time to assess our performance. Busy yourself at the cemetery for a month. And due to the nature of your duties there, I give you permission . . . no, I *require* that you wear civilian clothing to prevent soiling your uniform. And in the event that our inspection team sees fit to visit the cemetery, you are to, uh, busy yourself elsewhere. Do you take my drift, soldier?"

I took his insult as well, but I swallowed it. There was more at stake here than my pride. "I do, sir. And I'll see that the inspection team does not see me or identify me as a member of your regiment." I kept all anger from my voice. "But before I vanish, sir, I would like to give you some information about the Specks and the trees at the end of the road."

"Well, then, do it, soldier, and then clear out. The inspection team arrived last night. In a very short time, I'm to join them in the officers' mess for a special breakfast. I can't be late."

"Yes, sir." I suddenly realized that I hadn't formulated how I was going to disclose what I knew to him without admitting that I'd been going into the forest among the Specks. I thought of passing it off as a rumor I'd heard, but knew that would be a betrayal of trust. I'd told Jodoli and the elder that I would come here and present their case to my colonel. I had to do it. "Last night, sir, I was in the forest with Jodoli. He's a Speck Great One. We might call him a wizard or a mage. He's a reservoir of magic for his people."

I paused, hoping for some sign of interest. Colonel Haren drummed his fingers on the tabletop. "Yes, soldier, I'm sure he is," he replied sarcastically. "And this Great One told you?"

"The trees at the end of the road, the ones marked for cutting, are very important to the Specks. They hold the elder spirits of the Speck people. Their advisers. Like ancestor spirits. The trees are important to them. Holy." I kept explaining, trying different words for what I was trying to convey. His eyes had narrowed when I first spoke of the trees. With every description I added, they seemed to go stonier.

When my words staggered to a halt, he asked me sternly, "Is this your information? Is this ALL of it?"

"Yes, sir. Well, not quite all. The fear we feel at the end of the road, the discouragement that drenches this town: it's all Speck magic. If we stopped threatening the trees, it would go away. If we backed up and surveyed a completely different route through the mountains, one that didn't cut through their sacred groves, Gettys would be a peaceful place again."

He made a contemptuous noise. He shook his head, then gave me a painfully incredulous smile. "Soldier. If we stopped trying to build the road, Gettys would be a near-useless place again. A place to come to trade for furs each summer, and a place to leave again. Gettys' only future is if the King's Road is pushed through the Barrier Mountains. If it goes through, we become the last civilized stopping place on that route. If it's not, if we stop cutting the trees . . . pray tell, what purpose do we have in being here?"

I blinked, my heart sinking. "Then . . . you already knew the trees were sacred to the Specks? That they house ancestor spirits?"

"Oh, please. Yes, of course we know of their quaint superstitions. If you have more details on them, then take them to Dr. Frye. He will listen to them carefully, write down your every word, and send it off to the queen herself. He hopes to curry favor with her by supplying tales for her collection of native lore. Burvelle, I'm surprised at you. The last time we spoke for any length of time, you convinced me that your father was mistaken in his evaluation of you. You seemed enterprising and thoughtful. Now the town simmers with rumors of your whoring, to the point at which twice ladies have come to me presenting petitions to bring charges against you. I was still willing to give you the benefit of the doubt, but here you come to my door on the day of an important inspection to tell me tales of 'ancestor trees.' Try to think about it like an educated man, Burvelle. After all, it was believed you were academy material at one time!"

I held my temper with difficulty. "Sir, I think I understand this situation far better than anyone else. If we provoke the Specks by cutting those trees, they will rise against us. They already perceive that we are at war with them. This will push them into making it more deadly. You yourself warned me that I should not antagonize them. Cutting their trees will do far more than that!"

He laughed. "The Specks? At war with us? Yearly their trade with us increases. Do people at war with one another trade together? Deadly? Oh, come, come. You can't be serious. I told you what happened the last time we 'fought' them. It was a slaughter for them. Have you ever seen a Speck up close, soldier? They can't even bear to be out in the sun for more than an hour. They run about town draped in veils with flowers stuck in them. They have no weapons. They barely have tools! And you would have me fear a Speck uprising?" He cocked his head at me. "I've told you before. The best way to deal with them is to let them know what we intend to do, and then do it. Calmly. Without threats. Without violence. They will not be happy with us at first, but once they see that nothing bad comes of it, they'll accept it. We've been out here for years, young man, and I think that makes us better qualified to know how to deal with them. What makes you think you understand the situation so well? Have you had unauthorized contact with the Specks?" His gaze pierced me accusingly.

I was in it now. Might as well swim as wade. "Some, sir. Yes. I've spoken to them about this."

"And they told you that if we cut the trees, they would attack us?"

"Not in so many words, sir, no. But that was my understanding of it."

"Do they have weapons that you know of? Trained warriors? A strategy?"

Honesty made me look a fool. "Weapons, no, sir, not in the sense that we use the term. Warriors, again, no. But a strategy that demands neither, yes, sir, they do. They have the plague, sir. They've been using the plague against us for years. I believe they spread it with their Dust Dance. The infection is deliberate."

"Preposterous!" He spat out the word, and his mustache quivered with indignation. "The plague is indigenous to this country, soldier. Do you know what that means? It means that everyone who comes to live here gets it sooner or later. The Specks get it, too. It's a part of living here on the far borders. We know the plague will come with high summer. It always does and—"

I interrupted my superior officer. "And do the Specks always do the Dust Dance shortly before it hits?"

He stared at me for an instant. I read my answer in his outraged glare. They did. Dancing Specks flinging dust did not fit with his concept of an enemy attack on the fort. "Your father was right," he said stiffly. "You're a fool. You'll always blame your own misfortunes on someone else, won't you? I had thought him wrong. I had even considered promoting you. I should have known. Who can know his son better than his own father?" He took a breath and I saw a strange transformation. His eyes went from steely to pitying. "I don't suppose you can help it. You believe your own ridiculous theories."

As his insults left me breathless with rage, he nodded at me and spoke in carefully measured words. "Let me point this out to you, Burvelle. When the trees fall and the Specks perceive that no disaster follows, they will more readily abandon their superstitious ways and enter the modern world. It is to their ultimate benefit that we take down those trees. When the road goes through and trade follows it, why, think of what it will bring to them. If you want to help us with the Speck problem, speak to them of the benefits of the road. Encourage their natural hunger for what civilization can bring to them. But don't humor their superstitious fears.

"But for now, get yourself out of sight. I don't need our visiting dignitaries to see you or hear you, and I certainly don't need the females of Gettys stirred to wrath by your presence at this time. Off you go now. Dismissed. Good-bye."

With his final words, he had lost interest in me. He had risen, walked to a mirror on the wall, and was carefully smoothing his mustache with one hand as he shooed me out of the room with the other. I made one last effort. "Sir, I think," I began.

He cut off my words. "No. You don't. *I* think. *You* obey orders. Dismissed, trooper."

I went. I didn't speak to the lieutenant as I left. I didn't trust myself to say anything. The colonel had known. They'd all known. I'd thought I'd been so clever piecing it together. But they'd known of the significance of the trees and they didn't care, because keeping Gettys on the road east was far more important to them. More important than what it did to the men to be kept on such a discouraging task. More important than felling trees that held the ancestral wisdom of a people.

I found I was nearly shaking with rage. My heart pumped magic like a poison through me. It took every bit of control I had to refuse to let my anger focus on those I wished to punish. It would solve nothing, I knew. If Colonel Haren dropped in his tracks tomorrow, there would be another man just like him right behind him. As I approached my cart, I noted with displeasure that Sergeant Hoster was standing near Clove, apparently inspecting my horse's harness. I wanted a fight so badly. It would have been such a relief to put my fist in his perpetually sneering face. By a vast effort of will, I walked around the wagon to approach the seat from the other side rather than jostling Sergeant Hoster out of the way. "Good day," I greeted him coldly, climbing up on the cart seat.

"In a hurry, soldier?" he asked me. His eyes glinted bright, as if he were seeing something that delighted him.

"Colonel Haren's orders. He wants me to go immediately to the cemetery." I gathered up Clove's reins.

Hoster sneered at me. "He's not the only one who thinks you should go straight to the cemetery." He gave a "haw" at his own joke and then added cleverly. "Nice harness on your horse, soldier."

I tried to find the insult in his words. "It's just a harness."

"That it is. That it is." He stepped away from Clove.

I shook my head and drove away.

It took me longer to get out of town than I expected. The streets were thronged with people converging on the dais. Half of them walked in a Gettys tonic daze; the others glared at me as if they could not believe my stupidity in trying to get a horse and cart through such a crowded street. The sun was well up now, and the day promised to be a sweltering one. I thought longingly of the forest shade as Clove picked his way through masses of people that grudgingly gave way to him. I was uncomfortably aware of turned heads and stares, but seated on my cart, there was no way to avoid scrutiny. The colonel's remarks about the accusations against me had rattled me almost as much as his cavalier attitude toward the Specks and their trees.

We finally reached the gates of the fort. In the wider streets outside, there were fewer pedestrians. I was able to persuade Clove to a trot and we soon rolled out of town, leaving only our dust hanging in the air behind us. I wished I could get more speed out of him, but Clove was a creature of endurance rather than swiftness. We rattled along, and my anger burned inside me. I was furious with my commander, and soon that anger spread to include all my countrymen. My mind raced ahead of my body, planning how I would return to my cottage, unharness Clove, and immediately go into the forest in search of Jodoli. The news I must give him shamed me. Plans for how I could stop the road's progress and whom I could enlist in my cause vied with the creeping suspicion that I was about to do something treasonous. I thrust that consideration aside. I insisted to myself that stopping the road until it could be completely rerouted away from Gettys would benefit both the Gernians and the People. A dim hope came to me. After I'd warned Jodoli that we must take steps today to save the ancestral trees, I would find a way to speak to Dr. Frye. Colonel Haren's sarcastic suggestion might actually bear fruit for me if the queen herself could be swayed to our view.

Ahead of us in the rutted road, I saw a lady trudging along alone. It struck me as strange that on a day of festivities in Gettys, she was headed away from the town. Her

bonneted head was bent against the sun's heat, and she held
her blue skirts daintily free of the road's dirt. I admired her
tidy figure from behind, and then swung Clove wide so that
we might not choke her with dust as we passed. I thought I
had done well, but as I passed her, she shouted at me. It was
only when I looked over my shoulder that I recognized that
the lady was Amzil. I pulled Clove in and waited as she hurried up to us.

"Nevare! I was coming out to see you!" As she spoke, she
climbed up on the cart seat beside me.

I shifted over as far as I could. I was still aware that she
had to perch on the edge of the seat. I could not help notice
how prettily she was dressed. There was not a smudge nor
patch to be seen on the blue dress she wore. Even the white
cuffs and collar were clean as fresh snow. A wide black belt
cinched her waist, and somehow emphasized both the swell
of her hips and the lift of her bosom.

"Well?" she said tartly, and I realized I'd been staring
at her.

I lowered my eyes. "I'm sorry. You just look so pretty today. So clean and fresh."

A long silence followed my words. I gave a wary sideways
glance to see how angry she was. There were two spots of
red on her cheeks. At my glance she muttered a stiff, "Thank
you."

Silence fell until I prompted her, "You were coming out
to see me?" Whatever her errand was, I decided I needed
to dissuade her from it. I needed to get to the forest, and I
could not very well just walk off and leave her in my cabin.
Telling her I had no time for visitors seemed harsh, and setting her back down in the road to walk back to town even
harsher. "I have a great deal of work I have to do today," I
began. I tried to think of a gracious way to phrase it, but it
came out bluntly. "I don't have much time for a visit."

She gave a sniff and sat up a bit straighter on the seat.
"Well, neither do I, sir! I'm actually here on an errand. I don't
know why it would be of great concern to you, but Lieutenant Spinrek wanted to you to know that the Specks are going
to perform the Dust Dance today. He called me aside to give

me the news. He thought it important enough to volunteer to mind my children for me while I came out here to give it to you. I was not pleased to let him do it, for Mistress Epiny still goes green as glass at the sight of food, and the children were frantic at the thought of missing the music and the Specks dancing and all the rest of the festivities."

"The Dust Dance? The Specks are doing the Dust Dance today?"

"It's part of the welcoming ceremony for the inspection team. The Specks wished to perform for them."

Before she had finished speaking, I had slapped the reins on Clove's back. I turned him in a tight circle and urged him to a canter. "We have to get back to town right away. I have to stop them."

She gave a small shriek, then held tightly to the back of the seat with one hand while clutching at her bonnet with the other. She raised her voice to shout over the rattling of the wagon. "Slow down! It's too late to stop them. You probably won't even get to see them dance. I told the lieutenant that, but he insisted that I go and tell you anyway." Then, as we hit a hard bump, she abandoned her bonnet to its fate and clutched at my arm. "Nevare! Slow down! It's already too late, I tell you."

I paid her no heed. "It's life or death, Amzil. The Dust Dance is how the Specks spread the plague! Everyone who watches that dance and breathes in the dust will catch it. And from them, it will spread to others."

"That's crazy!" she shouted back at me. "Nevare, pull him in! Slow down or I'll jump. This is crazy!"

She sounded so sincere that I heeded her. As soon as Clove dropped down to a trot, Amzil let go of my arm and resumed her grip on her bonnet.

"Amzil, I know it sounds crazy, but it's true. It's how I caught the Speck plague. Spink . . . Lieutenant Spinrek caught it the same way. That's what I believe. I think it's why they do the Dust Dance. To infect us and kill us."

As the meaning of those words sank into my awareness, I suddenly felt doubly betrayed. Yes, it was why they danced, and it was especially why they danced today. They would kill nobles and generals as well as poor soldiers. The inspection team would be their targets, even as the academy had once been their target. Each time, I had unknowingly given them the information they needed to kill most effectively. I felt doubly betrayed by both my peoples, first the Gernians and now the Specks. They would find ways to hurt one another, and I would feel the pain of both sides.

Clove gave a snort, shook his head, and slowed to a walk. I let him. I thought of the only people I could protect and turned abruptly to Amzil. "Listen to me. Please believe how important this is. I'm taking you back to Lieutenant Spinrek's home. You'll have to show me the way, and I don't want to pass through any crowded streets. Once we are there, you have to go inside and *stay* there. Do you understand how important it is? You have to stay inside with your children and not go out into the city. By tomorrow, if I am correct, people will begin to get sick. Stay away from them. Keep your children away from them."

She was staring at me as if I were insane and possibly dangerous. I took a moment to get control of my voice. In a calmer voice, I told her, "Spink has these little bottles of water from his home in Bitter Springs. He thinks they may be a cure for the plague, or that they might prevent people from catching it. Ask him to set some aside for you and the children. And ask him to send a courier immediately to his brother, no matter the cost, pleading that Bitter Springs water be sent to Gettys in as great an amount as possible."

"Spink?"

The way she said his name made me wonder if she had heard anything else I'd said. "Lieutenant Spinrek," I amended, and muttered, "We knew each other a long time ago."

She gave a curt nod. Then, staring straight down the road, she asked me, "And how are you related to Mistress Epiny?"

"I—"

She cut me off while I was still deciding whether to act bewildered or to lie. "You look alike around the eyes. And she often speaks to her husband of her fears about what might have befallen Nevare." Her voice went hard. "I never would have taken you for a cruel man. She's with child and having a bad time of it, and you leave her in anxiety, both of you. I don't know who is more despicable, you or her husband."

"You don't understand. It would ruin her reputation to be connected to me. It would bring her great unhappiness. It's better that for now she knows nothing."

"So that when you tell her later, she can feel an even greater fool? Most folk around town don't know your name. They just call you the Cemetery Sentry. But sooner or later, she'll put it all together. She's not dim, that one, though you seem to treat her as if she is."

I dropped all effort at pretense. "My cousin is not dim. But in many ways, she is too quick to risk herself. I won't have her put herself in danger for my sake, especially when I do not think it would truly help me at all. All she could do is stain her reputation with mine, to no good end. I love her too much to allow her to do that to herself."

I had not expected to speak with such vehemence, and when I uttered my feelings aloud, I was surprised at the strength of them. I think Amzil was, too, for she looked both taken aback and chastened. After a moment, she said more quietly, "I think I understand you better now."

"Well. Good. And if we are finished with that, please let me know that you understood my earlier words as well. After the Dust Dance, at most a few days will pass before Speck plague sweeps through Gettys. I do not think we can stop it. Quarantine yourself and your children, and please do not let my cousin go out and risk herself. Remind her that if she does, she risks her child as well. That should get her attention."

"I did hear you," Amzil replied a bit testily. "And I will tell the lieutenant about the water and the courier. Mistress Epiny has told me of her journey here from Bitter Springs. I do not think you can expect that water to arrive soon." She shook her head at me. "If you thought it worked, why did not they immediately start bringing it in to Gettys? If you know the Dust Dance could spread the plague, why did you not warn everyone ahead of time?"

"We're not sure the water will work. It seemed to work for Spink and Epiny, and they did bring some when they came, as much as Epiny could manage, actually. As for the Dust Dance . . . we, that is, I believe it spreads the plague. I haven't had much luck in convincing anyone else of that."

We had reached the outskirts of Gettys town. The streets were still empty. Everyone, I suddenly knew, would have converged inside the fort to watch the welcome speeches and ceremonies. As we grew closer, my heart sank. Where the Speck tent village had been there was little more than trampled earth. This morning, Clove and I had ridden past it. Now it was gone. They had melted away, leaving no sign of where they had gone. I suspected I knew why they had gone. They'd be well away from Gettys before the deadly dust rode the breezes. "I think we're too late," I said quietly. "They've left. And Specks don't usually travel during the day, only in the evenings or nights."

"Nevare, I believe you," Amzil said suddenly. "Take me home. I'll keep my children in and do my best to keep Mistress Epiny there, too. I won't be able to do much about the lieutenant. But I've heard that folks who have had Speck plague once don't catch it again."

"Most of them don't," I agreed. "But some do. Such as Spink and Epiny."

As we were passing through the gate to Gettys, I saw something that chilled me to the bone. Seven Specks, draped in their encompassing network of vines, leaves, and flowers, were leaving the fort, walking swiftly. I could not see their faces or even tell their sexes, but their bare speckled feet were gray with dust. I wondered if it was the dust of the dance or of the road. I felt a sudden urge to leap down on them from the wagon seat and kill them all.

I could not see their faces, but as if they could feel the malice of my thoughts or sense the anger boiling the magic though my blood, their draped heads turned toward me. I stared at them, feeling coldness build in me. How many people would die from the dust they had spread today? Amzil put her hand on my wrist. "Nevare. Let them go. Take me home." The sudden urgency in her voice swayed me. I wondered what she had feared I would do. I could not stop what they had begun. And how could I pretend that they were any worse or better than my own folk? I had precious little time in which to act. A few people I cared about could be spared.

As we went through the gate, the sentries exchanged a glance and then waved me through. Despite their freshly cleaned and pressed uniforms, they were not behaving like real guards. They were too busy craning their necks to see what was going on down the street. Up on the dais, someone was talking loudly, and his every pause was punctuated by applause. I glanced back over my shoulder. The Specks were separating, each going a different way. Did they see me look at them? Perhaps, for they all sprinted away like startled rabbits. If my suspicions needed any confirmation, that was enough. I gritted my teeth.

"Go left here," Amzil said quietly. "We can get around the crowds that way. I want to get home as soon as possible."

She guided me and we threaded our way through the back streets of the fort. I'd never really explored the area where the officers were housed; I'd never had reason to. The structures dated from the fort's earlier days and were tidily built. Most of them seemed to have a fresh coat of paint, but that sprucing up could not completely disguise years of previous neglect. Wooden steps sagged, window shutters were missing slats, and the few gardens had the bare, brave look of fresh effort. The housing for the junior officers and their families was humbler and had not been as well built. "Pull in!" Amzil warned me, and at the corner of a street, I hauled Clove to a halt.

"I'll get down here," she said, "so Mistress Epiny does not see you dropping me off." Before I could start to climb down to assist her, she gave a little jump and landed in the dust of the streets. Her skirts billowed out around her as she landed, and for a moment I had a glimpse of her stockinged ankles.

"Keep the children in," I reminded her as I took up Clove's reins.

"I will," she promised and then, holding up a hand to bid me wait, she asked, "What are you going to do?"

I almost laughed. "I'm going back to the cemetery. I've got a lot of graves to dig. I may as well get started today."

My words startled her. "You really do believe the Dust Dance will bring on the plague in the next few days." Her brow furrowed. "Aren't you going to warn Colonel Haren?"

"I saw him this morning. I had my say then, and he didn't believe me. I doubt he'll believe me now. He'd only be angry to find I'd defied his direct order and come back into town. I'm supposed to be hiding out in the cemetery so his visitors don't see me. I'm an embarrassment to the regiment, you know."

She squinted her eyes looking up at me. "Do you still care about things like that?"

"Of course I do." I shook Clove's reins. "I'm a soldier son."

CHAPTER TWENTY-SEVEN

THE AMBUSH

I guided Clove back through the streets the same way we had come. My mind seethed and my blood simmered with both unfocused anger and frustrated magic. My peoples were set on killing each other off. The moment I recognized that thought in my mind, I realized how much the magic had changed me. Not so long ago, I had belonged to only one people. At one time I would have shared Colonel Haren's conviction that the road and trade would bring good to the Specks, and like him I would have rejected the idea that the trees could be anything more than trees. Yet the part of me that had been initially stolen and made Speck was now as integral to my self as the soldier son was. Every day, his memories surfaced more clearly in my mind. Removing those trees was the equivalent of burning all

Gernian libraries. The Specks might go on without them, but they would lose their roots.

Yet at that moment I did not feel torn between my two peoples; my selves were united in how furious I was with both factions and how desperately I wished I could withdraw from them both entirely. We rattled through the near-empty back streets and toward the gate. The sentries annoyed me by stopping me.

"Where you headed, soldier?"

I was in no mood for their sudden vigilance. They'd let me in unchallenged, but would stop me on my way out? "Where do I always go? Back to the cemetery. It's my post."

They exchanged a glance and a nod. "Right. You may pass."

I slapped the reins on Clove's broad back, jolting him up to a trot. I left the fort behind and rattled my way out of town. Every time Clove tried to drop down to a walk, I nagged him on. I wanted the noise of the empty cart and the jostling and the dust. The violence of it suited my mood. As I left the town behind me, I urged him up to a canter. The cart jolted and bounded, bouncing in and out of potholes. I passed two struggling trees beside a failed farm. A flock of black-and-white croaker birds had found something dead by the trees. They rose, screaming their displeasure, as I careened past them.

I knew I invited disaster and didn't care. The anger was building inside me and I longed to have an outlet for it. Everyone was acting in absolute certainty and righteousness. Was I the only one who could see how wrong both sides were? Destruction and death awaited everyone, and I saw no way to defuse any of it. The lack of a focus for my anger made it a churning, clawing dragon inside me.

Time after time, Tree Woman had insisted to me that the magic had chosen me because I was the one who could do something that would send my people away from these lands. Over and over, she had tried to wrangle from me what it was that I had done or was going to do. I'd always thought her eager for the destruction of my folk; now I wondered if she didn't believe that driving the Gernian away was the only way to save us all. Perhaps she was right. Perhaps the only way to avoid the coming conflict was to make the Gernians retreat from the land of the People.

But I knew of nothing I could do to cause that. The coming month would bring me dozens of plague victims to bury, and would see the felling of the Specks' ancestral trees. No one would triumph. The ancestor trees would fall and the Speck culture with them. The Gernians would fall to the disease the Speck had deliberately sown among them. Death, death, death for everyone. Magic thrummed in me, drumming through my veins with each beat of my heart, but I could not save a single soul from the misery ahead.

Clove tried to slow down again. Sweat streaked his back and flanks, and I felt shame for how hard I'd driven him for no good reason. The anger that had coursed through me suddenly subsided into hopelessness. I let him slow, and as the rattle of the cart decreased, my ears picked up the thunder of other hoofbeats. I glanced over my shoulder, and had a single, fleeting glimpse of mounted men coming up behind me, fast. I saw a muzzle flash.

Something was very wrong. I was breathing dust instead of air. A great crack had opened in my head, and light was pouring into my brain. It hurt. I tried to lift my hand to cover the crack, but my fingers only feebly twitched at dry dust. Every breath I sucked in pulled dust with it. I knew I should lift my head from the ground. It was too much trouble.

"Think he's dead?" someone asked me. I couldn't work my mouth. Someone answered for me.

"Good as dead. This could be big trouble. Damn it, Jace. Slowing him down is one thing. Killing him is another."

"He was trying to get away. You seen how he run that horse. Hoster said he might try to get rid of it if we didn't get it right away. I had to shoot." Jace was angry, not repentant.

"Calm down. No one's going to care if we prove he's guilty."

"I wasn't trying to kill him. When he slowed, it spoiled my aim. His own damn fault for turning to look back at us."

Someone else spoke. "I didn't bargain for this. I'm sorry I got mixed up in this whole mess. I'm going back to town."

"We all are," the first voice decided. "Jace, you drive the cart."

Horses' hooves striking the earth. Wheels turning. Then silence. I tried closing my eyes to keep the glaring light out of my skull, but my eyes were already closed. It just went on hurting and hurting. I tried to be unconscious or asleep. I failed. Lights bloomed across my vision and then faded. Pain burst and ebbed with the light. I couldn't make sense of what had happened to me. Trying to think hurt too much. Stillness without thinking still hurt. The intensity of the pain suddenly increased. The throb of my heart was like a wave slamming against the inside of my skull.

Several days of agony seemed to pass. Then I could move my hand. I put it up to touch my head. Blood. A flap of scalp. The hardness of bone beneath my wet, questing fingers, and some rough splinters. The rip of the bullet's passage was a ragged groove across the back of my skull. I was dying. Time stopped. It seemed impossible that dying could take so long. Perhaps time dragged only because it hurt so badly, and because I was waiting for it to stop. Dully, I began to count the throbs that corresponded to the beating of my heart. I reached twenty. One hundred. Two hundred. I felt my eyeballs pressing against my eyelids, as if they wanted to leave my skull. Five hundred. A thousand. I managed to turn my head so I wasn't breathing in so much dust. One thousand, five hundred. I heard the caw of a croaker bird. I felt the scuff of earth and the brush of its wings as it landed beside me. I braced myself to feel the slash of its greedy beak.

"You owe me a life," Orandula reminded me.

You can have this one. I no longer cared which god took my soul. I just wanted the pain to stop.

"Give me a life that is yours to give before you die."

The croaker bird had the voice of a nagging little old lady. I didn't have the strength to frame a thought in response to it. It didn't matter. I was dying.

Damn. I'd lost my count. I started over again at one thousand five hundred. I knew I'd gotten at least that far. A fly buzzed heavily near my ear. I lifted a hand and brushed it away. No distractions. My heart pounded in my chest, and I felt the throb of the moving blood in every part of me.

When I reached five thousand, I opened my eyes a crack. They didn't feel quite as tight against the lids as they had. I could see dust and scrub brush. I don't know how much longer I lay there before I gave in and admitted I wasn't going to die right away. The pain was still intense, and when I sat up, the world spun around me so violently that I was sure I was going to vomit. Three croaker birds took sudden alarm as I moved, but by the time I recovered from my vertigo, they had resettled around me. They were large birds, and their red wattles always made them look as if they had just finished a bloody feast. I'd never realized their eyes were yellow. "Go away," I told them feebly. I waited for them to answer, but none spoke. One hopped three steps closer and tilted his head to stare at me. I stared back.

After a longer time, I lifted a hand again to explore the wound where the bullet had grazed me. Blood was caked thick on the back of my head. My hand came away sticky and black. *Don't look. Don't think about it.* I surveyed the world around me instead. It was afternoon at least. There was no traffic on the road; everyone would have gone to the fort for the welcoming ceremony. No help was going to come to me.

After five attempts, I remained standing. I wasn't standing straight, but I was upright. I looked around. The road was there, but my distance vision was fuzzy. I couldn't decide which direction led back to the fort and which led to the cemetery. I could feel myself swaying. If I could just find the cart, Clove would probably take me home. I couldn't turn my head. I had to turn my whole body in a slow circle, looking for my horse and cart. It took me a very long time to realize that neither Clove nor the cart were there. I was badly injured, probably dying, and on foot.

And suddenly I didn't care

I walked. Not quickly. I followed the rutted road. The landscape was blurry. At some point I found I had to hold up my trousers. My belt had loosened, and I could not make my eyes focus well enough to tighten it. I clutched the top of my trousers and staggered on.

Slowly my equilibrium came back to me. I walked more steadily. My vision began to clear. I felt grateful when I saw the sign for the cemetery and left the main road to follow the trail leading up to it. I lifted my hand to the back of my head and felt about squeamishly. It was undeniably tender, but I no longer felt torn flesh or scored bone. The magic was healing me. I couldn't decide whether to be grateful or angry.

When I reached my cabin, I filled a basin with water and wet a rag. I gingerly dabbed at my wound. The rag came away dark with clotted blood and small tufts of hair. I dipped it in the water and rinsed it clear. When I wrung it out, I felt a splinter. I plucked it loose and looked at the tiny fragment. Bone. From the back of my skull. I felt ill. I dipped the rag again, squeezed it out, and washed all the blood, scraps of dead flesh, and loose hair from the wound. When I was finished, I could feel a hairless stripe of soft bare skin across the back of my head. I wondered if it would be a scar.

The healing had consumed a lot of my magic. I could tell by how my clothes hung loose on me. I moved my belt buckle two notches tighter. Then, carefully not thinking, I dumped the dirty water from the basin, washed it and the rag, and hung the rag on my laundry line to dry. I was hungry, I realized, and the moment I acknowledged it, my hunger flared to red and ravenous. I went back into my cabin and began rummaging through my pantry. I longed for a certain pale mushroom that Olikea had once brought me, and those hanging, thin-skinned berries. I longed for them above all else. But what I had were some potatoes and an onion and the end of a side of bacon. They would have to do.

I think my injured body recovered faster than my jumbled mind. I was frying chopped potatoes and onion with a bit of fat bacon before it dawned on me that someone had tried to kill me. They'd stolen my horse and cart. They'd left me for dead. I put a pinch of salt on the cooking food and stirred it again. What did I remember? Men on horses behind me. Long guns. The flash. I didn't even remember the sound, only the flash of black powder igniting.

Someone had shot me. Shot me! They'd left me for dead, and stolen my horse and cart. The bastards! And in that arrowing of fury, I felt the magic flare in me and then subside. Too late I regretted that surge of hatred and vindictiveness. I knew I didn't have the strength to call it back, and suspected it was already too late to think of doing it. I sat down heavily on the floor by the hearth, feeling as if I'd just burned the last bit of energy in my body. I wanted to fall over on my side and sleep. By an extreme effort of will, I managed to take the pan of food from the fire before it burned. Once I had it on the floor, I ate from it, using the stirring spoon, with the single-mindedness of a starving dog. When the last strand of translucent onion had been scraped from the pan's bottom and consumed, I crawled into my bed, pulled my blanket over me, closed my eyes, and slept.

And slept. I woke to a foreign dawn, blinked at it, and closed my eyes again. I awoke to darkness, staggered to my water bucket, and lowered my face to drink like a horse. Chin dripping, I stood in the closed darkness of my cabin. I thought I heard someone call my name softly, but I ignored it. I found my way back to my bed, fell into it, and slept again. Dreams tried to break into that rest. I banished them. I heard my name spoken gently, then with urgency, and finally with both command and annoyance. I pushed her away. She battered at the edges of my sleep, but I pulled it tight around me and would not admit her.

I rose with the next dawn, famished, my mouth dry and sticky. My body stank with my own sweat. I crunched through my last two potatoes raw, for my hunger would not wait for me to cook them. I heated what water remained in my barrel, washed myself, and got dressed in my other clothes. My head no longer hurt.

I went down to the spring. There I found the shallow prints of bare feet at the water's edge. So Olikea had ventured that far in trying to lure me back to her. A spike of desire pierced me. I longed for her warm willingness and the mindless pleasure she could wake in me with her body and her food.

No. Fervently and abruptly, I decided to end all my interaction with the Specks. I was not a Speck and I could not save them. This magic had been forced onto me. I didn't like what it allowed me to do or what it did to me. I would be prey to it no longer. Let it punish me as Buel Hitch had said it would. I no longer cared. With equal vehemence, I rejected my own people. I no longer wished to have anything to do with any of them. Even the thought of Spink and Epiny could not lure me back to being a soldier and a Gernian. I would end my life here, I decided, in this role of grave-digger. I could not save either people from their own foolishness. The best I could do, the only thing I could do, was to bury them. So be it.

In that frame of mind, I went to my tool shed and began to dig a fresh grave. I knew there would soon be bodies aplenty to bury. I might as well be prepared. I dug it with professional competence, a good deep grave with straight sides and plenty of room to lower a coffin. As soon as it was finished, I drank more water and went right on to dig the next one.

The thought of going to town and reporting that someone had shot me and stolen Clove and my wagon came briefly to my mind. I pushed it away. I found I no longer cared for anything much except my gravedigging. I found that my only thought on the subject was to hope that Clove was well treated by whoever had him now. I went on digging. I tried not to recall how the magic had felt as it had rushed out of me. I didn't know who had shot at me. Did that mean the magic could not target them with my anger? I feared what I had done, and then felt furious with myself for thinking about it. It wasn't my fault, I angrily declared to myself. I hadn't sought the magic, and I'd never wished for it. Those who had imposed it on me were to blame for all of this. Not I. I pushed the nose of my shovel deep into the turf and ripped out another shovelful of earth.

Neither Ebrooks nor Kesey came to the graveyard that day. I missed them, but I was glad they hadn't come. I would have liked their casual companionship if I could have looked at them and not wondered how soon they would die. I wondered if plague was already prowling the streets of town, or if the people were still intoxicated both with Gettys tonic and the thought that the road was moving forward again. Even now, I was sure the heavy saws and axes were biting deep into the flesh of the ancestor trees.

That thought made me ill, and for a wavering moment I was outside my body, reaching up to distant sunlight as I felt the inexorable severing of my connection to the earth and all it had been to me. I felt both the breeze that shivered my leaves and the deep vibration of the blades gnawing through me. A love of life deeper than anything I had ever felt rang through me, coupled with the anguish that it would end so suddenly. I jerked my awareness away from the magic's greedy clutches. I didn't care, I told myself fiercely. It was only a tree, and a Speck tree at that! But even that denial showed me how deeply I'd changed my way of thinking. Sickened and shaken, I dragged my thoughts back to my work. I drove the shovel deep into the earth again.

I worked until there was no light left in the day and then returned to my cabin. There was little left in my pantry, but I made a meal off the last end of the bacon, a few vegetables from my garden, and some hearth bread. After my day's work, it was less than satisfying, but I sternly told myself it was enough.

And then the long night stretched before me. I had nothing to read nor any way to occupy my mind. For a time I sat and stared out my window and tried to empty my mind. Despite my efforts, my thoughts returned to the looming plague, the felling of the ancestor trees, and my determination that henceforth I would be a part of neither people. After a time, I took down my soldier son journal and made the longest entry that I had written in some weeks. I poured my thoughts onto the paper, and when I had finished, I felt almost at peace. I waited a few moments for the ink to dry, and then leafed back through it. The entries I had made at the academy now seemed shallow and boyish, and the sketches I had made of my classmates were the scribbles of a child. As I paged through the leaves of the books, the entries grew longer, and the thoughts more considered. I'd been lax in my duty to be a naturalist as well as a soldier. There were few sketches, and other than an attempt at showing how the specks were placed on Olikea's hands, they were all of plants I'd seen. The soldier son journals I'd seen at my uncle's house had been terse accounts of battles and journeys over difficult terrain. In contrast, mine looked like a schoolgirl's diary. I closed it.

"*Nevare.*"

Olikea's call was a whisper on the night wind. I tried to pretend I'd imagined it. But it came again and with more urgency, like a doe's mating call.

"*Nevare.*"

Against my will, I felt stirred. I knew exactly where she would await me, in the trees just behind the spring. I gritted my teeth. She would have a basket of food with her, I knew. My will began to crumble. What would it matter if I went to her one last time? Didn't I at least owe her an explanation? After all, it was not her fault that I was caught so harshly between our peoples. Hurting her served no useful purpose; in a way, it was giving way to the magic, to let it force me to be cruel to her.

I had almost convinced myself; indeed, I was rising to go to her when I heard a sound that stood the hair up on the back of my neck. Hoofbeats. A horse was coming up the road to the cemetery at a canter. In a rush of wariness, I was sure it was someone coming to kill me. My attackers would know I had lived because no one had found my body by the road. They'd want to be sure I was dead before I could step forward to accuse them. I suddenly saw how stupid I'd been not to go to town to report the assault and the theft. If they killed me now, there would be no one to accuse them. They'd go free and I'd be dead.

I pulled my window shutter closed and fastened it. In two strides, I reached my door and slammed the bar into place. I took my disreputable weapon down from its hooks and checked the charges I'd prepared for it days ago. I readied a load and waited silently, the muzzle pointed at the door. Ears straining, I heard someone ride up to my door and then dismount. An instant later, someone pounded on the door. I kept silent. I didn't want to kill anyone unless I had to.

"Nevare? Are you in there? In the good god's name, open up! Nevare?" Spink rattled the door loudly and then gave it a good kick. For a moment longer, I sat still and silent. "Please, Nevare, be there!" he cried out, and there was such despair in his voice that I relented.

"A moment," I called, and set my gun aside and unbarred the door. The moment I did, Spink came pushing into my cabin. He seized my forearm and exclaimed, "Are you all right, then?"

"As you see," I told him, almost calmly.

He slapped his hand to his chest and breathed out heavily. I thought he was being dramatic, but when he straightened up, his face was pale save for two bright spots on his cheeks. "I thought you were dead. We all thought you were dead." He tried to catch his breath and failed. "I left Epiny caught between hysterics at the thought that you were dead and fury that you had been so close and alive all this time and I never told her. Nevare, I am in such trouble at home right now because of you that I could kill you, except that I am so glad to find you alive."

"Sit down," I told him and guided him to a chair. He dropped into it, and I brought him a cup of water. He was breathing as if he'd run all the way rather than ridden his horse. "Catch your breath and tell me what happened. Why did you tell Epiny I was out here? What made you think I was dead?"

"Amzil told me." He took another drink of water. "She'd gone out to do errands for us. She came running back, sobbing her heart out, saying that your horse and wagon had been found surrounded by dead men." He dragged in another breath. "Oh, and of course Epiny was not in the bedroom napping as she thought, but only in our kitchen, and the moment Amzil blurted out that 'everyone in town is saying that Nevare is either dead or the one who killed them all,' she came bursting into the room demanding to know what was going on and how there could be news of you that she hadn't heard." He ran his hand over his head. "From there, all was chaos. I was trying to explain, but Amzil kept interrupting me, and at the same time I was trying to get Amzil's story out of her, and when Epiny started weeping and shouting at both of us, Amzil got angry at me, saying I'd upset her now and she might lose the baby. So then Epiny started crying even harder, and all the children joined in the wailing. And Amzil threw me out of my own house telling me that I was just as useless as any other man she'd ever met and I should at least come out here and see what I could find of 'that big idiot.' Meaning you."

He took a deeper breath and dropped his head onto the back of the chair. Staring up at my rough ceiling, he added, "And here you are, alive and fine, and my life is in an uproar and will be so until you come to town and see Epiny. You'll have to now." Almost as an afterthought he added, "This whole mess is your fault, Nevare. You know that."

"Tell me about the dead men and my wagon," I said quietly.

"Meaning you know nothing about it?" he asked quickly.

"I know something of it, I suppose. Yesterday . . . no. The day before, I think, when I was last in town and sent Amzil to warn you about the plague . . . what was Amzil doing out of the house? Why have you left your home? Didn't she give you my warning? You need to keep quarantine! The Speck plague is going to break out any day now, Spink. It always follows the Dust Dance. It's how they spread it."

"No one has been sick yet!" he defended himself, and then added shamefacedly, "I told Amzil not to go. But Epiny has been so sick with this pregnancy, and there's some tea that an old woman in town makes that seems to help her. Amzil insisted on going for a fresh supply when we ran out. It was no good my telling her to stay inside. I tell you, Nevare, once there is a woman under a man's roof, he can just forget about being in charge of his own life. Two women, and he doesn't even have a life anymore." He shook his head as if bothered by gnats and then glared at me. "But you were explaining how your wagon came to be in a barracks stable surrounded by dead men."

"No, I wasn't," I replied testily. "I was telling you that on my way home, I was attacked. They hit me hard and I went down fast, so I can't tell you how many they were or what they looked like. When I came to, I was facedown on the ground and Clove and my wagon were gone. I managed to get home, spent a day recovering, and then got back to my work."

"And you didn't come to town to report it?" he asked me severely.

"No. I didn't. Spink, I expected town to be in the first throes of the plague. I'm surprised it isn't, but I still think it will come. And when it does I'll have the graves dug and waiting." I sat down in my own chair across from him and rubbed at my face. I suddenly felt a hundred years old. "It's really the only thing I can do for anyone," I added morosely.

"Well, I can see that you're discouraged and worried. We all are, Nevare. When the Speck magic isn't flooding us with discouragement, we're either drugged or simply seeing how senseless life on this post can be. But to not report the attack and theft now make you seem, well, involved somehow in those deaths. You know there were rumors about you. That was why I asked you to stay out here and out of trouble. And now people are saying—"

"How did they die?" I demanded suddenly.

"Well, I don't exactly know. Amzil said they were just sprawled all around your wagon, like they'd been gathered around it and then just died right there."

"Who were they?"

"Nevare, I don't know. I didn't hear the story firsthand, and between Amzil's blubbering over you and the hysteria that followed, I didn't get much information. Only that Sergeant Hoster was saying that you'd probably killed them all to shield yourself and that you should be arrested until we can discover what's going on."

"Hoster would say that. The man hates me, for no reason that I know. Do you think they will arrest me?"

"Nevare, I don't know! We still have the inspection team here, and the mysterious death of four men inside the barracks stable doesn't make any of us look good. Command

will have to cover it up, explain it away, or find a scapegoat."
He rubbed his face and then looked a stark plea at me. "You
didn't have anything to do with it, did you?"

If he hadn't asked me directly, I could have maintained
my deceit. But Spink had always had that honest, open stare
of a boy who wants to believe the best of his friends. Even in
a face that was beginning to show the care lines of a man,
that look still demanded honesty. If I lied to him now, I'd
know that I'd given up all hopes of ever being the man I
thought I'd become.

"I probably killed them," I admitted bluntly. "But I don't
know how. And I didn't do it on purpose."

He sat very still, looking at me. His mouth was a tiny bit
ajar, and I could hear his breath going in and out of it. He
looked as if he was about to speak, and then his face crum-
pled. "Oh, Nevare. No. I can't go back and tell Epiny that. I
can't. It will kill her. It will kill her and the baby and they're
all I have in this godforsaken piss-hole of a post." He leaned
forward, his face in his hands, and spoke hoarsely through
his fingers. "How could you do this, Nevare? Who have you
become? I've seen the changes in you, but I always thought I
knew the true heart of who you were. How could you kill
men in your own regiment? How?"

"The magic did it," I said softly. "It wasn't really me,
Spink. It was the magic." It sounded like a childish excuse. I
didn't expect him to believe me, but he didn't lift his face
from his hands or interrupt me. I found myself telling him
the whole story of what had happened to me in the last
week. I didn't mince words or find excuses for myself. I told
him everything, even going back to fill in the truth about
Olikea and myself. It felt good, cleansing, to be honest finally with someone. His shoulders sagged as I spoke, as if
he took on the burden that I shed. When I was finished, I felt
hollow and he looked like a man crushed beneath the weight
of a world. Two worlds, I thought to myself.

I got up quietly and filled a kettle. My throat was dry and
despite everything else, I was ravenously hungry. Perhaps
coffee could soothe that pang a bit. As I set the pot on to boil,

Spink finally spoke. "They've always known the trees were sacred to the Specks?"

I lifted a hand in a dismissive gesture. "That was the impression I got." I was surprised that he cared.

"Do they know that the sadness and discouragement that overwhelms us here is from Speck magic?"

"I don't know. They must suspect. What else could bring on a fear like that at the end of the road? They must know that's Speck magic."

He spoke in a low voice. "The doctor wants Epiny to take the 'Gettys tonic.' She keeps refusing. He says that if she doesn't, she will miscarry. Or that when the baby comes, she won't be a fit mother to him."

He fell silent. "And?" I prodded him.

"And he might be right," Spink said heavily. "Not that many healthy children are born here, Nevare. And the women who do have children seem . . . flat. Exhausted. As if they can barely care for themselves, let alone their children."

"But Epiny seemed to have a great deal of energy. The way she's organized all those women with whistles. Didn't you say she was trying to hold classes or lessons . . . ?" My questions trickled away as Spink shook his head.

"She starts things. Every day, she gets up, saying that she's not going to let it win. We both do. But by afternoon she is weeping, or we've had a quarrel, or worst of all, she simply sits and stares out of the window. This dark magic is devouring her, Nevare. It eats at me, but Epiny is more vulnerable to it. You remember what she once told us? That it was like a window had opened and she couldn't shut it? The sadness comes in that window and Epiny's life leaks away through it. I'm losing her, Nevare. Not to death, but to . . . sadness. Bleakness that never goes away. And for what? So that we can push a road through by the shortest possible route, regardless of what it does to the people who live here, or what they do to us in retaliation?"

He stood up slowly. The coffee had just begun to smell like coffee. He didn't seem to notice. "I've got to go home to Epiny. I'm not going to tell her all of this, Nevare, but I am going to tell her that you are here and alive." He walked toward the door.

"Spink—hold on a moment. Did Amzil give you my entire message? Did she tell you to send for more of your Bitter Springs water?"

He smiled sourly. "Nevare, you are so accustomed to life on the King's Road, aren't you? Bitter Springs is far more isolated. There is no regular courier run to my home. Sending a courier to Bitter Springs would cost me most of a month's pay. And my message would not reach my brother until weeks from now, if it arrived at all. Add to that the time it would take for a wagon with casks of water to make the trip. With great luck, it might reach Gettys before next winter's snow closed the road."

"So, you didn't send the message," I confirmed quietly.

He shook his head. "It would be pointless."

I was silent for a time. "How many of those little bottles of water do you have?"

"Now? I have three left."

"That's all?" I was horrified. "What happened to the rest?"

He shrugged. "Almost as soon as Epiny arrived, she began to give them away to people she met. I hid three, for she was determined to pass it all out. I've told her it may not be enough to help anyone. After all, I immersed her whole body in the water to cure her. She seems to think if they drink it at the beginning of the fever, it may cure them. As for ourselves, she believes that since we took the Bitter Springs cure, we are immune. I'm not so certain of that." He hesitated, then asked, "Did you want some for yourself?"

"I . . . no. Thank you, but no. I'm sure the magic protects me now."

"You speak of the magic as if it were a thinking entity."

"I'm not so sure it isn't. I still don't know what it is. But I don't think I'll need any of your water. If the magic can heal a bullet graze in three days, I doubt it will let me die of the Speck plague." A new thought chilled me. "Unless, of course, it suits the magic's purpose." I shook my head, refusing to let my thought follow where that might lead. "When I asked about the water, I wasn't thinking of myself, but of Amzil and her children."

Spink smiled. "Epiny has already provided for them. She and Amzil have become quite close. As for the children, they are almost like our own."

"I'm glad of that," I said, and was surprised at how grateful I felt.

He was quiet for a moment and then said, "For what it's worth, Nevare—I think she cares for you, too. Her terror at the thought you were dead surpassed the caring of a friend." He turned toward the door. "And speaking of that, Nevare, I must go. It's cruel for me to let them dangle in suspense while I tarry here, talking with you. I'll admit that I dread rushing back to Epiny's wrath. I fear her forgiveness will be slow in coming."

"Blame it all on me," I suggested apologetically.

"Oh, never fear. I fully intend to." The grin he gave me was a cracked imitation of his usual one. I was still glad to see it.

I spoke before I could lose my courage. "I'll come to town tomorrow, Spink. I'll come to your house. We can tell people that I went there to visit your maidservant, Amzil."

He folded his lips for a moment and then decided to speak. "Odd how easy it is for you to arrange a ruse once *you* decide to do it."

I bowed my head to the rebuke in his voice. I could imagine the scene he was returning to, and dreaded my own next encounter with my cousin. "I'll see Epiny and tell her that all the secrecy was my fault, not yours. And I'll go to headquarters and report I was attacked."

He glanced back at me. "And prove it how? You're completely healed of a bullet wound in less than three days. There's no evidence you can offer that you were attacked. What are you going to tell them?"

"I'll think of something."

He nodded grimly and left. I barred the door after he'd mounted and ridden away. I took the coffee from the fire and poured myself a cup. It wasn't what I wanted, but I sipped it anyway. It was hot and bitter and did nothing to assuage any of my hungers. While Spink had been here, I'd been able to call my thoughts my own. Now that he was gone, I felt besieged again.

"*Nevare.*" Olikea's call sounded closer.

"No." I said aloud. "I've had it with you and your magic."

CHAPTER TWENTY-EIGHT

COFFINS

I did not intend to sleep that night. I did not want to wake finding I had sleepwalked into the forest. I sat up in my chair by the fire. As the night crawled past, I drank mug after mug of steaming black coffee. The summer evening outside was balmy, so I let my small cook fire slowly die. I watched the flames falter and shrink until they subsided as a ripple of light over the dwindling coals.

From time to time, I heard Olikea call to me. With every summons, temptation flamed up in me, but I was determined. Covering my ears did nothing to muffle her invitation. The magic conveyed her call to me rather than the utterance of her voice. Was she in league with the magic or only the unwitting tool of it? Perhaps it was only that she wanted to use the magic in me for her own ends.

The last cup of coffee from the pot was thick and bitter. I'd worked hard all day and my body ached for sleep. The night had reached its coolest point, and I felt chilled. I longed to wrap myself in a blanket but resisted. Too much comfort would make me more susceptible to sleep. Dawn would come soon. I rubbed my eyes, stood up, and paced around the room. I yawned hugely and sat down in my chair again.

"*Nevare.*"

"*I'm not coming.*" I leaned my head back on the hard top of my chair and stared into the shadowed corner of the room. I could picture how irritated she would be at my refusal. She'd be standing just inside the new forest, just beyond the spring where I filled my water bucket, naked to the night, heedless of the chill and the settling dew. I had noticed something the last time I was with her; even in the darkness, I could sense the dappling on her skin when I ran my hand down the smooth curves of her back. There was a very subtle difference in the texture from dark to light. My mother had used to favor a fabric that had that texture. What had she called it? I couldn't remember, and that saddened me. Another little bit of my old life gone from me.

"*Nevare.*"

"*Leave me alone, Olikea. You don't love me. You don't even know who I am or where I came from. You're just the same as Amzil. She can't see past my fat to discover who I am inside. You can't see past my body either. But to you, it's what makes me desirable. It's probably the only thing that does.*"

"Who is Amzil?" It was a sharp, suspicious query.

"*Don't worry about it. She is just another woman who doesn't love me.*"

"There are many women in this world who do not love you." She puffed her lips at me disdainfully and lifted her chin. "Why should you care about one more?"

"There you are absolutely correct. There are multitudes of women in this world who don't love me. In fact, if we were looking for women who did love me, I think we could quickly narrow it down to two. However, one loves me as a brother and one as a cousin. Neither is very satisfactory to a man."

"Why not?" She stood just under the shadow of the trees. Her basket rested on one outthrust hip. I could smell the mushrooms, and the soft, heavy petals of a pale water blossom that tasted like sweet pepper. The necklace I had given her glittered around her throat. It was the only thing she wore. Her jutting breasts seemed to offer themselves to me, a warmer sort of fruit. For a moment, I could not think.

"A man wants more than kindly affection from a woman. He wants all of her."

She puffed her lips at me again. "That is a stupid thing to want. Only a woman can have all of herself. You should be happy with what any woman offers you, rather than to want everything she is. Do you offer all you are to any one woman? I doubt it."

That stung. "I would if a woman offered all of herself to me. It is hard for me to be with someone who holds herself back from me. My heart doesn't love that way, Olikea. Maybe among your folk that is how you love. But among my people—"

"Your people and my people are the same people, Nevare. Over and over I tell you this. Cannot you learn it? The People are the only people you have now, Nevare. And we offer you everything. So why do not you love us with this 'heart' of yours? Why do not you come to us for every day and every hour, and use the magic of the People as it should be used?"

"To do what?" I asked her. We had moved closer together. The cool mud of the spring's edge cradled my bare feet. The night did not seem so dark. There was light in the spring water that glinted up at us. The light in Olikea's eyes was twin to it. I smelled the startling tang of crushed fruit. It was a berry in her hand. She reached up to my unsmiling mouth to push it gently between my lips. Her fingertips lingered a moment on my tongue and then drew back, painting my lips with the stinging sweetness of the fruit. My senses reeled with the flavor, the scent, and her touch.

"This is a new taste for you," she whispered. "They grow only in our dream country. And only a Great One like you is allowed to eat it. I can taste it only when I taste it on your mouth." With sticky fingers, she hooked my face, pulled it closer, and lapped her tongue lightly across my lips.

A man can only bear so much. My dreams of true love and the fulfilment of a life shared dissolved beneath a wave of simple lust. I caught her up and pulled her close. She let the basket of food fall. I tasted the skin of her neck, breathed in the scent of her hair.

She laughed softly. "Remember, I do not love you as your sister does, nor as your cousin does. I do not love you as a plain-skin woman would love her man. So this—" and she touched me teasingly "—is not enough for you. Is it? You don't want this from me, do you?"

"I want it," I told her fiercely, imprisoning her in my arms. "I want it, but I want more than just this. Can't you understand that, Olikea? Are our peoples truly so different?"

"Our peoples? I tell you and tell you. You have only one people. There is only one people, the People. They are our people. All others are strangers. All others threaten our ways."

"I don't want to talk right now," I decided. I stooped and picked her up in my arms. She gave a whoop of surprise and flung her arms around my neck. I liked the feeling that I could startle her, that I could move her with my strength. It fueled my lust.

I carried her deeper into the forest. Magic surged in me with the heat of desire. I made a gesture, and moss and fallen leaves gathered themselves into a couch for us. Another motion of my hand, and a tree branch drooped to become a support for a vine that suddenly draped itself into a bower around us. Fragrant flowers opened to perfume the night. I banished the small stinging insects that had come to investigate us, and invited instead the little glowing moths, that I might better see what I touched. I lavished magic with a free hand. It was as simple and natural as the way Olikea opened herself to me, and as mutually pleasing. This night I led and she followed in that most ancient dance. In our previous times together, she had always taken the role of aggressor, and I had been astonished to find how much pleasure I could take in that. This night, I think she was equally surprised to find that a male could command her pleasure so completely. Discovering that I could render her near-mindless with bliss bolstered my sense of myself as nothing else had in the previous year. It spurred me to greater efforts, and when at last she lay beside me, slack in my arms,

I felt I had proven something to her, though I could not have said exactly what.

We dozed. After what seemed a very long time, she asked, "Are you hungry?"

I nearly laughed. "Of course I'm hungry. I'm always hungry."

"Are you?" She sounded concerned. She set her hand on my side tenderly. "You should never be hungry. Not if you would allow me to care for you properly. Not if you allowed me to feed you as you should be fed. How can you do all that the magic wishes you to do if you do not eat as you should? You must pay attention when I call to you, and eat every night of the food I bring to you. You must stay close by me so that I can bring you to the peak of your powers."

She stood up and stretched. "I'll be right back."

I lay where I was on the moss, trying to find thoughts that belonged to me. I hadn't intended to come here. Yet here I was, enmeshed with Olikea again, and listening to her scold me for not letting the magic have its way with me. I knew it was a problem, but I couldn't bring myself to care about it.

She returned and sat down in the angle of my body, her back against my belly. She leaned back on me a little and rummaged in her basket. Some of the fruit had been bruised in the fall. I could smell each separate one quite clearly. She offered me a lily leaf. "Eat this first. For your strength."

I took it from her and ate a bite. "So. You anticipate I will need more strength tonight?"

I was surprised when she giggled. "You might. Just eat it."

I obeyed and then asked, "Does each food you bring me ave its own virtue?"

"Here, yes. On the other side, sometimes food is just food. To eat. Here each one is a piece of magic. What you eat here is far more potent than anything you eat on the other side. It is why it is so important that you come here every night."

"What other side?"

"The other side of here," she said impatiently. She took another lily leaf, put an orange section of root in its center, and rolled the fleshy leaf around it. "Like this. Eat it like this."

I obeyed. The orange root was slightly sweet. Weariness fell away from me. I reached over and pulled her basket closer to me. "What is this one for?" I asked, taking a clump of pale yellow mushrooms.

"For walking the web more strongly."

"I don't understand."

She puffed her lips at me, and then made a dismissive gesture with her fingers. "Just eat it. Trust me. I know these things."

The mushrooms had an earthy flavor, rich and dark. She followed them with a double handful of berries so ripe and sweet that they burst in my hands before I could get them to my mouth. Each had a flat seed inside it, strongly piquant. As I chewed a mouthful, she said, "You should go now, so that you can come back to me on the other side before the light is too strong. You do not need to bring anything with you. Simply go and then come back to me."

I didn't understand, so I avoided the question. "The light doesn't bother me."

"It troubles *me*. And you need to be with me, so that I can show you the way to the deeper place. We think that one of the old ones will fall tomorrow. The magic will waken with great fury then. It would be better for us to be sheltered from that wrath."

"I cannot go with you tomorrow, Olikea. I promised my friend that I would come to visit him in Gettys. I have to keep that promise."

"No." She shook her head. "Tomorrow death sweeps through that place. It will only make you sad to see it. Come away with me."

Every word she spoke jabbed me like a small pin, awakening me to my other life and the dangers that threatened it. While I loitered here with her in satiation and contentment, my friends were in danger. The closeness I had felt to her was thinning like darkness before the dawn. "Were you there?" I asked her. "When your people danced the Dust Dance in Gettys, were you there, spreading disease with the dust?"

"Of course I was," she answered promptly. There was no shame in her voice, no regret at all. "You saw me leave by the gate. I thought you would come with me, but then I saw that you had *her* with you. So I left you."

I lifted her hand that rested against my ribs and looked at it. "With this hand, you threw the dust that will make all of them sicken with the plague?"

She twisted her hand from my grip, and then held it palm-up and fingers loose. She shook it like that. "It is the winnowing. The dust flies and blows and settles where it will. Some will walk the path of the winnowing and some will not. Of those who walk the path, some will cross the bridge and others will not. Some will serve the magic: they will cross, but come back to us, briefly, as messengers from that far place. Among our people, we honor those ones as worthy of a tree. They send down roots to one world and reach up branches to another. They stay among us then and grow, and wisdom grows with them. You, you bury your dead to rot, as if you care nothing for the wisdom of that world. The messengers who come back to you, you ignore and bury beneath the earth. We have tried to help you be wiser. We have tried to give some of your people trees so that they could grow in wisdom, but never does it work. The tree does not thrive, or one like you comes to tear them free from the tree and throw them back into a hole in the ground where they rot like bad seed."

I sat very still. She took another lily leaf from the basket, rolled it around an orange root, and passed it to me. I took it from her absently. I could almost understand what she was telling me. The little I comprehended frightened me.

Olikea took pleasure in her musing. "A few, a very few like you," and she patted me fondly, "pass through the winnowing a different way. No one knows what makes the dust change you. Perhaps it is not that the dust changes you, but that you have already changed in a way the dust cannot alter. Great Ones can cross the bridge more than once and return to stay among us as members of the People." She shrugged. "Perhaps it is because the magic knows its own. It is a thing to think on, sometimes, when one does not feel too much like sleeping. But it is not a thing to be troubled about, because it does not matter if we ever understand it or not. It is for the

magic to know. We can be content with that." She spoke
softly, contentedly, as if this was a philosophy of life. To me,
it was her justification for the slaughter of innocents. I felt
sudden disgust with myself that I had whiled away these
hours in animalistic pleasure while in Gettys men, women,
and children were beginning to burn with the sickness she
had sown.

"You can, perhaps, be content with that. I cannot." I rolled
to my belly, pushing her away from me in the process. She
made an annoyed sound. I got my knees under me and then
stood up. "I am leaving, Olikea. I will never come back to
you. I cannot be with you again. I cannot accept what you
have done to my people in Gettys."

"What *I* have done? You make this my doing? It is the doing of the magic. And perhaps it is more *your* doing than
mine. Perhaps, oh plain-skin Great One, if you had followed
the magic's calling more willingly, it would not have had to
be!" She sprang to her feet to confront me "If you had done
the task the magic set you, the intruders would be gone by
now, banished back to their own lands. You were the one who
was to drive the plain-skins back to their own lands. Jodoli
saw that clearly. We all saw that. For that task, the magic
marked you. And we have waited, we have all waited, and
I have tried to nurture you to your power, but always you run
away and deny it and refuse it. Jodoli humbled himself to
show you the danger that threatened the ancestor trees. He
has explained it to you in every way it can be explained. All
thought that when your own eyes beheld the danger to the
ancestor trees, you would waken to your task. But now they
teeter and sway, and tomorrow one of them will fall and be no
more! They are the oldest memories of our people, and tomorrow we lose them. Because of the intruders. Because they
wish to make a path for their horses and wagons to go where
they have never needed to go before. They say it will be a
good thing for us, but how can they know what is good for us
when they have begun by destroying our greatest good thing?
We have let them feel our sorrow. We have let them feel our
fears. Still, they are too stupid to go away. So they must be
driven away with harsher means. How can anyone doubt that?

But you, oh, you look at those intruders who live little short lives known only to themselves, you look at those treeless people and you say, 'Oh, let them stay, let them cut the ancestors from their roots, do not make them endure the winnowing, let them be.' And why? Because they are wise or kind or great of heart? No. Only because they look like you!"

"Olikea, they are my people. They are as dear to me as your people are to you. Why can you not understand this?"

She puffed her cheeks in a display of utter disbelief. "Understand what? They are *not* the People, Nevare. They will never be the People of this place. They must all go away, go back to their own place, and then all will be as it should be again. Except, of course, that with their tools 'your people' will have cut a hole in the sky of leaves and stolen from us the oldest of our elders. But for this, you care not at all! Will you say what all of 'your people' say? 'It is only a tree!' Say that, Nevare. Say it so I can hate you as you deserve."

I stared at her in shock. Tears were running down her cheeks. They were tears of fury, true, but up to that moment I had not thought anything I said or did would wring such impassioned words from her. I was a fool. I tried to reason with her.

"The Gernians will never leave here, Olikea. I know my people. Once they have come to a place, they do not leave it. They stay, they trade, and their towns grow. Your lives will change, but the changes will not be all bad. You could learn to accept it. Think of your own people. From us they get tools and cloth and jewelry. And sweets! Remember how much you liked the sweets? The Speck people like these things, and we value the furs that they—"

"Be silent!" She shrieked the words at me. "Do not tell me in soft words that our dying will not hurt! Do not tell me of trinkets to wear and tools to use and sweet things to eat." She tore the simple bead necklace I had given her from her throat and the bright little glass beads went scattering, littering the moss like tiny seeds of Gernia.

I looked at them, glistening orbs of red and blue and yellow resting on top of the moss like a dew of gems, and for an instant I saw the future. A hundred years from now, those shiny bits of glass trodden into the ground would still remain intact, but the forest near the cemetery would be gone. I felt a sudden sorrow that it would be so, but I also recognized the truth. "Olikea, it is inevitable."

Her hands rose as claws and she screamed wordlessly at me. I lifted my hands to defend my face from her nails. "Stop!" I told her, and to my horror, the magic obeyed me. She halted, straining against it, longing to rake me bloody, but unable to push past the boundary I had put there. For a moment she scrabbled against it wordlessly, a savage animal caged behind glass. Then she stopped. Breasts heaving, eyes streaming tears, she let her hands drop to her sides.

She took a ragged breath. When she spoke, I could hear how she forced the words past the lump in her throat. "You think you can do this! You think you can swell up big with the magic of the People and use it against us. You cannot. You will come to do what the magic says you must. This I know. Of this, I say to you, 'It is inevitable!' And you shake your head and make your eyes sad and do not believe me. I do not care. The magic will convince you. It will send you a messenger you cannot ignore, and then you will know. You will see." She crossed her arms in front of her and stood tall and straight, reclaiming her dignity. "I did not think you were so stupid, Nevare. I thought that if I fed you, you would see the path of wisdom and tread it." She fluttered her fingers dismissively. "You did not. But it does not matter. You will do what the magic had destined for you. You will turn your people back to their own lands. We all know this. Soon, you will know it, too."

She turned her back on me and walked away. Her stride was arrogant and free once more, not that of a woman scorned but rather that of a woman who had won and no longer cared whether I recognized that or not. As I watched her go, the dawn's light broke through the canopy overhead. In that sudden brightness, I could not see. I blinked frantically, but she seemed to be disappearing even as I stared after her.

I shut my eyes and knuckled them.

When I opened them, fingers of strong daylight had reached through the cracks in my window shutters to fall across my face. My back was stiff and my neck ached from sleeping with my head thrown back against my chair. I sat up, flinching as my neck bones crackled. Despite all my efforts, I'd fallen asleep. And I'd dreamed . . . something. The first thought that came to me filled me with dread. I'd promised to go and see Epiny today.

I groaned and rubbed the back of my neck, and then scrubbed my stiff face with my hands. When I lowered them I was stunned at what I saw. My fingers and hands were sticky and stained red from the fruit I had shared with Olikea. My mind wobbled as it tried to integrate the idea of dreaming myself into a world that left physical evidence of itself. The other side, Olikea had called it. And now I was back on this side. The strength of the sunlight filtering through my shutters told me that I had slept far past my usual rising time. I rose and opened the window to the day. It was sunny and fine, and the sun already stood high in the sky. I rubbed my face again, and then grunted in annoyance.

By the time I'd wiped the stickiness of the dream fruit from my face and hands, I had another distraction. The sounds of a horse and cart reached me through the open window. I wondered if someone was returning Clove to me, but a glance out the window showed me that was not so. A man with his face muffled in a scarf perched on the seat of wagon pulled by a swaybacked black nag. It took me a moment to recognize Ebrooks. Three coffins jutted from the open back of the cart. My heart sank. It had begun.

I went out to meet him. He waved me back. "Speck plague!" he shouted at me "Going though the town like a prairie fire. Here. Put this on before you come any closer." He tossed me first a small glass bottle and then a folded cloth. The liquid in the bottle proved to be vinegar. "Wet the cloth with that and tie it over your nose and mouth."

"Will it keep away the plague?" I asked him as I obeyed him.

He shrugged. "It's mostly for the smell. But if it keeps you from catching plague, well, you haven't lost anything."

As I tightened the knot in the kerchief over my face, I heard a terrible sound. It was like a distant scream, breathlessly and hideously prolonged. It ended with a monumental crash that shook the earth under my feet. I staggered a step or two from the impact and then stood unsteadily, dizzied from the experience. "What was that?" I demanded of Ebrooks.

He gave me a puzzled look. "I told you. Just vinegar. But some folk say it wards off the plague. Can't hurt is what I say."

"No, not that. That noise in the distance. The scream. That explosion."

He looked puzzled. "I didn't hear anything. There was some talk in town that the high mucky-mucks from Old Thares were saying that we were wasting time trying to fell those big trees with saws and hatchets. One fellow suggested drilling a hole and packing a black powder charge into the trunk and then touching it off with a long fuse. Don't know that they decided to do it, though. And I'm not sure you could hear if from here even if they did."

"Oh, I think I'd hear it," I said faintly. The world still seemed to shimmer at the edges. I knew what I'd heard. The ancestor tree had fallen. That piece of the past had been destroyed. I had a sense of a gaping tear in time, and a cold wind blowing through it. What had been known was unknown now. Names recalled, deeds of old, all gone, as if in an instant a great library had collapsed into ash. Gone.

"You all right, Nevare? You coming down with the fever?"

"No. No, I don't have the plague. I'm just—forget it. Forget it, Ebrooks." All would be forgotten. "Three bodies. It seems so sudden."

"Yes, well, the plague is always sudden. There will be more before the day is out. The colonel himself has it; they say every officer that was on the reviewing stand is down with it, and a good portion of the troops. The infirmary filled up last night. Now they're telling people to stay home and put a yellow flag out in front of their houses if they have sickness and need help. Town looks like a field of daffodils."

"But you're all right?"

"So far. But I've had it twice, and lived both times. Makes it less likely I'll get it again. Come on. No time for talking. We've got to get these ones planted before the next load arrives. Kesey was waiting on coffins when I left. Luckily, they had a batch of planks all sawn, just the right size."

"Yes. Lucky." I didn't say that was due to my foresight. What had seemed eminently practical when I had suggested it now seemed grisly and foreboding. I felt as if I'd been the croaker bird waiting for the dead to die. As if my thought had summoned them, I heard a hoarse cawing. I turned to see three of the carrion eaters sail in from the seemingly empty blue skies and alight in the branches of my newly planted trees, which bent beneath the weight of their heavy bodies. One of the croakers spread his wide black wings in alarm and cawed again. I felt cold. Ebrooks didn't even notice them.

"All those empty graves you dug will come in handy now. Time to show the colonel what you're made of."

"Is he very ill?" I asked him. I walked beside the wagon as he drove it slowly to the opened and waiting earth.

"The colonel? I reckon. He's never had it before. First year he was here, it went through the ranks like a batch of salts. Killed the commanding officer; that was when Colonel Haren got jumped up to commander. Well, the day he did, he all but went into hiding. You've seen how he is. Hardly ever leaves his rooms if he can help it. I hear he's got them all fixed up like a little palace in there. Comfy as a bug in a rug. Winter and summer, he keeps a fire going in there; I know that rumor is true, because I see the smoke all the time. Someone told him that fire fights off fever; burns it right out of the air before it can get to a man. Seemed to work for him, anyway. But maybe this was just his time for it. He come down bad, I hear, and none of those visiting officers are likely to go home. Well, actually, they will, but in boxes. Too good to be buried out here in the wild east with us common soldiers. They'll go home to their fancy stone tombs. Well, here we are. Last stop, folks."

His forced good cheer was already beginning to grate on me, but I didn't ask him to stop. I suspected that whatever feelings he hid behind that mask would be harder for me to look at. We worked quickly and efficiently to set each coffin in an open grave. The names were marked on each coffin. Elje Soot. Jace Montey. Peer Miche. The waiting graves were ones I had dug last autumn. Grass and weeds had sprouted on the soil mounded next to each hole. "I'll go get some shovels," I said when the heavy coffins were in place."

"Sorry, friend. I won't be staying to help you dig today. My orders were to come right back for the next load. Oh. Wait." He took a folded paper from his pocket. "Here are the names. Better note down who went in each hole if you want to make markers for them later." He watched me closely as I took the paper.

"Oh. Yes. Thank you, I'll do that." I took the list, scarcely seeing the names. "I'll see you later, then."

"I'm afraid you will, and often." He paused. "You didn't know none of them, did you?" he asked curiously.

"No. I don't think I did. And it's too late now."

"Humph. Well, I admit I thought you might flinch a bit when you saw those names. But either you're cold as ice or you never knew them at all. These fellows aren't dead from plague, Nevare. These are the ones they found dead around your wagon in the stable. Doctor still don't know what killed them. He wanted to keep them a bit longer, figure it out, but with all the folks sick and needing the beds, he told me, 'Just get them in the ground. We'll sort it all out later.' You didn't know nothing about them, huh?"

A chill went up my back. Ebrooks had been testing me with that list. I tried to speak slowly as if jolted by his news. "Someone found my wagon? And my horse? I got jumped a couple days ago. Hit on the head. When I woke up, I'd been robbed. My horse and wagon were gone. I managed to walk back here and didn't do much for the next day or so. You think they were the ones who jumped me?"

"Well. I known them a little. Never figured them for thieves. Not that they were gentlemen, either. Mean as a mad dog, that was Elje. And Peer just liked to see blood. Everyone knew that about him. None of the whores ever wanted his money. Still, I hate to see any of us go like that. They were all twisted up like poisoned cats. That's no death for a soldier."

A terrible tingling ran over me. In a fit of anger, I'd killed these men. It had been vengeance for what they had done to me, and yet it still bothered me. Horribly. Ebrooks was right. Execution by unseen magic was not a fitting death for any soldier. I felt as if I was made of wood as I lifted a numbed hand to wave a farewell to Ebrooks. He waved back at me and slapped the reins on the horse's back.

I fetched my spade and began moving earth down onto the coffins. The first few shovelfuls woke an empty thumping from the coffin below, but soon I was shoveling earth onto earth. I'd finished the first grave and was carefully packing the mounded earth into a smooth heap before it occurred to me how commonplace this had become to me. I hadn't even breathed a prayer over them.

Neither had Ebrooks. He'd behaved as if he'd dropped off a load of grain sacks. All my life, I'd always heard of our glorious military tradition of respect for the dead. After battles, our soldiers were always buried with pomp, ceremony, and reverence. The military cemeteries in the west were well tended, planted with flowers and trees and solemnized with ornamental statues. Not here. Here we planted our dead like potatoes.

Speck plague had made death mundane. Dealing with it had become something we did efficiently. Mourning would come later, when danger had passed and we had time for reflection. It saddened me, but on a deep level of familiarity, I understood it. It was no different from how I had been forced to bury my mother, sister, and brother.

I put my foot on the shovel and pushed it deep into the grassed-over heap of soil. The first shovelful of earth and gravel rattled down onto the coffin's wooden lid. It was the only music that would be played to memorialize this passing.

The day was warm, and sweat had long since soaked my shirt to my back. I toiled doggedly on. My head throbbed. My brief sleep of the night before had not rested me. On the contrary, whenever I allowed my mind to stray to that "dream," I felt even more drained of energy and purpose. I did not think that Olikea would make a threat she could not fulfill. The only way I could distract myself from that anxiety was to worry about Spink and Epiny and Amzil and the children. Had the plague descended on their house as well?

If it had not, if her mind was free to dwell on such things, would Epiny forgive me for not coming to visit as I'd said I would? I hoped she would consider my profession and understand. I lifted yet another shovelful of soil.

I promised myself that as soon as I finished the third grave, I would take a rest. I'd make a trip to the spring for cool, fresh water. I was thinking of that longingly as I used the back of the shovel to smooth the mounded soil over the last grave when I heard an ominous sound. It was the rattling of heavy wagons. On the first, driving it slowly, sat Kesey, his face swathed against the plague. The wagon rode heavy; there were six coffins stacked in it.

A soldier I didn't know drove the other wagon, equally large. Three other soldiers rode in the back, perched on top of a load of lumber. The second wagon halted near my shed. The men jumped down and began unloading their cargo. Kesey drove the other wagon slowly toward me. He hadn't even reached me before I saw Ebrooks drive up his horse and wagon, similarly laden. Kesey pulled his team in. "Give me a hand unloading," he requested gruffly.

"What are those men doing?" I asked, gesturing at the fellows unloading lumber.

He shook his head sadly. "The bodies are piling up at the infirmary. I can only haul six coffins at a time. But if the supplies to make coffins or the coffins themselves are already out here, then I can just bring the bodies. We can crate them up here before we drop them in the holes." He spoke with deliberate callousness. He climbed into the back of his wagon while I stood at the rear of it and shoved one of the top coffins toward me. I caught an end of it, surprised by how little it weighed. Kesey saw the look. "She was just a girl," he said. "Martil Tane."

"You have a list of names, then?"

"I do."

We lowered the first coffin and went on to the others, taking each one in its turn. The names were roughly chalked on the coffin lids. I put the list of the dead in my pocket with the first one. By the time we were finished with Kesey's load, Ebrooks was ready to deliver his. We went by the order of his list. I borrowed a pencil stub from Ebrooks to number the lists to match the graves.

Nine coffins awaited burial. I was relieved when Ebrooks and Kesey both went for shovels. Even with three of us working, it was heavy work. At one point, they walked to the shade of my fledgling hedge while I went to the spring for a bucket of water. We drank, put fresh vinegar on our masks, and cooled our heads.

"How bad is it going to get?" I wondered aloud.

Kesey lifted his mask and spat to one side. "The first few days are always heavy. The weak ones go down fast. After that, it's just steady for a while. Then, just when you think it has to be over, there will be another flurry of deaths. I think the people that have been taking care of everyone just get too tired and let go. Then it trickles off until it's only one or two a day until it finally stops. And then winter comes."

I wanted to ask him how many plague seasons he had seen, but could not bring myself to form the words. I looked at the freshly mounded graves, then toward my shed, where the ringing of hammers against nails had been a constant since the men and lumber arrived. A glance in that direction showed me a tidy stack of new coffins. As I watched, two men stood up and moved another one into place. There was something so implacable about the process that my heart turned over in my chest. It was almost like an odd sort of peace.

This was the Gettys I had not been able to see before now. This parade of coffins, this methodical burial of the dead, this was what had separated me from the veterans of my regiment, far more than my body had. This was the war they had fought without weapons every summer since they had been stationed here. They lived the year around knowing that when the hot, dry days of summer returned, disease would pick them off as remorselessly as any enemy marksman. Like any battle-hardened regiment, they looked askance at the newcomer, wondering how long he would last and if, when the battle were joined, he would fight or break. I had been green and I had not known it until then. We were at war with the Specks, and today marked my first skirmish. How had I ever doubted it? I had lived in the midst of this graveyard and never truly seen what it meant until then.

"Let's finish it," I said quietly, and picked up my shovel. With a grunt, Ebrooks stooped to take up his and Kesey followed.

I was smoothing the last mound with the back of my shovel when I heard the creak and clatter of another wagon coming. I looked up in dismay. The sky had begun to turn pink in the west; the light would soon be gone. Over an hour ago, the coffin-builders had left their yield and departed for town. Only the three of us remained.

I didn't recognize the driver until Kesey grunted and said, "More joy to come. It's Sergeant Hoster." Ebrooks uttered a muffled obscenity. I said nothing at all, but my heart filled with dread. Yet when they picked up their shovels and went to meet the wagon, I forced myself to trail along after them.

Hoster pulled in his team alongside the row of empty coffins and sat waiting for us to approach. His vinegar-soaked mask was crusted brown with road dust. "Got a few more deaders for you. The docs don't want them lying around the infirmary."

"Couldn't they have waited until morning? Night's coming on fast," Kesey objected.

"You don't have to bury them tonight. Just get me unloaded so I can head back to town. There's a double Gettys tonic waiting for me, and one of Sarla's whores, on the house." He scratched the back of his neck and then pretended to notice me for the first time. "Well, well. I thought you'd run off and joined the Specks by now. You would have if you were smart, Burv. But then you probably think you are smart. So smart that you think you covered all your tracks and no one can prove what you done. But I can, Tubs. And you won't get away with it. This outbreak of plague may give you a bit of a reprieve, long enough to dig more graves. But when it's all over, we'll still find time to deal with you. I promise you, in the end you'll be filling a grave up here. Justice will be done."

"I haven't done anything," I retorted, but even as I said the words, I knew them for a lie and could almost taste the untruth in my mouth. I'd killed those three men and now I'd just lied about it. Hoster laughed skeptically. "Keep saying that. See how much good it does you. Bet you're wishing you could bury me, aren't you, Fats? Shove me under a shit-pile like you did that poor whore. I'll admit one thing. I'd love to know how you done those men."

"I don't think he had anything to do with it," Ebrooks defended me suddenly. "He didn't even know their names. He said he got jumped and someone stole his wagon."

"You don't have to know a man's name to kill him, stupid. Now shut up and unload this wagon."

He had the stripes. We did as he told us. There were three bodies, loosely shrouded in sheets. The first was a woman. We set her in her coffin, and while Kesey put a lid on top, Ebrooks and I went back for the next body. The cloth came free of his face and I was shocked to recognize the barber who had shaved me when I first came to Gettys. I hadn't know him well, but having the plague take an acquaintance was a sharp reminder that it could strike much closer to me. No one I cared about was safe. I was setting the lid in place on his coffin when I heard Kesey exclaim, "Damn! Buel Hitch. I never figured him to die from plague."

Sergeant Hoster laughed. "I always thought a jealous husband would do him in. Or that Speck whore I heard he had." He lifted his mask and spat over the side of the wagon. "Get him out of there. I want to go home."

He drove off as soon as the body was clear of the wagon. I stood, stunned and numb, and let Kesey and Ebrooks carry the scout to his coffin. As they set him in, Kesey said quietly, "He must have gone down fast. He's still wearing his uniform." With unlikely tenderness, he reached down and tugged Hitch's collar straight.

"Or as much of the uniform as he ever wore." Ebrooks gave a small, fond laugh. "Damn the luck. That's a shame. That man had the spirit of the old regiment in him. Not many of us left like him. It's too bad to see him go like that."

I had picked up another coffin lid. As I approached the coffin, I wondered if I wanted to look at Hitch's face one last time or not. The choice was taken from me. Kesey had reached in and covered him over, and I found I couldn't bring myself to touch the cloth. I set the wooden-planked lid in place.

Ebrooks spoke quietly. "You keep good watch over him tonight, Nevare. Don't let no Specks come and steal him. He may have walked the line, and yes, we all know he crossed over it more than once. But he was ours, he was cavalla, and he ought to be buried here, not stuck to some tree somewhere."

"He had a Speck woman, I heard," Kesey added sagely. "She or her kin might come for him. You keep good watch, Nevare."

"You aren't going to help me bury them tonight?" I was dismayed at the thought of letting the corpses lie unburied all night.

"Tomorrow's soon enough," Kesey said, glancing at the sky. "Light's going. I don't fancy filling in graves in the dark. Ebrooks and me, we got a long drive back to town. We don't leave now, it'll be too dark to see before we get there. But we'll be back tomorrow. Probably with more bodies, may the good god save us." He shook his head at my shocked expression. "Nevare, you'll get used to it and more's the shame. When they really start dropping, there's no keeping up with it. You done your best to get ready for this, but before the week is over, you'll be digging a trench and covering them any way you can. And no one will think the less of you for it."

I could think of no response. I watched them mount the wagon. Kesey slapped the reins on the horse's back and they drove away. I was left standing beside three coffins in the gathering dark.

CHAPTER TWENTY-NINE

THE MESSENGER

I couldn't stand it.

The thought of going to my cabin, eating, and then trying to sleep while the dead lay in boxes outside my cabin was too much for me. I looked at the darkening sky and resolved to try to bury them.

The problem was moving the laden coffins to the graves with neither Clove nor my cart to help. The woman's body had been the lightest, so I began with her. I could not lift the laden coffin; the problem was not the weight. The size and shape prevented me from getting a firm grip on it. Dragging it was difficult and nearly disastrous. I crabbed along backward, dragging the coffin over the uneven ground. The hasty workmanship of the coffin builders was soon evident, as the flimsily built box began to give way. I stopped and, muttering an apology to the dead woman, removed the lid from the coffin and lifted her body out of the box.

I tried to be respectful as I lay her loosely shrouded body on the bare earth. I could not restrain myself from hurrying as I carried the empty coffin to her grave site and then all but ran back to fetch her body. Once I was at her grave, I discovered a new awkwardness. I could not lower the laden coffin gently into the earth by myself. I did what was expedient. I put the open coffin in the grave and then lowered her body into it. I cringe when I think of how awkward it was to straddle the coffin while I put the lid on it, and then step on top of it to clamber out of her grave. I had acted with the best of intentions, and yet I still felt as shamed as if I had deliberately been disrespectful to her.

The whole process had taken far longer than I had expected. I shoveled earth in the darkness, working to cover her coffin more by feel than by sight. When I stood beside her grave to offer a simple prayer to the good god on her behalf, I realized I didn't know her name. The sergeant had not give me a list. I cursed him for his callousness. Then I added a prayer for myself, that no matter how many bodies I buried, I would remain properly respectful to the dead.

Shovel on my shoulder, I went back to my cabin. The light leaking out from the shutters was a welcome beacon as I trudged past the freshly mounded graves. I wanted to put this day behind me, to rest, and then find strength to move forward through the dismal days ahead of me.

I planned to go inside, wash my hands, and then use one precious sheet of my journal paper to carefully make a record of the folk I had buried that day. I decided I'd record the woman as "unknown woman victim, blonde hair, of middle years, delivered to cemetery by Sergeant Hoster along with the bodies of Scout Buel Hitch and the barber whose shop was by the west gate." If anyone came looking for them, perhaps the date of death and that brief description would be enough. I realized I faced a long winter of making grave markers.

I wondered if I dared try to sleep that night. No. I feared

I'd dreamwalk again if I did. And I had to guard Hitch's body. My heart sank as I considered his death. I'd lost a true friend. I took a breath and closed my heart to the grief that tried to hollow it. I needed my strength for the next few weeks. Later I could give way to mourning. I pushed open my door.

In the same moment that I recalled my cabin should have been dark, I saw Hitch sitting beside the little hearth fire he'd lit. I froze where I was. He turned to me and grinned apologetically. His face had lost flesh from the plague, and there were dark hollows under his eyes. His voice was hoarse. "Come on in and pull up a chair, Nevare. We need to talk." The foul smell of the plague, familiar to me from my own experience with it, wafted to me on his breath.

I took two steps backward. Then I turned and ran to the two coffins I'd left by my tool shed. The lid from Hitch's had been kicked aside. It was empty except for a rumpled sheet in the bottom. I went back to my cabin. At the door I hesitated, then resolutely shook my foolishness away. He hadn't been dead. That was all. Dr. Amicas had been aware of such incidents; plague victims sank into comas so deep they were mistaken for death. The doctor had insisted on bodies being held overnight to prevent anyone being buried alive. Spink and I had both been "dead" for a time. I pushed my superstitious fears aside. "By the good god's mercy, Hitch, I'm so sorry. I thought I was imagining you there." I hurried past him to my water cask and began filling my kettle. "We all believed you were dead. It's only the sheerest luck that I didn't bury you tonight. I'm so sorry, man. Do you feel all right? I'm making coffee. Do you need water, food? To wake up in a coffin! What could be worse?"

"Not to wake up at all, I suppose. But worst of all is to have someone waste a man's last bit of time with idle chatter. Be quiet, Nevare, and listen. I'm here as a messenger. You were expecting me, weren't you?"

Olikea's angry words echoed in my mind. "It will send you a messenger you cannot ignore." Cold emanated from my spine and spread to every part of my body. I barely managed to set the kettle on the hob without spilling it. I was suddenly shaking, my teeth chattering with it. His grin grew wider, a merry death rictus. "Are you cold? Sit down by the fire, Nevare. I don't have much time. Listen to me."

"No. No, Hitch, you listen to me. Back at the academy, Dr. Amicas said some of the plague victims seemed to die but then they revived. That was why he wasn't letting the orderlies take the bodies out of the wards right away. You've just been in a very deep coma and now you've come out of it. You're disoriented and confused. You need to rest. The same thing happened to me and to my friend Spink. We both lived. Let me get you some water, and then I'll ride for the doctor— No, damnit, they stole Clove. But I'll go on foot. I'll get help for you. You just rest."

He shook his head slowly. "There isn't any help for me, Nevare. I made my choice a long time ago, or rather, the magic made its choice when it took me. After that, I had no choices. That's one of the things I've come to tell you. You have to understand this. You don't have choices when it comes to what the magic makes you do. It can turn you against your own people; it can make you do things you'd be ashamed to whisper to a demon. Sit down, Nevare. Please sit down."

I knew that I should insist on getting help for him immediately. Instead, I slowly sank into my chair across from him. He smiled at me, and for a moment he looked more like his old self. Then he looked down at his feet. They were bare, I suddenly noticed. They'd sent him to his grave without his boots. He spoke without meeting my eyes. "I'm going to tell you one of those things I wouldn't whisper to a demon, Nevare. Because I think it may be the only way to convince you that you have to do what the magic demands of you. And it's the only way I can clear my conscience. You've been resisting the magic, haven't you?"

"Hitch, I truly don't know what you are talking about. Olikea says the same thing. So does Jodoli, and so did Tree Woman. They all tell me that I'm supposed to do something that will send the Gernians away. They act as if I know what it is I'm supposed to have done by now. But I have no idea what they are talking about. If that's what the magic wants, then it should give me some clue of how I'm supposed to accomplish it. Because I don't think there is any action one man could take that would suddenly cause King Troven to give up his road to the sea and the Kingdom of Gernia to retreat from its frontiers. Do you?"

He slowly shook his head. "Well, I don't know of any. But then it isn't my task. It's yours." He gave me a ghost of his old grin. "I'll tell you one thing that was true of the magic for me. When it wanted me to do a thing, I knew clearly what it was. And I did it. It always seemed the most obvious choice to make. It made me want to do it more than anything else in the world. Even if it was something wrong, something that went completely against the grain, the magic made it easy, even desirable. Nothing ever made me feel better than just doing what it wanted me to do." He coughed a dry little cough and added, "I'll take that drink of water now, if you please."

His request comforted me. I'd been toying with the idea that I'd somehow slipped into dream travel and was only speaking to him on that "other side." To have him ask for something as simple as water made me more confident that we were still in my real world. I rose and went to fill my cup from my water barrel. When I brought it to him, he took it and drank it in long, smooth swallows. He lingered over that water as if it were nectar.

I spoke as he drank. "Your fever's broken, Hitch. Let me find you some food. If you drink a lot of water and eat some bland food and get some good rest, you'll be fine. You'll live. I know how vivid fever dreams can be. But you're back in the real world now. You're safe. You're going to live."

As he handed the cup back to me, our eyes met. He looked sorrowful. "Thank you, Nevare. And not just for the water, but for hoping I'll live. I won't, not in this 'real world' of yours. In that other world, well, yes, I expect to live for a good long time. In fact, it has been promised to me. Especially if you do the task the magic has given you. But my time here is ticking away, even now. So let me talk while I can.

"You're a good man, old son. You'd have been a good soldier, and I suspect you'd have been a damn fine officer, given

the chance. But then, so would I, if the magic hadn't taken me.
I hope you'll understand that what I did, I did because I didn't
have a choice. Soldiers kill in times of war, and sometimes
they do even worse. They're under orders. And everyone understands that a man under orders does things he wouldn't
otherwise do. When you think of me after this, think of that,
please. 'Hitch was under orders.' Will you do that for me?"

A terrible foreboding rose in me. I moved the bubbling
kettle off the hob and then slowly sat down in my chair
again. "Tell me what you did," I suggested quietly.

He shook his head, his lips pursed sourly. "You already
know, don't you?" He sighed. "I tried to warn you about it.
'If you resist the magic, then bad things happen to you,
things that force you to go the way it wants you to go.' I told
you that. Never say I didn't. It's like being a sheep herded by
a big mean dog. Run where it wants you to, and you don't get
bit. I've been bitten by it a few times. Did I ever tell you that
once I had a wife and a little girl? A real wife, I mean, a
Gernian wife, one who dressed in ruffles and set a fine table,
and played sweet little songs to me on her lap harp. Lalaina.
And I loved her, Never. Loved her, and our little golden-
haired girl. But that wasn't what the magic wanted from me.
It wanted me out riding the edges and doing its bidding, not
sitting home listening to sweet little tunes with a child on
my lap. I wouldn't leave them, though, not for the magic, not
for the world. So the magic took them away.

"The plague cut them down, and once my roots were
gone, the magic could roll me wherever it wanted me. Kind
of like what it done to you. A girl to marry and your mother's love and a father who respected you? Well, if you'd kept
all those things, you wouldn't be here now, would you? So
when you held onto those things too tight, whisk! The magic
took them away. See, that's what I'm telling you. There's
something you're still holding tight to, isn't there? If you
love it, let go of it. Before the magic destroys it, or finds a
way to make you let go."

"Epiny and Spink, you mean?" Amzil and her children
came to my mind also, but not from my lips. Not even then
could I admit to Hitch that I cared about them.

"I don't know who or what you cling to, man. I'm not the magic! All I know is that you stay here when the magic wants you to move on. So it found a way to make you move on. Don't hate me for this. I'm the messenger. But I came here on my own just as much as because the magic made me. Because, despite everything, I'm still a soldier son, like you. I've still got a bit of honor left." He shook his head ruefully. "Damn me. In a few more minutes, you're going to hate me, old son. I don't like the thought of that. But it's got to be, before I go. So before I make you hate me, I'll ask you a last good turn. Because I know that if you give me your word, you'll stick to it, even if you hate me.

"Never, will you do me a favor?"

"What kind of favor?" I asked him, suddenly suspicious.

He gave a croaker bird's caw of laughter. "There, you see. I shouldn't have warned you. A couple of minutes ago you'd have agreed first and then asked what it was. Well, it's something easy, Never. Don't bury me. That's all I'm asking. I'm supposed to get a tree. That's a high honor from the Specks. My own tree. And if they do, if the Specks come and take my body, let them have it. All right? Just let them have it."

The thought appalled me. I covered it as best I could. "I'm not going to bury you, Hitch, because you aren't dead."

He folded his mouth into a stubborn smile and shook his head as if my words amused him. "Just say you won't bury me, and I'll do whatever you ask, Never. Because I know you'll keep your word."

"Fine. I won't bury you." I felt I was indulging a child. "Now do what you said you'd do. Obey me. Go lie down. I'll bring you more water."

He rose slowly and when he did, I saw how the sickness had wasted him. His clothing hung on his body. He walked slowly to my bed and sat down on it while I got him water. When I handed it to him, he said, "Good-bye, friend. Good-bye. Because this is the part I do for myself, so I can die knowing that I warned you. So I say good-bye to you one last time as a friend, because in just a few moments, we won't be friends anymore. Will you shake my hand a last time, Never? Nevare. See, I'll even call you by your real name. Just shake my hand a last time, and then I'll tell you. It will make you hate me, but I warned you."

"Hitch, you're raving. Just lie back. I'll be back soon. Well, as soon as I can." I turned for the door.

He groaned. "Good-bye, my friend. Good-bye."

I feared he was becoming feverish again. He sounded so strange. My hand was on the door latch when he spoke.

"I killed Fala. I choked her to death with a strap I took from Clove's harness. And when it was done, I went to Rollo's Tavern and I got drunk. Good and drunk. Drunk enough to tell everyone that you were a nice enough fellow, really, but you had a bit of a mean streak, and a temper where women were concerned. And I hinted that Fala had laughed at you when you couldn't do the deed with her. We all had a good laugh about that one, a big porker like you trying to prong a tiny little thing like Fala. Everyone knew she'd never lie still for it. She'd mouth a man, but that was all. Did 'em all fast, that was our Fala. Yes. We had a good laugh. And then I drank some more, and threw up on Rollo's floor, and passed out and slept it off in the corner. And rode out the next day. And the worst part was that I felt good about all of it. Really good. Because I was doing what the magic wanted me to do. The magic wants you to come to the forest. And if you won't come because you're being offered sweet foods and sweeter flesh by Olikea and led that way, then it will drive you with whatever whip or spur it can find. Just like it drove you away from your home. There. I'm done. You hate me now, don't you?"

"I think I will in a moment," I said quietly. I was reeling from his revelation. At the same time, all of the pieces were falling into place for me. Hitch had taken me to Sarla Moggam's brothel. Had he arranged that Fala would volunteer to take me? It wasn't an unheard of thing, for one man to arrange a whore for a friend, as a favor or as a rough jest. I remembered the missing bit of strap from Clove's harness, and now I recalled, with a groan, how interested Sergeant Hoster had been in Clove's harness the last time I'd gone to town.

The three men who had attacked me? That was what they'd been after. Not to steal my horse and wagon, maybe not even to hurt me, but to get Clove's harness, and show the one new strap amid all the old tack he wore. I'd killed them for that. I wondered where that harness was now. Did Hoster have it? Did anyone else know its significance?

If I didn't flee Gettys and take to the forest and the Specks, my regiment would hang me for killing Fala. As Hitch had warned me, I had no choices left. Not if I wanted to live.

And Hitch, my friend Hitch, had set me up for all this. He'd framed me neatly. Who wouldn't believe that a whore would mock a fat man who couldn't perform with her? Was that a reason to kill her? Enough men would think so. And would they think me stupid enough to have throttled her with a strap from my own horse's harness? Yes, they would. I looked at the wreck of a man whom I had trusted. I'd saved his life. I'd called him friend. "You've ruined me," I said quietly.

"I know," he replied as softly. "And as a man and as your friend, I'm sorry about that, Nevare. Sorry beyond anything you can ever know. All I can repeat is that the magic made me do it. Maybe someday you'll understand what I mean by that, how it forces and lures a man to do what it wants.

"I'll only say one more thing, and then you can do what you want. Beat me back to death, if it brings you any satisfaction. I'm headed that way anyway. But before I go, let me tell you this. Whatever it is you're supposed to do, Nevare, you'd better do it. Do it and have done with it, and know that you did what was best for king and country, not to mention yourself. The Specks, they're determined to have us out of here. The Dust Dance plague and the fear at the end of the road and the despair that rolls out of the forest and fills Gettys: you might think that's awful magic, but the Specks think it's sweet persuasion. They were sure it would send us all hightailing out of here. But it hasn't. And you and I both know that likely it won't. But if you don't find a way to make it happen, well, then, all the Specks will say that Kinrove has failed and that it is time to listen to the words of the younger men."

I was scarcely listening to him. My mind was racing through solutions to my problem. I could leave tonight and seek refuge with the Specks. That solution held little appeal to me. I'd be abandoning all my friends, and they'd believe what Sergeant Hoster told them about me. I also didn't relish the prospect of Olikea flaunting that she had told me so. But a darker fear was that by giving into the magic, I'd be setting my feet on the same path that Buel Hitch had followed. I didn't want to become what he was now, a decent man distorted and tormented by the foreign magic that had infected him. I'd rather face a hanging than be herded like a sheep. I would not flee directly into the jaws of what threatened me.

I could see two alternatives. One was to keep laboring at the cemetery and hope that in the tragedy and the confusion of the plague, poor Fala's murder would be forgotten. Yet Sergeant Hoster had promised me he'd never let that happen.

The sole hope I had of remaining in Gettys and escaping the noose was the man now reclining in my bed, talking in a voice that sounded ever vaguer.

"The youngsters, they say they have to make it a war in the way Gernians understand war. Maybe they're right. They say that Kinrove's dancing has failed, that all it has done is consume the best and strongest of them. They're the younger generation, and they've got new ideas of how to deal with us. They don't want to give up what they get from us; they like the trade we bring. But they don't want us living here, and they're tired of waiting for us to go away, and they won't tolerate us cutting their ancestor trees. Some of them think the best solution would be open warfare, bloodshed that we'd understand, and taking what they want from us. You were the last best hope for avoiding that, Nevare. If you don't do whatever it is you're supposed to do, they'll bring war down on us. And there are two things you should know about that: there's a lot more Specks than the other scouts think there is. And they'd all be willing to die, down to the last child, to protect one ancestor tree."

His voice had become a hoarse whisper. His eyes were drooping shut.

"Hitch?"

He had stopped speaking. He turned his head slightly toward me but didn't open his eyes.

"Hitch, I'm going for help for you. Just lie there and rest. I'll be back. I promise."

He took a breath and sighed it out as if it would be his last. But then he spoke. "Don't fight it, Never. It all goes easier if you don't fight it. I'm not going to fight it anymore."

"Hitch. I'll be back."

A very faint smile curved his lips. "I know you will."

I wanted to run. I knew that if I did, I'd collapse long before I reached town. So I set off at the brisk walk that I thought I could sustain. The night was clear and the moon had risen. There was no color in the light it gave me, but the longer I walked, the more my eyes adjusted. That bit of moonlight and the feel of the road under my boots were enough to guide me.

I was tired to the bone. I'd had two solid days of hard physical labor, with only a sleepless night full of strange dreams to rest me. My back ached from all the digging I'd done. It was fear that drove me more than the desire to save Hitch's life. I wanted him to live, but only because I hoped I could persuade him to confess to what he had done. It was a thin thread of hope, but I still believed that I knew the heart of the man. He'd done terrible things, if I were to believe his words, but in his heart he was still a soldier son, born to duty. If Hoster did accuse me, I didn't think Hitch would stand idly by and watch me hang for something I hadn't done. Would he put his own head in the noose to save me? That was a question I didn't want to consider. I focused on the problem at hand; I had to keep him alive.

More than once on that long walk I cursed the men who had stolen Clove and my wagon. My big horse would have made nothing of this journey. When the lights of Gettys came into sight, I had to resist the urge to break into a run. I knew I had to pace myself. It seemed to me that more lights than usual burned in the windows for such a late hour. When I finally reached the town itself, I followed the main thoroughfare right up to the gates of the fort without seeing a living soul on the street. I passed three blanket-draped bodies set out in front of homes.

The annual invasion of the plague had created its own traditions for the town. The dead were put out almost as soon as they had expired for the corpse wagons that would make a circuit of the town three times a day until the plague season ended. People, I thought to myself, learned to cope; there was nothing so strange, so heartbreaking, or so horrifying that people could not eventually become accustomed to it.

The wooden walls of Gettys stood tall and black against the night sky. There was a lone sentry on the gate. A torch burned low in a sconce beside him, making inky shadows at his feet. He drew himself up straighter as I approached and then commanded me to "Halt!" When I did, he announced, "This post is under quarantine. No one may enter who is sick with the plague."

"That's the most useless measure I've ever heard!" I exclaimed. "There's plague both in and outside the walls. What is the use of a quarantine now?"

He looked tired. "Colonel Haren gave the order before he took ill. And now that he's dead and Major Elwig is raving with fever, there's no one to rescind it. I'm only doing my duty."

"And I'm doing the same. I've come in from the cemetery. And I'm not bringing any sickness that isn't already here. Scout Buel Hitch was sent out on a corpse wagon a bit prematurely. I think that if a doctor could come to his aid, he might recover."

He laughed. There was no joy in it, or even bitterness. He laughed because I so casually suggested the impossible. "The town doctor is dead. Both the regiment doctors are overwhelmed with the sick already. Neither will leave the infirmary to go to treat a single victim, regardless of who he is."

"I have to try," I said, and with a skeptical nod, he passed me through.

I found my way through the darkened post to the infirmary where I had brought Hitch on my first day in Gettys. Lanterns burned on either side of the entry. Outside it, a double row of draped bodies awaited the corpse wagons. I walked carefully around them and entered the building. The same boyish soldier who had greeted me the first day was asleep at the desk in the anteroom, his head pillowed on his arms on top of a thick book. Even in his sleep, he looked pale and frightened.

I knocked gently on the desk to awaken him. He lifted his head immediately, his mouth hanging slack. It took a moment for his eyes to focus. "Sir?" he asked me vaguely.

"Not 'sir,' just 'soldier.' I need a doctor for Scout Buel Hitch."

He looked sleepily confused. "Scout Hitch is dead. I logged him into the record myself." He gestured at the ledger he'd been using for a pillow.

"He revived at the cemetery. I think that he'll live if he can get a doctor's care."

His eyes widened slightly. He sat up straighter and looked more alert. "Lieutenant Hitch is a walker? Ah. Well, if anyone would be, it would be him. But I doubt he'll live. Walkers hardly ever live. They only revive for an hour or so, and then die again. Dr. Dowder and Dr. Frye argue about it all the time when Dr. Dowder is sober. Dowder says they just go into a deep coma, rally briefly, and then die. Frye says they really die and then come back. He wrote a big report for the queen about how the Speck magic makes them wake up a final time after their first death before they die their final death. She sent him a present for writing it. The big green ring he wears on his left hand."

"You seem to know a lot about it."

He looked a bit ashamed. "I don't eavesdrop. The walls here are thin and they often shout at one another. They shout a lot, about everything. Today Dowder wanted to bring the sick prisoners here so that they could treat everyone in one place. Frye was angry about that. He says that soldiers shouldn't have to die alongside felons. Dowder said that three infirmaries for two doctors is ridiculous. And he said that a sick man is a sick man and deserves to be treated as well as they can manage. They fight about the prisoners a lot. Almost all the prisoners who get sick die. They lime-pit the bodies from the prisoner barracks. Dowder says they should be given a decent burial."

I'd never even stopped to wonder why dead prisoners never arrived at the cemetery. Now I knew. Work on the

King's Road, die, and be flung into a pit full of quicklime. A sordid end for anyone. "Three infirmaries?"

"The officers' mess is an infirmary now for the visiting delegation from Old Thares. Every one of them sickened. Dowder says they're all going to die because they haven't been east long enough for their bodies to adapt to the humors of this region. Frye says they'll die because the Specks hated them the most."

I was beginning to think that I needed to have a long conversation with Frye. He was disturbingly close to what I perceived as the truth. I wondered if he might lend his weight to my plea that we stop cutting the ancestor trees to end our war with the Specks. Could he make Colonel Haren see that we truly were at war? Then I remembered that Haren was dead. I didn't have time to feel anything about that. Callously, I wondered if our next commander might be more open to the truth.

"I need to speak to Dr. Frye or Dr. Dowder. Can you take me to one of them?"

· He shook his head. "I'm not supposed to leave my post."

"Can I go in there and look for one of them?"

The boy soldier yawned hugely. "Dr. Dowder took a Gettys tonic and went to bed. You won't be able to wake him. Dr. Frye is spending the night in the officers' ward. You won't be able to get in there."

"Is there no one else who can help me? Or at least advise me what I should do for Scout Hitch?"

The boy looked uncertain. "There are orderlies on duty, but I am not certain how much they know. And some townspeople have come to help."

"I'm going to see if there is anyone who can help me," I announced.

He shook his head at my determination. "As you will," he conceded. Before the door had closed behind me, his head was pillowed on his ledger again.

The infirmary ward was dimly lit. A few hooded lanterns burned on small side tables between the beds, but the room was still shadowy and dim. I walked into a wall of smell. It wasn't just sweat and waste and vomit. The plague itself seemed to exude a sour stink of illness from the bodies it consumed, just as a fire gives off smoke as it devours fuel. My nightmarish memories of being confined to a plague ward slammed into reality around me. For an instant, I felt again the fever and disorientation. All I could think of was fleeing. I knew I couldn't.

I made the mistake of trying to take a breath through my mouth. I tasted the plague then, a foul miasma that coated my tongue and throat with the taste of death. I gagged, clamped my mouth shut, and furiously took charge of myself.

When I had first delivered Hitch here, the infirmary had been a clean, sparsely furnished room washed with sunlight. Now the windows were heavily draped against the night. Twice as many beds lined the walls, and litters had been brought in and set haphazardly on the floor. Each bed and pallet held a feverish victim. Some tossed and groaned; others lay deathly still, breathing hoarsely. The door to the next room was open. In that room, someone raved with fever.

Three upright figures moved among the fallen. A woman in a gray dress was making up an empty bed. A man was going from bed to bed, emptying noisome basins into a slop bucket. Closer to me, a woman in blue bent over a patient, applying a wet cloth to his brow. I made my way awkwardly toward her, stepping around the litters on the floor. I had nearly reached her when she straightened up and turned around. For a moment, we simply regarded one another in the dim light.

"Nevare?" Epiny whispered furiously.

I was caught. I could not flee without treading on sick men. I stood staring down on her. She had always been a slight woman. Now her face was even thinner. Her features were sharper than I recalled, and she looked as if she had aged much more than the one year since I'd last seen her. I suddenly recalled that she was in the early months of a pregnancy.

"You should not be here, in your condition," I rebuked her. Her mouth dropped open in shock. Then she reached across the patient who lay on the floor between us and seized my upper arm in a painful pinch. Keeping a grip on me, she walked me along the patient and then tugged me after her as she picked a path through the beds and pallets.

"Epiny, I—"

"Sshhh!" she hissed furiously.

Still not daring to speak, I followed her out into the anteroom and then out onto the dark street. The boy soldier at the desk didn't even stir as we passed through the room.

Once we were outside, she turned to face me. I braced myself for harsh words. Instead, she flung herself at me in an attempt to hug me. Her arms couldn't span my girth, but it still felt good, until I felt her shoulders heave in a sudden sob. Then she pushed herself back and looked up at me angrily. The lantern light picked up the streaks of tears on her face. "I shouldn't be nursing plague victims while I'm pregnant? But it's fine for me to be submersed in grief at such a time, I suppose! I thought you were dead, Nevare! For weeks I mourned you as dead, and you let me think that. And so did Spink! My own husband would rather keep faith with a friend than ease his wife's agony of fear. I will never, never forgive either of you for what you've put me through."

"I'm sorry," I said immediately.

"Of course you are! You should be. It was despicable. But being sorry doesn't change anything about the shameful thing you've done. And your own poor little sister, all this time thinking you'd gone to your death, imagining your body rotting unburied in a ditch somewhere. How could you do that to us, Nevare? Why?"

And in that moment, all my excellent reasons suddenly seemed shallow and stupid and selfish. I tried them anyway. "I was afraid it would ruin your reputation if people knew you were related to me," I said awkwardly.

"And I've always cared *so* much for my reputation and what other people thought of me!" she fumed at me. "Did you truly think I was so shallow as to put such things ahead of family, Nevare? You are my cousin! And you saved both Spink and me, at great risk to yourself. Do you think I would forget that, and shun you because of what the Speck magic has done to you?"

I hung my head. She had taken both my hands in hers, and that simple act of honest affection in the midst of her anger moved me terribly. I spoke simply. "Sometimes I think you need to be protected from your good intentions, Epiny. Now is one of those times. You may have the moral fiber not to care what others think of you. But what others think of you may well cost Spink a promotion, or you may find that other officers may not wish their children to play with yours. Think of what it would do to your status among the women you have championed if they found out you are related to a man they have accused of the two most heinous crimes that exist. I think you must know by now that I've been accused of murder. Until I can prove I am innocent, I do not think our connection should be revealed." I squeezed her hands affectionately, wincing at how thin her fingers felt, and then let them go.

"No, do not argue with me about this now," I cautioned her when she opened her lips to speak. "I'm on a desperate mission tonight. The one man whose testimony could prove my innocence has just escaped premature burial. He's what they call a 'walker.' He's in my cabin recuperating, but he's still very weak. I need to get a doctor to come out to see him. Or, failing that, I need to know what I can do to help him recover. My life depends on this as well as his."

She began shaking her head slowly before I'd even finished speaking. At my final words, a look of despair crossed her face. She spoke softly. "I don't know of anything you can do, Nevare, other than the obvious. Give him water and thin soup, if he will take it. I've seen one other 'walker.' A woman came into the infirmary tonight, trailing a shroud sheet. She begged us all to leave Gettys forever for the sake of her children. She begged us to make sure her children were taken safely west. Then she lay down and died again. Someone recognized her and went running for her husband. The poor man came racing to the infirmary in shock. He said she'd died hours earlier and he had put her body out. We had to tell him that she'd died again. Dr. Frye only made it worse when he tried to tell the man that his wife had never revived, that it had only been an evil Speck magic reanimating her body. I wanted to throttle the man."

"Dr. Amicas knew about 'walkers'; remember how he insisted on waiting before he sent bodies off to be buried?"

"Well of course I do! You were among those who 'died' and returned. As were many whom you sent back across the bridge. As was Spink."

"Where is Spink tonight? Does he know that you're here?"

"He doesn't. He was called away from our home early today. So many of the higher-ranking officers have become ill that the junior officers are being called in simply to keep some kind of chain of command functioning. He didn't want to leave us, but he had to go. Some sort of trouble with the prisoners. It was his duty and I understood that.

"When a runner came to our door tonight saying that a sick man was asking for me by name, I knew it was my duty to come here. The man in that bed in there has no one else. His wife died in childbirth the year after the regiment came here. I was shocked the first time I called a meeting for the women of the post to talk about improving our safety on the streets, and he walked in. I thought he came to mock us, or perhaps worse. But ever since then, he has been one of our staunchest supporters. He was the first man to join in our promise that if ever he heard a woman blowing a whistle for help, he would stop whatever he was doing and come to her aid. And he has kept that promise, more than once, even if the woman was a common prostitute. He has been faithful to our cause. So, you see, now that Sergeant Hoster is the one who needs help, I must return that faithfulness."

"Hoster?" I was shocked and amazed. It couldn't be the same man. "But I saw him just a few hours ago. He drove the wagon that brought Scout Hitch's body to the cemetery."

"You know how suddenly the plague can strike, Nevare. And taking bodies to the cemetery might be how he became infected. We know so little." She gave a sharp sigh of frustration. "And I should get back to him and ease his discomfort what little I can. He's very ill, the sickest man I've seen tonight. It's a shame to see such a charming, gentle man so stricken. I fear he may die, and I should be shamed if there was no one at his side when it happened."

My mind was reeling with that description of Sergeant. Hoster. It did not seem the right time to disillusion her. His deception of her made me despise him more than ever.

"I'll let you go, then. And you think there is nothing I can do for Scout Hitch?"

"Nothing except pray that he has a strong constitution. Wait. I'll give you one of the powders we've been using. Willow bark, feverfew, and a bit of sulfur steeped with simper leaves. We've been brewing it up as a tea. To be honest with you, I can't tell if it helps or not. I've been spooning it into Sergeant Hoster for an hour now, with no change that I can see. The only certain thing I know is that people who drank the Bitter Springs water as soon as the fever came on seem to be recovering. Slowly, that's true, but their fevers are not as extreme and they aren't hallucinating."

"Do you think Bitter Springs water would help Hitch?"

"If we had any left, we could try it. But I'm afraid I've given it all away. I doubt it would be of much help. The small quantities we brought with us only help if taken at the first sign of the disease. I had one extra bottle that I had kept in reserve. I sent it to Colonel Haren when I heard he was stricken. He died anyway. I think the disease was too well established in him to yield to so small a quantity of the water."

My last hope fluttered and died away. "Well. Can I get one of those powders from you for Hitch, please? And then I must be on my way back out to him."

"Of course. Wait here. I'll fetch it for you."

She went back into the infirmary. I was left standing outside. I tried to fit my image of Sergeant Hoster with the man that Epiny had described. Obviously, he showed such a very different face to the ladies. He'd always been a tyrant to Ebrooks, Kesey, and me, but what sergeant is not seen as a tyrant to the men beneath him? I tried to pare away his dislike of me to see what sort of a man he might have been. I didn't have enough to go on. Nevertheless, I had to admit to myself that I'd felt a flush of relief at Epiny's news that Hoster seemed to be dying. He was the one who most ardently believed in my guilt. Once he was gone, perhaps everyone else would let the matter drop. I could hope. I felt a twinge of guilt at hoping for the man's death, but consoled myself that the feeling was mutual.

Epiny appeared a short time later clutching two little muslin bags of herbs. "Steep one bag in boiling water, and be sure you squeeze it well to make sure that it reaches full potency in the drink. I've given you two. If the first one helps him, then give him the second one, and come back to town for more. But, Nevare, don't hope too hard. This round of Speck plague is the most vicious I've seen. It's worse than what you had at the academy and even worse than the sort that hit Bitter Springs."

"Epiny, I fear for you. What if you catch the plague again?"

"I don't think I shall. Everyone I've talked to says that if you've had it twice and not died of it, it won't bother with you again. Besides, I don't see you cringing and hiding from your duty. You're handling all the dead from this plague, and from what you've said, you've a sick man in your own home. Why do you think I should do less?"

I smiled regretfully. "That's a discussion that we have no time for just now."

She narrowed her eyes at me. "There are several discussions that are going to have to wait. Just because I've spoken to you civilly, don't assume that I'm not still furious with you. And hurt by what you and Spink have done. It's going to be a long time before I trust either one of you again."

"But Epiny, I—"

"No. Not now." She was adamant. "But when this is over, Nevare, I intend to give you no quarter. And I do not think that your sister will think kindly of you when she hears of how she has been made to suffer by your silence."

Her last words quenched me. I felt a selfish brute. Over the last few days, I'd allowed myself to forget about Yaril's plight. Betrothed to Caulder Stiet; if my father could force that on her, she was completely under his dominance. I discovered that I had been toying with the idea of fleeing to the Specks because I suddenly recognized how selfish that decision would be. No. I had to endure life at Gettys and make something of myself, and that included providing a home for Yaril where she could have some say in her own future. My resolve hardened. "I will do better," I said aloud, and the words surprised a feeble smile out of Epiny.

"You had better," she warned me, "for I can't imagine what you would have to do in order to do worse." She surprised me with another hug. "Hurry along. We both have to get back to our patients."

She had turned and was walking away when I called after her, "Are Amzil and the children still all right?"

She stopped short and turned back to me, and this time her smile was stronger. "They're fine, Nevare. And now that I know they're yours, I'll look after them even better."

"What is that supposed to mean?" I demanded, but the door had closed behind her.

I tucked the two herb bags into my jacket pocket. Then I went to the regiment's stable area and after a short search found Clove crammed into a stall that was too small for him. I found a hackamore that would fit him and strapped a blanket to his back for makeshift tack, and we were soon on our way home. No one saw us. It had been a long time since I'd ridden him that way, so the only pleasant part of the journey home was how swiftly it went compared to my long walk there. Even so, we did not gallop along, but went at a sensible pace through the moon-silvered darkness.

Light still glowed faintly from the windows of my cabin as I approached it. I dismounted, put Clove up hastily, and then, with a small shiver, hurried past the two coffins to my door. "Hitch, I've brought medicine for you," I called.

And stopped.

I didn't need to cross the room to know he was dead. He lay on my bed, one thin hand stretched out toward me as if pleading for understanding. His face had fallen on his bones, and his jaw hung slack and awry. When I did cross the room and touch him, he was still warm, but it was the fading warmth of a recently vacated chair rather than the warmth

of life. Still, I shook him and called his name and even bent
to put my ear to his chest, but it was useless. Scout Buel
Hitch was gone.

"Oh, Hitch. What have you done to me?" I asked his
empty shell. It offered me no answers.

He wasn't a small man, and I was weak with both weariness and despair. Nevertheless, I managed to carry him
from my bed back to the cold wooden coffin that awaited
him. I draped him again with his sheet, and set the lid once
more on the box. Then for a time I stood there, staring down
at it and wondering at what moment life became death. I set
my hand briefly on top of his casket but could think of no
prayer nor even a final word to utter. He had been wrong at
the end. I hated not him but the magic that had poisoned
him. I settled for "Good night, Hitch," and left him there.

Tired as I was, I still had a hard time bringing myself to
lie down on the bed where Hitch had finally died. It seemed
slightly macabre and more than a little unlucky to sleep in a
dead man's last bed, but I finally decided that my luck was
already so abysmal that I couldn't worsen it. I thought I
would have a hard time falling asleep, for my mind whirled
with worries and conflicts, but I think I slept almost as soon
as I closed my eyes.

I had no dream that night. I awoke when the dawn pried
its way though the cracks in my shutters. For a time I lay in
my bed, wondering how I'd face this new day. Hitch was
dead. I'd never realized how comforted I'd been to know
someone else who was as infected with Speck magic as I
was. While he had lived, there had been hope to clear my
name. That was gone now. If Hoster lived, I'd face a court-
martial. I pushed my fear down. I tried not to be the sort of
man who would hope for another's death.

I washed, cooked, and ate some porridge, and then
emerged to a fine summer morning. The sky was an infinite,
unclouded blue. Leaves on my hedge fluttered in the early-
morning breeze. Birds were singing, and the summer day
smelled new and alive. In anyone else's life, it would have
been a beautiful day, rich with promise. I went to fetch my
shovel to finish filling in the woman's grave.

The lid was crooked on Hitch's coffin.

I didn't have to look inside to know his body had been taken.

At one time, it would have been a hard decision. That morning, it wasn't. I carried the empty coffin and lid out to the next available grave, lowered it in, and buried it. By the time Ebrooks and Kesey arrived with the first two corpse wagons of the day, I had Hitch's coffin covered and had smoothed the mound over the woman I'd buried the night before.

"Looks like you got an early start on the day's work," Kesey observed.

"Looks like it," I agreed.

CHAPTER THIRTY

THE
APOLOGY

The days creaked by on corpse-laden wagons.
There was no respite from the parade of death that stopped
at my door. Every morning I arose to bodies awaiting burial,
and every evening I had to leave the dead in boxes outside
my cabin. All day long, the *tack-tack-tack*ing of the coffin
makers was a steady counterpoint to the scrape of my shovel
as I dug it into the earth. The bodies went from the wagons
to coffins and quickly into the waiting graves. Whoever
was in charge at Gettys sent us two more men to help cover
the graves. The empty holes filled at an alarming rate.

The gallows humor of the first few days gave way to an
unremitting gloom of spirit for all of us. We didn't talk much.
Most of my conversations were with Ebrooks and Kesey, and
limited to the logistics of our tasks. How many coffins we

had, how much wood was left, how many empty graves, how many coffins filled but unburied, how many bodies in the latest wagonload. I doggedly kept my tally of names, though often enough bodies came to the cemetery with little identification. Still, I logged them in as best I could: *Old man, toothless, wearing worn cavalla trousers. Child, female, about five years old, blue dress, dark hair. Mother and infant, in nightwear, mother with red hair.* The fourth day was hard for me. It seemed a day of dead children, and the little bodies looked lonely and abandoned, one to a coffin. Worst of all, mourners came that day, doggedly following the corpse wagons like hungry dogs hoping for a final bone. They watched us take the bodies from the cart and set them in the coffins, and their eyes seemed to blame me for taking their children from them. One mother, her eyes bright with fever, insisted that she must comb her little girl's hair before I could put the lid on. What could I do but let her? She sat the child on her lap for that final grooming, and smoothed her hair and straightened the collar of her little nightshirt before tucking her into the coffin as if it were a truckle bed. Her husband took her away after that, but late that evening, on the final corpse cart of the day, she returned to us. I wished I could have buried her with her child. I kept dreading that I would recognize Amzil or one of her brood, but I was spared that.

The only body that I selfishly welcomed with relief came on the third day after I'd visited town. Sergeant Hoster arrived with his arms crossed on his chest, his eyes closed, his hair combed, and his face washed. A shiny whistle on a chain was enfolded in his stiff hands. Pinned to his shirt was a note in Epiny's hand. "*Bury him well. He was a good man.*" She'd signed it with a simple "*E.*" For her sake, I did just that, though I privately thought that he had deceived her and the other women of the town with a fair face over a foul heart. The brief prayer I said over his grave was to the good god, and not for his mercy on Hoster but that Hoster's accusations against me might be laid to rest with his bones.

Occasional mourners brought their own dead to the cemetery or followed the corpse cart. Usually they were parents mourning children. I dreaded to see them come, for I knew the burial they would see would offer them little comfort. There was no music, no solemn prayers, no bouquets or memorial of any kind, simply the efficient lowering of a coffin into the earth and the shoveling of soil down onto it. Perhaps that was all they came for, to be able to return to Gettys knowing the body of the one they had loved had been safely consigned to the earth.

I lost no more bodies to the Specks, and never mentioned to anyone else that Hitch's body had been taken. Several times Ebrooks or Kesey spoke of how well I guarded the cemetery, for in years past the theft of plague bodies had been a horrific addition to all the other troubles of the plague season. I scarcely felt I deserved their praise, for I had done nothing to deserve it. I had no idea why the Specks were respecting our dead; I only felt vaguely grateful that they did, even as it gave me an ominous sense of impending disaster.

Sometimes I thought of Hitch and wondered who had come for him and carried him off in the night. I hoped he had his tree and wished him well of it, despite his betrayal of me. I knew only too well the lure of the magic and how strongly it could affect a man's mind. I told myself that I would never fall as low as Hitch had done. Yet as I looked back over my behavior of the last few months, there was much in it that was reprehensible. The worst, I think, was that I had let my sister suffer uncertainty for so long.

I threw caution to the winds. I would no longer wait for a secret letter to reach me through Carsina. I wrote Yaril not one, but three letters posting them days apart in the hopes that at least one might get through to her. I told her that I was alive, a soldier, stationed at Gettys, and dealing with the most current outbreak of plague. This I described to her in detail in the hope that she would immediately see how impossible it was for me to send for her. In the closing paragraph, I counseled her to consider all decisions carefully and to be true to her own heart. I hoped it would give her the courage to defy my father and refuse Caulder Stiet. I hoped such advice was not too late.

Kesey took the letters to town for me and sent them off with the couriers who daily rode west. He also took it upon himself to bring me food from the mess hall each day. It wasn't especially appetizing; the cook staff was reduced, and the food was usually a cold serving of soup and bread in a dinner pail that had arrived on a wagonful of corpses. But I ate it, and little else. Anyone else would have lost flesh on such a regimen of constant work and reduced food. I changed not at all.

I didn't return to town. Much as I longed to see Spink and Epiny, my days were too full of backbreaking labor to make me want to give up a night's sleep to a long ride there and back. I almost hoped that Epiny or Spink would come out to see me, but I recognized that we lived in dangerous times. I hoped that Epiny's nursing of Sergeant Hoster had not endangered her pregnancy, and that she was not suffering too much in the endless parade of hot days the summer had brought us. I was grateful that she had the sense to stay home and safe, even as I hungered for the sight of a friendly face and a kind voice. I had not known how much I missed Epiny before that chance encounter.

All I knew of Gettys was what I heard from Kesey and Ebrooks. Some of it was very bad, for the plague continued to rage as if the hot, dry days fueled it. The sadness that flowed from the forest into the town seemed to deepen. We buried suicides as well as plague victims, people who, having lost loved ones, saw no reason to continue. Kesey and Ebrooks told me tales of sordid crimes, too, of scavengers who robbed the dead left out for the corpse carts, and thieves who robbed homes before the eyes of people too sick to stop them.

Yet there was news that gave me hope and renewed my faith in my fellows. Gettys was a town that had known plague before, on a yearly basis, and had learned to cope with it. Those who had the plague in years past kept the town running. Several of the stores remained open, though the merchants allowed no one to enter. Customers had to shout their requests from the street, and then deposit the coin to pay for their purchases in a pot of vinegar outside the door before the shopkeepers put their purchases out in the street for them to collect. It sounded like a complicated process, yet most customers were grateful to be able to get supplies at all.

A different order emerged in the town. Men and women judged too feeble to be employed at any other part of the year were now in demand. These former plague victims could nurse families, care for livestock, and perform other chores for households where the plague was rampant. I saw a different side of Gettys. I had wondered previously why the regiment kept within its ranks so many soldiers who suffered impaired health due to previous bouts of Speck plague. Now I understood, as they became the backbone of the regiment during a time when the hearty and hale were either in hiding from the plague or succumbing to their first bouts of it. The plague that the Specks had thought would drive the Gernians away had, indeed, "winnowed" us, so that those who remained in Gettys were stronger than before. As the people here acquired immunity, they found a niche in the society. Surviving the plague in Gettys actually increased the chance that folk would remain in the town, for only there could they have their yearly season of strength.

The town and the fortress had immediately gone under "plague rules" from the time of the first outbreak. Public gatherings were forbidden. Alehouses and taverns closed their doors. Funerals were forbidden for the duration of the plague season. It was forbidden to touch the bodies set out for the corpse carts; only the men designated for that duty could handle the dead. Those men lived apart from the rest of the regiment for that time. Food was set out for them, but neither Ebrooks nor Kesey was permitted to go into the mess hall.

I suspected Epiny when I heard that the women had organized a system of taking hot meals to homes marked with plague flags. There was a grimmer duty for one crew of men. They knocked daily on the doors of plague houses, and then stepped back into the street to await a response. If there was none, the corpse handlers were dispatched, for it was assumed that the entire family had perished there.

But for every evidence of adaptation and cooperation, there were horrible instances of failure. A young widow fell ill and before it was discovered that she had died, her infant had starved in his crib. A former prisoner was caught sneaking into the homes of the ill to burgle them of valuables; he was flogged and then hanged in the town square. In times of plague, even relatively petty crimes were punished more drastically, lest others follow the example of the criminals.

The prisoners lived in conditions far more crowded and unsanitary than the military barracks. The plague burned through the place like wildfire. In the second day of the fever and fluxes, those of the prisoners who could offer resistance had rioted, believing that plague was only in their prison and that their guards were deliberately confining them in a death hole. They'd overcome their guards and almost a hundred had escaped. Several dozen had attacked the town, looting supplies from untended businesses, but most had simply gone to the stables, stolen horses, and ridden off. A lieutenant had rallied a small force of mixed soldiers to reestablish order. The prisoners who had been foolish enough to remain in the town were shot down in the streets, and summarily consigned to the lime pits behind the prison barracks. The ones who had fled were pursued, not for themselves but for the horses they had taken. The pursuit had been successful.

The upper echelons of our command had been devastated by the plague. Ebrooks told me one day that Major Morson was now in charge, but didn't know it, as he had sunk into his fever before death bestowed command on him. "But having an unconscious commander isn't much different from what we're accustomed to anyway," he added with sour humor, and I was forced to agree.

I lost track of time, not just hours but days. The plague season ran together into a time of endless work for me. By the third day, I had become so accustomed to the stench of death and decay that I scarcely needed the vinegar and rag mask, not that it had worked very well in the first place. There came a day when we ran out of both ready graves and materials to make coffins. We did what was expedient, which was to put one body in each coffin and another on top of the coffin in each grave in the final row of waiting holes. I logged their names as best I could, and told the coffin makers to join me in digging a ditch for mass burial. I was surprised when they grudgingly complied. That night, before I closed my eyes for sleep, I took a small moment of pride in how they, as well as Ebrooks and Kesey, had accepted my leadership. I had no stripe on my sleeve and less seniority than any of them. I recalled with regret how I had angered Colonel Haren. Had he truly considered me for promotion? Well, I thought grimly, the plague was forcing a change in command; I'd have a second chance to impress my superiors when all this was over and I once more knew who they were.

Nights brought me no rest. The row of unburied dead outside my small cottage was not even contained in coffins anymore, but only in coarse white sacking. The scavengers of the forest ventured forth to feast. I did what I could. I set pitch torches in a protective ring around the bodies. That seemed to keep most of the larger predators away, but nothing seemed to discourage the rats. Often it was only when we went to move the bodies to their grave that the rodents would scamper away, bellies bulging with human flesh. I hated them and killed them when I could.

The carrion birds had become a constant. Red-wattled croaker birds skirmished with crows over the open-pit graves. They followed the corpse carts and gathered in the trees, watching while we placed the bodies in the pit graves and covered them with a thin layer of quicklime and earth. As soon as we stepped away, the croakers would descend. Kesey brought out a shotgun and killed a dozen of them one day. He tied the bodies to tall stakes and set them around the pit grave. The bird bodies served as a deterrent to the rest of the flock, but they quickly rotted and stank in the hot sun, attracting both buzzing flies and wasps. Worse, they reminded me of the horrible little bird carousel at Rosse's wedding. The croaker birds seemed especially incensed by Kesey's murder of their fellows. They recognized him and would dive on him when he was driving the corpse cart, stabbing at his hat and croaking loudly. Every evening, other creatures ventured out of the forest to dig in the newly covered graves. Not even the quicklime we used in the pit graves deterred them completely. Every morning, I made a brief tour of our most recent graves to fill in little tunnels and holes dug during the night. I felt as if I were under siege. My growing hedge, lovely as it was, would never keep out such creatures, and I reluctantly concluded that Colonel Haren had been right; a stone wall was needed.

I had not slept well any night since Olikea and I had quarreled. I still dreamed of her, and dreamed too of the wondrous foods from that "other side." But I couldn't quite reach them. I walked there, but I walked there knowing it was a dream. The food I ate in those dreams was substanceless and unsatisfying. I would see Olikea, but always at a distance. If I called to her, she did not turn her head. If I followed her, as I inevitably did in those dreams, I could never catch up with her.

The days became weeks, and then a month. We toiled on, barely able to keep ahead of the dead. The stink of decay and the burning of lye in my nostrils became one sensation in my mind. Even when I heated water and washed with soap, I could not cleanse the smells of my profession away. The lime we sprinkled in the ditch graves drifted and made raw patches on my skin. Worst of all was the terrible hunger that burned in me constantly now that I no longer had the forest foods that Olikea had brought me. The food I ate should have been enough to sustain me; instead it was not even a taunt to the deeper hunger that devoured me from within.

And in the midst of death and stench and plague, summer blossomed around us. The days were lovely, long and bright under blue skies. Butterflies danced above the flowers I had moved into the graveyard, and songbirds sang in the trees at the edge of the forest. My "hedge" flourished, and smaller bushes sprang up in the shade my little trees provided.

The bony hands of the plague respected neither age nor rank. We filled one ditch grave and started another. We buried tiny babies and old men, delicate little girls and brawny men. That long hot day had brought the body of Dale Hardy. He was the rowdy who had put himself forth as the man to give me a beating the day that Carsina had said such foul things about me. The plague had taken him down swiftly, Ebrooks told me. He hadn't lingered to die of the fever but had choked to death on his own vomit the first day he sickened. I thought of how he had stood in the street and threatened me that day. I could have taken satisfaction in his death. Instead I only pitied him, felled in his prime so ignominiously.

It was late afternoon when we finished filling the second ditch. In an obscene way, it reminded me of watching the cook in my father's kitchen layer ingredients into a casserole. Instead of meat and gravy and potatoes and carrots, we layered bodies and lime and earth and bodies and lime and earth until we finally mounded earth over the whole of it.

"That's it," I decided when the mound was patted smooth as a pie crust. I took my vinegar mask from my face and wiped my brow with it. With the last bodies covered, the air smelled almost clean. "That's enough for today, boys. Tomorrow we'll dig a fresh ditch and begin again."

"Pray the good god that it's the last pit this season," Kesey suggested, and "Amen," both of my carpenters-turned-gravediggers responded.

"It has to stop soon. Doesn't it?" I asked them.

"It'll stop when it stops," Kesey replied. "The rains always end it. But sometimes it stops sooner. I heard a rumor in town about some special water that might cure it. Some spring water that a doctor back west has been trying on people. The courier that brought the news said he'd heard from the courier before him that they were trying to get some to us here, before the end of the plague season, to see if it really worked or not."

"Did you hear the doctor's name?" I asked, wondering if Spink had written to Amicas and if he had acted on it.

Kesey shrugged and shook his head. We had shouldered our shovels and were making our way back to the tool shed when we heard a sound we all dreaded: the *clop* and *creak* of a team pulling a laden wagon up the hill to the cemetery. "Can't they just stop dying for one day?" Kesey asked me pathetically.

"I think they would if they could," I replied, and one of my diggers smiled grimly.

"Those poor devils will just have to lie bare under the

moonlight for tonight," Kesey observed, and I shrugged. It would not be the first time that shrouded bodies had had to wait for a fresh grave. But like Kesey, I prayed it might be the last.

Ebrooks was the driver. He got down stiffly from the cart. "You boys had better help me unload if you want to ride back to town," he suggested, and we began our grim task. There were seven of them. Ebrooks, knowing my insistence, handed me a list of names. I thrust them into my pocket and helped the other men drag the corpses from the cart. Three men, a boy, and three women we laid out side by side. Kesey had brought a fresh supply of pitch torches from town. Ebrooks helped me set up a circle of them around the unburied bodies. Then the others climbed up on the wagon, bade me farewell, and headed back to town as the long-awaited night began to flow across the land. I hoped it would bring a little coolness with it. I kindled the torches. They burned straight, nearly unwavering, in the calm summer evening.

I went back to my cabin, washed my face and hands, drank deeply, and then turned to the cold meal Kesey had brought me. There was bread and meat and cheese. It was good enough food, and I devoured it hungrily but as usual felt no satisfaction in it. It was only food, and I'd learned that the hunger that burned me most was not a hunger for food. I forced myself to set aside a portion to break my fast the next day, and left my table as hungry as when I'd sat down.

I washed up my few dishes and set them aside. With a sigh, I took out what had become a ledger. I opened it to the current page, and unfolded the scrap of paper that Ebrooks had given me. He was not a lettered man; most often he depended on the family of the dead or whoever was on duty at the infirmary to write down the names for him. Sometimes there was only a tally mark on the page. I entered the names as he had given them to me. They'd go into a ditch grave tomorrow; there was little point any more in worrying about the order in which I wrote them down. And so I logged Eldafleur Sims, Coby Tarn, Rufus Lear, Joffra Keel, A Retired Soldier, Carsina Thayer—

I set down my pen. I looked at the name on the list, and

the name my hand had so obligingly written. Hadn't my Carsina been betrothed to a Captain Thayer? My nervous fingers scrabbled lightly against the tabletop. Carsina Gren-alter. Carsina Thayer. Many couples wed hastily in the face of the plague. My friend at the academy, Gord, had done so. It seemed likely that Carsina had wed her handsome captain. No matter how foolish or shallow the attraction had been, Carsina had meant something to me. My first romance, and my first heartbreak. And today her body had been unloaded from a corpse cart and somehow I hadn't even noticed. I rubbed my face and took up my pen again. Reddik Koverton was the last name, and I carefully entered it into the ledger. I blew on the ink to dry it and then closed it.

Did I want to look on her again, dead?

No. Of course not.

Yes.

However we had parted, whatever I had discovered about her, she had been my sister's friend, a longtime friend of my family, and the first girl I'd ever kissed. Her love letters to me at the academy were still bundled in with my soldier son's journal. Tears found their way to my weary eyes. I wouldn't bury her in a ditch, with strangers tumbled beside her and lime eating away her flesh. I'd dig her a separate grave myself; she would not lie in a common hole.

I put my face in my hands and sat like that at my table for a time. I knew that I was going to go out to look at her tonight. I could not decide if I was motivated by sentiment or morbid curiosity. It probably didn't matter. I took my lantern and went out into the darkness.

The circle of torches still burned. Nonetheless, I heard a squeak of alarm and then a rustling as I approached. Rats. I held my lantern high as I entered my torch circle. The seven bodies lay as we had left them. Of the three women, only one could be Carsina. I knew her by a single blonde curl that had escaped her shroud. Unlike the others, she was not wrapped in coarse white sacking. A fine fabric enveloped her, white linen with white lace worked along the edge of it, and someone had wound the sheet around her with care. I went down on one knee beside her and reached a hand toward her face.

Then I drew my hand back. It wasn't that I feared to see how the disease had ravaged her. I suddenly felt that I intruded. Someone had lovingly prepared her for the grave; who was I to loosen that cloth and look into a dead face that no longer belonged to me? Her name on the papers indicated that she had been a married woman at her death. I should respect that. I bowed my head and asked the good god to guide her into peace. Then I said simply, "Good night, Carsina." I went back to my cabin.

It was a warm night. The little cook fire in my hearth was down to a few coals. I gave it another two sticks of wood, more for the company of its light than for any other reason, sat down at my table again, and made my day's entry in my journal. I closed it and put it away. Too tired to change, I lay down on my bed in my earth-stained clothes. For a time, I watched the shadows mirror the dance of my little fire in the corners of my ceiling. I thought of the women I'd loved in my life, not just Carsina and Tree Woman, but my mother and sisters and Epiny, even Amzil. I tried to work out why I'd loved each one and which sorts of love were real, but came to no solid conclusions. I'd been born to love my mother and sisters, and perhaps I had to include Epiny on that list as well. Tree Woman I'd loved; I knew that without knowing the details of how my other self had bonded to her. I loved her still, in that other place. Amzil I loved perhaps for no better reason than that I thought she needed someone to love her. I even thought of poor, unfortunate Fala. We'd shared no more than an evening of closeness. Did the brevity of that relationship mean that I couldn't call it love? It had certainly been something beyond lust.

And Olikea? Yes. I loved her. Not as a good Gernian loves his good Gernian wife, not with romance and vows and a shared hearth until the end of my days. I loved her as I had come to love her forest, as a thing that gave me delight but never offered me mastery or any degree of control. I had no partnership with Olikea. She did not want me to provide for her or protect her. On the contrary, she had seen herself in the role of provider. I wondered if we could ever truly know one another, and concluded the opportunity for that was gone. I'd forsaken her in this world, and she'd turned away from me in that other world. We knew remarkably little of one another. But did I really know any more of Amzil than I did of her? I knew Amzil better only in that we shared a culture. She was still as great a mystery to me as Olikea was.

The shadows were fading as my fire died. I repeated my prayer for Carsina, and added one for my mother and Elisi as well. I thought of the women who had passed beyond my reach and the women who remained to me, and resolved that I would treat Epiny, Amzil, and Yaril better while I had the opportunity to do so. On that thought, I turned my lamp wick down as low as it would go and closed my eyes for sleep.

Perhaps my evening thoughts had paved the way to her. I dream-walked strongly that night, and my footsteps led me not in pursuit of Olikea, but to a stump in the old forest. The tree that had grown up from the fallen trunk of Tree Woman's tree stood straight and tall. I now recognized that my hedge trees were of the same kind, and that they were growing very well indeed; I touched it fondly, and felt an echo of Tree Woman's presence. I walked slowly to the stump and sat down with my back to it. "I miss you, Lisana. I miss you terribly."

"Oh, you are a cruel one," she rebuked me, but still she reached to take my hand. "To call me at last by my name at such a time. Did you know how hearing that from your lips would wring my heart? But it is too late, Soldier's Boy. I can do nothing to spare you from what is to come. You've brought it on yourself. Still, if I could, I would save you somehow."

She was not there in the old way she had once been. She was a dream within a dream. I could feel the warmth of her hands around mine, but I could not enfold them. When I turned to embrace her, I felt only the rough bark of her fallen tree's trunk. I drew back from her. If I could not touch her, at least I could see her. She was in the first guise in which I'd ever seen her. She was an immensely fat woman in her middle years. Her streaky hair tangled against the bark of her tree as if it were tendrils uniting her with it. And, of course, they were. Her eyes smiled at me; they remained unchanged regardless of what guise she showed me. And I discovered that truly her body no longer mattered to me. She was as dear to me in this form as she had been in those un-remembered times when we had first come together. She had folded her hands on top of her ample belly. Her hands reminded me of little cat's feet. They were small, and the skin on the back of them was sooty dark, fading to a lighter speckling on her forearms. I wanted to kiss them; the most I could do was hover my hand over hers, feeling a ghost warmth. "Why aren't you here?" I demanded.

She smiled in a bittersweet way. "Someone used iron magic here, and cut down my tree. It fell in both worlds; you have noticed this, perhaps?"

I lowered my eyes in shame. "But it did not kill you."

"No. But it weakened me. A hundred years from now, perhaps I shall have a quarter of the strength I once had. Then, perhaps, we can kiss and touch as we used to."

"It seems a very long time to wait."

She nodded, not in agreement but confirming her own thoughts. "And that is where our worlds do not align, Sol-dier's Boy. A hundred years from now, if our people prevail, the soil here will be a bit deeper, the girth of the trees will be greater, and little else will have changed. The same flowers will bloom, the same pollen will drift, and the same butter-flies will float among the foliage. I am happy to wait a hun-dred years for that. What will be here if the intruders prevail, Soldier's Boy? What will you wait a hundred years to see?"

I thought of the Gernian answer to that. A wide road up into and through the Barrier Mountains would lead to the land beyond and eventually the sea. The king was open about his ambition. Those lands were largely unsettled. Gernia could have a new seacoast with access to trade. Goods would flow from the eastern seaboard into Gernia. There would be growth and prosperity. New farms, burgeoning towns. None of that was bad. But I could no longer say with certainty that it was better than what was here now.

"People could live in prosperity and peace. The Specks would benefit from the trade. They would have everything they need."

She puffed her cheeks lightly at me. "We already have everything we need, Soldier's Boy. And we still have our forest and the ancestral trees. When we have lost our shady places and the land that loves us has been cut wide open to the sunlight, will we truly have everything we need? Or will we simply have the things that you think we need?"

I couldn't think of a response. A slight breeze or a ghost hand stirred my hair. I lifted my eyes to look into hers and asked, "What do you think I should do, then?"

"You know what I think. You have known from the beginning what I think."

"You say I should do what the magic wants me to do. And you say I should have done it by now. You've told me that over and over. But I truly don't know what that means."

"Perhaps the magic does not speak to you more clearly because you have avoided it so earnestly. Perhaps if you had not resisted its efforts to fill you, perhaps if you had come more promptly to its calling, you would know what you were to do. Now, I fear, it is too late for you to seek the magic."

"What do you mean?"

"I mean that I feel the magic reaching out to take you, Soldier's Boy."

"What do you mean?"

"Just what I said! Always you ask me, *what do you mean*? You hear my words. When you don't understand them, it is because you do not wish to understand them. It is the same way that you resist the magic. Why?"

I didn't even have to think of a reply. "Perhaps I want to have my own life, the way I envisioned it, the way it was promised to me! Lisana, from the time I was small, I was raised to be a soldier. I expected to go to the academy, to be well educated, to become an officer and distinguish myself in battle, to have a lovely wife and children, and eventually to return to my home and retire with honor. The magic took all of that away from me. And what has it given me? A fat body that is awkward and ugly to live in. A power that comes and goes, that I don't know how to use or control. What good has it done me?"

She looked at me sadly for a moment. She lifted her arms as if to display her body to me. "Awkward and ugly," she

said, and when she took the words to herself, it cut like a
knife that I had uttered them.

"I didn't mean—" I cried out, but "Hush!" she scolded
me. "I do not pretend that I don't understand what you say!
I know what you meant. What good has the magic done
you, you asked. I could say that through it, you came to
know me. And that you have come to know the forest in a
way you never could have before. But the real answer is
that the magic is not for your good, and so it does not matter if it does things that make you happy or not." She
cocked her head at me slightly. "Don't you remember, Soldier's Boy? I held you over the abyss and told you that you
must choose. I told you that you must say you wished to be
taken up to this life. And you said you did, and I brought
you here."

"But I did not know what I was choosing. I only knew that
I feared to die."

"None of us ever know what we are choosing when we
choose life. If certainty is so important to you, than you
should have chosen to be dead. That is a certain thing."

"Look at the life I am leading, Lisana. I'm a soldier in
name only; what I truly am is a gravedigger. Tomorrow I am
going to bury the woman I was once supposed to marry. Did
you know that? How cruel a fate is that? For her, as well as
for me, because if the magic had not intervened in my life, I
am sure Carsina would be safe at her home and awaiting me
still. I am lonely and alone, my body hampers me, I am always hungry—"

"And those are the things *you* chose instead of the magic."
She cut into my diatribe. She sounded angry.

"What am I going to do?"

I meant the question to be rhetorical. I'd asked it of myself
thousands of times with no answers. Lisana had one.

"You are going to do what the magic wants you to do. It
would have been easier by far for you to have lived with the
choice you made instead of fighting it. Now it comes for
you, Nevare. And no one can protect you anymore."

"You called me Nevare," I said.

"Nevare."

I was sitting up in my bed in my cabin. The echo of her voice saying my name was still in my ears. It was such a physical memory that it was hard to convince myself it had been part of my dreamwalking. I rubbed my eyes and sighed. Only darkness showed through the crack in my shutters. It was still night. I groaned. I doubted I would find sleep again that night.

My fire was nearly out. I forced myself to get out of bed and pad across the room to give it another stick of wood. Feeding it now was easier than trying to start another fire in the morning. I was getting back into my bed when I thought I heard a noise outside. I swung my feet back onto the floor.

Soft as the wind, someone spoke outside my door. "Nevare?"

"Who's there?" I asked. I stood up and took two steps.

My cabin door opened soundlessly.

I saw her nightdress first, a long confection of lace and white linen. Expensive and elegant, I thought inanely to myself. Doubtless her trousseau had been purchased in Old Thares from the most exclusive merchants. A flirtation of veiling pretended to hide the cleavage of her breasts, and a high collar of soft lace maintained a mockery of virginal modesty.

I was trembling. I lifted my eyes to her face. She had always been plump, with rounded cheeks. The disease had sculpted her face to sharper lines, and her lips were chapped. Dark circles ringed her eyes. Our gazes met. She entered the room, came to me, and took both my hands in hers. I couldn't move or speak. I was caught between horror and hope for her. Slowly, she sank down in a graceful curtsy. She bowed her head, and her flaxen hair fell forward to hide her face. I found my voice.

"Carsina?" I croaked.

She moved closer and rested her forehead against my knees. The hair stood up on the back of my neck. Her voice was husky and low. "I've come to beg your forgiveness, Nevare. Just as you said I must. I apologize for how cruel I was to you at your brother's wedding."

I took a step backward. I felt faint. Our quarrel at Rosse's wedding seemed to have happened a century ago. Yet at her words, my angry prediction to her came back to me, and I recalled too well the tingle of power that had rushed through me as I had uttered my harsh words. "Carsina. Please get up. Please." My mind was reeling. Carsina was a "walker." Could her life be saved? I'd failed with Hitch. Epiny had told me that most walkers died. But not all of them. I stooped down to offer her my hands to assist her in standing. She remained on her knees, her head bowed.

"You have not said that you forgive me." Her voice was low and hoarse.

"Carsina, I should be begging you to forgive me. I spoke angrily, never thinking that I would bind you to this. I am the one who is sorry."

Her voice was muffled. "I cannot rise from my knees until you forgive me."

"I forgive you, I forgive you, I forgive you a hundred times." I all but babbled the words. It went against everything I'd ever been taught as a gentleman to have her on her knees before me. "Please, please, let me help you get up."

Despite my offer, she tried to get up by herself. She swayed, and I barely managed to catch her before she fell over. I lifted her gently to her feet and helped her to a chair. "Sit there and rest. What a nightmare for you, to wake alone in a winding cloth in the cemetery among the dead. But you're safe now. Just sit and rest. I have medicine from the infirmary in town. Let me put the water to boil for it. It's feverfew and willow bark and, and I forget what else, but the doctors in Gettys are giving it to the plague victims there and they believe it helps. Just rest while I prepare it for you."

I moved swiftly as I spoke, putting fresh water in the kettle and setting it on to boil. I added more sticks of dry wood to the fire to send the flames lapping against the kettle's bottom. I found the little tisanes that Epiny had given me, wiped my mug clean, and put one in it. "Do you think you could eat a little something? Broth would be best for you, but I'm afraid I don't have any. I've some bread, though, and a bit of cheese, I think."

She looked pathetically grateful. "Water," she managed to say.

I hurried to my water cask and came back with a dripping ladle. She clasped it with both hands and drank so greedily that it ran down her chin. When it was empty, I brought her more, and she drank again. Where the water had fallen on her nightdress, the fine linen became nearly transparent. I tried not to stare. I tipped my water barrel to fill the ladle a last time. She drank it down, and then handed the ladle back to me with a small gasp. "Thank you," she managed to say.

"Sit still and rest. As soon as the water boils, I'll have a healing tea for you." All the anger I had ever felt at her had fled. I could not look at her without thinking of all the times she had been my sister's playmate and companion.

She covered her face with her hands for a moment, and then let them drop limply into her lap. "Tea won't help me, Nevare. You know that. I've only come back from the dead to beg your forgiveness. Because you said I must." Her eyes flooded with sudden tears. "And now I have to die again." She sounded terrified.

All pretense fled before her words. "Carsina, I'm so sorry. I didn't know what I was doing. Truly I didn't. And I won't let you die. Listen to me. Listen. I know you feel weak, but your fever has passed. Let me take care of you."

"You don't hate me?" She sounded puzzled. "After what I did to you in the street in Gettys? You forgive me for that, too?"

I am not as noble as others might be. I felt a flash of anger as I recalled that scene. A suddenly selfish thought quenched it. Just as she had accused me publicly, so could she also clear my name. If she lived, and if she felt kindly toward me. I chose my words. "You thought you had reason to fear me. You don't. At one time, Carsina, I think you loved me. I know I loved you. You are beyond my reach now, and in many ways I am beneath your notice. But I do not think we have to hate or fear one another. Look. The water is boiling. Let me brew you that tisane."

"Oh, Nevare, you are too good. And I am so ashamed now of what I said and did. But I *was* afraid. I hated coming to

Gettys, but my father said it was my last chance to make a good match for myself. He did not want to send me to stay with my cousin, for he feared for my reputation. He was so stern. He said I must not flirt or do anything that might invite a scandal, and that if I did, he would disown me. He was still angry because he had found Remwar kissing me when we both knew that Remwar had been promised to Essilee Cummors. But Remwar had said that he truly loved me and that the engagement was something his father had forced on him. We were going to run away . . . or so he said. Oh, Nevare, I have been a fool, over and over again. I lost your sister's friendship over Remwar, and he wasn't worth it. But you must admit that most of that was your fault. I still do not understand how you could have chosen to get so fat, and then to embarrass me like that at Rosse's wedding when I had been dreaming and planning for months about how fine we would look together, and how my green skirts would stand out when you spun me on the dance floor. I had so looked forward to that, and then you dashed all my hopes!"

I had forgotten how much Carsina could talk. "None of it was my choosing, Carsina. On that, you will just have to believe me." I had poured the boiling water for the little sachet of herbs. The sulfur in it immediately betrayed its presence. It reeked. "I'm afraid this isn't going to taste very good, but it's what the doctors at the infirmary are prescribing. Do you think you can drink it?"

"I want to live, Nevare. I'd do anything to live." Her eyes shone with the intensity of her desire. A moment later, I interpreted that glitter a different way. Fever. Her fever was coming back. As I handed her the cup, our fingers touched briefly. Mine were warm from holding the hot cup, but so were hers. I watched her put the cup to her lips, wince, and blow on the hot liquid and then sip from the edge. She wrinkled her nose and pursed her mouth at the foul taste but swallowed it down determinedly.

"That's right," I encouraged her. "But you need to drink it all, Carsina."

She tried another sip. I saw her grip on the cup begin to loosen and managed to take it from her before it fell. She looked at me with a gaze both desperate and unfocused. "My mother died of the plague, Nevare. I didn't get to say good-bye to her. My father wouldn't let me go near her once she got sick. Only the servants tended to her. And I had to wonder if they really did. She could have died alone." She blinked her eyes at me and then said unsteadily, "I'm married now. Did you know? My husband took care of me until I died. He kept saying, 'I'll be right here, Carsina, my sweet. I won't let you die alone.'"

"He sounds like a very good man. I think you need to rest now, Carsina. Do you want to lie down?"

"I . . ." She looked up at me, suddenly puzzled. "I want Jof. I want my husband. Where is he?"

"He's probably at home, Carsina. Let's put you to bed, shall we?"

"But . . . where am I? How did I get here? Please, can't you get Jof? He promised he would stay right by me." Her lips were a darker red, and two spots of color had begun to show on her cheeks. I did not think it would be a good time to tell her that she'd come here on the corpse cart, or to point out to her that Jof probably thought he had stayed by her side.

"Lie down and I'll see what I can do."

"I want Jof," she repeated, and she suddenly looked very young, a child asking for her daddy.

"I'll go and get him," I said reluctantly. I feared to leave her, lest she die as Hitch had. On the other hand, I could see that she was working herself up over her missing husband. "Can you drink the rest of your tea?" I asked her, and was tremendously relieved when she nodded. I handed her the cup, and she bravely drank it down. "I want you to lie down now," I told her firmly, and was rather surprised when she took the arm I offered and accompanied me to my bed.

"Lie down, Carsina," I suggested to her. She sat on the edge of the bed and looked up at me. She was breathing through her mouth. "You look like my first fiancé. Only fatter," she said. Before I could reply, she commanded me imperiously. "Fetch me a drink of water, and then please tell my husband to come in to me." Of her own volition, she lay down. I helped her lift her feet onto the bed and tried to put my blanket over her. She angrily kicked it away.

"Very well." I saw no sense in upsetting her.

My water keg was empty. I damped a clean cloth in the dregs and put it across Carsina's brow. She did not open her eyes. She was fading rapidly. I caught up my bucket and headed out to the spring. I'd fetch water first and then saddle Clove and ride into town to find her husband. I wondered how I'd locate him.

Outside my cabin, the pitch torches around the unburied bodies had burned low. Dawn would soon come. I started toward the spring with my bucket and then turned abruptly back to the torch circle.

No bodies rested inside it. A single shroud, probably Carsina's, lay in a tangle on the ground. The other six bodies were gone.

Horror and panic rose in me. The bodies had been stolen. I spun around, scanning the graveyard in all directions to see if I might see Specks still carrying the corpses away. What I saw was more frightening. The torchlight did not carry far, but it picked up the figures stumbling toward my hedge. Their shrouds trailed white behind them. As I watched, one fell away and the woman who had been wearing it stumbled on. Numbly, I counted them. Six. All six of them were walkers. Seven if I counted Carsina.

It was not a coincidence. It was the magic. Why? What could it mean?

I snatched up a torch from the ground and hastened after them. "Come back!" I shouted foolishly. "You need help. Come back." I ran after them, torch in one hand and water bucket in the other.

None of them paused or even looked back at me. The smallest one, the boy, had already reached the hedge. I saw him halt there. Slowly he tottered around. He reminded me of an arthritic dog walking in a circle before it lies down. Awkwardly, he sat down on the earth by one of my trees. Then he leaned back against it. He crossed his arms across his belly and was still. The foliage of the little tree rustled as he sat down against it. I saw the boy give his head a shake. Then his legs twitched, and the tree rustled more strongly.

As the others reached the hedge, they each selected a tree, turned slowly, and sat down against it. A horrible suspicion filled my mind. I recalled the body I had had to retrieve from the forest. "No!" I cried as I raced toward them. "Get away from there! Don't!"

The young trees shivered and trembled as if a strong wind were running through their branches, but the summer night was still and warm around me. The walkers twitched and jerked like puppets. One of the women cried out, a high shriek cut short. I dropped my bucket and torch as I reached her. I reached down and seized her hands. "Come away from there," I cried, pulling at her hands. She did not resist me, but neither could I budge her. She looked up at me, eyes open, her mouth stretched wide in a silent cry of pain. Her hands closed on mine and gripped tight with the strength of terror. I pulled with all my strength but could not lift her. Her legs kicked wildly against the earth. Not far from us, the boy gasped suddenly and then sagged limply against the tree that gripped him. Then something not his own muscles lifted his head from his chest and pressed it back against the tree. In the light of the torch guttering on the ground behind me, I could see black blood trickling from his nose and mouth.

I still held the woman's hands, and she still gripped back at me. "Please!" she gasped. I stooped, seized her shoulders, and with all my strength, I tried to pull her free of the tree. She gave a long, agonized caw of pain, and her head suddenly rolled limply forward on her chest. Her hands, which had been gripping my forearms, fell away. "No!" I cried, and again heaved at her inert body.

"No way to treat a lady," a voice rasped hoarsely behind me. "You scoundrel. You raping bastard!" I let go of the woman and turned, smelling earth and rot and quicklime.

Dale Hardy stood, legs spread, at the edge of the torch-light. He held my wooden bucket by the bale. "I warned you!" he shouted as he charged at me. As he came into the light, I could see that the quicklime had eaten half his face away. He could not be alive, I thought wildly, he could not be a walker. I took a stumbling step backward as he swung the heavy wooden bucket in a wide arc. It was coming too fast. I could not avoid it. It hit the side of my head, and I exploded into light.

CHAPTER THIRTY-ONE

ACCUSATIONS

Ebrooks and Kesey found me a few hours later.
When they arrived with the first wagonload of bodies for the
day, they were puzzled to see the dead torches and only a
single shroud remaining where they had left seven corpses
the previous evening. Thinking I had somehow dug a new
pit and begun to inter them on my own, they had walked out
into the graveyard. They'd found me, facedown, next to Dale
Hardy's body. As they approached, a whole flock of croaker
birds rose. They'd been feeding on the six bodies that were
neatly fastened by the swiftly growing rootlets to my hedge-
row trees. The whole area stank of rotting flesh and buzzed
with flies.

Kesey thought I was dead. He and Ebrooks assumed that
I'd gone down fighting with Specks who had come to steal
our dead. Blood coated one whole side of my head. But
when Kesey rolled me over, I groaned. He sent Ebrooks running to my cabin to get water.

"And that was when Ebrooks found Carsina's body in your bed," Spink said quietly.

He stood outside my cell and spoke to me through a small barred window. I lay on a straw-stuffed mattress on a narrow pallet and looked up at the dim ceiling. The only light came from a lantern fasted to the wall in the outside hall. Spink was the first visitor I'd had since I'd wakened in the cell a day and a half ago. They'd fed me twice, food on a tray shoved through an open slat in the bottom of the door. Grayish stuff in a bowl and a round of very hard bread with water. I'd eaten it. The two meals had been the only noteworthy events since I'd wakened there in the dark, head pounding with pain.

I listened to the silence of Spink waiting for me to come up with a logical explanation. Talking hurt. I didn't like to move my jaw. Thinking hurt, too. I made it brief. "Carsina was a walker. She came to me just like Hitch did. I tried to help her, but her fever came back. She asked me to get her husband for her. I was going to bring her some water first. I took the bucket, went outside, and realized that all the corpses we'd received that day were walkers. And they were all headed for the hedge. I ran out there and tried to pull one woman free of the tree, but it was already growing into her. I couldn't get her loose. And that was when Dale Hardy came up out of the pit grave, picked up my bucket, and hit me with it. And that's all I know."

It was my turn to fall silent. I waited for him to say he believed me. When the silence lasted, I waited for him to say he didn't believe me.

What he finally said was, "That doesn't sound good, Nevare."

"Just say it sounds like a madman raving. I know it does." I sighed and slowly sat up. "I don't remember any of what you're telling me. Only that bucket coming at me." The vertigo passed. I felt dizzy every time I changed position. I scratched the side of my head. Flaky brown blood came off under my nails. The magic did not seem to be healing me as swiftly this time as it had when I'd been shot. The answer came to me. The magic was severely depleted. If I didn't feed it, the next time death knocked on my door, it might come right in. At that moment it sounded like sweet mercy. "Spink, you shouldn't be here. No one connects you and Epiny to me. Go home. Let me just meet my fate."

"Before you sounded mad. Now you just sound stupid," he huffed. When I made no response, he sighed. "If you only sounded insane, it would be better for you."

I stood up slowly and came to the window. "What do you mean?"

"Captain Jof Thayer nearly went mad when he heard that the dead body of his wife was found in your bed. Captain and Clara Gorling are equally distressed. It looks . . . very bad, Nevare."

"What, that I tried to save his wife? What was I supposed to do? Look, Spink, I've been here a day and a half. And if it weren't for," I lowered my voice, "the magic, I'd be dead by now. No one gave me five minutes of care for my smashed head. The guard won't talk to me at all. I don't even know why I've been thrown into prison."

Spink swallowed. He started to speak, then looked around as if he'd rather bite his tongue out.

"Just say it," I barked at him.

"It looks *bad*, Nevare. No one will believe that all those people were walkers, not all at once. It looks as if you deliberately planted those trees and then, when you had the chance, shoved fresh corpses up against them to feed them. The trees had shot up almost three feet taller overnight, and blossomed! They had to chop them down to free the bodies from them. The trees had rooted into them so deeply that they had to bury them with pieces of trunk still attached to them. And Dale Hardy's body out there, pulled right out of his grave? From the damage that the quicklime did to him no one will believe he was a walker."

"Look at the grave. You'll find no shovel marks on it, at least, none that I made. If anyone dug him up, it wasn't me. And I don't think anyone did. I think he came crawling out on his own."

Spink gritted his teeth again. "A bit too late to look for any evidence of that sort. They put him back in the earth as quickly as they could. But it was no secret that he'd threatened you in the street that day. How people see it is that you took a macabre vengeance on both the woman who accused you and the man who wanted to defend her. You dragged his body out intending to give it to a tree."

"And then what? I hit myself on the head with a bucket?"

"Good point. But people in the town are too scandalized and horrified to think sensibly about this, let alone make allowances for claims of Speck magic. Nevare, they found Carsina Thayer's body in your bed."

I was baffled. "I told you. She was a walker. I tried to save her. I gave her water, and made her one of those teas that Epiny gave me for Hitch. I never had a chance to make it for him; he was dead when I got back to him. But I thought I had a chance to save Carsina. I took my bucket to get her more water before I left for town to get her husband. But when I went out the door, I saw the other walkers. I'm afraid they distracted me from my errand." Spink didn't deserve my angry sarcasm, but my head was pounding with the effort of talking. My jaw felt strange. When I touched it, I found lumpiness at the hinge. Had it been broken, and healed by the magic?

"They found Carsina in your *bed*," Spink said again, heavily emphasizing the word. Then, his face flushing dark scarlet, he added, "Her nightgown was rucked up around her waist."

It took me a moment. At first, his words made no sense to me.

"Oh, by the good god!" I felt as if I'd been punched in the belly. It had never even occurred to me that Carsina's body in my bed would be seen as anything other than an act of compassion on my part. I felt dizzy. Rumors that I could murder and rape had been hard enough to deal with. Adding necrophilia to the list sickened me. I said as much to Spink, and added, "I was rather counting on the fact that I'd tried to save Carsina to be to my benefit."

"You're facing execution, Nevare."

"I didn't do it, Spink. Surely I'll be given a chance to

defend myself? They'll have to admit that someone struck me down." A thought came to me. "My journal. My soldier son journal. Can you get it?"

"I already thought of that. I have it safe at my house. No one will know your secrets, Nevare."

"I wasn't worried about betraying secrets. I was hoping that it might be accepted as evidence. Surely if a man keeps a journal faithfully, he records what is true. There is a lot in there that I wouldn't want widely known, of course, but there is also much that will prove me an innocent man, if they allow it."

"Or a crazy man, Nevare. I don't think they'd let you pick and choose what your judge saw. Would you really want the whole thing bared to him?"

I thought of everything that was in there. My true name, among other things. The shame a court-martial would heap on my father. My unvarnished opinion of my father, hard things I'd said about Yaril, and my trafficking with the Specks. No. "Burn it," I suddenly decided. "I'd rather hang than have my journal become fodder for the yellow press."

"I wouldn't let that happen," he assured me.

Silence fell between us. The utter hopelessness of my position washed through me. "Why are you here?" I asked miserably.

He shut his eyes for a moment. "Epiny demanded that I come. She did something, Nevare. She did it for a friend, a deathbed favor. She had no idea what it would mean. Sergeant Hoster entrusted a letter to her. She promised that if Hoster died, she would deliver it to the commanding officer of the regiment and demand that the letter be opened and read in her presence, and the contents acted upon. Nevare, I swear she had no idea what was in it! When Major Helford read it out loud, she fainted there in his office. They came to get me, and I had to carry her home. She's been distraught ever since."

I didn't have to ask what it was. Epiny, my own cousin, had unwittingly delivered Sergeant Hoster's damning evidence against me. I spoke the heavy words slowly. "The letter accused me of Fala's murder. And it told where to find Clove's harness, with the one mismatched strap."

He stared at me. Then, "Yes," he said softly. His eyes were sad. I tried not to see the question in them.

"Hitch did it," I told him. "He confessed it all to me that night he walked."

Spink glanced away from me. His eyes did not come back to meet mine.

"Spink, I'm telling the truth. He told me he took the strap from Clove's harness and that he killed Fala with it because the magic forced him to do it. He'd set the whole thing up. He was the one who took me to Sarla Moggam's brothel in the first place." I suddenly stopped talking, as I recalled that no one there had seen us together. He'd entered before I had, and I'd probably left after he'd gone. *Oh, so neatly done, Hitch. You served the magic well.*

Spink spoke hesitantly. "I'm sorry, Nevare. I believe you. I do. But it all sounds so, well, so desperate. What possible reason could Scout Hitch have for killing that whore? You're accusing a dead man whom almost everyone on the post respected. He was a bit of a rogue, that's true, but I don't think anyone is going to believe that he killed Fala because Speck magic made him do it."

"But they'll believe that I did it for pleasure," I said heavily.

He closed his eyes before he spoke. "I am afraid that they will."

I turned and walked away from the door. I sat down on the bunk. The wood frame made a cracking sound. I ignored it. "Go away, Spink. Save your reputation. I don't think there's anything that anyone can do for me now. Go away."

"I do have to go. But I'll be back, Nevare. I don't believe the things they've said about you. Neither does Epiny. For what it's worth, most of her women are angry at her now, because although she gave Major Helford the letter, she has tried to say that it's all a huge mistake, that Sergeant Hoster didn't have the truth of it. But they found Clove's harness hidden in the stable, with the one odd bit of strap, and the strap they found around Fala's neck matches the harness perfectly."

"So, in addition to knocking myself out with a bucket in

the midst of dishonoring the dead, I'm now stupid enough to have strangled a whore with a strap from my own horse's harness? Think about it, Spink! Can you honestly picture any man planning such a murder? 'I think I'll take a harness strap from my own horse's harness, take it to town with me, lure Fala away from the brothel, strangle her with it, and leave her body where it's certain to be found.' Can anyone believe that I'm that stupid?"

The muscles stood out on the side of his jaw. He forced himself to speak. "Nevare. These acts you are accused of are so hateful that given even a scrap of evidence, they'll find you guilty. The whistle brigade is demanding that some-one be punished, and the only someone in custody is you."

My mind jumped back to what he had been telling me. "Epiny took my part? Publicly?"

He nodded grimly.

"Tell her to renounce it. Tell her to say that she has changed her mind."

"Oh, and of course she would do that if her husband com-manded it." Spink's voice was dryly sarcastic, but I saw something else in his tight smile. Pride. He knew Epiny would not back down. And he took pride in the fact that she would stand behind her convictions regardless of the conse-quences.

"Oh, Spink, I am so sorry. She will lose all her friends over this, won't she?"

"Not quite. Amzil has come forward to stand beside her. She has told everyone that you lived with her for nearly a month in Dead Town and never put a hand on her or demon-strated any sort of temper. Of course, as a former whore, her word counts for less, but she gave it nonetheless."

I winced. "Go home, Spink. You've done all you can and I need to think. There has to be some compelling evidence I can offer that I'm innocent."

"You'll have to come up with it soon," he warned me.

"Surely they won't try to hold a court-martial while the plague is still raging?"

"The plague has stopped. Just as if someone blew a lamp out. Some are hailing it as a miracle. I've heard at least one person say that it's the good god showing his pleasure that a vile criminal like yourself has been captured."

"It stopped?"

"Like magic." He smiled grimly. "Fevers went down. People rallied on their deathbeds. There hasn't been a death since you were brought here, Nevare."

"Like magic," I agreed sourly. I lay back on my protesting pallet and looked at the cobwebbed ceiling. "Go home, Spink. Tell Epiny I love her and tell her to stop defending me in public. Tell Amzil the same."

"That you love her?" He seemed incredulous.

"Why not?" I replied recklessly. "I can scarcely lose anything by saying it now."

"I'll do it, then," he said, and seemed almost pleased at the prospect.

As he turned to go, I called after him, "I'll be sent some sort of counsel, won't I? Someone who will help me present my defense?"

"They're trying to find someone willing to represent you," he said. If he meant the words to be reassuring, they were not. I wondered if they would still hold the court-martial if I had no representative.

If I had remained at the academy, I should have eventually had to complete a course that covered martial law and how it was administered. What little I had heard of that course convinced me it would have been a dry study. Little had I ever thought that any of it would apply to me. I closed my eyes for a moment and tried once more to be the boy who had set off so joyfully for the academy, so full of anticipation of a glorious career and a golden future. That future was to have included an obedient and doting wife, a woman raised in the traditions of being a cavalla officer's wife. Carsina. What had we done to one another? Then I clenched my jaw and admitted that she was little to blame for all that had happened.

If I wanted to parcel out blame, I had only to look at myself. Hitch had warned me that using the magic for my own ends would always extract a harsh price. If I had not put Carsina under a command to apologize to me before she died, she might have died quietly of the plague. I had sealed my own fate. At least hanging would be a swift end for a man of my girth. The physics of such an execution probably meant that my head would be torn completely from my body. Grisly, but much swifter than dangling and strangling. I shook my head and tried to rattle such thoughts away. I could not think of that just now.

And I could not think of anything else, either.

I was in pain from the blow I'd taken from the bucket. Feeling my face and the side of my skull, I became convinced that I should have died of such injuries if my residual magic had not undertaken to swiftly repair them. Tender spots convinced me that the least injuries I had taken were a cracked skull and a broken jaw. I was torn between being glad the magic had preserved my life and wishing that I had died a swift death. The healing of my injuries, though not as fast as my recovery from my bullet wound, was a liability to me, I slowly realized. It was likely that when I stood before the court-martial, I would appear fully healed and in good health. No one would believe that I had taken a deadly blow from a dead man. They would find some other way to account for me being unconscious.

My cell was a small bare room. I could see the cot, a chamber-pot, the barred window in the door, and the food slot in the door. Light, dim but constant, came from a lantern on a hook in the hall outside. It was very quiet. Either the other inhabitants slept a lot or there weren't any. Other than my visit from Spink and the guard on his regular rounds to check on me or feed me, I did not see a soul. With no pastimes and nothing to distract me from my predicament, my thoughts chased each other in ever-smaller circles.

I was going to die. That much seemed very certain. I hoped I could maintain my dignity. Just thinking of ascending the steps to a gallows made me shaky. I resolved I would not shake or weep or beg. Probably all condemned men resolved to go bravely; I hoped I'd have the strength to keep those resolutions. I dreaded my trial and yet longed for it, to have it all be over. I made and unmade final decisions a dozen times a day. I would ask that all my possessions be left to Amzil and her children. No, I would not mention her or the children lest association with me taint them. I would tell the court everything: who I was, how I had become infected with magic, the dangers of the Dust Dance, how I had consorted with Specks and been tricked into planting ancestor trees in the graveyard, and what the matured trees meant to the Specks— No. I would stand silent and say not a word and let them convict me. That would shelter my father and sister from further shame. I would tell them only of the walkers, and how I had tried to save Carsina. I wondered if they would think me a liar or a madman.

The days dripped by. A Lieutenant Roper came by to tell me my trial had been delayed until it could be determined if the town of Gettys had more right to try me for crimes against its civilian citizens than the military. He came to the door of my cell, imparted this to me, and left before I could ask me if he was my defense counsel. I feared he was.

My next visitor wakened me in what I thought were early-morning hours. A tall man with bloodshot eyes breathed brandy fumes into my cell as he gripped the bars of the little window in my cell door and shook it on its hinges. "You great fat bloody coward!" he slurred at me. "I ought to drag you out of there and rip you limb from limb for what you did to my beautiful wife. You desecrated the most gentle and honorable woman the good god ever made! You filthy dog! You unspeakable filth!" He shook the barred window again, working the heavy door against its hinges and the stout bolt that locked it. I wondered if he had a gun with him. I wondered if I would move out of range of its muzzle if he did.

When he had spent his fury shaking the door, Captain Thayer suddenly slammed his head against the wood of it. He rested it there, leaning on my door and breathing harshly. Then his breath caught. His ragged breathing gave way to the heart-wrenching sounds of sobs ripping out of him. Into the lesser noise of his weeping, I foolishly spoke.

"I did not dishonor your wife, sir. I did not touch her. Carsina was a walker; she roused from what we thought was death but was only a coma. I gave her tea and cold water. I was on my way to fetch you when—"

"You lying scum!" My words had kindled him to fresh

fury. "Don't you dare say her name so familiarly, you piece of filth! Hanging is too good for you! You should have to suffer as you've made me suffer!" He thrust his hand and arm between the bars and made groping motions, as if it could somehow stretch across the room and throttle me. It would have been humorous if his murderous intent had not been so sincere.

"Captain Thayer! Sir! Captain, please, sir! You should come away now." The guard who addressed him had a thin reedy voice. Thayer turned his head to stare at him. "Please, sir. You have to come away. I shouldn't have let you in at all. He'll come to trial soon, and you can confront him there. Sir."

Thayer seized the bars again and tried vainly to shake the door. The guard let him. When he finally gave up his vain effort, he sagged against the door, breathing hoarsely.

"Come away, sir. Justice will be done. Come away now." And with that, the guard led him away.

I suspected I had burned away whatever magic I'd had left. I ate the prison food, but the sophistication of taste that had allowed me to take pleasure in even the simplest of foods had fled my palate. It was a bowl of slop each day, with a hunk of hard bread and some water. I ate it only because I was constantly ravenous. As if to make its mockery of me complete, the magic that had kept me fat even in far more dire circumstances now failed. My clothing hung looser on me every day, and my skin began to sag. When I slept, I only slept. The dreams I had were fragmented nonsense or ominous nightmares of hanging. After the initial burst of healing that had kept me alive, my recuperation from the bucket blow was slow. My jaw ached and my head hurt most of the time. Sudden motion as simple as turning my head toward a sound produced dizziness.

And the waiting dragged on, day after day, with no one seeing fit to inform me of anything. The guard who fed me and checked on me refused to exchange a single word with me. I lost track of the days. Sometimes I dozed and thought only a few moments had passed, only to hear the rattle of an insipid meal being pushed through my doors. At other times,

I could find neither sleep nor true wakefulness, but lay on my cot suspended, feeling as if all time had stopped.

The waiting came to an abrupt end when I jerked out of such a reverie to find Spink once more peering through the barred window.

"I thought I told you go to away," I greeted him, even as I could not deny the relief I felt to see a friendly face.

"Well, you've been outranked. I'm here under orders."

"From Epiny?" I jested, and he almost smiled.

"If her commands could have gotten me through the doors to you again, I'd have been here a hundred times. No. From Major Helford. His search for anyone willing to act as your defense finally discovered me. And here I am."

"But . . ." Dismay filled me. "You're in supply. How on earth could they select you to act as my counsel? Do you know anything about military law?"

"They did not select me so much as work their way down to me. I'm afraid everyone above me who was asked begged off. Man after man said that he could not defend you impartially. As depleted as the ranks of our officers are, you should probably be grateful that you don't have Ebrooks or Kesey in this role."

"How do you know Kesey and Ebrooks?"

"I was given this task yesterday. I immediately rode out to the cemetery to interview them."

I'd sat up too suddenly. I closed my eyes to let the dizziness pass, then opened them and asked, "And what did they tell you about me?"

"That they had liked you. Not at first, but when they saw you doing your best at a task no one else wanted, and living out there despite the forest so close by, they came to admire your 'guts,' as they so elegantly put it. They said it was hard to believe you had done such a thing."

His tone told me everything. "But not impossible. They do believe it."

He folded his lips tightly and then gave a curt nod. "The evidence is against you. Every man who has held the post of cemetery guard before you has come to a bad end. Desertion or suicide. One man simply drank himself to death. They found him neatly laid out in the grave he'd dug for himself. Kesey and Ebrooks both think you went mad."

"How do they explain the injury to my head?"

"Self-inflicted."

"They think I hit myself in the head with a bucket?" I was incredulous.

"It's the only possible explanation, Nevare. And therefore, as unlikely as it is, they have to believe it."

I turned away from him. My hands went to fists. Irrational tears stung my eyes. Foolish as it was, I'd expected them to believe me. I hadn't thought their good opinions would count for much, but I'd believed there would be at least two speaking in my favor at my trial. To hear that even Kesey and Ebrooks could believe such evil of me destroyed all hope. "I'm going to plead guilty." I could scarcely believe I'd said the words, but the moment I had, I saw the wisdom in them.

"What?" Spink was horrified.

"I'm going to plead guilty and get it over with. I don't want a drawn-out trial with spectators flocking to listen to people say vile things about me. I don't want to stir things up until my execution becomes a social event. I just want to plead guilty and be done with it."

"Nevare, you can't! You didn't do it, you didn't do any of it!"

"Can you be sure of that? How do you know I'm not mad, Spink?"

"Because of your journal," he said quietly. I thought he sounded embarrassed.

"You read my journal?" I was outraged.

"No. Not directly. Epiny read it. She found it soon after I hid it, though she didn't tell me she'd found it until after she'd finished reading it."

"Oh, by the good god. Is there no mercy left in the world?" For one horrifying instant, every demeaning thing I'd written about Epiny flashed through my mind, along with my accounts of my sexual encounters with Olikea and every other stupid thing I'd recorded in there. Why on earth had I written such things down? They didn't belong in a soldier son's journal! And now Epiny had read them all. And through her—

"How much did she tell you?"

"Enough," Spink replied, his ears going pink.

Silence reigned between us. To have the last two people in the world who thought well of me know exactly what sort of man I really was overwhelmed me in a tide of despair. Execution would be a mercy.

"I'm going to plead guilty, Spink. If you have any regard left for me at all, burn that damned book and then forget you ever knew me." I felt a sharp pang of regret as I recalled the letters I'd sent to my sister. A heartfelt prayer went out of me that my father had been vigilant and had destroyed them unread. "Good-bye, Spink. If there's anything left of mine in the cabin that has value, sell it off. And Clove. See he goes to a good master. Use the money however you think best."

I heard Spink shift his feet on the floor outside my cell. After a moment he spoke almost calmly, the anger muted in his voice. "I thought you had more courage than that, Nevare."

"You were mistaken, then," I retorted.

I heard the rustle of paper. "There are certain things you should know. The town of Gettys wanted to try you. Major Helford decided that the military has more right than they. But he conceded to them that when you stand before your seven judges, three of them would be from the town. Now, they haven't given me much time to prepare. I have statements from Ebrooks and Kesey. Can you think of anyone else who might give a testimonial as to your character?"

I didn't reply. After a short time, he pushed on doggedly. "I have a list of questions here that I need you to answer. They'll help me to defend you."

I said nothing.

He cleared his throat. "Under what circumstances did you first meet Fala, a prostitute working in Sarla Moggam's brothel?" His voice was absolutely neutral.

I refused to answer.

After a moment, he asked, "On what date were you first betrothed to Carsina Grenalter, Nevare Burvelle?"

I came to my feet faster than I thought I could possibly do it and flung myself at the door. I tried to thrust my hand through the bars to seize his damnable list of questions, but he simply stepped back out of my reach. I was dizzy with my sudden motion and with the fury he had awoke in me. I clung to the bars to keep from falling and growled through my teeth, "Don't you dare reveal my real name at the trial! Don't you dare connect me to Carsina!"

"Nevare, it's your only chance. Tell the whole truth. All of it."

"I won't. If you even try to bring it up, I'll disrupt the whole proceeding. I'll attack my guards and force them to kill me right there." It came to me that that was an excellent idea in any case; it would avoid all the ceremony and suspense of a hanging. I think Spink must have seen that in my eyes. He suddenly looked very tired and defeated.

"I know you think that your life is in shambles and not worth saving," he said quietly. "But for a moment, I wish you'd stop being so selfish and look at what you are doing to Epiny and me. She loves you, Nevare. I can't fail her and then spend the rest of my life with her. She has already said that if we have a boy, she's going to name him Nevare. Does that mean nothing to you?"

"It means that as usual, Epiny is acting without a grain of sense. You should stop her. You have a duty to protect your son from his mother's foolishness."

There was a long, cold silence. He spoke formally at last. "Well. I will tolerate many things from you, but not insult to my wife. You may do as you please. I will put forth my best effort, and I will never have to apologize to my wife or anyone else for being derelict in my duties. Go to your death a coward if you must, Nevare. Good day."

And with that, he left me.

CHAPTER THIRTY-TWO

LISANA

For the rest of that morning, I laid on my pallet and wondered exactly what Spink would think he must do. It was good to know that he would stand by me as a friend, even when I chose to give up, but it was intolerable that he should defy me, for if he chose to betray my real name and then speak of my involvement with the Specks, he would ruin my family's name. Even if he won clemency for me that way, I thought grimly, I would emerge from my cell into a life I preferred not to face.

I reined my mind away from such thoughts and began to make my plans, feeble as they were. At the very first opportunity after I came into the courtroom, I would attack whoever was presiding. I'd have to make it a real effort, not just a dramatic show. I wanted to force them to kill me. I wondered if I'd be moved from my cell to the courtroom by armed guards. If so, a simple escape attempt might win me what I hoped for. Now that the magic had forsaken me, a bullet or two in the back should end it all. I shifted on my bunk, and the abused planks beneath me gave a final protesting crack before they collapsed onto the floor. I sighed, but did not bother getting up. After a time, I closed my eyes.

Sleep opened under me like a trap door.

I fell to my knees in the deep moss. Around me, the summer forest hummed with life. I blinked, for even the leaf-dappled sunlight was a shock to my eyes after the dimness of my cell. The rich, earthy smells of moss and earth filled my nostrils. A pale green butterfly came to dance around me, perplexed, and then suddenly lifted and wafted away on the foliage-filtered breeze. Slowly I stood and looked around me, then turned my feet to the path that led up the ridge to Tree Woman's stump.

I felt a difference in my presence in this place. I was not there under my own power but at her command. I was as footless as a ghost, as if I drifted over a path where before I would have felt the mossy earth beneath my feet. The cool breeze touched my face but did not move my hair or stir my clothing. When I came in sight of Tree Woman's stump, I halted, perplexed.

"And here he is," I heard Tree Woman say. But not to me. Epiny stood there beside her, leaning on Tree Woman's trunk, looking pale and sweaty and disturbingly real. She had been wearing a straw sun hat; she had pushed it off and it dangled down her back by the ribbon around her neck. Her hair had been pinned up as befitted a married woman, but it had come down messily in tendrils around her face. The dark blue dress she wore struck me as peculiarly shapeless and unflattering. Then I abruptly realized it had been cut to accommodate the growing child inside her.

"You cannot be here," I said to her. She peered at me, her eyes widening. "You can't be here," I said more loudly, and then she seemed to hear me.

"I *am* here," she asserted, an edge of anger in her voice. She squinted at me and then, with a small gasp, lifted her hand to her mouth. "You are the one who cannot be here. Nevare. You are *rippling*."

"It is only by her pleading that you are here," Tree Woman

rebuked me as she wavered into view. She sat on top of her stump, looking older and wearier than I had ever seen her. She was thinner, I realized. Depleted of her fat. That was disturbing. "You see what you have reduced me to!" Tree Woman rebuked me. "This is your own fault, Soldier's Boy, that I have so little strength to help you."

"I don't understand."

"He never understands anything," Tree Woman observed to Epiny in the voice of an older woman advising a much younger one.

"I know," Epiny replied. She sounded both exhausted and fearful. She was breathing heavily, and when she set her hand to the top of her belly, my heart tightened.

"You shouldn't be here. How did you get here?"

"I walked." She took a breath. "Uphill. And against the fear."

"I am surprised she managed it," Tree Woman observed. "She came into the forest calling for Olikea. She is fortunate that I answered instead of that one. *She* is still very angry with you, Soldier's Boy. I can imagine too well how she would have vented that anger."

"I don't understand how any of this can be," I repeated. "Isn't this the *other* place? Aren't I dreamwalking?"

"Yes. You are. And you have dreamwalked to a real place, just as your cousin has hiked here. So. Here we all are. And she tells me she would do anything, give us anything, if the magic will help her find a way for you to live." Tree Woman cocked her head at me and her eyes went cold. "Perhaps I should ask for her firstborn child."

"No!" I roared, but my roar had the strength of a cat's hiss.

Epiny had gone paler, but she said nothing. She looked at me and her eyes filled with tears. She bowed her head.

"She is going back to her husband right now," I announced.

"Oh, is she?" Tree Woman laughed humorlessly. "Stop giving commands. You are powerless here. And you are powerless by your own choice. Again and again, you refused to serve the magic. Repeatedly, you refused to answer Olikea's

summons so that she could build you up with the correct
foods. You have been like a small boy refusing to do his
chores. With your willfulness you have tangled the magic
until I begin to wonder if anyone can make it work again. But
some tasks must be done, and if the proper person will not do
them, another will be found. Your cousin has come here of
her own will. I do not know why the magic did not choose
someone like her to begin with. I think she will serve it far
better than you have."

"You can't do this! You can't take her instead of me!"

"Do you think not? She has strength, and a natural affin-
ity for this world." The woman on the stump looked down
on Epiny, and her smiled narrowed. "I recall the first time
that she and I fought over you. I was surprised at her strength
then. And on the day you cut me, she came into my world
and dared to challenge me for a life the magic had already
claimed. She took him back with her, and a man who should
have fed the magic has instead fathered her child. It would
suit me very well, Soldier's Boy, to see her bow her head to
the magic. It would be fitting if she lost what I lost."

I looked at Tree Woman. I still felt my love for her, but I
also felt the gulf between us that she could even threaten
Epiny so. "What can I do to persuade you to let her go free?"
I asked bluntly. "I'll give you anything to see her safely
home."

"That's the wrong bargain," Tree Woman replied. "She
has already told me several things she is willing to do to win
your life back for you. The only thing that is left for me to
decide is if we have any use for you."

"Let Epiny go. Help me to live and I will come to you and
serve the magic. Even if it means going against my own
people to do so."

Tree Woman cocked her head. She was quiet for a time,
but it was more as if she were listening than thinking. I
stood beside Epiny and tried to take her hand. She watched
owlishly as my phantom hand swept through hers. I put my
arm around her. She gave me a pale, tired smile and then
turned her worried glance back to Tree Woman. I looked
past the meditating woman to the new tree sprouting from

her prone trunk. Its leaves hung limp and motionless in the summer breeze.

Lisana focused her gaze on us again. "The magic will take both of you," she announced, obviously pleased.

"That wasn't offered!" I retorted angrily.

"Of course it was," she replied. "Epiny said she'd give anything to save you. You said you'd do anything to see her safely home. The magic agrees to both."

"That isn't fair!" I cried.

"What *would* be fair, Soldier's Boy? Shall we let her go, let you die, let the intruders cut down the ancestor trees? Let the road gash through the forest like your blade cut through my trunk? Cut the People loose from their roots as you severed me from mine? *That* would be fair?"

"I'm sorry I did that," I said again. I suddenly understood that Epiny's venture into the forest had reawakened all of Tree Woman's hurt and anger. Lisana and I had set our great battle behind us; we had even seen ourselves as victims of our own conflict. Epiny's presence tipped the scales a different way. She was my ally who had aided me in Tree Woman's defeat. Tree Woman felt afresh the ignominy of her defeat. Epiny was the living embodiment of my other life and my loyalty to it. She represented everything that kept me away from the magic. "Please, Lisana. Please let her go," I said simply at last.

"You ask that as if you think it were in my power. She came here howling out Olikea's name like a she-cat in heat. She is lucky that one did not come to her. Olikea and the others have fled into the mountains. They fear what is to come. When the magic is angered, all suffer. The People are converging on Kinrove's folk now. They fear his magic has ceased to work. The Fear his dancers make no longer holds the intruders at bay; the ancestor trees have begun to fall again. Kinrove is the oldest and fattest of our Great Ones. They will petition him to stop the dancing, and begin a war such as your folk will understand."

"There is no need for that!" Epiny broke in. She gave me a single sideways glance and then said, "I can do what you have asked of me. I can stop the men from cutting down your ancestor trees. And I will do it, if you find a way for Nevare to live."

For a long time Tree Woman regarded Epiny silently. Then she said, "I told you. The magic has accepted. It is up to the magic now, not me."

"But what are we supposed to do?" I asked.

"Whatever the magic wants you to do," Tree Woman replied.

"Lisana," I begged. "I have told you over and over again. I do not know what the magic wants of me. If I knew, I would have done it by now."

"You are the only one who can possibly know. I suggest you listen more closely to it," she replied stiffly. I suspected I had offended her by calling her by name in front of Epiny. She turned her back on both of us, and then, suddenly, she wasn't there. In the instant she vanished, I suddenly felt frail, a shadow blowing in a black wind. Then Epiny looked at me and set her hand on top of mine, which rested on her shoulder. Her fingers went through my hand; she clasped her own shoulder but I felt more stable.

"You're holding me here." I said, amazed.

"I'm trying to. I don't quite know how any of this works." She looked around fearfully. "Do you know the way home?"

"I might. It's a long trek through the woods. Do you think you're strong enough?"

She gave a strained laugh. "What choice do I have? I've read that phrase over and over in your journal, Nevare. That the magic leaves you no choices. Now I think I understand what it means." She turned away from Lisana's stump and walked back along the ridge and I drifted with her, a child's toy on a string.

"Why did you come here? Why were you looking for Olikea?"

"I thought . . . I don't know what I thought. That perhaps she would know a way to save you. Spink came home heart-sick that you had decided to plead guilty and be done with it. I waited until he left the house. And then I borrowed a horse . . ."

"From whom?" I cut in.

She was unfazed. "Very well. I stole a horse and cart and drove out to the cemetery and walked into the new woods behind your spring. The fear wasn't so bad there. So I thought I could do it. And I pushed on up into the old forest. But I could barely make myself go under those trees. So I stood there, and I called for Olikea. I think my shouts stirred something up, because then the fear flooded over me. Nevare, I have never been so frightened. My heart was racing and I couldn't get my breath. My legs just turned to jelly and I sank down where I was. I was so terrified I couldn't even run away. And it made me, well, angry. So I screamed for Olikea again. And then something happened. I was still very scared, but I felt I had to get up and walk. So I did. I walked and I walked, up steep hills and through brambles, and I was so tired I knew I couldn't keep going. But I had to. And finally I got to that stump. And when I saw your sword sticking out of it, the fear came on me so strong that I thought I would die of it. Because I knew that somehow I'd come to a place that we had all dreamed together."

She stopped walking. I halted, too, not because I willed it but because I was somehow fastened to her. She drew a deep and shuddering breath. "How did you stand it?"

"What?"

"The fear. Even though I know that it's something being done to me, I can't ignore it." She put a free hand to her chest as if to calm the pounding of her heart.

"Epiny, I didn't. The magic took it away, or I never could have ventured so freely through the forest. I don't know how you forced yourself to come here. Keep walking. I want to see you safely home."

"I wish you were really here. I wish you could protect me."

Those words stabbed deeper than any knife could. It took a little time before I could speak. "Epiny, I don't think you're in any real danger right now, other than exhaustion. Go down that way, to the left. See that little rabbit trail in the moss? Follow it. There's a stream down there. Drink some water and rest for a bit before we go on. I'm amazed that a woman in your condition could make this hike at all."

She followed my suggestion, but as she worked her way

down the steep path, she asked me, "So you are one of those men who think pregnancy is a 'diseased state'? You can't even bring yourself to say 'pregnant,' can you?"

"I was afraid you'd consider it rude." Even to myself, I sounded priggish.

Tired and scared as she was, she still managed a small laugh. "It's only rude because you think how I got this way is somewhat shameful. Well-bred women shouldn't be pregnant. Isn't that true?"

I thought over her words, and then had to laugh with her. "You make me think about how I think about things, Epiny. You're one of the few people in my life who can make me do that."

"If we both live through this, I intend to do a lot more of it. At this rate, I fear I will never have time to scold you properly for how badly you treated me by concealing that you were still alive. I want you to know I'm just putting it off until it's more convenient. I have not forgiven you."

"There, through those trees—see it? That's the stream." I forced myself to add, "I probably don't deserve to be forgiven for that. I don't expect it."

She halted for an instant and then stumped her way down to the stream, complaining as she went, "And that is probably the only thing you could have said that would make me instantly forgive you, no matter how much you deserve to endure my disdain and contempt for, well, at least months! Oh, how lovely! It's beautiful, here." She pushed through the foliage of a bush and emerged onto the mossy banks of a stream.

"It is. I'm surprised that you can see that through the fear." Something else caught my attention. "Epiny. Do you see the berries on that bush? The one we just passed?"

"I do." She ventured closer. "They're lovely. Such a rich color."

"Do you think there is any way you could pick some and bring them to me in the jail?"

"I've nothing to carry them in except my handkerchief." She walked past them to the stream. She sank down carefully onto the moss. She dipped the handkerchief she had just mentioned into the water and wiped perspiration from her brow and the back of her neck before cupping some water in her hand to drink. All the while, she never let go of my phantom hand pinned to her shoulder. "When I get back to town, I can buy you some berries at the market if you wish."

"Not like those," I told her. A faint but tantalizing scent wafted to my ghost nose. My mouth watered, and my suppressed appetite woke with a roar. "It's a special sort of berry. They facilitate magic."

"Really?" She stood up slowly and went back to the bush. "Such an unusual color," she said. She picked one. And before I could utter a sound of warning, she ate it. I felt her consume it. "Oh, my! I've never tasted anything like that!"

"Epiny, stop! Stop!" Her hand hovered over another berry. "I'm afraid if you eat them, the magic will gain more power over you. Don't eat anymore."

With just the one berry, I sensed a change in her. She did as well. She gripped my hand now, not her own shoulder. Some of her weariness had fallen away. Tree Woman was right, I realized. Epiny did have an aptitude for their magic. I recalled what Epiny had told me so long ago in Old Thares: that once a medium had shown her how to open herself to magic, she had felt it was a window inside her that she could not close.

"They're so delicious," she murmured. She picked a second berry.

"Epiny! No!"

"Just one more. It made me feel stronger." It was already in her mouth. I knew the moment she crushed it, for I felt a surge of magic wash through her.

"Epiny! For the sake of Spink's child, stop now! You cannot use this magic without it taking something from you. You've read my journal. Let me tell you what isn't in there, what I didn't have time to record. This magic, it grows in odd ways. You'll use it without meaning to. I made Carsina a walker! I forced that on her, by my foolish words spoken in anger at Rosse's wedding. I was too ashamed to tell Spink what I'd done to her. Carsina came back from the dead, forced to do what I'd cursed her with. I forced her to go on her knees and beg my forgiveness before she could die."

"Oh, the good god's mercy!" Epiny leaned over and spat. It was too late; I knew she had absorbed the berry's potency already. But the simple act showed me that she had the strength of will I'd lacked. She took a breath, and then straightened. "Show me the way home, Nevare."

"Pick the berries for me, Epiny. Even a kerchief full will restore some of my power." I felt tantalizingly more substantial. The smell of the two berries she'd eaten was on her breath. I longed to devour every one that remained on the bush.

"But you said they'd put me in the magic's power," she protested. "Won't they do the same to you?"

"I'm already in the magic's power. If you can get them to me in the prison, I may be able to rejuvenate enough magic to be able to help myself. Then you won't have to."

"But—"

"I've already given Lisana my word. Pick the berries for me, Epiny."

She stood a long time considering it. Then she spread her handkerchief on the moss and began, one-handed, to pick berries and drop them on it. When she had a goodly pile, she gathered up the four corners of her kerchief and picked it up.

"The way home?" she asked me again.

I made a decision. "Going home the way you came is far too long. Follow this stream," I told her. "It has to flow downhill. It will take you closer to the end of the road. From there, I think you can beg aid of the men working there. They'll put you on a cart and get you home."

It was a long and weary walk for her. The berries, she told me, seemed to have calmed the fear in her and lent her strength. Even so, my heart ached for her. She'd had the sense to put on boots before she stole the horse and cart, but her heavy skirts were scarcely the best hiking garb. I greatly feared that night would fall before we were out of the forest. I wondered if I'd misjudged the way until we heard the muted sounds of axes falling and smelled the smoke of burning brush. "We're nearly there," I said quietly. "All you have to do is go toward the sounds. The men working on the road will help you."

Her response was as subdued. "She took me to the end of the ridge and made me look down on what we had done to her forest. I don't pretend to understand completely what the ancestor trees mean to her. But for that moment, I felt what she felt, and my heart actually went out to her, Nevare. Different as we are, I still understood that all she wants is to keep things as they are, to protect her people."

"But we both know that things never remain as they are, Epiny. It's a lost cause already."

"Perhaps. But I've already said that I'd stop them from cutting the ancestor trees. Do you know exactly what they are?"

"I think that when a Great One dies, the Specks give the body to a tree. And that the tree absorbs the body, and somehow that person lives on as a tree."

"That's what Tree Woman is? Lisana?"

"I think so. We've never discussed it directly. There are so many things that she assumes I know, and—"

"But that's horrible! We're literally killing their elders when we cut those trees! By the good god's mercy! No wonder they think we're monsters! Nevare, when you went to Colonel Haren, you should have told him what those trees were! If only he had known!"

"Epiny. I know you've read my journal. I did go to Colonel Haren, the morning before the Dust Dance. I told him what those trees meant to the Specks and even warned him that if the cutting did not stop, we'd be facing a different kind of war.

"He dismissed my concern, and said that he thought less of me for having it. He'd heard it before. He saw it as silly superstitious nonsense, and said that once the trees were gone and nothing bad happened to the Specks, they'd see they'd been foolish and come around to our way of thinking. It was as if he believed that if we took their culture away from them, they'd instantly convert to thinking like Gernians. As if our way of seeing the world were the only real one, and that anyone, given the opportunity, would think like we do. I couldn't make him see any other point of view. Even if I'd told him that the trees were actually the Specks' ancestors, he'd have been unable to believe me. But, yes, we knew those trees were sacred to the Specks. We've evidently known it for a long time. And we keep trying to cut through there anyway."

"We've been fools! Couldn't someone, for just a moment, have believed the Specks knew the secrets of their forest better than we did? We've brought all this on ourselves! The fear, the despair, the Speck plague! It's all our own doing."

"I wouldn't go that far—" I started to say, but she interrupted me.

"So what did you try, then, to stop the cutting?"

"I—well, that is, what else could I do? I told the colonel and pleaded with him to stop it. He refused."

"Well, you should have done something more!"

"Perhaps I could have, if I'd had time. But on my way home, your friend Hoster's men shot me."

"He thought you were a murderer," she said. She sounded angry and embarrassed.

"I still can't believe you trusted that man!" I retorted. She stopped and looked up at me, and her eyes suddenly filled with tears.

"You should just say it and get it over with, Nevare. It's my fault that you're in that cell facing death. I betrayed you. I'm so sorry! So sorry."

"Oh, Epiny, I didn't mean it that way! You didn't betray me. All you did was what you thought you should do, keep faith with a man you trusted. And maybe by his own lights, he was a good man. If he believed me such a monster and a threat to the women of the town, then maybe he was justified in sending those men after me. It's all about what we believe, isn't it? Not just Gernians and Specks, but even down to individuals like Hoster and you. All we can do is what we think is right, driven by what we know, or what we think we know."

"Nonetheless, I feel it was my fault. And that was why I had to go to the forest today. To do whatever I could, at any cost, to free you from that cell." She was no longer meeting my eyes. She trudged on. The forest brush was getting thicker. She pushed her way through.

"Epiny, you don't have to do anything more." The ringing of axes came louder now. I could see the sunlight at the edge of the clearing ahead and smell the drifting smoke of the burning slash piles. The work crews were close. "Just get yourself safely home. And if there is any way you can get those berries to me, please do that. And then stay away from whatever happens next, knowing you've done your best."

"Would you go back on your given word, Nevare?" Her hair had tangled in a bush. She stopped and made an exasperated sound as she pulled it free.

"Of course not!"

"Then how can you suggest that I do that? I told Lisana that I'd do whatever I could to save the ancestor trees. I intend to keep my word."

"Epiny, I don't think that Major Helford is going to give you any more credence than Colonel Haren gave me. Less, because you're a woman."

"Such a comforting thing to say to me, Nevare!" I could sense her anger coming to a boil and felt helpless to stop it. I feared that when it bubbled over, we would all be scalded.

"Epiny, what can you do?"

She halted. We could hear men's voices ahead of us. I felt a sudden bolt of fear. I'd brought her here assuming that the work crews would offer her help. What if they didn't? What if they abused her?

"I shouldn't have brought you this way, Epiny. Most of the men on these crews are prisoners. And their guards don't strike me as much better."

"Actually, I think this is the best way you could have guided me, Nevare. It will give me the opportunity to see how they are working, and where, and what they are using. That is information that will help me stop them."

She was patting her hair back into order and brushing at her skirts as she spoke. She was tidying herself, I realized, before she walked out to meet the work crew.

"Epiny, what can you possibly do to stop them?" I asked in a low voice.

"I was thinking explosives," she replied brightly. "I've heard they've been using them to fell trees. Perhaps they'd work to make them *stop* felling trees."

"Oh, the good god's mercy on us all! Epiny, let that idea go. All you'll do is succeed at hurting yourself or others. Where would you get explosives, anyway?"

She turned and gave me a sly smile. "Have you forgotten? My husband is in charge of supply."

Then she lifted her hand from mine. All around me, the forest sparkled unbearably and then dissolved into floating dust. A moment later, I was staring up at the ceiling of my cell. I groaned and covered my eyes.

CHAPTER THIRTY-THREE

COURT-MARTIAL

They woke me early on the day of my trial. I was given a basin of warm water and a rag to wash myself. When I thanked the guard, he told me gruffly, "It's for the benefit of the court, not you!"

The water was filthy long before I finished. Just the caked blood from the side of my head had turned it a rusty brown. I wished for a mirror, then was glad I didn't have one. My hair and my whiskers had grown out. I hadn't changed my clothing since the day I'd awakened in the cell. Grave earth still smudged my knees, and my own blood stained my shirt and jacket. The cuffs of my trousers seemed to have picked up some very real burrs and thorns on my dreamwalk. I'd lost weight, but not in the way of a man who had worked it off. My flesh hung slack on my body; my face sagged. I suspected

that many people would flock to my trial expecting to see a
monster. Thanks to my confinement, I would look the part.

The last two days had been an agony of suspense. No one
had come to talk with me. I didn't know if Spink was too furious or too busy trying to collect evidence in my favor. In the
long lonely hours that had passed since I had "returned" to my
cell, my emotions had peaked and fallen in an endless series
of waves. Lisana had said that if I did what the magic wished,
I'd be saved. I'd promised to do anything. But the magic had
not asked anything of me. I'd sat, idle and hopeless, waiting for
something to happen. I tried to feel some spark, some turmoil
in my blood to suggest that the magic had not abandoned me.
There had been nothing. If the magic had given me a task, I
didn't know what it was. Nothing and no one could save me
now. It was time to meet my fate like a soldier.

Spink arrived by midmorning. When I heard his step in
the corridor, I went to the window of my cell. Over one arm,
he carried my spare uniform, freshly mended, washed, and
pressed. The glint in his eyes warned me that he was still
angry over my earlier comments about Epiny. What I had to
say to him today would please him even less, I thought. I
might have only one chance to bring up that topic.

So I greeted him with, "Epiny plans to use explosives to
stop the road crews from cutting the Specks' ancestor trees."

He stopped dead and stared at me. Then he turned to the
guard who had been outside my range of vision. "Bring this
man more water and a razor! He cannot be presented to the
court this way. We have the dignity of these proceedings to
consider."

"Sir, he may do himself an injury with a razor."

"And how much would the court care about that? Less, I
think, then having an unshaven bumpkin presented to them
as a soldier facing trial. Corporal, this is still our regiment.
Doubtless this man will exit it one way or another in the
next few days. Let's have him leave looking somewhat like a
soldier, shall we?"

"Yes, sir," was the daunted response. I listened to the
scuff of his boots as he left.

Outside my door, Spink gave a sudden sigh. "I shall hope

I can pass your greeting off as lunatic raving. How are you feeling?"

"Did you hear what I said?"

"I did. I hope the guard thought it was gibberish. And you obviously expect me to be surprised by it. Nevare, it grieves me that you don't understand at all the depth of love and trust that exists between Epiny and me. You think she has concealed this from me, don't you?"

I was left speechless. It had been inconceivable to me that Epiny would go home and confide her intentions to Spink. He was right. I had had no concept of the strength of the connection between them. But when I replied to him, I spoke to something else. "That isn't the only reason you're furious with me, is it?"

He spoke tightly. "No. It's not. In a very short time, Nevare, after you've gone to the trouble to shave and wash and put on your best uniform, we will walk under guard to the courtroom, where you will face seven men all intent on condemning you to a vile death. I'll put on a mimicry of a defense, not because that is my intent but because I literally have nothing to work with. After that, they'll condemn you. And tomorrow, as your friend, I'll watch you hanged. Then Epiny and Amzil and I will bury you. We've already decided that it's better that the children not attend any of this. It would scar them for the rest of their lives. We'll allow them to pray for you at home."

Slow tears formed in his eyes. He ignored them when they began to roll down his cheeks. He stood very straight, stiff as a soldier facing deadly fire. And as brave, I thought to myself. I tried to find a gentle way to ask my next question. "You'll keep Epiny safe, won't you? You won't allow her to do anything to endanger herself?"

His voice choked. "I'm afraid I already have. She's been in bed since she was brought home after her little stroll in the woods. She had—that is, we feared she was going to lose the baby. The doctor says her situation is still grave, but that if she stays in bed, she may still carry the child to term. Such is our hope." He took a deep shuddering breath. "For a short time, I feared I would lose Epiny and our

child, as well as you. I've had a very dark three days, Nevare. I know I should have come to see you and consult
with you on your defense. But it all felt so hopeless."

"It is hopeless for me, Spink. But if you keep Epiny home
and safe and she gives you a healthy child, well, then, that is
hope enough for me. Don't think you have to watch my execution. In truth, I think I could bear it better knowing that
you were not there. Please."

He'd gone paler. "Military laws demand it. I'll be there,
Nevare. Epiny wanted to be at your trial today. Only the
threat of losing her baby kept her at home. Amzil is taking
care of her. If there is an opportunity for her to testify on
your behalf, I'll send a runner for her. It was very difficult to
convince Epiny that there was nothing she could contribute
to your defense without putting you in deeper water. I've
been grateful for her weakness in one way—at least I know
she won't be running off to explode things." He took a breath
and then asked wistfully, "Is there no chance the magic will
save you?"

How peculiar the world had become. A year and a half
ago, we would have mocked such a fantastic idea. Now we
both tried to cling to it as a last hope. I had to shake my head.
"It's gone, Spink. I haven't felt even a tingle of it." I did not
add that with Epiny unable to fulfill her end of the bargain, I
had no chance at all. I would die tomorrow, her bargain with
the magic would be broken, and its ability to manipulate her
would be gone.

Spink spoke suddenly in an official voice. "Ah. Here are
your water and razor."

The guard commanded me to stand well back from the
door as he entered to give me the fresh water, a mirror, soap,
and a razor. Spink passed in my clean uniform. Then they
withdrew while I made myself presentable. I wadded up my
filthy clothes and tossed them in the corner with the pan of
dirty water. Not much chance I'd need to worry about having spare clothing anymore.

The mirror showed me that I looked even worse than I had
supposed. Haggard would have been an understatement. I
cleaned myself as best I could, shaved, and then got dressed.

The many-seamed uniform that Amzil had sewn for me hung oddly on my reduced frame. When I heard Spink and my guard returning, I stood straight awaiting them.

They both peered into my cell through the barred window. The guard's eyes widened. Even Spink looked rather impressed. "You look a lot more like the soldier I know you are," Spink observed. The guard made a derisive sound, but when Spink turned on him, he pretended to have been clearing his throat.

"Shall we go?" Spink asked me.

The guard shook his head. "Sir, we're to await an armed escort for the prisoner. They should be here shortly."

"Do they truly think I'm going to try to escape?" I almost laughed. "What would be the use of that? I'd still be inside the walls of the fort."

They were both silent for a moment. Then Spink said unwillingly, "The armed guard will be protecting you on the way to the courtroom, soldier. Feeling has run very high against you. There have been threats."

"Oh." Cold washed through me. The studied calm that I'd been practicing for the last two days suddenly cracked. This was real. This was now. I'd step out into sunlight, walk a short distance, and then stand before seven men who would condemn me to death. My legs felt weak, and I was suddenly terrified that I would faint. "No!" I forbade myself in a low rough voice, and the vertigo passed.

"While there is life, there is hope," Spink said suddenly. I heard the cadenced tramp of feet at the end of the hall. I recalled my resolution. They would be armed. If the opportunity presented itself, I would make a run for it. I could force them to kill me. I just had to find the right moment and the nerve to act. I had to be ready.

The men they'd sent to escort me were brawny fellows. The sergeant was half a head taller than me, and his steely gaze left no doubt that he'd happily shoot me down if I ran. I primed him for it, meeting his stare with an insolent smile. They formed up their patrol around me. Just when I thought fate had finally smiled on me, the sergeant produced a set of leg irons. As he went down on one knee to fasten them tightly above my ankles, he observed, "We promised the ladies of the town that there would be no chance you'd escape trial and the death that you deserve."

Having my solution yanked so neatly away from me paralyzed my thoughts for an instant. He clamped the iron cuffs tightly around my legs, just above the bones of my ankles. "He's too damn fat for the irons!" he observed with a guffaw, and then crimped them tight enough to make them latch anyway. I cried out in pain and anger as the iron crushed the tissue of my calves, but he latched the second one anyway.

"They're too tight!" I complained. "I won't be able to walk."

"Your own damn fault for being so fat," he observed. "Let's go."

It was only when he was once more standing beside me that it occurred to me that I should have kicked him while he was down. If I tried to escape now, all I would earn myself was a severe beating rather than the bullets in the back I'd anticipated. Another opportunity lost.

The patrol stepped out smartly around me and I trudged in their midst, taking quick short steps in a futile effort to keep up with them. The leg irons bit instantly and painfully. In three steps I was limping. I awkwardly double-stepped up a short flight of stairs. By the time the outside door of the prison was flung open and the harsh sunlight assaulted my eyes, the pain was such that I could think of nothing else. "I can't walk," I told them, and the man behind me gave me a firm shove in the back. When I tottered and nearly fell, they laughed. I jerked my head up and looked around me as I minced painfully on. Beside me, Spink's face was scarlet with fury, his mouth held so tight that his lips were pinched white. I caught a quick sideways glance from him, steeled myself to the pain, and walked on.

The short walk from my cell to the building where I would be tried was a gantlet of mockery. The only other time I'd seen the streets of Gettys so packed with people had been right before the Dust Dance. The crowd surged forward at the sight of me. A woman I had never seen before screeched the foulest invective I've ever heard before falling to the ground in a sort of hysteria as we passed. Someone shouted, "Hanging's too good for you!" and threw a rotten potato. It struck the guard next to me and he cried out angrily. This seemed to incite the mob, for a veritable fusillade of rotten produce was launched at me. I saw a ripe plum bounce off Spink. He kept walking, eyes straight ahead. The sergeant roared at the crowd to "Give way, give way!" and they reluctantly let us pass. The pain from my chained ankles vied with the flood of hatred that rolled out from the mob.

The courtroom was stuffy. I shuffled up a short flight of steps to the prisoner's box. A solid half-wall topped with iron bars separated me from the spectators but permitted all the gawkers a good view. Below and in front of me, Spink sat alone at a table, a small stack of papers before him. Opposite, at a larger table, sat a captain and two lieutenants. Behind them, seated on benches, an assortment of witnesses waited impatiently to testify against me. Captain Thayer, Captain Gorling, and Clara Gorling were seated in a special section. My seven judges sat at a high table on a dais in the center of the room. A line of guards held back the mob that had surged in to watch the proceedings. Folk who could not crowd into the room peered in through the windows. I thought I caught a glimpse of Ebrooks, but when I turned my head, he was gone. Other than that, the only soul I recognized was Spink.

I stood still and straight and tried to ignore the agony of the iron clamped tight into my flesh. I could feel blood seeping down my left ankle. My right foot buzzed and went numb.

The proceedings began with a lengthy reading of a document that said that the military would conduct my trial, and in the event that I was found guilty, the town of Gettys would have authority over my punishment for crimes against the citizens of Gettys. I listened to it through a haze of pain. We were momentarily allowed to sit down. Then we had to stand again for an extended prayer to the good god that asked him to help the judges to fearlessly render justice and condemn evil. I could barely stand upright for the wave of red pain washing up through me; my ears rang with it. When we were

finally allowed to be seated, I leaned forward to explain my
discomfort to Spink, but the officer in charge of the proceedings commanded me to silence.

I sat, agony rippling up from my legs, and tried to listen to
the testimony against me. The officer in charge listed my
misdeeds. The charges began with my rape of Fala, moved
on to her murder and my subsequent concealment of the
crime, my assaulting of respectable women on the streets of
Gettys, and my poisoning of the men who had managed to
claim my horse's harness as evidence against me and finally
reached a crescendo with a long list of my supposed crimes
the night Carsina had walked into my cabin. One woman
fainted when the words "necrophiliac depredations' were uttered. Captain Thayer lowered his face into his hands. Clara
Gorling stared at me with the purest hatred. Witness after
witness spoke against me as I endured the silent torture of
my leg irons. Once I leaned down to touch them, to try to
shift them on my compressed flesh, and the judge shouted at
me to sit straight and show some respect for the court.

The damning evidence piled up against me. A horde of
women testified, one after another, that they had witnessed
me terrorize poor Carsina in broad daylight on the busy
streets of Gettys. Others told how I had scowled at the noble
Dale Hardy when he had sought to protect Carsina's honor
from my scurrilous behavior. One claimed to have heard
me mutter threats against him as I left. A doctor I'd never
seen before testified that the manner of my ambushers'
death was such that poison was the only explanation. Sergeant Hoster's letter from beyond the grave was read aloud,
and Clove's harness held up so that all might behold the
telltale piece of less worn harness compared to the strap
that had been "pried out of the livid flesh about poor dead
Fala's neck."

Late in the afternoon, Spink was finally allowed to address the judges. I heard his speech through a haze of pain.
A runner was sent to fetch Amzil to testify. While we waited
for her arrival, Spink read aloud statements that both
Ebrooks and Kesey had thought me a good man and that I
tended the graveyard well. After a significant wait, during

which the judges scowled and the spectators shifted and muttered, the runner returned. He stated only that "the witness is unavailable." That sent a buzz of speculation through the courtroom. Spink gave me one stricken glance and then maintained his composure. With the judge's permission, he read a statement from Amzil. I wondered why she had refused to come, but when I looked around the courtroom, I realized it did not matter. My fate had been decided before I even left my cell.

The seven judges stood as one, and then filed out of the room to consider their verdict. I sat, sweat rolling down my face and back from the pain in my ankles, and waited. The spectators shifted, murmured, and then, as the wait continued, began to openly converse with one another. Clara Gorling spoke furiously to her husband. Captain Thayer sat silently and stared at me. I met his gaze briefly and then looked aside. The genuine suffering in his face moved me. He believed me guilty of the horrific crime. I found I could not resent his hatred of me. How would I have felt in his place? That thought put a new face on what was happening to me. I glanced about the courtroom. The eyes that met my gaze were avid with hatred, yes, but fear and horror were what sparked that hate. I lowered my eyes before it.

When the judges filed back in, the courtroom quieted immediately. I knew by the looks on their faces that I was condemned. As one by one they spoke the word "Guilty," I hung my head.

When they announced my execution by hanging, it was anticlimactic. I'd hang. My execution would bring a measure of healing to a town traumatized by my imagined misdeeds. And my death would free Epiny of her bargain with the magic. I took a breath and accepted my fate. I thought my ordeal was over.

But then one of the civilian judges stood. He smiled as he announced that the justices of the town of Gettys had decided that justice would be best served if the victims most wronged by my misdeeds were allowed to determine my punishment for my crimes against the citizens of Gettys Town. I stared at him in consternation. I'd already been condemned to hang. What punishment could they wreak on me beyond that?

Clara Gorling stood. Her husband and Captain Thayer rose to flank her. She was well prepared for her moment. She unfolded a small sheet of paper and read her statement from it.

"I speak for the women of Gettys. I do not ask this just for my poor dear cousin, but for all the women who live in Gettys." Her hand crept up to clasp the brass whistle that hung on its chain around her neck. "Gettys is a rough town. It is a difficult place for any woman to live, yet we do our best. We strive to make homes for our husbands and our children. We are willing to face the privations of living in such an isolated place. We know our duties as cavalla wives. And our husbands and loved ones try to protect us. Recently, the women of Gettys have banded together to try to protect ourselves. We have tried to bring the gentler virtues to this rough place, to make our homes havens of civilization and culture.

"Yet despite all our efforts, a monster has roamed free among us, raping, murdering, and—" she choked for an instant, but forced herself to go on, "dishonoring our dead. I ask that the honorable judges imagine the terror that the women in Gettys have endured. Hanging, my friends, is too good for this creature. It offers him too swift an end for his misdeeds. And so we ask that before he meets his end, he receive one thousand lashes. Let any man who thinks to perpetrate such evil against defenseless woman witness what his wickedness shall bring him."

Tears were running down her cheeks. She paused to dab at her face with her handkerchief. A profound silence held in the courtroom. Coldness spread through me. Clara Gorling took a breath to speak on, but suddenly sobbed instead. She turned abruptly to her husband and hid her face on his shoulder. The silence held an instant longer, and then gave way to cheers and applause. I heard the request spread to the crowd outside in a rippling roar of satisfaction. Then a terrible silence fell as all waited for the officer in charge to make his decision.

He commanded me to stand to receive my sentence.

I tried to. I placed my hands flat on the railing of the box before me and tried to lever myself onto my numb and swollen feet. I stood up, teetered for a horrid moment, and then crashed to the floor. A wave of hate-filled laughter greeted my mishap. "The filthy coward fainted!" someone shouted. My head was swimming with pain and humiliation. I scrabbled my hands against the floor but could not even sit up.

Two of the brawnier guards came to my box and hauled me to my feet. "My legs are numb from the irons!" I shouted at them. I don't think anyone heard me over the commotion in the courtroom. They hauled me to my feet and held me up while the officer confirmed that the town of Gettys wished the military to honor the request of the victim's next of kin that I receive one thousand lashes before being hanged by the neck until dead. When it was confirmed, he made it official, and then issued a lengthy apology on behalf of the cavalla that a man such as I had ever been admitted to the ranks. He deemed it a misplaced act of kindness by his worthy predecessor.

I think they judged me overcome by terror when I could not walk out of the courtroom on my own. The soldiers who dragged me from the prisoner's box from the courtroom, through the streets, and back to my cell were not gentle. Spink walked silently beside me, his face grim. The rejoicing mob closed around us, shouting curses and making the short walk from the courtroom to the prison seem endless. My chained ankles flopped and clanked behind me, and every impact was a clout of pain as they dragged me down the steps and back to my basement cell. My captors dropped me inside my cell. The sergeant knelt to retrieve his leg irons as I sprawled on the floor. I had thought nothing could increase the pain of that stricture, but when he undid the locks and jerked the embedded metal cuffs from my swollen flesh, I roared with new agony.

"Serves you right," I heard him say, and then consciousness fled from me in a red wave.

When I came to myself, I was still lying on the floor of my cell. I groaned and managed to sit up. I wondered how much time had passed. It was hard to reach the cuffs of my trousers to try to pull them up and see the damage to my legs. The leg irons had crushed and gashed the tendons above my ankle. The flesh above and below the imprints left by the leg irons was dark and swollen. Both my feet were puffy and tender. I tried to flex my feet and could not. I dragged my bulky body over to where my single blanket was mingled with the collapsed wreckage of my pallet, pulled my blanket free, put it around my shoulders, and leaned back against the wall. I was cold and hungry and I could barely move my feet.

I would die tomorrow.

That knowledge came to me just like that. All my petty concerns for cold or thirst or pain gave way to numbing awareness of my impending death. Yet I couldn't even focus on dying. All I could think of was the agony that would precede it as the lash ate the skin and flesh from my back. They'd strip me for the flogging. That was customary, as was tying the man by his wrists to the post to keep him upright. Details of what I would endure ate into my mind like acid. The mockery of the crowd. How they would dash me with vinegar water to revive me if I lapsed into unconsciousness. I would die a varlet's death, and I already knew that I would not go to it with dignity and courage. I'd scream. I'd faint. I'd piss myself.

"Why?" I asked the dimly lit cell, but received no answer. I tried to pray, but could not find enough faith to do even that. Pray for what? A miracle that would save me and return me to a life worth living? I couldn't imagine what could possibly happen to do that. I didn't know what to ask of god, nor which god would hear my appeal. I sat and stared at the stout wooden door of my cell. I would have wept, but even that ambition was beyond me now. I sank into a sort of stupor.

I heard the door at the end of the corridor open and then footsteps, and slowly lifted my eyes to the barred window. My bowels had turned to cold liquid. Was it morning already? Had I spent my last night in the world? My lips suddenly trembled like a scolded child's, and useless tears flooded my eyes. I wiped them hastily on my sleeve and stared stiff-faced at the window.

When Spink's haggard face appeared there, it nearly unmanned me. His eyes were red-rimmed and shot with blood. For a moment, we were both silent. Then he said hoarsely, "I'm sorry, Nevare. I'm so sorry."

"There was nothing anyone could have done for me," I said.

"They've allowed me fifteen minutes to speak to you."

"What time is it?" I demanded.

For a moment he looked puzzled. Then he said, "Evening is just coming on."

"What time is my execution scheduled?"

He choked for a moment, then managed to say, "Noon tomorrow, it will commence."

Silence fell. We were both thinking that no one knew when it would finally end.

And then, to say anything at all, I asked him, "How is Epiny?"

"Strangely calm," he said. "She encouraged me to come here for a final visit. She said I should tell you that she loves you and doesn't forget anything. I thought she was going to insist on coming with me, but she didn't. I didn't want to leave her alone. Amzil is off on some errand of her own, and the children are minding themselves. But she said she was well in control of her mood and insisted I should come to you. She said you'd want to know that we had heard back from your sister. Yaril received the letter you sent through Carsina. She wrote back to Carsina, but she also had the sense to write to Epiny as well."

I swallowed my words. I didn't say that I wished I'd never sent the letter. I'd told her that I was alive. By the time she read Spink's response that would no longer be true. I wondered, very briefly, if Captain Thayer had received my sister's letter; it probably would have puzzled him mightily if he had. I hoped that he had discarded it and would never plumb the mystery of what it meant. I wished to die as Nevare Burv, the gravedigger, not Nevare Burvelle, the disgraced soldier son of a nobleman.

"Don't ever tell Yaril how I died," I pleaded with him.

"I'll try to find a way to avoid it," he told me, but could not meet my eyes.

I cleared my throat. "Is she well?" I asked him.

"She is engaged to marry Caulder Stiet." His voice was flat as he announced this. "She says that she does not think it so evil a fate as she once did, that she thinks she can manage him. The actual phrase she used was that she found him 'tractable.' Your father had a stroke and has had difficulty speaking. She does not say that this has made her life less onerous, but that is what Epiny reads between the lines."

"Who is running the estate?" I wondered aloud.

"Yaril, by the sound of her letter. She mentions that a Sergeant Duril, her new foreman, was very proud to hear you'd become a soldier. He asked her to send his best wishes along with hers, and to remind you that you'd promised you would write to him."

And that was when I broke. I lowered my face into my hands and dissolved into tears. Spink was silent, doubtless embarrassed to witness this. I managed to calm myself enough to say, "Spink. You have to find a plausible lie for me. If it's the last favor you can do for me, please do it. Don't let any of them know how I died. Not Yaril, not Caulder or my father, not Sergeant Duril. Please. Please."

"I'll do what I can," he replied hoarsely.

I lifted my face in surprise. Tears ran unchecked down his face. He was not a tall man. He stood on tiptoes and thrust his arm into my cell window as far as the bars would allow. "I'd like to shake your hand a final time," he said.

"I don't think I can stand up, Spink. I'm hamstrung. Those leg irons cut into my ankle tendons badly."

He pulled his hand back and peered down at my feet. He narrowed his eyes in sympathy. "Those bastards," he said with quiet feeling.

"Lieutenant Spinrek! Sir?"

"What is it?" Spink scrubbed angrily at his eyes as he shouted back at the guard. "My time isn't up yet."

"No, sir, it isn't. But you're wanted right away. All the officers are being called to report. There's been a disturbance out at the road's end, some sort of sabotage. And—"

Before the guard could complete his sentence, a muffled explosion shook my cell. The guard gave a yelp of terror.

Dust sifted down from the ceiling. A sudden crack ran across the back wall of my cell.

The guard's voice shook as he called down the corridor, "That sounded like it came from the prison quarters, sir! Do you think it's an uprising?"

Epiny! I mouthed silently at Spink in horror.

"It couldn't be," he said aloud, but I heard the terrified doubt in his mind.

There was a second, smaller explosion. Dust hung in the air now, and I coughed. Spink looked in at me and our eyes met for a last time. "She sent you this," he said hastily, and vanished for an instant from my sight. Something wrapped in a napkin was thrust through the food slot in the bottom of my door. Then Spink bobbed into sight again. "Farewell, my friend," he said through the bars, and then he was gone. I listened to the clatter of his boots as he hurried down the hall.

I noticed that he had not said, "Good-bye." I hoped that he would be in time to whisk Epiny away from the scene of her mischief and get her safely home before anyone knew she was involved. And I wondered, with a sudden hope too sharp to bear, what else had she set in motion?

CHAPTER THIRTY-FOUR

SURRENDER

I waited until I heard the door slam behind both Spink and the guard. I could not tear my eyes from the napkin that rested on the floor of my cell. My nose picked up a tantalizing scent emanating from it. I grunted as I leaned forward over my belly and tried to massage my injured legs. It only awoke fresh agony in them. I gave up the thought of standing up and dragged myself over to the door to see what Spink had left. My hands trembled as I carefully unfolded the napkin to reveal a small pastry. I looked at the browned crust sprinkled with sparkling sugar as if I were beholding a treasure chest of jewels. My nose told me that it was stuffed with the forest berries from Epiny's kerchief. In a transport of joy, I devoured it. There were scarcely three mouthfuls to it, but when I had consumed it, a sense of well-being flushed through me. It muted the pain in my legs. I was tugging at the cuffs of my trousers, trying to see if the magic was healing my injuries, when I heard a peculiar sound.

I looked around, trying to discover its source. The crack in the wall was running. I watched it wander a crazy path across the face of the plaster. Bits of whitewashed plaster popped off and fell to the floor in a dusty shower, revealing the heavy bricks and thick mortar behind it. The engineer in me concluded that the building was resettling after the concussion of the nearby explosion. I decided that either the crack would soon stop, or the whole thing would suddenly give way and fall on me. It was difficult to care about either outcome.

More plaster flaked away. A chunk of mortar fell to the floor and shattered. I sat up and stared at the wall. Near the bottom, a brick shifted out of place as if pushed from behind.

I tried to stand and found that still sent agony shooting up my legs. Gritting my teeth against the pain, I rolled over onto my knees. I crawled to the back wall of my cell and put my ear against it. I heard small sounds, as if hungry mice were at work in the wall. Mice in a wall of mortar and brick, set below ground level? Tiny grindings and popping sounds came from the besieged wall. Plaster popped off the wall near the ceiling, and the crack ran along the top of the wall. At the same time, a dusty stream of mortar drizzled from between two lower rows of bricks. It cascaded down the wall, forming gritty little piles at the bottom of it. Then, as I watched in awe, one brick midway up the wall very slowly began to seesaw its way out of the wall. In fits and starts, it ground its way out from its fellows. When it protruded enough from the wall that I could get a grip on it, I seized it in both my hands and tried to pull it from its niche. It didn't budge. I let go and moved back to watch. The wall continued to shed crumbs of mortar and bits of plaster in a nearly continuous sprinkling. A second brick wriggled slightly beside the first one. Little grinding noises, pops, and cracks sounded.

The two bricks suddenly hinged out into my cell, and I smelled earth. A cascade of tiny white rootlets flowed out though the wall from behind the bricks. Clods of moist earth moved with the seeking roots, plopping down onto the floor. Sudden horror filled me as I recalled how the roots had emerged from the young trees and plunged into the bodies of the walkers. I hitched myself away from the wall, my heart hammering. I wanted to call the guard. No. Horrible as this might be, it would still be a faster death than being dissected by a leather lash. A third brick above the first two gave way and fell with a small thud to the floor. More roots emerged into the room and hung down the wall, a frill of white lace.

I took a deep breath and moved closer to the roots. I could smell earth clearly now. In the wall above the fallen bricks, a new crack appeared, zigzagging up the wall as it followed the mortar lines. The wall swelled in, and suddenly half a dozen bricks fell onto my ruined bed. Evening light and fresh air flowed into my cell through an opening about the size of my head. Hope rippled through me. The magic was providing an escape route for me. *At what cost?* I wondered, but found I didn't care.

On my knees, I crawled to the wall. I reached up and this time the brick I tugged on came out easily. The hole at the top of the wall gave me a ground-level view of a neglected, weedy alley behind the prison. I took bricks from the edge of the hole one after another, trying to drop them quietly to the floor. The roots continued their work, both pushing bricks and mortar into my prison and shoring up the wall so the hole didn't collapse on itself. When I judged that the hole was large enough, I took a deep breath, gritted my teeth against the pain, and reached up to seize a double handful of roots to pull myself to my feet.

And in that moment, faint as mist, I saw her. The specter of a skinny, very old Speck woman materialized before me. Her skin sagged from her bones. I recognized her eyes, and her dark little hands that she reached toward me. For a moment, I felt my face held between their phantom palms. Her smile deepened the wrinkles on her face.

"Lisana?"

"You didn't really believe I would leave you to die, did you, Soldier's Boy?" Her words were faint.

"What's happened to you?" I asked.

"I've spent my strength," she told me sadly. "It's taken me

all this time and used all my magic to grow my roots this far. Don't waste this chance. It's the only one I can give you." Her wrinkled hands slid away from my face.

"Lisana!" I whispered urgently, but she was gone. I bent my face and kissed the pale roots that now spilled in a cascade into my cell, framing my escape route. As I did so, I smelled a familiar aroma. It came not from the roots, but from the corner where I had discarded my filthy uniform and dirty wash water. I knelt down in the dim corner. The magic had kept its part of the bargain. Mushrooms were growing from the caked soil on the cuffs of my trousers. I could see the pale caps thrust up, open, and expand.

It took all my willpower to refrain from gobbling them at first sight. I forced myself to wait until they had reached full size and ceased growing. Then I snatched at them, cramming them into my mouth by the handful. I swallowed the half-chewed mouthfuls and immediately shoved more into my mouth. Magic and strength coursed through me. When they were all gone, I stood up. My legs still twinged with pain, but held my weight. I seized Lisana's roots, kissed them gratefully, and then hauled myself up and out of my cell.

I slithered on my belly out of the hole and into the alleyway. The night wind seemed a blessing. I lay there gathering my strength, formulating my feeble plan. I was out of my cell, but still within the fort. I was on foot and just able to hobble. Even if I managed to get past the guards on the gate, I'd never escape any sort of pursuit. All Tree Woman had won for me, I regretfully concluded, was the opportunity to persuade someone to shoot me when he caught me escaping. Compared to being flogged to death, it did not seem a bad bargain at all.

I sat up and tried to get my bearings. At one end of the alley, I could see flames in the distance over the rooftops of the buildings and the wall of the fort. That would be the prison. Evidently the explosion had sparked a fire. I could hear shouts in the distance. I wondered why Epiny had blown up the prison. A wry smile twisted my mouth. I wasn't wondering how she had done it or if she had done it. Only why. *Oh, cousin. May the good god keep you safe this night!*

A more immediate question came to mind. Could I stand? Leaning on the wall, I pulled myself up and onto my feet. As my feet flattened against the ground, pain bit into me and sweat broke out all over my body. The magic was healing me, but not quickly. I clenched my teeth tightly together and took three tottering steps toward the dark end of the alley.

From behind me, I heard the *clop, clop* of a slowly led horse. I glanced back over my shoulder. My worst fears were instantly confirmed. Someone was leading a horse down the alley toward me. In his free hand, he carried a long gun; I could see the silhouette of the barrel. I wanted to run, but resisted that impulse. I turned back toward him and tried to look menacing. "Give me your horse or I'll kill you!" I growled.

Horse and man halted. Then, "Nevare? Is that you? How did you get out?" Amzil hurried down the alley toward me. Patient Clove followed her even though she had dropped his lead rope. The pry bar she had been carrying rang loudly on the cobblestones when she dropped it. "Sssshh!" I hissed at her.

"How did you get out?" she demanded in a hoarse whisper.

"How did you know to come here?" I countered.

"I knew to come here after I got home and Epiny told me I'd blown a hole in the wrong prison. I thought they'd keep you with the working prisoners; I suppose that was a stupid thing to think, but when Epiny told me to blast out the east wall of the prison, that was what I did. I'd already set off the bombs she'd made out at the road's end. I blew up the culverts and two equipment sheds; it will be weeks before a wagon can get to the road's end. I thought the buildings would just fly apart, but it made a big hole in the ground as well."

She sounded very satisfied with herself as she peered up into my face seeking approval.

"You did that?"

"Well, yes. I had to. The mistress is still too weak to stand. Epiny said that if we stopped the road building, the magic would find a way to save you. But then she decided to help it along, just in case, by making a big hole in the side of the prison. So I did. Only then the master came home, to make sure she was still sick in bed, and told her that while he'd been with you, someone had blown up the workers' prison. Oh, I felt such a fool when I got home and she told me. And we didn't have any powder left. But I promised her that I'd take a pry bar and the horse and see what I could do to get you out."

I'd never thought Amzil could chatter like that, let alone speak so calmly of magic. Too much time with Epiny, I thought to myself.

"What are you smiling about?" she demanded. "You're not out of danger yet."

"I know. I'm just glad to see you."

"How did you get out?"

"Epiny was right. The magic got me out. Tree Woman tore down the wall for me." I shook my head in wonder, still moved by what she had done. "She rescued me, at great cost to herself."

Amzil scowled when I said that and then retorted, "Well, much good that did. She didn't get you out of the fort, did she? It looks like she's left the hardest part for us. And there's no time to waste."

"Amzil. I'll never get through the gate. But I want you to know I thank you for trying. That you would do all this . . ."

"You'll never get though the gate if you don't shut up and listen to me," she corrected me. "We only have a little time. We stole your horse and he's had a good feed of oats earlier today. Mistress Epiny said that would give him staying power. We put food and a bottle of water in your panniers. It's not much, but it will do you for a day or so. Now, this is the plan, or as much of one as we could come up with. I'll go first. At the gate, I'll find a way to keep the guards busy. Give me some time. Then, when you judge it's best, put your heels to the horse and gallop on through. A lot of the soldiers were sent out to the road's end to see what the first blast was about. Most of the others are busy at the fire, trying to put it out and round up the prisoners who escaped. So there aren't a lot of folk on the streets just now, but we don't know when they'll start to come back. We need to get you out of the gate as quickly as possible, and then hope the darkness will hide you."

I stood gaping at her. When she finally ran out of words, she scowled up at me and asked, "What are you waiting for? We're losing what time we have."

"Why are you doing this?"

She stared at me for a moment, lost for words. Then she said with indescribable scorn, "The mistress is right. You *are* an idiot. Let's go."

I took a step toward her and my legs folded under me. As I sank down, hissing with pain, she crouched down beside me. "What's wrong with you?" she cried in alarm.

"The tendons in my calves are badly cut. From the irons they used on me today. They put them on cruel tight."

She was silent a moment. Then she said, "I've seen what those can do to a man's legs. They did that to you on purpose, Nevare. To hurt you and cripple you." She sounded furious.

"I know."

Her pragmatism came back in a rush. "You'll have to get on your horse now and ride from here on. Makes you more obvious, but what else can we do?" She stood up, then suddenly crouched down again next to me. She seized my face in both her hands and kissed me on the mouth. I thought I had been kissed before. I was wrong. I reached for her, but before I could pull her close, she drew back from me. Her words were breathless. "The lieutenant told me—what you said. He gave me your message. And I, I think I love you, too. But we haven't got time to talk about it now."

"Amzil?" I said, too shocked to say more.

"Shhh!" she hissed at me, and stood up.

She brought Clove to me. He stood, patient as ever, as I dragged myself to my feet. My calves hurt less this time, but Amzil had to steady me as I lifted my leg to put my foot in the stirrup. I hissed with pain as I put my weight on that foot trying to get up onto my horse. The most humiliating moment was when Amzil put a firm shoulder into my rump to boost me up into Clove's saddle. I settled onto his back, feeling oddly whole again, even though Amzil had to help my other foot find the stirrup. "I'll go first," she told me hoarsely. "Stay well back."

She had just kissed me and said she loved me. And now she would go to another man to save me. No. "Amzil. Please don't do this. Don't whore yourself to the guards for me. Stay here. Clove and I will make a run for it."

"You'll never get through the gates if they see you. You just mind your own business about how I do things." She hissed the words, and I thought she was angry. "Give me a few minutes to go ahead. Be careful when you come out of the alley. Look around first. You're a hard man to mistake."

"Amzil, I—"

"Look, Nevare." She took a ragged little breath. "You have to let me help you however I can. You helped us with no thought of thanks. Now it's my turn." She was quiet and then added in a very low voice, "You know that I'd go with you if it weren't for my children. I can't just leave them. But if I didn't have them, I'd go with you now. You know that."

Her words left me speechless. "No," I said at last. I looked down at her, but her face was shadowed. "No, Amzil, I never thought you'd come with me. You take good care of the children. And take care of my cousin for me."

"I'll do that," she said quietly. Her hands moved up to her face. Perhaps she wiped away tears, or perhaps she just pushed the hair back from her eyes. She cleared her throat. "Everyone will expect you to run to the forest. Don't you do that. Go west. Don't stop in Dead Town. They'll look there for sure. Just keep going, as far and as fast as you can. If you want . . ." She hesitated and then plunged on, "Go to Darth. Mistress Epiny says it's on the road to Mendy. Within a year, we'll come there, the children and I. If you want, we'll find you there."

I was speechless at what she offered me. For a moment, the prospect of an entirely new life floated before me. We'd be starting with nothing. I'd have to find a trade to support us. It would be a hard life, but it would be mine. Almost as soon as the temptation formed in me, I felt the magic roil forbiddingly in my blood. Would I try to break my bargain with it? It would leave nothing standing that would keep me from coming to it. I could almost see the shimmer of impending doom it cast around Amzil.

"Amzil, you must not—" I grasped for words that would forbid her, words that would send her fleeing from me and the magic that marked her.

"There's no time now, Nevare. Later, we will have time for words. Now you have to listen to me. Wait here!" She leaned close and pressed her cheek to my thigh in a farewell embrace. Before I could touch her hair, she whirled away, lifted her skirts, and ran off toward the dark end of the alley. In a moment, she had vanished from sight.

I sat on Clove in the dark, my heart thundering with dread. Only a coward would let a woman do for me what Amzil was about to do. "I'm not going to her," I whispered to the night. "I'll keep my word. I'm coming to the forest and the Specks. I'm not going to Darth. No life with Amzil and the children awaits me." Childishly, I hoped the magic would hear and heed my words. My wayward heart yearned after the future Amzil had sketched. "No," I growled at myself, and tried to believe that as long as I went to the forest, the magic would leave Amzil untouched. What could I do about my creeping suspicion that it would burn every bridge behind me, destroy every person who might draw me back to my old life?

I sat on Clove in the alley because she had told me to, because she and Epiny had planned it so carefully that it seemed an insult to let my man's pride get in the way of their women's wiles. My hands became fists, and when I suddenly knew that I couldn't stand it, couldn't allow her to whore herself out to save me, fate intervened.

I heard pebbles rattle in the darkness. I turned to peer in the direction of the sound. In the dimness behind me, the guard poked his head out of the hole Lisana had made in my cell wall. He gasped and then shouted, "Help! The prisoner's escaping. Stop him, stop him!"

Startled, Clove lunged forward. I kicked him awkwardly and leaned forward, kneeing him on. I wasn't sure that anyone would respond to the guard's outcry. I wasn't going to wait to see.

Amzil had not gotten far. Clove and I passed her at a gallop as she hurried down the street. She shouted angrily at me as she scurried out of our path. I wanted to look back, to see her one last time, and didn't dare. I yelled encouragement to Clove, and the big horse pounded through the streets headed directly for the gates of the fort. Behind us I heard the guard ringing the alarm bell. I leaned low on Clove, urging him on.

There was a single man on duty on the gate that night. The sound of the bell had alerted him. He stepped out into the opening, peering toward me through the dim evening, perhaps thinking that I was a messenger sent on a desperate mission. He held his long gun across his chest at the ready. "Messenger!" I bellowed at the top of my lungs, hoping he would believe it. It bought me a few moments; by the time he realized I did not wear the garb of a courier and lifted his gun, I was on top of him. Clove's big shoulder spurned him aside, and we were through the gate. I heard his gun clatter as it hit the cobbles. I leaned in tight to my horse and urged him on. A few moments later, there was a muzzle flash behind me and a bullet whizzed past us. I was already at the limits of his range. He would not kill me tonight.

I glanced back over my shoulder. The fires at the laborers' prison made a red glow against the night sky, silhouetting the walls of the fort. The alarm bell was still clanging. Ahead of me, the streets of Gettys Town were deserted. Muted lights showed through a few windows, and welcoming lanterns still burned outside Rollo's Tavern. A few faces peered out the door, wondering what the ruckus was about. The guard fired another futile shot after me. I grinned as Clove stretched into a harder gallop.

I heard questioning shouts behind me, and to my horror, they were answered by other cries. My eyes picked out a mounted troop of horsemen coming at a trot down the street toward me. The troops who had gone out to investigate what had happened at the road's end were returning to Gettys. I reined Clove hard, but he was no cavalla horse, to wheel on his haunches and gallop away. The troops had spurred their own animals, and before Clove could even turn they had surrounded me. Gloved hands seized his bridle while other men clutched at me. "It's the cemetery guard. He was trying to escape!" someone shouted.

In the next instant, I was pushed and dragged from my saddle. Horses and men milled around me in the dark. Voices shouted angrily. My calves burned with pain as I stumbled and then tried to stay on my feet, struggling against hands that clutched at me from all sides. I could smell smoke and sulphur on their clothing. A fist hit my jaw, reawakening the old pain. I yelled and tried to strike back, but my arms were held. In the darkness, someone hit me in the belly, once, twice, thrice. The blows drove the air out of my lungs and I sagged down, gasping. Wild laughter fenced me. Someone brought the lantern from the tavern's door, pushing though the mob toward me. Someone else had found a torch. He reached me just as Captain Thayer seized the front of my shirt in his fists and dragged me up to face him. His eyes were wild with grief and fury. "You won't escape me!" he roared. In the lantern's bobbing light, I had a fleeting glimpse of a white-faced Spink trying to elbow his way to me through the mob. The mob surged closer to me; I could no longer see him.

Thayer was strong. When he hit me, I felt my head snap back on my neck. I fell backward into the roaring, jeering crowd. They seized me and pushed me back toward their captain. "Carsina!" he cried and hit me again, unholy joy lighting his face. I went down, tasting blood and bile. The torchlit night spun around me. I'd die here, beaten to death in the streets.

As I was hauled yet again to my feet, I heard a sound that froze my blood. "Stop! Let him go, let him go! He didn't do any of those horrible things. He's innocent! Let him go!" Amzil's shrill cries cut through the deep laughter of the men. The troopers holding me for their captain turned toward her. Someone laughed harshly.

"It's the Dead Town whore, come to rescue her lover!"

"Let her through! I want to watch them go at it!"

"No! Bring her to me!" someone else shouted. "I'll comfort his widow!"

I could not see what was happening. Men ringed her. I

heard her furious shouts and then a shriek of outrage and pain. "No!" I roared, but the men holding me only shook me roughly and laughed. I thought I heard Spink's voice raised in outrage, but the rough laughter of the men who dragged Amzil forward drowned him out. The front of her dress was torn, her breasts bared to the night and the harsh groping of jeering men. Two men gripped her roughly as they presented her to me.

"Hey, Nevare! Want to watch us do your woman before you die?"

"Let me through! Captain Thayer. Take charge of the men! Are we soldiers or scum? Let me through!"

Spink finally eeled his way past the taller men blocking him and into the circle of light. Captain Thayer looked down on him, breathing hard. He still clutched the front of my shirt.

"Sir." I heard the desperate plea in Spink's voice. "Take command. Restore order, or we'll all have to live with this for the rest of our lives!"

Thayer just stared at him. Then he let go of my shirt. Stillness fell over the mob. It had grown. Townsfolk had tumbled from their beds and come out into the street to see what was going on. They ringed the troop of uniformed soldiers, their eyes avid for blood and spectacle. Thayer's control of the moment teetered on a pin's head.

He hit Spink. The blow sent my friend flying backward into the crowd. The men behind him parted to let him fall, and then closed up the gap. I heard Spink cry out and knew someone had kicked him while he was down. Thayer turned back to me. His eyes glittered in the wavering torchlight. "Shall we do to your woman what you did to mine?" he asked me in a hoarse voice devoid of humanity. "Shall we rape her after she's dead?"

A roar went up from the gathered men. Months of fear and bleak spirits, suppressed anger, and the bestial impulses of deepest night spoke. "Let me do her while she's still alive!" someone shouted, and laughter rose in a night lit by fire and hatred. Thayer drew back his fist. A man stepped out of the crowd, fumbling at the front of his trousers, while another man pulled Amzil's arms back behind her and thrust her at him. For a horrible instant, our eyes met.

"Stop."

Blood sprayed out from my broken lips with the word. I did not shout it. But as I spoke it, I finally surrendered completely to the magic. It was the only thing that could save her. In that single spoken word, I gave up all hopes, all dreams, all futures I'd ever imagined for myself. The word was like lightning, and the power that surged out from me was its thunder as the magic rumbled through the crowd and filled the street. The power of the magic settled on the people like a light only I could see. They froze as they were, Thayer's arm drawn back, the man opening his trousers, Amzil with her head thrown back in a wild cry of fear. Spink stood as he was, blood running down his face, his hand gripping the shoulder of a man in front of him as he tried to get to me. All was sudden stillness. Only the flames of the torch still wavered and leaped.

I was shaking as I jerked myself free of the hands gripping me. The men who had been holding me let me go, their hands dropping to their sides. Thayer slowly lowered his fist, a puzzled expression on his face. Around me, the magic rippled and began to ebb. I summoned the power inside me and burned it furiously. "Stand as you are!" I commanded them. "And believe me."

I stepped forward to Captain Thayer. "You beat me to death. You avenged your wife. You were satisfied. And you went home. Now." I tapped his brow, and he blinked, then turned and walked away from me.

I reached through the crowd to seize Spink's hand and drew him to me. I spoke hoarsely. "I died tonight. There was nothing you could do to save me. But you did what you knew I would want you to do. You saved Amzil."

I led him unresisting to her. Then I tugged her away from the men who feebly gripped her. I gathered the torn remnants of her dress around her, and then stooped to kiss her mouth. She made no response to my touch. Her eyes were full of darkness and fear. I whispered to her. "You fought them off. They didn't take you. You know now that no man will ever take you against your will. You're strong, Amzil. Strong. You'll keep going and build a life for yourself and your children. Lieutenant Kester helped you get safely home."

As if I were posing dolls, I put Spink's protective arm around her shoulders. I gave them both a slight push. "Go home now. Go home. It's done. I died here. You did all you could for me. There was no way you could have saved me."

I watched them walk away into the dark street. Tears rolled down my cheeks, and as my heart yearned after them, I felt my control of the magic waver again. I instantly repented. "No," I promised the magic. "I sever myself from them. They are no longer a part of my life. I am dead to them. Let them go, let them be."

I took up the reins of the power again. I moved swiftly through the crowd now, touching men as I passed, speaking to them quickly. "You regret your part in this."

"You saw me die."

"You were there. You saw me beaten to death."

"You held me for your captain. You know I died."

I moved from man to man, repeating the lies that would become truth in their memories.

"The Dead Town whore escaped you. You're sorry for what you nearly did."

"You're ashamed of how you treated the woman. In your heart, you know you're a coward."

As I worked my way past the inner circle of men who had ringed me, I was kinder.

"You turned away, sickened by what you'd thought of doing."

"You tried to stop it from happening."

"You saw nothing."

"You never came out of your home tonight."

I did not stop until I had spoken a command and sealed it with a touch to every person on the street.

At the outermost edge of the crowd, I found Ebrooks. He crouched in the darkness, his hands over his face, his shoulders bowed. Despite my command that all be still, he was sobbing softly. I touched him gently. "You did what you could for me. After it was all over, you took my body. You buried it in a secret place. It was all you could have done. You bear no guilt."

I found Clove. I mounted him without difficulty. My injuries were healed. I rode him to the end of the street and then looked back at the frozen mob. I spoke a final command to them. "You don't see me ride away. You don't see each other, you don't speak to each other. Go home now!" I sat a moment longer, watching them slowly stir to motion and then begin to disperse. Then I turned again and slowly rode away. Behind me, I heard doors closing and horses slowly ridden away.

The magic had kept its promise. I would keep mine. I urged Clove to a quiet trot. The streets were empty and the houses quiet as we passed through town. When we passed the edge of town, I kicked the big horse up to a canter. The road unfurled before me, a ribbon of paler gray over the dusky land. Directly ahead of me were the hills and upon them the forest. The sun was a pale streak of rose on the horizon. I rode, not to freedom, but to the magic that now owned me.

Turn the page for a sneak preview of
the thrilling conclusion to
Robin Hobb's Soldier Son trilogy

RENEGADE'S MAGIC

Available now
wherever books are sold

The huge hooves of my big horse made a steady drumming as we fled. As we passed the last outlying farms of the scattered town that surrounded the King's fort at Gettys, I glanced back over my shoulder. The town was silent and still. The flames on the burning walls of the prison had subsided, but a dark smear of smoke still smudged the greying sky. The men who had fought Epiny's sabotage all night would be trudging home to their beds now. I kept my gaze fixed on the road before me and rode grimly on. Gettys had never been my home, but it was hard to leave it.

Ahead of me, light began to spill over the mountaintops. The sun would soon be up. I had to reach the shelter of the forest before men began to stir. There would be some early risers today, people anxious to secure good vantage points to watch my flogging and execution. My mouth twisted, imagining their disappointment when they heard of my death.

The King's Road, that ambitious undertaking of King Troven of Gernia, unfurled before me, dusty, rutted, pot-holed but arrow straight. I followed it. It led east, ever east. In the King's vision, it threaded through and over the Barrier Mountains and on, until it reached the far sea. In my king's dreams, the road would be a lifeline of trade for landlocked Gernia. In reality, his road ended only a few miles past Gettys, its growth foundered at the edge of the vale where the Specks' ancestor trees grew. For years, the indigenous Specks had used their magic to incite fear and desolation in the road workers and halt the road's march. The spell the Specks cast varied from a deep terror that made men crawling cowards to a deep despair that sapped them of all will to work. Beyond the end of the road, the forest awaited me.

On the road ahead of me, I saw what I'd been dreading. A horseman was coming towards me at a weary walk. The rider sat tall in his saddle, and that as much as the brave green of his jacket labelled him a cavalla soldier. I wondered where he was coming from and why he rode alone and if I'd have to kill him. As I drew closer, the rakish angle of his hat and the bright yellow scarf at his throat betrayed what he was; one of our scouts. My heart lifted a trifle. There was a chance he'd know nothing about the charges against me and my trial. The scouts were often out for weeks at a time. He showed no interest in me as our horses approached one another, and as I passed him, he did not even lift a hand in greeting.

I felt a pang of sharp regret as I went by. But for the magic, that could have been me. I recognized Tiber from the Cavalla Academy, but he did not know me. The magic had changed me from the slim and fit cadet I'd been. The fat, dishevelled trooper lolloping along on his ungainly mount was beneath the lieutenant's notice. At his current pace, it would be hours before he got to the town and heard of the mob that had killed me in the streets. I wondered if he'd think he had seen a ghost.

Clove cantered laboriously on. The cross-breed draught

horse was no one's idea of a mount built for either speed or endurance. But he was big, and for a man of my height and bulk, he was the only possible steed that could carry me comfortably. It came to me that this would be the last time I'd ride him; I couldn't take him into the forest with me. Pain gouged me again; he'd be one more beloved thing that I'd have to leave behind. He was running heavily now, nearly spent by our mad flight from Gettys.

Well outside Gettys, a wagon trail diverged from the King's Road and led up to the cemetery. Clove slowed as we approached it, and I abruptly changed my plans. The cabin I had called home for the past year was up that trail. Was there anything left there that I'd want to carry forward into my new life? Spink had removed my soldier son journal and taken it to his home. I was grateful for that. My journal held the full tale of how the magic had entered my life and slowly taken it away from me. There might still be letters in my cabin, papers that could connect me to a past and a family that I needed to abandon. I would let nothing tie me to either Lord Burvelle; let my death shame no one except myself.

Clove slipped into his ponderous trot as he laboured up the hill. It had only been a couple of weeks since I'd last been here, but it felt like years. Grass was already sprouting on the many graves we had dug for the summer victims of the plague. The trench graves were still bare soil; they had been the last graves to be covered, when the plague was at its height and we grave-diggers could no longer keep up with the steady influx of bodies. They would be the last scars to heal.

I pulled Clove in outside my cabin. I dismounted cautiously, but felt a mere twinge of pain. Only yesterday the leg irons had cut into my tendons; the magic was healing me at a prodigious rate. My horse blew at me, shuddered his coat and then walked a few steps before dropping his head to graze. I hurried to my door. I'd quickly destroy any evidence of my former identity and then be on my way.

The window shutters were closed. I closed the door behind me as I stepped into the cabin. Then I recoiled in dismay as Kesey sat up in my bed. My fellow grave-digger had been sleeping with a stocking cap on his bald head to keep the night chill away. He knuckled his eyes and gaped at me, his hanging jaw revealing gaps in his teeth. "Nevare?" he protested. "I thought you were going to—"

His words fumbled to a halt as he realized exactly how wrong it was for me to be standing in my cabin.

"Hang today," I finished the sentence for him. "Yes. A lot of people thought that."

He stared at me, puzzled, but continued to sit in the bed. I decided he was no threat to me. We'd been friends for most of a year before everything went wrong. I hoped he would not judge it his duty to interfere with my escape. Casually, I walked past him to the shelf where I'd kept my personal possessions. As Spink had promised, my soldier son journal was gone. A wave of relief washed through me. Epiny and Spink would know best how to dispose of those incriminating and accusatory pages. I felt along the shelf to be sure that no letter or scrap of paper had been missed. No. But my sling was there, the leather straps wrapped around the cup. I put it in my pocket. It might be useful.

The disreputable long gun I'd been issued when I first arrived at Gettys still rested on its rack. The rattley weapon with the pitted barrel had never been reliable. Even if it had been sound, it would soon have been useless when I'd expended the small supply of powder and ball I had. Leave it. But my sword was another matter. The sheathed blade still hung from its hook. I was reaching for it when Kesey demanded, "What happened?"

"It's a long story. Are you sure you want to know?"

"Well, of course I do! I thought you were going to be lashed to pieces and then hanged today!"

I found myself grinning. "And you couldn't even get out of bed to come to my hanging. A fine friend you are!"

He smiled back uncertainly. It wasn't a pretty sight, but I welcomed it. "I didn't want to see it, Nevare. Couldn't face it. Bad enough that the new commander ordered me to live out here and keep an eye on the cemetery because you were in prison. Worse to watch a friend die, and know that I'd probably meet my own end out here. Every cemetery sentry we've ever had has met a bad end. But how'd you get out of it? I don't understand."

"I escaped, Kesey. Speck magic freed me. The roots of a tree tore the stone walls of my dungeon apart, and I crawled out through the opening. I nearly made it out of Gettys. I made it past the gates of the fort. I thought I was a free man. But then I met a troop of soldiers coming back from the road's end. And who should be in charge of them but Captain Thayer himself."

Kesey was spellbound, his eyes as round as bowls. "But it was his wife—" he began, and I nodded.

"They found Carsina's body in my bed. You know, if not for that, I think the judges might have realized there was very little to link me to Fala's death. But Carsina's body in my bed was just too much for them. I doubt that even one ever considered that I might have been trying to save her.

"You do know I didn't do any of those things, don't you, Kesey?"

The older man licked his lips. He looked uncertain. "I didn't want to believe any of that about you, Nevare. None of it fit with anything Ebrooks and I had ever seen of you. You were fat and a loner and hardly ever had a drink with us, and Ebrooks and I could see you were sliding towards the Speck way. You wouldn't have been the first to go native.

"But we never saw nothing mean in you. You weren't vicious. When you talked soldiering with us, seemed like you meant it. And no one ever worked harder out here than you did. But someone did those things, and there you were, right where they happened. Everybody else seemed so certain. They made me feel a fool for not believing you done it. And at the trial, when I tried to say that you'd always been a stand-up fellow to me, well, Ebrooks shoved me and told me to shut up. Told me I'd only get myself a beating trying to speak up for you, and do you no good at all. So, I kept quiet. I'm sorry, Nevare. You deserved better."

I gritted my teeth, and then let my anger go with a sigh. "It's all right, Kesey. Ebrooks was right. You couldn't have helped me."

I reached for my sword. But as my hand came close to the hilt, I felt an odd tingling. It was an unpleasant warning, as if I'd just set my hand on a hive of bees and felt the buzzing of the warriors inside. I drew my hand back and wiped it roughly down the front of my shirt, puzzled.

"But you escaped, right? So me keeping quiet, it didn't do you no harm, right? And I'm not going to try to stop you now. I'm not even going to tell anyone that you come this way."

There was a note of fear in his voice that wrung my heart. I met his eyes. "I told you, Kesey. It's all right. And no one will be asking you if I came this way, because I met Captain Thayer and his men as I was leaving town. And they killed me."

He stared at me. "What? But you—"

I stepped forward quickly. He flinched from my touch, but I set my hand to his forehead as he cringed away. I put my heart in my words. I wanted to protect him, and this was the only way to do it. "You're having a dream, Kesey. It's just a dream. You'll hear about my death next time you go to town. Captain Thayer caught me escaping and beat me to death with his own hands. His wife is avenged. There were a dozen witnesses. It's over. Ebrooks was there. He might even tell you about it. He took my body and secretly buried it. He did the best by me he could. And you, you had a dream of me escaping. It comforted you. Because you knew that if you could have helped me, you would have. And you bear no guilt for my death. All of this was just a dream. You're asleep and dreaming."

As I'd been speaking, I'd gently pushed Kesey supine. His eyelids shut and his mouth sagged open. The deep breathing of sleep sighed from his lungs and in again. He slept. I heaved a sigh. He'd share the same false memories I'd left with the mob that had surrounded me. Even my best friend Spink would recall that I'd been beaten to death in the streets and he'd been powerless to stop it. Amzil, the only woman who'd ever looked past my fat and unlovely body to love me, would believe the same. They'd bear that tale home to my cousin Epiny, and she would believe it. I hoped that they would not mourn me too sharply or for too long. I wondered briefly how they would break the news to my sister, and if my father would care when he heard it. Then I resolutely turned away from that life. It was gone, over, finished.

Once I'd been tall and strong and golden, a new noble's soldier son, with a future full of promise. It had all seemed so clearly mapped for me. I'd attend the Academy, enter the cavalla as an officer, distinguish myself in the King's service, marry the lovely Carsina, have a fulfilling career full of adventure and valour, and eventually retire to my brother's estate to live out my declining years. If only I'd never been infected with the Speck magic, it would all have come true.

Kesey snorted and rolled over. I sighed. I'd best be gone. As soon as the news of my death spread, someone would ride out to tell him. I didn't want to expend any more magic; I already felt the aching pangs of hunger that using magic brought on. As soon as I had the thought, my stomach growled furiously. I rummaged hastily through the food cupboard but all the food looked unappetizing, dry and old. I longed for sweet berries warmed by the sun, earthy rich mushrooms, the spicy water plant leaves that Olikea had fed me the last time I'd seen her, and tender crisp roots. My mouth ran at the thought of such foods. Instead, I glumly took two rounds of hardtack from the shelf. I took a large bite and, still chewing the loathsome stuff, reached for my sword. It was time to be gone from here.

The sword burned me. It all but jumped from my hand when I let go of the hilt, as if magnetically repelled from me, and clattered to the floor. I choked on the mouthful of dry crumbs and sank to the floor, gasping and gripping the wrist of my offended hand. When I looked at my palm, it was as red as if I'd gripped a nettle. I shook my hand and wiped it against my trouser leg, trying to be free of the sensation. It didn't pass. The truth came to me.

I had given myself to the magic. Cold iron was mine no longer.

I stood slowly, backing away from my fallen sword and a truth I was reluctant to face. My heart was hammering in my chest. I'd go weaponless into the forest. Iron and the technology that it made possible was mine no longer. I shook my head like a dog shaking off water. I wouldn't think about it just now. I couldn't quite grasp all it would mean, and at that moment I didn't want to.

I gave a final glance around the cabin, realizing belatedly that I'd enjoyed living here, on my own, having things my own way. It was the only time in my life I'd had such freedom. I'd gone from my father's house straight to the Academy, and then returned to his domain. Only here had I ever lived as my own master. When I left here, I'd begin a life not as a free man, but as a servant to a foreign magic that I neither understood nor wanted.

But I'd still be alive. And the people I loved would go on with their lives. I'd had a glimpse, when the mob seized me, of a far worse future, a future in which Amzil's best hope was that the gang rape would leave her alive and Spink's that he would survive having his troops turn on him. My own death paled in comparison. No. I'd made the best choice, for all of us. Now it was up to me to move on, keeping whatever shreds of my integrity remained. I wished I wasn't going into my new life so empty-handed. I looked longingly at my knife and my axe. No. Iron was not my friend any more. But my winter blanket, folded on the shelf, I would take. One final glance around the cabin, and then I left, shutting the door firmly behind me on Kesey's rattling snore.

FIONA MCINTOSH'S

MASTERFUL EPIC FANTASY
THE PERCHERON SAGA

* * * * * *

ODALISQUE 978-0-06-089911-0

In the exotic land of Percheron, the fifteen-year-old heir to the throne, Boaz, must assume the mantle of leadership, guided by his trusted warrior adviser, Lazar. In the midst of roiling covert intrigue, a headstrong young woman is brought to Boaz's harem, inflaming unexpectedly strong feelings in both Boaz and Lazar. And, unbeknownst to all, the gods themselves are rising in a cyclical battle.

EMISSARY 978-0-06-089912-7

Lazar offered up his life to protect Ana, a prisoner in the forbidden harem of the great Stone Palace of Percheron, accepting punishment intended for the bewitching odalisque. Now, with Lazar's guiding hand absent from the city, Percheron has become a darker, more treacherous place, as the young Zar Boaz has to battle the machinations of his mother Herezah.

GODDESS 978-0-06-089913-4

While enemy ships threaten Percheron's harbor, heroic Lazar lies afflicted with the drezden illness. And Zaradine Ana has been taken prisoner by the mysterious Arafanz and his warriors, and is believed to be with child—carrying the heir to the throne, the unborn son of Zar Boaz.